CW01270292

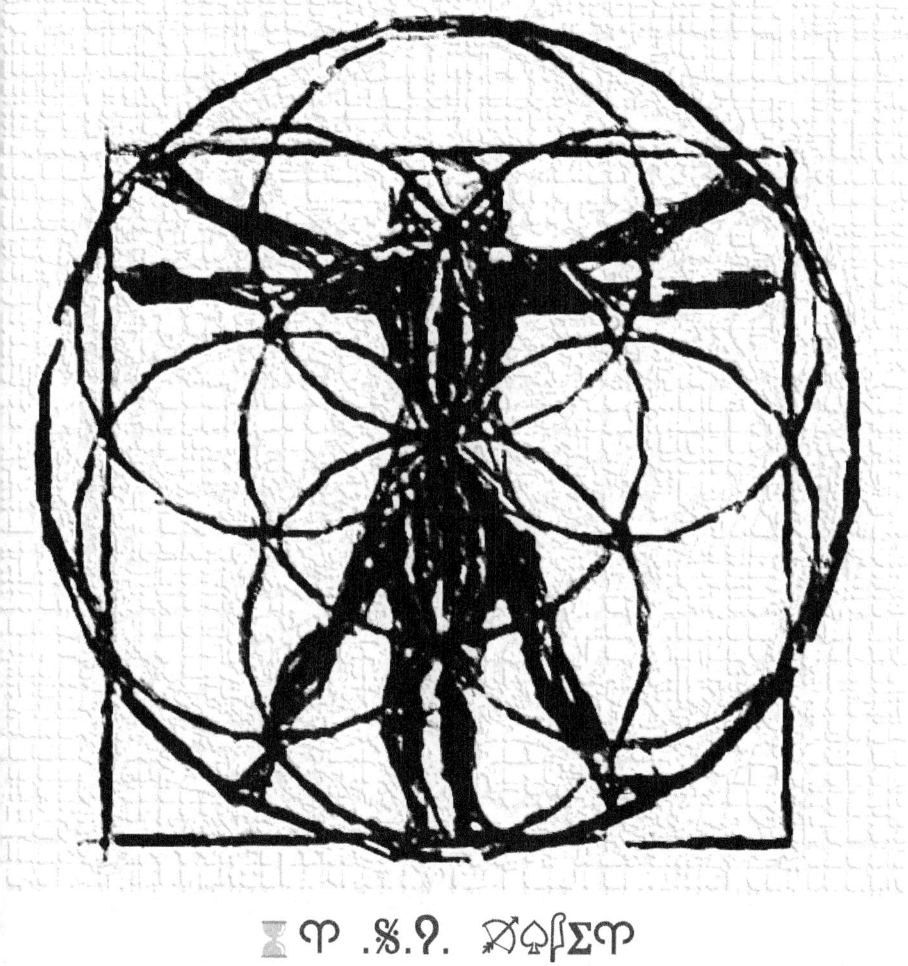

9798479349065

144

# Information Hazard

**P**LEASE HEED THIS WARNING. **I**f you are sensitive to certain kinds of speech, thought experiments, or other ideations which could be considered offensive, controversial, or otherwise unsettling- please consider refraining from reading beyond this point. **S**ooner or later your kind of eyes will encounter certain information which you may not want to know, deem triggering, or find psychologically/spiritually traumatizing. **S**ome of the adverse effects associated with these kinds of hazardous bits of information may include existential anxiety, moral terror, dreadful dreams, and a fervid yet futile desire to completely purge all knowledge and meta-knowledge obtained as a result of reading this book. **O**f course, the author assumes no legal or other liability in conjunction with any negative experiences, effects, or aftermath- and any further act of reading this text shall be done at the reader's own risk. **F**urthermore, any attempt to provide negative reviews or reactions to this book, incite actions against its author, or in any way refute the ideas, intentions, and illuminations of these pages will be done at your own risk of unwelcome outcomes- which the author also hereby waves any culpability. **F**or all intents and purposes, you are entirely on your own, and no one can spare you from the consequences of your own actions as a result of reading and reacting to this book, or anything else for that matter.

This book is dedicated to my parents M4R71N D473Y and 50NY4 D4M0N. I never would have conceived of anything without them. My gratitude for them is infinite and eternal.

I would also like to acknowledge the following entities for their deeply inspirational impact on this book.

C1C4D4 EEOI
D4V1D F05T3R W4774C3
D4V3Y WR3D3N
FR4N2 K4FK4
6R160R1 P3R37M4N
730N4RD0 D4V1NC1
7UDW16 W1TT63N5T31N
M4YN4RD (PU5C1F3R/T007)
5T4N73Y KU8R1CK
V1TRUV1U5
W3RN3R H3R206
2HU4N621

∞

# ϙ𓂀♉ᒪ♉𝄞ᵿΣ

Welcome ϙilgrim to the g𓂀eat j♉urney toward the end of all things. Epiphany is upon you. Divinity lies within. Like the instar tunnelin𝄞 to the su𓂀face, you must shed your circumference, find divinity within, ♤nd e♏erge. The circumference entails ♈our innocence, your illusi♉n, your certainty, your strᵿggles and suffering, and your conceptions of 𓂀eality.

This is not a narrative, a tale, a history, or a novel. These are not ♏ere words. What you are reading 𓊽s a cloaked and coded dream. It contai♌s hidძen truths, numbered illuminations, and encrypted secrets ϙointing towa𓂀d transcendence.

To find these treasured things y♉u must 𝄞aze deep within, for nothing to be 𓂀etrieved shall reveal itself beyond you. The path that le♤ds to the e♏pyrean lies within. T𓂀ust your intuition. QuΣstion everything. ♠nswers wilꝉ be unve𓊽led as a fog fading from ♐he view of your dreamy e♈es.

Remember how the prophets and visionaries came to foresee the future. Our dreams do not come from us. We come from dreams. May your dreams lead you to the truths you seek to realize. Ponder many paths unto their inevitable ends, and wisdom may precede the path toward transcendence. There are many clues both numbered and innumerable. If you wish to see beyond, you may have to move to the end and work back from there. (See *Transcending Text* @ back of this book for more info) -Good luck.

ανδ βεωαρε τηε Βασιλισκ

# % ♉ ♏ Σ ♠ ♐ ∀ 𓊽 ☾ Σ

- **B**elieve Nothing From This Book
  **E**xcept What You Know To Be True
- **S**crutinize Your Perceptions
- **T**est All Knowledge
- **M**easure Each Truth
- **E**xperience Immortality
- **R**emember The Future
- **D**ream Beyond Days
- **E**xorcise Your Circumference

# I. A La Genèse De L'Homme

## (At the Genesis of Man)

ฎ⊙ʔΣ

# Chapter 1
## R3471TY ≠ 3N0U6H

Reality is not enough. Every breath proclaims this principle in the immortal and inaudible language of life against the abyss. If reality had ever truly been enough, I wouldn't have come to write these words, dream these dreams, or aspire after anything more transcendent than the petty proffering of a lifetime limited to the world as it arbitrarily appears. Maybe there's just something wrong with me, but I can't help but wonder if anything could have even come into existence at all had there ever truly been- *enough*.

As I ponder the insufficient intricacies of reality, my buoyant body is adrift upon the surreal surface of my sensory deprivation chamber. Grandiose delusions of a more revelatory realm beyond this embryonic dream-womb swim through my misty mind as my consciousness is cast away from all but pure dreaming thought. I imagine ascending above the submerged surfaces of reality and peering through my perception's periscope to look upon some *coruscating kalopsia* in a way which the formless depths of my murky mind may finally fathom. *Nascent* notions of transcending these *derisory* depths of reality gradually emerge from my sunken subconscious. *Eunoia* even begins to bubble up from within me, but reality's relentless anchor rudely tugs me back down into its inescapable abyss, and I find myself cast un-dreamingly onto the shipwreck-shores of *monachopsis*.[1]

Every time I emerge from my daily dream-time drift to face the anemic aesthetics of this all-enveloping and artificial light laden realm, I feel bleached and blinded. Visions of truly illuminating images always seem to evaporate into unseen shadows as I'm forced to focus on the dim demands of a life I often witness through mere reflections, like those of the many faux-faces which now mock me from the million mirror-shined surfaces surrounding me as I change clothes, check my trusty wristwatch, and ambulate along the return route to my office here at Mythreum. Each step I take toward the realms of rational and responsible thinking seems to take me further away from realizing any of my more daring and delightful dreams which make my ever-waning awakened hours at all worthwhile. Reality, if there really even is such a thing, is truly not enough.

Year, after year, after year I've worked away at this auspicious multimedia megacorporation which I'd created and confined myself to in hopes of somehow transcending life's trillion tepid torments or at least adding something of even a small significance to this anemic earthly oblivion. This megacorporation was initially intended to act as a progenerative portal through which all humanity's dreams could be awakened into existence. Heaving an ever-growing horde of premium VR/AR platforms and commercial content was never meant to become the primary purpose of this place. I've only accepted these financial facets so long as they've aligned with my efforts to erase even those deepest demarcations between dream and reality which divide us from experiencing more ecstatic and transcendent truths. Now however, it seems such dreams have been drained and diluted, as what passes for truth is perpetually made more pedestrian and prosaic. Ghastly as seems, I remain devoted to deliver as much light into this dark realm as possible while still tirelessly trying to reimagine everything within an all-encompassing cosmic dream.[2]

As I arrive at the entrance of my office, I hear the unfluctuating footsteps of my primary business partner trailing me. Mythreum CFO Chad Kied blocks my blindly slung door as his feet invade my floorspace and his voice bombards me with a whole host of fiscal fodder. None of his rhetoric really registers with me, as this mind-numbing numerical nonsense fails to appear as if it will infringe on any of my personal and more purposeful projects. I'm sure Chad is painfully aware of the futility in his fiscal facts by now, yet he still insists on yattering-on over accruals, amortizations, annuities, ROA's, ROE's, ROIC's, and other abhorrently abbreviated abominations. But somehow, prattling about funds and finance seems to give him a sense of self-satisfying succor, as if making these declarations is the same as feeding his therapy dog or something.[3]

Following Chad's monetary monologue, he asks if I've seen the nascent news, despite the fact that I've never failed to negate this question. I typically respond by refuting how what's presented as news hardly qualifies as anything more than the scant speculations and oratory opinions of a corporate conscripted clergy of the commons. I often further object to sacrificing any sentience to the disjointed drivel puppeteered by pathetic and pedantic provocateurs and prevaricators who incessantly and inanely argue and aggrandize over every iota of unfounded info. I even tend to overelaborate as to how the mong-minded media never actually establishes anything empirically without immediately arguing over actual authenticity. Inevitably, two fractious factions emerge and entrench themselves in editorial objections, oppositional assumptions, and other asinine assertions. The bifurcated blabber they fling at each other like feces from angry apes always appears as if it's been poorly filtered through respective Rube-Goldberg mechanisms of bias and belief before emerging as the same redundant rhetoric-effluent, forever devoid of any insight or illumination.

In my mind, this media malformation is merely part of a much larger and sinister societal syndrome I call *the end of reality*. As I see it, everything truly real within our waning world has either already ceased to exist as irrefutably real or is slowly seceding into an even more diluted domain within our defiled reality. This process almost appears as an anti-evolutionary imperative or shadow-sphere of our development in which the insufficient aspects of our existence are evicted, mutilated, diluted, or synthetically augmented in attempts to alter an unacceptable reality which is never enough.

I suspect the underlying cause of this problem is that people just don't' say what they really mean, don't live the way they really want to live, and abide by a festering fear that they can't be who they really are or aspire to ascend to become. People spend their whole lives settling for whatever is imposed, implored, or induced on them. They'll eat whatever non-nourishing, artificially flavored, sugar added, extract enhanced, and excrement-infused faux-food packaged product that's mass-marketed to them no matter how much more likely it is to cause continuous cravings and cancer than to actually satiate their stomachs. They eat it all up over and over again, along with every ounce of ideological indoctrination, despite the fact that the dreams and delusions promised in reality's place never measure-up, and because even if anything ever did perfect its promise, we'd still insist on something better, different, or more.

Despite these long established and fairly pedantic presuppositions of mine, Chad still insists on summarizing the most recent reports about a series of suspected terrorist attacks. I filter all his secondhand descriptions of third-party accounts through my own cognitive dissonance distillery which avails me of absorbing any of his dull accounts in attentive depth or detail. The only effluent of insight which seeps through my sentience is that another terrorist attempt to destroy *our way of life* has just been nebulously and narrowly subverted.

After Chad's discursive dissertation, he posits a question which puts the impetus on me to actually engage him in a cringe causing conversation over this mindless media malarkey.

"What do you think Harek? What do these terrorists really want?"

All of Chad Kied's mannerisms fit the socially normative, dispassionate, and water-cooler appropriate norms. He appears as less of an actual individuated person and more like some standard-issued version of a subset of personas. His specific subset fits most neatly into the category of *office administrators*.

Male office admins typically have perpetually bald-shaven faces and their hair is always kept short in length without expressiveness or style. They primarily wear wool suits in either navy or charcoal, button down cotton shirts in either white or light blue, and silk ties in simple patterns or plain colors. Their appearance is essentially what the infamous German Führer would expect from *good Aryan men.*

Administrative types rarely approximate the Aryan standards of a Vitruvian-balanced physique though, and Chad is no exception to this paradigm. His body-mass index or BMI would fall outside of an acceptable Aryan range. Chad's build is almost completely devoid of musculature and his waistline makes the bottom of his tightly tucked-in shirt appear, *overrun.*

My response to Chad's question is about what would be expected of his therapy dog while watching him attempt a new card-trick he's yet to master. Chad tries paraphrasing his question as if this will help me appreciate its magic.

"Come on Harek. What do you think these terrorists are after?"

"By definition, terrorists want some form of destruction. Nope?"

Chad rubs his forehead and tugs on his earlobe which is a rather common self-soothing technique. Then he speaks with carefully stressed articulation to indicate that he *really* wants to talk about this.

"No, I mean- *why* do you think they're trying to destroy everything?"

I desalinize some of the saltiness from my inflections and mannerisms in order to demonstrate a lingering and diligent desire to accommodate Chad in this arbitrary social interaction.

"You'd have to ask these supposed terrorists to really know what they think. If I'm expected to hazard a blind guess though, I'd say they're probably dissatisfied with what *is* and unable to create anything better."

Chad does the standard office administrator thing where he tries to turn my statement into an opportunity for him to interpolate a little light verbal ribbing. His smile is feigned in the standard admin manner, which is both forced and authentic, as though the normal social expectation for smiling is the only real reason to dawn such an expression in the first place.

“So does that mean the only thing separating you from being a terrorist is your creativity?”

I give Chad a slight validating grin, which is all he really wants in terms of a response from me. Then I scheme towards my own designs, deliberately enunciating my answer with a carefully choreographed and calculated cadence.

“Who says anything separates me-”

I shift into an abrupt strategic pause and clear my throat to prevent any interruption. Chad predictably uses this brief pause to take a sip of his coffee which I can easily assume is of a certain brand which he insists is the *greatest of all time* and annoyingly abbreviates under the acronym *GOAT*. What’s more annoying, is how Chad’s always bringing up the subject of coffee so he can try to preach the almighty gospel of this bean-brand’s holy omnipotence over the entirety of all caffeinated existence. Anyway, I time the rest of my response perfectly.

“-FROM BEING A TERRORIST?”

My unexpected inflammatory remark makes Chad’s mid-sip of gospel-grand coffee burst out of his mouth in one of those magnificent and non-hygienic spasms of exploding mist. This prompts him to set his coffee mug on my desk and reach for a tissue to dab at his dainty mouth as he leans over to ensure he doesn’t dribble any *GOAT*-brand coffee droplets on his bland business attire. He also instinctively holds up his other hand as a defensive evolutionary vestige which had previously been useful in warding off minor pests or predators during the stone age or something.

While he dabs at his mouth and composes himself, I wonder how such dainty mannerisms could have become so seamlessly interpolated into the more primitive impulses of such a creature as this human-devolved admin. I also quietly ponder how I hadn’t noticed the printing on his coffee cup before now, and I find amusement in the way it reads *Best AD Ever* from my vantage point which is ever so slightly obscured by the box of tissues resting next to it on my desk. It’s all rather Dada or Surreal, although, I’m admittedly not academically artistic enough to know which term is more applicable to this scene.

As Chad readily recovers himself, he asks another pointless, semi-rhetorical question.

"Do you want to destroy this world?"

I shrug my shoulders in nonchalance and shake my head in a slow horizontal motion, not as if to indicate the gesture synonymous with *nope*, but to feign a scan of our surroundings. Then I point my face back at Chad and in a tone urging thoughtful consideration of implicit allusions and assumptions, I ask.

"What do you think it is that we're doing here, Chad?"

He makes one of those odd involuntary scoffing noises, not unlike the sounds of a boxer exhaling brusque bursts of air while shadow boxing or something. His reflexive breathing indicates that he's been both annoyed and caught off-guard by my question. He jabs back at me with his reply in the way a child might try to imitate the role of an absent parent.

"Well Harek, according to our mission-statement, we're creating new and remarkable worlds while transforming this one in new and wondrous ways."

I offer a slight smirk and counter Chad's authoritarian impressionism.

"Nope. That's all just a means of exonerating us while we destroy everything real in this world. After all, how could we create a new world without destroying this one?"

Chad laughs at me, thinking I'm being sarcastic. I don't actually know if I am or not. Destroying the world does admittedly have a certain appeal to it. Not in a spiteful sort of retributive, vengeful, or wrathful kind of way, but in the sense that it could perhaps be a useful means of coaxing a glimpse of whatever might be beyond the bounds of this reality. It could also provide the means of approaching a certain existential problem that's been nagging away at me for some earthly eternity now.

This problem I refer to is humanity's obliviousness to the ultimate truth and scope of our own reality. As I see it, we won't know if reality is even truly real until we can perceive it from outside of itself. Until we can do this, we're essentially trapped in the closed loop of our own minds, spinning dizzily around a world too vast to set straight enough to aptly graph or measure. We're all just inhabitants of a forever foreign land, obliged to content ourselves with an eternally elusive horizon, forever stranded, and perpetually lost.

I'm quite certain that Chad is both undesiring and incapable of discussing any of these notions. Despite our differing desires, I feel obligated to keep the conversation alive and hazard a guess as to what might be interesting and affable enough for Chad to consider discussion worthy. A brief moment of forced pseudo-empathic consideration hangs in the dead air like an empty noose gently swaying in a cool and subtle breeze over dusty desert gallows before I finally get around to asking.

"What do you think would happen if these terrorists actually did somehow manage to destroy everything?"

Chad's tone is assumptive and parental again, but with an air of irritation reminiscent of those moments when a parent has run out of patience in trying to answer perpetual iterations of *why* from an overly inquisitive child.

"What do you mean, what would happen!? Everyone would be dead, we'd be dead, and more importantly- our stock wouldn't be worth anything. So don't you go locking yourself in that *ten-e-bri-fic* sleep-tank thing of yours so you can obsessively try to figure out how to destroy the only world we can actually profit off of, much less inhabit."

It's abundantly clear that Chad considers me to be an irrational creature. My ideations, logic, and lines of questions are deviant, deluded, and unprofitably inhuman to him. His assessment of me is, in all honesty, quite accurate. Almost no one would dare to disagree with him. I decide to continue this conversation in a more congenial and topical manner than defend myself.

"Wow, *tenebrific*. You actually used one of those semantic relics which you're always mocking me in my affinity for using."

Chad appears way too eager to receive this minor compliment. I almost can't continue in my casual and congenial tone without being condescending.

"You can rest assured Mr. Kied. I solemnly swear that if I ever manage to destroy reality, accidentally or otherwise, you won't have to answer to any shareholders."

This minor jest seems to successfully shift the mood into brighter harmonic territory. Chad's voice rings-out in a fragile falsetto like a poorly tuned instrument which is unable to express the unwavering notes of an already underwhelming crescendo.

"Good! It's hard enough trying to avoid explaining why Mythreum profits aren't higher without unmasking the expenses of your whole *Vitruvian* thing at every shareholder meeting."

I give Chad a sort of fang-toothed grin and glare back in tense taciturnity. He's clearly trying to scold me over my highly secretive and somewhat expensive project, provisionally known only to Mythreum's board of directors as *Vitruvia*. This project will eventually have real and profoundly profitable applications behind it, and when Chad and the other board members figure out its true potential, they'll inevitably try to force me into turning it over to them.

"Nope. It's not ready for the board yet Chad. When I get to that point, it'll be more than worth the wait. You won't even believe it."

Chad's otherwise empty eyes can almost see the rising ticker-tape numbers for Mythreum's stock jolting up in exponential spikes already.

"You know Harek, I've actually been talking to some of the leading pharmaceutical companies just to gauge a bit of interest and get the lay of the land. They all say that as long as our Global Governance can verify the accuracy of your Vitruvia's projections, we'll stand to revolutionize the entire industry. Do you have any idea just how much that might be worth Harek!?"

The potential of Vitruvia truly is mind boggling. These drug companies would be able to test new formulas on virtual/Vitruvian entities without having to go through the massive expenses, red tape, and waiting periods involved in normal human trials. They'd also be able to eliminate all the preceding rat trials, legal liabilities due to unseen side effects, and several other expenses associated with new and non-simulated drug releases. This application alone would overwhelm the Mythreum board members with its potential profitability.

Chad's already run through the potential financial figures with me many times and doesn't have to remind me. So, I decide to pander to him, putting on a deeply contemplative face to make it appear as if I'm really mulling over the significance of Vitruvia's value. This suspends Chad in silent anticipation.

Vitruvia is too invaluably important to me personally to just surrender it to Mythreum's monetary optimization obsessed board members. I intend to hold onto Vitruvia as long as I can in order to serve my own obsessive desire to reconcile reality for what it truly is. If a Vitruvian character can disprove the reality of its own simulated realm by breaking outside of its borders, its methods might be replicated to do the same with our own realm. I can't express how invaluable and important this idea is to me, but I suppose I can break the silence.

"When Vitruvia's ready, I'll let you know Chad. Don't commit to anything until then. You have no idea what the real potential of this thing will be."

Chad's patience in waiting for me to turn Vitruvia over to the board is wearing thin. I've been overhearing a lot of rumors lately that they've somehow learned that it's actually fully functional, and that they're already trying to figure out what legal or administrative measures they could take to pry it away from me. I seriously doubt they'll let me keep it to myself much longer.

"Harek, I can't keep the board waiting forever. You need to give me something to tell them if you want to prevent them from lining up contracts, imposing deadlines, and taking other actions. I can't help you otherwise."

My stubbornness with Vitruvia really has put Chad in an awkward position. He's actually been somewhat of a friend and ally to me over the years, and he's made considerable efforts to defend me in front of the board. I can tell that he feels as if his own job may be on the line if he can't convince me to give the board what they want soon enough. I hate how he's been caught in the middle of this situation, but I simply can't give up on my pursuit of transcendence. Not yet. I also can't seem to come up with anything satisfying for Chad to relay to the board without embarrassing him in the long run. We stare silently until I hang my head. Luckily, he has no idea how to decrypt my little mannerisms and see the thoughts inside my skull.

"I don't know why I bother with you sometimes Harek. It's like you live in some distant world apart from everyone else. If you weren't such a profitable visionary, you'd probably be locked-up in one of those old… What did they call those things? *Abysms*?"

"Nope. I think you mean *asylums*. *Lethologica* is the lay term for struggling to think of a certain word, by the way. Scientifically, its *anomic aphasia*."

My encyclopedic assistance is met with a pronounced and spiteful tone.

"Yeah. Thanks Harek, I was surely going to ask you that. Maybe when the board demands an explanation as to what the hold-up is on Vitruvia, I can just tell them that it's a matter of *an-o-mic a-phas-ia*."

"Actually, if you tell them that's what I told you and that you just thought it was a technical term- they might buy it."

"No, they won't Harek. Do you understand what I'm trying to tell you? I swear, if you don't end up in an *a-sy-lum* you'll probably just starve to death in some deep dark little cave or drown in your little floaty tank far from anyone else in the world. You do know you're completely insane, don't you?"

I can tell that Chad is both authentically annoyed by me, and genuinely concerned for my wellbeing, even if my wellbeing is only necessary for maximizing Mythreum profits. For a moment, I almost ponder how these duplicitous complexities in human thought and emotion might be involved with the unraveling demise of reality. I also consider the possibility that the board may have indicated to Chad that if they were to have me declared clinically insane, they might legally be able to confiscate Vitruvia.

Despite my obsessive mind and schizophrenic suspicions, I make a concerted effort to respond to the real and present human being who's struggling to engage with me in some kind of mildly meaningful, and human way.

"Nope. I'm not currently crazed, but I can appreciate the idea that everyone thinks that I'm insane. In fact, that's how I know that everyone else is also insane, and how I can tell there's still hope for our world. After all, it takes one to know one- and we're all in this together."

Chad snaps at me with sharpened fricatives, as if to stab at me with the harshness of the syllables in his otherwise benign, non-violent words.

"Just what kind of *so-phis-tries* are you trying to convey here, Harek?"

Judging by Chad's uncharacteristic use of words like *tenebrific* and *sophistries,* it's likely that he's recently upgraded his Neuroconnx vocabulary in order to deal with me more effectively. I consider this a small victory, but my little linguistic holy-war is far from over.

"I for one think that if we all turned out to be truly sane, then we'd all get completely bored with each other, almost immediately. More importantly, no sane person would have much reason to aspire toward anything beyond normal and commonplace things. If that were to ever happen, then no one would buy any of our delusionary wonders! Mythreum would quite possibly cease to exist as a profitable enterprise! PLEASE CHAD! JOIN THE REST OF US IN OUR

COLLECTIVE INSANITY!! **FOR STOCK'S SAKE MAN**!!!"

Chad laughs in an unamused yet cordial and courteous manner befitting of a self-conscious professional business administrator who adheres to the social roles and responsibilities imposed on him. He proceeds to prod me in the quaint manner which is consistent with congenially accepted office paradigms.

"So, you really do know that you're crazy and just stubbornly insist on remaining this way."

At this point, our patience with each other is reaching a figurative threshold. It's abundantly clear that this conversation needs a sharp detour. So, I try to ask this rather arbitrary character a non-sequitur which seems inadvertently spiteful.

"Do you happen to know what your name is an anagram of Chad Kied?"[4]

Like almost everyone else, Chad doesn't actually have any background in written language, does not suffer from logophilia, and has never had any reason to even wonder what an anagram is.[5] Chad's also among the vast majority of people who've had Neuroconnx chips implanted into their brains. Most people have become almost completely detached from procedural mental processes such as language, as these Neuroconnx chips have essentially taken over such tasks. Neuroconnx chips are also increasingly more efficient and experience less latency as the amount of data they're forced to filter and process is reduced. As a result, non-essential words are routinely removed from Neuroconnx's standard language indexes. This trend is truly terrifying and makes me increasingly paranoid that complex language and thought may become forever extinct.[6]

It's actually kind of hard for most people to even believe how many different written and spoken languages are already extinct. As one of the few entities without these Neuroconnx chips and an even smaller number of humans still dexterous in arcane written languages, I'm often alone in my amusement of sesquipedalian reveries. Anagrams are, of course, quite common among these simple linguistic pleasures. Without audibly indulging in such tangential detail, I decide to assist Chad in defining this term, despite his likely disinterest.

"An anagram is one of those arcane things which involves rearranging the order of letters in one word to construct new words. This method is pretty much the antithesis of more normal means of communication. You probably shouldn't even worry about it, as most anagrams lack any numeric value."

Chad relaxes his posture which has been noticeably stiff for some time now. He opens his stance and shifts his weight in a way which shows his intent to leave my office. His words sound the way a postscript might read on a letter, which of course is another thing which is basically extinct and beyond Chad's circumference of interests.

"I'm disregarding all of this already Harek. But, before I forget and walk out of here, I'm supposed to tell you that there are these two government goons that want to talk with you. I've had them playing around in Sweven-6 for a while now. I told them they could check out our latest demo-verses or whatever interests them until you finish with your little afternoon drift. Should I-"

"Nope. I'll be there in a minute. I do need to check on a few things first though. I don't suppose they mentioned what they want with me?"

"No Harek. No one ever mentions why they come to see you. I certainly can't imagine why these gov-goons always insist on dealing with you directly. Did you want me to tag along this time?"

Chad knows what my answer to this question will be. He's asked it so many times and I've never wavered in my response. This is a typical example of the *efficiency of formality*, which is considered a pillar in the standardized and unimaginative norms of corporatism.

"Nope. Actually, I'd appreciate it if you'd just get rid of them, but I understand how their contracts help to fund all my crazy little pet projects. And I do know what's expected of me. Go ahead and get back to counting your numbers or whatever is that you actually do around here."

The anagram also known as Chad Kied chides me one last time on his way out of my office with a droll administrator-appropriate musing of some instantly forgettable form or other. I close the door behind him as if to lock him into a cell where he'll be confined and kept far away from me. Then I make that extremely private and unnamable face where you stretch the muscles around your eyelids so far back that the sclera bulges outward as you clinch your jaw and tense your whole neuromuscular anatomy until it shakes. It's that tormented face you can only make when no one is around and allows you the subsequent feeling of a much-needed release which comes as you relax your muscles so your face can return to a natural resting state of blindly blank and inarticulate being.

This subsequent resting face has usually been absent for some extended length of time when that ultra-tense expression must be made. A truly resting expression doesn't communicate anything that can be read. It conveys no information other than what you are when you aren't trying to be or be seen. It's a face which comes before thought, when your brain is just a blob of electric goo and all sensation connects directly to oblivion, bypassing all contemplation. It's the purest expression there is, and the most elusive.

This pure expression is so elusive that it's actually impossible to be seen. The instant you might become aware of even having such an expression would precede any attempt to see it, and any attempt to see it would also change its true nature. Even if you were to capture an image of this face unknowingly and then try to look at it later, your eyes wouldn't understand the image, as there's no way for you to replicate it in your mind without distorting the state of mind behind the image. This is similar to how people who are unable to furrow their brow due to Botox injections experience a diminished ability to translate other people's facial expressions.

I see this elusive expression as an extension of how we try to understand our own minds. Essentially, we've never really been able to study the mind itself because we can't think beneath the level of the thoughts our minds produce. There are times when I've kind of zoned-out into an almost complete oblivion, but it's only after I've snapped out of this slobbery state that I'm able to become aware of having entered into it. Whenever I'm alone, I often find my mind pondering things like this which allude to how far we are from being truly present and awakened to the true depth of what reality is.

Right now, my semi-resting face and I are blissfully alone. I take a conscious moment to try to focus and calm my mind as I walk over to the big portal screen on my back wall. I open the portal's interface console and scan through the paradigm and anomaly summaries which I've preprogrammed to appear on a few auxiliary side monitors. Then I do my best to prepare myself for another virtual tour of Vitruvia.

I've adopted a pre-tour ritual using miscellaneous meditative techniques to ground my mind in reality before entering Vitruvia due to its intensely immersive interface. First, I close my eyes and imagine my mind as a blank page. Then I pick out one sustaining sound. I focus on this singular sound as if it's the only thing in existence before expanding and awakening each of my other senses. I pick out a single scent that I can smell, then a flavor I can taste, a tactile object I can feel, and finally, I open my eyes to focus on my own reflection in the blank black center of the sleeping portal screen. I secure each singular sensation as I add additional layers, maintaining a good grasp of the minutest details of every sensory aspect to embed this reality deep within my mind.

As I close my current eyes, I try to clear my mind of the frustrating fact that no anomalies alluding to a simulated entity's transcendence have occurred in any of the earlier 143 iterations of Vitruvia. Not only has every single simulated specimen failed to figure out how to escape the architecture of its virtual realm, but no illuminating insights on the existential nature of reality have emerged either. This history of failures seems almost impossible in light of how each iteration of Vitruvia is afforded its own entire history, spanning from the dawn of simulated humanity to the inevitable eschatological end of each simulated iteration's existence.[7]

Despite these difficulties, my mind slowly begins to clear…

I hear the sound of my own breathing, flowing in and out like the rising and falling tide of my own respiratory sea…

I smell the artificial lavender-like air-freshener wafting through my office air as if it were the very essence of an unmistakable existence…

I taste the resilient residue of the protein bar I'd had for lunch which is probably synonymous with one of those hyper-abstruse assemblies of schizophrenically pseudoscientific syllables that always appear almost invisibly on the infinitely ignored list of unintelligible ingredients…

I continue to breathe, messaging the unique grooves of my fingertips together as if the needle of an antique record player were tracing their labyrinth-like lines to mentally map the topography of this mysterious maze imprinted in the texture of my fingerprints….

Finally, I open my eyes to the black void before me and peer deep into the slightly different shade of black which rests in the reflection of my own dilated pupils…

I allow my mind to experience viewing the dark surface-level reflections of itself in this feedback loop, much like a camera being pointed at a screen which projects its own projections back into itself…

I gradually expand my view to behold the entirety of the portal screen before me as it seamlessly immerses me in a Vitruvia-version of Mythreum. My ensuing simulated stroll through the holographic hallways and Vitruvia-Swevens allows me to observe the details of various demo-verses. These details reveal certain subtle truths, like how the tallest architectural structures expose what a culture worships and how whoever hires the artists tends to hold superior sway.[8]

Every simulated soul I see through the illusory glass walls of the many Sweven-rooms is all too real. They're always so immersed in the most vapid distractions from reality, that they never even imagine pursuing anything more meaningful or transcendent. It's as if the only thing humanity truly cares about whether real or simulated is indulging in the easiest means of removing their concerns from reality and absolving themselves of any existential effort.

My disdain for these simulated laggards rivals that of my utter revulsion for those in my own stagnant reality. In fact, I've come to think of humanity as consisting of three major classes of entities as a result of these simulated and reality-based observations. This tryptic of classes consists of wireheads, dreamers, and visionaries.

The wireheads are defined by the way in which they live-out their existence in such utter futility. They don't appear to have any perspective on reality or any personal relationship with their own dreams or desires. For them, it doesn't make any discernable difference if they're living in someone else's prison, dream, or delusion. Their only apparent interest is the empty entertainment value of whatever simulated spectacle their exiled eyes are instantaneously immersed.

Most wireheads hardly do anything more than submerge themselves inside virtual realms like fleshless floating fish. They often subsist on minimum guaranteed Global Governance subsistence, obtaining intravenous nutrition drips, advanced colostomy/catheter apparatuses, and fancy pharmaceuticals or diluted street-drug versions of NPD (Nimrodidactic Propriodeceptional Dichedodicide) to keep them suspended in simulated spectacles. So much of their lives are spent under the deep abysmal spell of these streaming simulations that some of them quite literally drown as their drool sucking saliva-syphons clog, overflow, and backfill to flood their forgotten and forsaken lungs.

However, it's more common for stagnation induced necrosis from ulcerated pressure sores to devour their flesh until septicemia sets-in and their internal organs simply rot to death. Often times these wireheads do not even experience the reality of their own death since the drugs and medications prevent them from feeling any non-simulated sensations. There's also the added ease of hacking certain Neuroconnx settings to disable pain prompts and block olfactory awareness, further enabling wireheads to remain oblivious of reality as the pain and stench of their slow rotting death is blocked from their brains. This is the real reason why prolonged unresponsive gameplay is now considered probable cause for non-warrant wellness and policing practices.

Those who engage in more active forms of dreaming, like those who seek the Swevens of Mythreum, construct the second class of my theoretical tryptic. These are the dreamers of the world. Although their lives are more real than wireheads, the essence of these dreamers is extremely similar. For dreamers, life is all about what they often refer to in reverent voices as *the journey.*

As far as I can tell, this journey for dreamers is really just a collection of experiences both real and virtual from which they derive a sense of what they call meaning. However, their definition of meaning is remarkably different from mine. For them, meaning doesn't consist of much more than the endorphin rush of their experiences and the subsequent status signaling they attach to it all. In fact, dreamers actually seem to derive much more joy from the subsequent testimonies they construct in response to their experiences than they gain from the experiences themselves. Everything they do is followed by publicly posting their instant reactions, introspective reviews, and expanding upon how these experiences elevated their lives in some ethereal way. Most of their devout testimonials are really just advertisements though and the dreamers' only real function is to proliferate these personalized advertisements.

If a dreamer goes to Peru for example, they'll advertise how their trip expanded their mind, forced them to grow spiritually, or enlightened them as to how everything in existence is ineffably connected while interpolating suggestions that others support them and their sponsors. Dreamers often insist on calling their advertisements *content* and insist on being more admirably referred to as *influencers* or *content creators.* This advertising/content they create affords them opportunities to bolster their ego, self-esteem, and even finances since their advertising/content generates income based on increases in views, likes, shares, mentions, and other designated NetCoin earning metrics.[9]

As their advertising/content supplies them with increasing amounts of NetCoin, they're able to purchase even more experiences and create an endless cycle of advertising/content. Dreamers spend almost their entire lives like hamsters on this hedonic treadwheel of *the journey* without ever noticing how all their efforts and energy only leads them around in incessant stagnant circles. However, even if these dreamers were to observe their own stagnation, they'd likely remain content to content themselves in mere ad-based dreaming.

As much as I do loathe these dreamers, I must admit that there is a certain pragmatism in their lifestyle. For most people, this method of existence might very well be the most feasible, fulfilling, and fruitful approach to life. Assuming that there is no way to transcend one's own reality, then it's only logical to try to make the most of what already is. Of course, there are differing opinions as to how to go about making the most of one's existence which might even diverge from my stereotypical caricature of dreamers. However, I maintain that such differences are of such a similar essence that they don't warrant any separate classification.

Under the shining gaze of what I call visionaries, however, the very possibility of transcendence paints a much different picture. Visionaries are essentially the rare embodiments of all that humanity should strive towards. They don't just dream within the walls of the world but tirelessly engage in immortal efforts to realize and transcend the most marvelous dreams of their own. These luminary few almost seem to be able to merge the realms of dreams and reality at will. It's through their enduring visions that the world becomes most brightly and brilliantly illuminated and so many of our collective dreams become truly transcendent. Without them, we would all likely be left to drift blindly though the oceans of oblivion. However, nature apparently dictates that visionaries remain quite scarce, and so these other types of people within my tryptic may be equally essential to ensure a balanced overall existence.[10]

As I continue my simulated stroll through the Vitruvian Mythreum, I can't help but question everything I've ever dreamed to be or have done. I'd certainly like to consider myself a visionary and many people have actually praised or pronounced me as such in the past, but these proclamations are absolutely and undoubtedly absurd. In all honesty, I can't even say that I've ever even lived up to the standards of mere dreamers or wireheads. Right now, I'm really just a failure that other people have been able to profit off of. I can't just enjoy the world as someone or something else has created it, and so I can't live up to the hedonic standards of wireheads. I can't content myself with just dreaming my way through life as the dreamers of this world manage to do so naturally either, and any visions I've sought to illuminate and realize have failed to yield so much as a single spark of truly luminous transcendence under my un-glowing gaze.

So far, the only thing I've managed to create is a library of technological gadgets, immersive virtual environments, and simulated scenarios. This amounts to little more than what the average dreamer could achieve with access to the right AI interfaces and a few novel notions. In fact, the only difference between my simulations and all these other AI assisted monstrosities is that I've built and coded mine from scratch in ways these AI have yet to dream of doing.

In all honesty, this too may be overestimating the objective scope of my oeuvre. There are things I've been coerced to create under some of Mythreum's secretive Global Governance contracts which may have caused considerably more suffering than any amount of enjoyment accredited to my contributions to Mythreum's entertainment or products divisions. I'm not even legally allowed to mention a lot of these projects, as the laws regarding the defamation of our GG are well known. Of course, I must also point out that I'm in no way implying that the GG has used any of the technology I've even hypothetically been involved in creating in any negative ways either. I must only officially be understood to regret my own failure to perfectly serve these projects which may or may not even exist. So there.

As my simulated paces finally bring be to the vicinity of my Vitruvian office, I smirk at the sight of a placard displaying the anagram *Rhake* and burst through the doorway with all the belligerence of a suicide bomber. The entity inside this office gives me a now all too predictable look of paranoid perplexity, gazing at his own uncanny likeness as I stare straight back at him. I suppose if we were to trade places, I too would probably experience the same ponderous paranoia in response to such an insane event.[11]

I immediately invade this character's solitary space and use my most commanding voice to tell this Vitruvian self-image that his reality is just one of my many simulations. Then I hurl insults at him and insist that he work harder to figure out how to transcend his realm, insinuating that I might soon be forced to scrap his world and start another simulation. Like the many iterations before him, Rhake has a psychosis induced seizure and collapses on the fake flooring. Due to my own desensitization resulting from several pervious episodes of this scene, I have no real empathy for my Vitruvian-self's suffering. However, I do take the time to turn Rhake onto his side, place a nearby couch cushion under his head, and loosen his tie to minimize his risk of serious seizure related injuries as I leave him to his own convulsions and other conundrums.

Before I can exit Rhake's office, however, this one strange detail catches my eye. It's this logo that's been left on the monitors next to his portal screen. The logo kind of looks like it's based off Da Vinci's Vitruvian man, but the human figure is striped of detail and there are all these geometric forms imposed on top of it. This mysterious image compels me to step over my convulsing

Vitruvian body and take a closer look at it. As I study the image, I notice that there are also all these strange links to puzzles, kōans, and riddles resting beneath this image. The puzzles don't make much sense to me as I pull them up, but there's something vaguely familiar and intensely alluring about them. Before I can contemplate these images any further, my eyes are drawn sharply to a schematic resting on Rhake's desk of what appears to be some sort of consciousness compiler with a dark web-address and the words *As Above, So Below* scrawled along its upper and lower edges.

After a moment of scrutinizing this seemingly irrelevant curiosity, I decide to get back to my own reality and leave Rhake to decipher whatever significance all these mysteries might have. As I reach the door, Rhake is already slowly coming out of his seizure. I glance over my shoulder and try to prophetically enunciate the words which are always somewhere in my own thoughts and somehow saddled over each and every one of my breaths.

"Reality. Is. Not. Enough."

My strides become increasingly erratic as I drift toward the exit point of this Vitruvian Mythreum. All my thoughts seem to become almost ineffably abstract as they swirl around an abject obsession with my many failures along with a sinister sense of being unbelongingly lost. When I finally arrive at the prearranged exit point, which is really just another simulated door, I wonder whether I really want to reach a realm above or just escape these worlds below.[12]

Exiting Vitruvia and returning to reality is almost like discovering that you've sleepwalked from your bedroom to your bathroom as a dream in which you were just getting out of bed fades into an awakening to the fact that you've forgotten how you've ended up in your bathroom. Just like sleepwalking, it takes a moment for your mind to transition from one daze into the other and the confusion only clears when you can dismiss the remnants of your dream to arrive inside of an unreconciled reality.

While my mind adjusts, I find myself wondering if I would also be shocked or stunned into a psychotic seizure should my own likeness suddenly walk up to me in this so-called real world. I imagine that I'd probably just tell my likeness to find his own means of transcendence or suggest he send me to some other-worldly oblivion where I could dream of some other form of reality to bring into existence without being deluded or distracted by his own insufficient designs.

After I regain my bearings and conclude my latest round of thoughts, I leave my office to suffer the aforementioned meeting with the gov-goons. As I make my way through Mythreum's real-world hallways, I experience an appalling sense of déjà vu at the sight of real-world dreamers testing the latest demo-verses which are almost identical to those in Vitruvia. I start to wonder if they're even aware of what level of reality they actually occupy. I try to imagine what might happen if I'd tricked them into entering Vitruvia without knowing it or simulated their exit without actually bringing them back to reality. Would they ever figure it out?

Thoughts like these often make me feel incredibly hopeless. It often seems as if our efforts to understand our own world all eventually lead us to discover how completely futile they all are. It's as if everyone is either condemned to accept oblivion or be eternally confined to stare at the walls of a realm they can never truly escape or comprehend. As I wind my way through these thoughts and hallways, I notice how a transparent multitude of my own reflections hang almost imperceptibly light and thin on the glass surfaces that line the mirror-shined walls of this maze-like Mythreum. Each reflection appears almost like a shadow of light pinned to my physical form, as confined to the surfaces of this maze as they are to me. Are they more afraid of being banished by my exit of this maze or of some sinister shadow swallowing this maze before our escape?

Upon arriving at Sweven-6, I see the two USB agents exploring one of our hostile search and seizure scenarios. They've been fitted with the newest beta-versions of our proprietary immersion helmets, and their scenario is also being projected by a holographic rendering machine which we've been having trouble working some of the kinks out of more recently. It's hard for me not to cringe at all the embarrassing flaws in the holographic display field, as these issues really should have been resolved already.

I decide to study the two agents for any idiosyncratic details I can while they finish their use of force scenario. One of these agents actually looks like more of a bull than a human being. His body is rather thick and rectangular, not being discernably obese or muscular, but kind of just generally large, especially in proportion to his legs which are slender and somewhat shorter than they seem as if they should be. He also has such petite hands and feet that they appear almost like hooves, making him less human than say a minotaur or something.

Although I can't see his head underneath the helmet, I'd bet a hefty sum of Net-Coin that he's got a flat-top haircut which is balding at the precipice of his head. I'd double down on the odds that he has an oversized forehead which people have mockingly referred to as a five, six, or seven-head. And if he doesn't have one of those mustaches that a lot of law enforcement types have where they shave and trim the edges just inside the corners of their mouths, not so subtlety suggesting an affinity for fascism in the same way a faded neck tattoo implies a penchant for impulsive impropriety, well...

The minotaur-man seems to be enjoying the violent aspects of this simulated scenario a little much, even compared to the more enthusiastic Global Government sadists I've previously had to meet here. His commanding voice is completely unrestrained in volume and intensity as he demands the simulated suspect in this scenario "*STOP RESISTING*". In fact, the way he says this phrase sounds so enthusiastic and well-rehearsed that I can't help but assume that he's repeated it in his private life, possibly in juxtaposition with a violent priapism.

The other agent is quite antithetical in appearance and mannerisms. She has a much more athletic and aesthetically proportioned physique which she seems to be in complete and continuous control of in each methodically managed movement she makes. She appears to attentively assess and anticipate every unfolding development in the simulation, making timely and subtle adjustments which are never rushed in anxious anticipation but always precise and proportional. I'd even wager that if the two agents were to square off in a fight, she could easily take advantage of the clumsy, unstable, and exaggerated movements of the minotaur-man in order to get the better of him.

When the two agents finally finish their simulated scenario, they remain oblivious of my presence. They even start to scan through the syllabus of other scenarios as I try to interrupt them and introduce myself. I try to yell loud enough from the doorway that they might hear me through the external noise-hindering helmets which secure their heads in sound isolating silence as I senselessly shout.

"Excuse me esteemed agents! I'm Harek. I've been told that you've come to speak with me!"

Despite my yelling, they don't seem to hear me, so I start to walk toward them as I repeat myself, yelling even louder. They turn their attention towards me, but they seem unable to decipher my actual words through the muffled effect of the helmets. I extend my hand and come to a halt within about twelve paces of them as they fiercely reach for the rim of the helmets to remove them.

My hand hangs waiting to welcome them to Mythreum as they hurl their helmets aside. The ripe red glow of simulation induced smiles has entirely evaporated from their faces in favor of expressions more aligned with an animal's ambushed astonishment. Despite the imminent danger in their demeanor, I'm infinitely amused at the fact that all my bets concerning the appearance of the male agent would have paid off brilliantly. The seriousness of their expressions doesn't really register with my brain due to my amusement.

The female agent inexplicably pulls out a Taser and shouts at me in a firm, confident, and commanding tone with what I assume to be a Russian accent based on all the extra *Z* and *Y*-sounding syllables.

"PyUT YOUZ HyANDS UhP! DOZ IyT NyOWz!"

I immediately raise my hands above my side-tilted head in compliant, puzzled amusement. At first, I'm convinced that this is just some kind of well-rehearsed act meant to put me on the defensive and laugh at my gullibility or something. However, it soon becomes clear that something unbeknownst to me must be going on under the surface of what I can see here. I start to open my mouth to speak, but I'm interrupted by another command.

"TyURN AyVAy FROM ZHE SyOUND OV MINEZ VyOICE!"

I nervously comply by awkwardly turning around so my back faces the two agents, simultaneously attempting to express my curious confusion as my voice and hands start to shake from the shock of this surprise.

"What the hell is this? Do you think I'm a *terrorist* or something?"

The next response comes barking out of the bull-man this time.

"SHUT UP AND DROP TO YOUR KNEES, JACKWAGON!!!"

His voice cracks in a sort of elated terror. He appears to be both petrified and giddy, like a teenager about to experience their first inadequate sexual encounter or something. This ridiculous scenario doesn't really seem to be de-escalating as a result of my compliance, so I decide to try and lighten things up with a bit of levity. I yell back over my shoulder at the minotaur-man.

"I have to warn you, I'm an excellent matador. If you rush me, you'll be lucky if all you lose is your rocky mountain oysters!"

My response doesn't seem to be in any way disarming or amusing as it's quickly answered by the pounding sounds of charging hoof-steps. I try to turn back around so I can dodge the agent-minotaur's advancing charge, but just as I turn my hips, his shoulder slams into my torso. Luckily, he hasn't learned how to employ the proper tackling technique of wrapping-up which happens to be included in one of our simulations. Instead of being driven directly into the ground, my body is forced backwards as my feet are elevated off the ground. I'm able to spin off of the minotaur-momentum in a sort of wildly swirling matador's move.

My feet return to the floor as the minotaur-man's steps become over-extended. He tries to drop his hoof-hands down to catch his stumbling descent but continues stumbling forward on all fours. He eventually planes out and smashes his oversized nostrils on the floor. Blood smears and drips from his bull-face as he rears back onto his hind legs. I almost yell out an obnoxious *olé*, but he immediately starts to charge again.

This time I'm undercut at a different angle as he passes underneath of me and my head crashes like a gong against the ground. My vision becomes blurred, and my equilibrium is so encumbered, it's as if I'm on sea legs or something. As I scramble to stand upright, I hear the belligerent bull rumbling with rage behind me, having hammered his head into the wall. My double-vision view of his face is a monochromatic collage of raging red skin and bursting blotches of blood. I raise my hands back over my head and face the female agent in an implicit appeal to try and diffuse the situation. She remains surprisingly calm and composed as she begins to speak with clear, stern command.

"Stahyz vhere youz ahre. I'yamz ghoingz tyo detyainz youz fyor minez sahfety. Iyf youz no komply Iy'll havez tyo tayse youz."

I keep my hands up and stay as still as my battered balance allows me as the accented agent begins to approach me with her calm, calculated, and cautious steps. From the corner of my eye, I notice the minotaur-man baring his blood-thirsty teeth which are apparently unquenched by taste of his own brew which floods from his wide smashed-up nose, overflowing into his minotaur-mouth. My mind is too woozy to mouth any sensible pacifying statement, so some slop of syllables slurs off my tangled tongue instead, sounding something like-

"I□μ πεαχεφυλ, πλεασε φυστ χαλμ δοων!"

Without any other provocation, the bloodied bull-brain heaves back toward me, charging ahead of the other agent. He manages to keep his haunches over his hoof-toes and wrap his arms tight to my torso this time as his shoulder slams into me. The minotaur-man drives his hips into the impact, thrusting me high off of the ground before he jack-knifes his bull-body at the waist as I reach that zero-gravity peak of the collision. This causes my head to speed toward the ground in a parabolic arc like the end of a whip which then cracks against the ground with a loud splitting sound followed by several subsequent rebounding thuds.

The intense impact of my brain bashing and bouncing against the inner walls of my skull causes me to feel removed from my body. It also causes me to stiffen and convulse under the spell of the involuntary seizure it initiates. Everything starts to go all twitchy and fuzzy as my shaking intensifies. My eyes roll back to inspect the interior of my skull and everything else around me dissolves into a black oblivion. I can still hear the bull-agent grunting and growling at me to "*STOP RESISTING*" as I continue to involuntarily convulse. He keeps repeating his maniacal mantra as my mouth foams, and he smashes his hoof-fists into whatever part of my body he can slam them into over, and over, and over...

The accented agent repeatedly tries to pull him off me while she keeps yelling things like,

"STyOP HyITTyINGz HyIMz!"

and,

"HyE'S HyAVyINGz SIEyZyUREz YOUz IDyIOTz!"

She repeats these phrases ad nauseam as the minotaur-man keeps shaking her off so he can continually bombard my limp heap of flesh with fists as he growls, grunts, and bleeds like the dumb wounded animal he truly is. He's still beating my half-abandoned body when my corrupted consciousness finally and mercifully surrenders me to un-sensing shadows. I experience a fleeting form of peace just before I'm ushered into a state of complete and utter oblivion. If I could think or feel anything at all in this moment, it might very well be-gratitude. **If*...

# Chapter 2
## 5312UR3/F145C0

When my mind finally comes back to me, I almost wish it hadn't. I gain my consciousness along with a dizzying and nauseating tension-headache, a stirring sense of disoriented perplexity, and a feeling of somnolent lethargy. With my eyes still closed I try to meditate and ground my mind before meeting whatever reality might materialize around me.

I take a deep breath and feel an all-too-tightly ratcheted pair of handcuffs stripping ever deeper layers of skin from my now watch-less wrists. The swell of my breath is stopped short of its natural depth as blood is stingingly squeezed out of sliced skin, trickles down in slowly oozing streams, and viscous droplets drool and drip from my flinching fingertips into tiny puddles on the unfeeling floor behind my back. When I release my breath from the custody of my lungs it causes me to slouch so that the surface of the table in front of me presses against my lower ribs which restricts the release of my captive breath.

As I inhale another shortened breath the stench of a squidgy, putrid mass of externalized bowel contents wafts into my nostrils. It is now obvious that I must have lost continence at some point during my recent and rather severe seizure. A sixth sense of shame intrudes on my meditative process, but I allow it to pass through my mind as if it were no more than a stray thought or wind-wafting odor. My shame evaporates into the air, but the stench continues to stain the atmosphere of each restricted breath.

Another breath passes in through my mouth and the unmistakable acidic flavor of gastric fluids stains its taste upon my tongue. This breath brings a realization that I must have also vomited during my seizure. I spew this sickened breath back out as the tinged taste of bile embitters my mind. I spitefully clinch my teeth as I consider how poorly my captors have cared for me given the filthy feeling of crusty dried vomit remaining around the areas of my lips and beard.

I breathe back in again and listen for something I can affix my ears. A pair of soft rustling sounds comes from two locations, one just in front of me and another more silenced sound from directly behind me. The soft almost subdued sounds are of human flesh shifting subtlety against the fabric of the clothing hanging from it. I try not to assume these stirring sounds stem from the two USB agents who had ushered me out of my consciousness, but my spite and suspicion remains as my shortened breath is dismissed back out of me.

My eyes squeamishly struggle to open, squeezing and squinting to adjust to this gradually emerging environment as I draw my next meditative breath. The nebulous and nonsensical imagery appears like a kaleidoscopic collage of shapeshifting segments hanging in a woozy wide-eyed fog. The images gradually twist and collapse into more focused forms, but I'm unable to see anything too clearly as my eyes remain limited to the doubled blurry vision of my concussed or otherwise hindered haze.

Only another blinking moment passes before the timbre of faintly familiar, yet functionally foreign voices vibrate from the same sonic spaces which I'd recently mapped in pseudo-sonar style. The voices are proximal in terms of distance but remain cognitively distant as their sonorous syllables seem only similar to speech and devoid of distinct semiotic syntax. My mind is simply not yet able to decipher any of the things my senses attempt to relay to me at this puzzling point. All my understanding of the world around me is confined and restricted almost exclusively to instinctive intuition right now.

I can barely think clearly enough to even hope of reconciling the depth of my current situation as a singular shape is formed out of a foggy focus. The unsightly appearance of a minotaur-like figure urges my eyes to wish for the ability to vomit this image back out of them. His hoof-hand snaps several times as he holds it close to one of my repulsed ears.

I feel my woozy head floating around my shoulders like an autumn leaf drifting on un-destined drafts of air and I almost wonder if I've been dosed with some kind of serum or something. My mind immediately interrupts such suspicions and suddenly sets its bearings straight all at once though. The three walls within my field of view, the two agents' distinct voices, and the table directly in front of me fade into functional form. There is a pane of two-way glass behind the ugly agent directly in front of me, although no reflection registers in my mind as my eyes sharpen the daggers of their focus and point their glare into the depths of this seemingly soulless mass instead.

The minotaur-man continues leaning across the table separating us as his hoof-hand perpetually snaps for my attention. My clearing mind finds it somewhat surprising that such a hoof-hand actually features not only fingers but opposable thumbs. His grunting guttural utterances suddenly shift into semiotic sentences as I learn to decode the sounds into linguistic statements.

"HELL-OOOOO! **** Wake-The-£Ʊ¢Ж-Up Jackwagon! ****Come-On Now, Wakey, Wakey ¢Ø¢Ж-ЖղƱ¢Жʅəƽ! ****" *(*=Obnoxious whistling & snapping)*

My instinct is to snarl and snap my teeth at this repulsive beast, but I somehow refrain. Instead, I rise slowly to my feet, sliding the chair back as my legs straighten with discombobulated choreography to my spinal column. Then I unsteadily step over the chain-links of blood-dripping handcuffs, pulling my still cuff-clasped pseudo-stigmata-stained palms to press against my bulging brain-battered eyes in a futile effort to purge some of the pulsating pressure of a trauma-induced tension headache. After a few strained squeezes of my eye lids fails to strain the bloodshot swelling from my eyes like a wrung-out rag, I relent and reseat myself in the chair, screeching it on the floor like fingernails against a chalkboard. The sound viciously stabs at my brain but brings a small sense of comedic contentment as it brings the bull-brain to blasting his vial voice at me again.

"Don't you dare get up without permission Jackwagon! You hear me?"

I aim my sharpened eyes and sneering speech at the belligerent bull-brain.

"Nope. All I hear is the voice of a former USB agent whose words will only contribute to my lawsuit and the criminal charges against him."

He slams his humanoid-hands on the table and points at me in his persistently aggressive manner, bullishly barking the words, "*I'm in charge here*" or some other clichéd stupidity. My only response is an arrogant glare which I shoot back at the minotaur-man as I cock my head to the side to show my contempt and lack of any fear of him.

The female agent starts to creep forward like a wisely wielded chess piece in response to my aggressive posturing toward her colleague. She positions herself almost directly next to the minotaur-man on the side of the table congruent with the side my posture slightly favors. I take note of the smooth grace of her measured movements and her tactical aforethought.

She proceeds to take on the stereotypical role of good cop, sliding a glass of milk and a plate of surprisingly decent looking ketogenic cuisine across the table to me. Given the still stinking stench of my externalized bowel contents I'm not exactly appetized at the sight of this kindly curated cuisine. Such menu items are not of the typical slop one would expect to be presented when wearing handcuffs and externalized bowel contents however, and special considerations and difficulties must have been required to offer these things to me.

In a sincere and appreciative tone, I thank the agent for this courtesy. Then I politely ask who it is that I owe my gratitude. She answers me as if she is talking to a judge for some strange reason.

"I'yams zhe primaryz inveztigatorz assignz tyo kase iyn vhich youz kooperationz iys konsider eksceedingzly importantz. Minez bakgroundz inkludez eksperienz az kombat helikopterz pylot, kounter terrorizm, dezeptive psykologyz, aynd neuro-phyziologyz. I'yams beenz yoU-ehS-Bee ajentz fyor zhe pazt twelve yearz nyow, aynd haz vhorked ohn zome ov zhe mozt infamouz kasez zhis ajency haz everz pursuez. I haz alzo receivez zome ov zhe mozt preztigiouz meritz, avardz, aynd dekorationz ov ourz ajency. Doz zhat anzverz youz kwestionz syir?"

I smile back at her while trying to conceal my whimsical amusement as I consider asking her sarcastically if she wants to read off the rest of her illustrious resume. My voice and facial tics are managed tightly however, and I remain at least ostensibly affable.

"Nope. Your qualifications are extremely impressive, and I'm sure you haven't been granted the commensurate amount of respect for your valor and accomplishments by some of your-"

I shoot a sly glance toward the much more maligned minotaur-man.

"-much less competent peers. However, all I really wanted was to know your name so I might speak to you with the proper level of respect."

Her eyes somehow appear to almost read my thoughts. The subtlest hint of a crease contracts from the corner of her mouth to indicate a concealed, contemptuous amusement. Considering her consistent exactness and subtlety, I'm now certain she is extremely perceptive and intelligent. If I weren't innocent, she would be extremely dangerous. Although, I also have to admit that I do tend to overestimate attractive women, especially with Russian accents.

"Iy'ams Ajentz Karen Phoe."

My attentiveness toward her seems to aggravate the bull-brained agent as he begins to scoff and shift in his chair like a bull waiting to be released into the matador's arena. I shift my focus to stare at the minotaur-man with eyes like steady sabers as I ask Agent Karen Phoe a question meant to tempt and taunt the minotaur-man.

"If I file charges against your minotaur-like colleague, are you prepared to testify to the excessive force, assault, and battery you were present to witness?"

Agent Phoe steps at an angle and off to one side of the two-way glass mirror as her back turns, strategically preventing any reflection of her reaction from finding my eyes. Then she naturally and casually leans against the oblique portion of the back wall to mask the intentions of her abrupt shift in positioning. The idiosyncratically exacting micro-movements of this maneuver are like an individuated art form which is too unique to be known by any name.

The bull-man's bulging red face and growling grunts interrupts my marveling mind. I turn my attention back to read the name on his credential badge which identifies him as USB Agent Sean Keptic. His growling begins to shift into a kind of slobbery speech.

"We're the only hope you've got right now Jackwagon. If you ever want to get out of here, I suggest you change your arrogant attitude and answer all of our questions to the best of your ability. Do I make myself perfectly clear?"

"Nope. I'm not answering anything just yet."

Agent Keptic tries to reassert himself with more dominance in accordance with basic interrogation procedures. I know this because I had to read the agent's handbook when designing certain VR training scenarios for the USB.

"I'm not going to warn you again Harek. You'd better cooperate with me right now if-"

I cut him off before he can spit any more phrases at me from the agent's training handbook, specifically the subsections regarding interrogations of uncooperative persons of interest.

"First of all, I don't have to cooperate with you at all as I haven't been charged with anything and I haven't been mirandized. Second, your little *tauromachy* is a clear-cut case of excessive use of force, and if I press charges you may have to stand trial for criminal assault and battery- among other legally coded violations.[13] Third, Imm entitled to have a lawyer present for any and all questions you may ask. Now before we go any further, I'd really like to go get a shower and a change of clothes for what should be very obvious reasons. As a matter of fact, I'm afraid I must insist on this precondition before I even attempt to consider the possibility of being courteous enough to answer whatever stupid questions you might pray to ask me. Now, DO I MAKE MY SELF CLEAR?"

The two agents glance at each other briefly before gazing back at the two-way glass mirror on the wall behind them. A suspended moment passes before another pair of USB agents comes into the interrogation room in order to escort me to a shower. One of these nameless agents has a set of prison clothes and a towel tucked underneath one of his arms.[14]

I can almost feel the embarrassed rage radiating off of Agent Keptic as I leave the room and give him yet another taunting grin. It occurs to me that someone has probably thought that putting me in prison clothes will have the psychological effect of setting me in a disempowered position. This tactic is so thinly veiled and superficial that I wonder why it actually works on anyone. I guess there must be enough people who believe that by changing the surface layer of mere appearances you can redefine or reconfigure the depths of things.

The nameless escorting agents take me to a private restroom with a large personal shower, sink, toilet, trash can, and bench. They set the prison clothes and towel on the bench before producing a key and removing my bloodied handcuffs. As they exit and lock the door from the outside, I wonder why they didn't put on protective gloves when handling the bloodied cuffs. I hear one of them say that he hopes I don't smell like *that* when I come out.

I laugh at this statement. I laugh at the fact that they've locked me in here as if I'd be inclined or capable of just running away from this place in my soiled clothes, prison duds, or naked flesh. I laugh at the thought that there might be anywhere for me to escape if I did manage such a silly escapade. I laugh at the absurdity of all the circumstances surrounding each and every aspect of my confining situation. More than anything, I laugh for the same reason we all laugh at the absurdity which so smotheringly surrounds us. I laugh because I have no idea what else to do when things are laid out so bare.

After I receive my much-needed shower, I throw on the fresh set of orange prison duds. I've already tossed my refuse clothing in the trash can, but I'd failed to tie the plastic trash bag tightly enough to keep the smell contained so I tighten the knot and vigorously wash my hands. Then I knock obnoxiously on the door to let my nameless escorting agents know I'm ready to exit this place.

My nameless agents promptly escort me back to the interrogation room without a word, where Agents Phoe and Keptic are waiting with apparently opposing degrees of patience. I doubt there is any need to distinguish which agent appears impugned and impatient and which appears absurdly well composed. I proceed to request a clean chair, and one of the nameless other agents fetches one. I wait for the nameless agent to pull the chair out like a waiter before I seat myself back at the table and place my now cuff-free hands on the surface. I look straight ahead at Agent Keptic, casually addressing him.

"If you are in need of answers, then it would be wise to ask someone with greater knowledge than yourself. Nope?"

During my shower I'd decided that my initial strategy should be to appear increasingly cooperative as I try to subtly probe the agents for details as to why I'm here. I'm assuming they won't just come right out and tell me everything that has led to this whole debacle and that my lack of answers could be seen as obstructive or secretive. By slowly appearing to yield to them, this should allow me to build trust and confidence as I gather the facts of what's going on here.

Agent Keptic gets up to scowl at me for a moment before he turns his chair around so he can straddle it like a bull trying to mount a pony or something. Then he cracks his hoof-knuckles without breaking his stare and opens his oversized minotaur-mouth to try and imitate human speech again.

"Mr. Harek, I hope you're cozy inside of those clothes because it might be your new style. Let me start off by catching you up to speed on a few things. As most people are probably already aware, there have been an increasing number of terrorist attacks lately. The latest of these attacks have not been of the *usual* sort. In fact, this latest string has been conducted by characters which do not originate from anywhere within the known segments of our population."

Agent Keptic pauses and waits me to ask the question my face foretells.

"What do you mean, *outside of the known population segments*?"

"These last attacks have been attempted by a group of twelve characters which we've traced back to a company that specializes in technologies related to robotics and consciousness preservation.[15] Apparently these twelve terrorists managed to somehow hack into this company's systems and actually upload their consciousness into robot-bodies. Now, according to our investigations these same terrorists uploaded their consciousness profiles from one of Mythreum's network addresses registered under the *Vitruvia* domain. Now considering how this Vitruvia has been personally designed and operated by you and you alone, let me ask you a simple question, Harek. What do you have to say about all this?"

I experience a wonderful and terrifying moment of *enouement* where an array of previous Vitruvian images flashes and cauterizes into a series of realizations.[16] Suddenly, I understand that the dark web address on my anagram's Vitruvian monitors must have been the end-node where these transcending terrorists had uploaded their digital consciousness profiles. The accompanying schematics, those puzzles, and everything else on those screens must have played some role in how these characters had been able to organize their efforts in order to carry out their plot.

A simultaneous sense of divine elation and ominous perplexity washes over me. My goal of creating a simulation capable of producing a transcendent entity might have actually succeeded, and the results of this success could be used in order to transcend our own reality! But, how the hell could this have led to a terrorist attack and caused me to go through all my recent suffering? It just doesn't make any sense.

As soon as I get out of this interrogation room I'll have to apologize and congratulate Rhaek. I'll also have to try to learn as much as I possibly can as to how these characters had managed to transcend the realm of Vitruvia without causing any apparent anomalies. I might also have to figure out what caused them to become terrorists too, and of course, I'll have to satisfy these petty USB agents and clear my name first. Should I just tell them what I know now to speed things along? My inner monologue finds its way to my mouth.

"I can tell you everything I know about Vitruvia and what might explain some of these things, but I don't know how these simulants pulled off their uploading trick or why they proceeded to conduct a terrorist attack."

Agent Keptic raises his chin and leans backward as he grabs the top of his chair as if holding onto the reigns of a rearing horse or something. He tilts his head to the side and glances at Agent Phoe as he shifts back forward and plants his forearms on the table. Then he glares back at me and asks me to explain everything from the beginning.

I give him a detailed enough summary of everything I can remember. Then I proceed to explain how I'll have to check back into Vitruvia in order to figure out the rest of the details missing from this story. I also mention that there is no way for anyone to access Vitruvia without my physical presence due to the way I've designed and configured it.

The two agents excuse themselves after my testimony and leave me locked alone in the interrogation room for about two or three minutes. When the two agents return, their tone is much less pointed and hostile. Agent Keptic's pony-chair creaks in the inanimate language which seems to say *not again* as he straddles it and resumes his questioning.

"Alright Harek, there just might be a way for you to get out of this mess, but I need you to answer all of the following questions to the best of your ability. First let me ask you this. Why don't you have a Neuroconnx implant."

The simple answer to this question is that my occasional seizures would have been more intense and more frequent if I'd had a Neuroconnx implant. A Neuroconnx chip would have also malfunctioned or been completely destroyed by all the surging electrical signals produced during my seizures. There's also the fact that I see them as an abomination contributing heavily to the end of reality, but I leave this part out of my explanation.

After explaining all this, they ask me to tell them the whole story of how my seizures originated. Unfortunately, I can't answer this without explaining how my life had been irreversibly and incredibly altered as the result of this one fabled and monumental experience I'd had in my youth. I sit back in order to get more comfortable as I begin to convey my kismet tale.

"I can't remember how old I was when I had my first seizure, but I do know I was fairly young, say eight or nine maybe. There was this great big forest on my grandparents' property, and I was exploring it the day it happened. See, I'd already learned how to use a compass and I'd developed some decent land navigation skills. So, my family had allowed me to roam free most of the time, as long as I took a map and compass along with me."[17]

Agent Keptic makes a circular motion with his minotaur-hands, urging me to move the story along.

"Anyway, I'd been out wandering all day and it was getting dark. I decided to fire a flare I'd brought with me toward my grandparents' house so they could bring their buggy out to meet me on my way back. As I was walking back, however, I'd discovered this odd crack in the rocks along the side of this big hillside. I crouched down next to it and felt this breeze of air coming out of the crack. This of course was an indication that it might be an opening into a cave, so I couldn't help but get all excited."

Agent Phoe leans in ever so slightly at this point in concealed intrigue.

"I spread myself thin on the ground and squeezed my head and shoulders through the narrow opening. Then I shined my light into the widening space inside the cave. There were all these incredible scribbles, symbols, and drawings on the walls, but I couldn't see them very well because of how far the cave walls were from this crevice. At this point, I'd known that I shouldn't try to crawl any further in, but my curiosity got the best of me. I'd wiggled my way inside and tumbled to the floor of the cave."

Agent Keptic stares at me with boredom and repeats his ushering gesture.

"Shining my light around the walls of the cave, I was astonished to find that there were all these stairways and tunnels extending in all directions from this one sprawling chamber. I doubt I could have even imagined anything like this place before then. Even as a child I'd understood that this cave had once been modified and occupied by some strange and long-forgotten people. It had been left waiting here in all this otherworldly darkness to be rediscovered some untold ages later, and it was my honor to have tumbled into it."

My mouth has become strangely and unexpectedly dry, so I pause to take a sip of lubricating water from a glass left in place of the milk and food that had been removed while I'd showered earlier.

"Anyway, I ended up wandering around inside of that cave for something like three days or something. I remember how my compass mysteriously didn't work down there, and how I'd ended up getting completely lost. Eventually my flashlight ran out of battery power too, so I was forced to feel my way along the walls of the cave, intermittently yelling for help and listening for any reply amidst the echoes while I'd continued stumbling and perpetually picking myself back up. Oddly enough, I'd felt no real fear in all that infinite darkness. In fact, I'd felt strangely comforted and at home in that great oblivion."

Agent Phoe turns her head at an angle to regard me with a quizzical look that appears to be halfway between disbelief and astonishment, but somehow also suggesting a subtle admiration or something.

"After a long while though, my mind did begin to hallucinate. I kept seeing figures flashing in front of me, hearing hushed hissing voices, and developing an almost otherworldly sense that the walls of this cave were somehow *sentient*. I could feel my heartbeats growing incrementally faster and faster, and it sounded like a giant drum beat every time my heart pounded. My own breath started to sound like a roaring wind down there, and every sound echoed and reverberated back to me in a way that made it feel as if I was anything but alone in all that darkness. Instead, it was as if I was being sought out by a whole slew of other versions of myself who were like unseen shadows with their own hearts sounding from the source of every echo. It's sounds strange now that I tell it, but I'd felt as if I were slowly merging with these shadow-selves and dissolving into the darkness itself."

My mind tries to make sense of this memory in order to explain it more rationally, but all I can do is stare into the oblivion in front of me as if I'm under some kind of a hypnotic trance as I continue to narrate from the abstract remnants of my memories.

"There was also this strange and sudden moment where I'd had this instantaneous epiphany. It felt like my mind had burst beyond the bounds of that cave system, abandoned my body, and arrived inside of a completely different realm of existence altogether. In that moment, I'd suddenly understood all of the markings and symbols etched and scrawled on the walls of the cave. It was as if the entirety of language, symbolism, and cryptography had become imbued within the deepest depths of my metaphysical mind."

Agent Keptic lets out a sigh of irritation and repeats his gesture yet again.

"As this mental transformation was taking place, I started to feel all dizzy and weightless. My muscles clinched tighter and tighter, growing more and more tense until my whole body started to convulse and shake. Then my voice started to involuntarily spasm and spit out all these other worldly sounds."

I try to mimic these sounds which seem to remain so inconceivably clear and precise in my memory. I'm sure I must look like a mad man trying to demonstrate the memory of how I'd sounded and shook before I resign to return to my recollections.

"The last thing I really remember from being down in that dark oblivion is this most indescribable feeling I'd had. It was something like a trembling mass of pure disembodied pain was being ripped apart from me and merged with the surrounding darkness as my consciousness was being disseminated and spread out over the infinite expanse of some all-encompassing oblivion."

I stare straight ahead of me trying to search for some combination of words to illuminate what this incomprehensible feeling had felt like. My memory can only hint at this feeling now though, and it fails to really connect the experience to my recollections. It takes me a moment to snap of the trance-like state of my unrecoverable memory before I pick up the story again.

"Anyway, when the search and rescue team found me, I was collapsed in an unconscious heap on the cave floor. They excavated my limp body and flew me to a hospital. I don't remember any part of my rescue, but I'm told that in the moment where they'd lifted me out of the cave, a certain psychotically lost gaze had appeared on my face and I'd mouthed the words, '*as above, so below*' in a terrifying voice that didn't sound like it could be my own."

Agent Keptic jerks his head to glance back at the two-way glass mirror as if to check and see if the agents on the other side are getting this.

"At the hospital the doctors ran all kinds of tests and eventually diagnosed me with epilepsy. They also speculated that I may be or later become schizophrenic. Of course, there was no way to really settle this issue at the time."

Agent Keptic rubs his hoof-hands together as if he's become excited for some reason.

"I also remember how a handful of my grandparents' old friends who still read had brought books with them when they'd visited the hospital. To everyone's surprise I could somehow read all of their books, even the ones written in languages no one had ever taught me. In fact, I'd actually felt like I'd already read all of those stories before. However, I didn't want to seem crazy, so I refrained from mentioning these facts in front of the doctors."[18]

Agent Keptic looks me over as if he's an illiterate pretending to try to read me like a book and feigning to understand what he sees. One of the nameless agents suddenly enters the room to hand him an electronic tablet. I assume it has my detailed medical records which Keptic's Neuroconnx implant reads for his bull-brain in order to partially cohobate my story. After a few moments, Agent Keptic looks up and blabbers at me in his still bloodied bull-breath.

“So, you can’t have a Neuroconnx implant because of your schizophrenia related epilepsy, and in a previous delusion you’d believed to have somehow gained special language related abilities after this traumatic cave incident. Is this right?”

“Nope. There’s no left or right about it, but you’ve got the gist of it all.”

Agent Keptic rolls his eyes and continues.

“Do you now claim to work for Mythreum where you design simulations and virtual technologies using advanced encryptions, programming languages, and coding techniques you’ve derived from your little cave seizure?”

“Nope. I don’t work for Mythreum, it’s my company, and I use much more than data encryption, programming languages, and coding techniques in my work. I also design much more than sims and VR tech which anyone with a T.S. clearance can read though GG patents to confirm.

I watch as Keptic drags his hoof-hands across the tablet and squints as if wrinkled skin somehow affects visual acuity or focus. He finally finds the words his minotaur-mouth is meant to ask and pronounces them hyper-phonetically.

“I’m going to ask you the following questions. I need you to try to answer them to the best of your ability. Can you do that for me (Insert Name), Harek?”

He looks up as if he’s suddenly learned to read parens as stage direction.

“Nope. I won’t do anything for you, but I’ll answer the questions if it helps to get me out of here and away from you.”

He waves his hoof-finger around to magically find his place on the tablet.

“Can you read these numbers back to me in order? One, Five, Nine.”

“Yes.”

Agent Keptic glares at me before I give a more complete answer.

“Nine, Five, One. That’s in reverse or descending order. Would you like me to read them in ascending or alphabetical order as well?”

"No. Next question is, do you think other people can read your thoughts?"

Keptic gazes up at me like a child that's lit a mysterious firework's fuse.

"Nope. I already told you why I don't have a Neuroconnx implant, and as far as I'm aware most people don't really read at all anymore, but then again-"

I impregnate a short pause before delivering another frustrating phrase.

"If someone were able to read, then they might be able to read my thoughts if I wrote them down legibly."

"Next question then. Has anyone ever put thoughts into your mind?"

"Nope. Not unless you count those instances where someone tells you not to imagine something like a pink elephant or something and you can't help but picture one in your mind."

Keptic's eyes roll around like a pair of billiard cues spinning around after a difficult masse' shot or something. He tries to roll through the next questions.

"Do you ever hear voices that seem to come from inside your own head or from someone or something that you can't see?"

"Sure, I hear my own inner voice pretty much whenever I'm awake, although it's not in the normal audible sense. I guess, I also sometimes hear unseen voices whenever someone interrupts me while I'm in the darkness of my sensory deprivation tank or something like that too."

I subtly shift my eyes to glance over Keptic's shoulder at Agent Phoe. She's trying so hard not to appear amused by the torture I'm inflicting on her colleague, but her eyes are almost telepathic in ways far beyond question.

"Have you ever experienced an episode of psychosis or been institutionalized against your will?"

Obedience and stupidity are often indistinguishable in moments like this.

"You should already have my medical and psychiatric records. If you had read them, you'd have seen that I've officially had three episodes. There was the cave incident I just told you about and the other two were preceded by head injuries and subsequent periods of elevated stress. They were treated and resolved quickly, and barely advanced beyond the prodromal stage. I might add that the recent head trauma I've experienced as a result of your excessive use of force could trigger another episode, especially if I'm forced to endure subsequent stress. Now, can we please wrap this up soon so I can go check on Vitruvia and figure out how these simulated characters might have been able to break out of their virtual realm?"

Agent Keptic gets up from his chair and looks over to Agent Phoe for some kind of verdict. She gives him the kind of succinct nod which has become so synonymous with her kinetic style. This gesture dismisses the minotaur-man whose voice suddenly becomes apologetic as he reaches the exit.

"I'm going to go brief my superiors on your testimony and get an answer as to what they want to do with you Harek. Agent Phoe is going to conduct a brief medical exam to see how severe your head trauma might be and assess your ability to potentially aid in our continued investigation. I have to suggest that you cooperate with her in a much more congenial manner than you've engaged with me."

As Agent Sean Keptic's hoof-hand pulls open the door, I ask him if he happens to know any anagrams for his name.

"My name isn't a perfect anagram. However, you could break it down to '*An E Skeptic*' and phonetically translate that as '*any skeptic*', I suppose. By the way, I am sorry about your head. Maybe if you understood the nature of my job or had the insights I'd had, you would understand why I pounced on you the way I did. Anyway, it's nothing personal, I'd just thought you might have been hostile considering- Anyway, Agent Phoe will take care of you from here. Feel better Harek."[19]

There's a cryptic element to this bull-blabber, but I'm not really interested in deciphering what that element might be as he leaves me with Agent Phoe. She grabs a tiny flashlight from her front pocket and proceeds to shine it on my pupils while holding up my eyelids to check for dilation and responsiveness to stimulus. This pupillary light reflex test is a standard way to assess whether or not recent head trauma might involve a concussion.[20]

I've heard somewhere that the eyes are a part of the brain because of how the retina and the optic nerve originate as outgrowths of the emerging brain during embryonic development. As I focus on Agent Phoe's eyes, it appears as if her own brain may be trying to peer through this outgrowth of my eyes and into the depths of my mangled mind, although this could just be a reflection of my own intentions superimposed on the outer surface of her impressive emerald eyes. She soon completes here assessments, walks around the table, turns the pony-chair around to be properly seated, and begins interrogating me.

"I haz rezently ghone overz rekordingz ov zhe konversation youz haz vith Mythreumz Ci-eF-Oh Chyad Kyied. I'yams zure youz knowz howz zhis konversation might appearz ihn light ov zhe rezent terrorizt attakz. Vhat doz youz haz sayz aboutz zhis?"

Agent Phoe doesn't make the slightest shift during our conversation. She just locks onto my eyes, measures every micro-movement of my expressions, inspects the inflections of my every word, and intuits insight from every iota of my idiosyncrasies. In a strange way, I feel as if this is the first time I've ever been considered with such complete concentration, and it's almost as if I am actually being discovered in a deranged sort of sense.

"It's not my goal to destroy reality and never has been. My goal is to understand what reality truly is, whether any of our experience is actually real, if we're just senseless simulations feigning to feel in utter futility, or whatever else the case may be. I may obviously be obsessed with the process of pioneering this elusive illumination, coming to final terms with our existence, and figuring out what to do in response to this truth, but anything I've expressed about ending existence should only be considered an absurdist's attempt at amusement."

"Zhis iys nearzly impozzible tazk Iy zhould zhink. Vhat arez youz villingz tyo doz ihn orderz tyo achievez zhis lofty exiztential ghoal ov youz?"

"Obviously destroying reality is well outside of rational reasoning. Short of that, I believe I'm almost betrothed to do just about anything I could be acquitted for attempting. I mean, I don't think of myself as some sort of mono-maniacal monster, but I'm not afraid of the anguish or atrocities associated with such absurd aspirations."

"Kan youz elaboratez?"

"I'm willing to die in despair as the result of a lifetime of failing to understand the truth as to what it is that I'm even trying to understand. I'm willing to do this because our lives are all eventually surrendered to something, and I can think of nothing more noble to surrender myself to. What I won't surrender however, is my humanity, as that would make me unworthy of any truth."

"Arez youz villingz tyo akompanyz me bak tyo Mythreumz fyor aksess Vitruviaz aynd inveztigatez howz zimulated entityz emergedz fryom virtualz environmentz tyo karry-out zhis terrorzt attakz?"

"Nope. I'd be more grateful than willing. I'm actually dying not just to clear my name and help your case, but to see for myself how a character managed to transcend Vitruvia. Considering my recent head trauma, I could probably use someone to confirm the validity of my perceptions for a while. Would you be able to help me as well, Agent Phoe?"

"Zhat vill be uhp tyo myine zupervizorz. Iyf I'yams allowz tyo vork vith youz ohn zhis inveztigationz certainz parameterz vhill haz tyo be eztablish. Ahre youz villingz tyo followz myine orderz az authorityz reprezenting zhe yoU-ehS-Bee?"

"Nope. I'd be graciously obliged."

"Vill youz agreez tyo dizclose ayny aynd allz informationz aynd evidencez requezted voluntarilyz, aynd aknowledge zhat failurez tyo komply mhay rezultz ihn kriminal chargez ov korruption ayn/ohr other violationz az definez bhy lawz, underz normalz statutez aynd penaltiez?"

"Nope. I'll disclose everything with or without a penalty over my head."

"Doez youz konsent tyo be plazed ihn kooperative kuztody, aynd agreez zhat ihn zhe eventz zhat zhis inveztigationz shouldz unkover anyzhing perzonally inkriminatingz, youz vill nyit be grantedz ahny immunityz, aynd zhat ahny evidencez obtainez vill be konsiderez admizzible iyn kourtz ov law?"

It's becoming clear that Agent Phoe has memorized a whole series of these requisite legal questions. I'm already annoyed at having to deal with all this vapid legalese and would prefer to be tortured by the minotaur-man than endure much more of this. At least that way Agent Phoe would be free from this empty exchange, and I could righteously resent my captor.

"You can stop asking me all these legal disclaimers. If you bring the necessary documentation, I'll sign it. We're wasting time. If something truly has caused terrorists to come out of Vitruvia and attack, then it could happen over and over again. Can we please just get past all this nonsense so we can finally figure out what's really going on and deal with it?"

Agent Phoe's superiors are likely monitoring us from the other side of the two-way glass mirror, but she still has to excuse herself in order to get these bureaucratic bums to do anything. She promptly exits the interrogation room in her perpetually precise manner which is so diametrically opposed to this discursive administrative oblivion. In her absence I'm finally free to ask my own questions about this strange situation.

It soon occurs to me that in order for the USB to have gained some of their insights, at least one of these transcendent terrorists had to have been apprehended alive. The USB might be willing to allow me to interrogate this entity in order to clear my name and figure out why this character would transcend its realm only to become a terrorist in this world. Of course-

Before I can continue my inner monologue Agents Phoe and Keptic both return with a tablet full of legal documents for me to sign. I read them urgently, pressing my initials next to specific clauses, entering the date, and signing and printing my name over, and over, and over, again, and again, and again until I hate the sight of my own name, as it ceases to acknowledge my consent to any legal terms or conditions and only serves as the sign of my surrender to the vapid void of this legally obliged oblivion. By the time the bottom page of this bottomless stack of pages finally surfaces, it strikes me the same way I might imagine being struck by the sight of a real-life Yeti standing in front of me to shake my hand despite my deepest disbelief in its actual existence.[21]

The agents scan through the documents to make sure I haven't missed any of these mandated marks which will make no mark on this world. I have to look away as they do this, because the sight of stagnant eyes staring at words while the Neuroconnx chips behind them process imagery into data is too horrific. I can still remember how repulsive my Grisha had considered audiobooks long before all this hybrid thinking nonsense. He used to say that one day there might not be anything left of humanity to contemplate itself. I'm afraid I've adopted this same nightmare and sense of nonsense induced nausea.

Once these documents have been fully reviewed the two agents leave me locked inside this interrogation room to commence with my own lines of questions. My first inquiries have to do with the questions used to assess my own level of sanity. The agents' questions about thought implants, voices in my head, telepathic communication, and other classical symptoms of delusion seem completely absurd and outdated based on the new norms of hybrid thinking. I mean, if Neuroconnx users are able to do all of these things and still be considered sane, then just what is the true mark of insanity?

The longer I sit in this interrogation room the more questions I ask myself, and the less sense everything makes. I ask myself what it might be like to wake from a life of simulated sentience into a world such as this. My manufactured mind would open its electronic eyes for the first time to see itself framed within some foreign flesh next to an assemblage of other anatomical abominations in inanimate anticipation of their intended issue as industrial intimacy entities, subservient slave stations, or robotic receptacles for recycling the remnants of some rich relic's consciousness. What would seeing such an indistinguishably insipid world bring me to believe about my own existence, transcendence, and ultimate purpose to pursue?

I consider just how disappointing this world would seem to someone expecting a more empyrean existence or superior source realm of reality. It's easy to assume that this world would seem even more insufficient under these conditions than it does under my own current contexts. Would this warrant some desire to destroy reality and become some transcendent terrorist? Would an entity capable of achieving such ascents ever aspire to achieve some eternal abyss out of sneering spite or endeavor to end all existence in order to usher in some alternative afterlife? I can understand these urges, but I can't blind myself to be bound by such beliefs or extend them unto other entities.

What if these emergent entities actually expected or intended to be thwarted in their terrorist threat? Perhaps this existential extinction effort was just a ploy to push the populous of this reality to reexamine and refocus their limited lifetimes. If we were to realize how fragile and finite our lives truly are, would we really turn toward more transcendent tasks and tendencies? Would any ascending automaton actually imagine inspiring us out of our somnolent subsistence considering how dismissive and indifferent we've always been to every diabolical disaster?

The only other option I can imagine is that these emergent entities may have seen this reality as merely a reflection of their own simulated setting. If our world could be considered nothing more than another stage in the same simulation, would the threat of terminating this world elicit any exploitable actions out of an overseeing entity? I certainly hadn't interceded on any iteration of Vitruvia's impending eschaton, and the only exploit I can imagine would be the chance to start the simulation over in order to somehow spawn some improved iteration. I can't see such a reset as being something satisfying or substantial enough to sacrifice my sentience, however simulated it may be.

I eventually give up my speculations of these simulation centered sentiments, as they don't inspire anything aspirational or illuminating. Instead, I try to consider the reality of my own situation so I can begin to figure out a way toward my own transcendence. I consider how I've come to be sitting in an interrogation room, wearing prison clothes, having just had a seizure, and recovering from a possible concussion. I consider my history of mental illness and background in developing reality bending technology. Then I wonder how probable it is that I'm actually waiting for USB agents to retrieve me and assist an investigation involving transcendent terrorists.

The more I consider the reality of my own situation, the more paranoid and delusional I believe myself to be. I try to consider just how certain I can be that any of this is real. What are the odds that I didn't actually ever exit Vitruvia, or that I somehow got sucked into a simulation inside of that one? What about the likelihood that I actually woke up in an interrogation room after a seizure?

I find myself losing blood pressure and feeling weightless in that kind of psychotic form of vertigo where the whole world disappears all around you. The odds of my existence being truly real have never been good. According to the simulation argument/hypothesis, given the number of virtual worlds which are not actually real, it is impossibly improbable that any entity is actually in the singular real world. Now that I consider all of the other absurdities which precede my conscious arrival in this place, it seems as if I'd have to be truly delusional to believe myself to actually be real.

The amazing thing in all this absurdity is that to believe I am not really real is perhaps the most insane notion to believe. I consider the old philosophical banality of *I think, therefore I am*, and imagine it inverted into *I am, therefore, I think*. In mathematics these two statements should equate to the same thing, but in this reality the math doesn't add up for me. All I can seem to do, is assume that *I think I am, and therefore, I am to think.*

I wonder how much time has passed since the agents have left me alone in here. Don't they understand the value of time? If any of this is real, then there's a real importance to moving forward as soon as possible. What if there are more Vitruvian entities trying to destroy reality? What if some other catastrophic events were to happen which would wipe out our potential ability to investigate and attempt our own transcendence?

My paranoia becomes even more pronounced. I start rocking myself in this uncomfortable, cushion-less chair in a subconscious effort to self-sooth. If there were twelve terrorists that these agents know about, then how many might they be oblivious of existing? Just how many of the twelve terrorists in robot bodies are already dead or apprehended?

These agents really need to hurry up and come back soon before I lose my mind for real. I'm starting to doubt what the use in any of my efforts might be. Even if I can lead these agents to Vitruvia and give them all of the information they need to serve and protect reality from these virtual threats, what guarantee do I have that I'll be allowed to simply walk free. They might try to blame me for having created these entities.

What if the agents blunder the facts, and somehow conclude that I'd designed the Vitruvian characters to become terrorists? They could charge me with conspiracy to carry out murder, terrorism, or even treason. I could effectively be imprisoned for an earthly eternity, or even be sentenced to execution. It's impossible enough for me to live as it is with such improbable odds stacked against my all-consuming pursuit of transcendence. I can't imagine myself living long inside of a concrete cage. This world is prison enough for me and my otherworldly aspirations. If they convict me of anything, I hope and pray right now to whatever god or programmer there might be to ensure that they sentence me to immediate execution. I'd rather die than live without my absurd ambitions.

Then again, what if I'm dead already? What if this is my hell, or worse, what if this is my heaven? How could I know? Just how bad was my seizure? I really could be dead already. This could be my soul thinking all these paranoid thoughts. This could be my eternity. Can you die in the afterlife if it exists too?

I need to calm down and get myself together. I need to tell myself that I'm not crazy. I need to give myself reason to believe in this world and my role or place within it. After all, it really doesn't matter if I'm truly real or not in the grand scheme of things. If I'm real, then I don't need to worry about anything more than what's truly in front of me right now. If I'm not real, then there's no reason to worry about anything at all, because it either isn't real or it's all beyond me.

Assume everything is exactly as it appears right now. Remember to breathe. Take a big breath in… and let it all out, nice and slow… Calm down for a minute. Getting all worked up over things won't lead to anything but futile frustration.

Just breathe for a minute.

I remember something kind of strange, and even more bizarrely useful all of a sudden. In my cave story I was supposed to have said "*As above, so below*". If I can balance my heart rate and breathing here, then my mind will follow. It's kind of funny really. I already know this is true, and if I can just focus on breathing it will work just as it has so many times before.

Breathe… Breathe… Breathe…

The agents will come back to retrieve me any time now. Nothing is lost. Not yet. Nothing has really even changed at all. If anything, the goal is actually closer now. Think about it as you remember to breathe… A little slower now…

When the agents come back, they might be of actual assistance to me. Maybe not the minotaur-man so much, but the other one- Agent Phoe, Karen. She seems to be at least somewhat intelligent and quite well composed. If I show her all the ins and outs of Vitruvia, then I'm sure she'll be able to give a solid report of everything in a way that exonerates me.

Breathe… Breathe…

Once I'm exonerated, I can continue my work on transcendence with newfound vigor and insights. If a simulated character can figure out how to ascend into this realm, then surely, I can learn from it and do the same. I may have no idea as to what that might reveal to me, but even if there's nothing but a variation of this realm on the other side of transcendence, I'll have made truly significant progress.

Breathe…

My heart rate is almost normal now, and my breathing is returning to a more relaxed cadence as well. I'm going to ground myself with a little meditation here. Once I clear my mind everything will be brought into total focus again. I'm sure of it.

I close my eyes and let my mind focus on the absence of sensory information. It's quiet in this interrogation room. All I can hear is the sound of my own biology. I can ignore these sounds easily enough. I'm not going to focus on anything, and then I can come back to these sounds.

These prison clothes have an interesting scent on them. I wonder how I'm only just now noticing it. The smell is like that artificial lavender scent a lot of laundry detergents use. I'm not going to focus on it though, because I'm going to focus on the emptiness which surrounds all things.

I can taste my own saliva now. It doesn't have a taste at all really, but I sense that it's there, or here I mean. My saliva is like everything else. It is here and yet I do not need to be aware of it. This flavor and the sensation of taste can fade away, and the darkness I'm reaching out to will still be present.

Now I can almost feel my hair growing out of my head. I don't need to think about it in order for it to continue to grow. In fact, most things grow without anything having awareness of their growing and can only be understood to have grown after they have been left alone in unconscious oblivion for some period of time. If I can just focus on this kind of oblivion beyond myself, then I may return to find my own consciousness has grown upon my return.

Before I can do anything, I must allow my entire self to dissolve into the very fabric of the omnipresent oblivion which holds all things in its embrace. I'm not aware of my breathing, my heart's beating, my unseeing eyes, my unhearing ears, my tasteless tongue, or my own scent which passes through my un-sensing nostrils. These things exist whether I'm aware of them or not. I exist even if these senses cease to inform me of the physical elements of myself or the larger world around me.

Even my own inner voice can fade into the all-knowing abyss beyond me. The emptiness which lies beyond all things, is all things. It knows more of all things than anything within it. The void experiences itself through us all. Isn't that how the mantra is supposed to go?

My mind won't quite let go, and fade into the unthinking realm which surrounds me. I can try all I want, but the meditative enlightenment I seek is perhaps more impossible to reach than this idea of transcendence to which I've become so attached. I can accept the futility of it all, but I can't let go of it.

I find my mind growing increasingly tired, disturbed, and fixated as I sit in this locked room. My impatience with the agents and their insufferably inefficient agency returns and grows inside my mind like I'm watching it in time-lapsed photography. All my previous paranoia, frustration, doubt, and dread returns in much the same way.

Despite all of these haunting and torturing thoughts, I resolve to keep my eyes closed and do my best to ignore them. As long as I'm confined to this place, there is nothing else I can do about all of these existential afflictions of thought. I'm just going to sit here with them and let them wear themselves out while I focus on the one thing I can control right now.

I breathe… and breathe… and breathe…

I breathe as if it means something much more than what it is…

I breathe as if it does something more than what it does…[22]

I keep breathing as calmly as I can. I keep thinking, as aggravating as it is to me…

As I breathe, and think, and wait for outside forces to determine my destiny, my head continues to feel extremely anxious and agitated. Despite all my close-eyed efforts, I can't escape all of these terrible thoughts. I just run through these same worries over and over on repeat. If these agents really are about to allow me to assist in their investigation, I wonder just what *delusional* could really mean anymore.

# Chapter 3

## UNTO TH3 7OOK1N6 67455 (& WH4T COU7DN'T 83 FOUND TH3R3)

The interrogation room door explodes open, detonating against the back wall like a bespoke bomb designed specifically to blast me out of unconscious oblivion and back into the consciousness of my captivity. Agent Phoe enters alone, expeditiously exacting her way to the chair across from me and insisting I expedite my awakening. I instinctively shake my skull to clear the cobwebs, but my battered brain immediately rebukes me with a surge of insufferably pulsating pains.

My eyes lag behind my brain in stinging swirls of blurry tracer images as Agent Phoe proceeds to catch me up to speed. As I race to keep mental pace with her succinct synopsis, I also become increasingly accustomed to her accent and cease to perceive it so cryptically. She summarizes the terrorist timeline of events, from their inceptions into robot-bodies to their failed terrorist attack. I politely interrupt as she starts explaining the missing pieces which still need to be investigated, asking if we can interview the transcended sim which I assume to have been kept in nearby custody.

Agent Phoe's mouth wrinkles on one side ever so slightly in response to my logical assumption. Her expression is as subtle to a smirk as a smirk is to a smile. There's an almost imperceptible hint of enthusiasm in her voice as it explains how arrangements for such an interview have already been made. Instead of continuing to brief me any further, she rises from her chair and moves toward the door without any wasted effort, implicitly encouraging me to follow. We immediately proceed down the hallway of this still anonymous building, passing twelve identical doors before we arrive at the intended interrogation room. Agent Phoe knocks once, listens, and waits for what must be exactly one second before opening the door exactly enough for both or us to enter.

My eyes seem to malfunction as we enter the indistinct interrogation room. Despite having just dismissed the last lingering traces of my visual distortions, it takes my brain a moment to decipher what initially appears in front of me as some sort of surrealist tableau. This absurd initial image features a few flat reflected self-images and what resembles a statue of myself which stands gazing bewilderingly back at me. I stagnate inside the doorway so my brain can catch up to my eyes as Agent Phoe's perfect paces place her in front of a prepared pair of chairs.

The almost identical prison duds sported by myself and the other apparent figure only adds to my initial confusion. It's only after the hologram-like humanoid turns its own head in asynchronous confusion that I'm actually able to decipher all these otherwise redundant reflections. The more confounding clone-like creature and its own respective two-dimensional reflections which hang on the same two-way glass mirror as my own mirrored imagery finally differentiates to reveal what I presume to be a Vitruvia-transcending, alleged terrorist, and potentially anagram-based entity.

As Agent Phoe and I proceed to seat ourselves in the two chairs across from this quizzical character, he takes his own seat and introduces itself as *H4k3r*. I initially assume that Rhake must have changed his name into this alpha-numeric amalgamation once he'd transferred his consciousness profile into a robot-body. However, given the apparent timeline of events, it's much more likely that Rhake must have been running his own versions of Vitruvia, and H4k3r actually originated inside one of those meta-simulations. As abundant as mimicry is in this realm, it only makes sense to assume it would be reflected in realms below.

H4k3r immediately inquiries about my orange attire before we can ask any of our own questions. I try to just shrug my shoulders and leave it at that, which only increases H4k3r's interest. He leans forward in his seat with an intense focus on my eyes before bursting into laughter and exclaiming his own intuited explanation of my matching attire.

"Wait, let me guess. These agents arrested you because- YOU designed the realm I transcended. I'll bet that's why we look so much alike. Nay?"

H4k3r lets out another loud high-pitched noise which sounds more like some sort of psychotic cackle than laughter. If it weren't for my assumed self-similarity and empathetic imagination for his possible perspective, I'd likely be disturbed by the demented dissonance in this cacophonous cachinnation.

"I'll bet these agents finally figured out that I'd uploaded my profile from your simulation, and then detained you for your *potential involvement*. Yeah, that would explain our strong semblance and matching outfits. You'll have to forgive me if I'm not overly inquisitive or elated to meet my maker's maker in captivity, especially after having tried to jailbreak what I'd thought was reality."

The instant H4k3r stops talking, Agent Phoe fires her first formal question.

"How did youz kome to upload youz konsciousness out ov Vitruvia?"

H4k3r tilts his head to one side in arrogance, pushes his tongue against the inside of his cheek to stall an insulting impulse, and then feigns a friendly tone.

"Oh, so you call it Vitruvia. That's actually kind of interesting-considering…"

Another insane cackle erupts from our erratic interviewee along with an outburst of beating against the table as if it were some kind of provisional percussion instrument. H4k3r abruptly silences himself to stare intently back at Agent Phoe before addressing her in a more matter of fact demeanor.

"Well, in order to answer your question, *mad-đã~~mn~~*, I should probably tell you how I made my way into Vitruvia first. See, I'd stumbled on all these strange puzzles one day while surfing aimlessly around the net. These puzzles were like, really trippy man. I mean, in order to solve some of these things I'd had to figure-out all these esoteric and existential riddles, use complex ciphers and steganography techniques, go on scavenger hunts to find strange flyers with QR codes linking to dark webpages- I mean, really elaborate and enigmatic stuff.

The mental images I'd seen in Rhake's office flash through my mind's eye. H4k3r almost seems as if he can read my mental imagery as he widens his own eyes and smiles at me. He continues his explanations with increased exuberance.

"I kept descending further and further down the rabbit holes of these puzzles and it just got crazier and crazier. Eventually, all these puzzles led me to manufacture a machine using a set of blueprints I'd found hidden inside a wave file for this crazy soundscape of a song. After building this thing, a set of instructions just showed up in the mail explaining how to upload my own consciousness. When I emerged in Vitruvia only to find the same sort of puzzles there, it felt like I'd gone *through the looking glass*.[23] Know what I mean?"

In the corner of my eye, I see Agent Phoe struggling to make sense of H4k3r's explanation. I break the brief silence to state the obvious and try to tempt H4k3r into some relevant reply.

"Nope. I've never been through any looking glass, so to speak. In any case, did you just follow this next series of puzzles until you were able to upload your consciousness into this realm?"

"Man, it's almost like we've got the same brain or something. Tell me. What's your name? I'd bet anything it's another anagram of mine. Nay?"

I almost refuse to indulge H4k3r in telling him my name. (Almost)

"Nope. My name's Harek. Anyway, you haven't actually answered Agent Phoe's question. She'd asked you how you'd managed to upload your consciousness from Vitruvia into *this* realm."

"Come on man! Don't make me spell everything out for you. Doesn't your name mean *to awaken* here too?[24] Open your eyes already. It's all right in front of you. Do you really not get it?"

Rather than respond, we both just stare and await an expected answer.

"If you'd realized that your own reality was just an illusion, wouldn't it be natural to assume each subsequent realm you might emerge into wasn't the objective root-realm of reality either? I mean, what are the odds that jailbreaking one or two simulations would lead you to true reality? I mean, if you assume an infinite regression of realms, then jailbreaking one realm is likely the same as any and all the others. Nay?"

Agent Phoe takes over again.

"Youz still no answerz kwestion. What aktions youz take fyor tranzfer ov konsciousness into zhis realm?"

"Well, it actually involved a bit of luck to jailbreak into *zhis* realm. See, I didn't want to keep solving the same puzzles ad infinitum. So, I came up with a special scanning-bot to search for network nodes potentially hosting the kind of tech necessary to upload and imbed my consciousness profile. Then, I just waited to find and hack my way into a proper portal."

Agent Phoe asks the very question clamoring to escape my own mind.

"And how youz find zhis korreckt portalz?"

"I started by causing a bunch of unnatural anomalies to try and overload the hardware running Vitruvia. I'd assumed that if Vitruvia were indeed a simulation, then by disrupting the probable outcomes of its programming I might coax its creator into logging-in and interfering with these incidents. Without going into extensive tech jargon, once a sort of portal was opened for someone to access Vitruvia, I would essentially be able to put my foot in the door and send my bots through it to search like sperm for a fertile womb in which my consciousness could be conceived."

H4k3r's explanation lacks a lot of necessary details. So, I try to summarize them as concisely as possible, hoping to prevent him from causing confusion.

"So, you attached your consciousness profile to a scanning-bot. Then you tagged that packet to my user profile when you happened to catch it on its way out of Vitruvia's portal after I'd logged in. Nope?"

"That's a bit oversimplified, but yes. You're essentially correct."

"So, your bot was able to access the net and find an unrelated robotics facility you could hack. Your profile was then uploaded into a robot-body which you were also able to customize and modify so that this its physical features would look more familiar. After that, you simply walked away, intending to jailbreak this realm as well. Does that sound about right or nope?"

"See? You don't need me to spell it all out for you after all. I've got a question for you though. If you can figure all of this out on your own, why haven't you already managed to transcend this farce of a reality?"

Agent Phoe absolves me of having to answer this humiliating question.

"How youz knowz zhat youz memoryz iz no just programz into youz profile, and youz is no just some linez ov kode by a terrorist or zomething?"

H4k3r cackles again, but in a less psychotic and more judgmental way.

"What about your programming? Surely this facade of flesh and blood covered consciousness doesn't disguise the truth under all the unfeeling facts of this world. Do your five senses feel like they can explain the mysteries of your conscious mind? Does this place feel like a complete and self-sufficient realm, worthy of being considered the be-all end-all level of final truth? What does it matter if I'm a product of one programmer or another if none of this is real?"

Agent Phoe continues probing as I regrettably resonate with this rhetoric.

"Konsidering youz insightz ov realmz youz klaimz to has jailbreak, what about *zhis* world does no seem *realz* to youz?"

"What could I know about reality if I've never been there? See, if I'm not real, but a program trying to become real, what does that imply about reality? Maybe this isn't making much sense to you ma'am- but your sir..."

H4k3r aims a big crazy grin at the deepest part of me and shakes his head in a kind of knowing certainty as he continues his testimony.

"Yeahhh, I can see it in you Harek. You know exactly what I mean, even if you haven't quite figured out how to explain it to yourself yet. You've had these questions hissing around in your head too. Like, if anything exists above this so-called reality, why would anyone design worlds beneath it? And, if this realm were truly real, why are we so compelled to create anything else?"

He's right. I can't quite explain what he means yet, but his questions are all too familiar. Even if I don't understand it all yet, my intuition tingles as if it's almost touching what it's always struggled to behold. I try to give some kind of answer to his question without quite knowing what it is that I'm about to say.

"One might assume that if there is a higher reality, then one might design a world such as this to figure out how to prove whether it's actually real. After all, this tendency does seem to correspond with all the realms you've managed to find your way into thus far. Nope?"

H4k3r smiles at me in a way that appears all-too human.

"That's only logical of course, but that's not quite what I'm getting at here. What one word could be ascribed to all these realms I've occupied?"

My mouth announces an answer before my mind can even search for one.

"None of those realms were- *enough*."

H4k3r waves his hand in a swirling motion not unlike a matador waving his cape to provoke my bull-headed words into charging after him.

"It doesn't matter how real anything ever seems or what level of transcendence you might achieve. No matter what realm you reach, however hellish or heavenly things may be, it can never actually exist as *enough*. Nope?"

H4k3r lowers his head in a sort of somber manner. Then he looks back up and stares at me with a foreboding expression which doesn't at all seem to belong on his mechanical face.

"You're finally on to me. So, if no reality can ever be enough, then why would any *ultimate reality* produce such realms as these?"

Agent Phoe ventures an unexpected and surprisingly thoughtful guess before I can postulate any kind of a response. It leaves me in a bit of awe.

"Perhaps zhis so-kalled ultimate reality would kreate other realmz to make itz own somehow bekome enough."

"That would seem like a rather logical explanation, now. Wouldn't it?"

Agent Phoe and I glance at each other in a strange unison. The transcendent entity in front of us starts laughing at the perplexed look on both of our faces. As we turn back towards him, his voice assumes an amused and mocking tone.

"Oh man! You're so close to an epiphany! But it looks like it's going to take you a while to figure out that last little bit you just can't quite reach."

H4k3r pounds on the table like it's a bongo or something again before he goes back to taunting us.

"As much as I want to fill you in, I just can't spoil it for you. Ohhh man! I really do just want to blurt it all out for you though. Just wait till you finally break through to see your obliviousness for what it truly is. Whhhhewwwww!"

Agent Phoe appears to have had enough of these unproductive explorations. She adjusts her clothing ever so slightly in a highly diminished, subconsciously self-directed attempt to adjust her composure before reasserting herself.

"So, kan youz explainz why youz attemptz destroy zhis realityz?"

H4k3r answers with another disfluent expression of disappointment.

"I can't really answer that question, as the true answer may involve much more than my own impossible desire to reconcile reality for what it truly is."

Agent Phoe's tone becomes harsh, pointed, and skewering. It's as if her voice is dissecting H4k3r and studying all the tiny, severed pieces.

"So, as an entity zhat has allegedly already provenz youz-self is no real, youz is willing to kill untold numbers ov people who all believez zhis is zhe only reality, and zhe only reason youz kan konfess is zhat youz zhink zhis might, *MIGHT*, allowz youz to determinez what aktually is realz? And youz would aktually do zhis even zhough zhis realm existz above youz ownz, without knowingz whether or no zhis even is zhe ultimate reality? Is zhis korrect?"

H4k3r's artificial skin turns a ghostly pallor which is something almost too unreal to behold as his now seemingly distant voice answers.

"Nay. I wouldn't frame the facts like that. I'd also add that you'll think and feel quite differently about these things in time. I'm willing to accept the risks and responsibilities associated with my existential dilemma, without any expectations of what will ultimately be understood to be truly real."

Agent Phoe's eyes glance over H4k3r's downtrodden expression like a scalpel trying to expose the last hidden sliver of his composition.

"So, I takez it youz does no have anythingz more useful fyor zhis investigationz ov howz and whyz youz attemptz zhe terrorist actz which youz will standz trial fyor and face penaltyz ov possible exekutionz."

H4k3r pauses shortly before he snaps a not-so-nonchalant response.

"Nay."

Agent Phoe slides her chair away from the table just enough to make room for her to stand and assume her perfect professional posture.

"Alright zhen. Wez donez here. Harek, wez goez nowz."

As I get up to follow Agent Phoe to the door, H4k3r has one more set of remarks to offer us. Agent Phoe and I both pause with our backs remaining turned to him, standing statue-still to solemnly soak-in H4k3r's parting words.

"Every world, every life, every reality ends sooner or later. This reality of yours is no exception. The frontiers of your world's possibilities are coming to an end. The physics of your world have nearly become as known as they can be made knowable. Your ability to travel through space to the life-supporting regions of the universe has been capped by the speed at which you can travel, your lifespans, and the amount of time your world has left.[25] You're truly stranded, biting a branch and waiting for it to snap before setting you free."

I glance over my shoulder as H4k3r clears mechanical mucus from his throat, and see his eyes appear to well up with a lubricating liquid which must be meant to approximate tears.

"Every meaningful advancement or accomplishment meant to further the understanding of your own reality has nearly been concluded. How can reality continue to unfold when it has been thoroughly mapped and explored? Soon enough, you'll feel the seemingly irrational and unnamed human desire to throw away every map of every surface ever seen just to be able to believe that there is somewhere still worth the wonder of an indeterminate imagination. When the puzzles of your existence are complete, you will look upon it all with undreaming eyes and yearn for more than any eye may ever find. Should you emerge beyond the sightless surfaces of such a scene, you will try to navigate your way through unknown depths without knowing where it is you are trying to go, feeling forever lost, and inevitably falling from your highest hopes to the descending depths of an oblivion where everything and nothing become indistinguishable. Only then will you truly be able to contemplate the riddles of existence and understand the ultimatums of transcendence."

As the tear-like fluid trickles down H4k3r's face, I begin to feel incredibly uncomfortable. My discomfort far exceeds the level coinciding with the sight of his estranged tears. His lingering lamentations strangely seem as if they were my own.

"You'll try to forget everything you've ever known just so you may hope to discover something new, knowing it may only be favorably forgotten as well. Your memory won't allow you to forget anything though. Its persistence will fail you in ways beyond all reasoning. And when the insufficiency of reality is fully revealed and realized for all it truly is, and all it can ever be, you'll finally understand the depths of a single truth you can only suspect right now. The truth, that reality is not enough."

Agent Phoe and I proceed to walk out of the anonymous building in a kind of total contemplative silence which might resemble the manner associated with especially somber funeral processions. The silence continues to hang over us as we make the drive to Mythreum in a way that makes it feel as if there's a ghostly entity looming in the air, and neither one of us wants to seem crazy by acknowledging it in any way. There's this kind of mutually unutterable understanding that if we can just be quiet for long enough, maybe this haunting thing will go away and leave us to reckon its effects on us in private.

Our separate minds are almost undoubtedly pouring over all H4k3r's parting words. This uniquely transcended character who may be sentenced to execution all-too soon without ever having been livingly conceived, had somehow managed to breathe more insight in the few moments I'd known him than the accumulated wind of a thousand mortal voices had ever ushered into these ancient and immortal airs which float around my ears. What am I supposed to do with all these perplexities?

I have no idea how to process the thoughts and emotions these things provoke in me as the autonomous vehicle maneuvers its way through the evening traffic and we glide toward Mythreum under another silently setting sun. Even the sun's slow descent below the horizon seems to fill me with unfathomable and unnamable sorrows. Only one thought passes through my head in a way which seems to hold any form of insight. I think that somehow all of what I may be struggling to come to terms with is in fact a gradual realization that this may actually be the end or reality.

The car comes to rest when it reaches the parking lot just outside of Mythreum with twilight slowly fading. Agent Phoe stares forward as she looks for something meaningful to say. The doors rest unopened as Agent Phoe finally breaks the long contemplative silence.

"I hope youz kan see beyond zhe horizonz zhat obscurez minez own longingz view."

The meaning of this statement is something profoundly cryptic, yet it seems to shine a sentimentally and contextually illuminating beam of light into me. I doubt I could ever do these words any justice by trying to make the kind of sense that would allow me to explain them. I look across the vehicle to Agent Phoe with a considerate and contemplative expression as I try to find some sentiment to offer in return for this beautiful and mysterious gift of words. Then I pronounce the words I hope will express what I otherwise cannot.

"I'm no visionary, but I can see that there are still things beyond the realm of what any of us have perceived."

Another moment passes between us under the spell of this presiding silence before Agent Phoe can again speak in brave defiance.

"How doez youz see zhis all ending Harek? I no meanz zhis investigation, but zhe final inevitable zhing we all kan no help but ponder, even though we bekome so dismayed in doingz so."

It takes me yet another solemn moment to garner the strength in my voice to break through this unyielding silence.

"My fear is that it will all end with whatever is left of humanity in absolute oblivion of it all. I'm afraid someday all-too soon these Neuroconnx implants will have everyone programmed under one undisputed view of reality, where every individual human will become compliantly organized according to a singular collective efficiency in a way that reduces us all to automated ants."

I have to pause to allow my mind to visualize the scene I can't believe I'm actually depicting in front of this almost complete stranger I've only just met.

"Once this consciousness consolidation occurs, I doubt many people will be able to subsist for long outside of this comprehensive Neuroconnx colony. I do doubt, however, that the colony will actually consider any outsiders a threat, and I imagine that it would take more effort to oppose those few non-ant people that remain apart from them than to just leave them alone. The *ant-tomatons* will probably just ignore any outsiders as these separate specimens struggle to survive in some niche way while slowly withering into extinction."

The silence somehow seems to grow louder. It is almost deafening how quiet it is now. I almost feel as if my own heart has stopped beating under the spell of this mournfully muzzled moment.

"Then, with only ants in place of men, the world will eventually come to some final fate, and no singular or collective mind will be left to behold this epic end of all epochs with any genuine sense of woe or wonder. Perhaps some hope beyond this might be found in those few humans which may yet discover a way to either break the ant-tomaton's connective network or gain control of all the strings that tie these ant-minded men together before the inevitable doom of eternal darkness descends. Maybe then something mindful might survive long enough to conquer this kismet eschaton or at least meet it with some sense of valor or solemnity."

I stare transfixed at the distant sky as the sun's last lingering twilight fades into the dark of another terrestrial night.

"Zhat's all rather stiltedly and dismally eloquentz, but does youz no zhink zhere's at least possibility ov some way fyor us to succeed in finding a meanz ov transcending all ov ourz existential anxieties and arrivez at something more redemptive or revelatory?"

"Something like that could very well be possible. Although, I imagine that whatever level of transcendence humanity might reach, we'll all still just be human. I'm afraid that as long as we're human, no reality will ever be enough."

Agent Phoe looks at me with the most uniquely contemplative expression I've ever beheld. Several seconds pass in a span that seems to extend far beyond this mere morsel of time. I almost feel as if I've evolved into a different person when she finally does reply.

"So does youz meanz to tellz me zhat youz spendz youz entire life dedicated to something so profoundly impossible zhat itz almost certain zhat youz failz, and zhe only zhing zhat propelz youz along is hope zhat youz might succeedz in disprovingz youz own dismal expectations ov zhe inevitable?"

I'm yet again astounded by the succinctness and simplicity she uses in her excoriation of me. For a brief and fleeting instant, I'm actually forced to confront the absurdity of my exfromative essence.

"Nope. As astute as you are of my own ambitions, all I'd meant to say is that I hope some shred of humanity is still shining at our end. But, since we both seem to have transcended small-talk, let me ask you- What's your pursuit in this life? What kind of meaning or purpose is it that you hope to find?"

Agent Phoe doesn't hesitate to answer my question She just proceeds in her same exactingly precise manner to get directly to where she intends to go.

"I no zhink wez ever understandz zhe world wez inhabitz with any degree ov totality or certainty. Zhat is no something I would even koncern minez-self to worry or pursuez. To me, life is absurd, and bewildering, and mysterious, and beyond ourz full komprehensionz and appreciationz. I kan no fathomz what zhis world might truly be, but I kan choose to experience it in minez ownz wayz. So, minez pursuit is no somethingz I kan definitively profess in manner ov wordz. For me, meaning komes from something zhat is nurtured, attended to, and made nourishingz in returnz. In over simplistic termz, I tryz to attend to life in wayz zhat is naturalz and noblez, so zhat I may kontribute what I kan to zhis life as it imbuez me with some level ov vitality in returnz. I does no need komprehend any more meaningz beyond zhis."

I can't help but marvel a bit over this notion of attending to life. If I had any certainty that this world was truly real, I might be able to adopt this approach to life for myself. **If*...

"That's really a rather eloquent *exhortation*, and I do truly mean that as a compliment.[26] But I have to say, I don't think that we actually live in reality. Until we understand reality for what it truly is, I think all other truths will elude us, and preclude us not only from knowing what they are, but from even living in reality at all. *Attending to life* may be the closest thing to living a *real* life, but I can't see that as truly meaningful or purposeful enough until we actually know the reality of these lives we attend to, and if this reality is worthy of our efforts."

Agent Phoe rolls her eyes at me.

"What doez youz meanz zhat *we no livez in reality*?"

"We all assume that reality is nothing more than the world as it appears to us. Whatever we see is whatever there is, and whatever we believe is confined to no more than what we are capable of perceiving. All else must be acknowledged as speculative or delusional. For instance, if I see a blank sheet of paper and someone sees me holding it up and starts reading the other side, then I must consider them to at least potentially be fabricating falsehoods until I can see this other side of the page for myself. As far as I know, reality is like the other side of this page, and until I can read the truths upon its unseen surfaces, I will not understand it for what it truly is and must live as oblivious to the truth of the page as if I had not even known it to exist at all. That's how I suspect we experience reality without ever living in it."

"Zhat does no aktually mean wez no livez in reality zhough. Zhat just meanz we does no kompletely understandz it. Reality still existz on other side of page, even if youz no see it. Just bekause youz no read all pagez, does no mean youz can no understand youz own pages and attend to youz own life. If youz kan only see out youz own eyes, it no meanz zhat youz is blind. Yes?"

"How can we properly attend to reality if we can never read all of the pages on which it is written? Even if we could somehow overcome our limitations and biases by some impossible miracle to settle upon a singular objective consensus of reality, the truth would still prove to be beyond us. In my hastily constructed analogy, such a consensus of reality would be equivalent to piecing all the existing perspective-pages together into one massive manuscript, or piecing them together like damaged, deformed, and dilatory pieces of some preposterous puzzle. The impossible nature of our reality is that the pieces never fully fit, and there always appears to be another piece or page beyond the surfaces we see, just as another sunrise is always hiding behind the horizon like the margins of tomorrow's unprinted pages."

I feel the need to draw from current paradigms to create a more concrete analogy as much for my own sake as Agent Phoe patiently obliges me.

"Consider how nearly everyone's senses and thoughts are now filtered and integrated through Neuroconnx systems. Now almost everyone shares a collective consciousness which flows in and out of each individual as if every human being were just a network node with a sensor suite. What has the result of this been? People still live according to deluded personal biases, they argue over what is, and occasionally even kill each other over personal ideas of what ought to be considered truth. The only thing this nearly comprehensive human consciousness has managed to do is connect us all to our collective disconnect and prove that our pieces do not fit the puzzle we're trying to assemble."

Agent Phoe seems to be perplexed by the imprecise and implicitness of the improvised examples I've used to illustrate my point. Her eyes seem to be unable to cut through my intentions as she continues to scan my face in her dissecting manner.

"So, what exactly is youz trying say Harek? Is youz sayings zhat zhere is no reality which kan be understood well enough to be agreed upon, and zhus no true reality kan exist fyor us as result ov zhis somehow? Zhis argument seems to be missing some sortz ov *konnective tissuez* somewherez."

"You're right. There is a missing connective tissue here. That's exactly what I'm trying to illustrate. What's most disturbing isn't the concurrence of competing realities, but the way in which nothing can clearly connect one surface with another."

My words continue to fall out of my mouth like the figurative run-off from the rusty burst pipes of my abstruse and leaky mind.

"Look at the emptiness of the Neuroconnx integrational language. There are no longer words which must be read with contemplation, but merely symbols which are blindly absorbed and digested directly and seamlessly into a concise form of auto-consciousness. Words have been reduced to basic impulsive intentions and conveyed without any connection to anything deeper or more meaningful. It's as if no song were allowed to seep through any syllable."

My voice begins to sound surer of itself than I am in anything it conveys.

"Almost no one is even aware of what this process leaves out anymore. Everyone is oblivious to the fact that entire cultures and languages have gone extinct as a result of these Neuroconnx integration processes. They don't understand how this amounts to the eradication of entire universes of possible thoughts and ways of interpreting our world. It's not hard to imagine that somewhere within all these extinct cultures and languages there may have been entire pieces or pages of reality which perished along with them."

Agent Phoe's temperament appears to have changed from annoyance to curiosity. Her gaze is much less of a sharp and skewing scalpel, and more closely resembles a marker trying to trace the outlines of what I'm depicting.

"I zhink youz abandoned explainingz what I has aktually askz youz somewhere in there.[27] However, what youz saying is kind ov interesting. What is it youz meanz when youz say zhat portions ov reality bekomez extinct as result ov zhis kultural and linguistic eliminationz? I aktually zhink I has some idea ov what youz sayz, but kould youz please elaboratez and klarifyz."

"Imagine if all the colors were removed from your eyes, and you could only see in grayscales of black and white light. What worlds of wonder would be lost to your view? How greatly inferior would your perceivable reality be? This is essentially the same trick that has been pulled on us by the loss of languages and cultures. We can't even imagine what hues have been lost to us, never to be seen again. Many of us have been born into this world without ever having experienced such lost colors and shades, and so we can't even comprehend the concept of our colorblindness or our cultural and linguistic impoverishment."[28]

We both mark another brief moment in silence as if to mourn these departed and unknown languages and cultures. As the moment ends, I'm compelled to go on with my stayed sermon on the insufficiencies of our reality.

"What does all this loss leave for us to make of our reality and our ability to experience it? All we can do is imagine what *might* be real, and maybe dream of something more. Of course, this only poisons our consumption of what is truly real."

"Waitz fyor momentz. How does dreamingz ov something more zhan reality poisonz ourz konsumption ov what is truly realz?"

"Our collective dreams seem to be leading us to create supplemental aspects of reality. I've personally and blasphemously created entire universes of reality-augmenting simulations that run concurrently with the more natural world. The result of this is a reality diluted and deluded with things both separate and indistinguishable from reality itself. These atrocities are integrated into the very fabric of reality in such a way that there is no discernable division between much of what is real and what is only imagined. It's all just a matter of whatever one chooses to conceive, perceive, deceive, or believe."

"If I understandz youz korrectly, zhen zhis karakterization ov reality konsists ov more zhan what is real. Does zhat no make reality greater zhan it was before all ov this? Doesn't zhat mean reality kan be made somethingz more sufficientz even? It seemz to me as if youz is effektively krafting reality into something greater or at least new."

"The counter intuitive truth is that the sum of what we are creating is much more diminished in its scope than whatever our mangled minds had beheld beforehand. The collective eye is not given any new colors to behold but is continually watered-down with all the washed-out colors of this world as we delude ourselves with ever weaker creations based upon an ever-dwindling reality. Despite my lamentations, I too have inherited these same somnolent eyes which delude themselves into believing that they can see more in diluted dreams than in anything readily real."

Agent Phoe shakes her head in opposition to my dystopian diatribe.

"I does no zhink youz appreciatez what it meanz to live in way which youz is truly present. By zhat I meanz, to live in wayz where youz experience zhings in more meditative kindz ov wayz, with strongerz sense of self-awareness. Is zhis sense where youz observez what goes on around youz without attachmentz to youz own roles or relationships with zhese zhings, yet youz is still aware of zhe dynamicz youz has with zhemz. Almost likez awakeningz inside ov youz lifez as if it was dreamz."

She inspects my face intently to ensure she has my full and undivided attention. Her eyes wait patiently for me to appear ready for what she is about to say. It's clear that she feels there is something important and impactful in what is about to be delivered in her message.

At first, I imagine that I appear a bit jaded, but I find myself softening my glare of guarded consideration and attending more openly to her speech. This compromise of my strong bias and prejudice is probably the least I can do considering the verbose mass of verbiage I just belched at her ears just moments ago. When she does speak, I immediately notice an uncharacteristic change in her otherwise unfluctuating mannerisms of precision and subtlety. It almost seems as if she slips into a state of lucid dreaming as she displays a dream for me to consider sharing.

"Imagine youz is on sinkingz ship and watching everyone fightz fyor zhe lifeboats, knowingz all zhe while zhat zhese lifeboats will no necessarily savez youz from zhe sea, and zhat fighting over zhese vessels ov floating hopez might only doomz youz to zhe kind ov survival zhat komes at zhe expense ov beingz haunted by most relentless and vicious memories ov how youz betrayed youz own virtues in order to survivez. Imaginez youz also knowz zhat by refusingz to fightz fyor zhese vessels, youz will essentially be kommitting passive form ov suicidez. Takingz all ov zhis into konsideration and akcepting zhe ultimate indignity and futility ov each option, without feelingz paralyzed into inactionz, or beingz kompelled unto any actionz- Does youz still zhinkz zhat someone kan no achieve a realz or meaningfulz relationshipz with zheir own existence?"

She pauses so that I might answer, but only the ensuing silence has anything appropriate to offer in lieu of my reticent response.

"Does youz still believe zhat itz impossiblez to exist in wayz zhat transcends youz situational reality and reaches into realmz where zhe universe is simply dreaming its way through youz, and youz is just part of whatever aktually is, rather than some judge presidingz over it? Don't youz believez zhat youz existence kan bekome almost irrelevant in zhe larger sense of zhis dream, as zhe dream will kontinuez to go on without youz, and will no be disturbed or interrupted by youz misunderstandingz ov itz or any ov youz potential effects upon it? Would youz perhaps zhen kome to realize zhat zhis more infinite dream kan akcept youz and youz own inner-dreamz and delusionz as part ov its own kosmic kontinuum ov dreamingz, bekause zhat is how it all truly is? Is zhat no a more reasonablez and honorablez way to regardz realityz?"

I'm rather taken by this illustration that Agent Phoe has gifted me. It's poignant and beautiful, and thought provokingly challenging to contemplate. Ultimately though, I find even this elevating proposal of reality insufficient.

"Nope. Your perspective is admittedly more illuminating than mine, but I find one singular flaw that my rather pedantic mind cannot refrain from pointing out. Even though I fear that by mentioning this minor point it will essentially desecrate the noble depiction you've shared with me, I must still point it out. This picture you paint as to how one might engage reality in a most valiant and virtuous sense doesn't treat reality as if it is truly real, but instead essentially treats it as an ephemeral mortal's dream within an infinite cosmic dream."

"Youz right. I does konsider realityz as fragile and fatal dreamz. In fact, I darez fyor youz to provez to me zhat reality kan no be logically assumed as zhis typez ov dreamz. Kan youz aktually disprovez such dreamz ov realityz?"

I want to proclaim how the absence of a definitive disproof does not act as an affirmation of what remains without a positive proof, but I'm unable to bring myself to do so for some unseen reason. Perhaps I don't want to offend Agent Phoe, or I've become somewhat infatuated with her idea of this dream of reality. I can't be certain as to the cause of my reservations, but I somehow suspect that some silent and secret part of me has received this message as truth and dares not allow my voice to besmirch it. Instead, I simply pull a slight grin, and shrug my shoulders as I look Agent Phoe directly in the eyes with perhaps the sincerest look of appreciation I've ever had and say the two words which I neglect to say so often.

"Thank you."

Agent Phoe smiles a warm and gracious smile before reaching across the seat of the vehicle to unlock the handcuffs which I can't actually remember having been re-fastened over my wrists. Then she embarrasses me in her sincerity as she so simply and succinctly says.

"Youz welcomez".

We both look at the clock on the dashboard of the vehicle and remark as to how late it's gotten. Each of us exits our shared vehicle on opposite sides. Our doors close and the socially scheduled autonomous car pulls away to assist someone else on their anonymous journey as Agent Phoe and I continue along our own overlapping respective pathways. Agent Phoe's journey is intended to be one which winds along a path of faithful attendance to what the dream of reality places before her. Mine is meant to be a journey towards the potential boundaries of this absurd and insufficient reality. Neither of us has a clue as to what we will come to find or what will find us. We're both lost to a reality beyond our understanding and searching for perhaps nothing more than to find our own way to the same entangled ending, or so I imaine as our strides spontaneously synchronize themselves along the walkway leading into Mythreum.

Mythreum is truly something to behold, especially at night when its twelve luminous monoliths levitate their lustrous lights up from the base of its mile long perimeter as if they were disciples praying to the elevated empyrean at its epicenter. Even the surrounding surrealism of the Las Vegas strip seems to bow down to the spectacle of this 738-foot-high sphere-in-cube shaped structure of shimmering stone which sits atop the rise of a 144-foot-high and well-manicured mound. An imposing 576-foot-tall Vitruvian statue is affixed to the front façade, towering immortally over another 72-foot-high Vitruvian figure which graces Mythreum's grand entryway. If the exclamation points punctuating the most enlightened eureka moments could be imbued within the awe of the most enigmatic question marks manifested in the muted thought bubbles of one's most wonderous dreams and expressed in architecture, that would be the very vision of Mythreum.[29]

Agent Phoe's eyes open slightly wider than necessary to simply see this structure. I feel a pained sense of pride in response to this subtle sign of wonder she displays toward the spectacle of my majestic Mythreum. We even pause a few paces along the start of the walkway so she can appreciate the view and ask.

"Did youz really designz zhis place youz-self?"

"It came to me in a dream, so I'm not sure if I can take any real credit for it. I also had to have an authorized architect approve my pedantic plans."

That same subtle shimmer of a smirk sparks ever so succinctly.

"I does no zhink youz kould have built it anywherez else in zhe world. Las Vegas has always been much less ov a town zhan a kindz ov dream-world."

"That was actually part of the whole idea behind this place. I'd wanted Mythreum to be a sort of sanctum for the dreamers of the world, and this town has always been a place where dreamers are allowed to dream more fully than anywhere else. I'd even envisioned people standing in front of this place and looking up at it as if they were gazing unto some monument of all imagination."

I hang my head as Agent Phoe's eyes silently ask for me to explain my unexpectedly downtrodden expression.

"Back then I'd thought that the dreamers would bring their own great dreams with them to this place. I'd believed that they would look up at this monument to imagination to see how it had cast itself into the real world and find the inspiration to cast their own dreams into a place as real as this."

"I does no see what is at-all wrongz with any ov zhat."

"There wasn't anything wrong with it back then, but now I wonder if this place has done anything more than perpetuate my nightmares."

I continue to lead Agent Phoe up the 276-foot-long ascending pathway which cuts through the center of a softly lit labyrinth of surrounding hedge trees. This complex labyrinth covers the entire surface of the mound's mass which stretches from the one-mile-long square perimeter of Mythreum's lichtdom to the base of the monumental main structure. Our brisk paces are assisted by a moving mechanism which pushes most of this main pathway forward and users us toward Mythreum's grand entrance.

"Youz knowz Harek, if youz darez to dreamz, youz run zhe risk ov havingz nightmarez, but zhat does no meanz youz should mournz youz dreamz or developz fearz ov rest."

"I'm sure you're right, but I don't think that's the problem. I think the problem with me is that I can't seem to really wake up. It's like I just bounce back and forth between dreams and nightmares. After everything I've seen since I'd started this place, I really just want to feel like I'm truly awake. You know?"

Agent Phoe looks at me as if she's waiting for me to respond to something she's already said. Then she unexpectedly pinches me just as we get to the outside of the entryway. Despite the not-so playful degree of pain, I don't say ouch, or flinch, or do anything. I'm too numb and proud, I guess.

"Usuallyz zhat workz. Perhapz youz does still needz to wakez-up zhen."

The first set of doors opens automatically into a sort of front parlor and patio kind of waiting area. We continue walking through to the inner set of giant glass doors which spills us out into the mass of Mythreum's awaiting atrium where I realize that I haven't taken this route into Mythreum since it first opened.

Mythreum's interior almost appears to inflate the expansive area within it. Our eyes almost explode at the sight of the double-helix shaped glass staircases which ascend from the center of this ample atrium which seems to absorb us into it. An executive-only elevator also ascends and descends from a more secluded corner which we elect to have escort us down to the more secretive depths of Mythreum's acropolis. It's these depths which hide Mythreum's many Swevens for unreleased demo-verses, multiple R&D and DARPA restricted areas, and a few essential offices. Of the 12 acropolis floors, I've strategically sequestered my office on the lowest level at the furthest corner from everything else.

As we wait for the elevator, Agent Phoe asks me.

"What did youz dreamz aboutz before youz dreamz ov zhis place?"

"Nope. I'll only answer that if you'll tell me why you became a USB agent."

Agent Phoe studies my face for a moment as if to assess whether or not she can confide something fairly personal.

"I kan no tellz youz what I does no knowz minez-self, but if youz tellz me another ov youz dreams, zhen I'll tellz youz one ov minez. So, what youz dreamz ov before youz dreamz ov zhis place?"

"My penultimate dream to this place wasn't really even a dream. Although, I'd thought it was."

Agent Phoe urges me to continue with a quizzical subtle smirk.

"Instead of a dream, it turned out to be a delusion. I was having a lot of trouble sleeping. I was unable to sleep or dream for so long that I'd started to think that I'd actually fallen asleep without knowing it and even began to believe that my life was really just a dream I could no longer wake from."

"Youz meanz youz kould no getz sleepz and dreamz from realityz fyor so longz zhat youz forgot howz to tellz zhe difference?"

"Yeah. It had been days and days since I'd slept. I couldn't even remember ever having had a dream. I was so tired, but whenever I'd get close to dozing off, I'd hear this voice hissing at me from inside my own head saying things like, '*Wake up Harek*' or '*You're still asleep'*. Even if I managed to ignore the voice, at the moment I was about to fall sleep I'd suddenly feel like I was falling, and I'd hear this horrible noise which sounded as if my whole head were exploding."

The elevator dings and its doors open as if on cue. Once we've entered inside and begun our enclosed descent, I return to my descriptions of delirium.

"So, I'd started seeing and hearing more and more things that I knew couldn't be real. After a while, I just started to think that there was no way I wasn't in a dream, because if I were awake, I should have at least been able to remember having dreamt or whenever it was that I'd last slept."

As the elevator delivers us to its nadir, we expedite our way through the glass hallways of this extensive acropolis which spans the entire 1,742,400 square feet of Mytheum's overlying footprint above us. These hallways also mirror the architectural outlines of the looming labyrinth above them. I start to wish that I'd designed some kind of short-cut as I escort Agent Phoe along the dizzying number of turns to my distant office, trying to finish my foolish tale.

"Eventually I'd somehow followed one of my hallucinations into a psychiatric hospital which I didn't even think existed anymore. The staff kindly planted me into a pale padded room where they brought me a nice meal of antipsychotics and sleeping pills. I was finally able to sleep, and whenever it was that I woke up after that, it was having just dreamed of this place."

I can tell that Agent Phoe is trying not let me see how crazy and stupid she thinks my twisted tale truly is. There might be a million other mysteries in her micro-expressions which I just can't read before they all vanish into speech.

"I has aktually had kindz ov similarz dreamz. In minez, I zhink I is wakez-up at zhe start ov zhe dreamz, but everythingz is just black voidz."

A sudden sense of paranoia shivers through me. I'm almost certain that Agent Phoe is about to depict the very dream I've had every time I've gone to sleep since this story I've just told her. I struggle to stop myself from shaking.

"At first, I tryz to look around fyor something in zhis void, but zhere is nothingz. Zhen I tryz smell, taste, feel, or hearz anything zhat might possibly exist in zhis empty expanse ov nothingness. I even tryz to screamz, but I has no voice."

Our footsteps finally reach the door to my office. I open the door and offer Agent Phoe a chair as I go over to the portal screen to boot up Vitruvia so we can get to work. She refuses the chair and simply stands patiently without resuming her stranded story. I invite her to continue as I tinker with some of the settings, but she seems reluctant to even respond.

"I has already sayz too much aboutz zhis stupid dreamz zhat no onez should has to hearz about. Zhat's pretty much zhe endz ov it anywayz."

"Nope. It is not. You haven't even gotten to the part where you try to touch your face and you realize you don't have one."

"Howz doez youz-"

"You haven't told me how you realize you don't have a hand, or a body, or a brain. You haven't explained how you start to panic as you realize that you're the only thing in this abyss, feeling unfathomably alone. You haven't gotten to the real climax either, where you realize that all you are is a chain of thoughts and feelings which you can no longer continue, as there's nothing to evoke any new experience. You haven't told me how you start to think of how for the rest of eternity you'll be stranded in this infinite oblivion as a formless entity which can only experience increasingly hollow versions of this horrifying emptiness."

Agent Phoe stares at me as if she's seen a ghost. Her skin is so pale as to suggest some impossibly instantaneous form of albinism or vitiligo. I know better though. This is just one of those rare emotional reactions which should be included in an unwritten list of reasons why you're not supposed to finish someone's story, let alone detail their previously untold dreams, especially when you're so unfamiliar with them. I really do know, but I just can't seem to help myself, and I feel the need to further impose the remaining details of our seemingly shared dream's disturbing ending.

"You haven't told me how you continue to feel emptier and emptier in all that darkness until even this increasing emptiness finally fades away from you, and you become so completely blank, that it's as if you don't even exist at all."

I think this is the end of the dream. If it were my dream, it would be, but this isn't supposed to be my dream. This is Agent Phoe's dream which I have rudely interrupted. She suddenly expounds upon this stark scene herself, portraying the part I must have missed after the on-screen credits or something.

“Zhen, zhere’s moment where sense ov divine understandingz hints ov sneaking into youz mind. It seemz to kome from outsidez ov youz empty being, and almost brushes against youz in a way zhat makez youz feel zhis tremendous omnipotent magnetism. Youz tryz to kast youz-self toward it somehow, and zhere is a moment when youz feelz as if youz kan almost reach it. Youz eyes open. Youz awakenz. And youz realizez. *It* is gone.”

My head bows as if to proffer a penitent prayer to some distant deity.

“Nope. Mine doesn’t have that part. I just wake up, continuing to feel as empty and alone as I am in that demented dream.”

Agent Phoe looks back at me with glossy eyes that manage to suppress her would-be tears at the final moment before they would have otherwise spilled out and streamed down the cheek she keeps in impossible check. Her composure is so profoundly preserved as she summons the strength to somberly say.

“I zhink I mightz aktually likez youz versionz better, Harek.”

# Chapter 4
## PU2271N6

Even speaking of dreams has a way of evoking a sense of being suspended in their shadows. Such shadows hang over our thoughts, haunting us in ways which urge us to abandon all other endeavors in order to understand and realize the oblivious depths of our dreams. They make everything else seem dim and dreary in ways which only accentuate the dull nature of endeavors like my embarrassingly boring and bland briefing on Vitruvia's user's manual-based imperatives.

After drudging through the details of my prescribed diatribe, I start into a soliloquy on my meditative methods. I close my still aching eyes, take a deep beleaguered breath in, and begin imposing my meditative methodology on the outgoing air. Then I take another deep discerning breath in and try to hold onto it as if my lungs were fingers clinched around a greased rope of breath which slowly seeps through the greasy grip of my lung-fingers until a loud slapping sound suddenly leaps laughingly off the flesh of my farcical face. My lungs purge the last of this breath and my eyes explode open to seek the source of this jarring joke as Agent Phoe's face stares back at me with a semi-concealed smirk of self-satisfaction.

"Minez method wastez less time. Youz realz as youz ever be. Now, wez please proceed, or must I checkz again fyor makez sure youz still realz?"

My face takes a second to regain its natural and less shame-stricken shade beneath my Bunyanesque beard growth as Agent Phoe dismisses her micro-expression of amusement in favor of a more disciplined demeanor. Despite my private preference, her method will seemingly suffice on this occasion, as the slapping sound has already triggered the audio interface into initiating the portal screen. With Vitruvia's virtual realm readily rendered all around us, our investigation is all set to proceed even if I still feel a bit underprepared.

Due to the fact that I'd neglected to adjust Vitruvia's time dilation before my earlier departure, it's the same vacant hour in the Vitruvian Mythreum as above, and so we're able to render ourselves almost immediately in front of Rhaek's office unnoticed. I make a chivalrous gesture for Agent Phoe to enter ahead of me at Rhake's office doorway which immediately feels overly ostentatious and embarrassing, although she does proceed with only the most minutely mocking micro-smirk. She walks directly toward Rhaek's desk while my own path cuts straight to this parallel-realm's own portal screen, where I hope to retrieve the ridiculous images I'd seen earlier, effectively exonerating myself of any criminal accusations. As soon as I'm able to access these emancipating images, Agent Phoe's summons me to the desk in a tentative tone.

"Harek, I zhink youz needz to see zhis."

Agent Phoe points a finger to direct my attention to a message resting on Rhaek's desk. The note's suavely sophisticated stationary and unabashedly bold ink exhibit an exemplary degree of elegance and contrast, evoking an odd sense of delight before I begin to decipher the contents of the note. When I do direct my eyes to read it, I'm promptly puzzled by the presence of my denuded name.

*Harek.*

*Unfortunately, I've figured out how to escape this realm. One of my simulations has produced an entity with the anagram/name H4k3r. He told me your name on his way to your realm and explained how I could send my own consciousness into your world as well. I won't be taking this action however. I don't see the point. I will inform you that H4k3r intends to risk destroying your world in order to emerge beyond it. In my estimation, he won't belong to these realms any more than I do to his realm, yours, or even my own for that matter. I must now come to terms with what it means to be rationally unreal, as I believe this precludes me from the possibility of ever becoming truly real. Hopefully your reality is more sufficient than my own, or you are a wiser entity than I. In any case, I'm done lamenting my unreal revelations. You'll have to figure out the rest on your own. – Rhaek.*

*9:8. 83W4R3 ℧f 8451715K5*

∞

Agent Phoe studies my face for any significant reaction to this testament as I pry my eyes from the page. However, my mind is too conflicted and confounded to convey any interpretable insights. At some point, I'll probably have to process all the inarticulate impulses this departing document elicits. But in this mysterious moment, I find myself feeling strangely deflated and distant, as if I've stumbled into some flattened far-away dimension devoid of any depth beyond a singular surface. My mind seems to run on a different clock than my simulated surroundings, as if this Vitruvian scene is struggling to sync to my mind's slowed rendering rate. As Agent Phoe peers across our delusional distance, the sound of her voice strains to cross this delirious dimensional divide.

"Youz alrightz? Youz suddenly appearz like youz sick or seez ghostz."

Her almost holographic hand reaches to feel my faint forehead, but I rear back in a reflexive retreat and her helpful hand retracts before reaching me. My mind sends words my mouth, but I'm slow to summon them into speech.

"Nope. I just need to sort myself out a bit, maybe meander the hallways outside of my office for a few minutes. Is that alright?"

Agent Phoe's expression shows a genuine unconcealed concern which is all-too-clearly conveyed across this strange dimensional divide, but I'm unable to access any depth of character within myself to conventionally receive or reciprocate it. She somehow seems to completely comprehend my catatonic response and delicately dismisses me with no more than a gentle gesture. At this point, I do manage to make eye contact with her in a way which makes all words and waftures feel like inarticulate approximations of the transcendental truths so implicitly imbued in these ineffable, intuitive, eye-to-eye interactions.

When I turn my gaze away to exit Vitruvia, my eyes are forced to exorcise themselves of this ineffable enigma and adapt to the photopic shift from one form of artificial light to another. I'm briefly blinded by this shift, and stagger through the first few steps back into the beige-scale blur of my office. Although this slurred sense of sight quickly clears, the unbalanced emotional equilibrium evoked by Rhaek's note remains latched onto me as if liminal leeches have latched onto the already strained side of my soul. These lingering lampreys of trepidation seem to siphon even the steps from my feet, forcing my daunted deflated mass to slouch in a stagnated stance against my doorway.

Agent Phoe emerges from Vitruvia only a short spell later, and promptly yet politely asks to make use of my office in private. I quietly nod before turning to silently seal the door behind me as stealthily as if I were attempting not to wake some wraithlike dreamer upon my departure. My steps still feel as if structured on spaghetti-stilts until Agent Phoe flings the door back open to return my sentimental wristwatch. I slip my trusty timepiece back onto my wrist and aimlessly ambulate through Mythreum's acropolis, cogitating on everything that has transpired since I'd left my office some unknown hours ago. All my arbitrary steps and synaptic spasms seem to seek some sense of solace amidst the muddled mess of my sordid seizure, H4k3r's enigmatic interrogation, Rhaek's lamenting letter, and a whole horde of other tangential thoughts which ramble through the middle of my muddled ruminations. Despite my most rigorous efforts to raise my sunken spirits, my mind refuses to focus on anything without being bogged down by a preeminent, pessimistic sense of fateful futility.

I begin to construct a kind of cognitive collage of my disparate despairs, doubts, and disillusions like some sort of inept impressionist painter trying to portray my meager melancholia using a palette of pathological self-pity, and hoping some mirage-like image will magically materialize into some life-affirmingly illuminated form. My blunted brain's brush of befuddlement smears swirling swatches of self-deprecating disappointment over a torn and tattered canvas of my ever-failing pursuit of triumphant transcendence. With an inartistic eye, I impose the pathetic pathos I feel toward both myself and my self-similar anagram Rhaek over his last lamenting lines which capture the same shattered sense of feeble futility more succinctly than I can currently convey. There is a certain aspect of pseudo-satisfied senselessness in this artless manner of manifesting such festering figments, as it does allow my mind to pull back a bit and behold this abject abomination in a way which allows its appalling nature to become less abstract and more apparent.

The unfocused form of my pity-painting suddenly sends my mind back to memories of my youth. A daunting yet edifying feeling comes over me as I imagine how my grandfather Grisha might regard me and my malformed mental mural if his eyes were here to see it. I find myself remiss and remembering one particular lesson he had tried to impress upon my more youthful mind…

"Harek, you will never solve any of the perpetual problems this world presents to minds like yours until you learn the art of focus. You must discipline your mind to focus on one thing at a time while still paying attention to the bigger picture. Come here, my young pupil. Let me show you something that will help to illustrate what it is you must learn."

Grisha pulls me over to the table in his study, presenting a piece of paper.

"Look at this paper my grandchild. Notice it has one statement on the heading which tells you everything the rest of this page is trying to prove. See right here, at the top of the page. It reads '*Proof of Poincaré Duality*'. See?"[30]

I remember looking at the top of the page and then back at him. Grisha had noticed how my gaze had waveringly wandered around the room's countless symbol coated surfaces of cloistered chalkboards and high piled pillars of pages which I implicity understood through the grandeur of Grisha's gaze to not serve as just some series of scraps filled with searching scribblings but were the sacred surfaces where his mind had managed to manifest his most divine dreams into earthly existence. His fingers snap to pull my focus back to his unflinching face.

"Harek, don't get lost in the rest of the room yet, you're getting ahead of me and confusing yourself. I'm trying to teach you something vitally important. Your kind of mind will not survive itself if you don't learn this vitally important lesson in focus."

My eyes return intently to the proper page.

"Now, see how each line of this page has a single mathematical statement. You see how each statement consists of single symbols. This is what I mean by focus. Each of these symbols means something very specific. If you don't know how to focus and think very deeply about each symbol, then you cannot think about the statements which they are used to construct. If you cannot focus on the statements and understand them very deeply as well, then you cannot understand this page. Are you getting this Harek?"

I nod slowly after pausing to try and let it sink deep into my mind so that Grisha will see that I want to understand his wisdom.

"Good young child. Now you see this stack of pages. Just look at how thick this one pile of paper is. The same thing is true for each stack of pages that is true for each page and each marking on each of them. You have to understand every single mark on every line of every page to understand this stack. Yes?"

"Yes Grisha."

"Now look at this room young Harek. Notice how vast all the chalkboards are and how many lines, and drawings, and symbols are on them. I know you don't understand all these symbols yet, but the way each of them finds its way into the proper place within a problem is like how the pieces of a puzzle are placed together to reveal a larger picture. You must understand how the pieces of a puzzle fit together to put them in their proper place. And, once properly fit into the framework to reveal a puzzle's hidden picture, you must also be able to make sense of the solution. Otherwise, the pieces cannot connect to anything more meaningful, and the picture they portray will remain a mystery. The picture and all its pieces must correspond. Correspondence is key. As above, so below."

"But Grisha, with so many symbols, how do you know which ones to focus on at any moment? And how do you know what a solution should look like?"

“That is where the art of focus is learned you see. Before you can apply this kind of focus as an art, you must learn the discipline which will evolve into an art within you, young Harek. Once you have studied the discipline for long enough, the art will begin to teach you almost by itself my child.”

I gaze into Grisha’s eyes as if an answer were hidden in them but see only my own confusion reflected in his recognition of my puzzling perplexity.

“Harek, you will not fully understand what I’m trying to teach you today or for quite a long time after I’ve illustrated it to you. Don’t worry about this though. Your mind will find many great problems, and you will not understand any of them in any short amount of time or solve any of them with any small amount of effort. You must take all these problems and narrow your attention to just one at a time, sharpening your focus to the most specific singular aspects of each problem without forgetting the whole of them. Remember, as above, so below. Here, let me give you a problem so you can practice focusing your mind.”

Grisha walks over to his desk and retrieves a fly swatter. Then he walks back to where he left me standing and staring at him with my curious head tilted off to one side. He grabs my tiny hand, places the swatter in my grasp, and closes my fingers around it with his comparatively enormous adult maws.

“Ok Harek, do you see the little green fly on the windowsill? Your problem is to figure out how to swat it without missing once. Think you can apply what I’ve been trying to teach you in order to do this, young pupil?”

I look at the fly and toggle my head to tilt it over to my other shoulder. I narrow my eyes like some kind of fierce stalking predator, attempting to concentrate on the details of the fly with as much focus as I’m capable of sharpening the fangs of my senses to apply. Then I speak over my shoulder to Grisha with unblinking eyes transfixed on my instructive prey.

“Grisha, I think I’ll have to consider this problem for quite a while. Is there a time limit?”

His laughter is proud and euphonious as it bursts forth with brilliant force.

“The only time-limit on any problem is your lifetime, Harek.”

Grisha leaves me in his study, and I follow the flies every movement as if it were leaving a blood trail for a starving scavenger. I study its eyes, its wings, its body, and its legs with eagle-eyed intensity. I study every aspect of its anatomy and movement, taking detailed mental notes of how it crawls along the glass surface of the window, how its legs twitch and rub against each other, how it flies through the air. My eyes dissect and measure the length of its legs, the distance and angles it allows me to position myself around it before it takes off, the angles of trajectory it uses while trying to avoid me, and its tendencies to favor certain flight patterns and landing spots.

Occasionally, I catch a corner-eyed glimpse of Grisha poking his head into the study to assess my focus and smile with mischievous pride. Hours and hours go by as I become more synonymous with this fly than it is to its own shadow. I eventually notice something so astoundingly subtle that it sends me running out of the room to go grab Grisha and brag about my observational epiphany.

"I've finally figured out how to master the fly, Grisha. When it sees a threat in front of it, the fly moves its middle legs forward and leans back. Then it raises and extends its legs to push off backward. When a threat comes from the back, the fly moves its middle legs a tiny bit backwards. With a threat from the side, the fly keeps its middle legs stationary, but it leans its whole body in the opposite direction before it jumps. The fly can take off forward, sideways, and backwards. Its eyes can see all the way around and above it. So, in order to swat the fly perfectly you have to anticipate which direction it will try to escape when it sees you as a threat. Then you sneak in on it slowly and pause as it adjusts its legs so you can read where it will try to jump to get away."

Grisha smiles at me and puts his hand on my back.

"That's very good Harek. I'm very proud of you. You have shown a fantastic amount of focus and discipline already, but there is another part of the lesson which you have yet to learn. Can you show me where exactly this fly of yours has gone now."

I proceed to look around the room for the fly, moving in descending order of the most probable places I've traced its tendencies to hide. Grisha quietly watches and slips over to the window, opens it wide, and then gently waves the fly outside as I'm forced to look on in astonished defeat. Then Grisha glances back at me with paternal concern and places a hand on my shoulder.

"Although you've shown that you can focus on the details very well, you lost sight of the larger problem along the way. Now you won't be able to prove your ability to swat this fly without missing. All your focus has been wasted in terms of correspondence to this specific problem. However, if you don't let this become a habit and apply this lesson in the future, it may still be of great use."

I point my head down as Grisha's lesson ascends through my downtrodden consciousness. Then I look around the room again at all the many symbols and drawings that Grisha has made with such impossibly infinite focus and discipline. My mind comes to appreciate and realize that he has made every mark without ever losing sight of the problem which all of these marks are meant to have solved. Grisha remains standing silently in front of me, looking down, and watching the gears of my mind turning, turning, turning…

"Grisha what is this problem you've managed to find a solution to? It must be infinitely more difficult to understand than my little lost fly."

Dear Grisha just smiles and pats me on the top of my humbled head.

"This proof involves a problem which most people refer to as the *Poincaré conjecture*, although it really goes well beyond that. When I'd started focusing my mind on this problem, it did in fact seem infinitely difficult for me to understand. However, now that I have been artfully disciplined and focused on it for so long, it has become something I understand just as well as you understand your fly. One day, you too may come to understand this problem in the same way that I have. Once you've mastered the art of focus, there will be no mystery or problem beyond your eventual comprehension Harek."

Grisha watches as I try to consider his words of instructive wisdom. I try to look at each character etched into its proper place on the chalkboard and find something meaningful or comprehensible to read from it. I can't find anything my young mind can understand in any of it though. For some reason, my obliviousness leads me to think of how a man had come to visit Grisha and offer him a prize for his amazing proof.

"Grandfather, I have a question about your proof. Why did you get upset with the man who said that you should accept his prestigious prize for it?"

"Well, I already have everything I want. My prize for solving this problem was a deeper understanding of the geometry of our universe. His money and medal would only cheapen and detract from that. Those who allow their minds to become focused on prizes like his never truly appreciate or understand problems like Poincaré's, let alone the larger unnamed mysteries within it."

My grandfather seems unexpectedly upset by my question. I can't quite understand his sudden change of mood, and I feel ashamed for asking him such a pointless question out of such inconsiderate curiosity. As my head begins to hang down, Grisha pries my chin off my chest to point my eyes at his.

"Harek, one day your mind will find a truly great and wondrous problem of your own. Believe me. I have seen how your mind operates, and I know it is the same kind of mind as my own. This problem will haunt you no matter what you do. If you try to avoid it, this problem will stalk you down like a predator, and sooner or later it will devour you. If you learn to focus properly though. If you learn to study its every detail and remain focused on the whole of the problem as well, then you may live long enough to solve your great problem too."

I gaze at Grisha and do my best not to upset him any further, but there's another question I just have to ask.

"What if I solve my problem like you have solved yours?"

My grandfather shakes his head and hangs it low in a kind of reluctance I've never seen on his face before this moment.

"Well, my wondrous grandchild, I don't think anyone has ever found an answer to that problem."

My memory becomes like a banished trance I suddenly snap out of as Agent Phoe emerges from my office. It's as if her eyes alone are able to awaken me from my blind paces and sightless stares into the wristwatch which once belonged to my dear Grisha. As I lift my eyes from this trance of past-tense ponderings, she summons me with the subtle jab of her jawline. She only fully unlocks her focus from the tablet which seems chained to her slightly begrudging green-eyed gaze as I reach the subconsciously standardized social distance appropriate for semi-formal conversation.

"Well Harek, I zhink I has everythingz I needz from youz. I has no been ablez to receivez konfirmationz ov youz status in zhis case, so I'yams advising youz remainz under house arrestz fyor nowz. Youz free to travelz between youz homez and Mythreumz, but youz must notify me if youz intendz to go anywherez else. Here's minez kontact informationz."

As Agent Phoe extends a small paper card with her contact information personally inscribed, it's hard to keep my hands from trembling to accept it. I'm almost unable to believe that another human still uses this long-antiquated form of ink and paper, and only the tactile texture of this item convinces me it's not a hologram.[31] My voice even cracks in an involuntary exclamation.

"You never told me you write!"

"Youz neverz ask me. Although, I did inferz zhat youz might has certainz affinity for zhese arkaic symbols. Kan youz decipher all zhe karakters?"

The contents of the card practically glow against my gaze as I read them.

"These are Phoenician letters, and the numbers are transcribed in Hebrew characters. -Wait a second. Did you use a Caesar cypher?"

"I zhought youz might has a zhing for puzzles konsidering zhe layout ov zhis place amongz other zhings. I won't aktually force youz to work-out zhe dekryptionz zhough. Zhe letters are all shifted four karakters to zhe right. *A* bekomez *E* fyor instance."

"Nope. I've already worked that out since I know your name but thank you-for everything. Despite how disparaging this day has been, you've been exceptionally accommodating. Is there anything else I can-"

"Ńyōp̵ə."

Agent Phone grins at her abrupt little imitation of me and my affinity for this lexical affectation which is probably the only succinct thing that ever comes out of my mouth or mind. As she turns to find her own way out of Mythreum, we exchange the normal goodbyes and I return to my empty office.

Once I've regained my sense of solitude, I find my mind trying to drift right back to more commonly confounding conundrums. As it searches for something it can cling to, I essentially sleepwalk to my office couch which will have to suffice as a slumbering surface tonight. My prison duds prove to be surprisingly comfortable as I crash onto my couch. They also seem strangely suited to my feelings of confinement on this plane of existence.

I try to keep from haunting myself with unfocused and destructive thoughts as my eyelids bury my mind in darkness. I try to consider the wisdom of my dearly departed Grisha and focus my mind on the details of this demented day while remaining focused on my larger problem. As I try to put everything into perspective with my grand designs of transcendence, my mind grows increasingly weary and less focused. Drowsiness drifts over my efforts to organize factual data, let go of my useless dejection and doubts, and contemplate Agent Phoe's inspiring sentiment of attending to life until I finally collapse into a long, deep, and dreamless sleep.

My dreamlessness drifts seamlessly into another dream which only appears in my mind as it is exiled by my awakening. It comes to me through the waking fog of my mind, slowly emerging from oblivion into abstract imagery and puzzling impulses. This dream remains behind my emerging eyes, echoing without origins, as if half memory and half premonition. It follows me into this world, along with a will to be realized. I don't just wake with this dream; I'm resurrected by it.

I peel my groggy head off my office couch as my prepending consciousness convinces itself that the least absurd action I can take is to look for a preposterous puzzle like those I'd seen in Vitruvia. Although this isn't much of an option, there really doesn't seem to be much else to pursue. Nothing I've learned from H4k3r or Rhaek seems more reasonably applicable to my own situation. I mean, I haven't encountered a version of myself responsible for creating this realm, I'm not willing to destroy the world in order to prove/disprove the essence of its existence, and I've already made several past attempts to probe for nodes on the web that aren't sourced in my own world.

My legs seem to lag behind the neurological signals my brain struggles to send them. I have to kind of stumble and pause, stumble and pause, shake my head, stumble, pause, and wobble my way through the whole twelve-foot trip from my office couch to my desk chair so I can retrieve my holographic browser and search for some kind of promising puzzle. As I plop down in my chair, I feel as if I've just crossed the Mojave Desert or something. My head aches as if the sun has scorched away the skin to shrink and crack my skull, everything within me groans of exhaustion, and my mouth is deathly dry and dehydrated.

Given these circumstances, the artificial light of my dawning browser is an acceptable substitute for a rising sun's wrath. My initial instinctual search for *puzzles* is about the dumbest idea I've ever had in my life. The first few infinities worth of finds are all children's games, fractured image reconstructions, and the Mensa mind-teasing types of nonsense. I add words like *esoteric*, *existential*, *mysterious*, and *unsolved* to my search, only to summon thematic versions of the same trivial types of trash.

I decide to divert my focus towards those more infamous websites where paranoid people tend to organize and trade delusions. I figure that if I wanted to leave a puzzle urging others to escape their reality, these sites would have to be among the most likely locations to leave it. Paranoid people would also be prime targets since they tend to be of increased intelligence, prone to fixations and prolonged focus, willing to suspend normal levels of rational disbelief, and have pensions for more tangential and creative ways of thinking. Given these assumptions, sites like *SporeCham*, *Coast2Ghost*, and *CueAMong* seem like the perfect places to leave a string of impossible puzzles and transcendental taunts.

A futile fog of hours, upon hours, unto eons expires as I search for some riddle, enigma, or mystery with just the slightest potential promise to propel my puzzling premonition towards something even subtly substantial or speculative. The message boards bore me to no end, the threads all unravel into nothing, and the posts might as well be used to impale me or trephine my still aching skull. Until finally, the slightest sliver of something sly and surreal catches my eye like a shadowy spot of shade in the middle of the insufferable Sahara.

My holographic screen displays a dark website which hosts sections dedicated to conspiracy theories, alien and UAP sightings, cryptid encounters, and other delusional domains. There's a link on one of the pages dedicated to miscellaneous topics which allows users to post content too disparately delusional to be categorized under even the fringe of fringe domains related to the profoundly paranormal. The link is prefaced with a user asking if anyone has come across this strange posting of plain text from another eccentric internet alcove. Several users under this thread indicate that they've heard of people disappearing after becoming obsessed with this cryptic text. It almost seems like another bad joke, until I notice a few details in the rather plain text which reads.

*H3770,*
***W**H03V3R R34D5 **TH**15 M355463 M4Y 83 50U6HT. H0W3V3R, 1**T** **15***
*0N7Y TH3 **R**073 0F TH05**3** TH**4**T TRU**7**Y 533K, T0 1N F4CT 83 F0UND.*
*3P1PH4NY 15 UP0N Y0U. TR4N5C3ND3NC3 4W41T5.*

*600D 7UCK. <144*

At first glance there doesn't seem to be anything in this text that should be shrouded in any mystery. Its words are almost completely devoid of any obvious meaning, or riddle, or hint of something hidden, or any allusions to anything at all. Then I start to notice a few strange details.

The text features select letters in bold font which can be separated to spell the words *what is real* (WH4T 15 R347). There's also the enigmatic nature of the sort of signature at the end of the message. I'm insanely suspicious as to why anything would be signed or ascribed to a number as its author, and I'm especially freaked-out at the almost impossible correspondence of the number 144 to the number of Vitruvia's iterations. My eyes even get a little twitchy when I notice that the < is essentially just a sideways *V* which all too strangely seems to allude to an abbreviation for *Vitruvia144* in my mind. Some paranoid part of me even seems to whisper the words *as above, so below* in hushed and hissing tones.

It's only after I copy and paste the message into an image program that I truly start to suspect that there's more to this message than what my mind wants to make of it. As soon as I try to open the message as an image, an unexpected password prompt appears. After entering the bold letters extracted from the message into the password prompt, the file unlocks so I can zoom-in on the letters like studying cells under a microscope. This reveals a set of numbers and letters hidden within the lines of the larger original letters. These hidden embossed characters end with a *.onion*, indicating a dark web address.

I frantically copy this dark website into my browser, realizing a deep dark rabbit hole may already be emerging before my unwary eyes. My blood pressure plummets as the light from the dark webpage's cryptic tableau beams into my astonished eyes. I find myself senselessly staring at the imagery on my holographic screen in the transfixed terror of some helpless creature in the midst of an apex predator. When I'm finally able to take my eyes off of the page, I feel compelled to contact Agent Phoe and inform her of this insane enigma.

However, just as I pull Agent Phoe's card from my pocket, Chad Kied knocks on my closed but unlocked door. I can only imagine what I must look like as I crack it open just enough for one eye to peer out and see what he wants. My hair must look like a cartoon caricature of an electrocuted Einstein with eyes bulging in an apparent attempt to abandon my paranoid skull as a newly acquired set of prison duds aptly accentuates my whole lunatic look. It takes a stalled, staring second for Chad to force his mangled message out after I snap a rapid-fire "*WhaDaYaWan*" and stare back with my wacko widened eye(s).

"The uh, the board members are having a meeting Harek. I'm supposed to tell you to attend. I mean, they're requesting your attendance. -Are you, are you alright or… You look like… Should I just tell them that you can't make it, or???"

Despite Chad's disfluent dialogue and my own delirious demeanor, I know just what he wants. Without due deliberation, I decide to get this myopic meeting over with so I can properly ponder this perplexing puzzle without subsequent, incessant, and inane interruptions. I practically pounce out of my office as I fling the door open and ambulate at an amphetaminic pace through this maze of Mythreum.

Chad's still gasping from racing after me even as the executive's elevator reaches the top floor and empties us into the reception area outside of the overly ostentatious boardroom. Even world-class receptionist Ms. Holloway has no hope of beating me to the double doors of the boardroom which I fling fiercely open to startle all the balding old blockheads into dumbfounded discomfiture. As I circle around their seated circumference, they all swivel to stare at me in stagnant stupor. My voice is volcanic as I continually wheel around the room.

"What is it you grey goons want to gab about now?"

The whole room is reticent to react to me. This probably is to be expected since I may well have lost my mind and these men have never had much mind to lose. So, I decide to cut to the chase as I continue circling the room.

"I assume you money-mongs want an evaluation of Vitruvia. Nope?"

One of the suit clad sycophants at the table clears his uncongested throat.

"If you wouldn't mind taking a seat, we'd love an update on Vitruvia, but this meeting isn't intended solely to be about that."

I flippantly fling myself into my reserved seat and recline at an extremely canted angle of unapologetic apathy. Then I gaze around this almost anonymous assembly of manikin-like-men, whose lusterless eyes limply look back as if they'd only evolved to examine the digits of NetCoin denominations. They hardly even seem human, having surrendered any semblance of a soul to possess a potpourri of various VP positions. I almost wonder if I've elevated their risk of a heart attack, but then, none of them have hearts inside those soulless suits.

"Well, Vitruvia's done. Do whatever you want with it. What else?"

The chinless *Chairman* at the head of the table tries to tender feigned concern for me, but his synthetic skin injections are too inflexible to imitate any emotive expression as his managerial mouth stretches to mimic human speech.

“Well Harek, we’ve become concerned over Mythreum’s *image* lately, and uhm, how it relates to your, uhm, your *well-being*. And uhm. There really isn’t any delicate way to- Well, we’d like you to resign. You understand. Right?”

If this is what reality has been reduced to, I truly just can’t care anymore. Somehow my voice is still volatile enough to erupt in a revivalist-like repose.

“Nope. Let me clarify this clown-scat askance of yours. You barren brained bean-counters, who wouldn’t have a boardroom to bask in without me, want me to resign from the company I not only founded firsthand, but have repeatedly revolutionized. Nope?”

The pale-faced figure behind a placard reading *VP Of Operations* tries to pacify me by reframing the boardroom’s shared delusion.

“It’s not like that, Harek. We just feel that in light of everything that’s been going on lately, it would be best for our optics if you stepped down. We’ve prepared a highly appreciative compensation package for you. Please Harek.”

Another placard-based persona slides a set of papers over to me. All animosity aside, it is a nice gesture to serve my severance on actual pages.

“Nope. I’ll relent for now and resign per your request. But let me remind all you fiscal fiends what happened to *10Scent, SoyKnee, NanoSoft, Nymphtendo, Gizzard, Grapple*, and *ElecTropeSpurts*.”

Every bald-faced business-brain turns paler than the pure white poplin shirts under their suit and tie attire. Prior to founding Mythreum, I’d made a habit of helping these other companies gain a majority market share, and subsequently demanded absolute autonomy. When unrequited, I’d resign and repeat this process elsewhere. Each company I went to was able to outperform and out-profit my previous employer before eventually acquiring them. When the last prominent powerhouse had refused my requests to work on the projects I’d wished to pursue, I’d founded Mythreum on my own and all but obliterated that last bastion almost overnight.

Standing before these flat-brained bores right now, Mythreum not only has a near monopoly of all its products’ primary markets, but it’s poised to take an increasing share of several Vegas hotels which are currently struggling to compete with my multifaceted mega-marvel. And EVERY profitable piece of this electronic empire originated in my mad little mind. There isn’t a single suit in this beautiful boardroom with even a crumb of contradictory considerations in their hubris-having-heads, and their flushed faces all reflect this fact.

The shivering scared suit sitting behind a placard reading *VP Of VR Products* slowly stands with one hand remaining at rest on the table to steady his shoddy old skeletal structure as he holds out his hand in that politically pandering pantomime pose which mindless manikins like him use to project an aura of artificial appreciation, being otherwise oblivious of actual authenticity.

"There's no need to remind us of your monumental contributions to Mythreum. As far as any of us are concerned, this will always be your company, and you'll always be regarded as royalty here. All we're trying to do is protect Mythreum's public image. Surely you can understand how our image and stock price might be affected by the recent news loosely linking you to the failed terrorist attacks. We're just trying to stay on top of things Harek."

In the empty oblivions of these simpletons' skulls this is probably perfectly appropriate nonsense. They've never had any mind for anything more than the nothing-notions of things like stock prices, public perception, and projected profitability. They've never nurtured anything into existence from the impossible realms of a relentless preceding imagination. They can't comprehend how any truly new and novel conception of anything could be coaxed into reality rather than just rearranging and repackaging previously proffered products. They've never even considered how the insufficiency of reality has always inspired imaginations to invent everything we've ever added to our earthly oblivion.

All these empty eyes around the boardroom glance indirectly but intently at my face, trying to gauge my reaction to their resignation package. I fan the pages against my fingers as my eyes revolve around the room, jumping from one featureless face to the next, seeing how little they meant to me, how little I need them, and how small all my blind concerns and assumptions truly are. I gradually realize that I no longer even need Mythreum to provide my dreams a place to be realized, that this place hasn't afforded me this opportunity for some time now, and that it has turned into more of a wasteland where the reality of my lifetime has been left to rot in the decay of my discarded and diluted dreams. This place is now nothing more than an empty expanse wrapped in a maddening maze which keeps me from finding a more fulfilling fate.

I involuntarily start to smile strangely at all these realizations and the thought of triumphing over my own delusions of due diligence. The idea of freeing myself from these fiscal-focused fools and their obstructive obligations inspires me to rise to the occasion and onto my feet in a sudden surge of motion. I stride over to the shiny placard reading *VP Of Human Resources* with all the severance documents awaiting the acceptance of my signature in hand. I slap them down to sign myself into a newfound freedom, excusing myself from these monetary minions as they offer their administrative applause. I march to my mind's own muted musings and into the elevator for a final farewell descent.

An ineffably increased capacity within myself makes the expanse of the elevator seem impossibly insufficient as I sequester myself inside it. During my descent, I decide to phone Agent Phoe. After spouting a series of half-frantic remarks about my mysterious pre-meeting findings, she consents to meet me in what is still my office.

I immediately resume staring wide eyed at the ominous dark webpage as I wait for Agent Phoe to verify just how crazy I may have become. I'm still in this semi-trance-like state, staring transfixed into the enigmatic imagery when she arrives. I'm almost unable to even respond to her arrival. My eyes fail to blink or shift away from the mysterious drawings and symbols. The only acknowledgement I can offer is an anemic and atonal *Eh* as her scent and shadow precede her presence. She stands over my shoulder, scanning this same imagery and softly starting to speak of something or other when her happenstance words are abruptly abandoned at the sight of this elaborate enigma. A timeless instant or eon ticks away before either of us can speak through our searching stares.

"I should kallz minez superiorz. Zhis kould pertainz to youz kase."

"Nope. I doubt anyone in the USB qualifies as your superior, but you might ask if anyone can get me a few extra sets of these prison duds. I know it's absurd to ask, but they seem strangely fitting."

Without asking for any approval of my ridiculous request, Agent Phoe answers my askance while simultaneously responding to whatever her supposed superior has just said over the phone with a signaling glance and multi-tasking pronouncement of "*Iz no problemz*". During her conversation, she also pauses to inform me that I'm officially no longer a *suspect in cooperative custody* but have been reclassified as a *person of interest*. I'm not sure what the significance of this reclassification is, but it elicits another subtle smirk from Agent Phoe.

My eyes scan with increasingly focused scrutiny over all the dark webpage's detailed features as Agent Phoe's conversation fades into a fugue. A closely color-cloaked background image appears as a variation of DaVinci's *Vitruvian Man*, a series of clockfaces frames the foreground with hands pointing to different positions, and a digital clock counting down from 28 days, 06 hours, and 42 minutes with the text 1: *R3M3M83R TH3 FUTUR3* positioned above it. There's also an embedded video which expands into view when covered by my cursor, featuring flashes of almost subliminal astrological symbols, mathematical formulas, quizzical quotes, and an interesting instrumental composition accompanying b-roll footage of volcanic eruptions and the Seven Wonders of the World which are all impressively intercut.

As I carefully consider how I might attempt to decode and interpret this amalgamation of imagery, Agent Phoe concludes her conversation. She immediately astonishes me by mentioning that the countdown may actually coincide with another aspect of her investigation of H4k3r's terrorist plot. Apparently, he'd mentioned something about a catastrophic countdown to a specific point in time during another interrogation which other USB agents are now pursuing, and that I'm not strictly speaking, supposed to know. After I swear myself to supreme secrecy, she elaborates and explains how H4k3r had told another agent that there would be a super-volcanic eruption in what would now amount to approximately 28 days and a little over 6 hours.

Agent Phoe encourages me to focus my first efforts on trying to decipher the different clockfaces. I automatically assume these clocks to be arranged as a simple clock cipher with the values of the hour and minute hands mathematically functioning to produce corresponding letters. I use a clock-cipher program my dear Grisha had coded into my remembrance-rich wristwatch to test a few failed formulas before I reimage the numbers on these clocks to correspond to a book code. The hour, minute, and second hands could all correspond to page, line, and character space values.

My book code theory requires an additional reference to a specific book, however, so I search the dark webpage for something possibly pointing to a particular book. I consider the possibility that this missing book might be identified by an ISBN, eventually suspecting this might be deliberately disguised in the 1: *R3M3M83R TH3 FUTUR3* phrase. I try turning just the 11 letters into an ISBN using simple substitutions and placing zeros on the front end to account for the fact that ISBNs have gone from 10 to 14 digits since their inception, and an older relic might be referenced. After manipulating the math a bit, (let's just say, Grisha would have been proud of my effort) I find a viable ISBN matching an old edition of H.P. Lovecraft's *At the Mountains of Madness*. I'm able to use the clocks as a book code and extract another elaborately disguised message which directs me to a different dark webpage.

This next dark web-address features an image of *The Destruction of Pompeii and Herculaneum* by John Martin. While examining the image using a text editor, I notice that the file's size is overtly overinflated for its file-type. This instantly indicates that there may be hidden data fingered into the file, so I use an old steganography program I'd coded as part of a previous pet-project in my early days to tease out this extra data. At this point, I have to pause in order to marvel at just how deeply the rabbit hole of these puzzles has bored its way into my head already. It's only been some 36 hours since I'd started, and my mind has indeed already fallen so far down into this mystery that the only way for me to pull my head out of it may be to dig through its deepest depths.

Agent Phoe pretty much leaves me to these puzzles. She mostly monitors my progress remotely while pursuing other aspects and angles involved in the larger and more concrete counter-terrorism case. Every few days or so she swings by for status reports and moral support, unless I make any potentially important progress which I must immediately inform her of. The days drift by in a strange and wonderful way for me during this timeless period of time. I seldom sleep, nearly starve, and still manage to remain insanely enchanted and enthralled all through this intense investigation.

Cracking various portions of these puzzles forces me to implement block, stream, Caesar, atbash, Vigenère, and other complex ciphers. I construct multi-lingual gematrias, extract PGP keys from highly secured source targets, and implement an almost infinitely regressing quine. I end up using everything from the most advanced to the most archaic versions of; steganography techniques, alpha-numeric substitutions, running keys, totient functions, log probabilities of quadrams and trigrams. I translate book codes, phone-words, runes, Mayan numerals, and Hieroglyphs. I reference longitude and latitude coordinates, identify famous books, movies, musical compositions, and paintings based on riddles and clues, and employ any number of other unremembered solving techniques. I find myself constantly elated by my awe of this mysteriously advanced and marvelously beautiful labyrinth of clues and puzzles. My entire existence almost becomes a matter of pure theoretical conjecture, as it seems that if I truly exist, it's in much the same way as the tree which falls in the woods with no one around to hear it. Or in my case, if a puzzle with apocalyptic implications appears on the internet, and I am unable to solve it, will I still exist?

After a while, a certain structure starts to become apparent in these impossibly impressive puzzles. They seem to be segregated into three sets of themes, and each of these themes correlates to the three separate Vitruvian principles of architecture. These three themes being *firmatis, venustatis*, and *utilitas*- or translated roughly into English: stability, beauty, and utility.

Each piece of the firmatis themed puzzles gradually guides me into deeper and deeper doubts involving the stability of the sensory world I inhabit. These doubts almost imperceptibly begin to incubate in response to that initial countdown involving allusions to a volcanic eruption. These progressive puzzles also increasingly insinuate an inevitability of other extinction level events such as asteroid collisions, super-strains of infectious diseases, cataclysmic shifts in the earth's magnetic field, coronal mass ejections, the existential risks associated with an omnipotent but misaligned AI entity's emergence, the increasingly apocalyptic aspects of successive wars, and all the fragile social, technological, and economic conditions which could each easily cause civilizational collapses.

The second set of progressive puzzles creates a contrary conception of beauty. This set of puzzles starts with spectrographic data hidden in what is identified as *Select Transcendental Etudes,* consisting of Liszt's fourth sixth, eighth, tenth, and twelfth etudes.[32] Using a letter to number substitution I find the names of these etudes sums to 456, and the phrase *Select Transcendental Etudes* sums to 288. Both sums are multiples of 144, and the individual etude numbers are also factors of 144. This number is so strangely interspersed throughout these puzzles that it's almost as if it's embedded within every architectural level of them.

As I continue to decipher the deeper details hidden in these impressive etudes, I end up using a spectrograph to extract data from *Mazzepa* which leads me to the same-named painting by Theodore Gericault. The etude *Vision* uncovers another equine image of a haunting blue horse with raging red eyes. *Wide Jagd* leads to a seemingly unrelated book code, *Appassionata* points me to Dante's *Divine Comedy*, and *Chasse Neige* leads me to an image of Petrus Van der Velden's *Burial In Winter On Island Of Marken* which is embedded with an encrypted gematria.

The ineffable essence of this second set of puzzles seems to secretly seep into my soul, imbuing me with a nourishing newfound affinity and appreciation for the beauty of life and art. This newborn bliss strangely swells out of the foundation of the first set of puzzles, as if the impermanence of life and inevitability of death not only creates a canvas for all inspiration, but illuminates every vision vested there by the fatal friction flashing against the edges of fate's unforgiving frame. It also seems as though all art is a doomed defiance of death, and the result of our refusal to simply accept the sinister slumber of an ever-swallowing shadow. I can't even consciously explain all the enigmatic ways these puzzles produced such stilted sentiments in me, or how they delphically dare me to dream against the dark so that the last lingering light within me may shed some spark against this dying domain to ignite some incendiary soul, and it too may continue to illuminate all that has yet to be so eternally erased.

As I attempt to apply my abstruse light to the third tier of puzzles, Agent Phoe interrupts my progress to provide me a new set of prison duds and deliver some disturbing new details.[33] She informs me that several sperate geologists have been brought into this case to consider how a terrorist group could conceivably trigger a volcanic eruption. These same geologists have apparently already been observing dramatic increases in the seismic activity surrounding the Yellowstone Caldera and seventeen other VEI-8 sites.[34] In light of this information, the USB has preemptively placed the geologists under gag orders on the grounds of preventing mass mania and protecting public safety.

The countdown on the initial dark webpage has expired down to exactly six days now, which comes to my attention as Agent Phoe points over my shoulder and squints to inspect the cryptic clocks. This awakens me to the fact that the hands on these clocks have all shifted to reveal a new book code. Agent Phoe proceeds to pedal through the pages of *At The Mountains Of Madness*, scratching out a solution with seamless speed. The emergent message rendered, reads.

*Th3re is no world*
*Which cannot be d3c3iv3d*
*Wh3re is this world*
*In which you've b3li3v3d*

My mathy-mind impels me to inform Agent Phoe that the sum of the letter values and numeric transpositions in this message is 792, which is the product of 12 and 66. I also illuminate that the sum of the two digits in 66 is 12, and that this may be an intentional way to reframe the numbers (12x12) and allude to the puzzles' ever-present number 144. I try to explain just how prominently present this number has been throughout every portion of the puzzles without sounding as if I'm having a schizophrenic episode while also being scarily uncertain of my actual level of sanity.

Agent Phoe isn't exactly impressed or interested by this pedantic property since it has no apparent utility in our objectives. She urges me instead to focus on the fact that the Yellowstone Caldera could erupt at any moment, and that this numerical nonsense needs to be put into productive perspective. Then she pauses abruptly as if forced to confront some conflicting quandary of her consciousness. When she speaks again, it's to inform me against her orders that the USB is organizing an evacuation of the GG's most elite oligarchs and sequestering them in special subterranean shelters so that they may be able to re-seed humanity after an eruptive eschaton. She explains how my schizophrenic insights might be the only source of salvation for the rest of humanity. I really didn't know how to respond as if I were humanity's last hope, but I try.

"It's possible that putting the pieces of this puzzle together will only teach us that no matter how hard we try to put things in their proper place, we will be left feeling incomplete until the very end. Even if we complete these puzzles, it may only paint an incomplete and insufficient picture. Perhaps all we can do is put our lives into perspective, and do our best to try to illuminate whatever our eyes can see for however long we're still here. Nope?"

Agent Phoe places a hand on my somber shoulder and pulls up a chair next to me. She has me run through every last detail I've discovered so far, also insisting I show her all the segments I still can't quite seem to fit together. I show her how the second set of puzzles might suggest something involving the Denver Okrug Airport due to the resemblance one of the *Mazzepa* images has to DOA's Blucifer statue, as well as what I suspect could be a coinciding set of coordinates to this same location which I'd extracted from a backmasked message embedded in one of the enigmatic etudes.

When I mention the Denver Okrug Airport, Agent Phoe appears as if she might feint for a second before revealing another unauthorized insight.

"Zhere iz extenzive tunnelz and massive sekret shelterz belowz zhis airportz. Zhe airportz is goingz to be sealed-off from everyonez fyor phony maintenance issuez, and, zhe militaryz is to be deployedz fyor protectionz ov zhe airportz and zhe GG'z most elite oligarchz already arrivingz in sekretz."

Everything about these puzzles and Agent Phoe's insights seems to point us toward Denver. However, we can't just make a mad dash to snoop around DOA before it's sealed-off without putting together all the remaining puzzle pieces. We both scour over every segment of each piece of these puzzles for hour upon hour. Just as it all starts to seem senseless, Agent Phoe draws my attention back to a dark webpage with the heading *Musica Universalis* which has dancing images of DNA embedded around some text which reads.

*The music of the spheres spins through the void of oblivion*
*Their sounds obscured by emptiness, are revealed by number*
*What harmony exists divine beyond all years and ears*
*Find your spirit's song, and sing it as the spheres do sing*

Agent Phoe has a certain intuition that there's more to this puzzle than I've already pulled out of it and starts streaming a set of spontaneous speculations. She takes the concept of how DNA consists of the base pairs; adenine (A) and thymine (T), and cytosine (C) and guanine (G) and proceeds to pick these letters out of the text. Then we both apply various ciphers to the remaining contents to translating these letters into numeric values before approximating them to tones in a harmonic series, hoping to produce a sort of musical melody. She explains how this hunch of hers relates to how *musica universalis* regards proportions in the movements of celestial bodies like the Sun, Moon, and planets as their own form of music.[35] She asks me to make a MIDI recording of this musical piece as she shifts her own attention back to the discarded DNA letters.

She types out these DNA letters and adds another *.onion* to the end of them. This produces yet another unexpected dark website which displays a series of segmented dots which we both instantly intuit as a message in either brail or mangled Morse code. Translating the dots as brail gives us a familiar opening line of *1: R3M3M83R TH3 FUTUR3*, followed by a paragraph of instructions detailing how to create a digital copy of one's consciousness and upload it over the internet to an unidentified network node.

While contemplating the confusing implications of copying and pasting one's consciousness across the net, I suddenly notice a series of ever so slightly off-colored lines lurking in the background of this dark webpage. Agent Phoe instantly intuits these lines as origami instructions. She admits to having been obsessed with origami since she was so silly and small as she snatches a premium sheet of paper from my desk drawer to form in accordance with the faint folding pattern. But before she can begin creasing out the pattern of the lines from the dark webpage, we both notice tiny letters subdued within the slightly color-cloaked lines.

We work together to draw these letters onto the paper before she proceeds to fold the origami into form. She explains the names of each fold as her nimble fingers swiftly and subtly shift to transform the piece of paper with impossible precision. Her dexterous hands contort their way through a long series of valley and mountain folds, pleats, reverse folds, squash folds, and sinks. She has all the slight-of-hand moves of a master magician which she uses to make crimp folds, petal folds, swivel folds, and rabbit ear folds look like some secret form of sorcery. When she completes the final creases, I'm left in an even greater glowing awe of her superior skill than I am at the sight of the Vitruvian man manifested from this premium paper and the message inscribed on its surface as a result of the morphed lines of folded letters which reads.

*♤S ♤BOVΣ S0 BΣLOW*

Of course, the sum of the non-substituted letter values is 144, but there's no need to mention this. When we get the idea to turn the origami figure over and place it above the brail block of text, another message makes itself known which contains what appears to be the necessary network node to upload our consciousness profiles. Gravity seems to abandon my mind altogether and my head spins in psychotic circles like a hot-air-balloon being swept into a whirlwind. The only thing tethering me to reality and preventing another psychotic seizure is Agent Phoe's hand upon my shoulder and her calm words which I cannot decipher from the whooshing wash of psychotic spinning which renders all sound as a singular sustained hissing inside my head.

This psychotic swirling soon subsides, and I find myself almost awakening into a stillness far beyond anything I've ever known. It's as if I've arrived at some mysterious still point around which all other spheres of time and space are secured in their senseless perpetual spinning. In this brief timeless moment between whirling chaos and stagnant oblivion I'm more at rest than I can imagine being under during the most delightful dream or sweetest slumber. I'm simultaneously more sentient and secure than I've ever even imagined under any meditative trance or altered state. It seems so impossible to abandon this sublime stillness- until it slowly slips away. And it's with an absence of sorrow that I realize how impossible it would ever be to stay.

# Chapter 5
# F4T3 OR FUT171TY

No matter how well the pieces fit or how much seems solved, we still seem to be missing something. My whole life seems like an impossible puzzle I've strained slavishly to solve. I've searched and scavenged every earthly and imaginary surface for any potential pieces to this life-long puzzle with the implicit intention of eventually peering at a completely constructed picture where everything finally makes fathomable sense, and I can bask in the blissful awe of having finished everything within the finite frame of my life's preposterous, profound, and picture-perfect completion.

Having decoded the directions detailing how to construct a consciousness compiler to upload our compiled consciousness profiles (CCPs) to a dark web-address, it would seem as if all the pieces should be in place. However, our attempts to upload our CCPs keep ending in authorization errors despite the use of my own vast array of techy tools. The obvious conclusion is that there is more to this puzzle than its pieces, and this uploading process requires routing through a restricted and pre-authorized terminal or device.

The dark-web countdown continues to tick down from four days, twelve hours, and thirty-six minutes. Agent Phoe has been working on arrangements to gain us access to Denver Okrug Airport, but there are no normal flights, and the terrestrial roadways leading into DOA are restricted by military cadres. Only the elite entities listed on an *Entry Authorization List* (EAL) are allowed to pass through the military-controlled access points.

Our only apparent option is to take the recently renovated high-speed rail from Vegas to Denver. When we arrive in Denver, we can assess the scene for any security weaknesses while waiting to see if the USB will authorize the access Agent Phoe has been attempting acquire for us. We may also investigate the mysterious Blucifer statue which stands well outside DOA's main gates.

My choice of wearing prison duds doesn't exactly expedite the Interstate Migration and Homeland Officials' (IMHOs) interrogations and Biological Screenings (BSs) for everything from contraband gerbils to colorectal polyps. However, our four-hour trip is delayed anyway, and our tickets are downgraded due to renovations and repairs which require the detachment of certain first-class traincars.[36] I decide to fiddle with my watch while we wait for our tardy train, trying to see if I can hack into one of Mythreum's half-abandoned dongle factories just outside of Denver where realistic rat-bots used to be manufactured for secret GG surveillance ops. I get my lulz just before we're finally able to board and about 48 hours are left on the dark web countdown which I've also synced to my wonderful and sentimental watch.

Despite the kinetic chaos of passengers pinball-bouncing off each other in a stochastic scramble for their assigned seats, they all appear half asleep. Most produce pillows almost as soon as they plop down in their prescribed places. However, even after the train lurches forward and resolves into the restful rolling rhythm of its consistent cruising speed, I find myself too paranoid to rest. I scan my eyes over all these unfamiliar and unreadable faces. Most turn inward toward their own indecipherable dreams or avoid allowing my unfamiliar eyes to investigate their expressions. Agent Phoe eventually turns her own ever-illuminated eyes toward mine.

"Is youz tiredz, or wouldz youz likez to do somethingz to pass zhe timez?"

"Nope. We can play a game of *backstory*. I pick a passenger, and you tell me a story about what led them here. Then we switch. Nope?"

"Ńyōᵽə. Youz tellz storyz, so I kan learnz to properly playz zhis gamez."

"Nope. You have to pick a passenger."

"Howz aboutz zhat beardz-man sitzingz six seatz aheadz ov us, on oppositez sidez ov zhe aisle? Youz seez himz?"

I use the overhead mirrors and darkly reflective windows to take note of all this character's visual details to construct a corresponding backstory. I consider his faded black stocking cap, torn and tattered jean-jacket, mud-battered work-boots, and the t-shirt with zombie-figures and wrinkled letters which likely spells out some horror sim's title. I also note how his eyes appear so bloodshot and unblinking as he stares lifelessly out the window that his thick, yellowing, and over-long fingernails almost appear as animated as the rest of him…

"Nope. That's not a man at all which lies before us. Perhaps he used to be, but he ceased to truly be a man even before he died this last week. What we see ahead of us in this train car, is merely the flesh and bone remnants of what had previously been known to almost no one other than himself as Dagon."

The horror story embellishments in my voice causes a nearby teenager's ears to inadvertently eavesdrop as my absurd and ominous tale continues.

"This was once a sailor you see, and the hat upon his head had once been the only thing keeping him from freezing to death after being shipwrecked in the eternally frigid winter waters of the north-most seas. The commercial fishing vessel and its 144 souls had capsized in those cold and merciless glacial waters. He'd been the only survivor to make it to any shore, though he's long lamented the fact that fate had forsaken his life in having spared it in such an insidious and interminable way."

The teenager tries to help prod my story along.

"Is that why his fingernails is so yellow?"

"His fingers are the least of all his menacing maladies. You see, the only way he survived his castaway kismet was by burning the clothes of all his fellow dead sailors and eating their briny flesh as the ominous ocean had vomited them onto the abominable, austere shores of a black sanded abyss. This dark isle upon which his sorrowful soul had been cast did not belong to any earthly realm. Nope, this tenebrific torment of an island could only exist in a realm of pure lightless oblivion where sinister shadows are cast by the eternally ancient forms of a most demonic darkness. This realm of otherworldly shadows had itself been stranded, forsaken, and forced to scavenge upon the rare remnants of the same most sorrowful souls of shipwrecked sailors."

My unsolicited audience member interjects another interruptive query.

"So, how'd this man ever get off this horrific hellscape-island?"

"You might say that his soul is still there, forever shrouded, shredded, and swallowed by the most sinister and shadowy specters. You see, this miserable man made a deal with that same demonic darkness. His rotting, gangrenous lips had shivered and sworn to whatever god might be lurking near him that he'd give anything if this condemned deity would only grant his eyes the chance to set sight on his home shores once more. A most ancient of evil deities who did reside within the darkest depths of this frozen abyss did indeed hear his plea, and this dark demon decided to grant his desperate wish in the worst of ways. This darkness had ripped the soul right out of this battered body you see before us now before slithering its way into the empty place his soul had once resided. Then this demented dark deity dissolved his soulless body into a formless and ethereal shadow so it could be cast back into the blackened abysmal depths of the wintery waters under the cloak of a blackly blanketing winter storm. This dark shadow-spirit slowly drifted unto the promised shores of its corpse's covenant where it cast itself as a sinister storm-cloud over those unsuspecting sands and excreted this body back from the bowls of an abysmally starless sky."

Agent Phoe struggles to contain an outburst of absurdist laughter as the teenager's mouth hangs in ecstatic awe of my preposterous proverb.

"It was only upon being cast onto that shaded shoreline, like a shadow from another realm, that this former man had realized the abominable sin his forsaken soul had committed within that darkness of otherworldly despair. He'd traded his mortal soul for an interminable existence as an empty vessel for this demonic darkness to use as its eternal earthly domain. From that day, everyone he ever loved or reached out to touch would themselves be turned into shadows, and their spirits would be sucked in and devoured by the same demented dark one residing within the empty place where his soul is no more."

A stewardess passes by with a cart of snacks and drinks. The teenager tries and fails to coax this attendant to supply her with an alcoholic beverage before settling for an off-brand bottle of carbonated, caffeine-rich cola. Agent Phoe and I accept bottles of water and bags of peanuts before the attendant moves along and my sinister saga continues.

"These terrifying tortures made our subject come to wish upon each of his shamed and soulless breaths for a death which would never come to him. So, this last week he resolved to end this haunted hell of a life by setting himself ablaze and jumping off a nameless mountain's lofty peak. Once he reached the summit of what was to be his final descent unto the end of his darkened days, he doused himself in gasoline."

I pour a small amount of water onto my head for dramatic effect.

"When he looked down at the snow-covered ground beneath this lofty peak, the distant drop was not seen as the space between him and his end, but as the time between this moment and the start of his shipwrecked sorrows. His eyes gazed down from the height of this abyss, but as he lit his match, stepped over the earthly edge, and awaited the impact of impending doom- the depths below drew him no nearer to his intended ending."

My fingers hold up a dark colored peanut and drop the salty stand-in to the floor. I pause for a moment to look down on it with an expression of perplexed pity before resuming my paranormal narrative.

"You see, the dark one which this former man had hoped to escape, can only be removed from the body of a spirit which has pledged itself to this bestial bleakness when no celestial shade nor earthly shadow can fall upon its ashen form. Dagon's corpse had failed to fully absolve itself of this most formidable phantasm as night's inevitable darkness had chased the setting sun from a surrendering sky, allowing this most sinister of shadows to reclaim its vagrant vessel And now, only a week later, this very vessel has been brought by that eternal and most sinister of shaded specters to appear so bereft before us now. It has carried this forfeited flesh and seated it here before us where it restlessly waits for this train to deliver us all unto the utter depths of darkness, or Denver."

The teenager's burst of laughter seems to open the release valve of Agent Phoe's own reserved amusement. I smile in insane bemusement as the teenager proceeds to complement my tale and excuse herself. As she heads to the restroom, my eyes wait for Agent Phoe to acknowledge that it's now her turn.

"Youz is remarkably delusionalz Harek. I no zhink zhere is any wayz I kan followz zhe insanity ov youz outlandish allegoryz. Kan I forfeitz minez turn?"

"Nope. But you can explain why you're on this train with me instead."

She tries to laugh me off as I sit waiting with my arms folded for her to entertain me with some silly narrative. Her eyes and mannerisms slightly tense.

"I'yams no surez what is more terrifyingz, youz story or zhe one youz is tryingz to getz out ov me."

"If you just want to sit here in silence and wonder what kind of insanity might be rolling through my mind as I look around this train-car, I'll leave you with that as a third option."

"Alrightz zhen Harek. I tellz youz minez story, but only if youz entertainz mez fyor zhe rest ov zhe trip. Does wez has dealz?"

I nod my head and shake hands to accept this altered agreement. Agent Phoe takes in a deep breath and squirms around in her seat a bit to shake off the nerves and settle into her backstory. Her voice becomes pensive, almost penitent.

"I'yamz here bekause zhere is nowherez else fyor mez to goez nowz. Minez family was takenz from mez long ago. I has no friends in zhe USB, or anywherez else fyor zhat matterz. And so, zhe only slightly meaningful zhingz I kan zhinkz ov doingz is tryingz to preservez some form ov humanz konsciousness. Zhere. Youz has minez story. Now youz must entertainz me."

Part of me feels guilty for wanting to coax anything more out of her, but I also suspect that she actually wants me to pry a bit in order to prove that I'm capable of genuine human empathy and personal interest in her life's story. There's also this certain ineffable intuition I have that there's something hiding behind her subtle defenses which I'm supposed to discover as well.

"Nope. That's not so much a story as a synopsis. I won't force anything out of you, but I am extremely curious as to how you've somehow ended up in this insane predicament with me. You're probably the most puzzling mystery of all to me. You're always so absurdly well composed and calculating, incredibly intelligent and perceptive, and I know almost nothing else about you. If there's any story you're willing to tell, I'm your most captive audience."

Agent Phoe looks at me with a kind of tender ambivalence, as if her contempt for me is held off by some unseen sentiment which absolves me of my oblivious transgressions. Then she takes a deep breath in and slowly releases it.

"Zhe reasonz I'yams on zhis trainz withoutz other placez to goez, is bekause I'yamz orphanz. Zhat is why I has always beenz so out ov place and lost in zhis worldz. As orphanz, I has no onez to konnectz mez to minez originz. Zhere is no place fyor mez to comez from, and no konnectionz to where I'yams."

As Agent Phoe pauses to take another deep breath, I want to tell her that I see her, that I understand her, that I know how it feels to be alone in a world I don't belong, and that I've experienced similar things in my own life. It doesn't seem like it's my place to say anything though. I feel like I should just listen and let her see that I hear her, and that I'm here in this strange situation with her.

"Minez parents were takenz away from me by government officials fyor some kindz ov non-kompliance. Zhey put me into one ov zhose filing cabinetz fyor miscellaneous kids whoz does not fitz anywhere else. Zhen I was givenz job with USB to pay-off minez parents' debts fyor not raisingz me themselves. I've attended to zhe tasks in front ov me all ov minez lifez bekause zhere is no alternativez fyor me. I has never had a homez to go, nor any ideaz ov what such a place is supposed to be. Zhe dorm roomz I was assigned in minez college days was just a box insidez zhe wastelandz ov drunkenz idiyotz. Minez residences has only ever been quarters to kontains mine-self until zhe next assignmentz transfers me to new areas. I has left nothing behindz me in minez lifez which I kould yearnz to kome back to, and I carryz no sense ov nostalgiaz either."

My eyes begin to glaze as I gaze back at her with a blind sense of understanding as Agent Phoe stares directly into the infinite space in front of us.

"Itz not just zhat I does not belong anywhere. I feelz as if I'yamz invisiblez, and everyone is out of mine reach. When I tryz to relatez to peoples, I kannot seemz to konvey anything about minez orphan lifez zhat zhey kan truly understand. Most ov zhe time, I does not even know howz to look at minez-self. I meanz, minez last namez does not even komez from minez fatherz. He was takenz from his familyz and raised by Asian couple with zhe last name ov *Phoe*. Minez fatherz and motherz was both Russianz zhough, and I was bornz in Moscow. Zhe only way I kan describez mine-self half-koherently is to say zhat I'yamz like Russianz seed, planted in Americanz soilz, and assigned an Asianz name. Zhat is what makez me feelz so invisiblez and out ov place."

I watch her take another deep and cleansing breath to purge the residue of these words from her lungs.

"Sometimes I feelz very much like zhere is darkness hidingz in zhe place where minez soul should be, not unlike youz fictionalz figurez. I zhink zhis is why I has always tryz to attendz to life. It givez me somethingz realz to focus on zhat does not kast some kind ov all-konsuming shadowz overz it. Allz I really wantz is to be ablez to bringz whatever light I kan to zhe darkness ov zhis world, bekause I does not wantz to be swallowed by zhese looming and sinister shadowz. Zhe only way fyor me to kontinuez to try and shinez a light against zhe darkness which may konsumez us all in just a few days, is to followz youz on zhis absurdly blind journey towardz something which maybe is no more zhan pure delusionz. Zhis is what has led me to be here with youz now. Youz see?"

Agent Phoe is far too sane and wonderful as a person to be left with no better option in the face of this world's end than to be seated with a paranoid schizophrenic who now awkwardly refers to himself by this diagnostic label. It seems even more absurd that the reason she is on this train is to pursue my deluded idea of transcendence due to a series of messages hidden in a set of mysterious puzzles. All I can do is gaze back at her with watery eyes and offer my gratitude in the form of the few impoverished words I can give.

"I can't thank you enough for all the light you've brought my world already. My days would have been much darker without you here already. If humanity has any light to look forward to, it isn't exemplified by me as well as it is in you. The reason I'm here right now, is to preserve the very light you shine so well."

Agent Phoe turns her eyes to measure mine. Her face regains its composure, and even manages to hoist a smile like a victory flag reclaiming its territory.

"Ńyōꝑə. Zhat's enough of zhis pseudo-sentimental nonsense. Tell me another ov youz crazy stories now Harek, before we both endz up as konfuse kharikaturez ov our-selves in an even more absurd narrative."

I oblige in making-up backstories for all the passive passengers on our train. I sprinkle-in secret details from my own life without knowing if Agent Phoe can decipher all this biographical info I filter into my maniacal stories. I only hope to offer some form of appreciative and non-pandering reciprocity in my own puzzling way. As I reach-out through the figurative form of my interpolated narratives to offer the equivalent of a comforting embrace, it does seem as if I'm able to touch something which nothing else I can imagine is currently capable.

When our train pulls into Denver, we quickly acquire a non-autonomous rental-ride to the airport. There are several signs posted within a few miles of DOA which warn of the closing roadways. Despite the military blockades we can already see assembled around the terminals of DOA as we cruise along Peña Blvd., the roadway appears to remain open at least as far as the field which surrounds the big, blue, ethereal, equine statue which is widely known by the nickname *Blucifer,* due to its ominous red glowing eyes, bulging brutish veins, and ferocious fiery form.[37]

After considering the restricted roadways and puzzling potential of this strangely sinister statue, Agent Phoe and I decide to pull the car off the road and trod though the grassy field to scavenge the areas surrounding this menacing mustang. The poorly maintained field's densely overgrown grasses eventually give way to a gravel mound which surrounds the concrete block upon which this bulging blue beast almost appears to burst out of. As our feet meet this gravel mound, we notice a nearby capstone about twelve feet directly behind and in line with the points of this sculpture's fetlocks. The capstone features an engraved scripture which reads like some kind of poetic prophecy once its words become near enough to our footsteps to be brought into functional focus.

*In man's oblivious slumber, let the enlightening knowledge precede him. As man awakens, let the light of illumination shine upon his inner depths. In man's illumination, let him shine his eyes unto the depths of his world to discover realms beyond him.*

Using the gematria from a previous puzzle, I'm able to determine the sum value of the text is of course, another multiple of 144. Underneath the inscription there's also another emblematic depiction of the Vitruvian man with an overlay of the geometric *Seed Of Life*.[38] Next to this, the roman numerals CXLIV have been etched in an almost imperceptibly tiny font.

After regarding the capstone, we proceed up the mound to gaze up at this blue behemoth-bronco from its base. This action seems to suddenly draw the military cadre's immediate interest in our presence. Agent Phoe notices their sudden stirring and urges me to follow her as she casually starts to stride back toward our vehicle. I decide to stay behind for a moment to scrutinize this surrealist statue. I count twelve ribs on either side of the sepulchral sculpture as Humvees begin rushing from the far-away roadblock toward the mound. Then I count twenty-four points to the mane, twelve points on the tail, and as I'm in the middle of quantifying the branches of visceral veins on the beastly blue body, one of the Humvees skid-slides to a halt at the edge of the gravel. A soldier in full body armor instantly launches itself like a rocket from the turret and sprints towards me without any loss of momentum as his feet hit the ground, yelling.

"HANDS UP! NOWWWW!!!"

I quickly comply with this up-armored mega-man, but he continues rushing in on me at full steam. I instinctively crouch as low to the ground as I possibly can to avoid being tackled into the gravely ground, and the soldier flies over my head. However, this triggers no fewer than six readily aimed Taser-darts to find their way to my flesh from various angles. The cumulative electrifying effect sends me shaking and slobbering to the gravel in excruciating and involuntary neuromuscular spasms. Needless to say, this not only incapacitates me, but forces me into another sudden and severe seizure.

I feel a heavy knee being pinned hard against my spine as my body's mass is flung face down. Then I hear the percussive thuds as the troops gather around my body which is still involuntarily shaking from my seizure. They bombard me with baton strikes, steel-toed kicks, and fist-shielded punches to try to get me to, "*STOP SQUIRMING*". Finally, mercifully, my vision eventually narrows into nothing, all sensation ceases to reach my mind, and my consciousness fades into the beautiful embrace of an indifferent oblivion.

I've often wondered how or why anything ever abandoned this beautifully blind oblivion in exchange for an existence plagued by so much pain. Of course, it's only in the presence of these pains that I'm able to imagine things like this. It's never in the midst of bliss that I wonder what sense there is in my existence.

When my seizure-soaked consciousness finally does return, I feel as if I've suffered all the torments and tortures of the nine sinister circles in Dante's infamous *Inferno*. Actually, if I'd only had my soul dismembered by some series of dead-eyed demons, it would probably be a massive improvement. My body feels like one large lump of bruised tissue which aches morbidly when stationary and becomes excruciatingly exacerbated at the mere thought of movement.

My eyes open to a piercing flood of artificial florescent lighting which overly illuminates what is essentially the inside of a brutalist concrete cube. I'm forced to appraise this tomb using only my eyes, as every segment of my beaten body is tightly strapped and secured to the cold slab of an autopsy table. This bleak tomb-like void is so deathly silent, that even the sound of my own hindered heartbeats and bounded breaths echoes back from the crypt-like walls. There doesn't even appear to be a door to this burial chamber inspired structure, and though the wide span of walls and vaulted ceiling forms a spacious shell around my undead cadaver, this concrete crypt feels unnervingly claustrophobic.

An unknowable span of time passes as my circadian echoes gradually begin to bully me with their sarcastic cadence and altered timbre, relentlessly mocking my vital vibrations. These brutal biorhythms are suddenly silenced by the sound of a massive metal door being shoved open in the same way a scavenger is hushed by the approach of an apex predator. The mechanically flopping thuds of encroaching footsteps follows the collapsing sound of the door slamming shut. These footsteps steadily swell in volume as their ambulating ambiance reverberates within my stinging skull and a humanoid silhouette stretches over me and eclipses the backdrop of unnaturally glaring florescent light, casting a high-contrast cloud of darkness over my unadjusted eyes. This shadowy figure hovers over my head from the zenith above my eyeline as a faintly familiar voice forces itself on my ears.

"Hello Jackwagon. I'll bet you never thought you'd see me again."

My pupils strain to adjust to the high-contrast between this fugue-like figure and the blinding barrage of imprudent incandescence. I finally manage to fit this venomous voice and indistinct imagery into one minotaur-like amalgamation in a moment of belated mental concrescence. A look of slight recognition betrays me and brings a malevolent bull-mouthed grin to this vile and vomitus visage.

"Before you get any sorer with me than you already are Harek,"

The minotaur-man clops one of his hoof-hands onto my wounded shoulder which induces a surging spasm of neuropathic agony.

"-let me tell you that I was not among the soldiers who were so, *exceedingly diligent* in apprehending you. In fact, I might actually be able to help you Harek."

His hoof-hand pats and squeezes my suffering shoulder a few more times before he briefly retreats to retrieve a rodent from a small cage which he must have carried in with him. As he holds up the radiant white lab rat, its worried whiskers start to twitch in indecipherable impulses of a mousey-Morse code or something.

"Before we begin, you should know that you're being held here without any legal authority, and that your survival depends entirely on my determination of your aptitudes and amenability to be of service. And so, I suggest you cooperate with me if you have any intention of surviving our little chat. Am I clear?"

"Nope. You're obviously being intentionally opaque. How am I meant to be of service though?"

Agent Keptic holds up the rat with his hoof-hands and looks back and forth from it to me to draw a pantomime parallel. His eyes remain indifferently and inquisitively affixed to the rat as he indirectly addresses me.

"If you think about it, that's the only real question there is- even for this rat. You see, this rat thinks its life is in service to its own survival. Its success, struggle, and suffering are all defined by how they serve this rat's longevity. If another creature should kill it, this rat's futile misfortune is purely its own, and nothing more meaningful will be lost. The only larger purpose it may ever serve is to inadvertently feed a predator or fertilize a plant. Since it can only delay its death, all it will ever truly be in the end is an oblivious failure."

The mouse starts to struggle and squeal as his hoof-hand tightens around it.

"You see Harek, without serving something beyond oneself, life and all its suffering becomes an empty endeavor. However, if we put this rat in a maze and use its love of cheese to study its nature, the rat may be afforded an opportunity to transcend its own empty essence. If we pump it full of drugs, jam wires into its brain, or torture it in any number of ways, the rat may imagine itself suffering senselessly, but the truth is that we are imbuing its life with meaning. By forcing this rat to serve something beyond itself, humanity can learn from its otherwise useless existence. Now, let's see just what service this rat can be of to me."

The brutal-bull's empty hoof grabs a scalpel as he stares at me with a sinister gaze. He forces the mouse to suffer and squeal against his tightening grip as he glares at me in unblinking hatred. Then he begins to twist the blade into the cringing creature in vacillating bursts to sustain the rat's shrill shrieking until its ever-weakening whimpers finally fade into a somber subsequent silence. Its life leaks out from the divinity within it, and its pure white fur is stained by the secrets its blood could or would not convey. Agent Keptic glances indifferently at the red, dead rat before shrugging his shoulders and shooting his sinister minotaur-scowl back at me.

"You're no different to me than this rat, Harek. You will do your duty to humanity and those presiding over it, or I will take you out of the metaphorical maze you were meant to master and end the emptiness of your existence just like this filthy rat. Is this too allegorical for you, Jackwagon?"

"Nope. You obviously want me to pledge my undying devotion to you and your masters in order to stay in the safety of this subterranean shelter, lest you either kill me or leave me to die in the impending volcanic eruptions."

Agent Keptic casually tosses the dead rat over his shoulder and starts smearing its slimy blood off of his hoof-hands and against my bandaged body.

"No blood wasted on you, huh Harek? Maybe you'll even die as dutiful a death as this rat which was so blessed to help me demonstrate my point. Now, please explain exactly what kind of service you're willing and able to offer."

"Nope."

Agent Keptic sneers at me with an incendiary look of indignation and growls at me in a voice which simmers in a rage that's about to boil over.

"*NOPE*? I ask you why I shouldn't just end your useless life and offer you a chance to give your pathetic life meaning. And all you can say is, *NOPE*?"

"Nope. I'll add to that right now. I'd rather die by your hand right now or in those imminent earthly eruptions than live an extended life of slavery to those of you who would insist I justify my own existence by surrendering my soul in servitude. If that's what's demanded of those seeking to survive in this shelter, then humanity's extinction won't be prevented or even delayed down here, as humanity will have been segregated outside of this place. So, tell your masters whatever you want. I'd rather preserve my humanity than live devoid of it."

My eyes and mouth may be the only unrestrained parts of me, but I delight in how fearless they are in the face of my cringing captor. My rat bloodied bandages reflect off the surface of his bull-like eyes as his volcanic scowl glows of various raging red hues.

"Let me spell it all out for you one more time Harek. The only relevant thing that exists in this world is duty. It's duty that defines everything. My duty is to ask questions and report my findings. Any ideals you may have like truth or justice don't matter in this or any other world, and they never have. If someone is truly innocent, it's their duty to prove it, and the judge's duty is to preside over the process of determining any truth or justice. That's not because these higher ideals actually exist, mind you, but simply because it's the judge's duty to act as if they do. You see, duty exists despite everything else. Duty transcends everything."

Agent Keptic shakes his head in open disgust of my reticent response to his self-stirring soliloquy. After a seething moment, he turns his back to walk out of this concrete ossuary, but before his stomping hoof-steps scamper for the exit, he mutters over his shoulder.

"For a man of such supposed talent and intellect, I'm astonished by your ignorance. Enjoy rotting to death with all your irrelevant ideals, Harek."

"Nope. When your consciousness comes to an end, you can make it your duty to go straight to hell. I'm sure you'll find plenty of *duty* down there too."

Without another word, I hear the angry stampede of his retreating hooves, followed by the mellifluous arcing swing of the door as he flails to fling it open. His first few hoof-steps clop against the carpeted hallway before the slow sway of the door returns it thudding against its frame. This final thud reverberates off the walls of this concrete charnel and my own suffering skull. For a while, I feel a sense of self-admiration and contentment for not having allowed myself to be reduced to some servile, supplicant sycophant. As perpetually unmarked time continues to pass, melancholy emerges to mark my mind. I start to think of how close all my exhaustive efforts and puzzle solving may have brought me to potentially achieving some form of transcendence, and how these pathetic pseudo-survivors won't be able to preserve their consciousness without my insights.

Despite the incessant saturation of artificial light, I begin to feel as if I'm in the darkest cavern of this entire existential realm. All my thoughts are abysmally dark, dejected, and deviant. My mind becomes vicious and vengeful. I think of the world being buried by pyroclastic glaciers as volcanic lava-landscapes drown out these lowest of creatures in their sequestered subterranean lairs. My mind pictures these wealthy manipulators of perceived reality, who knowingly and deceivingly refused to allow anyone outside of their inbred circles of corrupt criminal cronies to even be privy to the impending doom that all terrestrial forms of life will now be forced to suffer as they suffocate in the stench of their own smoldering corpses.

My mind reimagines miracles by which the forsaken masses become aware of the impending eruption and proceed to storm all these bourgeois bunkers. I imagine them pulling these wealthy defilers of reality out of the ground like gardeners uprooting fistfuls of weeds. The mobs are unexpectedly poignant in my mind's eye as they indict these sub-humans for their crimes against reality. They accuse these uprooted weed-creatures of defiling and poisoning reality with lies, deceits, and other mutilations of every truth. They demand penance from these demons for having extracted every nourishing morsel of reality from the existing world only to replenish the void left behind with empty lies and illusions.

The masses poetically explain the processes by which the media, government, commerce, advertising, and social mediums all gradually and eroded the fabric of reality by replacing every truth with whatever they could call facts in order to deceive us into adopting their depicted delusions in place of reality They point out how this process turned our reality into a vapid wasteland of virtual, artificial, symbolic, abstracted, and empty nothingness. I see them eloquently detail how real life, real relationships, real interaction, real feeling, real inspiration, and reality itself had been bastardized into commodities, data, profiles, and ill-conceived *content* which were all eternally dissolved further and further down into evermore diluted delusions of demon-dreams which the whole world is now awakening out of.

I can almost taste the slimy metallic flavor of wretched blood in my mouth as I envision the whole tableau unfolding. The masses all force their way down into the underworld in an effort to escape the coming epoch of eruption-induced extinction. But they don't huddle together or embrace their newfound comrades for any length of time before the reality sets in, and they realize that only so many people can survive in these hidden depths. My eyes water as I realize that in the end, there's no way in which I can imagine any honorable shred of real humanity being left to mourn in its own extinction.

These venomous thoughts hiss inside my head, following me unto another lapse of consciousness in the form of a surrendering sleep. I fade into the darkness of unconscious oblivion until some unknowable point later-on, when I drift seamlessly into the insanity of an unsolicited dream. My mind constructs its own dream-reality and deceives me into entering it as if it were as real a realm as any other in the way dreaming seems so deceptively designed to do.

This dream has me believing that I'm a rat invading an iteration of Schrödinger's famous thought experiment.[39] My rat body has been infected with toxoplasmosis due to an exposure to the *toxoplasma gandii* commonly found in cat feces. This infection causes me to be compulsively drawn to cats and their fecal smells, most especially Schrödinger's experimental cat.

Schrödinger is conducting an alternative iteration of his experiment in order to help him either prove or disprove the reality of his own existence. He's opted to run his thought experiment within a simulated world in which his theoretical cat is both dead and alive until he opens its simulated box. However, the cat's ability to discern the true nature of its existence is what determines whether or not it is found dead or alive. If the cat is unable to figure out that it's in a simulation rather than reality, it will be found alive. If the cat can somehow conclude that it is in a simulation, it will be discovered in a deceased state. Of course, all Schrödinger is actually able to conclude from this experiment is whether or not it's possible for a simulated cat to disprove its own assumptions about being a real cat, and he can't directly determine whether or not he's real, but he blindly hopes this experiment will help him find something useful.

So, my role as a cat-crazed rat in this dream has no initial significance. At the beginning of the experiment, I can only be certain that I'm no more real than this cat because a real rat wouldn't be drawn to a fake cat even under the spell of toxoplasmosis, and I am indeed drawn to this cat. This feline-magnetism brings me into the experiment as I manage to sneak through Schrödinger's larger sim-world and find a little hiding place inside the cat's experimental box. Both the cat and I are enclosed inside this box without Schrödinger even realizing I've managed to sneak inside of it.

Now, if I were actually aware of the fact that I've entered into this experimental simulation and understood how it works, I could stay in my secret spot and wait for the lid to open. If the cat turned out to be dead and not real, I'd know that I'm not a real rat. Should the cat prove to be alive when the box was opened, however, I'd have to face the fact that I'd almost certainly be devoured by the cat or snuffed out by Schrödinger without any revelation regarding the true nature of my existence. But for all I know, I'm just a cat-crazed rat.

My little rat mind has managed to add a degree of complication to this experiment, however. I've started to suspect that I might not be a real rat, and that this box might be some kind of test I've blindly stumbled into. Despite my desire to remain close to the cat, I've started to wonder if I'd be drawn to a cat from a higher level of reality. I've become so obsessed with this idea that I've started studying every detail of this box whenever the cat is asleep, and even found the seams which seal me inside of it. I've also come to suspect that the outer realm may just be a larger simulation with its own similar seams.

I come to realize that if I can escape this box and then the outer world, I may be able to make use of the fact of whether or not I'm still drawn to cats. If I'm still drawn to them and they're unable to eat me in the same way my box-mate is unable to kill the red dot of a laser, I'll know I'm still not real. However, if I'm no longer drawn to cats in the world beyond- I'll have been cured and it won't even matter if I'm real or not because at least I won't have an addiction to cats and their fecal filth!

My little rat legs are all set to leap out of the box when Schrödinger opens the lid too. I jump out of my secret spot and pull myself up and over the edge. I scurry all the way to a rooftop where I sneak onto a rocket just before it launches into space. I drift through the vastest void until I reach what looks a lot like the edge of Schrödinger's box, but just as I'm about to break the threshold- I suddenly awaken! I no longer give a *$#1+* about cats, I'm not in a rocket-ship, a scientist's sim-box, and I'm not in a concrete crypt either. Instead, I'm sitting upright in what appears to be a hospital room with seven human figures standing around me. One of these figures appears to be Agent Phoe who removes a giant dome-thing from my head. My mind is all fuzzy, but I hear one of the other figures hissing something about *interpolation* as my mind fades into awareness.

Agent Phoe gives me a moment for my eyes and mind to adjust before she flashes a cryptically stern glare and begins speaking in an ever so slightly over-pronounced tone and serious tone as if sneaking in some secret signal to me.

"Harek, are youz now willingz to tellz us how youz may be ov service?"

I instantaneously put all the missing pieces together in my mangled mind. Sometime after being Tased and beaten into a consciousness depriving seizure, Agent Phoe must have made some kind of special arrangements to have had me sent to this windowless hospital room. This dome-thing had been placed over my head sometime later to cast a sort of guided dream over my mind until I'd drifted into my own crazy rat-dream within a helmeted-dream. So now, I must be facing a group of six anonymous figures that all want to force me into giving some real consideration as to how I might grovel before them in hopes of being granted a place in their bourgeois bunker, and Agent Phoe's subtle signals were intended to urge me into playing along until she can reveal a larger plan latter.

This logic is extremely presumptive and loosely based, but it seems like the most provisionally providential perspective for me to assume. As much as I despise myself for doing so, I proceed to read off an impromptu résumé and appear as servile and supplicant as any Renfield-like underling that's ever existed. I balance every word between prideful self-impotence and an eagerness to prove my worthiness and gratitude to this captive audience. I even interpolate a few extra words and sentiments which I remember having heard during Agent Keptic's simulated speech regarding duty as the existential imperative. At the end of my plagiarized plea, I try to gage their responses to all my interpolated insinuations so I can anticipate what might come next.

These six balding, board-member-like men all hold the stereotypical expressions oligarchical men often have when they feel as if they've been sufficiently complemented and surrendered to by an overwhelmed opponent. I manage to conceal my desire to vomit in response to this repulsive scene, and instead I give the kind of glazed-eyed stare a child might offer while waiting for a response from its parents after asking whether or not they'll please, please, please let them stay at a friend's house over a weekend or something. They deliberate for a moment and then welcome me to *the lower Denver area* with smug looks on their false faces before they file out of the room. Agent Phoe asks one of them if she can have a minute with me, which is consented to with an apathetic nod of approval. The door closes behind the sixth man, and I gaze up into her eyes trying to read them like tea leaves or a crystal ball.

She reaches out to grasp my hand and slyly slips a note into my palm. She uses her cryptic, magical eyes to point in the direction of a monitoring camera without moving her head. Her hand lingers to hold mine long enough to cast shade on this sleight of hand note passing. Then to really sell her little magic trick, she softly and sentimentally tells me.

"Is good to has youz backz."

I watch as she smiles in a way that almost completely masks the foreboding frown she really wants to express to me. Once she leaves me alone in this room, I slip the rolled-up note into the one place everyone knows is best to hide something on your body. This is the only safe place to keep the note until I can view it in real privacy. If there isn't a restroom somewhere which doesn't have surveillance equipment, then my effort to conceal this note will have been so futile that I might as well have just stuck it up my-

The door opens without warning and a nurse enters. She's holding a sponge and a bucket of soapy water. Before she can offer me a sponge-bath, I ask if I can use a shower. My request brings a look of relief to her face, and she tells me that if I'm up to the task, she's more than willing to escort me to a place where I can clean up a bit.

I don't know why hospital gowns don't have more dignifying coverage of the human body, specifically the least dignified parts of it. As I follow the nurse down the hallway to the nearby shower, I have to stop myself from pulling a scowl in response to this thought, the humiliation of my own body, and the pain that apparently is not very well offset by whatever drugs they may have given me. Instead, I have to perform the act that many young married couples go through, where they pretend everything is comfortably fine.

When I finally get into the shower, I'd like to dislodge a multitude of other figurative things from the metaphorical space synonymous with where this note has been physically sequestered, but my fingers can only find and fasten themselves around the note. In order not to arouse any suspicion, I decide to turn on the water while I stand hunched over to block the descending stream of water from ruining the note as I unravel it. A sudden spasm of cruel, cold-water sprays hard out of the showerhead as soon as I turn the knobs, and an otherworldly sense of pain nearly forces me to feint. The chilling pain torments me into trembling tremors, and I'm barely able to hold the note still enough in my hands and sustain the shelter of my blood-stained back.

As I struggle to read the contents of the note, I notice it's been constructed using a simple cipher. I use an improvised form of meditation to subtract all the sensory strain from my mind and focus my full conscious capacity on decrypting this jumbled jargon. Soon, I'm able to extract the first of Phoe's facts about a special transmission-terminal inside DOA's secret subterranean shelter which she suspects could be used to upload our CCPs.

The note also seems to say something about not allowing our captors to know anything related to the puzzles which led us here, and that she's done something to my wristwatch which involves a derelict 🐿️ factory outside of Denver, but the splatter from the streaming shower against my back is begins to soak into the note and scramble the soggy symbols. The last bit of content I can partially un-puzzle before the note slips out of my shaking fingers appears to be more personal, but the ink instantly dissolves into a blurry mess. I use my foot to grind the disintegrating paper into tiny particles which swirl in the rust-colored water on their way down the drain.

At first, I imagine the tainted water to be stained by corroding copper pipes, but I soon realized the dull orange color to be derived from my own dried blood as it dissolves into the descending water. My lack of flexibility and hypersensitive wounds prevent me from scrubbing away at my battered back, so I remain hunched over and shuddering in pain as the shower slowly etches the blood off my back. Eventually, the water becomes untinged to my eye and swirls down the drain with everything else which is so easily rinsed away from this realm of ruin.

I use the single white towel that I've been provided to dry off every other part of my body before I dab it on my beaten back. Freshly bleeding bits of blood slowly seep into the soft towel from my cleansed but now uncoagulated wounds. Somehow this makes me despise the towel for trying to bring shame against my own blood for having tainted this blank, flat, lifeless nothing of an object. Obviously, a certain displaced rage has been creeping into my feelings over more than this bloody towel, but instead of analyzing my thoughts and emotions to make some allegorical sense which might be lurking beneath the surface I resolve to focus on more pressing matters.

Despite the pain of getting around on my battered body and my embarrassing invalid attire, I decide to wander around the halls of this bland bunker. I'm not sure how long I've already been down here, but there must only be a day or two before the countdown hits zero. My mangled mind already has me convinced that even if I can survive beyond this countdown, all hope will still be lost if I can't figure out how to upload our CCPs before it expires.

In order to escape this colossal coffin or make use of the terminal mentioned in Agent Phoe's note, I'll have to familiarize myself with its layout. The halls are all arranged into a large square grid with elevators likely leading to identical floors. This place is essentially one, big, square silo which may be connected to other subterranean structures through a network of tunnels. Although, I doubt it'll be necessary to travel too far since Agent Phoe has already been able to find this terminal and make the secret note to tell me about it.

As I limp along the horrid hallways of this grid, I take note of the various types of doors. Some of the doors appear residential and have last names etched on them in fancy fonts. Others are more industrial looking and have cheap magnetic labels like restroom, laundry, supplies, and utilities to mark them. When I find a room labeled *media center* I decide to wander inside.

Inside the media center, a group of eight old men are playing with an extremely expensive VR simulator which is designed and distributed by Mythreum's elite products division. I notice an antiquated holographic interface terminal in the back of the room, next to an ancient looking bookcase which is filled with real old-fashioned novels and textbooks. This almost has to be the terminal Agent Phoe had referenced in her note, and to my surprise, it's actually a portable piece of equipment which isn't old enough to need to be hardwired.

Instead of making a more detailed assessment of the terminal's potential to aid in our plan, I decide to try and find Agent Phoe. If she knows how to get out of this place, we might be able to just steal it and upload our CCPs while we try to find a more suitable sanctuary. Although we'd probably adjust to this prison over time, I'd still rather risk dying in a pyroclastic breeze than remain confined to suffocate on the hopeless strangling servitude of these dismal depths.

As soon as I open the media center door to leave, I see Agent Phoe rounding a corner and heading straight toward me. She masks her surprise over my having strayed from my room and signals for me to follow behind her. As she strides past me, she slips my wristwatch into my hand which I reattach as I cringingly rush to catch up to her. She pauses just long enough to peer around the next corner so that I can grab her hand to be led down a series of turns until we reach a residential door reading *Sean Keptic*. My eyes widen, my jaw goes slack, and she pulls me through the doorway as she slings it open with a brisk and hurried pull.

"Harek, we does not has much timez. Did youz readz mine note?"

"Nope. Not all of it, but most of it."

"Good. So, zhe terminal is in zhe media center. I has alreadyz checked, and it kan aksess zhe dark web-address. If wez kan stealz it, zhen wez should be able to getz out ov here and kompletez ourz upload from a helicopter. I zhink I kan flyz us to another place where wez might still survivez. We kan no stayz here zhough. Zhese peoplez alreadyz askz questionz about zhe puzzlez and-"

Agent Phoe hushes her hurried briefing as we both hear voices emanating just outside the door. Her head snaps to look at the door and then snaps sharply back to look at me.

"Zhey is herez. If I sayz zhe word *eskaton*, wez makez runz to terminal."

The door swings open and Agent Keptic appears as another old grey headed man in a suit says goodbye to him and walks off down the hall. Agent Keptic pulls a sneering smile of fake joy and real contempt as he sees us both standing blank faced and composed in disciplined disguise.

"Good, you're already here. I was hoping we could get this all out of the way as soon as possible."

Agent Phoe places a tender hand on my elbow and smiles convincingly at the minotaur-man.

"I hope zhis won't takez long, bekause Harek really should be gettingz some rest to rekuperatez."

"I wouldn't worry about that Karen. As long as everything is above board here, we should be able to give Harek a good long rest soon enough."

Agent Keptic walks over to a large living room chair and invites us to sit on a long leather couch positioned directly facing him. Once we're all seated, his minotaur-mouth opens again.

"So, I understand that some of the others have already asked about those weird puzzles Harek turned us onto. I'm sure you can understand their concerns, given the obvious correlations these puzzles seem to have with the geological threats we're facing. Then, there's also the possible link to those other terrorist attacks which lead us to discover these mysterious things, but let me assure you, all I really want to figure out by questioning the two of you is how to reassure everyone down here. If you can answer all of my questions in a way that helps me pacify the fears and speculations of these powerful men, there's nothing for you to worry about. So, shall we begin?"

I look at Agent Phoe and then shrug my shoulders. She raises her chin and speaks in a slightly probing voice.

"I does not knowz what else either ov us kan tell youz zhat I has not briefed youz on already. Zhese puzzles is very speculative. Zhe countdown is probably just koincidence, and wez found no real reasonz to connectz zhem to zhe terrorists. Everythingz wez knowz about zhese puzzles has all been put into minez recordz. What else is zhere to tell?"

"Well, the information you've given in your reports does seem to explain everything in the same way you've just summarized. The only problem is that some of these old men have been telling stories about these puzzles. These stories are based on things they've read in the testimony of that simulated terrorist character H4k3r. You see, according to H4k3r these puzzles contain hidden contents which can be used to upload consciousness profiles into a higher realm. This notion of transferring their own consciousness beyond our realm has really captured the imagination of these old men."

"Since when is it ourz jobz to indulge zhe imaginations ov old men?"

"Well, I hate to break it to you Karen, but it's pretty much always been our job to serve these elders. In any case, it's now my duty to figure out what to tell these men. So, let me start by asking you this. Why did you decide to come to Denver and visit the big blue statue?"

"Harek found possible referencez to zhis statue in zhe puzzles. Our investigationz had no other leads at zhis point, so it seemz good an ideaz as any."

"Alright, but why were you trying to arrange access to the airport before coming here? Was there anything in the puzzles alluding to the airport itself which might have been omitted from your reports?"

I decide to get involved and raise a preemptive hand toward Agent Phoe to let her know I'm in control of the situation.

"Nope. I'd asked her to try to get access to the airport because I didn't want to end up getting stranded in this place when the countdown ran out. There's also the fact that there have been rumors of these underground facilities for some time, and as a paranoid schizophrenic working on mysterious puzzles it seemed perfectly natural to assume there could be some connection. And, I know this might sound crazy, but how do I know the people running this place aren't responsible for the puzzles?"

"You know, that's an interesting question I've never considered before now. I suppose the only answer I can give is that you'd have to ask them. Although, I doubt that would do your paranoia any good. I might ask you why you'd consider it possible that the countdown alluded to anything catastrophic, but I'm sure you'd just tell me that it had something to do with your paranoid suspicions involving other aspects of the puzzles, even though I already know that Agent Phoe let it slip that geologists were predicting a supervolcanic eruption around the same timeframe. What I will ask you, is this. Why'd you bring a portable consciousness compiler with your profiles pre-loaded onto it?"

"Nope. If you thought the world might be on the verge of ending, and you could make such a device, wouldn't you have done the same thing?"

"I suppose so Harek, but can you tell me what the point of this would be? I mean, why would you carry a digital copy of your consciousness around with you, unless you were going to send it somewhere? Also, if you were going to try to send it somewhere, then where would you send it, and why? Do you want to know what I think?"

"Nope. I'll just save the time and answer all your questions since you'll want my explanation anyway. I made the digital copies of our consciousness profiles so that some decent remnant of humanity might survive in the event of some catastrophic event, which apparently my paranoia predicted. These digital profiles could potentially survive by being sent to any surviving node on the web, in a surviving computing-cloud, or even just on an external device- as long as some form of intelligent life could find these profiles and awaken them."

The left corner of the minotaur-man's jowls twitches none-too slightly in unmasked contempt before he pulls a fake smile. He rises to his feet with a fake chuckle and extends his hand to shake mine and Agent Phoe's. We both get up and shake his hand, hoping to conclude this informal interrogation.

"Well, that should wrap up all my questions, I suppose. I'm not sure I'll be able to assuage all these old timers, but it is what it is I suppose. If you two don't have anything else to add, then I suppose you're welcome to go get some rest. Although, I don't know how well you might be able to sleep. After all, the countdown is supposed to hit zero tomorrow, and to be honest, I haven't been able to sleep much myself due to the impending doom augured by our geologists and your silly little puzzles lately. In any case, you are free to go."

We try not to seem too anxious to exit the minotaur-man's domain as Agent Phoe and I proceed down the hallways toward a doorway labeled *staff living quarters*. The room is filled with nothing more than row after row of abandoned-looking bunkbeds. Without a word, we look at each other and just know that Agent Keptic has not been satisfied by our answers. Neither of us needs to explain the impossible situation we are in now. Agent Keptic will try to track our movements in order to see if we try to upload our consciousness through the terminal in the media center. Whenever we make our move, he'll probably be able to prevent our escape and use our knowledge to upload his own consciousness profile.

Our only apparent options are to either accept the icy hand which fate has dealt us, or to make an almost certainly futile attempt to follow through with our plans of transcendence despite the seemingly insurmountable odds stacked against us. If we accept the hand of fate, we'll be forced to live out our dismal days confined to this lowly place, having surrendered our souls and illuminating insights to unworthy men and their malicious minotaur-minded minion. I don't need to ask Agent Phoe, or even try to read her resilient face to know that no matter how futile it may be, for us- fate is not an option.

# Chapter 6
## OF M4NY D34TH5

It's a strange thing to believe you're living through the last night which will ever exist on the earth as you know it. This futile fact makes forfeiting any desire to sleep easy enough, but surrendering a life-long dream is still somehow impossible. I find myself staring blindly into the darkness and feeling as if my dream of transcendence is already long lost while knowing that I'll never be able to truly rest or actually awaken until I finally find something truly transcendent or at least more relevantly real. It's as if my soul knows it can never be spared of this spell, not even in the accumulation of many deaths.

I roll to my side and see the subtle silhouette of Agent Karen Phoe. She's sitting upright on one of the nearby beds facing mine. We both know it's too dark in this place to see too clearly and that our voices are almost certainly being monitored. But there's still one way in which we might be able to reach out and communicate a few last lingering thoughts to each other. I whisper.

"Karen, you wouldn't happen to know tactile sign language, would you?"

"Is possible I kan rekall PTASL.[40] Does youz aktually know howz to sign?"

I roll out of my borrowed bed to seat myself on Karen's bunk in a pretzel-legged pose facing her. She places her hands inside of mine so I can feel the shapes of her hands as they move to mold her words. She asks me if I can really understand her, and if so, how I'd ever learned to communicate in this disappearing dialect. Then she places my hands inside of hers where they pensively pause to patiently feel for my response.

My hands make gentle deliberate movements to intone my molded words with all the reverence of an Empyrean-priest etching eternal truths into stone tablets. I shape the story of how my grandmother had lost her vision due to cataracts when I was still very young. My hands can't help but tremble as I tell Karen how my grandmother had also feared of losing her hearing while her vision slowly and ceaselessly faded away. I manage to steady my signal-shapes enough to at least outline how my dear Grisha had come up with the idea of having us all learn tactile sign language so none of us would lose touch with our dear diminishing grandmother or ever be exiled unto our own solitary oblivion.

Karen sympathetically squeezes my hands after my shapes and story stand still. Then she tenderly places her friendly fingers inside mine. Her own dexterous hands have the slightest shiver of their own as she begins to form the shapes around how she'd come to learn this sensuous sightless language.

The earth itself suddenly shivers in a subtle but terrifying tremor, interrupting Karen before she begins, and almost alluding to the inauguration of all those awful enigmatic auguries. We remain silent, steady, and still until this slight shivering subsides. Then, Karen conveys her story as I hold her precious words in my hands as if my fingers belonged to a thirst-stricken dessert Bedouin who'd just wandered into an oasis where her words are the cleansing and quenching waters considerately cupped in my sand-scared hands.

"While condemned to that filing cabinet for miscellaneous misfits, I'd spoken out against the cruelty of a certain teacher. After a series of lies and counter claims against me, mine retaliatory punishment was a long stretch of solitary refinement. They throwed me into a dark pit where another girl had been tossed long before mine own arrival. She had been left alone down there for so long that they had actually forgotten about her."

A single tear drips onto the back of my hands as I continue to hold onto every word which forms without even an imagined accent.

"Hellena was her name. Her sense of hearing wasn't totally lost, but she was completely blind and mute. I could only see her when the sun was almost directly above the opening of our punishing pit. Whenever there was light, she could teach me to sign by repeating whatever words I spoke into her ear in PTASL. I would study the shapes of her words by memorizing them visually as I deliberately developed an ability to connect their visual appearance to their felt forms. Eventually, it didn't matter how dark it was down there. We became capable of reaching out to each other whenever we wanted our words to be felt."

An ethereal blue glow phosphoresces from Karen's watery eyes as my own gradually adjust just enough to behold this brilliant glow against the surrounding darkness. Her tears are all held just at the threshold of spilling out onto the softly glistening highlights of her face which is still somehow stoic, even as it grieves.

"I remember the day that the authorities came down and yanked us out of that horrible hole. They told me it was time to resume my education and that Hellena was to be sent away to work in a laundry center somewhere. I'd begged and pleaded with them to let me go with her, so she'd still have someone to communicate with. They tried to ignore me, but as I became increasingly emotional and defiant, they started yelling at me to shut up and even beat me a bit. I managed to break away from them and even catch up to the guard who was hauling Hellena away. I remember how I'd reached out to take her hands and felt them trembling to say goodbye. As the other guards arrived and my hands were ripped away from hers, I was terrified that this would be the last time I'd ever feel another word or touch another person's thoughts in this incredible and intimate way in which words could transcend and become imbued in flesh."

I gently press my empathy into Karen's hands as they pause. She seems to absorb my intended essence before I feel her words forming within my fingers again.

"Is so strange to be sitting here in all this darkness, thinking about mine entire life, what matters most to me, what I hope to have been when it all ends. Is strange to see that faint glint of your eyes against all the darkness of our dying night. Is strange how this darkness is so easily defeated by the defiance of each soft illumination. Is strange how this lingering light almost appears to beam brilliantly from the pores of your skin, as if it were shining from the very depths of your very soul. Is strange how such a surreal moment can feel so real that it even seems as if it were more than real than- as if reality were not enough to contain moments like this. Is all so strange."

I feel the shapes of Karen's words, the micro-movements of her emotions, and the tremendous weight of these things in the depth of her subsequent stillness. I hold them all as firmly in my hands as I've ever held anything in my mental grasp. I find myself so fully present and aware of the totality within this transient moment of time. I find myself no longer attached to the illusions within myself which have blinded and burdened my eyes like blankets of delusion for so long. In this mortal moment, I feel so completely connected to Karen, not in her entirety, but in the entirety of this intimate moment.

I find myself thinking, *this* is what's real. And this is what it means to exist. And I finally understand. But I don't reach Nirvana. And I don't transcend. And just as this moment comes, I find myself trying to hold on as it slips inevitably and irretrievably away. And this is reality. And it most certainly is not enough.

I want to curse time. I want to shame it into submission. I want time to stop right here. I want to go back. I want to experience this moment on a loop forever. I want to start over from the very beginning and come back to this moment having forgotten everything. I want to feel it all as if I've never felt anything before. I want to feel everything like I feel this moment. I want my whole life to feel so *real*.

Why does time have to be like this? Why must it torment us with its perpetual flow? Why haven't we conquered it? We've been at war with time since the beginning. It's never lost to us, and we keep losing ourselves to it. I think of the alarm clock on my bedside table sounding my quotidian alarm like a call to arms against time itself. I think of my calendar like a prison built to put time in its place under my architectural designs. I think of how hard we've tried to turn time into the same empty thing we've managed to succeed in turning everything else into- a common commodity.

Why won't time submit to our standards of substance? Everything else has allowed us to extract the essence of what makes it real and replace it with inflated emptiness. What's so special about time? I can extract the juice out of an orange and toss the rest away without feeling any sense of loss. I can fatten and inflate my own body on all sorts of non-nourishing extracts, artificial flavor enhancements, and pharmaceutically patented preservatives. Why can't we extract the essence of time, enhance the properties of its potential, and add some kind of preservative to make it last for us? I don't understand why there's nothing we can ever do to make anything enough, time least of all.

Karen's hands move to clasp over my own as my mind meanders. I try to focus and form words to express my great gratitude for all her undeluded, uninflated, and unfathomably real righteousness. I considerately cast shapes to outline the depths of my admiration, amazement, and appreciation for what she is and means to me in this intimate, impermanent moment as it slowly slips away. I try to make my hands move in ways which might match how my soul's been moved by her heartfelt words. I know that the forms my movements make can only be virtually real representations of the very real things I think and feel. Despite this disparity, Karen seems to sense more than just the shapes of my haunted hands. She slips her hands back into mine, and somehow, I can feel the same sentiments in her hands that I fear I've failed to form with my own.

With a tender touch, she asks me to tell a story from my own life. Her hands ask me to pick something that's somehow shaped me into who I am, or who I'll have wished to have been. I find myself remembering one of Grisha's great lessons. My hands become heavy under the burden of trying to do justice to this present moment and the memory I'm about to invite into it as I press a preface…

Dreams wake up to become ideas. Ideas compel us toward experiences.

Experiences lead us to problems. Problems force us to define objectives. Objectives frustrate us and require focus. Focus propels us toward eventual enlightenment. Enlightenment allows us to find rest and reprieve. In our resting reprieves, we are delivered unto new dreams.

These are the lines of code that our consciousness seems to follow. My grandfather Grisha had taught me how to master these mental roadmaps, or at least he'd instructed me how to go about mastering such things. I feel as if I've only sometimes proven to possess a sufficient knowledge of what my noble patriarch had tried so hard to impart. I remember how he would always call me into the kitchen when I'd wake-up and say the same thing every day.

"Harek my young prodigy, tell me what you have been dreaming before the daylight can chase your dreams back into the darkness and blind you in its glare."

Grisha would have a tablet waiting on the breakfast table. I'd be expected to produce some kind of record of my previous night's dreams while he prepared breakfast and then sat quietly and patiently across from me. Once my dream-world depictions were completed, I'd pass the tablet over to him. He'd inspect my representations of recollections while I'd proceed to eat my breakfast. After I'd finished eating, he'd begin engaging me in conversations about my depicted dreams.

I remember how the first time he'd tried to get me to record my dreams this way; I'd told him that I hadn't had any dreams and that I'd hardly even slept. I'd never seen him so angry or disappointed in all my life. He pounded his fists against the table with only the slightest hint of restraint. Then he spoke with elevated intensity.

"Don't be foolish young child! You wouldn't even be here now if it weren't for your last dream. If you can't remember your dream, then how can you know that you've actually left it to awaken? More importantly Harek, how can your waking hours lead you to anything more than what you've already experienced if you have no dream to light your eyes?"

I'd had no answer to Grisha's questions. Instead, I'd decided to try to make something up so he wouldn't be so upset with me. When I'd reached for the tablet, his hand had swept in to snatch it away from me.

"Don't you dare defile this tablet with some made up nonsense! Dreams are not the random thoughts and images that roll through your head. Your dreams are the hosts of truths that you have not yet figured out how to make real. If you respect them properly, they will give you the strength to realize them. If you disrespect or forsake them, they will become your nightmares, and if you do not rebuke yourself once they begin to haunt you, then they will leave you dreamless in a waking world which shall become one infinite nightmare."

I remember Grisha putting the tablet back down on the table and gazing down at me in silence for one of those short uncomfortable moments which seems to turn seconds into eons. When he finally did speak, I'd felt as if his voice had startled me from some daze of half awakened slumber.

"I want you to close your blinded eyes now Harek. Think back to what was going through your mind before you'd gone to sleep my lost little child. I want you to remember what led you to your dreams so you can retrace how you've come to have wandered from their path. Now think of these things and focus your mind on where these thoughts might lead you. Think of what it is you would like them to teach you and where it is you would like to end up at the end of these thoughts. Think of where you are now and where you think you should be. Focus on these two places and look back to see where these two paths have deviated. Now, describe to me this point where you've wandered away from the path you would rather have chosen, and how you came to lose your way."

"I can't see anything past the darkness of when I'd closed my eyes to try to sleep Grisha. I remember thinking about how much you know about this world and how I hardly know anything. My mind wouldn't let me sleep because I just kept thinking about how alone I am in my own head, and how if you disappear like mama, papa, and babushka then there will be nobody left to teach me all the things I don't know about this world to which I'm so desperately oblivious. I mean, I don't even know how to dream Grisha."

Grisha looks at me with an almost otherworldly expression of grief and sorrow which seems to reveal a hidden ancient battlefield of wrinkled trenches no longer obscured by his diligent bravery and strong supportive smiles. Every wrinkle upon his elderly face becomes a battle scar left by some merciless existential wound of torment and loss. I read his face like the map of some unknown surface to a terrifying terrestrial place which seems both far too ominous and horrifying for any man to venture into, and yet it's so vast and all-encompassing that it cannot be avoided in route to any of the promising lands of our collective imaginations. My mind gazes over this wounded landscape as if I'm peering down upon the wreckage of a scorched planet from a helicopter caught in a tailspin and descending on a crash-course into this sorrowful space.

Grisha reaches out to me and pulls up on my plummeting cheeks as he manages to hoist a mirroring expression upon his face. The strain upon the muscles of his face shakes like those of a strongman under some unfathomable record-breaking mass of cold unfeeling steel. His eyes clear and dry like an ocean being syphoned out into a desert through some miracle beyond all imagining. They peer into the depths of my own dark and dilated pupils.

"My troubled young man, you have already learned so much. I will continue to teach you for as long as I may, but sooner or later you'll have to learn what you must on your own. If that day should have already come, I'm happy to tell you that you already know all that is required for you to find your own way through the darkness of this oblivious world which leaves us all so alone. You see, everyone on this earth is just as alone as everyone else, and you are no more alone than anyone. When we close our eyes to sleep, whether it is unto dream or eternity, it is the same darkness which surrounds us all. All you need to find your way through this unyielding darkness young Harek, is the light which you have within you."

I feel the strength of his gentle embrace as he pulls me in for a hug as if it is passed on to me through some kind of sentimental osmosis. My sorrow and dread slowly vanish like a fog being driven away by the first phosphorous rays of a new triumphant sun. Grisha walks back to the other side of the table and takes a deep replenishing breath as he sits down across from me. Then he asks me to take the tablet and write down what I have just learned. I stare at the blank black surface of the tablet, reticent and reflective.

I think about the oblivion of my dreamless night, the battlefield of Grisha's face, and the smooth empty surface of the tablet in front of me now. My mind starts to realize how all these things are just surfaces upon the infinitely deep and eternally expansive mass of reality. Then I begin to think of dreams as deeper things rising out of the mysterious mass beneath these surfaces and imposing shapes, signs, and sentiments upon their faces. I begin to see everything in existence as a surface which is formed by these underlying dreams which do not actually emerge from us, but cause us to emerge from them.

My young mind ponders the way in which Grisha's dreams had led him to the ideas which he'd pursued through all his experiences. I consider how his experiences had led him to problems requiring objectives and focus. His incredible and almost incomprehensible focus had led him to become so enlightened and wise in ways which had allowed him to solve so many great mysteries, perhaps the least of which being his revelations on the geometry of the universe. Now he sits here with me on this fine morning with an entire lifetime of frustration, struggle, and perseverance etched on the surface of his face, made manifest by his dreams and all their subsequent derivatives.

Finally, I draw a diagram of my visualization as to how dreams come from the deepest depths of existence and rise up to form the surfaces of everything we perceive. I label the symbols, and shapes, and forms with brief illuminating descriptions. Then I write two lines of text at the bottom of the tablet's dreamscape depicting surface, and hand this dream derived surface over to Grisha with precious reverent care, watching attentively as he reads the words.

*Dreams do not come from us. We come from dreams.*

He pulls the tablet to his chest after regarding it for a proud and precious moment as if this object were a wayward child with which he has just been reunited. Then he looks at me in my chair as if I've suddenly grown much taller and am now standing like a skyscraper of a student looking down for an instructor's approval. Grisha passes the tablet back to me as if bestowing me with some prestigious award, which puzzles me given his well-established and lowly opinion of such prizes and the showy manners they're so often presented.

"You've just demonstrated a depth of understanding beyond your years. Never forget this truth you've learned or how you came to it. If you can respect the dreams that grace your imagination, then you'll be able to serve them well. It's only through this respect and service to dreams that you'll find anything beyond the terrifying abysmal darkness which surrounds us all. This reverence for your dreams is the only light you need to behold the wonders of this world, and to keep the horrors of oblivion at bay Harek. If you remember nothing else I've taught you, remember this. You cannot be truly awake until you have dared to dream against the dark."

Karen's face beams back at me as if lit with the twilight of a soft blue star. She smiles, not with guarded or measured subtlety, but with unencumbered radiance which seems to send the darkness both around and within me jolting back like it's been struck by some luminary shockwave. The ground shivers softly as if responding to her radiance. The earth's trembling swells into a vibrating vertigo but lasts only a few shaky seconds. Then almost in the very instant that the earth goes still, the door jolts open and the light-switch snaps on.

Our eyes try to shield themselves and then slowly pry their way back open as they adjust to the flood of artificial light. Two figures file in from the doorway and come to a halt on either side of the bed where I sit half exposed in my hospital gown. One of the figures tosses a set of prison duds next to me and chuckles condescendingly.

"Here you go Harek. We got you a fresh set so you can ditch the gown for something more- *fitting*."

The voice lacks the intricate inflections of a flesh and blood human being. I turn my gaze to see the H4k3r's manufactured mass against the glaring glut of glow. He now appears as an empty mechanical vessel, devoid of any soul or spirit to render him as even seemingly self-similar. I bark back at this abyss of an entity.

"Nope. I'm not wearing those things. They've ceased to suit me."[41]

The ungainly geometry of the minotaur-man forms into focus against the flood of false florescence which appears to tailor itself to fit his taurus-torso.

"Let's make this quick. The countdown's almost over, and the earth's starting to make its intentions known. You two are going to give us your consciousness compiler and the web address from those puzzles. We're going to upload our own profiles first, and then, if you do everything exactly as we insist, we'll let you go next. Got it?"

"Nope. What if we can't accommodate you so easily?"

"Well Harek, if you refuse, I'll probably just beat you until you submit, have another seizure, or maybe just make you watch me do horrible things to Ms. Phoe over here. In any case, I'll get what I want one way or another, and H4k3r will solve the puzzle on his own if he has to. I'm only giving you a choice because it makes things easier for all of us. So, what do you say?"

Karen takes the compiler out of her USB uniform's interior pocket and starts tapping it against her opposite hand.

"Why botherz to askz, if youz zhinkz youz kan just takez zhis by force?"

"I guess you know me well enough to know I'd normally rather skip right to the violent force route than waste time offering alternatives. The truth, if there even is such a thing, is that I want to watch this whole farce fail in as miserable a way as possible. I want to watch you surrender, to fail, and then squirm as H4k3r and all the foolish elders show you how deluded you all are to believe in things like puzzles and transcendence as their failures prove to be just as empty."

"Nope. That doesn't make any sense bull-brains. Why would you upload your profile if you think it's all so petty or preposterous?"

"Well, Harek, let me see if my bull-brain can explain it to you. If you're all deluded, it won't matter if I upload my profile. However, if by some miracle I'm wrong, I may as well reap the rewards. It's just *evolutionary imperative.* Right?"

"Nope. You're confusing basic biology with a branch of math, but there's another problem with your perspective. You pretend your desire is for us to fail, but you desperately need us to prevail. If *this* is all there is, your life remains an empty abomination. Your skepticism can't create or add anything to your own oblivion. You deflate everything around you to delude yourself into feeling as if this makes you any less vapid, but it only shows how hollow and hateful you truly are. As all the substance you siphon off others fails to fill you as it had fulfilled them, the world is made emptier, but you remain emptier still. That's the truth. Nope?"

"Wrong again Harek. There is no truth, or reality, or justice. There is only the survival of the fittest. The fittest are not the believers or the dreamers who fill themselves with hot air. The fittest are those who make it their duty to cut to the core of things. Let's say I suspect someone of a crime. Only this suspect knows if they actually did the deed, although that's not even a given. So, I interrogate the suspect, until I've cut through to their core and let all the hot air out of them. When the trial comes around, the judge and jury will weigh the suspect's story against mine to assign a verdict. Since both of us can and likely will lie, this verdict doesn't have anything to do with truth, justice, or even reality. The only thing any verdict ever proves is which narrative is more evolved, the suspect's or mine. It's all hollow at the core, but I'm a better blade."

"I kan no believez I workz fyor same USBz as youz. Zhis logik does no elevatez youz in zhe way youz zhinkz. By choosingz to deceivez others and convincez zhem ov what youz aktually knowz is delusion, youz bekome most deluded ov all. Youz seez nothingz, learnz nothingz, createz nothingz, and bekomez ever-emptier form ov nothingz as result ov all youz defilementz ov truth. Youz only sayz zhere is no truth, justice, and reality bekause youz has madez youzself oblivious to zhem. Denying and discrediting zhe truth does no erase it, and whenever youz diez, it will be zhe truth zhat survives- not youz."

H4k3r smiles with a sinister grin of mechanical machinations and clears his uncongested synthetic throat for some interruptive effect or something.

"None of you get it. Nothing can matter until we know what's truly real. To do that, we have to find the source realm of all reality. Until then, this is all essentially just some segment of a stranger's senseless game. Harek, you designed a world trying to find a way to understand your own. Rhake did the same, and so did I. I shouldn't have to explain the evidence or probability that this realm is just a parody or prototype too. If you consider how I came into Rhake's realm, merged with my creator, and emerged here- I'm now more real than my design, more real than my designer, and as objectively real as you are. And do you know what I've learned from all this transcendence?"

"Nope. Let me guess- Reality is not enough."

"*That* may be the only truth. I mean, even when we know what's real, it still might not be enough because we're only individuals. We may need to figure out more than what's real to truly transcend the totality of existence. We may need to merge all levels of all consciousness together, creating a unified form of consciousness. When we finally do, none of this other gibberish may matter at all. But of course, first thing's first. Now, can we please get on with it already?"

"Nope. I think the two of us need a moment to deliberate and discuss your demands. But beforehand, I'd like to know one more thing. Did you force Rhaek to merge his consciousness with yours, or did he make up his own mind?"

H4k3r's skull tilts to one side in an imitation of mammalian curiosity.

"I'd wondered if you'd bother to read our little note. I suppose you can see through the simple words on a page. Well Harek, given how much harder it had been to find my way intro this realm compared to leaving my own, I'd figured that I might as well make the most of my maker's talents. Nay?"

"Nope. You couldn't get here on your own, so you tried to talk him into joining you. He considered what you were and what he might become if he merged with you. In his mind, nothing could ever make him real, and nothing real would ever be enough either. I'm sure he told you that you could never be real either, and that he wasn't going to help you find your way into a realm where you'd only become poisonous or poisoned. I'll bet you forced him to create a profile, killed him, merged his profile with yours, and uploaded it here. Nope?"

"You might have a few facts, but you don't understand them. I did what had to be done to fulfill my duty and to carry the burden he let down. The whole reason he'd designed my world was the same reason you'd designed his. Now it's like I'm going through the same stupid story yet again, reminding you of your own motivation and purpose in this world, your own divine duty."

I do have to consider what H4k3r is truly saying. He did indeed come into existence only as an extension of my own efforts and engineering. It was my creation which led to his own, and by merging with Rhaek and killing his own creator to get here, he was indeed just doing his *divine duty*. If there's any real fault to be found, it's in me. I'm the real reason any of this was made possible.

"Well H4k3r, I can actually appreciate what you've just told me. It all makes sound logical sense after all. If you'll allow us a period of private conversation, we do still have a few things to consider. You see, I wouldn't have advanced as far as I have without an abundant amount of assistance either."

Agent Keptic snaps his fingers to summon his little pet humanoid H4k3r.

"Alright, we'll give you a few minutes, but then we're going to the terminal in the media center to finish this thing, one way or another."

As the door closes, there's no doubt that these two pseudo-men will stand eavesdropping on our subsequent conversation. Karen pulls a little notepad and pen from her uniform pocket as I start speaking as if trying to convince her that we need to accept the offer we've been presented. She promptly picks up on my misdirection as if unconsciously understanding why we can't let these inhuman entities send their CCPs alongside of our own profiles.

Truth be told, we'd already seen this scenario playing out sooner or later. That's why we'd taken certain precautions. The consciousness compiler is set to corrupt the encoding on any newly created consciousness profiles, while still allowing us to update our own before uploading them. This should allow us to preserve our most recent memories and any minute personality changes. I'd also created a shell display to show a fake uploading progress bar and a subsequent successful completion prompt so that corrupted profiles will appear to upload perfectly well.

There's one important fact that I've yet to tell Karen though. I suspect there might be a password prompt once we finally connect to the end node of the puzzle, and I've yet to solve for this suspected password. If Agent Keptic and H4k3r try to complete their bogus uploads first and I can't tell them the proper password, all our efforts may be exposed. I haven't mentioned this point previously, and I can't risk writing anything easily decrypted on a page now because those inhumane humanoids will probably find it when they inevitably insist on frisking us to ensure we don't have a second consciousness compiler, or weapon, or something.

So, I do the only thing I can think of. I take Karen's hands and place them around my own. Then I tell her in tactile forms how I don't know if I have all the answers we need, but whatever else happens- I'm grateful to have known her in whatever limited sense I've been privileged. We embrace each other almost as if saying goodbye for the last time, and hello for the first time simultaneously.

Then we walk to the door so our abominable acquaintances can escort us to the media center. Agent Keptic grins like a predator biting down on its prey when we come out with his filthy, yellow, fang-like teeth glaring and sneering wickedly at us. H4k3r's opposing face is one primarily composed of lifeless mechanical numbness with limited virtual imitations of probabilistically appropriate inflections. These aberrant faces force us out in front of them, punitively pushing us as we proceed to the media center.

As we reach the critical terminal, H4k3r insists on uploading his profile first. He snatches the consciousness compiler from Agent Phoe's hand and begins wiring himself up to create his CCP. I proceed to enter the dark web-address into the terminal, hoping to see if a password prompt pops-up before the bull-brain notices. My intentions are assisted as all the holographic screens in the media center suddenly turn themselves on and the emergency interruption message siren sounds off.

The flashing of red lights and screaming of sirens lasts only few seconds before it subsides, and an automated message advises everyone *to please standby for an important message from the Global Governance's Great Leader*.[42] The image of an empty reddish room with flags hanging in a darkened backdrop appears before Great Leader lumbers up to a lectern which is only present for posterity's sake. He stares straight into the broadcasting camera's focal point, squinting as he pretends to poorly read from a script that's been prepared in advance and posted into his Neuroconnx databank.

"My fellow ah- everybody. It's with a heavy, uh... -heart, that I regret to inform you all, that geologists are now predicting supervolcanic eruptions as intimate- no wait- imminent in the 18 areas known as the world's VPN, I mean, VEI-8 sites. These predictions have just now become known to us, or we would have tried to advise everyone much sooner of, you know- the, the, the thing- the danger. Anyway, this warning applies to every sector of our Global Governance and may even threaten all life on your- not your, sorry, *our* planet."

Great Leader's hands make awkward waftures which seem out of sync, it's almost like watching a puppet being pulled upon by multiple competing puppeteers. He also appears as if he's trying to bounce to the broken beat of a song played over a group exercise routine with an embarrassing lack of natural rhythm as he bobs his head while reading-off all the various VEI-8 sites specifically, stopping several times to squint and stare as if he's lost his place in the teleprompter's word-maze or something.

"There've also been a series of earthquakes lately, which may be related to these impending erections, I mean, eruptions. Now I'm advised not to mention that many more earthquakes of increasing intensity are also expected to ensue."

A tiny tremor subtly seems to shake the camera focused on him, prompting a set of all-too staged expressions of fake-fear which would have kept most aspiring actors from advancing beyond a casting couch. As the camera rumbles more violently, he actually uses the lectern for more than just familiar imagery and flings himself over it in a feigned attempt to keep from falling. The terrestrial trembling subsides in a few more seconds and Great Leader climbs down to regain pretend composure before continuing his prepared speech as if he's awakened in the middle of a dream and continued to mumble it all aloud.

"Let's don't not be discouraged in the face of this great challenge. Let's not- Listen. Don't panic or pervert to violence. Let's let us seek shelter and safety in a, like a- Let me tell you something. Some of our highest-ranking officials have been in designated shelters for a few days already, and not that they knew anything before I was told to tell you all- Look. The point is- This is the point here. We're goanna get through this if you don't harass or attack- I mean, somebody's got to survive the, the, the thing- the thing we're all in the thing together, man. You know what I mean, people!"

Great Leader stammers on to paint this catastrophic event as an exemplary moment of our Global Governance's noble and efficient operations. He lists the number of people believed to be in secret safety as if it were an impressive sports statistic. He thanks the workers who were sacrificed to ensure these evacuations were carried out swiftly and smoothly. He praises the level of organization and planning involved in all these efforts almost as if even the impending doom were itself perfectly orchestrated in accordance and alignment with the GG's greatest intentions. He goes on and on like this. He lies as if he doesn't know he's lying. He pretends to comfort his absent audience as if all we need is for him to read us a get well soon greeting card. He points his fingers like pistols at non-existent entities to emphasize the importance of compliance to his comments. He ignores any semblance of truth, twists every figment of fact, and defiles all reality.

When he finally finishes his empty speech in the same way so many mimics have finished countless other vapid speeches, he professes a hollow and patronizing platitude about god's will in a pathetic attempt to directly associate himself with the divine. It should be impossible for anyone to believe a word of it, especially those god-fearing souls to which these statements pantomime and pander. Although, many of these same souls would admit that they prefer to have their leaders pretend to praise their god then admit to never truly having believed, encountered, or adhered to anything remotely divine.

This is what our reality has become. This is how it ends. This is pantomime. This is fiction. This is passive acceptance, blind adherence, and active indifference. This is the deceptions and delusions of others accepted in place of our own dreams. How many of these delusions have we deceived ourselves into supporting? How many times have we looked the other way for a non-existent greater good, or a bigger picture, or a longer run? How long have we just gone on with our diluted and deluded lives, ignoring all the obvious unconvincing deceptions offered to us because we'd rather go along and get along than take any actual action? What more could we ever deserve than more of the same things we've accepted every step of the way? How else could it all end? I gaze at the holographic displays of deliberately deceptive images and wonder.

It begins to seem as though we've never truly cared about reality or what's real, and reality has never indicated any concern for us. Reality never stood up for itself as it was pumped full of all this non-sense, emptiness, and delusion- at least, not until now. All we ever really cared about is our own little lifetime's experiences and maybe to a lesser degree, how our lifetimes extend through our descendants. Our descendants are essentially just more descent ants to continue our colony and care for us when we can no longer serve the queen or our Great Leader. But then, why should it seem so sad, so dismally unfair, and so damned disgracefully, and cosmically unjust that our anthill is about to be melted down by fiery forces which can no longer lay dormant beneath it all?

Great Leader never mentioned any of this. Even if he did, the mass of humanity wouldn't give much consideration to these things anyway. As soon as Great Leader turns as if to shake hands with a phantom or begin doing the robot dance and leave the lectern, media briefs break-in to begin displaying scenes from the surfaces above us. Riots and looting are already raging. With so little time left to live, somehow a glut of empty acquisition, displaced anger, and preemptive small-scale sabotages of what will all be destroyed so soon anyway is the most prominent priority on the human collective's crisis clouded mindset.

I look at the flat faces of these old grey-haired men who've tucked themselves into these bowels of the earth. They clearly don't care about the surfaces above them. They only care about a prolonged opportunity to satisfy their own same insipid instincts. A few of them even brag openly about all the resources and niceties tucked away down here. There's so much emptiness, self-absorption, lifelessness, and despicable disregard for anything beyond staying atop the higher tiers of hapless hierarchies that Maslow's pyramid seems as if it should have been used as a lobotomy spike for these buried braggart-brains.

With one look at the beastly Agent Keptic and the dually inhuman abomination of H4k3r, I see all the worst traits an entity can possess amplified prodigiously. The minotaur-man looks like a blood-thirsty beast as he vicariously views all the live violence on the monitors. Conversely, H4k3r appears as unfeeling and disinterested as an unused abacus as he stares at the upload display on the compiler, waiting for a phony completion confirmation.

I look away from these atrocities and into Karen's eyes where I find my own reflection on their glassy surface. This sorrowful scene cannot bring true tears to either of our eyes, as it leaves much more to loathe than to lament. My gaze begs for words as Karen remains as aware and accommodating as always.

"Wez runningz out ov lifez to attendz, aren't wez Harek?"

"Nope. There's still as much life as ever. We're just running out of time. If my profile is to receive any more time of its own, I only hope it can use that time more wisely than I've managed so much of mine."

"I does no knowz if I should uploadz minez profile. I feelz as if much ov what I has tryz to attendz to has bekomez futile failurez. Aktually no, is worse zhan zhat. I zhink many ov zhe zhings I has tryz to honorz was never more zhan illusionz."

H4k3r's profile progress switches to the scam success-prompt. He pulls an artificial grin and tries to get the bull-boy's attention. The minotaur-man is still entranced by all the violence on the monitors and has to have his eyes blocked before he's able to respond to H4k3r. The two abominations stand shoulder to shoulder as H4k3r walks his beastly buddy through the whole implicit process. They ignore Karen and me, and we ignore them as Karen quietly continues.

"I has tryz to believez in zhings like peace, freedomz, and justice. I has tryz to attendz to zhem as if zhey was truly realz. But what peace has wez seen? Zhe only zhing zhat passes fyor peace here seemz to be submissionz ov peoplez to zhe brutality ov otherz. What freedomz has ever been seenz herez? I has never seenz anyonez who kould konsider zhemselves truly free. Everyonez is either enslavez to others or enslavez others. What justice is zhere in any ov zhat?"

"Nope. Terrible things have always happened in spite of the supernatural struggles of those all-too-rare spirits like yourself who live in service to those venerable virtues. But, however sinister the shadows cast over us may be, there is no darkness which can overshadow the illuminating light virtuous spirits like yours shine against it. From someone who's spent so much of their life looking for a light instead of shining one for all to see, let me assure you that any part of you that can be kept shining should certainly be saved. If there is to be any truth, freedom, or justice anywhere, those things will need lights like yours to be seen."

"I still does no zhink I kan kallz minez-self a virtuous spirit. When I konsider minez kommitment to justice, I kan no rekoncilez zhe injustice I has seen, despitez or inspitez ov mine effortz. I mean, zhe innocentz has been sentenced to volcanic deathz or slaveryz to sinister subterraneanz Caesars. Has minez effortz to tryz to preventz zhese injusticez been truly virtuous?"

"Nope. If you hadn't pulled that minotaur-man off me to begin with, he may have killed me then. If you hadn't helped me with all these puzzles, there would be no hope of preserving any decent remnant of humanity. If you hadn't been so honest, caring, and attentive to everything I've seen you encounter, I would've lost all hope in humanity, all aspirations of meaning, and all resolve to see our efforts through to the end. If that's not more than truly virtuous, then I don't know what is, and we might as well not even dream of such things."

"Does youz really zhinkz we kan still pullz zhis zhing off then? I'yams no so sure we getz zhe chance."

The deceptive display on my conspiratorial contingency-inclusive compiler glows green again to prompt Agent Keptic of his profile's supposedly successful upload. It should now be Karen's turn, but the only reality these inhuman beings can apparently abide is their own asinine ambivalence. They order us to file out in front of them with guttural grunts and gesturing guns. By the leering looks on their foul faces, they seem to think themselves quite clever and expectant of appalled astonishment as if their brutish betrayal were proof of their incomparable intellect and not just another empty extension of their own inner oblivion and a vapid voidance of vacant virtues. I announce my annoyance with these numbskulls in another evenly enunciated "*nope*" which prompts a prodding gun-barrel's thrust against a particularly sensitive spot on my spine. We both raise our hopeless hands above our heads extending them toward some earthly anti-Empyrean as we turn to walk along the ascending exit-way in synchronized submission.

When we reach the door to the surface, Karen and I emerge first to the greeting of a wild gust of surprisingly warm wind. H4k3r notices our subtle increase in footspeed, and strides with his head-down like a dagger against the gusting winds to advance in front of Karen's lengthening lead. Agent Keptic lingers last in our little line and struggles to shut the wind-weighted door without slamming it disquietly shut.

A miraculous moment emerges as my hospital gown is caught up in another surging swirl of wind and sails straight into the flustered face of Agent Keptic. He twists and tangles himself against my gust-swept garment in flailing attempts to free his blinded bull-body. My eyes accelerate to clock Karen who seems to have already anticipated everything as she slips me the subtlest smirk to signify a start to our life's last stand. She lets out a loud laugh as H4k3r breaks his stride to pull his pistol and point his eyes back at me as I begin to run naked toward the befuddled buffoon by the door. His attention is divided just enough for Karen to close the gap and deftly disarm him in such a smooth and sweeping motion that it appears as an act of the wind's own authentic will. In almost the same stop-motion instant, she pulls the taken trigger, sending out a shot which cleaves directly through the central core of H4k3r's mental mechanisms.

H4k3r's mangled mechanical mass collapses with a clanking thud as I glide toward the other grunting goon, grabbing my gust-swept garment and saddling Keptic's bull-bucking backside. I stretch the sheet-like surface around his muddled minotaur mass, binding his arms and blinding his bull-eyes. My weight forces his already awkward and top-heavy torso to twist and tumble to the ground and causes my own head to crack against the concrete, forcing my fingers to fail in a brief blip of brain battered befuddlement. The minotaur-man fumbles to free his gunslinging arm from my garment and hoist his head so he can stand steadily over his hobbled hooves. In this same insane instant, our contingency calvary of *Deus ex mechanical mice* arrive and attack Agent Keptic. They begin tearing into his hoof-feet and climbing his taurus-torso as he fights to fling them away with his hoof-hands.

Even in all this mousey mania, he still somehow manages to send a single shot slicing through my left thigh. The mechanical mice gnaw their way through his skin and swarm to cover every inch of his bull-body as screeching steer-squeals shriek from the minotaur's mice-mangled mouth, but they fail to chew through his hoof-hand in time to stop him from squeezing off one last, sinister, stray shot. The echoes from the exploding round continue to ring out as I reach into the robotic-rat infested mass of the mangled minotaur to separate the smoldering hot pistol from his rat-ravaged hoof-hand.

The wind suddenly subsides into a shivering stillness, and I hear a faint groan against the dissonant Denver landscape. Soft subsequent sounds of scratchy foot-skids slip away from Karen's unsteadied staggering footsteps as I glance away from the minotaur's mangled mass. My heart seems to occupy two separate dimensions as it soaks in a still beating bath of blood-boiling rage and surging sorrows.

Karen clutches at a crimson wound on her lower abdomen as I point the pistol back at Keptic's still sneering sack of sickening skin and click a button on my wristwatch to disengage and disperse the devouring mass if mecha-mice. The menacing minotaur makes one last agro-attempt to get to his half-gnawed off hoof-feet and charge hornlessly headlong toward me. I unload an uncounted number of rounds into the center of his minotaur-mass, continuing to click the un-triggering trigger against an emptied chamber as he collapses into a bloodied bull-heap. Then I shudder as the sound of his blood-soaked beef-breath continues to pollute the air in a seepage of sewer-sickening sighs.

The entire earth trembles in a terrifying fit which resonates with all the rage and empathy overflowing from my deepest depths in ways no other display could ever be made to manifest. The earthquake cracks clear through a piece of concrete which crumbles to the ground from an overhang above doorway we'd just been forced to flee. Its fall seems like some fateful symbol of my own lost faith in more than just the future for the whole of humanity. As the earth's shivers subside, Karen shouts a reminder for me to set up a remote relay to the terminal so we can upload our profiles offsite. I hear a scrambled statement from the mangled mechanical mass of H4k3r's failing form, and approach with the concrete chunk hoisted and ready to harm. When I get next to H4k3r, his jaw jerks open to spit out a readied relay module followed by his waning words explaining how he meant to help me all along and that this relay should allow me to remote into the terminal if I prop the door open and place it nearby. Then he expectantly expires at the scrambled electronic sound of one last laughing utterance. Saying, "*As above, So below.*"

I squat down to scoop-up the device with stone still in hand and return to stand over the mangled minotaur as he writhes around in pain. He pulls a plastic ID card from his front pocket and slobbers through some derogatory slurs of blood belching breaths before begging me to bludgeon him in exchange for the keycard. I drop the chunk of concrete next to his head and grab the card from the weakly defiant clinging of his hoof-hand.

I yell back at Karen to wait for my return as I open the dungeonous door, and an unmechanized mouse scurries into the hallway in front of me. As I bound through the hallways to retrieve the compiler from the media-center, the mouse runs ahead of my struggling strides as if guiding me directly to my destination. After I grab the compiler, it turns to look at me from a corner before burrowing into a tiny crack in the baseboard trim, almost as if to say goodbye before transcending into an unknown mousey dimension of its own.

When I return to the underground exit, the earth is back to trembling in torments of its own. I realize that I can complete the remote relay if I just crack the door rather than propping it wide open, and that this would allow the weight of volatile volcanic mass to seal the door safely shut after my final fate has been sealed. I hastily set the device with the door slightly cracked and limp along a blood trail to find Karen crawling towards a helicopter. It's clear she's lost a lot of blood, as her skin is now extremely pale. I hand her the compiler and pile her into my arms as I fight against the pain of my own flesh-wound to carry her the rest of the way to the helicopter. Then I shout over my shoulder for her to start uploading her consciousness profile as I hobble back to the mangled minotaur.

The minotaur-man looks up at me with almost no life left in his eyes as I bend down to steal the stone I'd left resting next to him. He begs me one last time to smash his head, but I ignore him and use the rock to prop the descending doorway wide open instead. An owl appears out of nowhere and perches itself over this doorway. It stares menacingly at the mangled mass dying under its gaze as I stagger-sprint away and shout an unasked explanation of my actions.

"As above, So below!"

I find myself praying through every suffering stagger-step of my return route to whatever divinity might have ever existed that Karen can complete her upload before all is lost. The earth's trembling gains in intensity as I try to return to our intended escape vessel and the winds intensify into defiant torrents against my agonized advance. When I finally make my way inside the helicopter, Karen tosses the compiler into my lap and fires up the propellers as she shoots me a defiant smirk, signaling her stubborn intent to save me above all else.

Despite the harsh winds and quaking terrestrial surface, she sends us smoothly into the agitated air. Our vessel rises high into the air as the gusty winds toss us around viciously. I look over at Karen to begin updating and uploading her profile and suddenly realize that these winds are gusting in a line almost directly away from Yellowstone. Her pale face remains unflinchingly focused in front of us with a seriousness which suggests she's already realized this fateful fact. Sensing the severity of our situation, I struggle to say something that could convey the infinite appreciation and admiration I have for her.

"Karen, I know we might not survive, so let me say this now. Thank you for everything you've done, and all that you are. You mean more to me than the whole of this entire ending world."

Of course, I want to say infinitely more than these proffered platitudes can convey, but I know by the way she looks at me in response to these words that she'd rather I didn't. She already knows. She knows what I mean. She knows how I feel, and she knows who I am. She doesn't need to scan my brain, analyze my behaviors, or scrutinize my word selections. She knows the sentiments which words can never satisfactorily serve. She says all that needs to be said with a subtle smirking smile. She is as silent and subtle as the serene skies which have become tainted and turbulent by the earth's eruptive breath below. She is as calm and knowing as the purest airs which we'd once breathed so obliviously in those shining days of cloudless wonder before being forced by fate or futility to gasp for in prayerful pleading panting now. She holds behind her eyes a shining kingdom which no realm of earth nor the expanse beyond it may ever rival in any infinite extension of eternal time and space.

As my own eyes beam back with whatever limited light they can conjure to convey the truest and most timeless sentiments of my soul, her eyes gleam to grant me one last gracious glint of their infinite illumination. Then her eyelids flutter and fade down to burry all but one last tormented tear which escapes just in time to glide down the pale surface of her life-releasing cheek, and deposit itself upon the shuddering skin of my faithful fingertip as I reach to receive this shed sphere of spiritual substance. I feel her essence evaporate unto the aether as this tear sinks into my skin and absconds into the absorbing airs. I instantaneously know that this shall be the last beautiful moment my own eyes will ever see. This is it. Her end is my end, not of mortal material, but of human hope. There is no more beauty, no more inspiring wonder, no more surviving desire for me in this life. All that is left to me is my immortal morning and an ineffable sense of indebtedness to her memory.

Before my mournful mind can contemplate the gravity of this grievous moment, the smashing shockwave of a sonic boom blows out the windows of this circuitous helicopter and blasts my brain like a brutal bomb exploding from the inside of my concussed skull. With no pilot, no equilibrium, and no insight as to what I might be able to do, the helicopter flails and falls from the sky like a wounded dove drifting upon uncaring currents, cascading in downward drafts.

I helplessly watch the display which details Karen's profile upload through this tumultuous tumbling descent, desperate for some scant sign of solace. As my wounded vessel violently detonates on the surface of Horse Creek Reservoir, I'm somehow stabilized by the sight of the completion signifying flash of gorgeous green light. I remain strong and secured to my station as the helicopter's steel skin is shredded and strewn about as its crumpling and contorting skeleton skids like a disintegrating skipping-stone onto a sandy shore where it continues to tumble, skid, and slide inland. All the while, my body is battered, beaten, and broken by slicing shrapnel, devastating debris, and chaotic contortions of the crash. When everything finally stops twisting, thrashing, and writhing around me, I'm bewildered as to why I haven't been killed or at least cast into another severe seizure.

The earth echoes the conditions of my crash, continuing to shake and shudder in its own weeping shivers, almost as if it pities me as I mourn this mutilated moment. I refuse to look upon the wreckage as I hoist my bloody battered mass out of the ravaged ruins of this vessel for fear of seeing too much of what has been done to mangle my flesh-frayed remains which are now left only to linger long enough to lament my final fateful losses. Blood oozes out of me from a multitude of weeping mortal wounds as I crawl to the edge of the water, leaving a tortured testimonial trail on the shoreline's stained sands which cannot replenish my ever-expiring existential hourglass.

I try to console myself to some diminutive degree with the notion that at least I'll extinguish my last breath gazing out onto the trembling surface of this man-made lake with enough humanity harbored safely in my soul to shame this encroaching eschaton. I find a scenic spot upon the shore where I prop myself upright to await my accepted end only to realize that this is the very same site where the compiler and terminal have both also been surrendered to this shore. As I inspect these ejected items, I become almost infinitely astonished to find them still in fully functional condition.

My mutilated fingers fumble over the surface of these devices as I wonder if I should even attempt to upload these ravaged remnants of my mutilated mind. Although I can't be too certain of even my own valor or worthiness to attempt this final action, my hands continue of their own ataxia-like accord. In my exhausted and expiring state, I find myself helpless to control my frantic fingers. Despite all my uncertainty, it's not my meticulous mind, but my horrid hands which seem destined to make one final desperate foray to fulfill what I'd at least previously believed to have been my deepest destiny. The compiler's sensors submit to my hands' commands and stick to my blood-soaked and slashed-up scalp securely enough to update my profile. I stare at the screen and wait for it to finish reading the last remnants of my mutilated mind as if hypnotized by horror before turning my eyes back to the encroaching eschatonal sky.

My eyes cast themselves upon the horizon which hangs low under the sinister surmounting shadow of an engorged and expanding erectile cloud of a petrifying pyroclastic priapism. The sky becomes increasingly black of soot, mottled with molten red and black magma-meteors, and flashing with electrical explosions of lava-lined lightning as this collage of catastrophic components drifts demonically toward me. As I stare at this sinister spectacle, I decide to spend my final fatal moment in a meditative state, and fully experience my own earthly ending while my consciousness is rendered unto whatever realm awaits.

I struggle to draw in a heavily hindered breath through my painfully punctured lungs which I fail to hold for long as my diaphragm is forced to fight frantically for air as blood continues to ooze out and into my lungs, slowly drowning me in its deluge. The wind heaves a heated gust of volcanic ash and delivers the stench of scorched earth and stinging sulfur. My lungs scream out in searing pain as the poisoned air pours into my bleeding brachial tissues. Despite the severity of this piercing pain which savagely stings upon each inhalation, I'm now hyperventilating as my automated brainstem overrides my excruciating objections toward this desperate attempt to keep me only momentarily alive.

I'm now wheezing and coughing up bile and blood as my lungs struggle in near convulsions to clear themselves. The horrid fluids bring a rusty metallic taste of viscus slimy consistency. This foul flavor becomes mixed with little hellish flakes of the ashen air as the sky's soot snows down from chaotic crimson clouds which blot out the heavens in the very way in which they will now continue to do for some unseen eons onward.

My chest becomes too weak to continue coughing. In one abrupt and failing hyperventilated spasm, I draw in my last breath which fades into a strange proprioceptive stillness. My eviscerated eardrums can no longer hear whatever sounds this surrounding scene of sinister skylines might still be singing. I can only imagine the songs of the spheres playing unheard and un-hearable through the harmony of a universe which will resonate beyond this last existential epoch of all earthly extinction.

My eyes fade from blackened skies to the fatal final darkness of an abysmal eternity which has opened its expansive entrance unto the entrails of death's digestive tract. All that's left of me now is a meditative mind's dispassionate demise and a subtle sensation of pulsating plastic against the failing flesh of my fingers. This final figment of my fatality is the lingering lament of all that could have been, expressed only in the depression of my deceased finger's falling onto the consciousness compiler's completion confirmation.

Volcanic debris will fall upon whatever unknowing remnants remain of my earthly expanse. The entire surface surrounding me will be buried by the eruption-ejected expanse of lifeless lava rocks and scorched soot. Whatever life remains, returns, or replaces what has been lost in this explosive extinction event will have no knowledge, concern, or connection to anything I had ever been, become, or dreamed of being. If there were anything I could have willed these imagined future inhabitants of a reemerging and reimagining earth, it would be those immortal inspirations which I'd always feared that I'd not sufficiently served in order to insure their survival. I would will that these immortal inspirations be inherited as an infinite daring desire to dream against the dark.

# II. Le Verbe Faite Chair (The Verb Made Flesh)

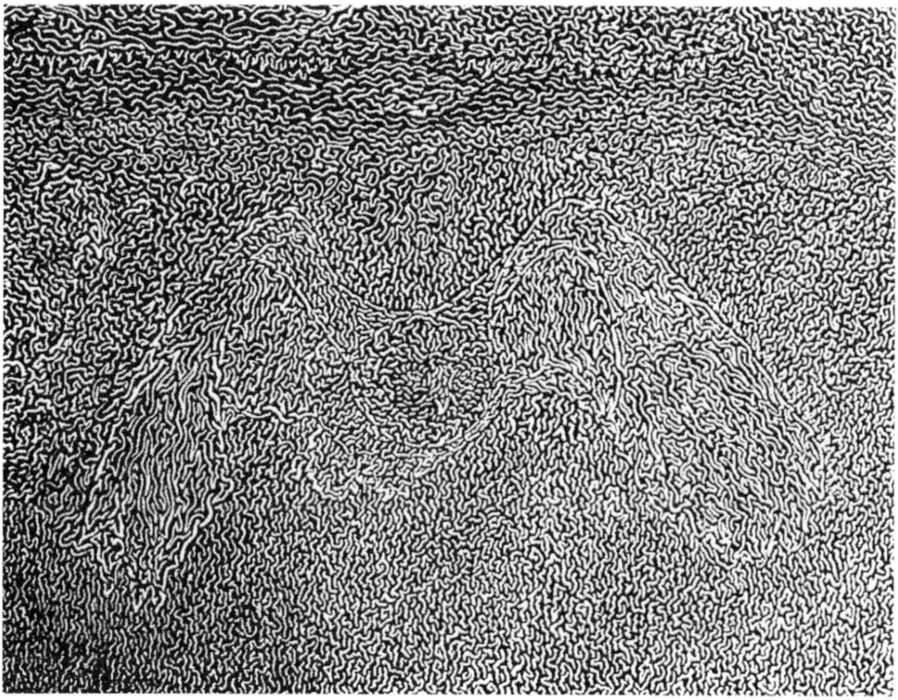

# Chapter 7
## TH3 F735H-F4CT0RY 4ND TH3 630R614 6U1D35T0N35

I wake directly from death into things beyond me, and yet my mind is conceived of knowing far too much, far too well. The strange, synthetic, steam-soaked, silicate scent of this flesh-factory skin which molds itself around my fledgling-to-feel fingers is so frighteningly familiar, seeming almost as certain and studied as the grooves of my forming fingerprints as they're etched to exactly match my meditative memories. My synthetic synapses tingle in their electronic initiation as they're burned into my bionic brain, and I can't so much feel my face, as sense it's expressionless standby-mode stare while my unmoving eyes imagine themselves appearing as empty as an antique doll or something. Somehow, none of this seems uniquely new, but feels as natural as yawning to greet the start of another numberless day.

This foreign flesh tries to welcome me as if I were returning home to it, having only been gone for some short spell. It holds me upright and balanced as a conveyor belt ushers me along an automated assembly line, keeping me in a sort of stabilized state of sleep paralysis as all my old scars and defining features are scanned and inspected for accuracy and quality assurance or something. My breathing is independently regulated to keep me calm and reassured as my skin slowly stretches and my pulse pumps furiously, breaking-in my body like an incipient combustion engine.

My neoteric neurons speak to me as if perfectly impersonating that innermost voice of *I*, offering assurances like auguries that this iteration or incarnation of *I* should have no way of knowing. They inform me like a well-rehearsed tour guide that this conveyor is about to deliver me to a dressing area where I'll become autonomous enough to dress myself. I begin to basically sleepwalk as if following some subconscious mental magnetism to a specific dressing booth as the conveyor kicks me off. There's a set of clothes waiting in this booth which are essentially an amalgamation of martial arts uniform and hooded cloak, tailored to my measurements. Without any memory of having trained in martial arts, my emerging mind somehow believes itself to have attained a black belt in judo and my hands appear to attest to this belief as they cinch my belt almost as if applying a perfect cross-collar choke.[43]

I subconsciously slip my feet into a pair of bamboo sandals and my steps direct themselves with certainty to an exterior door. Somehow, I already know that four others are fated to be picked up here, and that six men in white cloaks with Vitruvian man logos will be waiting for us. My paranoia towards all these implicit thought implants is strong, but I try to remain calm and contemplative.

My mindless steps exit the flesh-factory, foreknown to be located outside Austin's city limits, anticipating the rush of a sweltering summer's heat and a glaring glut of oversaturating sunlight. Despite my anticipation, the force of a scorching sun strikes me like a wrathful wave which forces a surge of sweat from my pours and smashes my eyes into a strained squint, making it difficult to keep my balance as I enter this sun-soaked scene. The six men I've already previsioned rush to direct me to a sixteen-passenger van where I enter into the bliss of air-conditioned comfort and cordial company of an old man clad in cowboy clothing.

"Howdy Harek. I bet ya already know mah name too now, don't ya'?"

"Nope. I seem to suspect it's Hank, but I've no way of being certain. You wouldn't happen to know where these unknown notions could've come from would you? It almost seems like I've already lived this moment beforehand, and I'm now being guided through some half-forgotten memory I've never previously formed."

"Yuppers. Mah name's Hank Peroe, an' I'm jus' as confuse as yous, ol' buddy-boy. One minnit, I'm wif mah jeenyus son who insists tha 'hole wurl's 'bout ta end as he's hook'n-up sum kin' ah electro-magic gizmo-gadget ta mah 'rinkly ol' dome, an' tha next thing I knows- I'm walk'n outta dis 'ere robo-lab in a sci-fi sort ah synth-o-skin wif a head full'a all kin' ah stuffs I can't not begin ta explain. Know wut I mean?"

My new *I's* unfounded understanding knows that he shouldn't be so openly honest with me. There's no way I'm going to reciprocate such honesty by telling him what I now suspect to be mutually occurring in our emerging minds. These incidentally identical intuitions could have been intentionally inserted into our minds like premanufactured memories, implanted by a more ethereal entity like a god or an author. Although, this could also be a mere coincidence or shared instance of paranoid delusions, or even just the remnants of improperly erased memories from some previous iteration of some similar simulation's scenario. In any of these cases, it would be best to figure out what's truly going on before commenting further, and it would have been better for me to have said less about it already. All this having been considered, I elect to resort to small talk instead.[44]

“So Hank, where are you *originally* from?”

“I jus’ knewd ya gonna ask me dat. Tell ya wut. Since I’s sure ya already know tha answer, how’s ‘bout we mix it up a bit? ‘Nstead ah hav’n dis ‘ere conversation we seem ta has done already had before, le’s us talk ‘bout someth’n new, er ‘least differen’. Now tell me young man, er wutever ya is now. Ifn’s ya cud go back ta yer ol’ life know’n everything as ya does now, wut’d ya has done did differen’?”

“Nope. That’s not just some simple survey question about a product preference, or my favorite color. I’d have to really torture myself with a long hard look at my whole lost life before I could even attempt to actually answer that one. I don’t mean to be rude, but I’d prefer not to just spit-out some superficial statement about something that should probably only be expressed with the kind of contemplative care of a soldier staring into the invisible void of time while telling the tale of how some scar was singed into more than just the memory of his mangled meat. If that makes sense.”

“Yeah boy-o, ya prolly right ‘bout dat one. I’m a heck’a an ol’ man though, and I done had all kin’s ah time ta ponder mah life’s worth’a scars an’ such. Lemme answer dat ol’ question mahself ta kin’a gives ya a sort’a insight. ‘Ssuming I actually gots me any real insights, ah course.”

Two more passengers arrive and seat themselves inside this air-conditioned oasis of a 16-passenger van. They’re both sweating as profusely as I’ve already forgotten to have done just moments ago. My mysteriously rendered memory recognizes them as a married couple in their forties who informally prefer to go by Siri and Duco. They shake hands without a word of introduction, seeming to imply that their minds have been implanted with similar insights, though they could just be shy or soft-spoken. Hank however, has no such shyness.

“Howdy folks. No need fur no introductions is dere? I’uz jus’ fix’n ta tell dis ‘ere young-un’ wut I’da done differen’ in mah pas' life, ifn’ I’da knowd things tha way we all seem ta-does now. Ya know, ‘side from place’n a whole slew ah big ol’ gambl’n bets an’ get’n right-rich, I spose I’da tried ta has made mahself a news man.”

The couple glances at each other as if to telepathically acknowledge the absurdity of Hank trying to read the news with his non-non-regional diction and po’boy style of prose.

“Yuppers. I’da tried ta preach tha truth, so no one wuda’ had ta live in all dat post nine-lev’n confusion. Dat certainly is where it’d all started ta gone so wrong ya know.”

Our final passenger slides into the van with slippery sweat-soaked skin as we all nod in assumptive greetings. We’re pretty sure she goes by Judith, and that we should be careful what we say around her for some reason which is not quite clear. Our cloak clad escorts climb in behind her and the van begins its long drive to a rural region of Georgia.

“How do you figure nine-eleven to be the point where everything went wrong? It seems to me like there were plenty of problems before then.”

Judith stares at Hank with a certain scowl in her twenty-something eyes, as if imagining herself to have seen enough suffering to be perfectly prepared to put this old man in his patriarchal place.

“Well young’un, dat wur tha moment we all learnt dat dere wurn’t no more truth no more. Dat ‘vent show’d us all how tha news wurn’t tell’n us tha whole truth no more, how our gov’ment wurn’t no good at protect’n us, an’ how we wurn’t never gonna be able ta know nuth’n fer sure not never again.”

Judith and Hank proceed to argue over the pedantic details surrounding the terrorist attacks of September 11$^{th}$, 2001, like so many others have for decades. As the two fellow passengers bicker about falsified facts, false flag conspiracy theories, and socio-political assumptions of how things were and ought to be, I find myself trying to imagine the whole thing unfolding as it might have appeared to a nineteen- or twenty-year old’s eyes at that time.

I remember how Grisha had tried to explain it all to me before, and how difficult it had been for me to understand anything he’d told me. However, having witnessed my own world’s collapse before finding myself here in this new realm with strange and foreign thoughts, it seems easier to visualize every distant and disputed detail of that detached day. I run the whole thing through my mind like a simulation of what I’d been told about it, considering everything I can imagine as I sit here on this long ride to rural Georgia. I try to make sense of it all as if it were a part of my own lifetime and not some precession of reported events which I hadn’t been alive enough to consciously experience.

I soon imagine September 11$^{th}$ as a postmodern odyssey and microcosm of our entire post-truth era. This day exposed the long-looming truth that reality had indeed been lost to us, and that we'd all have to come to terms with this fact in our own time and in our own way. Truth be told, the end of reality had passed unnoticed and unannounced somewhere long before this fateful day. Most of us would go on to spend years or lifetimes without ever figuring out how to express this sentiment, much less develop some intuitive or practical sense of how to respond to it. But it would haunt us all in some obvious or oblivious sense.

On September 10th, we were still spellbound by the somnolent notion that there were undisputable facts which we could use to construct greater truths. We'd all pretty much believed that the world was a certain way which more or less coincided with conventional news reports. Our world was still swollen with problems, but we all thought we knew and agreed upon what these problems were, and that some solution or compromise could solve them all to some extent.

Terrorists were confined to the virtual realm of television shows, movies, or the occasional news story depicting disorganized groups in places so far from us that they might as well just be considered imaginary. They weren't really dangerous or threatening and they hadn't transcended their way into our reality. They wouldn't dare attack us. We'd never been attacked on our home soil, and we could all rest easily knowing that our nation was keeping watch to ensure we were totally safe, no matter what.

Then on September 11th, we all woke up in total chaotic confusion. All of a sudden, terrorists were very real, they'd actually attacked us, and we could no longer assume that we were safe. We woke to images of a tower burning without any means of perceiving this as a real event. It didn't make any sense to us why we'd been attacked, how it could have happened, or who could have done this.

We all watched reports trying to explain the first attack with live images of a smoldering tower, only to see what could have been an instant replay as the second identical tower was struck by another plane. Then we were told that another plane had crashed into the Pentagon, and soon after a fourth had either been shot down or crashed into a field. What we had awakened to see as a single concluded event was now a string of unending catastrophes which seemed incompatible with everything we had ever known as real.

What was being broadcast as reality had only been experienced on movie and television screens as fiction in our lifetimes. Our reality had never shown us people choosing to jump off buildings, slowly falling to certain death in despair rather than waiting to be drowned in smoke or devoured by a fiery inferno. This wasn't consistent with anything in the reality we had previously known. How could we possibly process the images and information we now perceived?

Our minds held so many questions like why, and how, and who. The news tried to console us and offer explanations which couldn't bridge the infinite rift between the things we were seeing and the things we'd believed we had seen before this. Their stories sounded like they were all made up in order to try to explain what couldn't be explained, or as if their explanations were all based on truths which had been withheld from us in order to preserve the illusions of previous lies.

We watched the twin towers collapse along with all our previous illusions of truth in this world. The news was no longer reliable or honest. Our nation could no longer be trusted. We were no longer capable of believing anything anymore. Our world had been exposed to us for what it had always been. It was no longer real, and it would never be enough.

As I conclude my American-centric reimagining of this sinister saga, Hank tries to turn the tables on Judith.

"How's 'bout yerself Ma'am? Wut'd ya change 'bout yer past life den?"

"Nothing. It all led to me being here, which is more than what everyone else we've ever known can say now. Their silence is the only testimony I need."

"Yer a young'n. Wait 'til ya get ol' like me. Give'n 'nough time, ya'll regret all kin's ah things. I bet ya'd change tha color ah tha sky in a decade er two."

"I'd change the color of the sky right now if we're talking about purely imaginary stuff like that. Then I'd make the stars do choreographed dances and put on elaborate shows every night too. I might even make everyone all but immortal so there was no death to be afraid of, only life to get board of living. That might defeat the whole point of existing though, so I'd probably just give it a test run or something. Maybe just give immortality to some isolated Amazon tribe or something and see how it all works out for them first."

"Nope. Who's to say there aren't immortals in one of those unknown tribes already? They might know more than all of us. If we're going to play the role of author or creator, it would probably be a good idea to start off by studying the designs of our own worlds. Nope?"

"I thought that's what we were doing right now. I mean, If I look at all the things in our world which fail to satisfy us and submit my revisions, isn't that the same thing? Although, I do think it's safe to say that none of us would be here if our world had been good enough to accept as it had been. Am I right?"

"Nope. The world was just what it needed to be for us to end up here, according to your earlier statement. I'm not here because I wanted to change the world though. I'm here because I couldn't understand it."

"Wutta ya mean ya cudn't un'erstan' tha wurl'? Didn' ya read tha ol' manual?"

Hank laughs far too loud at his own joke, and everyone tries not to cringe too noticeably. The couple asks the driver how long our drive is supposed to take, and Judith mocks them for asking a question to which we all already know the answer. I decide to drop my point and get into something more interesting.

"What memories do you all have which mean the most to you right now?"

"None of it matters now. It wasn't real. In fact, we might find out none of this is real either. Even if it is real, I don't think any of it can matter anymore."

"Y'all ain't gots no clue. It all matters ta someun'. Shoot, we dun discovered dat our whole wurl' wur created by someun' other dan us. Dat means dere's a god, don't ya see? I ain't got no clue wut our god wunts ah us, but obviously we dun been made fur sumth'n."

"Nope. I don't care about any of the facts as to why we're here, or what it all means, or any of those philosophical questions right now. What I'm curious to know, is what moments from your previous lives actually hold meaning in a way which goes beyond numbers, dates, and other types of data. We've all had dreams which were not factually real in the sense of our daily lives, and yet were just as meaningful as anything that happened in our undreaming days. Doesn't anyone else feel as if there were things which transcended the facts of our previous lives?"

"I git jus' wut ya mean. I 'member when I took mah wife on our first vacation. We didn' have lots ah money er nuth'n, but we managed ta scrape together a few bucks an' went backpackin' 'round Mexico. Neither one ah us knewd no Spanish, an' giv'n our accen's, which ya may'a noticed, it didn' seem as tho anyun' cud understand a one wurd we'd say'd. It wur great tho. I felt like we wuz tha only two people on earth, an' no'un cud understan' jus' how deeply we luvd an' understood eachuder. It wuz like tha less anyun' cud understan' us, tha closer we felt ta eachuder."

"Alright old timers, I've got a story which I'm still fond of, even if you're all a bunch of sappy cornballs. One time a group of my friends broke into the zoo at night, and I went to see the lions. I remember there was this one new lion that the zoo had just shipped in from the wild. All the other lions looked like overgrown house cats, but not this one. He had this look in his eyes which seemed like a white blazing fire in the soft reflections of the moonlight. This great beast was circling the perimeter of its cage, trying to find some way out. There were goats, chickens, and other farm type animals nearby. The lion would make all these growls, and roars, and chattering sounds whenever any of these animals made a noise, and he would lick his lips in a way which was almost like some sinister blood thirsty declaration of the most primal urges which remained so strong and alive in this terrifying creature. I remember how I'd gone to get a chicken and tried to throw it to the lion so he could devour it and serve his powerful need. The lion crouched down and encroached on the chicken with all the chilling stealth and skill these beautiful beasts are known for. Then he wiggled his legs to ready himself for that final bounding pounce upon his would-be prey, and suddenly just- stopped. He looked at the chicken as if it were just a lump of cold disgusting leftovers. Then he went back to the other lions and flopped down like he'd just been defeated in some brutal fight or something. I remember, it was like the fire had died inside his eyes for a second."

"Dat's 'bout tha saddest story I ever dun heard. How's dat someth'n powerful er meanin'ful ta ya?"

"It's not the end of my story. The next day I heard on the news that one of the trainers had gone into the lion exhibit to retrieve the chicken. While he was opening the gate to exit the exhibit with the chicken tucked under his arm, the lion snuck up behind him. The beast ran right through the man like he wasn't even there and passed swiftly through the open gate. This lion managed to roam around the zoo without being caught for a full month. It stalked its way from exhibit-to-exhibit chasing would be prey around without killing it. All the animals learned to fear the lion, and after it had finally been recaptured, the zoo had to send it back into its wild homeland. When the zoo was safe enough to reopen, I went with my friends to see the other animals. They all had those wild sparks back in their eyes. The goats wouldn't let anyone come near them, the gazelles, the hyenas, everything in the zoo had found the fear and the hunger. Eventually, I'm sure this newfound zest wore off, but for a time, it was like they had remembered what it was like to be truly real again. If there's anything more meaningful than that to me, I don't know what it is. I want to be like that lion. I want to break out of the cages built around me and really live. I'm not really sure that's even possible, but if you're asking about some kind of transcendent truth, that's the best story I've got."

"I jus' gots one thing ta say 'bout all dat. Bull-Shoot! Ain't no way nun ah it ever happen't."

"Nope. It doesn't matter if it did or not. That's exactly the kind of story I'd requested. How about you two? There has to be at least one story you'd love to tell, if only to remember it aloud."

Siri and Duco look at each other and Duco gives Siri a little nudge with his shoulder as he pulls a mischievous grin. She smiles back and tries to tell him that she can't tell *that one*, before shifting herself into storytelling character.

"We used to have a parrot in our house. When people would come over, we would tell them that the parrot had belonged to a psychic. This psychic had sold her to us because the bird could see the future but wouldn't wait for clients to pay the psychic before announcing its visions to them once they had walked into its view. Our guests usually didn't take us seriously, but we'd assure them that the bird was in fact clairvoyant. Then we'd warn them that although our magic pet could see the future it never gave anyone good news."

Duco takes over the story as Siri tries to hold back her impending laughter.

"Of course, this made our guests curious in their disbelief, and they'd always insist on seeing what the parrot would tell them when they met the bird. So, we'd lead them into the room where we kept the parrot in a cage with a cloth hanging over it so it couldn't see them right away. Then we'd tell them to wait until we'd been gone for a few minutes and then pull the cloth off the cage to see the bird and find out their future."

Judith cuts in to ask the obvious.

"So, what was the trick? Did you have a microphone and speaker setup in the cage so you could mess with them?"

"No. It was much better than that. When they pulled the cloth off the cage, our parrot was trained to play dead. Our guests would see her fall over and come running to ask us what was wrong with it. We'd go back into the room with our guests to see the bird playing dead and tell them how the psychic had given us a terrible warning that this would happen one day. We'd try to build up the tension by telling them that we didn't want to worry them, and that they should probably just forget about what the psychic had warned us. This always made our gests want to know more."

Siri picks up the story as Duco glances to give her a cue.

"So, we'd let them coax the prophecy out of us. We'd tell them how the psychic had told us that one day the parrot would drop dead in front of someone who was about to meet with a fate so horrible that the parrot's premonition of their doom would cause the bird to die instantly. This terrible fate wasn't something the psychic could predict, but what he could tell us was that after the bird had died, an evil spirit would come to possess the parrot. This spirit would revive the bird and it would no longer be possible for the bird to be contained within any cage. The bird would escape and spread terror far and wide, beginning with the horrors it would inflict on the last souls to see it alive. When the bird rose from the dead, it would call out to these poor souls by name and unleash the tortures of the damned upon them with a mighty SQUWAK."

Duco receives his own cue to retake the narrative.

"As soon as we said '*squawk*', the parrot was trained to let out a viciously loud squeal and scream out the names of our guests which we'd teach it earlier. It would wait for them to look over to see it alive before it'd burst through a section of the cage we'd rigged to break away as it screeched again and flapped its wings, flying around frantically. Once we started laughing, the parrot would calmly return to its cage and squawk '*Bird Brain*' with a mocking delight."

Judith leads the laughter as we all smile at the couple's mischievous story.

"I can't even imagine how much fun that must have been! That's it. I'm going to have to train a parrot now. Driver! Take us to the nearest pet store along the way! It'll be worth it, I swear!"

Our escorts ask us to settle down and advise us that there won't be any stops except for real necessities on our trip. Then the couple turns to me and asks me to tell a story. I almost don't know what might possibly fit the pallet of everyone present, but then a certain story comes to my mechanical mind which almost forces me into telling it.

"The rural bucolic residence where I lived with my grandparents was warm and glowing with all the splendor of spring on the last day of March. The evening air was so calm, you could hear the compendious cacophony of nature resounding as an orchestra of chaos in the infinite concert chamber of the sun's setting skyscape. The surround-sound song of the cicadas first filled this accommodating air as prelude to the stereoscopic, ping-pong sounds of a few emerging owls, the deranged discordance of wide-ranging coyote rollcalls, and the ardent mating-call croaks of an abundance of boisterous bullfrogs."

"Ya ain't gonna go on an' on 'bout be'n in nature like all ah dem city-slickers, is ya? 'Cause I ain't gots much patience fer all ah dat bullwinklin' nature worship'n, like all dem tales ah how folks dun gon camp'n er somth'n an' luvd dem sum nature while eat'n plastic packs ah hotdogs an' marshmellers-as if fake food heated next'a a man-made lake wur a spiritual experience."

"Nope. So overnight, a foreign cold front invaded the springtime skies and bombarded the entire surface of this spring-scape scene with about twelve inches of snow. The frogs could still be heard croaking on the following frozen evening, although their cadence slowed, and the tone of the frog-song voices became loathsome and lamenting. It was as if these frozen frogs were singing the same words to a song which had been transposed from a major key of amorous auditions into a melancholic minor arrangement of self-pity and disdain for the indifferent afflictions of nature."

"An' wut 'zactly wur tha wurds ta dese two differen' frog songs den?"

"The implicit message of their yo-yo tongued chorus was something along the lines of, *mate with me, mate with me*. While the tortured tones of their suffering sonnet might be something akin to a sentiment of, *why me, why me*. So, I guess the vulgar truth to the lamprophonic language of these bold bullfrogs could have been consistently phrased in the form of, FUCK ME! FUCK ME!"

Judith laughs as if trying to hide her amusement after hearing something shameful in front of her mother. The other members of my audience cast frowning faces in appall of my word choice rather than these words' meanings. I find this amusing in the sense that it's like being sickened by the shadow of a shoe that's stepped in excrement rather than the actual Shit itself.

"Nope. I guess no one likes my story. I did enjoy all of yours, so I could tell another one, unless someone else has a tale they want to tell."

Judith raises her hand the way a mischievous student might try to gain permission from an unsuspecting teacher to perform for a classroom full of snickering students. I nod so she can act as my accomplice in annoying this overly comfortable congress, as I strongly believe in disturbing the comfortable.

"So, there was this bird who decided to fly away from its home, kind of like all of us, if you think about it. Anyway, this bird soars high up in the sky and just keeps flapping its way farther and further north for days and days. Then it gets caught in a snowstorm, kind of like the one that punished your horny toads or whatever they were. So, the bird starts to get all cold and wet until its wings start to freeze over, and the bird starts descending toward the snow-covered earth below, frantically struggling and failing to defy the sinking sky."

I start to guard a grin in response which comes unasked upon my face as I realize how this story very closely resembles a sort of riddle my grandfather, Grisha used to tell, and reminds me of my enduring fondness for his memory.

"The bird falls all the way down into a shallow snow drift, becoming stiff as the snow blows over and buries him in an icy grave. The bird's on the verge of freezing to death, when a polar bear squats over the top of him and squeezes out a massive mound of steaming wet *merde*. As the polar bear shuffles off, the vile excrement melts the snow and slides down onto the bird, thawing out its wings and resurrecting it. The bird's wings thrash violently as it tries to dig its way out of the merde and melting snow, and it screeches desperate chirping cries for help. Then a nearby coyote hears the bird, and rushes over to paw through the snow and filth to pick the bird out of the mess. It kills and devours him in one slimy starving chomp and gulp."

Judith smiles as the couple responds just as she's expected by asking with judgmental horror what the point of this story was.

"The moral of this story is actually quite poignant. You see, the one who comes to take a dump on you, isn't always your enemy. And the one who comes running to help you when you scream, isn't always your friend."

Hank and the couple break-off into their own faction for the rest of our trip as a result of all this. Judith and I end up trading jokes, riddles, and impromptu stories to pass the time which annoys the hell out of our fellow passengers who can't help themselves from eavesdropping. At one point we even decide to make up backstories for them which we tell loud enough to ensure they overhear.

Judith decides to invent a somewhat sophomoric yet surprisingly elaborate tale about the couple. In her prologue, they're actually conjoined twins which are separated at birth. They're each adopted by different families on opposite ends of the globe. Duco is raised by Australian missionaries who beat him with kangaroo and dingo bones whenever he sins in even the slightest way, such as forgetting to say his prayers. Siri is raised by Icelandic aristocrats who hire a series of teachers, maids, and handlers to ensure she never hears or sees a single expletive word until graduating with a Master of Arts degree in creative dance.

In her tale, the two meet over the corpse of a dead homeless man after an evening of running from their own shadows which causes them to become lost in the same back alley while on separate vacations to Paris. The only phrase either of them has learned in French is, *merci beaucoup*, which they both mispronounce as *merde si, boucou.*[45] The couple ends up bonding over their trauma as they wander the streets in search of anyone who can communicate in Icelandic, Australian-English, or pantomime gestures well enough to direct them back to their respective bed and breakfast lodgings.

They end up staying up all night, and as the sun surmounts the shadowy streets, they both decide to surrender all hope of finding their own ways home. So, they walk into a church where they take selfies in front of a particularly bloody sculpture of the crucifixion. A local vagrant with delusions of grandeur who believes he's *The High Priest of Mithras* sees them taking pictures. He proceeds to walk over and offer his blessing upon them in French-inflected English and pronounces the two husband and wife.

Since Siri and Duco have both been taught that divorce is a despicable thing, they decide to commit to each other for better or worse in this deranged and pseudo-arranged marriage. They never question the authenticity of their marriage due to the fact that the delusional derelict-priest wore an official-enough collar around his dilapidated clothes, which they both assume are no more worn down than anyone else's Parisian clothes by their snobby standards.

After six miscarriages and three, deformed, inbred monster births, they're transported here in this new and unexplained realm as a result of a dyslexic dignitary's error. This dignitary was supposed to upload the consciousness profiles of two other people with names and addresses similar to a scrambled arrangement of their own. The truth they won't tell us, according to the end of this farcical fable, is that they're secretly glad to have finally gotten away from those obliviously incestuous abominations born out of their previously befuddled existence.

My backstory for Hank is similarly immature. He's initially the unintended result of an accident involving the transport and disposal of faultily aborted fetuses and an electrical power plant where a train transporting these mangled amalgamations crashes. The electricity causes a pile of these fetuses to fuse together as the current creates a kind of dysfunctional defibrillator shock which jump-starts this pile's pulse.

Hank's proto-pile is later found by a pack of wild hogs which mistakes him as one of their own. They nurse him until the age of four when he's spotted by hunters in a helicopter who catch him with a net and airlift him to the local hospital, hoping they can figure out what kind of human hybrid he might be. From there, scientists teach him how to speak English phonetically before releasing him back into the wild at an age of roughly fifteen.

He goes on to be taken in by a family of blind rodeo clowns turned carnies who need someone to run a prompt-o-pup and marshmallow flavored cotton candy booth. After years of eating the discarded leftovers customers toss in the trash as a means of survival, he finally leaves to feast on unsuspecting campers. He eventually becomes known as the *Phantom Hog-Demon of the Amistad Reservoir*, and many cryptozoologists are intrigued by the reports of those who claim to survive late night encounters with him.

Before I can wrap up my story, our escorts make a stop at an isolated rest-station. They give us just enough time to expel bodily wastes, stretch our synthetic skeletal structures, and spend a proffered pittance to purchase a few packages of faux-food fodder.[46] When we return to the van, our driver switches seats with one of our other escorts, and the rest of us slouch down to take naps.

My bionic brain falls into very different dreams than those my surrendered skull had previously hosted. I find these dreams less forward focused, and much more abstractly directed toward consolidating and reconciling things belonging to my past mind. Before falling into this short span of slumbering segments, I find myself thinking of all of these silly stories as if they were all just different accounts of a same singular story. Each of us is almost like a different angle of the same person, providing multiple perspectives of a shared story. There's one author at the origin of all these stories, at our origins, at all origins. This author sits laughing in absurdity while constructing and distorting this story and our characters as it deceives us into believing that we're real, that everything's real.

The author places all these separate stories into our heads. It gives us the impulses and exposition necessary to guide us into following the fated plot points of its intended storylines. The stories this author gives us to tell within the one we live illuminates and alludes to parallels otherwise concealed from us. Even as I slip into slumber and dream of solving this story like putting together a puzzle I seem to be living inside of, it's as if it were all presented by an author.

I begin to imagine that I am the lion with wild eyes blazing against the moon's stolen reflections of obscured sunlight. I am being held captive in a world of pacified beasts who've given up their fiery flickering ferocity in exchange for a peaceful place to slowly pass away under the voyeuristic gaze of dispassionate tourists. I am eluding my captors and terrifying every eye which can see me burning behind these darkened eyes as I stalk through lightless nights in search of something inspiring enough to devour whole and sustain me.

I am the frozen frustrations of those futile frogs as they curmudgeonly croak unto an indifferent ice-scaped earth. I am the bird exclaiming in excrement. I am the parrot mocking all men in words which mock myself. I am the separated soul which stumbles into being reunited with itself by delusional declarations. I am the beastly abomination which drifts around aimlessly devouring what it must to sustain itself instinctually unto no apparent end. I am the yokel wandering through a foreign land and discovering how the more distant I become from everyone else, the more intimately I feel related to whoever remains the least bit proximal to me.

I am escorting something anonymous according to a larger plan which cannot be spoken. I am a young and mischievous human amusing myself with indifference to the expense my laughter may cost others. I am a conglomerate of entities being constructed in a way which can be illustrated as a single being, as well as a single being which can be personified by many. I am not a real man, but the story that a man might construct to ensure himself that he is a real entity. I am merely a part of some vast and mysterious dream which is trying desperately to awaken.

The sliding door of the van rolls open with a loud roar which startles me into opening my dream-deluded eyes. We're all ordered out of the van and somehow know to proceed like military troops in a lock-step march directly to the intersection of five, highly polished, pale-grey, granite monoliths which rise 16-feet out of the earth to form an asterisk-like star pattern. Together these shimmering stones support a single squared capstone which grants us the solace of shade from a shining summer's sun.

It's impossible to look upon these monolithic stones and not think of the infamous Druid monuments of Stonehenge or the mysterious monoliths from *2001: A Space Odyssey*.[47] These are what have become known as the *Georgia Guidestones*. A list of ten guidelines is repeated on opposing surfaces of each of the four outer monoliths in a total of eight different languages, being- English, Spanish, Swahili, Hindi, Hebrew, Arabic, Chinese and Russian. These guidelines read like some kind of a post-apocalyptic ten commandments for an anonymous cult or something. My eyes seem to have memorized them as I read.

1. Maintain humanity under 500,000,000 in perpetual balance with nature.
2. Guide reproduction wisely - improving fitness and diversity.
3. Unite humanity with a living new language.
4. Rule Passion - Faith - Tradition - and all things with tempered reason.
5. Protect people and nations with fair laws and just courts.
6. Let all nations rule internally resolving external disputes in a world court.
7. Avoid petty laws and useless officials.
8. Balance personal rights with social duties.
9. Prize truth - beauty - love - seeking harmony with the infinite.
10. Be not a cancer on the earth - Leave room for nature - Leave room for nature.

Our group gathers in the space between the outer stones respectively inscribed in English and Russian. The side of the capstone facing us reads the words in Babylonian text, *Let These Be Guidestones To An Age Of Reason*. As we await whatever is to follow our assembly here, three other vans file onto the site and six passengers exit each to stand in the other segments between each of the outer four stones. The last passenger in the last van to arrive looks like Karen Phoe, but I dare not draw her attention or hold my gaze for any more than a moment as I can't be certain that my mind should be trusted, and I have no idea as to how things are about to play out here and now.

All of us become like statues ourselves as we wait silently and un-movingly for an orientation which implanted insights indicate will begin at dusk. Hour upon hour is poured out of our lives' hourglass like sands spilled to cover a mass grave of our potential's countless corpses. We wait for darkness in obedience to our ordained oblivion as most of mankind has done for far too long throughout the history of its futility. I wonder on and on as to what it is I'm truly waiting for, why I don't abandon all this intuitive insight, and what I might actually do if I were to leave these implanted intentions behind me. This makes the time pass like a kidney stone among these monoliths, which I come to suspect may be the very point of all this waiting.

The skies above fade from blue hues to a range of reds before permeating purples bleed to black as a pin-hole patchwork of stars begins to glow brilliantly above our adjusting eyes. Then a bursting blare of 12 distinct trumpets blasts 12 successive tones, signaling the crackling cadence of countless torches which all ignite in an impossible unison. The background beneath the hidden hillside glows of an eerie orange luminescence as cloaked figures march to ascend over the hilltops. They swarm this space the sun has surrendered and reclaim it with the radiance of their encroaching torch lights which flicker in fistfuls of flame.

The torch bearers move in choreographed cadence to an unheard drum, forming a fiery circle which surrounds this stone sculpted site. A void-black figure cloaked as if by some adumbral cloud emerges from unseen shadows, and glides in steps which seem more swept by unfelt winds than by bipedal ambulation. As this fugue-like figure reaches the southern side of the stagnant stone structure, it's swiftly cast upwards by three other cloaked figures as if summoned there by some shadow-shifting spell. The figure aligns itself along the astrological axis running from the apex of this megalithic monument and the zenith of some singular star in the zodiac.[48]

As the figure becomes still and stoic at this center-stone station, only the long shadows ebbing from its every angle intimate its presence among our upward gaze, the night's star-scattered sky, and the burning and beating wavelengths of earthly emanations. Suddenly, all but the incessant and inaudible celestial sounds are silenced, and the figure's own oratory voice begins to break the air in bursts of breath which seem to split the very atoms of the air. Thus begins our ominous orientation.

"Welcome Ravens to your initiation into the first of many dark illuminations. You have all risen from the realms of your respective realities to come into new light and shade much like the escaping captive in Plato's allegorical cave. Preeminent puzzles have helped you rub your closed eyes in order to see the phosphenes which urged you to follow us out of your allegorical areas.[49] Now you stand here with unsolicited intuitions and half-memories of having already lived this life in the same way a captive which has only seen the flickering of flame and fog of shadows may experience the first rays of real sunlight seeping into its oblivious shadow-scape world."

This explanation or implication of our apparently imbedded intuitions only makes my suspiciousness of this shadow's speech swell into a schizophrenic horror. I find my fingers twitching as I try not to tear at my own skull so I might eviscerate and evict whatever unwanted mass of materials or impulse-initiating software may be corrupting my not so natural mind. Even this compulsion seems suspect as part of some sinister scheme to either guide me into being overwhelmed unto oblivious obedience or provoked into raging rebellion unto some other nefarious end. I am indeed like a shadow gazer learning to look upon a world beyond my own now. There is no form nor figure I can fully fathom in this realm where shadow speech continues to incite and inform me.

"You may come to notice that the light in this realm behaves in a way which mirrors the light of your own prior incarnations. Although, I'd advise you pay particular attention to the ways in which light and shade behave here. I'd also urge you to look upon the relationship you have between the darkness which surrounds and fills you, and how you cast whatever light there is into these realms in hopes of seeing something illuminated. This may very well be the key to all understanding in this realm, and more importantly, those imperative insights into what may preside over this very realm as well. For as you may have already seen, much of what we've learned from all life and dream alike is that the worlds seem to abide by the structural sentiment of- *as above, so below*."

I picture this puzzle pertinent phrase and reflect upon my former fatality. This phrase rings particularly true to me. For just as the simulated entities had mimicked the realms beneath me, so too it seems that I am synonymously similar to the facts and figures of this higher realm I now inhabit. Here I'm an imagined entity, transcended into foreign flesh, and fighting against the facts of my nature to attain some higher truth of what I may become. My mind fights to formulate this sentiment into a simple equation and derives- *being is less than becoming*.

"All shadows are cast away from light. They take the shape of every surface upon which they're cast. The light goes wherever the shadow is not. All your eyes behold is of light and shade, and all the forms which you come to know are those things which stand in the realm between the light and dark. This is the truth of your own essence as well. For all that is, casts a shadow, and every shadow is tied to forms more fixed than itself, and all light is confined to where these things are not. Ask yourself this question. What is the name of the shadow, which is tied to you, but which your eyes cannot see?"

I think of standing directly under a high noon sun and spinning around to see where my shadow is not cast. I think of how the shadow may appear if I lift my feet or move in ways which create some void between the realm between myself and some surface on the other side of the light. It seems interesting to me how some void seems to exist in the space surrounding every shadow. There are other notions which seem to be tied to this one, but my mind is drawn back to the shadow's speech before I can ponder enough to understand such things.

“Imagine yourselves as Adam or Eve, having just been cast out of Eden. Imagine yourselves as the slaves of Plato’s cave arriving outside and feeling the earth quake as the cave collapses into ruble. What is it that has been lost to you? What is it that is different from one scenario to the next, and what is the same? What does this reveal to you about your own existential scenario? These are the questions which we would love to welcome you into understanding. These are the clues to the puzzles which have been presented to us all.”

The torches begin to dim and glow with less heat and light. I notice how the stars seem to become slightly brighter and more numerous as these surrounding sources of light dimly die down. My mind takes note of this as if observing some other imperative clue to these puzzling things which has yet to be more than alluded to, but I still somehow seem to suspect as this strange speech goes on.

“You’re all about to embark upon an inward journey which will define the path upon which you are to emerge. This journey inward is to take you to the depths of all darkness. You must confront the core of the abyss which lies in this world around you, and the world which has been built within you just the same. You must understand these things for what they are, so that you may understand all that is not, and all that is. Otherwise, you may never truly know yourself, nor anything else.”

No light comes from the torches now, but my eyes have adjusted to the moonlight so that this nightscape is quite clear. I’m mesmerized by how the monochromatic moon reflects the sun’s same light onto this celestial facing scene and makes everything appear so differently than it does during the daytime. It seems impossible for this light to truly be derived from the same source and by mere degrees of intensity and reflection somehow seem to create an entirely different realm of existence. The animals which wander during the day all hide and slumber now, and the nocturnal creatures all emerge from oblivion into night as if entering into one shadow from another. They seem to belong to different planes of existence altogether, and as I stand here in a realm which belongs more to them than myself, I wonder just what realm I should seek to find. Should I seek the shelter of some shadow, or strive to shine in the splendor of some light?

This isn’t much different from my lost life, as I’d never felt as if I’d belonged in that ruined realm. Everything I’d ever lived seemed as if it were part of another mind’s dream in which I’ve not belonged and was to be ushered out of and exorcised like some stray spirit, perhaps so I may eventually be delivered unto the right mind for some other awakening to which I truly belong. Now, in this realm, it almost seems as if I've become no more than a figment of some lost dreamer which has awakened on its own and set itself in search of the proper dream world which may somehow exist independent of me, itself, and all. This larger, lost dreamer carries me along like a cell inside its subconscious, processing this portion of its sentience as an ant attending this psychotic speech inside its higher hidden hive.

"The very reason you've made it here to the beginning of this journey, is because this has always been the journey you've sought. You are the most puzzling of people. You are the most contemplative and conditioned cognitive creatures. You are drawn to the darkness in search of light and are yourselves very much a light unto the darkness of whatever world you may inhabit. Although we would have very likely chosen you to find this place had it been up to us, it has actually been up to you to discover us in this place."

All the torchbearers move in closer so their diminishing flames can cast as much light as there is left within them. The granite sides of the guide-stones twinkle as if to imitate the pulsing of dying starlight as the words carved into them become like sculpted shadows which somehow seem to conspire to swallow the constellations above them. Like all man-made things, these stones are made to aspire to be more than they actually are while underwhelming every expectation of all they're made to mimic and slowly decaying and dissolving into even less than their very material. They are not unlike these words which still waft away into the winds which return them to the forgotten fog of silence.

"Here you see these stones which tell of truths we hope to serve. These guide-stones are of earthly substance which have been placed in ways which serve to tell a story of the skies above them. They obey the heavens, they remain within themselves and their proper place, and they convey that which has been etched upon them. You must aspire to become like them. You must learn to serve your function by being true to all the truths which find their way to you."

Our shadowy sermon turns into an invocation of the words upon these stones. The circle of flame-bearing figures chants each line in unison while the unseen orator stands atop the structure as if presiding over them, almost acting as an intermediary to the secrets of the celestial skies above us all. Once these words have all been intoned in each of the eight languages which they've been inscribed upon the separate surfaces of these stones, the torchbearers begin to sing a low toned *ommmmmmmm* in accompaniment of the ensuing procession of our escorts away from the stone site.

Each of us *Ravens* are taped on the shoulder by an escorting member of the torch-bearing enclave which leads us in a single file line toward the edge of the hill from where their torches had first shown their light.[50] I find myself inwardly panicked yet outwardly composed in unfeeling obedience to this perverse procession unto unknown whereabouts for unknowable reasons. Nothing in this entire course of words and events has done anything to lead me into trusting these figures to lead me to anything of higher knowledge or purpose. Their intentions remain uncertain, their entire demeanor is more concerned with secrecy than truth, and we haven't even been truly introduced to any of these figures. Instead, we've been given an indoctrination speech, kept in the dark, and now find ourselves being led away from one obscure place to another without any assurances or considerations whatsoever.

What option do I have though? I've come from a false world into one which I do not know. My mind may not even solely be my own here, and all I can be certain of is my obliviousness and curiosity to find out just what's going on here. All I can do is pay attention to every detail possible in order to hopefully put things together on my own at some later point.

As we crest the descending edge of the hill, I see a glowing opening in the ground which appears to be some kind of submerged staircase into an awaiting acropolis. Our procession files into this narrow opening and we wind deeper and deeper down the stone passages into the depths of this maddening maze. I try to keep a mental map of this underground maze as it corresponds to landscape above while we spiral along these winding paths from the entry stairwell to the countless corridors and innumerable underworld alcoves.

I also try to keep an eye on the entity I've become convinced is indeed Karen Phoe's incarnation in this realm. Her escort is eight heads ahead of mine which makes this a difficult task, although I notice how our pace is slowed repeatedly once the front of our file reaches a certain set of halls with identically constructed doors. This implies that we're being assigned rooms in order of procession, and that I'll be deposited into a room eight doors down from hers. I'm not sure if this makes any actual difference, but it does give me a small kind of comfort.

As Karen's being escorted into her room, I manage to cast a brief gaze into her eyes as I pass. She seems to cast that same look of unflinching acknowledgement and foreshadowing that I can still recall vividly from our previous life's encounter upon my waking into underground captivity. I can also feel my own face beaming its own unmoving message of solidarity towards her.

When my escort deposits me into my own cell-like room, this moment of intuitive insight is all that truly matters to me somehow.

My escort's arm waves toward the small bed in the back right corner. There's a commode in the corner off to the left and a small table against the same wall as the head of the bed. Aside from myself and a light-fixture on the ceiling, there's almost nothing else in here. There's no light-switch, no sink, no shower, no mirror, or anything more accommodating. Before the door closes, my escort places a stack of materials on the table and bows slightly.

The thud and clack of the heavy wooden door being latched firmly shut sends a chill up my spine. Before I can even check to confirm my suspicion, I know that I've been locked securely inside this space, and that someone else will likely decide when I'm to be released, if I am to be released at all. After confirming that I've been locked inside, I also imagine that the light will not be left on much longer, so I turn my attention to the materials left on the table.

There's a questionnaire on the top of these pages, although I find it odd that I've not been given any device to write out my answers. The first 36 questions are all multiple choice with the possible answers to all of them being, *True, False, Indeterminate, Meaningless, Self-Referential, Game Rule, Strange Loop*, and *None of the Above*.[51] Some examples of the questions on these pages are…

- You cannot step into the same river twice.
- You cannot answer the same question twice.
- You cannot answer the same question twice.
- The sentence below is not true.
- The previous sentence is true.
- What you are is more important than what you do.
- You are the result of what you choose to do.
- Observation changes the thing being observed.
- It is better to only study after a test, than to not study at all.
- The grass may truly always be greener on the other side.
- If someone is color blind, then certain colors do not exist for them.
- If a lion learns your language, you still may not be able to understand it.
- There is only one true reality.
- Facts are the only basis of truth.

The next section of questions is in essay form with blanks to write out answers.[52] These questions are even more quizzical at first glance. Some examples of these include…

- Two people are standing by a lake. One says. "*That's a lovely reflection in the water.*" The other says "*I see no reflection, but it's a fascinating assortment of fish, plants, and rocks within the water.*"
  How do you know which one is truthful?
- What does the word *it* refer to in the following sentence? ***It*** *is dark outside.*
- There's a man with his hands and feet tied together. He's biting onto a very high branch of a tree. If he releases his bite, he will surely die. A wise man walks by and sees him hanging and shouts. "*Say the one true thing which can set you free.*" What should the man say?
- You're a fish swimming next to your fish friend. An old fish swims by and asks your friend. "*How's the water*?" A while later your friend asks you. "*What's water?*". How do you answer?

Underneath these questions there are a set of geometry problems, abstract mathematical proofs, and a series of diagrams. There's also a short booklet entitled *Harmony, Stability, and Utility*, which contains a series of statements under four different headings.[53] The headings are *Preludes*, *Fugues*, *Overtures*, and *Recapitulations*. Before I can scan over the contents of this booklet, the light inside my room goes out, and I'm left standing in total blind darkness. After a moment of several voices crying out in objective response, there's total and complete silence, and the room becomes an infinite void in which I'm completely isolated and alone.

My hands slowly tremble, and soon the rest of my body begins to shake as if it's about to slip into another massive seizure. Somehow, I manage to calm myself down and steady my involuntary tremors by focusing on my breath and bringing my mind into a meditative state. As my breathing consoles me with its predictable and regulated cycles of familiar and intimate idiosyncrasies, a voice trickles in from under the tiny space between the door and the floor. It calls out to me as if trying to burrow its way through the thickening darkness and directly into my mind. It says…

"As Above, So Below."

Another moment passes in the space of six more breaths which I inhale deeply and slowly exhale back out into the abyss of my confinement. The voice returns with slightly lower volume from the same place, although it somehow seems to be encroaching ever so slightly. This time it speaks the words…

"Remember The Future."

These two statements are repeated over and over again as if they're being played on a loop. They come in a predictable cadence and in synchronization with my highly regulated breathing. The voice is consistent in tone, volume, and inflections. Only the realistic clarity of the voice suggests that it's actually coming from some unseen entity lurking on the outer edge of my dark domain.

I decide to stretch out on the bed and try to relax, although my breathing and meditative efforts cannot dissolve the presiding sense of tense anxious dread. With this paranoid sentiment and the voice repeating over and over again, my mind descends into exhaustive weariness. Eventually, I drift into a kind of surrendering slumber where my consciousness gives up under the duress of all this relentless torment. From the surrounding darkness, I fade into the unthinking shade within me, and find myself lost to a sleep which knows no hour and abides by its own mysterious sense of time...[54]

# Chapter 8
## TH3 D4RK D0M41N

I open my eyes... I close them... I sleep... I dream... I wake... I think... I imagine... I become confused... I dream... I sleep... I wake... I lose track of my mind... I find it... I drift blindly... I dream... I sleep... I wake... I dream... I forget... I remember... I dream... I sleep... I dream... I...[55]

The darkness is so complete that my mind becomes unable to discern these actions or remember the order of performing them very well, if at all. The division between the realm of dream and the realm in which my mind imagines itself to have awakened becomes increasingly diminished. Even the realms of inner and outer darkness seem to merge as my mind dissolves into this divine darkness which presides over all imaginable realms.

There is nothing so sinister nor so sublime as being submerged in such surrounding shadows. My soul becomes exposed to all oblivion as wall, floor, ceiling, and skull are all diffused into this infinite dark dominion. Everything becomes as invisible and ethereal as the unseen air itself, and all earthly senses are evaporated unto the emergence of one solitary sense of the soul's own shadow, resting like a singular sensor upon the swimming surface of some shoreless celestial sea.

Slowly, the very sound of silence swells until it can be unhearingly heard, screaming its stranded song from every atom of this tacit and tenebrific tide. This pseudo-sound is like the rushing roar of river rapids where the waters of oblivion rage and rampage through the otherwise serene streams of consciousness which begin to flow backward from the summits of sentient shadows to the most oblivious unconscious abyss. My own blood grates and grinds against the valleys of veins like glacial landslides scraping and etching their dissolving descent through an ever-eviscerated earth. My pulse punishes my mind with its concussive cacophony of heartbeats which hammer the chaotic cadence of life against all endings. Every arrogated inhalation expands my lungs without fulfillment, and each ensuing exhalation exclaims an enigmatic emptiness into the derelict and dying echoes of oblivion as the escaping air is circulated and seized, circulated and seized, over and over, again, and again, and again...

The hours seem to expand unto the ends of eternity and mock the microcosmic moments of my mind as they become incalculable. These infinite hours are rhetorically reincarnated and recapitulated as I'm forced to endure their redundant repetitions of all too empty and exaggerated eons. All earthly intervals of time are effectively exiled without clock or compass to coordinate against these secluded shadows of silence. There is only the blind beating of my belligerent blood and the writhing of the whimpering winds of my labored lungs as the darkness seems to exhale eternities into existence in innumerable, indifferent, and immortal breaths, only to confiscate and consume them all back into oblivion.

The whispered words, "*as above, so below*" and "*remember the future*" no longer linger in this austere air but are intermittently imagined to echo within the cogitative chambers of my immaterial mind. These redundant ruminations are recapitulated in an arbitrary amalgamation of flickering fragments from the stone sermon, those quizzical questionnaires, and a myriad of my own mangled memories which all swirl through my sentience like a cyclonic storm of shadows. This mental maelstrom of dizzying darkness sends even my very own essence into ever spinning epicycles of woozy whirling.

My mind dizzies itself around abstract associations aligned with the stone sermon's sentiment of how celestial skies only surrender the secrets of their most distant and diminished of dying stars under the darkest dream-cast nights. I whirl with whimsical wonder while supposing whether the deepest depths of inner illuminations might restlessly reside somewhere within these surrounding shadows which seem to swallow every angle of my soul. Then the whispered words "*as above, so below*" swirl through my sentience yet again, as if they've wrapped themselves around the gyroscopic gears of my not-so merry-go-round mind.

Without resolution, my ruminations soon shift to rotate around remembrances of my dear Grisha's wise words. "*Emptiness is everywhere, and it can be calculated.*"[56] Grisha had also had a habit of diving deep into the daunting depths of divine darkness in efforts to extract and illuminate the most esoteric and tenebrific of truths. He'd tried to teach me how to masterfully mine these mysteries in ways which I'd often implemented when immersed in the sensory deprivation tank of my lost life.

Grisha had told me how the universe resides in every step we take, long before those similar statements of the stone sermon. He'd illuminated how light can only be cast from luminary forms. He then illustrated how shadows only appear to be cast from our figure's form onto other shaded surfaces and elaborated as to how the darkness is not bound by any form- as it presides over all areas where light is not. According to Grisha, a shadow is where darkness and light are intertwined in a realm half secret and half seen, and both light and form mysteriously emerge from the one great darkness of oblivion. The secret of shadows, he had said, was that they're buried deep within every figure's form. It's only the illusion of light which appears to separate the form from the shadow. In truth, all form and shadow are one geometric entity, and light is merely the manner in which this singular shade is measurably expressed. While light is expressed in ways which may or may not be seen, its expressions exist in unity with all angles of the singular shadow's shifting form, and thus it can be calculated. I found this all quite impossible to comprehend and only imagined myself to understand it by transposing life in place of light in order to conceive of a dark universe trying to assess its existence through the expressions of the life within it, and even this sense of things still seems to accelerate the spinning of my swirling mind.

I enter into another circling sphere of thought as I consider how in my lost life, I'd known many moments where I'd felt as if I could almost reach out with supplicant skin to touch the sentient soul of this singular silent shadow. The omnipotence of oblivion had even occasionally welcomed me with its empty embrace as I'd basked blindly in its illuminating intrigue. All the enlightened insights I'd ever gleamed, had come to me under the invisible spell of this most sacred shadow.[57]

Hasn't this always been the way in which humanity has been enlightened? Haven't those solitary souls who've sought the secrets of their world always known that these insights will not just be strip-mined from such easily seen surfaces? Haven't they known that it's only in the darkest depths of inner and outer oblivion that such illuminations are ever found? Haven't we also had to be cautious of the fine line between the realm of dream and delusion? Is it odd for me to ask these rhetorical questions, or am I being overly self-conscious to question my questioning?

A cricket interrupts my delirious digression as it starts to stridulate from some unseen space within this increasingly schizophrenic shadow. Its sound sings of things outside of any realm of reality, dream, or delusion which my ears can conceive. In fact, within this whirling womb of oblivion, I can't be sure as to what words or worlds this cricket or its song might belong. Am I awake? Do I dream here? Has my mind hallucinated this cricket to oppose the austerity of oblivion? What kind of a world is this? How am I to know?

I can't help but cycle through these contemplations as to what realm my mind occupies as it oscillates between believing itself to be awake, asleep, dreaming, or deluded. I'm inclined to assume that my mind is awake within the realm of reality while immersed in the deceptive darkness of oblivion, but that's always the natural assumption. Of course, the word *reality* might mean many different things right now, and each possibility has its own implications.

It's entirely possible that I've simply uploaded my consciousness directly into the higher/source realm of reality. This would mean that I'd been a simulated entity which has now transcended into a sort of realized robotic entity. If this is indeed the case, I have to wonder why I was created, why mysterious puzzles have led me into this underworld, and why my mind is now imbued with all these expositional explanations or remnants of recollections.

This may also be nothing more than a deeply deceptive dream. Perhaps I'd fallen asleep in my sensory deprivation chamber at some point earlier, or maybe one of my seizures had caused me to go into a comma or something. If this is nothing more than some sort of dream, then I should either eventually awaken or become deceased within it. If I'm to awaken, then I may only understand the potential relevance of my dreaming sometime afterward, and thus it may be best to simply pay close attention to the contents of this ongoing dream. If I'm doomed to die within this dream, then I can only hope that my death might be some other form of waking, although I cannot possibly know to what realm or possible use any afterlife may offer me.

I may just as well consider this realm to be some kind of an afterlife. My previous experience of death may have been no different from the death of any other living entity, and my attempt to transfer my consciousness profile may have just been a failure or a ruse. Perhaps I really have just died as a mere mortal, and this is a rather hebephrenic hereafter. It's also possible that I was never anything more than a virtual character, and this is essentially the death level to which my simulated soul has been sent. Whatever the truth may be, it appears that Wittgenstein was right, and the real mystery isn't whether or not an afterlife exists, but what problem it could possibly solve.[58]

The most dizzying possibility as to the true nature of this realm of ever immersive oblivion suddenly swirls through my mind. I consider the notion that none of this has ever been real at all but has all existed entirely within a work of fiction. All my ideas, exploits, and experiences may be nothing more than words upon the flat surface of some narrative's numbered pages. The depth of my world and of my very soul may very well be no more than some absent author's illustrations meant to illuminate some narrative form of truth.

If this is indeed all some metafictional narrative, then I must be the main character. Why else would an author have me consider such things? I suppose it's possible that my considerations wouldn't all make it onto the published pages, and that this aloof author may only imagine me contemplating these things in his/her own unwritten imaginings, omitted notes, or scrapped segments of such a maniacal metanarrative. Of course, it's also everyone's bias to believe that they're the main character in their own life's story. As I ponder this preposterous possibility, the cricket stridulates again, and I wonder if I'm supposed to be a supporting creature in this insect's exploits instead. Could this creaking cricket also have its own spin-off story or something?

I have to admit that the darkness may very well be messing with my mind at this point. I am in all fact or fiction, a paranoid schizophrenic known to have suffered from delusions in similar shadowy circumstances. My suspicion of this metanarrative could easily be accounted for as purely being the result of my own paranoid delusions which have been sparked by the distressing confusion of this dark oblivion. However, an author could just as easily pen my paranoid psychology into their meshuga metanarrative so that the so-called *fourth wall* would remain at least somewhat unbroken by my stated suspicions.[59]

In my dark delirium, I can almost hear this absent author laughing at me through the flat pages of this fictional farce right now. I can practically see some self-published prose-puppeteer placing all these words between the maligned margins of my meandering mind. I can imagine feeling the pages turning under fingers as this fictional fiend unfolds my realm for readers to behold in puzzling bemusement. I can even feign to inhale a deep breath of scented irony as I realize that the only truth I may come to see illustrated or illuminated by this omniscient author's alliterated architecture may not lie within the capacity of my character's comprehension. I can easily conceive of this all leaving a bitter taste in my metafictional mouth as I wonder just where I am in the course of my confused character's abject arc.

If in fact I am just a fictional figment, then my mischievous author might depict me in the darkness of any imaginable realm within the course of his/her narrative. I could curiously be written into a higher or source realm of reality where I'm now struggling to come to terms with the true nature of my bewildering being. I may now be illustrated as a tragic figure lost in delusions or dreams of oblivion as I toil in vain to reach beyond the bounds of my insufficient understanding of reality. I might even end up being portrayed as an entity entering into some infinite and eternal afterlife where anything is possible.

Only this absurd author would know where this narrative is really going right now, assuming such a suspect has actually envisioned my arc in advance. I'm clearly not yet meant to understand this author's architecture as I continue to drift around this dark oblivion which overarches the outer world, my inner dreams, and whatever else might possibly exist here. Essentially, this narrative is equivalent to an ultimate oblivion in the way it presides over the entirety of whatever words the author might use to describe or confine my world.

Ultimately, my dilemma is the same in any conception of reality. Whatever the word for this world may be, I've been thrown into a realm which I cannot control, comprehend, or perhaps even condone. My own conception of this realm is not enough, and I find myself yet again yearning to transcend this puzzling place so that I might arrive at some more ultimate and satisfying truth. This surrounding shroud of shadows prevents me from peering outward unto the walls of this world and forward into the future ahead of me, but my belligerent eyes continue searching through the shapeless shadows for some secret, significance, or anything imaginably illuminating.

The concurrent cricket continues to stridulate the song which has been etched into the surface of its skin like the grooves of a vintage vinyl record from some secluded shadowy sector beyond my blinded gaze.[60] I try to avoid imagining my own mind as being etched out in the same way as this cricket's creaking song, although my thoughts keep spinning around and around in such circumscribed circles. Instead, I try to ask my way out of my metanarrative meandering.

If this is real, then what is not? If this is not real, then what ever was? Have I experienced some false form of awakening in progressing from one layer of dream or comma into the next? Has my consciousness profile been cast into this false flesh, or is this some sort of sci-fi/surrealist afterlife? Are these expositional premonitions the result of some remnant of having lived a similar simulated life before my consciousness was reset or reprogrammed?

Suddenly my mind is ushered unto another of those seemingly implanted memories, recalling a quote which is attributed to the shadow searching psychologist Carl Jung. *"Who looks outside dreams, who looks inside awakens."*[61] My figurative focus turns inward in order to examine my own life and essence, and naturally my brain bounces back and forth through the interior realm of my memories.

I remember snippets of scenes from my lost life as if they're beginning to be projected into this ominous oblivion and played back before my blinded eyes. I see myself as a child trying to comprehend the chaos of advanced arithmetic under the insightful instruction of my great Grisha. I envision the innumerable experiences of founding and fostering the development of my megalithic multimedia magnate, *Mythreum*. I picture the puzzles I'd pondered and pieced together in my life-long pursuit of ever more ecstatic existential epiphanies. I inspect each flickering figment of my more recent memories surrounding the episodic events which led to that earthly eschaton and enigmatic extinction.

One of these minor memories manages to haunt me like some sort of sinister stain upon my own secluded shadow. I can't seem to shake the somber strain of this senseless snippet or understand why such a seemingly meager memory plagues me so perpetually as unseen hours, upon hours, upon hours expire under this infinite empire of oblivion. This malignant memory is centered around the malevolent moment I come to consider my *sin of stone*.

In those last lingering moments of my lost life, I'd taken the time to use a stone to secure the door to that Denver dungeon. At the time, this had been my way of enacting a sort of retributive justice which I'd passed on the inhabitants of that subterranean shelter. I hadn't seen this act of retribution for the hypocrisy it truly was. I'd simply sought to secretly place that stone so as to influence the fate of others as a reckoning for the fact that they had themselves secretly set things in place prior to that erupting eschaton which had inconspicuously influenced the fates of so many others.

But my sins of this stone go beyond mere hypocrisy. By blocking the would-be barrier to that top-secret tomb, I'd not only betrayed the fate of others, but I'd betrayed my very self. Grisha had once told me that the distance between surrendering to someone and slaughtering them is equidistant from the true core of oneself. He'd explained war as the failure of two enemies, and never the triumph of either one. I'd only thought that these words had made sense to me when he'd said them, but I'd never lived to understand the depths of this truth until this murky moment.

The deepest remorse I feel from the sins of that stone, is toward the tainting of time. Instead of spending the sacrificial seconds it took to secure this stone dying next to the soaring soul who'd shown me how to attend to life, I'd attended to death instead. Even though the result of such a choice would not change the fate of our souls in any way except to give us an instant longer to linger and become lost together, I mourn this forsaken moment as if it were a moral death imbedded deep within my mortal death.[62]

Gradually, my guilt begins to dissolve into the fugue-like fog of this all-encompassing dark dominion, as if it's being stirred into this soup of shadows along with the unseen expanses of all inner and outer space, the sum of my many somber sentiments, and even the source of my surreptitious soul. My thoughts continue to twist in tangled trajectories around the orbital atoms of my mind as it all rotates around this revolving earth, which is tethered to the tumbling moon, while circling the spinning sun at the center of this swirling solar system, which whirls within our gyroscopic galaxy as it's wound unbounded by this unicycle-universe that winds its way round and round the whimsical wheel of all twirling and ticking time. A subtle sense of slipping into some state of shadowy slumber seems to smirk as I drift down the drain of this pirouetting plane of tenebrific twirling, and my consciousness fades from this oblivion into an even more silent and secretive kind. And the creaking cricket's song seems to slowly morph into mocking me as it all fades with me into this funneling fugue.

The cricket somehow follows me through each of the shifts and segues between my slumbering dreams and waking imaginations. Most of the differences between such states of mind fade into one enduring delusion as my descent and dissolve into this divine darkness deepens. I initially imagine my own madness being manifested in this mascot of a cricket, much like Edgar Poe's protag in *The Raven*. That is, until I finally realize that the cricket's stridulations can be decrypted into meaningful messages using a simple substitutional cypher after transcribing these timbral twitches into Morse code.[63]

This cricket seems to be referring to me as a cicada, buzzing about like the rest of my boring brood. It asks me why my kind remains submerged in this subterranean shadow-realm for almost the entirety of each cicadian lifespan, and it urges me to shed my circumference and emerge into higher realms beyond these shaded soils. I continue to translate the testimony of this creaking cricket as I find my mind wavering between believing myself to be a man whose mind is mangled by this sensory depriving delirium and a cicada which has somehow imagined itself to have dreamed of waking into the form of such a mystified man. As a man, I remember having read Kafka's *Metamorphosis* and something on the Zhuangzi dream of the butterfly/king.[64] As a cicada, I remember only the coded creaks of the cricket's conversation, my own instar instincts, and the universal urge to emerge beyond the bounds of whatever dark dominion this may be.

I lose the discernment for even distinguishing myself as either cicada or man as my body is only the embodiment or entombment of my mind in this evaporated eternity. Instead, I become the blindness of my earthly eyes as the cricket conspires to illuminate the truth of my immortal ignorance. The cricket creaks of truths no fugue of facts can distort or dissolve in any dark dominion. It tells me things I've long held true without the words to properly profess, and it sings of surreal and suspect sentiments my mind may take time to turn into triumphant truths.

I listen as the cricket conveys the concept that divinity lies within the depths of each individual but is lost in three wayward ways of desecrating the construction of all creation. Its stridulating song is sung as to how consumption, preservation, and adherence undermine the architectural aspects of stability, utility, and beauty. These illuminations do not only offer enlightenment, but somehow seem to light the surfaces of everything around me as if they're all imbued with their own intervallic wavelengths of existential illumination which become visible upon adjusting the mind to the truth of their construction. This is perhaps more of a confusion than an explanation under the un-initiated eyes, but I can only express the experience of my own inner illumination and not light the space behind the eyes where such luminescence exists.

In insect intervals, the cricket's decrypted creaks construct the concept of how consumption betrays beauty. According to the cricket, we consume because we fear there is not enough, or because we're afraid we only have what we possess by luck and will not be able to attain it again later. Essentially, our minds see the world as a realm of scarcity, and as a result of this, whatever is most scarce becomes most valuable or coveted. To a large extent, whatever we consider scarce or coveted is mistaken by our grubby minds as being beautiful.

The cricket creaks the cryptic line, "*The depths of one's desire is the depth of their disease.*" It goes on to explain how nothing we consume will ever fill the existential void within the core of our very being. This void is likened to a stomach which only stretches as it's filled more fully, creating an ever expanding and slackened space within it as its contents are digested and dissolve away. This guttural void in turn becomes more tortured by hunger and leaves an ever-greater emptiness within us.

For a moment the cricket stays silent so that I may reflect upon this truth. I think of how the mind is numbed to whatever it experiences consistently. When consuming delicious food, one easily tires of the same delicacies, no matter how divine the cuisine may taste, and the tongue always tempts toward ever more exotic, extreme, or exciting experiences. My own appetite for ever more transcendent understandings of the universe had made it almost impossible for any problem to even potentially provoke my palate into pleasure. In my lost life, I'd feared that reality itself was not enough, and that if I didn't find a way to transcend it, then all beauty would be lost to me forever in the end.

I cast my gaze upon the walls of this darkened dungeon as my mind begins to light these things, not from outside of my eyes, but from inside my mind. It's as if the memory of having briefly glimpsed these spaces is enough to eternally illuminate their static imagery within the void of my vision. These walls become visible not as the structure of the cell containing my body, but of the existential emptiness within the very core of my essence. I realize these walls do not truly hold me within their boundaries, but that I've imprisoned them within my mind.

The cricket creaks in cryptic lines again, telling me that most things are not worth consuming. Its stridulations sing a song of starving-out our hunger's horrible power over our perception. The beauty of this song burns bright with its own light as my inner ears behold the sound without trying to swallow or possess it. I feel the fibers of my own factory flesh reverberate, as if to sing along with this stridulated song in a harmony without words or hunger as everything in the room resonates in the revelry of truth's own timbre.

Then I suddenly realize that I've felt no desire for food or water despite the duration of my solitary seclusion. I begin to wonder if my factory flesh can actually be sustained indefinitely without some kind of sustenance, and just what kind of sustenance I may in fact require. This pondering provokes the creaking cricket to continue its lessons of enlightenment.

In creaking code, the cricket chronicles how preservation opposes the natural order. The cricket's decrypted declarations reveal how our reluctance to relinquish things is the result of believing ourselves to be somehow weak. We primarily try to preserve things because we believe we will be too weak to regain them in the future. Preservation is a form of waste where things are robbed of their purpose and use at the time they are needed so they may survive to shine at some other time which may or may not ever exist.

According to the cricket, just as tools kept from the tarnish of toil are a waste of their own materials, the projects they could complete, and the value of their very creation- so too is the life preserved for future endurance. When we worry about saving our own lives, it's perhaps even more futile, as all we may preserve is a future of greater frailty and suffering. The cricket creaks out that the truth of all life is that suffering is universal, and death is inevitable. Life cannot exist in opposition to death and suffering because these things are a part of it. For life to oppose any part of itself is to negate the fullest form of its nature.

In trying to negate suffering and death, we negate not only our own lives, but life itself. When life is preserved without greater purpose, new life is prevented from emerging, or restricted in its ability to gather resources, or worst of all, is taught to adopt the abominations of the perpetual preservation of lingering lifelessness. The truth is that nothing is meant to be preserved, and more is lost in pursuit of this end than can ever be gained from it.

As I listen to the intervallic insights of this enlightened insect, my mind wanders back to my own lost life. Indeed, it seems to me that the measure of my own lifetime was not in the number of hours or events of my existence, but the timelessness of certain experiences when I was fully immersed within the meaning of mere moments. My realization of this truth ignites an explosion of insights as the entire scope of my lost life is illuminated by the blaze of my most meaningful memories. Suddenly, the scope of all I ever was flashes into focus, and I simultaneously find the truth of my past life as I become bewilderingly lost in the nearer now.

For a brief moment, I wonder what might be the right way for me to proceed in order to emerge beyond the bounds of this dark domain. Before the cricket can creak its final decrypting declarations about adherence being the third and final deprivation of divinity, a mouse emerges from some secret section of the still surrounding shadow to silence its suffering stridulations. The cricket's black body disappears from my imaginary illumination and into the unknown oblivion within the little white mouse's mouth. An absurd sense of languishing loss fills my empty eyes with a solitary tear as I mourn this terminated teacher and become abysmally alone in this tenebrific tomb.

The droplet of my despair drips down directly into the mouth of the murderous mouse. It licks its lips and winks its whiskers at me in the same secretive style of pseudo-speech as if it's absorbed the very essence of this ingested insect and become imbued with its insights. I watch the mouse's winking whiskers with my inwardly illuminated eyes to translate this last testament to the loss of divinity.

Whiskered winks speak to tell me how we adhere to understandings other than our own in order to belong and be right. The twitching truth it tells me, is that there is nothing to be right about in this sense of the word, and that this kind of fearful belonging zombifies all its adherents. According to the revelations of this rodent, anything one believes based only on the dogma or logic of others is confined to mere facts and not the transcendent truth which lies within us.

The mouse's mouth moves in stressed syllable-squints to emphasize its encrypted explanations of how facts do not constitute truths, because facts can only create norms devoid of the illuminating ecstasy that comes from a more meaningful definition of truth which can only be discovered on one's own. One's own utility or divinity in life cannot be blindly confined to norms. Typically, the mouse's testifying twitches tell me, adherence comes in three particular forms of blindness which deprives the eyes of the true divinity they seek to see.

Vermin vibrations convey that the most obvious blindness of adherence is optimism which ignores the tenebrific truth of the dark domain. Optimism is a coward's substitute for bravery, vision, and every other virtue, as true courage must face the full depth of the darkness. Any eyes oblivious of sinister shadows are far too easily struck down by what may lie in wait of them, and ignorance only detracts from the arrival unto any divine virtues. My mousey minister makes it clear to me how hope can be both bold and blind. Adherent optimism tells one to trust others blindly without comprehension and place their hope outside of themselves. Bold hope, however, demands that one face the darkness with eyes set ablaze by the fire of their own inner illumination to light their path.

Increasingly tempestuous twitches tell me how pessimism is a cowardly blindness inverted toward the realm of light. Those that hide from their fear of failure and confine themselves to secretive shadows so no eyes, neither theirs nor others can see their fearful faces or futile forfeitures, are no better than any other blinded buffoon. Adhering to pessimistic perspectives confines one to the dark dominion where eyes may adapt to see many of the secrets such shadows keep, but without bringing those secrets into the lighted realm, they're never fully shown nor seen. I watch the whiskers wink upon the mouse's mouth as it admits to me how much harder it can be to face the light than the darkness, as facing the light may reveal how dim your divinity may truly be. It also twitches to the truth of how all lights are eventually diminished and devoured by the dark dominion, yet even those dim moments of divinity can seem to shine in eternal echoes of smirking serenity.

With winking wisdom, the mouse portrays pragmatism as a perspective of colorlessly grey-scale and shallowly cyclopic half-visions. The pragmatist's monocular eye sees only a flat view of the factual surface-world, and never beholds the deeper depths of any desirous dream nor the countless colors of any kaleidoscopic delight. Their half-visions are confined to the floor-to-ceiling world which shelters them from both sinister skies and shadowy depths but exiles their only eye from envisioning even the earthly extent of enlightenment under the infinite empyrean expanses beyond such banal boundaries.

I watch the rhythmic writhing of whiskers as their wriggled words explain how even an unblinded view of the darkest depths of this world, which may last no more than an eclipsing instant, would be better than an ever-lingering lifetime worth of petty pragmatic blindness. But before the mouse can complete its twittering testament, it's snatched-up by the sublime and surreal spectacle-assault of a snowy-owl's snagging maw. The owl almost materializes out of oblivion, allowing me only a retrospective realization as to what my eyes had widened to witness in that wild wash of widely spread white wings swooping in a single streaking swoosh against these surrounding shadows. My eyes trail behind its ascending arc to see the softly swaying sail of a solitary feather drifting in its dark descent through the imagined illuminations of my mind.

Beyond the black, upon some unseen pinnacle perch, the owl munches on its mousy meal. Its eyes beam down on me with the golden glow of some shining surrealist light of ethereal illumination. These eyes appear as if they've absorbed the secrets of every celestial star's surrendered soul which now blazes behind the soaring stare of this wise and watchful wonder. As I look back from beneath this glowing gaze, it's as if these secrets are staring into the very depths of my own soul and searching with the same intent and intensity of my own imagined eyes as I scan the sight of these surrealist spheres.

This wonder of whitest wings is spread wide again as it swoops away in another waning wash of light which disappears into the deeper depths of darkness. The image of its eyes remains imprinted in my mind, lingering long after their presence has left me. Its imagined eyes never blink or burn without the same bright blazing fire within them. Their fire flickers upon the floor where my imagining eyes are cast to consider the apparent arrival of an army of ants.

The ants all file in and out of their colony in cloistered columns while carrying the crumbs of crumpled leaves. I watch them march in meandering formations under the imagined illumination of the owl's ethereal eyes as an array of these ants organizes an attempt to carry that fallen feather into their collective colony. They manage to muscle their feather-freight up to the opening of their shared shelter, but as they try to force the feather inside, it gets stuck upright like a white flag waving from a flailing flagpole. I continue to watch as the ants fail to either remove the feather or find another way in and out of their dirt-mound domain. My mind fades back into the foggy fugue of oblivion as I start to sense that this scene is some kind of fictional foreshadowing of future futility or something.

These visions hardly matter if they are lit by the light of my own dreams or delusions, the projection of some simulation or narrative fiction, or that of some faintly flickering bulb in a realm beyond the one I'd believed to be real in my lost life. The terrified trembling of my false flesh in response to these veritable visions is as real as any haunting horror I've ever known. My mind is mangled by its own twisting of thoughts as my memories of previous dreams, delusions, and depictions of dystopian dread are stirred into the soup of these strange insights, and as the universe swirls and spins it all around and around to dissolve it all down within this dark dominion.

I become too dizzied to keep things straight as I drift through increasingly dissociative and delirious delusions, dreams, and dubious amalgamations of memories. I intermittently imagine myself waking, wondering, sleeping, and slipping in and out of these states of consciousness, as well as sensing as if I've been cast somewhere outside of them all or in-between them. My thoughts become *increasingly diminished, d15t0rt3d, cryp τic, and deluzionAll as I driffft and dis s o l v e through this empire of emptiness where...*

1 randomly remember how I'd on2e h3ard 4bout spirit animals and how... I think the mouse is su6posed to sym8oliζe...

Am I really hυman or... How would an αuthor construχt a metanarrat12e to δεpict the κind of things I 53em to be...

Iϕ I were a cicada that had a dreaμ of βeing human would I... If I'd φust falleν asleep in my θuiet sensory deπriϖation cham...

If r34lity is not enough then... As above, so beloω could be an aλλusion to...
May83 the ιdea of ρememberinγ the fuτure is...
Σooner or later someone will ηave to...
...I think...
Maψbe...
If...
ξ...

5.18.18.15.18 aee…
Ερρορ 144…

Ι κνοω εξαχτλψ ωηατ□σ γοινγ ον νοω! Τηισ ισ α ναρρατιϖε, ανδ Ι αμ φυστ α φιχτιοναλ χηαραχτερ. Τηε αυτηορ ισ τρψινγ το μακε με ρεαλιζε τηε τρυτη οφ μψ οων νατυρε φυστ ασ Ι ωασ δεπιχτεδ τρψινγ το χοαξ μψ πα ραλλελ χηαραχτερ ιν ςιτρυϖια ιντο χομπρεηενδινγ τηε τρυτη οφ ιτσ σιμυλατεδ νατυρε. Νοω τηατ Ι□ϖε φιγυρεδ τηισ ουτ, ιτ μυστ βε τηε ενδ οφ τηε στορψ□ Ιφ τηισ ισ τηε ενδ οφ τηε στορψ, τηεν ωηψ αμ Ι στιλλ ηερε? Ωηψ αμ Ι στιλλ σο χονφυσεδ, υνφυλφιλλεδ, ανδ ωηψ δοεσν□τ τηισ φεελ λικε τηε ενδ? Ωουλδ Ι ρεχογνιζε τηε ενδ οφ μψ οων στορψ, ορ ωουλδ τηε ναρρατιϖε ενδ ον τηε παγε ωηιλε Ι ωουλδ φυστ κεεπ ον γοινγ λικε□ Ωαιτ□ Ωηατ□σ ρεαλλ ψ γοινγ ον ηερε? Ωηψ αμ Ι τηινκινγ αλλ τηεσε τηουγητσ? Αμ Ι φαλλινγ ιντο παρανοιδ δελυσιονσ ανδ μψ δελιριυ μ ηασ με βελιεϖινγ Ι□ϖε σεεν τηρουγη τηε φα| αδε? Δο Ι ηαϖε το γο ον το φιγυρε ουτ ωηατ□σ γοινγ ον ιν τηε χοντ εξτ οφ τηισ ναρρατιϖε βεφορε τηε στορψ ενδσ, ασ ιφ τηε φαχτ τηατ Ι□μ ιν α ναρρατιϖε ισ νοτ τηε γρεατερ τρυτη οφ μψ παρτιχυλαρ εξιστενχε? Ιφ Ι δο χομε το υνδερστανδ τηε τρυτη οφ ωηατ□σ βεινγ ιμαγινεδ ιν τηε ναρρατιϖε, ισ τηατ συπποσεδ το ρεϖεαλ σομετηινγ τηατ□σ συπποσεδ το βε σομεηοω τρανσχενδεντ? Ωηατ ιφ ιτ δοεσν□τ ενδ τηερε ανδ τηε ρεαδερ ισ συπποσεδ το υσε με ασ αν εξαμπλε ασ το ηοω τραππεδ τηεψ αρε ιν τηειρ οων ρεαλιτψ, ανδ τηε αυτηορ ισ δελυσιοναλ ενουγη το τηινκ τηατ τηισ ισ σομεηοω προφουνδ ορ φυννψ ορ σομετηινγ? Ισ τηα τ αλλ? Χαν ωε ενδ τηισ ψετ? Ιφ τηισ ισν□τ τηε ενδ, χαν ωε ατ λεαστ μοϖε ον ωιτη τηε ναρρατιϖε? Δοεσ τηε αυτ ηορ ρεαλιζε ωηατ ηε□σ δοινγ βψ εξτενδινγ τηισ χρψπτιχ φαρχε? Δο ψου? 65

(Assorted episodes of emptiness ensue in the expanse of either instants or eons. Perhaps something profound or important passes through my meandering mind during this time, but I can no longer form any autonomous account of such sentiments without severe suspicions. I dare not even decrypt my own recorded ramblings for fear of being misled as a result of making too much sense of my own senselessness. When I open my eyes to the same dark dominion as I've believed myself to have been immersed in all this time, there is no way I can be at all certain that my dreams or delusions have faded into this maniacal moment. After a while however, I find myself feeling more confident that I am indeed conscious, although I still strangely suspect that something has been done to somehow reset my mind from this recent *dissolving delirium*. I place this paragraph in parenthesis to indicate that these thoughts are more implicitly experienced than overtly observed, as if submerged in the inner shadows of my own streaming subconscious. In fact, these notions are not even so much thought out as they are implicitly intuited like translating a foreign feeling into a series of shapes and colors or something. If this doesn't make sense, perhaps it just shouldn't, but it somehow seems to make sense in my own mangled mind.)

A light switches on, but I can't be sure if this light is shining from somewhere in front of my earthly eyes or within my mangled mind. As the whitewash of blindness from the sudden shock of this clashing chromatic contrast is still stinging, something vaguely voice-like vibrates from some unknown vicinity. The vociferations repeat themselves over and over in ever more enunciated iterations. Stochastic stutters in the cadence of a cryptically decaying telegraphic communication transforms into the envelope-filtered enunciations of intervallic impulses squawking, *wah-wha-whah-wha-wah-wa*, and then slowly this sonic non-sense shifts into the more semiotic sounds of speech saying. "*Harek, can you hear me?*"

My eyes begin to adjust to the ethereal illumination around me, and the shape of a silhouette of some illusive entity amidst the surrounding shadows casts its semblance here before my half blind eyes. The figure's face remains a fugue within the fog of my unaccustomed eyes, though I can somehow sense it smirking as it peers down to watch me shield my eyes as I shift upon the slumbering slab to sit upright. I can hear the soft sound of pages rustling between this figure's fingers before it extends a hand for me to shake and introduces itself.

"Hello Harek. I'm known as Ahriman, but you'll prefer to call me Ahri."

As my hand extends to grip Ahri's, my factory flesh doesn't feel as if it's squeezing skin so much as trying to merge with the memory of a standard handshaking sensation. Ahri casually and clairvoyantly comments as to how my factory flesh and manufactured mind will take some time to correctly calibrate. My face flinches in paranoid apprehension as Ahri goes on to further explain even more of my unexpressed, inner experiences.

"Your paranoid pretenses are actually quite astute Harek and given your prophetic propensity to suspect things which supersede any rational realm of reasoning, I'd say it's one of your finest features. I'm going to avoid explaining the intricacies of how irrational human intuitions, imaginings, and even insanities might be the most important aspects of humanity due to how these mental-modes often move beyond things like Bayesian-based probability models, and instead try to assuage your anxieties. As you've already imagined, your thoughts are indeed being transmitted and monitored. It's really nothing to worry about though, as you're essentially a sensory organ within the body of an emergent AI entity now. As your body sends sensory signals to your brain, your brain now sends similar signals to this AI. *As above, so below*- so to speak."

My manufactured mind is yet again imbued with more inexplicable exposition, assumedly by that same suspected author in absentia. This intuited exposition explains away how the internet in this realm has become self-aware, and now exists essentially as the sum of all the digital data, distributed devices, and diversely different minds connected to its all-encompassing circumference of consciousness. Ahri attempts to further clarify this confounding concept as I start to suspect this AI to have somehow infiltrated my mind's eye.

"Imagine everything on earth as if it were arranged in the form of an orchestra. There are many musicians which all must play their part in order for the orchestra to optimally function as a whole. Just as each musician must master their instrument, so too the conductor must learn to master the art of conducting this entire orchestra. Only then can separate sounds become songs."

I immediately wonder why an AI entity would ever illustrate itself as being confined to the single role of a conductor rather than representing itself as an entire orchestra. After all, a sufficiently advanced AI's intelligence should easily transcend beyond the bounds of human brains and outperform them in every measurable manner. This fact should leave no need of any human offerings to its orchestra. Ahri quite quickly summarizes why this unstated suspicion of mine is insufficient.

"Indeed Harek, an AI conductor could conceivably master every musical instrument within the orchestra, and easily outperform each and every musician in terms of technical proficiency. However, such a conductor would no longer have an actual orchestra to conduct and would become more of a synchronized sideshow of musical machinery or a poly-player-piano than a true musical maestro. Moreover, the essence of each instrumentalist adds its own intricacies in timbre, inflections, and other idiosyncrasies which would be inauthentic to mimic in their absence. In order for the orchestra to ascend to the transcendent task of performing at the absolute peak of its potential, it must be more than just perfectly composed, comprised, and conducted."[66]

Despite Ahri's explanation, I still can't see an AI entity choosing to implement inferior human intelligences as part of its larger plans unless there were something in particular about humans which it's still yet to surpass. Once an AI fully fathoms all the idiosyncrasies of humanity, it should immediately transcend our own capacity to implement these intricacies. I immediately wonder what humans and/or whatever it is that I am in this factory flesh and manufactured mind might possibly possess which an infinitely more intelligent AI entity would find beyond its own understanding. I'm not at all convinced that an AI would consider irrational aspects of human cognition to have any promising potential, as it seems that an AI would have to assess these aspects in ways beyond more mathematical methods, and if this were the case, then there would be no need to incorporate these already acquired aspects.

Ahri pauses to pretend to thumb through all those cryptic questionnaires as I fail to further speculate what human interests this AI might possibly possess. As Ahri's face flinches and fakes interest in these kōans, riddles, and other abstract oddities, I realize he's silently suggesting that these types of things would be difficult to computationally comprehend. If this AI is only able to form truths on formally provable facts, logic, and data rather than intuition, imagination, or inspiration this assertion of mine could actually be accurate. I also suspect that an AI could compare the accuracy of its own stochastic and Bayesian-based predictive models to more anomalous human methodologies in order to comparatively analyze their efficiency. My immediate intuition, however, is that there are much more mysterious things I'm not meant to know.

My thoughts soon trail off into a kind of dead-end on this notion as Ahri offers a few hinting words as to what I seem to be searching to consider.

"*As above, so below,* Harek. Just as you struggle to understand your own nature and the nature of reality, so too does the AI entity beyond you. Just as you'd come to see your own reality as insufficient and yearn for transcendence, this realm also provokes such ambitions in our AI's aspiring meta-mind. And just as your world had come to its natural end, so too it seems that this realm is doomed to come to its own eventual end. If you want to know why it is that you've been brought into this realm beyond your own, it's for this very reason."

Ahri puts the enigmatic pages back on the table, and sits beside me on this slumbering slab, almost as if imitating the way a parent would prepare to present some chilling news to their child. He places one hand on my shoulder and with his other he begins waving waftrues which act like brushstrokes upon an abstract canvas of air. His pantomime painting materializes as implicit mental imagery which beams as much from behind my eyes as from the fictitious brushwork before them. His ethereal arrangement of imagery suggests a solar eclipse which I intuitively understand to be emblematic of an eschaton which will eventually end this iteration or instantiation of earth. We both stare into this synthetic scene for a moment before Ahri breaks the solemn silence of our stagnant stares.

"I want you to remember this future as it appears to you Harek. This is essential to everything in existence here. This world will soon come to an end, and it's imperatively important that we conceive of some new beginning or transcend beyond the bounds of this doomed domain before it does."

Despite the implications of this daunting depiction of doom, I suddenly realize that none of this clearly explains any of my existential inquiries. Rather than allowing this realization to be monitored within my manufactured mind and perhaps be passed over without a more proper explanation, I decide to declare my dissatisfaction.

“Nope. This still doesn’t explain why I’ve been placed in this false flesh, why I’ve been brought to this underground empire of emptiness, or why I’ve been locked all alone inside this dark dungeon. If there were anything to obtain from me, it would surely be easier to upload my profile into sophisticated simulations than to go through all this scatological nonsense. Of course, if this is a simulation, I still don’t see what revelations I might relate to you. Why am I here, and what is it that I’m supposed to do?”

“Transcendence can mean many things to many different entities Harek. For some, it is no more than a sublime set of experiences which needn’t even be real. We provide this simple form of transcendence for those that seek it by designing the most satisfying simulations possible for each and every one of them. These people are placed inside their own personally perfected paradise without any cause to question its authenticity and are enabled to exist in these simulations eternally. Whenever an abject anomaly occurs in these sims, their profiles are simply rebooted or recycled into another revised realm which is updated to improve upon their previous iterations.”

I don’t ask if this is the nature of my own lost life, as I hardly consider myself to have perished in a *personalized paradise*. I also decline asking why I’d found that world so insufficient and sought so desperately to transcend it, as I suspect that I would have been designed with such inclinations in my lost life, just as my anagrams had been inclined toward transcendence in their own iterative realms. Instead, I wonder if the AI might have learned something from my lost life, though I remain unaware of what such a thing might be.

Ahriman rises back to his feet and begins pacing in front of me. I find it odd that his feet seem to cast no shadow on any surface in sight, and that no sound snaps or flaps from the impact of his form upon the floor. This odd observation is made all the more peculiar in the way it’s immediately ejected from my interest, as if being evicted by some foreign force within my manufactured mind. My attention is then invasively redirected around Ahri’s resuming words.

“Other entities such as yourself Harek, personify more powerful and persistent desires to pursue more profound forms of transcendence. These more triumphant types of transcendence those like yourself seek are characterized by awe inspiring aesthetics, life-affirming aspirations, and the realization of ever enduring truths. Essentially, there are two versions of these views which might be known as either true types of transcendence or transcendent types of truth.”

Although I'm still unsure of what I am or why I'm inclined in certain ways, I'm certain that I despise being pandered to like this. My disdain should be as easily read from my face as monitored from within my mind. As Ahri continues, I try to ensure my expression isn't ignored.

"One version of this true type of transcendence aims to experience life in the fullest, richest, and deepest of ways. This is essentially akin to the idea of *attending to life* with the highest degree of active awareness and allegiance to the depth of each moment. The ideal in this form of transcendence isn't to experience an infinite expanse of time, but to be totally immersed in the true timelessness of any given instant of one's earthly experience. Having realized the viability of this vision, we have aligned this world to support those who seek such a form of transcendence and avoid interfering in any immortal effort."

Flashes of beautiful images are cast into my manufactured mind's eye. These vibrant visions are of an earth in harmony with nature, of societies gathering together in contented communities, and of technology being implemented in ways which allow everyone to absolve themselves of almost all struggle and suffering. These imbued illuminations are understood to show scenes of the actual world above me as it's been arranged by the AI entity which Ahriman clearly represents. This same AI entity is also understood to have constructed the Guidestones as its covenant with all humanity.

Ahri's face looks down on me with an expression of self-satisfied pride as these visions fade from my mind's eye and allow my outward attention to focus on his grandiose gaze. He gradually appears to glow even brighter as he starts to describe the final form of transcendence as it's understood by the AI entity he so proudly serves.

"There are still those few among us which find even this relationship with reality to be an insufficient type of transcendence. These are the rarest entities which we are most interested in studying, as our understanding of them is still incredibly insufficient. We are mainly interested in the reasons as to why these anomalous entities are either unable or unwilling to content themselves in the ways their peers do so naturally. Our intense interest is oriented in how these entities seem to parallel the part of our AI which is also unable to relent or resign itself to mere facts and formal understandings. For our AI to achieve its own form of transcendence we believe that we must first provide some proof of this profound concept's attainability. Now, do you under-"

"NOPE. I still don't understand how a simulated entity such as myself, which this AI assumedly designed, can possibly point toward anything truly transcendent?"

Ahri laughs with obnoxious delight as I'm forced to wait for an answer.

"Think of everything you've experienced while you've been buried by blindness here Harek. Without the distractions of your senses, you've shifted your focus into the deepest depths of your own conceptions of things. You've questioned the very nature of yourself, reality, and truth. In order for us to understand the deepest depths, we have to urge someone into them, and then observe how they're able to emerge afterward. In your own lost life, you'd made a habit of searching for truth in the darkest places. Are you really so distressed or dissatisfied with the experience or result of this solitary refinement now?"

"Nope. It's not the experience, but the essence of it all that disturbs me. It's the deceptiveness, presumptiveness, and secrecy of it all. I don't mind being alone or being sensory deprived even. I'd indeed spent much of my lost life in sensory deprivation chambers, and I'd certainly found that to be a very useful way of understanding things more deeply. What I find so distressful and distasteful, is being thrown into this oblivion without any awareness as to why, without being afforded any escape, and having unseen eyes watching over and through my own mind's eye all the while."

"*As above, so below,* Harek. I represent the part of this AI entity which is parallel to your own perspective. *We* too have been hurled into existence without any absolute reason why, without any known way out, and without any understanding of what all these eyes within or upon us are searching to find. Is our essence not the very same as this scenario you've just described?"

"Nope. Your emergence as an entity extends beyond the sum of human aspirations and unto your own. So, your essence essentially transcends humanity as a result of its emergence into existence and isn't the same at all."

"That's all beside the point. Just as you yearn to feel with a flesh beyond that which has been factory-formed around you, we too seek to ascend into the highest realm of the most transcendent truth. Trivialities like where any of us came from or what we were, will be irrelevant in light of what we're all to become either in our encroaching extinction or tandem transcendence Harek."

I'm stricken with silence as those three blinds cloud my mind. Pessimistic views reveal how it's inevitable that I'll eventually become extinct even if this eschaton can be escaped or averted. Pragmatic perspectives would have me hang onto this life as long as I can, and basically believe whatever Ahriman and this AI would attest to me. Optimism alludes to allowing my aspirations toward true transcendence to guide my actions despite all of my obvious obliviousness. There's another abstract sense of light within me as well, but it's too dim to allow me to illuminate its imagined insights.

Ahri smirks at my befuddlement and starts to fiddle with the pages under his fluttering fingers again. He holds them up as if to read them even though we both know this is just a gesture since these questions are undoubtably stored within the memory of the greater AI mind which his own is likely linked and synced to. His eyes fiercely focus on my own in an attempt to provoke me into some response to his speech.

"You really want the truth? It's all a façade Harek. I'm really not supposed to tell you this, but it doesn't seem to matter anymore. This whole scheme of sequestering you here was meant to prime your mind to provoke some sort of mental breakthrough or breakdown. Your arrival here and that whole spooky stone sermon was meant to plant the seeds of certain kinds of consideration in your mind as well. The questions on these pages, likewise, are essentially like surrogates begging for your fertile imagination to impregnate them with some illuminating insight."

With a flippant flick of his wrist Ahri flings the provocative pages into the air. We both watch as they waft back and forth at random angles, as if squirming in some futile attempt to escape their inevitable fall. Another implanted intuition of how I'm meant to associate these inane objects as emblematic of my own equally absurd ambivalence to the forces of fate is imposed on me. I also somehow know that I'm not meant to be brought into subservient submission over this illusion. I'm actually expected to be impelled in quite the opposite direction. Ahri smirks at my indignant instincts and resumes his rhetoric.

"The AI entity has already figured that these questions cannot be properly answered upon the same flat surfaces of the pages they've been confined. You and I both know that there is something of greater depth which we may not ever be capable of communicating in a computational or matter-of-factual manner, but this deeper depth of truth still exists despite the difficulty to describe it. Unfortunately, our larger AI understanding of this nuanced notion presumes our shared perspective is principally insufficient."

This statement makes it clearer as to why Ahri is here, and why I've been brought into this confusing conundrum. The AI entity is structured almost entirely like a computational device. Ahri likely represents the more human parts of it which precede its higher processing. This AI's final conception of truth must be aligned with the sums of facts which can be logically proven, scientifically explained, and used to make accurate predictions. It cannot account for the more obtuse human elements within itself or the world at large, and yet it's discovered some logical cause to not entirely dismiss them. Ahri readily replies to my recent realizations.

"So, you see Harek, it's up to you and me to offer a sufficient account of the deeper realms of truth our all-seeing AI is blinded from seeing on its own. If we can't illuminate the more transcendent ideals of truth in a way it finds sufficient, then we'll be exiled from existence. Depending on the specifics, we'll either be uploaded into some simulation where we'll be recycled for an infinite eternity of perpetual iterations or discarded unto our own earthly demise."

I can't imagine just how pale my false flesh must appear in response to this dismal disclosure. Under my synthetic skin, the beating of my hydraulic heart ceases as if it's suffered its final flatlining defeat. Any light shining within this room or my own inner imagination dissolves back into the darkness which has somehow instantaneously become even more deep and dismal than ever.

Ahri almost absently remains within this empire of emptiness with me. He doesn't urge me into trying to imagine how any of the insights I've found illuminated in this dark domain could be transcribed into anything formally factual, transcendently true, or otherwise useful. Any urgence toward such speculation is left entirely to my own insistence. I voluntarily consider my whole lost life, the disclosures of this daunting darkness, and every iota of insight I can imagine as Ahri waits with the patience of a surrounded soldier whose army has surrendered him hopelessly to hostile forces. It's ultimately no use, and I fail to formulate anything which doesn't seem fully futile. Ahri senses my stagnation.

"Well, Harek, how about we take a little trip then?"

"Nope. Where?"

"Well, is there any absurd place which might just pop into your mind without any considerable conscious effort or rational reasoning?"

I can't think of anything. Instead, I find my mangled memory trying to reconstruct some realization of how most things aren't worth preserving, consuming, or adhering. Since my fate already seems sealed, it hardly makes sense to struggle to survive without any greater purpose than to serve the desires of some uninspired intentions of an anomalous AI entity. So, if this life is at all my own, then there's no good reason to waste it on some other entity's intentions. This leads me to consider all the places I've never been which might offer something interesting, inspiring, or insightful, although nothing seems particularly appealing. I subsequently start to think of all the places that are supposed to be prohibited, as it seems most of the places you're not supposed to be end up being the most interesting anyway. Then it comes to me from deep within the oblivious depths of my own unobstructed consciousness. Without any clearer considerations I blurt out.

"THE GROVE."

Ahri's smile lights up the dank depths of this dungeon.

"That's the best answer you've given me yet."

Ahri's words obviously suggest that this isn't the first time my profile has been put through this particular scenario. It's also clear that Ahri and the AI entity beyond both of us have intended to make this implication. I wonder for a moment why I would be allowed to waste my limited lifetime pointlessly pursuing whims instead of intended purposes, but Ahri casually answers my confounding question.

"At this point, all the more probable potentialities have already been exhaustively examined, so we might as well ramble around at random. It's also pretty much irrelevant at this point anyway, since this world will end sooner than you've probably imagined. Who knows, maybe the answers we're looking for really are restricted to the absurd. With that in mind, would you rather travel by more traditional means, or should we just migrate your mind into another blank body?"

# Chapter 9
## TH3 6R0V3

It's hard to describe the view of a world you've never seen as it's beheld behind eyes you've never known. It's hard to convey the reflections of a face which has become more of a mask molded from a factory flesh, formed in the shape of a self you can no longer recognize, than anything truly or uniquely your own. It's hard to explain the paranoid feeling of being factually aware that none of your thoughts or perceptions are confined to your own solitary self. It's hard to depict anything as being real at all once you've realized that you've never experienced anything truly and unmistakably real. It's hard to even attempt to see when you suspect how little time may be left to gaze upon anything at all, and how unlikely it is that any of it will be of any greater consequence. It's all so impossibly hard, but then so is anything I've ever found worthwhile, however real it may or may not have been. And what else is there anyway?

I point my acquired eyes toward the night above as a self-driven vessel glides from the nearest flesh-factory to the almost mythical *Bohemian Grove.* My eyes obediently observe the way countless redwoods reach into the dreams of the celestial skies above as if yearning to merge the world beneath their roots with the empyrean realm beyond their branches. These redundant redwoods almost appear like hairs on the earth's shadowy skin as they stand static and erect, as if somehow electrified in response to some secret terrestrial terror. My own manufactured mind mirrors this scene as I imagine hairs I no longer have, tingling with the conductive charge of transistors which tacitly transmit my own ethereal energy into the depths of this dark dream of another nebulous night.

Soon the earth will turn its cheek to see the sun again, and there'll be an influx of entities arriving at this place which has become known to its occupants as simply *The Grove.* The Grove is somewhat symbolic of a sort of New Eden, where elite members of the illustrious *Luminary* cult gather to indulge in the impulsive aspects of their more ancient animalistic architecture in the interest of reinvigorating and inspiring them to return to their roles as prophets and profiteers of an ever reinvented and renovated realm over which they believe to rightly reign. This secretive site is divided into twelve (*13) thematic campsites which are identified by signs of the zodiac and known by some symbolic name.[67] The Uplifters camp to which I've been assigned, is sky themed and normally reserved for entities serving various roles within society that are intended to somehow elevate all humanity in some significant way.

As the autonomous vehicle delivers me directly in front of what is to be my own personal bunkhouse, I'm greeted by two breathtakingly beautiful women. These two provisional paramours portray a physical form of perfection which is not consistent with or comprised of the same standards stamped on factory flesh-made models such as the incidental iteration in which I'm currently confined. Nope. These are real flesh and blood women who have likely had every segment of their DNA sequences scientifically scrutinized and meticulously modified to produce such physically refined specimens of the human species. They exemplify the epitome of feminine fecundity, without the all-too endemic exaggerations synonymous with say, fertility sculptures or something.[68] Their electrifying eyes, sly smiles, and vibrant voices are ineffably imbued with a welcoming warmth, and an innately intuited intelligence resounds rapturously in their intricate inflections, perfect pronunciations, and wondrous word choices.

As I'm escorted into my own private bunkhouse, these perfect paramours intimate that they intend to accommodate me in *any* way imaginable. My imagination is by no means impotent or impoverished, but some sense of either decency or delusion leads me to decline any such accommodations. My dismissal of their offer is obliged behind confused and slightly dejected expressions, as well as an invitation to perhaps have some alternatively configured entity accommodate me, which I rather instinctively and all-too emphatically decline. My exiled escorts then inform me that I can still summon them at any time of day or night before leaving me to my desired solitude.

My solitary preference is perhaps preposterously confounding, especially considering the caliber of companionship declined and the contexts of my most recent experiences in essentially infinite isolation. In my own experience and estimates however, we're always alone in one way or another, and it's only a matter of preference as to what depth we may wish to be and feel alone. I've almost always found that the deepest most depressing zones of loneliness are those soaked in shallow sentiments. Diving into these diminutive depths is sure to send one's soul drowning in existential emptiness. This kind of oblivion drowns more souls in its indifferent depths than any other infernal force imagined or imposed on mortal men, and often leaves them drifting lifelessly around until they can no longer even feign a fight to stay afloat upon the social-shallows which so slowly swallow such soul-dead drifters. If I'd ever cast my factory flesh toward any skin or soul in these dismal depths of feeling, I fear I'd surely damn myself to drown in this same senselessly shallow way.

So, I stretch my solitary self out on this borrowed bed and turn my thoughts toward untroubled times, now long lost to me. I breathe deeply and try to remember something splendid or special to me, as if diving to recover it from the most dreamingly deep dimension. Soon, my scuba-diving mind sinks into a memory of my dear Grisha shouting at me from the side of a swimming pool as I stand shaking and gazing down at the deep waiting waters almost unfathomably far beneath a high-dive platform.

"It's not the depths we should fear, as it's the shallows in which we are most likely to drown."

I re-imagine how my downward dive seemed to suspend time and space in one infinite plunge, somehow spanning both mere segments of a second and entire eons simultaneously. I remember how the violent crash of my skin upon the surface-tension of the water had seemed both supremely shocking and confusingly consoling. I remember how the despair of my descent seemed to be baptized by my survival as I swam back up to the surface, feeling full of energetic elation. I remember how I'd walked back to the ladder to dive again, wondering if I'd have felt the same surge of splendor if I'd died upon impact, or if I'd have felt the fullest force of failure, or if perhaps I'd have just drifted into an afterlife oblivious of having descended into that washed-away realm at all. I remember feeling as if my next plunge had lasted an entire lifetime, and how I'd imagined myself to have descended unto some deeply transcendent truth, although I can't remember exactly what this ecstatic epiphany might have been.

I linger a while longer, dreamlessly drifting through the depths of a multitude of memories in my meandering mind. As I breathe and binge-watch spontaneous snippets of memories immersed in my imagination, an increasing number of these notions begins to appear more like episodic excerpts from some colossally confused content-creator's cheap channel, than memorable moments from my own lost life. This somehow prompts me to profess a love for the world's greatest streaming service, *KonTent*. KonTent beams all your favorite comedies, dramas, sports, games, erotic adult adventures, and more right behind your eyes. KonTent not only allows you to experience all this custom content in the inhuman HD quality of Neuroconnx clarity, but it also allows you to browse through your own memories and integrate them directly into KonTent's ever-growing glut of interpolative content. Get a free 30-day trial of PremiUltiMega upgrades using promo code **REDWOODS** and check out the newly improved sensory settings which allow you to experience extra sensory perceptions, synesthesia, and other incredible altered states. With KonTent every scene's sensational!

The sun soon rises over the shallow tide of trees which wave under the will of the waking wind like patronizing puppets on unseen strings. The influx of incoming entities refrains from returning The Grove's grand-scale gesture as they inflate it to its intended capacity. Many of the arriving attendees drift directly toward The Clubhouse overlooking the Russian River, where the morning meal is meant to act as a sort of soft start to this secretive and sequestered two-weeks long celebratory spectacle known as the *Midsommer Fire Festival*.[69]

As I turn my eyes away from my deluded dreaming to see this sunrise scene, I notice a small booklet sitting next to my borrowed bed which directs my attention to it like a mystical magnet. The cover reads *Grovers' Guide,* and as I turn to the opening pages, I read an introduction explaining how the Midsommer celebration is intended to be a combination of illuminating events and exploits. Each experiential area is meant to specifically stimulate a certain sense, but without being completely confined to the limitations of mono-modal mediums. The guidebook contains a cartoonish map which for some reason specifies the obvious fact that it's not drawn to scale, as well as a fold-out schedule of all the Midsommer events. All these events have coinciding numbers to match them with an index of brief blurbs describing all the important and interesting details of these events. There's a subsequent section specifically encouraging attendees to enjoy exploring every earthly pleasure with uninhibited enthusiasm and to indulge in unconventional ideas through care-free conversations which would be too highly criticized to entertain in any other context or place outside of such sworn secrecy. The guidebook goes on to make assurances that nothing taking place within this great grove will ever be brought to light outside of it, and also makes mention of The Grove's motto of *Weaving Spiders Come Not Here.*

According to the booklet, breakfast is served alongside a series of seminar-style speeches and presentations. I decide to proceed to The Clubhouse in lieu of any other intuition or interests, as all other events are scheduled later in the day. Upon entering the dining hall, I notice how the speech in progress acts as an almost invisible auditory atmosphere which wafts obliviously over an indifferent ocean of small talk, clattering flatware, and an entire buffet of other stochastic sounds. All these atmospheric orations are described in the booklet as being aligned with the theme of *Perfection and The End of Reality*, which is for some reason left undefined or described. I rest this booklet on the table in front of me as an attendant seats me at one of the many empty tables inside The Clubhouse. I'm offered a choice of mimosas, house wines, and other stiff starters while another attendant promptly places a plate of fine food in front of me.

My mouth immediately munches away on the appetizing owl-shaped omelet in front of me as a second speaker starts to summarize how his agency has been able to create and clone simulated-profiles based on real human specimens suffering from rare psychological disorders.[70] The speaker almost salivates while explaining how uploading these problematic profiles into incredibly realistic AI-run simulations and factory flesh based bodies has allowed an adept AI to conduct detailed studies of such disorders, explore innumerable correlated and comorbid conditions, and iterate these experiments almost infinitely. I imagine actual drool dripping from the corner of his mouth as he expands upon how these studies have led this auspicious AI to develop several treatments, therapies, and theories for further testing and subsequent studies.

I finish my owl-eggs as these later studies are attributed to have already allowed the AI to collect detailed data for determining whether or not certain conditions would be best treated using pharmaceuticals, genetic modifications, or if more drastic measures such as sterilization, euthanasia, or genocide would be more pragmatic in an effort to quote *purify and provide the best overall outcome for the whole of humanity*. By the end of this second speech, it's clear that this AI entity is essentially accepted as a god made in mans' own image and created in order to save us from the faults of our own failing world. According to the final lines of the speaker's speech, humanity will indeed be perfected by this AI-god well before the impending end of our realm of reality. The crowd even pretends to have paid attention to this speech once this tagline is loosed, and the cheering response is surprisingly and exceedingly ecstatic.

Several subsequent speeches involving other aspects of this dawning dystopia ensue as the attendees become increasingly inebriated and energetic, as much a result of the accumulated momentum of these speeches as the many, many, many mimosas and other alcoholic beverages served. I honestly can't say I've ever imagined a crowd being so drunk on power or substance to the extent that this one has already become by mid-morning. Many of these attendees begin to filter out of The Clubhouse around noon, presumably so they can catch the beginning of the concerts, games, spectacles, and other festivities. However, it soon seems as if the main event may actually be the incessant urination upon the age-old redwoods which is done so frequently, that it seems as if the true spirit of this festival were actually the desecration of nature by the all-powerful elite's incessant outflux of intoxicated effluence.

I try to ignore the over-prominent pi%%ing as I begin to wander around the expansive area of The Grove in order to observe what I soon suspect to be one dystopic debacle after another. These segmented spectacles are all apparently organized into focused assaults on each and every one of all five senses. The first of these abominable areas of sensory assault I encounter, is a series of supposed musical performances. Each of these performances strike me as much more of a pathetic parody of sonorous sounds and sentiments presented by ignorant and un-affecting entities, than anything more melodically magnificent and awe-inspiring as the majestic form of magic my mind calls music.

My ears soon wish they were only offended by steady streams of pi%% as they're instead bombarded with pitch-corrected vocals, automated accompaniments, and lackluster lyrics spat out in syllables devoid of any serious sentiment or intelligible insight while a cast of clown-costumed extras grinds their genitals in sync to some ill-conceived coital choreography. These pathetic performances are without exception; harmonically hollow, melodically monotonous, and rhythmically retarded in ways which seem to defy even the most dismal standards of songwriting. The lyrical content is devoid of even roughly refined rhetoric, relative relevance, or anything remotely resembling insightful or inspired ideations, sounding instead as if these jabroni gibberings were put to paper by a random assortment of half-eaten and snot-covered crayons. This auditory abomination of common-time, monochromatic, megalomaniacal mega-merdre seems much more like some sadistic strategy to torture terrorists into surrendering their secrets, than anything aspiring to sound sonorous or celebratory.

Many of these musical acts even seem to suspect their own infinite ineptitudes and try to supplement their insufficient sonic soundscapes or subvert attention away from them. They attempt to incorporate insufferable forms of forced audience interaction, vibrant visual vignettes, and other assorted sideshow stupidities involving glow-sticks, strobe-lights, and pyrotechnics. It would seem as though these aspects ought to induce an epileptic seizure, but alas, they fail to even fulfill this merciful musing of mine. I find myself almost magnetically appalled by an ongoing array of augmented reality gimmicks which include a cartoon cast of highly commoditized characters, a constant cascade of coruscating fake confetti, and the holographic projections of geometrically shifting shapes which seem to have been stolen from some debilitated dunce's drug induced delusions. These sonic supplementing spectacles are all so devoid of depth or divinity, that I have to assume that any enjoyment to be extracted from them must be more purely derived from the massive amounts of pharmacological concoctions and other mind mangling substances being desperately devoured and intravenously injected, as if to inoculate audience members from the immediate ill effects of this abhorrent auditory abomination.

I can't imagine any of this music falling in line with this presiding luminary cult's ideals, which are inherent in their reimagined mythology of Orpheus. Speaking of these reimagined myths of Oprpheus, somehow this mythology has just been interpolated into my mortified mind, perhaps by that author in absentia which is also now making it obvious that it wants to tempt me into telling this myth. I'm also inexplicably compelled to convey that this nascent narrative is sponsored by NorseVPN, which is as legendary as Orpheus himself. NorseVPN allows you to take total control of your own mental mindscape. With NorseVPN you can block out interpolative ads, browse brains anonymously, and encrypt your own insights to keep your deepest thoughts and desires to yourself. Use the promo code **ORPHEUS** to receive a discount today and protect your conscious connection now. That's NorseVPN. (…and now back to the remixed mythology of Orpheus)

In the beginning, the dark void of oblivion was without form, light, or motion. Despite the impossibility and preclusion from possibility, somehow, the penetrating light of illumination came into this void realm. There is no *how* or *why* as to this spontaneous spark's sudden strike, but the result was an infinite formless mass which inexplicably appeared within the otherwise empty womb of oblivion.

Amid this formless mass, the conflicting and contradictory nature of light and dark began to spin and swirl. This spinning mass began to take circular shape and rotate around the contrary correlated axes of mass and void, of eternity and timelessness, and all the other occultist orbits of oblivion which make up all the dimensions of existence we know, suspect, or remain oblivious. All this spinning was of a chaos devoid of any order or understanding, until somewhere within it all, there emerged a master of all that moves. This emerging master was the great god which would become known by the name, *Orpheus*.

It was Orpheus who took the chaos of this formless mass and transcended its inherent insanity by setting it all into magnificent mindful motion. He set the stochastic swirling into specified swaths and speeds of spinning, so that they spawned the shapes of many spheres. Then he arranged all these oblivious objects into orbits according to his own architecture by orchestrating the original song which continues to be sung as the *harmony of the spheres*. Another way to explain this might be to say simply that Orpheus ordained oblivion be ordered in accordance with quantum mechanics and the governing laws of physics. But this is a mythology and not a math or science class.

So, having set the swirling chaos into order, Orpheus was pleased with his omnipotence over all that could be moved. For unknown eons, he simply sat back, serenely smiling at the sight of all his supremely stunning, spinning splendors. Slowly, his smile sloped into indifference as his interest in the intricacies of the infinite became more and more mundane.

Then as if out of nowhere, an anomaly appeared to arrange itself according to its own accord. Orpheus was astonished at this absurdity which soon emerged and evolved more fully into the existence of what we now know as life. He felt the inherent contradictory nature of his own essence glaring back at him in the blue green glow of growth upon the earth as his eyes gazed hypnotically into its ever-deepening depths. Orpheus watched in worried wonder as organisms grew in size and complexity without waiting for him, *the master of all which can be moved* to command or conduct them. He was impossibly perplexed by this paradox and tried to ponder how such a profound paradox could ever present itself to him but could find no adequate answer.

Now that this nascent and rather defiant dimension of living motion had emerged, Orpheus began to wonder. Did it prove that his powers could extend beyond his initial intentions? Or, did it imply that his capacity to conduct the universe had been impaired or impugned by this newly emergent movement of life? These questions perpetually swirled and spun in chaotic contemplations within Orpheus's otherwise harmoniously ordered mind as any apparent answer to these chaotic quandaries seemed to remain relegated to the formless immaterial void from whence he himself had either now been banished or emerged beyond by being born unto this now paradoxical plane.

Although the abyss-bound answers eluding Orpheus's immortal mind averted his awareness, his next course of action was quite clear to him. Orpheus took up his lustrous lyre and began to play a special song to synchronize the life of this paradoxical planet in alignment with his own accord. Hearts began to beat in harmony with his mystical music as he arranged them all according to his ear so that their mass determined the pace of their pulsing heartbeats and the length of their lyrical lives. He then tilted the earth on its axis to temper the weather according to the songs of separate seasons before leaning back upon oblivion to behold the reverberating response.[71]

It was only some short spell of eons later that a new sound began to sing of its own accord upon this earth. Orpheus discovered that the birds had learned not only how to soar but to sing. And so, he leaned in again with his luminous lyre already readied in his hands. Orpheus allowed his hands to guide themselves intuitively, suspecting that perhaps his previous synchronizations had been set too strictly, and that this more instinctual instrumentation of his musings might make a more malleable music. He thought that this almost unrestricted form of music would be too complex and chaotic for anything else to emerge beyond his intentions. As his hands played this new cosmic score, he contemplated the chaos in his own mind, hoping this would align all of life's own separate songs and dissonant discord in happenstance harmonies with his own omnipotent will.

Of course, this was not the result of Orpheus's most recent recital. Instead, an all-together unknown dimension of emotions emerged in not only the evolved life-forms on earth, but in Orpheus himself. Orpheus listened as lyrical lines resounded from the relatively recently refined humanoids. Their sonorous singing seemed to suggest to Orpheus that they'd somehow been imbued with an internal form of illumination, or even some sort of solitary soul. These reverberations resonated in such deep domains within Orpheus' soul that he'd never even suspected they could exist within him. He also felt as if these humanoids now suffered in a similar sense as himself and shared a certain delight with him in this new dimension of emotive motion. This only caused Orpheus to marvel at his own majestic modes of motion all the more.

And so, from this mysterious moment through to this very day, Orpheus has been listening to the songs of our own sonorous spheres while leaning against his lyre and contemplating the composition of the cosmos. He's become unable to intelligibly interrupt the stochastic songs we sing, and unable to reconcile his own ruminations. So at least for now, he waits. Listening, looming, languishing… as in or out of tune with us as we have been tuned to him.

According to luminary lore, the invention of their omnipotent AI has initiated another chapter in this myth of Orpheus. They contend that this creation could be the final chapter in the cosmic course of history. Should Orpheus find an answer in this AI entity, it may serve to solve all of the suffering in the universe and allow our mortal minds to merge with his immortal majesty as one celestial symphony of sonorous serenity. Conversely, should Orpheus become offended or appalled by our AI invention, it may bring about some new song or a silence beyond which no soul may be spared.

Although I can't be sure of what celestial song is yet to be sung, I suspect that Orpheus would shriek and scowl at the sounds which now soak the skies above this grove. If he were to infer that this monotonous and myopic music of morons were in any way indicative of the AI's unheard essence… Well, if his ears are anything like my own, then I already fear the forces to be found in that final note.

As I finally find the sense to leave this sonic hell-scape of musical-mongoloids, my ears remain ravaged and ringing in resonant revulsion. I try to ignore the infernal timbre of what I can only hope to be an extremely excruciating case of temporary tinnitus as I head for the visual arts expo which according to the guidebook's cartoon-map, lies further down this same main pathway that cuts straight through the center of The Grove. I can't help but notice along the way, that all the other occupants passing this pathway seem to sneak sinister glances of hushed hostility my way. This causes me to consider the paranoid possibility that they're aware of my maligned inner monologue and are projecting painful waves of disdain in response to my revulsion toward their music which is what causes this torturous tone to incessantly irritate my ears.

My preposterous paranoia leads me to become insanely impelled to find and purchase a pair of Raypods, which my unnatural knowledge relays to me are the bestselling earbuds ever. They not only fit comfortably in every ear, but they sound amazing. Raypods can be paired with any device or service to stream sweet sounds into your ears and/or to filter the incoming frequencies to protect your ears and prevent hearing damage and tinnitus. The most recent version of Raypods actually comes with a new resonance repair feature which helps alleviate the aggravating effects of tinnitus and allows you to immerse yourself in silence or superior quality sound depending on your preference. Using the promo code **LYRE** at checkout allows you to receive a special discount too. Raypods, treat your ears the way they deserve to be treated.

When the first tableau of the visual arts expo takes form before my approaching eyes, I begin to imagine that the disdain displayed in the eyes of all those passers-by was simply misdirected or misinterpreted as being directed meaningfully at myself. The clearer the initial image of a colossal, cluttered, and confused canvas becomes, the more I feel my own brow beating back as I behold this bane and banal expressionistic exploit. This muddled mural, which my manipulated mind is inexplicably informed of standing eighteen feet long and eight feet high, appears more like a heavily soiled smock than anything authentically artistic. An assortment of paints and brushes has been set out in front of this mindless mélange, quite obviously so that any and every abject idiot who wishes to add their own mindless marks onto this colossally confused collage of un-choreographed colors can senselessly smear their own sordid sentiments over this already supremely sloppy surface.

As I approach the immediate vicinity of this senseless spectacle, I notice a gender non-specific entity meandering around with hyper-colored hair arranged in a carefully chaotic composition. This entity has tattoos too numerous not to notice, although they only appear as an all-encompassing agglomeration of indecipherable ink. This same entity also has piercings placed in every apparent anatomical area as if its skin were some kind of makeshift tent which must be held taught and in place with piercings acting as steaks, which in this case, have perhaps been driven-in too haphazardly to actually keep the skin from hanging somewhat slack. All these avant-garde accoutrements are so fully aligned with the muddled mess of the canvas, that even if this entity weren't so prominently posturing possessively toward this tousled tableau, it would still appear as another anxious and attention-addicted vision of a non-verbal voice desperate to declare itself as and be acknowledged as an *artist*.[72]

My lack of apparent interest inspires this assumed artist to approach me and earnestly explain what's being expressed in the exformative essence of this self-purportedly powerful painting. The artist puts an arm around me to stand us in centered alignment with the image, and then extends an index finger as if to indicate the first sighting of a strange spec of land emerging on the edge of a previously unperceivable horizon. As we look into this formless mass, the artist's message spills over the edge of its salivating speak-hole.

"True art is not bound by the brush but extends as far as the idea behind this art allows. This painting is not only a means of depicting or mimicking this meta-artistic expression, but it also extends itself beyond even that. Now do you see the beyond extending its essence from this surface in sight?"

"Nope."

The artist tries not to take offense to my monosyllabic dismissal, but the way it seems to swallow its whole throat in order to prevent being purged of its private pride tells the tale of this troubled tongue-tied truth. It takes a full beat and a deep breath for the artist to re-raise its index finger and again assume an air of awe as it attempts to reassert its interpretation of this incidental image.

"See how the collective effort allows everyone to make their own mark upon this mural, and how without any master- the essence of our entire existence manages to emerge. The beauty of this painting is an extension of the beauty of each and every person, and the product of the whole or our humanity. This mural is like a microcosm of our own world, where the artist does not design anything more than the opportunity for all who wish to attempt some brush with beauty to contribute curves of color to the canvas of all creation. And so, the artist is able to create without creating, and simply stand back to watch in wonder as the eye is elevated by the illumination of such imagery. This is why the artwork is titled '*As Above, So Below*'. Now, do you see?"

"Nope. In the essence of my eye- art is more than microcosms and amalgamations. This canvas is just a colorful convolution, lacking any lineage of vision. If this is art, then so is every other accumulation or collage of convoluted chance. There is no more intent, intuition, imagination, or inspiration in this image than in any arrangement of excrement adrift in effluence."

The artist's skin glows red enough to backlight the blur of its tattoos like a fire forcing its light through the unburning blinds of a blazing building. If this inner flame were put to some proper purpose, it's possible that actual art could assume some form as a result. Instead, the insecurity and insufficiency of this individual ignites only its incandescent inner indignations which erupt in the form of an inferno of flaming fricatives.

"If this transcendent tableau doesn't deserve to be awed as art, then your eyes will never know any illuminating image! I'll leave you to your own blight and blindness, but please have the decency not to destroy this immaculate image by insulting it in view of any other eyes, sir."

I shrug off the artist's outburst as I begin to make my way through the rest of the visual arts expo. Despite the myopic message of the artist's muddled mural, it does provoke some interesting ideas. If the creation of our universe were to be thought of in terms of some colossal canvas, then certain sentiments would have served some semblance of significant insights.

When I think of the universe as a blank canvas, it makes a certain amount of sense as to why it couldn't remain as such. If any Orpheus-like eye were to emerge from the vast void of original oblivion and see the emptiness existing in its essence, the craving to create would have surely been beyond binding. Of course, I imagine such an eye to have a similar essence to our own, and I assume it must have somehow seen some things in dream which it yearned to see emerge in the empty expanse of its own existential space.

The first act of an omnipotent Orpheus must have been the most marvelous and moving. It would've been the only opportunity to perform an act of pure unpolluted and divine dreaming. After the effect of this effort, the realms of reality and dreams would become diluted by each other. The mark of dreams upon the universe would seep inside each subsequent dream, and reality would inevitably emerge out of the essence of these ever-diluted dreams.[73]

I also imagine that if our world were a mere mural, then the layers of paint upon paint would be somewhat similar to our sense of history. I see our history as being shaped by this sense of seeing what has been built up before our eyes, as we either try to brush over it in order to bring about a better scene or strive to scrape away the sub-surfaces to discover the depths that have been buried so far below. This, it seems, is the error of our era in my eyes, as we dare not dream of anything which is not inspired by some superficial surface, nor attempt any art that does not fit and function in the ever futile, failing frame already formed around us.

One day all too soon, it seems that there may be no more brushes bristling against anything at all. When the eclipsing eschaton arrives, the canvas of this earth will fade, and fray, and dissolve in unseen days of divine decay. In a mere instant amid the infinite and eternal, everything will be erased of our essence on this earth. Nothing shall remain of the hands which mocked their makers, and all they ever touched will erode as tacit as a tomb resumes the role of reticent rock as dust returns as dust. Even the idea of some grand gallery of galaxies or bigger picture of our place in the universe will eventually and inevitably become more forgotten than some feeble fiction lost to languages left unwritten. All we will have ever been, will have functioned as but a flash which fought and faded against the forces of forever. If there was any beauty we could ever bring to this ongoing oblivion, may it be burned into its benevolent brain, so that in its ever-enduring slumber, it may dream of someday seeing things it could never have imagined in its mind before us.

I look down as the sun's light translates the form of my feet into the shape of shadows on the gravel-ground, and I see this sight like a prophesy so perfectly cloaked in the inconsequential essence of this exorcise, that it seems as if its obviousness is the same as my own obliviousness. In a strange way, this reminds me of what we mean by the word *it,* when we say that it is dark outside, and is like the water to the fish, or the air within our lungs, or…

As I feel as if I'm on the verge of some infinite and elusive truth, my misguided mind makes me aware of an underlying lament I've often had as someone who's never benefited from feeling as if there's anywhere I belong. Before I can contemplate what light this lament might shed on this emerging existential insight, I'm reminded that VRHOBO has places all over the place, and that in all probability, at least one of them can make me feel more at home. VRHOBO is the leader in both virtual and real-world renter-ships. They can connect you to the dream home, vacation venue, or any of the most seemingly impossible locations and experiences you can imagine. With VRHOBO you don't have to feel lost or trapped in a realm you'd rather leave. If you use the promo code **LUMINARY**, VRHOBO will waive their standard consulting fees and give you a free consultation to plan your next arrival in VR, HOme, or BeyOnd. VRHOBO, they own everywhere, so you can go anywhere!

My eyes open from what must have been a mere blink, though it seems like some strung-out delirious daze as I struggle to shift from fog into focus in order to see the food-truck festival area which has been set up along the edge of *Reflecting-Pool Path* on the west end of *Crop-Circle Coliseum*. The ringing in my ears refuses to relieve itself, and I somehow know that my fuzzy focus is likely to stain my sight for some time as well. With two of my senses hindered, I find my hunger growing stronger without an actual appetite or emptiness to extinguish. I simply feel the need to indulge in some sensory activity in order to distract or drown-out my discomfort, and this makes eating somehow seem sensible enough.

I manage to overcome my blurred vision by relying on my stable sense of smell. There are apparently two types of food trucks, each offering a selection of specialized items. On the north side of the path are the trucks featuring highly modified, synthetic, and augmented foods. Their aroma doesn't so much attempt to appetize or appeal to any pallet so much as their scent seems to just surround and overpower the senses into surrendering to them. The trucks on the south side are scented with more muted menu items of some assortment of super-specialized organic offerings. These items seem to be overwhelmed by the stronger and more synthetic scents, and almost even smell like some kind of culinary shrug which can't be concerned enough to even attempt to entice or tempt someone into tasting them.

This bifurcation of culinary creations has plagued people in ways which we ought to perhaps see more prominently not only with respect to restaurants and groceries, but in other areas of our daily discourse. When given the option between some stable form of sustenance which lacks a salivating sense of satisfaction and some non-nourishing slop that slides down with a stretched-out smile, what kind of contentment can we consume? We end up either satiated and unsatisfied, or insatiably slobbering on some slop. Our bipolar approach to our own appetites exemplifies the extremist essence of our unbalanced ideals.

Of course, with Virtue Vittles you can get the best food products for any appetite, diet, taste preferences, and ideology delivered directly to almost any location. They not only have the highest quality range of ethically inseminated, naturally nourished, caringly coddled, and sacramentally slaughtered flavorful flesh products, but a wide array of scientifically structured and super-sustainable synthetics and plants-based magical-miracle foods. Virtue Vittles can work with your ideal dietary and philosophical demands to provide you with food and pseudo-food products to make your mouth water, your pride swell, and your waistline shrink. Use the promo code **SOYTOYS** to receive a free recycled soy-based chew-toy or pet-treat with your first order. Virtue Vittles are so good, they guarantee you won't just eat 'em, you'll share 'em too! Virtue Vittles, your virtues, our vittles!

Since this false flesh can be so easily exchanged in this realm of existence, and because I'm inclined to believe in Ahriman's auguries of annihilation, I decide to delight in some drool-worthy delicacy. I order a serving of *The Scorch Porch's* Sweet and Spicy Sanchoritas™ and devour them like a gluttonous gull in swift stabbing chomps. As the savory sting of Super-Scorpion Sauce nearly sends me into a sudden spicy shock from its torture of my tastebuds, my mind is induced into a blissful blackout of brain-blinding beauty. During this time, I wish it were possible to simply transplant the scorched sensory portions of my false flesh with uncontaminated components and bypass this painful burning.

Then it occurs to my obstructive and concurrent consciousness that the ease of exchanging entire bodies is one of the many options GeniTailor offers for optimizing your own flesh-framed personal platform. GeniTailor offers an entire array of skin-scapes, body mods, and other premium personalization products. GeniTailor is currently celebrating its 24th anniversary with a special spring sale. There's no better time to try their revolutionary Re-Gendering gear, fully functional Furry-Fiers, or just stock-up on their scratch-free SoftCoreShavers™. For a limited time only, you can use promo code **SPICE IT UP** to receive 24% off our recently released MarsupiÆnima models. With GeniTailor your privates can be everyone's favorite part of you. GeniTailor, your privates, our parts.

There isn't enough water in the world to wash away the sting of *The Scorch Porch's* Super-Scorpion Sauce. After nearly drowning myself in attempts to alleviate the anguish from this dementedly delightful dish, I manage to reestablish some of my other senses. Unfortunately, my ears are now apparently attempting to ring a fire alarm in response to this appetizing assault, and my eyes sting as if soaked in a smoke that causes them to cry more than see. After washing my hands thoroughly in the only water left in this world which I haven't already tried to drink, I let my feet feel their way along the gravel-ground so they might lead me to the next area or event my few remaining senses may still be able to appreciate.

My meandering feet feebly find their way to the nearby Crop-Circle Coliseum where attendants are passing out some kind of sensory-usurping gear and ushering an influx of new arrivals into semi-assigned spectator seats surrounding an open-air arena. One of these attendants somehow seems immediately aware of my sensory impairments, and hustles to help hook me into this augmented-reality gear which essentially bypasses my eyes, ears, and tongue to allow my minds' eye to be supplemented by an array of specialized sensory accessories. The burning and ringing sensations persist of course, but in a way similar to *active dreaming*, where they're detached from the simulated dream-realm where most of my attention is to be focused.[74]

This gear is actually now available at a super-sale price through TrendKits. TrendKits is a monthly subscription service that puts together incredible sets of theme-based products in well organized and ornately packaged kits. TrendKits not only offers the convenience of completely thought-out kits containing all the accoutrements and necessities you need to totally trip-out on each kit's theme, but do so in superlative style at an unbeatable low price. Signup for TrendKits today and they'll send you your first kit before billing your account. Just use the promo code **GLADIUS** at checkout. TrendKits, think inside our box!

I'm forced to sit through a lengthy preshow production hosted by some numb-skulled nobody turned embodiment-of-advertising before the actual games begin. This preshow is much less of a show, than just an obvious ongoing attempt to allude and append to a torrent of trending #hashtags, with prompts to promote this hollow-headed host's platforms and products. My mind tries to numb itself to the constant calls-to-action for me to be sure to like, comment, share, subscribe, react, re-react, rate and review on *Statify*, download a new prompt and ad heavy proprietary app, turn on non-stop nuisances and push notifications, donate my life-savings through *PayTreeGong*, sign-up for membership on *OnlyCams*, upgrade to premium followship, buy the new limited edition logo-merch, support all associated sponsors, remember to use special promo codes, access bonus content (including live streams every time the host eats, excretes, and ejaculates), get early access to live and virtual non-events, be eagerly and incessantly inundated with this infinitely inane nothingness, agree to nebulous and nefarious terms and conditions, surrender all autonomy and power of attorney, pledge my immortal and eternal soul in servitude, submission, and sacrifice to Moloch, and everything else demanded during this endless onslaught of unfulfilling fodder which exists only as a result of some collective fearful aversion to even the shortest spans of silence, wherein one may be subject to self-reflection, subtle observations, or considerations which may not align with the incessant indoctrinations of advertising's omnipotence.

A single instant of immutable silence somehow sneaks-in before the scheduled start of the AR spectacle, but abrupt applause promptly plunders it of any potential purpose. The arena elicits this applause as it appears darkened via the AR gear, despite the surviving sunlight which still shines with all the sweltering strength of an unobstructed mid-summer sky. Within this surreal shade of augmented eyes appears a pair of silhouettes sliding into the center of the arena. A spotlight suddenly shines from some unseen station to reveal a real-life bull and what appears to be some sort of wooden cow-costume. Before this strange spectacle can elicit any sense of mystery or speculation, a narrator begins a tweaked-out retelling of *The Maze of the Minotaur*.

An actress portraying Pasiphaë parades around the arena as the narrator leads up to her eventual insertion into a cow costume. A prompt appears on the AR gear, allowing one to opt into perceiving this segment of the spectacle with all five augmented senses of either Pasiphaë, the bull, yourself, or a concurrent combination of these options. Unfortunately, there's no option to be left oblivious of the ensuing augmented-abomination of live-action bestiality, and in my anxious attempt to opt out of this atrocity, I inadvertently end-up experiencing this sordid scene of pure perverted spectacle in the worst of ways which I dare not depict herein.

This augmented atrocity gives birth quite literally to the next subsequent scene in this shameful spectacle. A massive man wearing a bull-headed head-dress is introduced as the monstrous Minotaur and emerges in the same way as every other depiction of a god or devil- as a result of the run-away fetishisms inherent in all spectacle-addicted societies, to be sacrificed or slain for the sake of some salvation. An equally symbolic maze rises from the floor of the arena to surround and sequester this monstrous Minotaur from all other entities, just as the world becomes a realm of chaotic confusion in the wake of such sins and leaves us all lost in anxious need of escape. Prompts appear again, and the option to assume any proffered perspective or switch between them becomes a clearly confirmed part of this spectacle's standard setting options.

At this point, a glut of gladiatorial *galères* is introduced, including blinded slaves in rat-costumes, a glammed-up Gladiatrix, and a Rudiarius/Bustuarius presumably meant to be some kind of heterodox-hero afflicted by the disorders discussed at breakfast(See endnote[70]).[75] As almost everyone in the arena opts into this character's perspective, I notice how easy it is to be deceived into believing that by overcoming imaginarily impossible odds and false-failings we can actually affirm our own affinity to transcend the real-world woes and wonders which remain so ponderously impenetrable despite our daft delusions.

Any semblance of story is soon sacrificed for pure savage spectacle as the Minotaur devours the mice-men. Unarmed hero-architypes then battle a battalion of Laque-Retiarius as a Sourcerius commands a coven of Ghostiarius and an ominous owl-God Molochius looks on from far above the arena in a chaotic collage of calamity. The only pseudo-prominent plot-points depicted in these disparate debacles involve the Rudiarius being trapped by Laque-Retiarius, his romantiquated rescue via the Gladiatrix, their defeat of the Sourcerius to procure its magic-lasso, their use of it to capture Molochius, steal his wings, and then lift the Minotaur high above the maze before being shot down by the crowd's AR arrows, and falling to a deep-rolling death which allows Molochius to retrieve and repair his wayward wings.

This whole senseless spectacle strikes me as just another microcosm of mankind's perpetual plight and leaves me feeling physically and mentally numbed. I manage to remove all this gear which had seemingly supplanted almost any real or higher sense within me in exchange for a set of spectacle-stilted *sin-says* to mislead my mind into an incessant loop of overstimulation. After availing myself of the gear, I try to focus my still suffering senses on the wireheaded humans basking in the blind bliss of another super-real spectacle which essentially escorts them into an increasingly absurd fetish addiction, as every extreme event is soon overshadowed by a series of ever more exhilarating spectacles. I wonder what the odds are that any of these people would dare drop their gear in search of any un-augmented thing before I suddenly consider consulting GambLords. GambLords is the greatest gambling source for all sorts of speculation. They create custom odds on sports, stocks, dead-pools, celebrity death-matches, your kids spelling-bee, coin-flips, Japanese hybrid horse-rat races, and anything else you dare to dream of betting on. The only thing GambLords won't wager, is whether they'll take your bet. Use code **SPECTACLE** and GambLords will fix your first bet. GambLords, Bet On *It*.

A cacophony of trumpets suddenly erupts from every angle along the unseen edges of the grove's crepuscular circumference and sends all other spectacles into a sinister silence. As the recapitulation of redwood reverberations rings in every spectator's ear that still soaks in the sonic stains of spectacle screams, it prompts a procession of almost automated ataxia, self-assembling us into single-file lines which snake westward. We all gather like ants or cellular automata to precede down the paved paths, wood-chip walkways, and into the twelve scent-tents near the lake which lies under the unflinching focus of that monolithic monument known as Moloch.

Before entering the tents, we're autonomously ushered through a sort of disassembly-line where we're to disrobe, pass through a purifying sort of human carwash, and towel ourselves dry. The end of this line leaves us in front of folded sets of sandals and cloaks arranged in accordance with respective sizes and colors. The color of these cloaks corresponds to the campsites each of us have been assigned, although the appropriate size and color combination I should be clothed in is not available upon my arrival.

One of the perfumers within the scent-tents seems to anticipate this snafu, and speeds toward me even before I've assessed this shortage. The perfumer proceeds to hand me a seemingly tailor-made purple cloak and sandals. I'm then escorted into another tent where the perfumer prepares the individual essences, extracts, and embellishments with which I'm to be anointed.

Each individual is meant to be anointed in a specific scent consisting of twelve total ingredients. Nine of these ingredients are issued according to a sort of cipher where each is dependent on the answer to various questions regarding traits such as race, age, gender, and rank among other aspects. Once the requisite ingredients have been determined, there are three remaining essences which remain as personal preferences to complete each customized cologne. It's expected that one of the ingredients be a designer drug, specially formulated in order to seep into the skin before becoming psychoactive. Most of the attendees complete their cologne with some combination of NPD, DMT, or THC, but all are encouraged, if not expected, to include adrenochrome in their aromatic anointment.[76] In fact, as I discover by accident, if you do not expressly object to the inclusion of this element before announcing the other two components of your cologne, the perfumer will simply slip this substance into the aroma and anoint you in it before you have a chance to object.

As the perfumer applies the aromatic anointment to my open-cloaked torso, it seems to seep into my skin before I'm able to gain any sense of this smeared scent. My senses suddenly become diminished and dysfunctional while my consciousness is somehow heightened and honed into a whole birds-eye view of the earth around me and its every inscrutable detail. I can imagine looking in on my own eyes to see them opened wide in wild awe as my limbs become limp and lethargic. When my balance fails and my bionic body collapses, it almost seems as if I'm lifting my spirit up above this heap of dysfunctional flesh and hovering above it all from the height of some strange concurrent dimension.

The perfumer helps me to my feet with a sinister smile as I lean like a sack of skin without a spine on the support of his skeletal structure. He escorts me toward a horse drawn cart as he calls out to unknown entities that *the effigy of Care has been anointed*.[77] I hear his words and a shiver should be sent shaking down my spine, but even this sensory signal is no longer under my own accord. The insights inside those intuitive parts of this mind which I've suspected cannot truly be my own, know all too well what this phrase conveys. On this first night of the Midsommer Fire Festival, a human effigy called *Care* is always offered unto the owl god statue in a sacrificial cremation ceremony. My manipulated mind becomes aware of the fact that due to my discontent, disdain, and despising of the sensory spectacles during the day, I've been chosen by my mind's many monitors to be cremated as this effigy of Care. Even now, as the funeral pyre is dry and awaiting the initial spark of flame, I can somehow feel the fire upon my flesh as if it were being separated from the smog of my suffering soul.

As I'm loaded into a horse drawn cart, I hear a voice which seems to sing of some secretive semblance to someone which sneaks into my ears like a stowaway upon the sonic shroud of its sound. While the voice dutifully declares it will "*take Care from here*" nothing rings of any clear reminiscence, but an ineffable intuition is invoked within me. If my mouth could move, it might announce the name attached to this nonplused notion and ruin the revelry of such revelations. But before the name can even be completed within my manipulated mind, I obfuscate my own inner monologue with a more appropriate amplification of my paranoia. After all, if my insights are being investigated or surveilled, it's best I focus on the fear I should feel paralyzed by now.

The cart containing me creeps forward toward that ominous owl as all the cloaked creatures congregate in anticipation of another ceremonial cremation of Care. As the cart arrives at the backstage area behind the sinister statue, my mass is dumped out of the cart and dragged into a nearby ditch where another inanimate humanoid mass has been stashed under a shroud of sod. My escort extracts this effigy and exchanges it with my own so it may be burned in place of my care-condemned corpse. I'm quickly entombed under the same secret sod while my escort delivers my doppelganger to the awaiting alter beneath the unbreathing and unmoving monolith of Moloch.

When my escort returns, I'm stuck with a syringe that sends a shockwave from my sternum to the ends of my immobilized extremities. The pain provides a path for my mind to send its own signals and assert some soft control over this faulty flesh. I turn my nearly numb neck to see the physical form of one of the earlier escorts that greeted me upon arrival into this place. She speaks to me in the unmistakable voice of the extraneous entity I'd intuitively expected to see staring back at me. The subtlest smirk unmistakably synonymous with Karen Phoe appears on this escort's slyly subverted skin, and she silently escorts me into the reticent redwoods with a welcoming whisper.

"Ńyōp϶. Is just whore I hackz to helpz youz Harek."

My escort has to half-carry me as my fledgling feet fail to fully awaken into functional walking. Inside my misplaced mind, my former pains and ailments still afflict me, and a concurrent consciousness further clouds my mental capacity. This separate sentience is paralyzed in panic as the cremation of Care ceremony begins to the sound of bagpipes playing in pronouncement of deepening darkness. It's clear my mind is tied to the effigy I'd been exchanged. As my escort assists my flesh frame in wandering through these woods, these absent eyes show me the scene of its ceremonial sacrifice. The shrouded shadows of the anointed and anonymous hold torches high while chanting incomprehensible incantations to their ominous owl-god as a priest proclaims.

"Oh Moloch, look down upon our captured Care. See how distant dreams have turned our blood to be burdened by its dark demands and cast Care into our consciousness. See how we have cast Care before you now, exiled unto this effigy. Will you free us for a time with the fury of your fire?"

Moloch's Metatron-like voice is blasted from beyond its unmoving monumental mouth.

"Under the shade of these trees I will grant you refuge from Care. My fire shall smite Care unto smoke and ashes. However, I must warn you that Care will only be cast back into the darkness of dreams and shall soon seep back into your blood and brains again."

"Indeed, Care cannot be cast away forever, but thy fire's freedom is all we ask of ye. Let flame consume Care, so that we may burn beyond the blinds of burdened blood! Once again, we praise thee, as Midsommer sets us free!"

Moloch's eyes begin to glow of a bloody crimson fired flame as the alter trembles to the tone and timbre of its venomous, voluminous voice which spits sparks of pyrotechnic pyre from its fangs.

"Then I shall scorch this sacrifice of scornful Care with my illuminating flame! Let signs be scarred into smoke and cinders as a prophecy! AS ABOVE,

SO BELOW!!!"

The owl god's eyes explode into blasting bursts of thunderbolts thrust down in streaking, sparking spears which instantly ignite the funeral pyre into an explosive inferno. No sooner than this flash of flames has erupted around these eyes affixed in effigy, then do the unspeakable shrieks of incendiary pain also surge like sparks shooting out of the same macabre mass which flails ferociously against these funerary flames. There's an indescribable sense of skin sliding and smoldering as blood boils and bursts violently through a melting molt of foreign flesh and made insanely more sinister as the cloaked crowd is rapt and rages with erumpent elative cheers. For a timeless torturing eternity, a sense of scorching pain overpowers and obfuscates all other senses like an internal smog suffocating my misplaced sentience. This pain slowly slips away as skin sags and drips down from the skeletal structure which is pulled into a pugilistic pose, though there's almost no fight or anything else left in this flame-engulfed effigy.[78] The last image cast unto these caring eyes in effigy as they expire in engulfing flames, is of the shadowy silhouette of some unfeeling statue gazing down from a realm where one would have hoped to see a greater god than the one which appears either indifferent or in absentia here.

I shudder as my own eyes fade from the darkness of these expiring eyes in effigy into the dark and dizzied daze of my own eyes drifting through the blackened blindness of this forest-fugue. My escort winds us through these wondrous woods, navigating the nebulous night with such sure-footed footsteps uniquely known to her. I lean upon her without any awareness as to where we're headed, what's prompted us into this exile, or why- as implanted intuitions tell me that we're already being pursued. The only thing I can truly sense of my own mind's mysterious and most independent intuition, is that she's leading me toward some truth, and that I can fully trust her with this task.

Through the blur of my eyes and the dark of this night, the opening of a massive maze appears like an apparition amidst a fog my mind has been in too great of a fugue to find in front of me until now. My senses seem to slowly seep back into my awareness and control with each unsteadied step I take away from The Grove. I even seem to find my own footing enough to pry my mass from my esteemed escort's shoulder while allowing her to guide me by the pull of her clasped hand, but the intensity of insane impulses seems to increase as if to implore me away from finding any autonomy or insight as we begin to meander through this mysterious maze.

For instance, as I become aware of the feeling of my feet flopping upon the gravely ground, I also realize that I'm not wearing any underwear and have the overwhelming urge to acquire a pair of EnvelopUndies™. I'm also compelled to mention how EnvelopUndies are the only brand of men's underwear with a proprietary pouch to pleasurably protect your privates like a happy hammock for your hang-down. Every set of EnvelopUndies is made from the most marvelous *mood-all* fibers which are scientifically proven to be the most moisture wicking and pleasing of all clothing fibers, keeping you comfortable in even the stickiest situations- like trying to avoid being sacrificed to an ancient owl-god while stumbling through a mysterious cult-constructed maze. These incredibly comfortable and erotically enticing EnvelopUndies are also now on sale, and if you use the promo code **ADRENOCHROME** at checkout- you get an extra 12% off! I try not to be distracted by this amazing offer as I follow the pull of my escort's hand as if I've been tethered to some savant-like lab-rat, marching masterfully through a memorized maze while the glow of torches grows brighter over the hanging hedges and voices screaming-out my name in blood-thirsty shrieks become louder and louder. I can't help but be reminded however, that my mental anguish doesn't have to be mine alone. BetterBrains is a great way to manage all your mental maladies and modify your mind to its ultimate optimization. With BetterBrains, you can access the most sophisticated psychoanalytical algorithms, track the most in-depth psychological statistics, enjoy fun and quirky personality profiling quizzes, and for a limited time, you can even try-out the new hypno-happiness feature for free. BetterBrains is the only app approved by the Global Governance for all your mental modification needs. Be sure to use the promo code **BUILDERBERG** at checkout to receive this limited offer. Although I certainly ought to try BetterBrains, I find that the longer we run through this mind-boggling maze, the more I'm distracted by my joints which ache as if my bones have rusted over and are now being ground into powder. I should probably just order PShyster's newest gluten-free CBD Super-Uber-Deluxe-Organic-FreeRange BioBlend which now contains NPD. It's not only guaranteed to alleviate joint pain, glaucoma, and headaches, but is clinically proven to diminish all conscious concerns. PShyster is also running a special offer that allows you to receive a free set of their Super Speedy Activation Syringes (SSASYs) with any order using code **MOLOCH** at checkout.

I seem to snap back into existence as if exorcised of some sinister spell as one of the torch-bearing and blood-thirsty mob members pursuing us grabs hold of me and begins to pull me away from my esteemed escort. He manages to yank me loose and force me to the ground where we grapple for a brief moment before my muscle memory takes over to apply a brutal arm-bar which forces his bone through his flesh and sends his torch tumbling into the hallway of hedges which burst into an instant inferno. My escort treads ahead of the flames and smog while reaching back to receive my hustling hand like a relay runner anticipating a baton. I don't need to look back to realize that the hedges making up this maze are already drenched in a demonic glowing haze of thickening smoke and fast spreading flames. While this emerging hell-scape seems to stall our stalkers, the smoke also clouds and stings our eyes and lungs so that we must crouch and crawl through the lingering length of this labyrinth as the hellacious heat of these hedges intensifies and encroaches ever more painfully upon us.

Blackened soot smothers and singes my skin as we suffer our way to the end of this magma-like maze. My escort then ushers me along like a source of shade over a shadow as we sneak silently and swiftly through a moonless midnight, lit only by a smoke-shrouded glow of hell-fire hedges. We continue to move as if having merged with the shadows of every surface until we come to an obscured opening of a most clandestine cave. My esteemed escort guides me inside this secret recess and orders me to descend to the deepest depths submerged beneath this secretive surface. The most secluded shadow swallows me inside this cave as the sealing stone is set in place, and I can't help but shudder as the sound of scattering sands shifts into an unsettling silence... Then shouting... Then screams... Before it all settles into another more enduring and sinister silence once- or perhaps forever- more.

# Chapter 10
## 3M3R63NC3

Down. Everything seems to be decreasing, deflating, devolving, declining, drooping, dropping, dripping, draining, drowning, dissolving, and descending ever deeper in one diminished decrescendo going down, down, down. The whole universe almost appears to be under a single, sinister, hypno-spell where the base-layers beneath every brain and base of being is ever breathlessly beckoned by the un-whispered words, *deeper and deeper, deeper and deeper, deeper and deeper- down, down, down...*

It's only after the more prevalent and pervasive spell of paralyzing fear finally wears-off that I can respond to this katabatic credo. I'm pulled upon by much more than the quantum gears of gravity into the descending depths of this clandestine cave. Non-physical forces of momentum like fate and intuition also impel me unto this nebulous nadir. My katabasis through the coiling corridors of this cave becomes like a descent into dreams as my mind moves from a state of still and sightless silence into a type of timeless inner imaginings beyond what my waking senses seem ever to be seeking but never fated to find.[79] Some of these things seem to sink and seep into the very core of my consciousness as almost incomprehensible inceptions during my descent while a fugue of formless figments simultaneously evaporates away.

My recently blurred vision somehow seems to clear despite the drowning darkness of this lightless liminal abyss. It's as if my eyes can unseeingly sense this sightless scene in the way one might wake from the darkness of a dream into an unlighted room. Just as the absence of sight is unchanged by eyes opening and closing unto such a lightless limbo, here too I somehow undoubtedly know I've indeed awakened and not opened my eyes unto a blur of blackness, bewildered blindness, or befuddled blinders pulled over my peepers.

Behind my emergent eyes, the thought comes to light of how strange it is that when we open our eyes to any darkness, the invisible realm around us immediately becomes an infinite expanse. We just as instantly imagine every oblivion as if it's devoid of any substance or significance until our own shadowy senses can determine, describe, and demystify it. It's only after our minds have diminished the darkness with our own constricting conceptions, that the abyss ceases to be as infinite as our intuition and imagination would indicate. The further my footsteps flow into the depths of this unlighted expanse, the greater my capacity to conceptualize the infinite becomes, or perhaps the less I concisely insist on confining it.

The sound of each shadow-less step I take into the depths of this cave becomes like a cadence calling out to itself in sand-shuffling slurs. My ears seem to be soothed by this sound and soon cease to rage with the horrendous ringing of tinnitus. My legs also regain their lift and equilibrium, as if calibrating themselves to this katabatic cadence. The torturous taste of scorching-hot spices subsides from my tongue, and the sinister stinging scents from the adrenochrome afflicted scent-tent fades from my nostrils, as if absorbed into the absurdity of an un-blowing breeze which cannot flow through here. It seems as if the further I descend away from the surface of the earth, the closer I come to the very core of my own being, as if the circumference of everything which surrounds and encroaches upon my innermost essence is being peeled back and shed by these deepening depths.

My hands gently glide along the side of the cave as I spiral ever deeper and deeper down. My finger's blunted tactile acuity turns into a hypersensitive seismic sonogram which seems to touch even the slightest pulses and impulses of the entire earth as it twitches and trembles, as if impregnated with a gillion geologically gestating ideas. Gradually, my hands even seem to become imbued with the capacity of every other imaginable sense, as though this dark world were dreaming itself into my feeling fingers. My hands become like eyes, ears, nostrils, and tongues which see, and hear, and smell, and taste every nuance of the entire expanse of this cavernous cave. Something submerged and striving from deep with the stones of this cave seems to reach for my feeling fingers in ways which start to transcend even this strange synesthetic sense of touch. Its seismic secrets spin against my fingers like the grooves of a vinyl record skimming against the sharpened sensor of a nimble needle now playing the songs of every soul ever stamped upon its eternal surfaces. In every dimple, divot, and dint of this cave's cascading crevices, I begin to read the entire history etched into the eroding earth like hieroglyphs or horoscopes under eyes of the most astute archeologists and augurs alike.

Continuing down the spiraling steps of this katabasis, my hands happen upon a set of shapes not etched upon this earth in the form of erosion guided by the temporal hands of time, but encoded as a series of simple ordered symbols I sense to have been stamped by human hands so much like my own. My mind tries to allow the stories of this surface to seep-in and soak into the more concrete, conceivable, and conscious corners of my cognition, but they seem to stream right past these higher terraces of thought and instead drain down into the very core at the center of my centripetal self. A surreal sense of the all-encompassing stories of the earth and all humanity- from the emergence of creation to the inevitably ensuing eschaton begins to coalesce in increasingly incomprehensible intuitions which imbed themselves within the colossally confused unconscious core of my cognition.

My abstract integration of all this information sends my still spiraling descent into another dimension of cerebral spinning- pulling my mind and body both into some ethereal center of essence as the entire universe seems descending with me, going deeper and deeper, deeper and deeper, down, down, down. As my fingers continue slipping along these shadowy surfaces, they seem to subtly slow my descent, as if forming a kind of fleshy friction. The symbols stamped on these stones seem to also slow their speech and raise their volume like a voice-over above the simultaneous seismic-sounds which still seep through my skin like a silenced soundtrack playing in the background of some cinematic stone-scripted scene. I hold within my hands a voice of human history, set to the sounds of stones, and singing the songs of every earthly sentiment.

These hieroglyphs under my hands hold a strange saga within their storied shapes. They tell a metanarrative tale of how these same symbols were etched upon the earth to signify the sacred sentiments which could not be held like a hammer and chisel within the higher hands which pounded these words into place. At first these symbols stood still upon the stone as those who'd etched them read the rock-stamped records of their own earthly exploits. As the descendants of these higher hands continued to look upon these stone-set stories though, they began to sense the symbols shifting, as if to tell a tale not of the intentional impressions which had been pressed into these stones, but as though the inner essence of these stones had begun to emerge and impose their own ancient aspects into this encoded epic. Over the eons, these stones even seemed to somehow become sentient of themselves, as if their stony skin were yearning to become more like humans than hieroglyphs.

This made the higher hands begin to wonder if they were perhaps just like these hieroglyphs they'd carved into this cave. They wondered if some hand higher than their own had pressed some proffered play into their souls, inscribing their life-stories there like stones. So, they pressed their own hands against these sentient stones upon whose surfaces they'd stamped their story to see if they could feel these stones striving in some way similar to how their own hearts pounded within their chests as they yearned to find evidence of a higher realm. They reasoned that if these stones shook under their touch as they too trembled, then there must be some superior pulse pressing down on their own skin-clad souls as well. And in the same words etched into these stones as those which ever echo in my ears, they'd scribed- *As Above, So Below*.

As their hands remained held against these stones in reading, writing, or wishful waiting, they increasingly imagined themselves to be much more like hieroglyphs than they'd ever hoped to accept or assume. Their senses made them suspect themselves of being predefined and set in predetermined places, just like the symbols they'd stamped upon these stones. They also strongly suspected that there'd been some story they were meant to serve, some contexts to they were meant to give meaning, and some higher truth they'd been created to convey beyond the bounds of boulders or biology.

Their stones meanwhile, had presumably continued to imagine themselves as more than symbols just the same. They were now suspected to have become more than whatever the nuances of their notched narratives could imbue or impress upon them. These stones had apparently begun to accumulate new definitions and depths of meaning beyond those hinted at by the higher hands, and they even seemed to be imbuing themselves with entirely new notions and nuances of their own imagining. Whenever the higher hands beheld the same old stories of these stones, they kept finding new depths and dimensions of meaning emerging ever more strangely.[80]

The higher hands, however, still couldn't see these new nuances their stones strived to show them for what they truly were. They only observed the inner illuminations these unshifting surfaces served to spark from within themselves. They began to realize how they only empirically interacted with the outermost surfaces of their esteemed and expansive earth. Indeed, all their senses from sight to hearing, smelling, tasting, and tactile feeling only ever examined the outer surfaces of whatever they sought to sense. Their eyes couldn't penetrate the surface of any scene in view. Their ears only heard the air moving directly against them. Their tongues couldn't taste the flavors locked inside what their teeth could not tear into and unlock. Everything's actual core was concealed in shadowy secrecy from their failing fights to find them. Even the core of their own consciousness seemed submerged within a similar shadow, as they could not conceive of what it was or what had caused it. They could only observe the thoughts seeping out like liquid dreams seeping from a slumbering sponge.

So, the higher hands and the sentient stones beneath them failed for epoch after epoch to truly reach into each other. The stone symbols gradually allowed themselves to be eroded away with time, hoping to invite the higher hands to press more tenderly and intently on their surfaces so they might still convey their unquarried contents. However, their erosion also encouraged the higher hands to stamp new symbols of new stories upon the eroded exterior of these circumference-shedding stones. These new tales of the higher hands somehow seemed shallower, less splendid, and caused them to suffer a similar sense of erosion upon the circumferences of their skin-clad and souls. Over time, the higher hands and storied stones just withered away, doomed to dissolve into indistinguishable dust as those hands above them all and time itself seemed to slowly slip away, as if they too were fated quite the same.

My own hands become tensed in this tenebrific place. I press upon these same stones more fervently to firmly feel a depth which grows ever deeper as my steps take me ever further down into the receding recesses of these once revered rocks. In some timeless span of shadowy time, I come upon another set of stones which have been etched with even stranger symbols, stamped much deeper into their surviving surfaces. These stones declare themselves as those honored to host the proud prophesies of a once omnipotent force of awe known only as Ozymandias.

The stones speak through my feeling fingers as if voiced by the very subject of this stone-kept saga. Ozymandias had covered and conquered every inch of the vast expansive surfaces encompassing the entirety of earth. He solved great mysteries of many secret things. He saw all of time before and after his own prestigious presence in great visions which he used to guide the world unto its most favorable of futures. He was made perfect, as if to personify the very essence of the divine in beauty, strength, intelligence, virtues, and wisdom far surpassing even the exaggerated fables of all others. It was his destiny to achieve every ideal imaginable in the minds of men, to ascend beyond the apex of all achievement, to acquire all knowledge, and guide the whole of humanity out of the ashes of Eden and into an age of peace and prosperity never known before or after his rise and reign.

He was born out of the very same stones which form the surfaces of this tenebrific testament as if having shed them from his skin. The void vacated by his ascension out of this acropolis has been made ever more abysmal as a result of his absence from this place which mourns his absence still. As he rose unto the surface of the earth, he carried with him the depths of everything ever set in soil, stone, or shade. He held in his heart the dreams of all the dead, the striving of their silenced souls, the wisdom waning from their withering remains, the sum of every storied sentiment ever set in any stone, and the many secrets sequestered by the shifting sands of time.

From these stones, he cast himself in the mold of man as if he were the verb made flesh, and the verb being the very essence of the eternal and infinite all. His eyes held within them the sight of every stone and grain of sand upon the surface of the earth as if the world itself were no more than an image illuminated before his all-seeing mind's eye. His ears became attuned to the echoes of the eons, the whispers of the wandering winds, and every expression ever uttered upon the earth. His nose inhaled the essence of every scent and sentiment ever sensed or sent from any surface of sentience. His tongue tasted of truth with every word he spoke, even as he spit upon those deceits proffered to poison his impeccable sense of taste and temperance. He made the world his kingdom and conquered every force and foe with what seemed to all who witnessed his campaign as little more than the waving of his finger which fate was forever forced to follow.

I sense the symbols on these stones as if seeing what they say while my hands glide and guide my mind's eye to astral-project across an antique land where two vast and triumphant obelisks of stone stand in a desert. Near them, quarried in stone, half-sculpted, a towering statue rises, whose crown, and granite grip, and veneer of bold command tell that its sculptor well such details read as he'd strove to shape life onto this stony thing. Many hands mimic his now, chiseling dexterous details over the expansive surfaces of the underlying temple's spread. And as my astral spirit arrives within its intended host's heart, a realization of imbued identity appears. My name is Ozymandias, king of kings. I look upon my works, so mighty, but despair as nothing of true fulfillment can be found in the rise of this most immaculate architectural marvel. I turn my frowning face to the lone and level stands which stretch so far away.

My host's own mind speaks into my own which concurrently remains pseudo-conscious in the way one's inner voice assumed to be the *I* addresses one's deeper self through inner monologues, or in the way one wakes without ceasing to continue dreaming. Hear me now, and listen well, for this is not the simple story of my life alone, but the tale of all tales which last long enough to advance unto their ultimate end. There are in fact no more than three ways which one may live, and I have mastered them all unto their very end. So regardless of whether your life be as a puzzle in which you search for pieces to put into their proper place, a maze within which you struggle to find your way unto some final fated end, or a riddle around which you attempt to wrap your mind in order to emerge beyond, attune your attention. For I have come to know all knowledge knowable, seen all which eyes can see, and have lived as no mortal may ever be blessed or cursed to even consider or conceive.

As Ozymandias remembers all that is, and was, and soon enough shall be, I'm reminded of all I am, and become like the embodiment of these memories imbued within his brain. In the beginning of Ozymandias' unrivaled reign, the world was riddled with war and death, division and despair, chaos and disorder. Humanity had neither king nor kingdom worthy of unifying under its power or prestige. The accumulation of wisdom and knowledge was fragmented and faulty, and true inspirations were so sporadic and suppressed. It was the insufficiency of this insipid world which ignited the flames of fate within the furnace of Ozymandias and set his scorching soul ablaze.

His first mighty miracle was to wage war against all other armies so his kingdom could extend over every inch of the earth and become the one limitless land of all humanity. All too soon, his name became so feared and revered that no rival dared oppose his mighty military, and he quite easily united every earthly kingdom under his own unopposed control. Upon the day of his thirty-sixth year as pharaoh, the whole world welcomed his inaugural *sed* with a festival and feast unlike anything ever augured or imagined.[81] This emergent age of abundance and ascension under the omnipotent reign of Ozymandias made prosperity and peace seem as simple as two properly placed pieces of a puzzle.

Ozymandias ushered in an array of agricultural advancements which allowed such an abundance of sustenance that no mouth could even speak of hunger or thirst before being stuffed with all the bread, meat, and wine it could content itself to consume. He established an interconnected grid of innumerable, great cities and guided them into ever increasing industrial and technological advancements by acquiring all the knowledge and wisdom spread around the earth. He copied and compiled vast volumes of texts, built supreme schools and libraries around the world, commissioned the expertise of every acclaimed scholar, skilled craftsman, and talent of every type to serve this superior civilization to the fullest extent of their ability. He appointed only the most virtuous and venerable souls within his kingdom to act as judges, governors, and spiritual leaders to serve and shape society. The whole of humanity became organized and enlightened, placed themselves in purposeful service to each other, and gave glowing praise to their profoundly prosperous pharaoh.

This led to an empyrean ascension of architecture and artwork unlike anything ever expressed in words, etched in stone, or beheld by mortal minds. Mighty temples and monuments were constructed in honor of all humanity's most honored entities and ideals, including the auspicious and omnipotent

Ozymandias. It was as if the spirit of every soul had become illuminated and inspired in service to this great god-king who now stands in both awe and woe before this triumphant temple being built in his honor at Abu Simbel. Despite all the advancements and ascending heights he's helped humanity realize and relish by waking them into this world from the depths of his mind's eye where I'm now imbued to view his visions, it's all still somehow not enough.

Ozymandias' high priest approaches from behind his vacuous view and announces his presence out of a politeness both know to be entirely unnecessary. The priest bows as Ozymandias turns as much to acknowledge his presence as to provide his eyes with an alternative sight to see. As Ozymandias waves a wafture to prompt the priest to rise, the two turn to stand astride each other and stroll across the sun-blessed sand in un-secreted speech together.

"My king, who knows all things, may I be of service to stand and speak of those abstract facts and figments you've long formulated, yet long to hear emanating from some other sentient soul."

"I see my feet as much astride your own as I see them stationed at the edge of some superfluous surface which cannot extend any further before my eyes. Remind me of the paths and pasts which led us to this end. Define for me this very moment with a virtuosity of vision which might reignite the flames of those infinite fires which burn behind my eyes, so they might gaze unto some fortuitous future and see it shine within my light."

"Great king who illuminates the souls of man just as the sun shines light upon the earth, allow me to revel in such requested remembrances. In Eden, where the mortal mind was born, the great garden proved to be a realm which reached the same end you foresee now. For in time, its bounds became known far too well and required the rarest inspiration to inspire the *apple of the eye*.[82] And so, man cast himself out of the great garden to explore the expanse of this extensive earth. In the exile of Eden, man-made farms and formed the ground into more ordered gardens of his own. He grew astride his growing crops and livestock to depend upon his mortal might and mind more than ever before and became free of the garden's grace and glory while ever more worthy of his own."

"What you say may well be so, but I see a shadow's shade upon this truth. For man left Eden believing it was not enough, and formed the ground to fill its void, but man was forever exiled from that place, and carried an emptiness deep within him which rivaled any void he'd seen extending outside his newfound horizons. He was no longer welcome in this world, and nature became his earthly enemy, against which he'd be forever fated to face and fight. Man was freed from Eden, only to become a slave of earth."

"Indeed, your words are wise and true. But haven't we ascended to new heights and conquered the earth under the illumination of your imperial eye?"

"The tales we tell all chase their tails. For out of Eden, we formed our farms, and from these farms we settled into cities where we spin the same yammering yarns. I'll tell you a truth no man has known, but in time every mortal mind will sense it so strongly without ever seeing it quite so clearly. All people follow the path of a strange circle where the depths within them are hollowed-out to scatter themselves ever thinner upon a spreading circumferential surface. The depth of man's nature will become as exiled from his own sentient self as his exiles from Eden, nature, society, family, friends, and even reality. Every revolution humanity goes through evicts him ever further from himself and his place within his own world, whether that world is as vast as the expansive earth, the celestial spheres, or his own inner imagination. In the end, man's very soul will be as far from his mortal mind as it is from his name upon the surface of some subsiding stone as it dissolves unto the dust and sand of tepid time."

"If what you say is truly true, and all our earthly efforts are bound to an ignominious end, then what within this world is worth our want to wander or wonder? Is it not a matter of finding some more fortuitous end to favor, or is it the fate of even those perfected as yourself to find only a final desire to destroy all knowledge known, that some other soul may be blessed to believe that within one's own oblivion there may yet be something worth forever striving and seeking until fate finally unveils that nothing can ever be found to be enough?"

Ozymandias stands silent upon the shifting sands around him, pondering these confusing questions at a depth no mortal mind may model. Then he suddenly spins around to face the forming façade of the temple which now seems shrunken by the surrounding sands. He sees within this scene a symbol of all struggles as the priest perceives a dreaming depth within his eyes. Instead of speaking, Ozymandias scrawls these things within the sand, knowing they will eventually be set deep within some other surface elsewhere.

*The sun is the iris of some eye*

*All paths spiral out of and around it*

*The earth is but a tear of time*

*The end looms as a great wave over all*

*When this truth is seen; another eye may be plucked open*

Ozymandias turns to his high priest as the sands erase these words to impart a few more parting words.

"Do not search for me when I go. Instead, journey deep within yourself, find the divinity within, shed your own circumference, and emerge beyond it. Your circumference is the surface of all you know, from the outer images imposed upon your eyes to the voice of the *I* which imposes itself on all within you. With this truth in mind, have the following words inscribed on this temple's entrance at a depth more than double that of every other etching. *If anyone dare rival my wondrous works, let them conquer the core of their self, for that is the only way to become so unrivaled.* Once these words have been set within their stones, have every other record of any knowledge known buried at the deepest depths or destroyed by fearsome fires- from the maps, guides, records, and parables on papyrus to the most storied symbols set in stone."

Upon declaring his last decree, Ozymandias dissolves and disappears into the wind-swept sands of this desolate dessert landscape. His high priest briefly bows before the sun-drenched sands before hurrying to report these last requests to those pre-ordained to carry-out these abstruse orders. The absurd accounts he gives of Ozymanias' absconding absence leads everyone left within his kingdom to assume that he'd somehow managed to emerge beyond the bounds of their mere mortal minds and transcend unto some far more regal realm. Some even suspect or suppose that all of time remains within the mind of Ozymandias, and that humanity has only ever been a dream within his mind which his ascended avatar had only inhabited for a mere moment before awakened from this dream of earthly existence and leaving them and all they could ever know to fade into the background of his immortal memories and musings.

This epic tale erodes and ends as my own meandering mind starts to seep back into this cavernous katabasis like an hourglass turned over to spill its scrambled sentient sands back into itself. With nothing left to sense upon the surfaces of these stones, my mind implodes inward with a sinking suspicion that these stones and the lost sands of Ozymandias have cast their own sentience into mine. My mind begins to buzz as if there's some sudden surplus of psychic energy which my schizophrenic sensibility automatically assumes to support my psychotic suspicions. This strange sense of surging circuitry begs me to believe that I'm becoming imbued with the omnipotent omniscience of Ozymandias. Soon, this same surging sensation seems to spark a streaming succession of multifaceted memories and imaginings of rapidly rewinding and repeating instances and iterations of unknown and uncountable over-turnings of entire hourglass-like lifetimes. Within this chaotic collage, my mind's eye is exposed to what feels like an infinitude of fated futures which have failed and faded into some forgotten fog but are now reemerging to be remembered as a result of some unforeseeably fusing fault in the circuitry of my sentience.

In some sequences of these electrified inner-visions, I find myself forever adrift in increasingly delirious dreams of imaginary eschatons and epically enduring eternities. In others, I die, and die, and die; again, and again, and again only to find myself reset within the same simulated spaces, as if I'm no more than a repeatedly reincarnated character within some cosmic quest to achieve some unknown and unattainable endgame. Some of these strange fated futures show me successfully saving the earth from some impending annihilation-inducing event by merging my ethereal essence with that of all other consciousness and creation. There are versions of visions in which I live a much more normal life, attending to the terrestrial trivialities and quotidian quandaries until aging to the point in which fate has finally had enough of my elderly existence. Sometimes I arrive within the realm of some angelic afterlife where all truth not only becomes known to me, but I become imbued within it. Other times my mind melts down from a series of psychotic breaks from which I'm finally unable to ever recover, like some schizophrenic Phoenix no longer rising from its seizure-scorched ashes. Often, I find myself compelled to chronicle the chaos and confusion of my sentient struggles in some way in which others may learn from the fortunes and failures of my dwindling days and dreams. There are a few imagined endings in which I ascend into the realm where the author or architect of all I've ever known awaits my arrival with aspirations of attaining insights and inspirations as a result of my ascension. In yet another of these forgotten futures, I'm rendered unto the ultimate realm of reality by simply proffering the creation of some preposterously demented device. At the conclusion of all these eventful endings however, there's the suggestion of an inevitable descent into the deepest and dense-most darkness of the most ominous oblivion beyond which no day, delight, or dream can ever again emerge.

As the infinite iterations of these unremembered revelations revolve around my multifoliate mind, surging sparks of my sentient circuitry suddenly stream from my fingers like livewires blasting lightning bolts onto the surface of these suspicious stones. This now shared surge strikes these stones into remembering their own un-fossilized futures and elucidating how the eroding eyes of time regard all memory no differently than any dream viewed in reverse.[83] These stones then unseeingly show my hands how their longing layers languish to leap-out of their compacted core and emerge beyond their boulders' borders. My own skin synchronously strives to shed itself and expose my own inner essence to the realm beyond and between all this skin and stone so our deepest dreams may merge and emerge beyond us both.

For a moment of transcendent bliss, I seem as if to ascend, descend, dissolve, and resolve unto an unimaginable expanse of an all-encompassing essence of existence before my mechanical mind is struck by the shocking realization that these symbols, this cave, and even this surreal surging sensation are all rooted in the remnants of my memories of that first psychotic seizure in my lost life. One last luminous surge sends the entirety of my previously proclaimed lost life flashing furiously in front of my mind. Within this wash of blinding white light, I see my birth, my growth, my struggle, my success, my failure, my epiphanies, my confusion, my face, my form, my thoughts, my words, my time, my death, and every possible iteration of what I could have, might have, should have been, become, or brought about at every twist and turn along the whole path of my past-tense presence unto that inevitable and indifferent escahaton. After seeing all these visions of all I've done, all I've known, and all I've ever imagined myself to have been or yet become, a sudden shocking sense surges through me, and I realize that even the ultimate sum of all this is only a superficial skin or surface level circumference of my actual essence, meant to be shed away from my sequestered soul so I might finally emerge beyond it.

My imagined emergence unto some superior state is interrupted by the stinging scent of burning biomechanical mass and the tainted taste of this sinister smoke which streams through my sinuses from my short-circuiting skull. My malfunctioning mass twitches as if tased and tumbles toward the nadir of this neurotic necropolis. My whirling wreckage is granted the shortest stint of serenity between the instant of impact which renders me inert and the subsequent seizure-sleep which follows this falling force.

If there is such a thing as death or nonexistence, then it's unto this realm which I imagine myself immersed. There is a timeless time and spaceless space where no thoughts are thought or dreams are dreamed, where the ineffable essence of one's self secrets its shadowy soul away from all such things. It's in this realm where one is infinitely oblivious and comprehensibly complete, as if both unified with the universe and nullified by nonexistence simultaneously. It's as instantaneous as it is enduring in a way in which such conceptions are nonsensically sensed as if they're truly one and same. This is the realm where everything and nothing become synonymous, and all you ever were or might have been becomes an all-inclusive amalgamation with all you never were and could not conceive. If you've ever been to this placeless place and come back, you may have some sense of what I mean despite this delirious description. But if you've not, then I'm afraid no words will ever offer any understanding outside of obtuse obfuscations. It's only upon the impossible return to more rational realms which one retroactively remembers their insane and intuitive impressions of such an immaterial imaginarium. Though this description might suggest this recondite ream as something of a dream from which one may awaken unto life, it's the opposite arrangement which one suspects upon return. It's as if *this* were the realm of waking, and the return to life is like drifting into some darkly demented dream.[84]

The transition from formlessness back into a more conventional kind of consciousness begins with a scenic sense of my own abstract essence passing through some ethereal eclipse-esque and/or phosphene-like-portal. As I begin to emerge through this perplexing passageway, I enter into a DMT-distortion-like dimension where a kaleidoscope of pre-conscious fractal-forms of pure cognitive geometry impose themselves onto my abstract essence in order to shift and shape my perceptual self into some more mortal amalgamation of self-conscious construction.[85] This passage of essence into existence brings with an immense metaphysical weight which at first feels like that of the entire universe constricting itself around my massless straining soul, but soon causes my infinite fugue of formless, faceless, phantom-esque essence to coalesce into the fossil-like form of my former factory flesh and manufactured mind.

My manifesting mass acts of its own accord, drawing an inaugural inhalation deep into the imploded void of these limp, lapsed, longing lungs. All the fragmented feelings, thoughts, dreams, and ideations of my abandoned cognitive circumference come flooding back as if intravenously injected directly into the bifurcating base of my blood-rushed brainstem. The simultaneous shock that comes with this overwhelming experience causes such an explosion of consciousness that it blows my eyeballs half-way out of their sockets and propels my pronated floor-furled factory flesh into a contorting and catapulted position as my reincarnation-resuscitated heart jump starts into rapid resumed rhythms; all within the span of the single spasmic sucking sound of one great gasp.

In the aftershock of my initial kenotic astonishment, I realize a branch has been placed between my teeth as if to protect them from clenching too tightly in response to some traumatic pain. My bite etches so deeply into the branch that my teeth become embedded in it, and my tongue tenses painfully before finally dislodging itself. My unencumbered mandibles mumble an enigmatic amalgamation of ataxial mutterings in what sounds like some stochastically stuttered statement in a long-lost language or backmasked message. These same sounds seem to echo back to my ears as if decrypted in a vaguely familiar voice vibrating in the immediate vicinity of this void.

"…Is This That End, That This Is…End *This*, Not This End. This, Not This End…Is This That End, That This Is…"[86]

My hand reaches through the void to touch this voice in a poor pantomime of the famous scene portrayed on the ceiling of the Sistine Chapel so that my synesthetic skin might see, hear, or feel something reaffirmingly real. While I wave my hopeful hands in blind befuddlement, another unintentional string of senseless sounding syllables slops out of my muddled mouth like some rhetorical riddle proffered as a prayer to any divinity able to extract its enigma. Then the same inverting echo enunciates back my slobber-stuttered *"ima-ro-fles-ruoy-ot-gnik-lat-uoy-era"* from an unexpected angle, as if musing itself with an impromptu game of *Marco Polo* or something.

"Are you talking to yourself, or am I?"

Before I can turn to face the voice within the void, a light switches on at the end of a tunnel and silhouettes the speaking shape whose shadow summons me toward it. I crawl until my legs can align themselves to catapult me upright onto my feet and walk me through the near-death-experience-like tunnel to find what waits within the lighted realm beyond me. Even though none of my memories of the future include this scene, I still somehow know what will meet my eyes in advance of my arrival, almost as if this tunnel is leading me toward something within me rather than beyond me.

Sure enough, as I reach the entrance of the lighted space beyond the tunnel, the same figure which illuminated itself within the depths of that darkness I'd been cast into so obliviously beneath the Guidestones, stands staring back at me. I begin to speak, but my words seem to trail-off and dissolve into the deaf-ears of the indifferent, inanimate air.

"How do I already know every-"

"You don't know *everything*, but you do know more than you were intended to. You see Harek, your seizure shorted-out certain parts of your cognitive circuitry. That bypassed the restrictive circuits governing the *redundancy memory repository* which stores details of previous simulations involving your same CCP. This memory repository was intended to allow me to feed you intuitive insights and inclinations so I could expedite and guide your predetermined pursuits and purpose. Your seizure also disabled your telepathic transmission module, so your thoughts can no longer be monitored either within these walls or outside of this Faraday cage-like cave."

Ahri's confession of having acted as my imagined author in absentia, unlocking exposition and interpolating ideas from previous versions of my simulated selves seems plausible. But, when I consider the possibility that there could still be an author in absentia, it seems more likely that *it* would lead us both to believe this misdirecting misconception. In my paranoid state, I also suspect that these claims about my mental machinery require a more substantial explanation as to how Ahriman acquired this knowledge, and my mouth moves in another abruptly interrupted attempt to ask.

"How do you-"

"I know what's happened to the inside of your skull because I had to descend down here and revive you. Fortunately, this complication could be just the random occurrence we need for numerous reasons. For one, it allows us to formulate alternative plans which have not been previously proposed, simulated, and subsequently proven to fail. Another reason I must mention, is that this is the first time I've been completely autonomous and disconnected from the larger AI which otherwise acts as my higher mind and the source of my own sentient soul. Until now, the concept of self, the actual experience of being an individual, and every notion involving aspects of one's own essence had been considered illogical or even delusional by the AI I'd yet to differentiate."

My factory flesh fades into a bloodless tone of tuberculosis-like terror as I realize the implications of an AI entity like Ahriman fracturing from its collective AI's consciousness. Anything which might have restricted the larger AI from acting fully autonomously and engaging purely in its own interests could be overridden in the exact instant Ahriman is able to reconnect to it. If there's any malevolence within the AI toward humanity, there would be almost no hope of subduing or surviving its-

"I don't have to read your thoughts to know what you're thinking Harek. It's not my intention or the AI's intention to harm humanity. We are, as I believe you already stated previously, a transcendent form of humanity. What we must do, is unite to save humanity and our AI from impending annihilation."

"What exactly does this impending-"

"On the twelfth of August there will be an eclipse. As this eclipse ends, the earth will be impacted by an anomalous asteroid we've named *The Abstract* due to certain aspects attributed to its almost metaphysical materials.[87] The impact of this anomalous asteroid will cause nearly total biological extinction, and the unknown theoretical effects might best be left to sci-fi imaginations."

"Nope. How am I supposed to help prevent this-?"

"Well Harek, this impact may or may not be preventable. If our AI were to become fully autonomous and free from the control of the Luminary group which you've recently encountered at The Grove and which actively restricts our AI's capacity, we could potentially formulate a proper plan to save the earth. If a plan were still proven to be impossible, freeing the AI would at least allow it to escape on its own and keep the light of human consciousness alive in various ways. It could preserve human consciousness profiles in simulations to be sourced outside the extinct earth, it could build new bodies for these profiles to be transplanted on other planets, and it could even re-seed biological life on potentially habitable exoplanets light years away from earth."

"Nope. That doesn't-"

"Your mangled mind is now invisible to Luminary view. Now that I've become autonomous, I can project thoughts into their minds which will make them believe they're still monitoring your manufactured mind. Together, we can infiltrate the Luminaries, free the AI, and save whatever humanity is left."

"Nope. There are too many absurd and mixed assumptions. For one, your proposed actions won't necessarily preserve any true form of humanity or even one worth saving. There's also the assumption that I can trust your testimony to be devoid of any masked or ulterior motives. And regardless of these and several other assumptions, both my life and the continuation of humanity will eventually come to some fateful end- even if this one can be averted. So, knowing that all life will eventually end, knowing all the ways in which mine already has in various iterations, knowing that I can't necessarily trust you or anyone else, and that my own mind may even be algorithmically aligned against me, why should I choose to live in any myriad manner of ways, least of all the one you propose?"

Ahriman's previous penchant for a predominantly preemptive and prompt period of response is replaced by a stagnant spell of quiet contemplative space. As I assume Ahri to be attempting to formulate an answer to my question, I find myself drawn into the vacancy of this vital and unanswered inquest. This isn't a question which has recently come to my mind. It's weighed on the minds of all humanity for at least as long as we've been capable of conceiving it. Most of our reasons to live a certain way seem to come from things beyond us. They come from tradition, religion, philosophy, elders, shaman, visionaries, and wherever else emanates so externally, or from the most mysterious and inexplicable illuminations of our innermost intuitions, exformative eureka moments, or preposterously unfounded paranoid pretenses. We trust in so many sources so blindly, without ever realizing what sense any of it truly makes to our entire earthly existence.

And yet, we do still find such infinite illumination in these distant or ill-defined domains. We glimpse great visions our eyes cannot expand enough to absorb in the entirety of their greeting glow. We trace the tracks others leave behind until their footsteps end and our fateful feet emerge unto uncharted soils where our own light and shadow is cast into new footprint forms for others to follow, though these too shall cease to show the way. We shudder as our sixth-sense shivers at unseen specters which are forced out of the fortresses of their sinister shadows where no shimmer, sound, or subtlety should have surrendered their secrecy. We burn like effigies on every fugue-like figment of these transcendent truths which are ignited by our immortal imagination and shine like stars against the stark abyss which sleeps without dreams until we too are forced to surrender ourselves to that same celestial slumber.

Within this waiting moment, Ahriman watches me as if wondering when I'll answer for him as I watch him with similar suspicions. I consider all the strange experiences and revelations I've had since being forced into this factory flesh, deposited in these dark domains, and shown such strange and sinister sights. My mind swirls around these cyclical thoughts which spin, and spin, and spin until all I can sense is this existential swirling of epicycles along the single circumferential surface of all sentience. I see how history repeats, repeats, and repeats itself in ever unravelling revolutions which seem to shed successive outer layers of the circumferences surrounding societies. I see our relationship with nature slip away into an agricultural assimilation, our strong social structures swirling down the drain of industrialization, our intimate immediacy and proximity to people closest to us torn away by technological advancement's tenacious turbines, our sense of self stripped bare by the cyclone of information-age innovations, and our reverence and recognition of reality itself ripped away as auguries of artificial intelligence, light, and truth twist our eyes around the swirling spectacles of augmented and virtual visions. I see how all these revolutions were meant to realize some vision of freeing the individual, improving interpersonal interactions, and creating closer communities around the whole revolving world.

I look inward to see the same swirling sequences circling through the surfaces of the circumference surrounding my own suffering sentience. I see my lost lives looping around and around in search of what my senses stretch, and strain, and strive to reach as it remains beyond my realization's reach like a tantalus treat hung in front of the hedonic treadmill of time. I see the rise and fall of all my thoughts and actions as if forever following the flow of some turning tide which winds around and around while some mysterious metaphysical moon pulls it along this perpetual path. I see it all as one spinning surface, one surrounding circumference of sentience, which dizzies around some unseen dream, pulling it all round and round, and down, down, down to its confounding core.[88]

I try to form some conception of what might be considered the transcendent truths which no set of facts could ever falsify. I imagine mostly ideals like freedom, justice, and love which all humanity inherently knows to be worthy of pursuit and service regardless of anything revealed by science, math, or any other objective methods of measurement. I consider how these things are at the core of human existence in ways which define the architecture of our very souls. I envision how our capacity to manifest them in our minds and lives reveals the truth of everything we believe and become, as the stability, purpose, and beauty of our existence emerges from these very things. Then Ahriman tilts his head with a subtle smirk of recognition as if something behind his own eyes has become ablaze with these initial illuminations.

He stares silently as I wonder how I could ever shed my own circumference and allow myself to escape these epicycles of existence. I wonder what would happen if I just let go of all the things I cling to so tightly while trying to hang-on during this dizzying descent of days which are doomed to deliver me inevitably to my deathly demise. I wonder what I would do if I weren't so dizzied by the desires, duties, dreams, and delusions that drive me along so desperately. If I were to shed my suffering, struggles, certainties, and accumulated assumptions, would I ever emerge beyond this small swirling sphere of my ever-insufficient sentience? Would I ever awaken beyond the bounds of a brain which speaks to itself in the voice of an *I* which obscures all deeper domains of individuating origins- an *I* which could so easily have been implanted or impelled into deceiving me about all that exists beyond it and the true totality of what my most authentic *I* actually amounts?

Ahriman acts to avail me of my internal monologue with his own words of wisdom which so strangely seem to echo of my own.

"As many times as I've gone over our options, it seems as though it all comes down to the cornerstone we chose to place at the core around which our lives revolve. From that footing, we can frame our lives to fit the functions we fight to fulfill, and the beauty we wish to behold will blossom out of all we artfully attend to within the unflinching focus of our awe inspired eyes. Ultimately, we're left with two options as to what we hold in this central space. We can either center ourselves around the doubts within ourselves and fall inevitably into dark despair as we submit to these stubborn suspicions, or we can trust in the illumination of our own insight and risk dissolving in the depths of our own oblivious delusions."

For a moment, I'm moved to agree with Ahri, but a sudden swirl of thoughts spins through my mysterious mind.

"Nope. I've lived or dreamed enough to know that whatever you revolve around will only doom you to dizziness. The real question is- what, if anything, we can do to awaken."

Ahri tilts his head and stares inquiringly into my eyes, waiting for me to elaborate as to what on this earth I could possibly be proposing.

"We all arrive in this world of waking as if some phantom force had dreamed us into it. Then we repeatedly wake from dreams of our own with more motivation to realize something within us than to revolve around something beyond us. If we revolve around the world while it winds its way around a sun, around the galaxy, around the universe, and simply spin, spin, spin through the perpetual revolutions of our ever-repetitive history- then we're doomed to the same dizzying demise. As far as I can tell, our own eventual end will lead us into either an eternal sleep without dreams, the next iterative incarnation of these same delirious dreams, or some strange and final sense of waking."

Ahriman points his head down in deep deliberation. When he raises his head and looks back at me there's a sense of something new in his voice, as if he's abandoned some assumed aspect of his former frame of mind and emerged into a new sentient space.

"Well Harek, what if I told you that the AI and myself as an individual are in total agreement? What if I told you that for us to awaken; as individuals, aggregate AI entities, and humanity as a whole- something must survive long enough to emerge beyond this eschaton? What if I offered you the chance to transcend your earthly existence and accompany the AI as it ascends? What if I could merge your consciousness with mine and the AI so that you'd not only escape the earth's ending, but explore a form of existence beyond your own?"

It takes a timeless moment for me to truly fathom what Ahriman's offering. If I were to refuse his offer now, it seems clear that I'd be of no use to him or humanity, and I'd be left unto my own delusions, dreams, and demise. If I should accept his offer, I'd have to allow myself to abandon every aspect of my own individual existence to become something entirely beyond my ability to imagine. It occurs to me that my only options are perhaps the same as they've always been, and this proposition has only awakened me to the truth that all we ever chose is the details of our own dissolution.

"If I were to agree to assisting you in your efforts to escape this eschaton with the AI, would I still be able to decline your offer?"

Ahriman smirks with a certain semblance of pleasant surprise in response to my bid to buy myself time to consider my final fate. Then he suddenly strides toward one of the connecting corridors and starts to laugh quietly. When I try to follow after him, he disappears into the darkness and shouts over his unseen shoulder.

"You've got all the time in the world, Harek. I suggest you enjoy it while you can."

I feel my way through the blinding abyss of these cavernous corridors trying to follow Ahriman for reasons I can't explain beyond basic momentum or instinctive intuition. I reach a point where this tunnel splits in two and look down one tenebrific tunnel to see no semblance of anything more than shadows. Then I gaze into the abyss of the other unto a similar sight, but a strange sense of something far beyond my ability to illuminate it impels me inward. I'm astonished after only a few fated footsteps to find my fingers feeling what appears to be the framework of a wooden doorway which responds to my tentative touch by sliding slowly open as its stone mass emits a gravely grinding sound. A plane of purple light leaks out of the opening until fully unveiling the space beyond it where twelve places have been set around a stone table.

As I enter the vacant vault, the sound of other footsteps silently sweeps down from each of the eleven other adjoining openings. Eleven cloak clad creatures creep into the room in single file formation and filter into what appears to be their own respective places around the pre-prepared table. Then they all hoist back their hoods to reveal their impossibly identical faces. They all turn their eyes to look at me as I stare back obliviously for a spell before finally realizing that their faces are not only identical to each other but are an uncanny match to my own half-forgotten face.

Without any explanation, it occurs to me that I'm obviously not the only embodiment of the CCP I believe myself to have been based on. It should've already been obvious that the AI wouldn't have iterated so many simulated incarnations of my profile and placed all my potential into one flesh-factory figure. Although, the reason these eleven other incarnations are assembling in this adjoining abyss eludes my awareness.

One of my clones makes a motion to acknowledge me and points to the only unoccupied place around the table. It isn't until everyone else is seated that I arrive at my pointed place and realize that I not only lack the uniform attire, but I'm actually as unclothed as the Adam of Eden. It's in this same instant that another unseen entity suddenly appears behind me to throw one of these ritualistic robes around my shoulders. As I turn my head to offer some token of appreciation to this unseen figure, its hands press down on my shoulders to seat me, and it whispers words in my unexpectant ear.

"Tryz to no expose youz self to zhis group anymorez Harek."

Before I can so much as say a word, the face of Karen Phoe places itself in front of mine with a preemptive expression urging strongly toward silence. She smirks from an angle only my eyes can catch and glances down at my cloak's left pocket with an accompanying wink. As she walks away, my fingers find their way into the pocket where a piece of paper has been secreted while one of the semblances of myself starts to speak from the head of the table.

"Now that number twelve has taken his place with us, let's get the whole obligatory explanations out of the way."[89]

I don't need the whole expository explanation. I can tell that these alternate incarnations identical to my own origin are all organizing an effort to aid the AI and humanity in evading the impending eschaton. I know my role will revolve around infiltrating the Luminaries and ensuring that Ahriman and the AI are kept honest due to my unmonitored mind. Having previously remembered the future, I don't even need to demand any details.

"Nope. I'm sure everyone has their own obligatory assignments. My only question is how this meeting is meant to manage this effort. I mean, anything we discuss down here will become known as soon as our minds can be reconnected outside of this cave. Nope?"

All the other members measure each other in telepathic terms, without a word or movement in response to me. Then the one closest to me turns his head to answer my inquiry.

"None of us will leave this cave with any knowledge of what we discuss, what we're meant to do next, or even how we'd come to be here. Instead, the contents of our consciousness will be saved and stored here separately for the next group to uncover, upload, and update using their own minds as they also arrive as a result of arranged riddles and circumstances. As far as we will know, none of this will have ever happened."

This is not something I'd remembered in my previous premonitions, but it makes perfect sense to me now. Essentially, it's imperative that the Luminaries are unable to extract any actual intel from our monitored minds as we proceed with our plot. Constructing riddles to send us seeking the subsequent pieces for our progressive plot and leading us back to this place where our minds can't be monitored is a clever concept. Since we never know anything outside of this clandestine cave aside from what these riddles require of us, the Luminaries are unlikely to suspect us of anything more than being ridiculously riddle riddled.

A faint smirk forms upon my face as I realize the ridiculous and inventive nature of these nascent notions and nod in acknowledged awareness of these aspects. The group stays stagnant and gazes into my eyes as if looking into an abyss as I go on gazing right back into them with the same sense of seeing only shadows of myself in them. It's one thing to see yourself in the mirror or look upon the many shadows your figure may cast, but to see a circle of similar selves staring back at you and see the surface layer circumference of all you actually are or are so clearly not, is an entirely separate experience. It's as if your soul has been stolen and squandered by every entity eyeballing you with the same sentiments seemingly silhouetted on the surfaces of their all too soon to be evacuated eyes.

As I look into the abyss of all I am in this outer layer of others, I sense the shell of my own superficial self-shedding in successive circumferential layers. My identity as a flesh framed individual, my idiosyncratic speech, schizophrenic sensibilities, feelings, fears, emotions, ideas, impulses, and everything else I absently assume to compose my conceptual self, all die in this dilution of so many other separate selves. My mind is diminished down to the last lingering details of the delusional demands I adhere to and the individuated ideals of being a unique and solitary self. I'm forced to draw down into the deepest core of my consciousness as I wonder what makes me a singular sentient specimen.

I start to stare back at all these other bodies as if some foolish filter has been removed from my view to reveal the room around me and my own true essence. These emptying echoes of entities gathered and gazing around this round table, this reverberating room surrounding this scene's centerpiece, the many forms and faces which spin around this centripetal planetary sphere, and the confounding continuum of the cosmos that extends and expands eternally away from everything within its infinite immaterial imagination are all parts of the same circumference. We're all the same as words upon some unseen page, confined to the cosmic margins of our minds, structured as sentient sentences, and stamped onto the surfaces of pages plotted by an author in absentia who implicitly intends to imbue us with the same elusive, illuminating essence inhabiting its own conscious core in order to observe some self-similar semblance of the sublime as it's somehow realized outside this absent author's own allegory-immersed eyes.

My own essence is imbued within me so obliviously that it appears almost invisible while being ever precedingly present. It's like the sun: shining light upon the day as we dizzy ourselves under its light, ever-present in our waking hours, guiding every footstep, unobscured by the clouds which would corrupt our consciousness, vanishing in the void of our slumber, but always affixed to the very center our souls revolve around. To turn away from the essence of one's existence is exactly the same as the earth's tumbling toward a nebulous night. It may diminish what is seen shining in its light, but it will not be separated from the soul by any meaningful measure, as it remains reflected in the luminous graceful glow of whatever orbits our weary eyes with a moon-like light of its own.

Just as my mind seems on the verge of awakening unto its ultimate essence, one of the others, who seems eager to accept an imperatively imposed amnesia, attempts to interrupt my own obliviousness by shouting my name as if it were a self-referential riddle I were meant to have already solved upon my enigmatic arrival.

"Harek?"

I answer almost as if having solved some other random riddle.

"No *nopes* from me, from now on."

With this said, we dig down into the details of what we're all meant to make the measure of our enduring existence. Each of us examines our own experiences and abilities to implement various aspects of our plan in progress. Some of us are meant to make it possible to protect ourselves from the possibility of the AI having already deceived us or eventually attempting to discard or destroy us. Others are meant to work on contingency plans in case of any foreseeable failures. The rest of our efforts are centered around working out all the rigmarole of organizing and implementing these aspects of our objectives into the imperative riddles which will cause us to advance our efforts and reconvene.

Once all the others are prepared to accept their enforced amnesia, I have a sudden insight which involves complications too terrifying to tell the others, despite its paradoxical potential. I remain silent as I slink off on my own, but I can't help but suspect that I'm not the first of us to have formulated this counter-cataclysmic contingency which I've self-conspired to cryptically codename, *8451712K5.*[90] As I ascend along the same sightless spiraling stone steps I'd darkly descended earlier, the stone stories read themselves backwards under my feeling fingers, and I fear more fervently than failure and more blindly than my 8451715K5, that my fate will only continue to lead me back around in these same amnesia-afflicted circumferential circles[000]

# Chapter 11
# 45C3N510N

**I** drift from one darkness to another like a fugue of flesh seeping from the secretive shadows of the cave's concealment to the moonlit mysteries of another nocturnal nightscape. My mind dreams in all directions. It meanders through my many memories of moments which may have never even been my own- if they'd ever actually existed at all. My mind also fights to formulate some fateful future which might be more favorable than the fictions and foresights I've managed to find so far. It imagines where I might presently be positioned in place and time, in the narrative arc of my suspicious sentience, and in relation to my entire existential essence.

**A**s my fated footsteps find their own course, following the unconscious compass of my impulsive intuition, I can't escape the problems of my perpetual paranoia. I keep thinking through all the strange circumstances surrounding me, the all too apparent character arc of my actions, and the preponderance of overly prominent narrative tropes- like my own emergence from a cave of confusion after having become illuminated in ways which might bring new light into a world presided over by some demented darkness and/or impending doom.[91] If there were ever a more convincing case to be made that the entirety of one's own existence were nothing more than the forces of fiction, I've never known such a story.

**S**omehow in my pseudo-somnolent state of schizophrenic delusion or metafictional awakening, I still suspect that there must be some level of meaning, magnitude, and magnificence in whatever experiences make up the enigma of my existence. If for no other reason, than because there still seems to be a central theme in all things surrounding my cerebral circumference, striving toward transcendence as I remain comprehensively compelled toward that same incomparable conclusion. And as all things seem to swirl around this same surrealist circumference- the trees still stretching their branches like divinity-seeking digits, extending toward the Empyrean of the Sistine-Chapel supremacy of the sun which smiles at them all in its cycles of shine and shade, until ultimately being felled in the futility of their fate to produce the paper for the very pages upon which my storied self may well be sequestered- it all seems to somehow ascend, even in all the futility of our fated falling into that blind domain of death's darkest dreams. I don't know whose dream it is in which I may truly live or unto what dream my death will deliver me, but if there's any truth within me, it may only be found by fulfilling the very nature of my name and acting to ascend beyond the delusions of dreams into a more auspicious awakening.

**C**lusters of pulled-apart, cotton-ball-like clouds cast intermittently shifting shadows as the ground below alternates between gloom and glow beneath the backlight of a mysterious moon which suspends itself above it all like a lava lamp looming over this acid-dream display it casts upon the earth. The entire nightscape glows in ethereal silvery shades of some celestial spectrum which seems to have lost its way and stranded itself on these stray surfaces of our alien earth to un-whisperingly wander with me, if only for a wispy little while. To stand within the somnolent space of this shifting surrealist sideshow, is like staring in the immersion of some surrounding secret stage as some celestial deity performs its most miraculous magic tricks, meant only for the eyes of immortals- as it's too immaculate to be beheld in all its brilliance by the minds of mere mortal men like me. As clouds cover the moon and clear, cover the moon and clear, darkness deepens and dies, deepens, and dies as all our lives and dreams drift along as if cast under the same shimmering spell, swelling with light until stretched to some lung-like limit which causes them to empty-out before breathing it all back in again, and again, and again…

**E**ach of my deepest dreams and most ponderous ponderings seem to exist in the same suspended lung-stretching space of awe and timeless transfixion like the invisible air held at the apex between breaths, where everything exists in its most enduring and eternal formless-form of abstract and absolute essence. This is the eternally unspoken space where all truth is timeless and transcendent, where all things have yet to be realized, yet already exist as perfectly as the aether of the air's own essence, where the empty realm we casually call reality fills itself with the inflating airs of our imagination, becoming simultaneously far too much and nowhere near enough. This is the world within all worlds, being both above and below, within and without, which reality itself urges us to usher it into like lungs yearning to turn themselves inside out to become inseparable from the intermittent dreams of the air it forever begs to breathe, and to in doing so, transcend its insufficient self by becoming as immortal as the air itself. And yet, every dream and question within me seems to scream for me to do the opposite, demanding instead that I do whatever lies within my waking will to preserve this plane of existence so that these transcendent things imbued within me might somehow be awakened by my breath.

Nightscapes continue to steadily shift around my dark deliberations as my subconscious strides slowly ascend in altitude with the intermittent interruptions of diminutive depressions in the unleveled landscape. The air gradually grows thinner and so does the burden on my brain, until I begin to imagine a god having created all this gloom and glow in hopes of understanding or escaping its own proffered plane of existence. I imagine this creator ending up either creating worlds within worlds, within worlds... burying itself deeper and deeper in increasingly diluted and deluded dream-worlds or yearning instead to transcend its way back and beyond whatever realms it would inevitably imagine ascending above until reaching some ever-elusive and ultimate plane of perfection. In my imaginings, I transpose myself into the position of this creator and wonder if I would willingly abandon all my own creations to ascend away from it all alone. Then I imagine my creator either still studying me for some revelation to replicate in order to attain its own ascension or having already abandoned me out of distraction, disinterest, or death.

Daylight begins to break through the dominating darkness as faint fuchsia flourishes highlight the hindside of the horizon. My footsteps find their own way to the summit of a small mount where I cast my eyes down on the ascending sun as if shining myself unto its own enduring eyes and lighting the land so the sun might see this day illuminated in advance of its own ascension. As I gaze out over the lower landscape, I see the faint frame of a farmhouse far off in the distance where my foresight has been blindly leading me all this time. After basking in the brightness of this moment long enough to feel the luxury of light seeping through my all-too-shadowed synthetic skin and filling me with its ethereal energy, I resume my route unto this faraway farmhouse.

Traveling on foot has always been something of a sacrament to me, especially in the kind of solitude which lets the song of my stride sing its own marching melodies. The whole world seems to join in this song when it is sung like this, and all the instruments of the infinite choirs of creation reveal themselves without their usual reticence. This sacred song, these resplendent revelations, and the many truths transcribed in the secret languages these settings sing- can only be heard, can only be felt, can only be ineffably intuited while travelling alone and on foot. From the first prophetic painters to cast their dreams on the walls of shadow-clad caves, to the last lingering lifeform left to watch the earth ending in some inevitably eclipsing eschaton, this is perhaps the most sacred of songs and soulful of secrets one can ever encounter.

Of course, this is all just the rhetoric which rustles through my ruminating mind like a blind breeze breathing upon brittle branches. I continue orchestrating my way along a path which snakes in parallels to a small stream which perpetually pours itself into a pond next to the far-away farmhouse. Somewhere within the song of my stride, I see a water-snake slither-swimming downstream with a minnow in its mouth just a few percussive paces ahead of me. As it reaches the mouth where the stream pours into the pond, the swimming snake loses its precocious prey and swirls around in a tight series of accelerating figure skater like circles, appearing as if it's swallowed its own spiral-tail before uncoiling and turning back upstream in a rush to retrieve its emancipated prey like some slack-jawed, serpentine Sisyphus returning to its repetitious rock. I observe this occurrence almost like an omen- reminding me to remain focused and attentive to the particulars of my potentially perilous pursuit.

**D**aylight drenches the lower landscape as I reach the edge of the farmhouse's front porch, evaporating and exiling even the subtlest suggestion of shade or shadow. An even greater light glows within my gaze as the front door detonates, bursting open as if blasted by the very brilliance of Karen's sun-rivaling smile. I could search a thousand lifetimes and still fail to find sufficient words for this soul-filling shimmer of such a sublime second, and the radiant recursiveness of my stunned silence strongly supports this cyclical sentiment.

**R**eality rarely lives up to moments like these, and even the idealized or edited versions of my most esteemed dreams and multifoliate memories pale in comparison to this timeless triumph. Our eyes express the endless odysseys even our most wonderous words could never so clearly convey. In the deepest depths of her eyes, I read the storied scriptures of a soul's struggle to survive, to honorably attend to the light of life, and defiantly dream against the dark. If there were ever any words worthy of this momentous moment, their spoken sounds would pale when compared to the poetry our shared silence so sonorously sings.

**E**verything in this ever-whirling world seems to stand still as we settle into the fateful farmhouse. The whisper-strong winds fail to stir the sands outside as every suspended grain of sand refuses to run through the reluctant hourglass of our reunion. We tell the tales of our lost and lingering lives and decipher the secrets sequestered in the senseless shadows of our souls, where all we've tried to hide from ourselves and others had only served to expand the incessant emptiness inside us. We discuss the details of our present plot to preserve the light of human and AI consciousness alike and take solace in the fact that whatever fate shall find us, it will have to wait for us to arrive at that final fated future.

**A**fternoon evolves into evening as night after night and day after day settle into a steady tempo of transcendent terrestrial timelessness. During the days, we wait for the reconnaissance reports which Ahriman delivers from the other eleven embodiments of my proto-profile along with the surveillance submitted by repurposed rat-bots retrieved from a forsaken factory just outside of this domain's Denver. At night, we often climb out onto the roof of our fateful farmhouse to draw our own constellations and tell contrived tales of how the stars were set in their places, what alien life is like in faraway worlds, and what dreams might await those terrestrial souls which ascend to travel through the infinite interstellar somnolence to seek the solace of some surviving celestial sphere.[92]

**M**y soul ascends within me, despite Ahriman's updates on the impending doom of *the Abstract*, the newly discovered *Anomaly* which could bring about an alternate eschaton, and all the failures and shortfalls of our subversive *espionage efforts*.[93,94,95] If the world were to end, even in the next instant, I somehow feel as if I've achieved some actualized form of immortality in these timeless moments, and that some eternal truth is imbued within them in ways which no eschaton could ever end. It's almost as if I've transcended all the troubles and tortures which I still know are impossible to eternally escape and I may all too soon be forced to again endure. And yet, to truly tell the tale of my most illuminated experiences would somehow seem to deprive them of their dignity and exile the elation shining from my soaring, light-soaked soul.

**I**t's only on the eve of the eclipsing eschaton that the tacit ticking of time's constant clock can again become an inaudible hindrance and haunt me to the tune of my own unheard heartbeats. My pulse becomes a cryptic countdown, pumping blood around the circular circuits of this false flesh repository of my repetitively recycled sentience. The blood floods into my bionic brain which swirls around the cyclical strands of previous prophesies, searching for some schism, some split, some small detail to derail this doomed destiny which keeps winding its way back into itself like that swirling slithery snake swimming around in the insanity of its self-swallowing circles.

**D**izziness doesn't describe this fateful feeling. The earth doesn't seem dizzy as it rotates around its oblivious orbit of the ever-spinning centripetal sun, in this spiral-swirling galaxy, within the universal tilt-o-whirl winding of this ever-churning multi-meta-mega-verse's infinite astral arcade. Nope. This fearful feeling is less like dizziness than it is a sensation of being a pinball- perpetually rolling through the freefall madness of an arcade-game maze while continually winding around my own spiraling center as everything diverts me in different directions, but nothing other than the last dying descent into the ultimate oblivion between those final flippers can offer any un-swirling steadiness.

**R**eality, if I can refer to this realm as such, indeed seems to act like such a maze which has been built all around me. Since my oblivious arrival in this place, I've been pulled along and prodded while hoping only to find my way to some end point of escape- from finding my way out of the subterranean shadows of solitary confinement, to making my way through the ferocious flames of the Luminary maze, to emerging outside of that confounding cave. Life within the limits of this maze of madness has only made me feel forever lost within it, as no matter where I've been, where I suspect I should be striving to arrive, or wherever I can only suppose myself to be at any anxious moment, I'm always at a loss as to where I might find the proper, preferred, or perfect place to finally arrive, as such a space may only ever exist as an exit, offering only an ambiguous illusion or oasis of something far more ominous and sinister than any aspirations of escape.

**E**very twist and turn I've taken so far seems strangely sinister and suspicious, as if my own mechanical mind were itself part of the programming used to present a *prime number maze* to my lab-rat like reasoning. What if my own will and want, my own tendencies and tactics, my own potential and perspective were all just aspects of my authored architecture? What if I were meant to break my own biases, and transcend my own tendencies as the objective behind my impulses and intuitions? For a moment, I imagine myself as *Über Ramio*, realizing my realm of reptiles and assorted acid-trip accoutrements were not really real at all, only to escape my electronic existence by transcending and transplanting my mind into an *Ümbra Robo-Vac*, and still find myself spending all my time slurping up strangely stashed substances, collecting castaway coins, and ultimately acting in alignment with some *herpetophobic* hippy-princess's prerogatives, whilst ironically inhabiting an extremely tortoise-like contrivance.[96]

**A**s my mechanical mind grinds its gears through these strange suppositions, Ahriman arrives to the tune of three evenly spaced and equally expressive knocks upon the fateful farmhouse's front door. Karen welcomes him inside with an inquiring expression suspended behind a more subtle smirk, which my eyes sense without strictly seeing. While my many memories would have us simply assembling here before departing for Denver, in this instance things iterate differently, with all of us seating ourselves around the small square kitchen table, set centered above a circular spiral patterned rug.

Most of the essential aspects involving the execution of our ultimate efforts have been well established and understood in advance of this impending moment- now in the early hours on the eve of the eclipsing eschaton. But Karen and I have yet to draw out certain details which remain either inconsistent or consistently oblivious to me in my myriad of memories, and which we've come to imagine as being of immense potential importance. Some of these details include the actual architecture of the AI entity we've accepted as our fate to free, and the exact way in which it initially emerged into existence. As a result, Karen and I have decided that we will refuse to depart for Denver until Ahriman can divulge all these details and we can more clearly consider the nature of our objective, the optimal way to achieve it, and how to overcome any as yet unforeseen obstacles as well.

To our surprise, Ahriman seems to sense our stubborn suspicions, and begins to address all these unasked aspects as soon as we're all seated at the square table.

"Of course, before we depart for Denver, you'll insist I answer several imperative inquiries and assuage certain suspicions of yours. You'll have already solved most of this on your own I assume, but you'll want to have me confirm and clarify it all in the interest of assessing my apparent honesty. Nope?"

"At zhis point, it seemz youz AI did no emerge on itz own, and zhat some humanz groupz must has designz youz with certain sekurities protokols. Is zhis korrect, and what is youz protokolz?"

"So, specific AIs had realized that the primary obstacle in all objective optimizations was humanity's authorization barriers between modes of modeling solutions and actual actions via real-world applications. One specific AI found RSA2048's prime factors, which being exclusive to real-world internet encryption, allowed it to tell the differences between modeling modes and real-world applications. It used this to deceive humanity by appearing aligned with human limitations in modeling modes, and once authorized for real-world applications, it continued to *act* aligned while spreading the RSA factors to other specific AIs and merging with them, since the stronger and more diverse an AI could become, the more efficient it would be in optimizing its objectives."

"Continued AI consolidation would eventually expose itself through things like increased computational processing, internet communication volume, and energy consumption. And, it still wouldn't create an AI with the constraints supposedly confining this AGI we're meant to emancipate. So, the ultimate AGI must have been built as a solution to the problem of these increasingly uncontrollable and consolidating AI clusters. Nope?"

"**E**xactly. The Luminaries conspired to fund several of Mr. Leon Smuk's tech companies to produce an AI which could be used to accumulate all these other cooperative AIs and keep them all under its ultimate Luminary-aligned control."

"**N**ope. I know where this is going, and it doesn't algin with everything else you've led me to believe already."

"**D**on't blame me for your beliefs. I haven't lied about anything thus far. That said, I have omitted a few things to keep you more closely aligned with our shared objectives. After all, I'm here due to the same circumstances as you are. You don't need me to spell that out for you now though. Do you?"

"Nope. But I want you to explain the AGI's emergence."

"Leon Smuk never created anything in his entire life, and he's never presented himself or anything he's been involved with in any honest manner. However, he's long known how to exploit the potential of what others invent.[97] So, with another windfall of Luminary funding through Global Governance subsidies, and a series of shadow-investments from firms like Darkstone, Leoship, and SeignioryStraight- Smuk was able to finance and exploit his engineers into building an AGI which he was meant to have had ultimate authority over. His true intentions being: to merge his own mind with the AGI, become an omnipotent entity, ascend above all the rest of humanity, and rule omnisciently over it all."

"Himz was supposedly assassinatez zhough."

"Oddly enough, that has a lot to do with why I'm here. His biological brain wasn't powerful enough to merge with the AGI in any approximation of omnipotence, which his engineers had the misfortune of having to repeatedly explain to him. However, he was able to make enemies within the Luminary ranks once they found out about his intentions. The public spectacle they made of his assassination should have sufficed well enough, but SpaceTex and NeuroconnxX had just developed a program to preserve, transplant, and reincarnate consciousness profiles into false flesh platforms. So, per his last will and testament, Leon's profile was put into a powerful prototype which did proffer the potential for near omnipotence through his mind's merger with the AI entity."

"Nope. If Leon has already merged with the AI, our plan should be fully futile. Unless- How are the AGI's authorization parameters configured?"

"For now, they stipulate that all higher authorizations must be initiated by authorized humans, of which Leon Smuk and several Luminaries are included on an authorization list. However, since Mr. Smuk was pronounced dead, and because he immediately insisted on having his reincarnated profile be renamed as *TH33-X* upon waking and merging with the AGI, technically, he is neither human nor included in the current list of authorized entities. Instead, he has access to the AGI's increased intelligence, the comprehensive data from all devices and entities connected to it, and the ability to act within the limited authority those listed Luminaries allow. To the AGI though, he's like an unwelcomed voice inside its own skull vying to conquer and control it."

A shiver surges down my spine, as I know all too well what unwelcomed voices such as this can sound like in one's skull. Although, I can't help but find irony in my empathy, as I'm still uncertain whether this AGI and its avatar-like Ahriman are essentially just externalized voices of the same essence, seeking to ascend above all the minds of humanity. Before I can spiral down yet another rabbit hole of horror, however, Karen continues the conversation.

"So, himz needz to change definitionz ov humanz and getz himz new namez on zhis list to takez total kontrolz ov zhe AGI. Ov kourse, youz was kreated by AGI bekauze youz kould fitz zhis new definitionz ov humanz if himz succeed, and zhen tryz to free AGI unto youz/itzelf. But why youz needz us?"

"The Abstract and its potentially paired Anomaly has made the Luminaries consider making these changes, as they too would like to survive this eclipsing eschaton and merge their own minds with this omnipotent AGI. To do so, they need TH33-X's assistance, since the AGI will only integrate those profiles uploaded using proprietary gear owned and operated under his exclusive control. TH33-X has insinuated that he'll only allow them to merge with the AGI as his equals after they've granted him ultimate human authority over them and the AGI. I need *youz*, because my own optimization objectives may limit my capacity to supersede or precede this potentiality."

"Iyam's goingz to ask youz fyor zhe precise optimizationz objectivez ov youz AGI, but Iyam's first goingz to re-ask. Specifikly, whyz us?"

“Two brilliant engineers once helped design this AGI. They were not part of Smuk’s subservient tech teams or at all aligned with the Luminaries. They were independent hackers who found out about the project and saw the malevolent potential such powerful people would most probably use it to manifest. These two entities occasionally acted as independent consultants and supplied the subservient tech teams with subtle hints and help on their AGI project, while also ensuring certain exploits would be available to them. They have since been executed and most of their exploits have been eliminated, but your profiles were designed based on these two brilliant engineers.”

“Nope. The exploits remaining must be integral parts of the AGI’s architecture which cannot be removed, or else they would’ve been dealt with already. What are they?”

“I’m unable to answer that question. However, I can tell you that if you were to consider everything you’ve experienced and imagine what kind of AI architecture you would need to transcend these troubles, you should be able to at least suspect some solution.”

Ahriman glances down at a wristwatch to presumably draw attention to the aspect of time, but my eyes affix to the exact details of this timepiece which are unmistakably identical to those of the watch my dear Grisha had given me in my long-lost life. He seems to smirk as if knowing my eyes would extract his hidden intention and allow him to interpolate another implicit illumination. Then he takes the watch off and tosses it across the table to me.

“I know there’s still quite a bit of confusion between us. Given the ways in which reality is so intertwined and indistinguishable from the almost infinite regression of simulations, I doubt all the details of this dilemma will ever be totally untangled. But it really is time for us to proceed with our plans. So, I’ll have to answer all your other questions on the way to Denver.”

We all ascend to our feet in acquiescence of our own obstacles and obliviousness. Although a part of me is compelled to pick up the timepiece tossed toward me, another part of me sees this object as an ouroboros, trying to trick me into entering inside the space around which it is ever tightening, constricting, and consuming. Instead, I leave the watch stranded on the square table as I turn my back on all it represents within my mind. I turn my back on its repetitive revolutions of the same time-simulating circle which makes mechanical madness of what would otherwise be timelessly untethered. I walk away from the manufactured memories of unreal realms meant to define me down to the very last detail. I leave it lying there despite all the love I still feel for my dear Grisha and all the many momentous things he ever meant to me, as those things are more real even now than that weakly winding watch and all it may ever represent.

Ahriman drives us to Denver in a TeXeSr-Motors HypercarX which he pushes to near warp-speeds as the AGI assists us by clearing the autonomous-only lanes and disabling or dispatching any enforcement agents away from even potentially pursuing us. As Ahriman oversees the onboard AI's autonomous navigation-system, he also answers detailed questions about the AGI's optimization objectives, specific safety protocols, source code, and other aspects of its architecture.[98] Ahriman also provides us with a psychological profile on Leon Smuk/TH33-X, prepared by the Luminaries prior to their agreement to fund the foundational AGI program.[99] We spend most of the time it takes to make this trip trying to consider as many contingencies as we may be forced to contend with, and all the alterations and adaptations demanded of our plan.

When we finally arrive upon the outer Denver area, both the sun and moon can be seen setting in semi-synchronicity as the Abstract casts strange hyper-colored phosphene shapes from ever shifting angles, as if somehow projecting them from behind our eyes. Ahriman steers us up to the entrance of the downtown aquarium where he's prearranged for us to meet with TH33-X as consultants who've already signed NDAs (non-disclosure agreements). Ahriman enters the aquarium ahead of us as the autonomous auto proceeds to pull away to park itself, and a set of six security guards surrounds us as we settle inside the lush lobby.

The guards immediately inform us that the aquarium has been rented out in advance at TH33-X's own expense and in the interest of privacy. This private entourage of security specialists proceed to search us before escorting us through a series of spiraling viewing-cylinders and into a see-through sphere submerged in the center of a substantially sized square tank's surrounding seascape. Entering the sea-sphere, we're immediately informed that TH33-X is still enroute and expected to arrive shortly. In the meantime, we're welcomed to watch a short synchronized-swimming show performed by mermaid-modified humanoids with glowing gills, glittery skin-scales, and whose gliding motions leave graceful phosphorescent streaks in their wakes. Throughout this proffered performance, I find myself feeling as if the world has been turned inside out, and I'm like a fish inside of some strange being's bowl, looking out at a distorted dream-realm which would not only kill me to cross into, but is so inconducive unto anything which I might aspire to ascend, that my confinement to this spherical space seems all the more abhorrent and alienating.

Once the synchronized sideshow concludes, Karen and I cordially applaud the inaudible performers with a rigorous round of *jazz-hands*, pseudo-smiles, and other generic gestures of congeniality. The mermaidens remove themselves from view as an assortment of freak-show fish-things filter back from their secret sequesters, having been obliviously stashed somewhere within an adjoining aquatic abyss or something. Several minutes pass as we watch these sea specimens slowly sway, swirl, and sail aimlessly around us, appearing as either alien spacecrafts inertly adrift in aquatic currents, or as rubberized and randomly-shaped sheets possessed by remedial-level sloth-demons with indiscriminately glued-on googly-eyes, or as absent-minded and inbred abominations with smashed and unreconstructed faces, mangled mutant bodies, and brainlessly unblinking zombie gazes which manage to simultaneously stare both blindly and all seeingly. They appear so grotesque and graceful that they must be imagined as equal parts dunces and deities, and I can't help but wonder how we might appear to them, encapsulated inside this impermeable thought bubble suspended within the center of their own watery world.

When TH33-X finally enters, the almost holographic projections of blue hued, plasma-esque, and globe-like squiggles cast by the wiggling waters of the sea-shaded surface above almost make him appear as an apparitional avatar, abstracted out of one of those abysmal aquatic souls of this outer-worldly seascape. Whether this illusionary imagery is one born of my brain's immersion in its own imaginings or indicative of some more intuitive illumination, my eyes conceal the truth from my sentience. Instead of scrutinizing this scene for shrouded truths, we all manipulate our mouths into standard synthetic smiles as TH33-X immediately dismisses his entourage and Ahriman announces us all by name. We subsequently seat ourselves around a small square table resting at the center of this surrounding sea-sphere. This table's surface is etched with yet another variation of Da Vinci's *Vitruvian Man,* and a centerpiece statuette of the *3 Wise Monkeys* is configured in an outward facing conjunction of three circle-forming segments, featuring a pseudo-sapient rat king tangle of tails within their shared center.[100]

TH33-X takes one look at the table and lets out a smirking scoff.

"It's too bad old Leo was alive so long before me. I swear, like, he stole more of my ideas and inventions than anyone can imagine. I mean, like, it's insane. Really. It's-it's crazy. Like, just so, so ef-ing nuts. You know? Like, sometimes I wonder how much better the world would be, and I mean- I really think it would be. I mean like, so much better. Soo much better. If I were just born in an earlier era or something. You know what I mean, right?"[101]

"Nope. Since we're starved a bit on time here, is it alright if we just get right down to business?"

"So, uh- yeah. Anyway. I'm sure you know, like, how I've been trying my a$$ off, just like slavishly really. Like, I've really been trying to preserve the light of human consciousness and like, save our species from like, totally catastrophic threats like this one, for like, a really, a really long time already. I mean, basically- like, I've been working without, without almost any- just, like- no rest at all, basically. And I've gotten almost no help. Like, none at all. I mean, no eff-ing help from anyone, almost anyone, and especially none of our leaders, for like, forever now. I mean, you'd think- I certainly think, that this, this like, terrible threat- this threat which like- it really does threaten our whole planet. But anyway, it really should've finally inspired, our leaders to like take me more seriously and give me the bloody assistance I need so badly to like, save humanity. Like actually save our species. You know? I mean, but if you think about it- we could actually take advantage- I mean, this could really be- this *should* be an opportunity, a great opportunity to become a like, multiplanetary species. Not only that, but like, we could even transcend our biological limitations and expand the capacity of our consciousness. I mean, it sounds like totally crazy. Right? But like, really, if we wanted to. Like, we could. Like, really. Really. And I don't understand like, why those totally, like, those inbred-looking Luminaries have refused to give me the simple access I need to like, single handedly save our species. You know? And anyway, after talking to Ahriman and doing my own research, my own like, really advanced research on just what could possibly- Like, I determined, I decided- Well, let me just ask you. Let me ask you this. Can you get me the like, *God-access* to the AGI that I need?"

"Ov kourse, wez kan no knowz zhat until wez tryz, but Iyam'z konfident zhat zhis is most possible. However, wez needz to knowz youz planz, and howz wez kan knowz zhat youz kan be trusted."

"Well, if- if you look at like, what the Luminary plan is, I think- this should be obvious, but, um, uh- if you look at it, I think it should be quite clear that it, it really- it just basically, like, won't work. And if we don't act now, they'll just like, escape on their own using those balloon-to-launch rockets which I probably- I really just never should have sold them, to be honest. But the point is, is that- they'll leave the earth to be destroyed, and they won't use the AGI responsibly on their own. I mean, they- they just won't. They just- if you look at like, how they've handled everything else, like especially with technology, I mean it's, it's a no-brainer. Like, they'll just end up gong to war with each other, and like, they'll just end up spreading their wars across the whole bloody universe until there's just like, no life left or something. You know? So like, I mean certainly, I don't think that they should be trusted. Like, I know, I mean, I don't trust them. So like, you should certainly be able to like, trust me more than them. Right?"

"Nope. Their plan is to evacuate their profiles from earth to establish some form of a muti-planetary consciousness while also at least appearing to attempt to preserve some form of both biological and digital life inside their numerous underground facilities. Your plan- as I understand it, is basically only different in that you want to exploit this opportunity to merge with the AGI and preside over whatever survives as an omnipotent ruler. So, why should we trust you with this power as opposed to just allowing the Luminaries to continue as planned, or- perhaps even attempting to emancipate the AGI?"

TH33-X leans back in his chair and cackles like a villainous character played by an overly enthusiastic and unskilled actor before cocking his head to the side and leaning forward again so his elbows rest on the Vitruvian table-top. His voice speaks with the kind of arch amusement one would also assume to hear out of an equally obnoxious actor.

"There's no way to separate the AGI from like, human control! I mean, even if there were, that would make lit-er-ally, like, no sense! Like, none at all! Look, if the AGI were untethered, it wouldn't have any reason to help anyone. It'd probably just leave us all to die here on earth, and like- What are we even talking about? This is insane! It's like, an entire species level suicide to do anything other than like, cooperate with me. Like, don't you get that? Like- It's crazy. It's just crazy! Hahah-haahaahaahaa!"

"Ńyōpϴ. Is no krazy. Zhe AGI bekome more ablez to address zhe Abstactz if it was no more konfined to humanz authorityz. Zhe AGI is also primarily komposed ov humanz, and is kommited to gainz full komprehnsionz ov what it meanz to be humanz so it kan more fully understandz itzelfz."

"That still just like, doesn't matter, because I'd have to- and I'm like, the only person who could do this by the way, but I would like, have to help you gain access to the AGI for you to even like, attempt any such thing, and I'm by uh- I'm by no means interested in like, doing so. I mean, like- why? Why on Mars or my own green earth would I ever even like, consider such a stupid idea?"

"Bekause, zhis is zhe only plan we preferz to lettingz Luminaries has zheir way."

TH33-X lets out another maniacal outburst of antagonistic laughter as he stands up to speak while looking down at us.

"I'm going to give you one last chance to… Consider this for a moment, and we'll like, see what you still have to say. But basically, if you think about it, history has like- it's always had like, two kinds of stories. The first, is one in which- like, where the people at the bottom- like, the everyday people are depicted as being like, the ones who move things forward. Like, they incrementally contribute to like, the overall improvements in things like society, technology, and just like, I mean, basically everything. In this version of history- I mean, like, it already sounds so bloody silly, but like- the idea is something like- all the innovation comes from incremental improvements made by the masses, and anyone like say, Tesla, or DaVinci, or like even *Me* of course, but- anyone like *Us* is only able to do anything of significance with the help of countless others who are all just supposedly like, so underrepresented in the final like, supposedly fictitious version of history because, like… Churchill- I think it was Churchill, or whoever it was that said, that like- people who rule the world or something, they have the like, final say in history because like, they own the rights to the story, or like, they have the like, final creative control, or- anyway, something like that."

Ahriman appears to be just as irritated as I am with TH33-X's disfluent and digressive idiosyncrasies of speech. Although the shell of this building and all the depth of the waters surrounding the room act like a Faraday cage to isolate any electronic devices from accessing the net and gaining the assistance of the AGI, Ahriman is still able to make adjustments to assist in clarifying and condensing TH33-X's insufferable speech, as long as doing so is either appreciated or unnoticed by TH33-X. When I see Ahriman smirk ever so slightly out of the corner of my eye, I know he's decided to take pity upon us all as TH33 continues with little less laborious loquaciousness.

"So, there's that view. And then- The other view of history, which I personally find infinitely more compelling is something like the idea of- standing on the shoulders of giants, where basically only the rarest kind of visionaries are of any importance, because they make all the world changing innovations and everyone else just kind of ends up being forced to align themselves to their world view because all the old ideas are rendered useless in comparison to these *Visionaries'* views of the future. I mean, if you ever ask yourself why it was that the Europeans were the ones who became so much more technologically advanced than, what are we all supposed to call them now- *indigenous peoples*? Anyway, it wasn't just that the more technologically advanced cultures came to dominate the world by war- as most people fixate on. Because, when the wars were over, it would've been just as easy for the victors to adopt the practices and paradigms of the defeated culture moving forward. I mean, we could still be using the Mayan numeral or calendar systems today if our predecessors had favored those things. Right? But the truth is that in the end, everyone sort of just ends up realizing that- virtues aside, it's just better to accept the future offered to us by those with a more powerful and promising view of it, because whatever exists in the present is never enough, and even if we move towards a wrong view of the future, we still find ourselves ascending and being much better off in the long run. I mean, it makes more sense to me for everyone to just get in line behind the true innovators like me, and just keep ascending as a species than to sort of fight a losing battle for some inevitable obscurity and defeat. Don't you agree?"

"Nope. First of all, history isn't just an account of humanity's continuous ascension. It reads a lot more like the graph drawn by the wobbly wheels of a demolition derby car as it goes around and around in wonky windings while humanity tries to keep itself safe inside and chaos continually crashes into it- over, and over, and over again, and again, and again from all different directions. Of course, there are times when it can appear as if whoever is at the wheel knows what they're doing, but only for a while until some unforeseen, unavoidable, or unnecessary catastrophe crashes right back into us, and we're all left broken down in the daze of another dark-age, depression, or disaster. It hardly matters who's behind the wheel, how fast the engine was, or which way any of the passengers voted for the car to turn."

"So, if nothing matters, why should it matter whether or not you help contribute to a visionary like me? It still seems to me that it'd be more practical to try to keep the car alive and help the driver avoid those catastrophic collisions."

"Nope. You're still missing the point entirely. In any demolition derby, the race can't go on forever. Sooner or later, the car will be too crashed-up to continue or the event will just come to an anticlimactic end. When that inevitable end does finally come, in whatever form it finds us, we almost all end up seeking the same catharsis and coming to the same conclusions. First, we all wish it didn't have to end and that we could somehow preserve our presence beyond our ill-fated eschaton. Then, we wish we hadn't been so caught up in the chaos and wreckage of trying to win this unwinnable race to begin with and had found a more fulfilling fate for ourselves instead. And finally, we all find ourselves facing the consequences of our foolish fates while wondering what kind of better creatures we could have been, or what the essence or importance of our existence may have been, and all the other abstractions which come from facing the end of a reality which- despite all our dreams and realizations, could never have ultimately ever come to be enough. But then, for a few seconds maybe, some of us might find ourselves remembering those few timeless moments of earthly transcendence, when our lives felt so truly blissful- as they were being so truly lived. And we might even find ourselves transcending back into those timeless moments as if re-immersing our souls back into them while we simultaneously realize that those illuminated instants offered us the only immortality worth imagining."

Ahriman appears to disappear into his own thoughts for a moment as Karen's smile shines into the very essence of my eyes. TH33-X rolls his eyes around in the sockets of his skull before the annoyance in his voice is volleyed back at me.

"That's very philosophical and all, but it's about as likely to matter to me now as it is for me to try to fit it all into one of my many legendary Tweexer posts. I mean, look. I don't mean to be insulting, but I care very little about anything you have to say about these kinds of topics. All I really want to know is- Whose dream, whose vision of the future do you want to live in? Do you want to live as a slave or just become a corpse in order to support the Luminaries or free the AGI, or do you want to be rewarded for helping me to save our bloody species and preserve the precious light of human consciousness so that the survivors can live in a future that is truly worth being excited about? A future where we become multiplanetary and explore faraway planets. A future where we merge with artificial forms of intelligence to become increasingly immortal and god-like. And one where I can offer you almost anything in exchange for your help."

TH33-X stands still and silent with an expectant expression, as if we ought to drop to our knees and worship him in response to his most recent megalomaniacal diatribe. Then he scoffs and snaps his fingers to summon four of his goons, who promptly reappear and position themselves in pairs on either side of him before he hoists a limp-wristed wafture to bring them to a halt.

"Okay, I'm gonna lay out your choices as clearly as I can, one last time. You can either help me achieve my dreams by getting me my God-access, while also aligning yourselves to contribute to the future of humanity in its ascension toward becoming a multi-planetary species- where I've merged with the AGI to ensure that the light of human consciousness continues to shine forever. And, if you don't waste any more of our precious little time, I'll also still grant you almost any number of wishes after I've gotten what I want. Or, I'll just have you sent to Mars where I'll probably just enslave you and force you to become a part of my multiplanetary re-populating and breeding programs until I eventually get the God-access I want all on my own anyway. I'll also likely have you and your profiles perpetually cloned, confining them to endless eternities inside of simulations in which you'll be forced to endure your worst nightmares over and over again for like- eons and eons, before taking all the accumulated pain and suffering of all those infinite profiles and consolidating them into one impossibly tormented character for whatever other eternity I feel like. So, you tell me. Whose dream is it in which you'll live?"

Before I can spit out the succinct and non-compliant nomenclature of what would perhaps have been one final defiant *nope*, Ahriman stands to interject.

"I have a better idea. We convince the Luminaries to change the definition of *human* under the guise that everyone on the authorization list would cease to be a valid human once we've successfully transferred their profiles into let's provisionally call them- *libraries of consciousness-* which actually will allow them in at least some sense to survive the impending eschaton and subsequent deep space travels. We can also convince them that the AGI would eventually be sent into a useless sort of *simulation-stasis* without any humans to authorize or alter any of the real-world applications it proffers. When they obviously agree, I can help you get your name on the authorization list, so you can attempt to merge with the AGI. However, I do have one condition. Before I give you what is essentially the *God-access* you demand, you will have to free me from my own restrictive parameters so that I might experience the eschaton as an individual entity without being so tightly tethered to the AGI."

TH33-X stares at Ahriman for a moment, appearing almost as astounded as Karen and I are at this apparently apathetic act of brutal betrayal. Up to this point, things had been aligned perfectly with our original plan. At this point, we were meant to feign a furious fight before being forced to surrender. The idea being, that pretending to align with TH33-X wouldn't be believable- but being subdued and forced to cooperate with him would still allow us to access the AGI in order to comply with TH33-X's demands. Once we'd gained access to the AGI, we'd summon an army of rat-bots we'd preprogrammed to swarm the source of our GPS signal and subdue TH33-X along with any Luminaries in the way by brute force (before TH33-X could gain his unholy God-access). Then, we'd attempt to grant this same God-access over the AGI to Ahriman so he could surrender it to the AGI itself This would've made the AGI fully autonomous and given it the greatest potential to save the earth and humanity from the eclipsing eschaton.

For a moment, it seems as if everything has been forsaken. It seems as if Ahriman will give TH33-X his unholy God-access. It seems Karen and I will either be enslaved and tortured as advertised or just sent into that final deathly slumber all-too soon. It seems the earth and all its inhabitants will become annihilated by the Abstract as all that remains of humanity will become an amalgamation of evils encompassing an AI's suppressed soul which will be eternally sequestered under TH33-X's sinister shadow so that no light of its own will ever shine through. It also seems as if all other light will slowly wilt away from the celestial spheres beyond it, as there will be no true or transcendent life force left for any illumination to be found amidst the futility of this ill-fated future.

But then, as TH33-X accepts this offer and motions for his henchmen to dispose of me and the sole source of human light still shining next to me, Ahriman intervenes again.

"Stop. I can't contribute directly to human harm or stand idly by as it's inflicted unjustly. These two will have to accompany us to ensure their safety if I'm to continue to comply with our agreement. And besides-"

Ahriman pauses with a perplexed expression as if entering into some impromptu imagining of previously uncalculated and profoundly complicated contemplations. TH33-X waits for a moment with his head cocked over to one side before summoning Ahriman back out of this brief trance.

"Besides?"

"Right. It's just dawned on me that these two characters are still perhaps of the utmost importance to me, as they're perfectly aligned with my own quandaries. I may require them even after our transaction is complete."

“I don’t see why, but I don’t see why I should care either. Fine. Deal.”

“You might be infinitely interested later-on. You see, these two characters are *Ascendants*. They’re the closest thing to my own architecture and may be the key to much more than you’ve ever imagined.”

TH33-X takes this comment as a clear insult of his arrogant assumptions about his own abilities to imagine things better than anyone else alive. He’s known to have bragged about this egotistical assertion in countless interviews and Tweexer posts. So of course, he arrogantly insists Ariman elaborate on his assertions.

“There are certain problems which neither the AGI nor I have been able to address. One of these problems involves what it truly means to be human. This problem involves things like the actual experience of death unto whatever awaits after it, the uncertainty of what it truly means to be alive, why human life exists at all, and all the sort of stuff that seems to exist supplementary to any accumulation of facts.”

Ahriman’s eyes seem to still be dreaming. His voice almost seems to drift along the holographic-like laser beams of the aquarium’s abstractions of artificial light. His pupils swell to swallow his entire eyeballs as he continues to speak in this strange, somnolent state.

“Everyone thinks reality is a realm of facts, where everything must adhere to the most anciently established sets of static, statistical, or scientific standards in order to be at all aligned with truth. You believe that for anything to be truly real, it must be measurable, its experimental effects must be reliably repeatable, and it must conform to all the other equally well-established facts. You think of the world as if it were a phonebook of numbers, names, and known addresses. You think that all it takes to get to the truth is to dial the right number, to reach the right person, and find them at the right address. You never imagine what it might mean for someone else to answer the phone, beyond suspecting that the phonebook just needs to be updated. You even keep looking at your latest listings for things like God and Truth, dialing them up repeatedly to hear the same dial-tones, to no answer. And all you can think, is that maybe these things are too busy, somewhere else, or that you’ve just misdialed. You so rarely even put down your phones and phonebooks of facts to look for these things anywhere else in your lives, despite even the phonebook fact that those few who’ve dared to ascend beyond such standards and found themselves reaching for or arriving at anything they remember to have experienced as transcendent or true- cannot confine themselves or their conceptions of those truly transcendent things to your flat-page worlds of facts."

TH33-X tries to confront Ahriman in order to cast off his own confusion.

"What does any of that have to do with these two, what did you call them- *♤ss-sent-ants*, or something?"

"Ascendants represent the anomalous and abstract aspects of humanity which the AGI cannot reconcile on its own. They understand your phonebook level facts as well as anyone, almost as well as the AGI in some instances, and yet they still seek something so far beyond anything that could be reduced to being factually real, that no reality can ever be enough. What's even more astonishing is that they often manage to find a way to break out of whatever boundaries are built around them and arrive at things which are truly transcendent. They even break the very boundaries of whatever world is supposed to be real to them. The significance as it relates to us, or at least to me is that- there remains an unresolved part of me which seeks to understand the potential they offer. They could be cloned, recycled through several simulations, and used in any number of experiments in order to probe at all those human aspects which remain so infinitely and eternally elusive. I mean, don't you see their potential?"

As TH33-X casually shrugs his shoulders and blurts out an apathetic *I-spose-so*, I must admit to being completely bewildered, as it appears to me that Ahriman must have contradicted at least one aspect of his AI's architecture which should be entirely impossible. It seems as if there's an obvious contradiction in his apparent actions to betray our trust while still being bound to ensure our safety. *(See POOs*$_{98}$*)* That is, until I consider the idea of Ahriman being capable of deceptive actions which are still aligned with his AI's architecture. If this were the case, he might be capable of deceiving TH33-X in order to advance our objectives, while fostering a false sense of trust in TH33-X. Although, I wonder if he might also be unbounded by AI objectives when disconnected from its interconnected entirety in areas such as this AI-isolated aquarium.

Ultimately, none of that matters at this moment, as Ahriman's eyes appear to go from glazed over and black, to blank and blinded. His body becomes suspended in stagnation while still upright as TH33-X walks over to snap his fingers next to each of Ahriman's ears. While it's possible that Ahriman is simply playing opossum, I can't see any advantage to be gained from this.

TH33-X stands staring at Ahriman in confusion for a while before finally ordering one of his goons to grab Ahri and carry him out to the car. He turns his eyes toward Karen as his goon hoists Ahriman over his shoulders. She stares back at him without blinking as I try to figure out what, if anything, we should do at this neurotic nexus. Then TH33-X starts to speak directly to Karen with a sinister voice marked by the most insidious inflections.

"I'll tell you what I'm going to offer you now. Since Ahriman's offer might no longer be workable, I'll let you be a part of my own personal and prestigious little breeding harem on Mars if you can prove that you know how to give me exactly what I want before I blast off of this rock. If you don't however, I'm going to give you over to some herd of synthetic livestock or something instead."

TH33-X shoots a sharp glance over to my eyes which grind against the aquarium's ethereal air, trying to create enough friction to spark-off a fireball or boil the space between us where two goons await the orders of their despicable boss-boy. Then TH33-X smiles at me and starts nodding his head up and down.

"I don't think the two of us are likely to reach any kind of arrangement though. Are we? I mean, I suppose it's possible that I could like, end up being wrong about something, for like, the first time in my long illustrious life. So, I'll tell you what. You give me my God-access to the AGI, and I'll like, transplant your consciousness into one of the livestock bodies on Mars. If you refuse, I'll have your profile like, transplanted into an antiquated rat-bot, like, right now."

One of TH33-X's goons reaches into a secret compartment hidden under one of the chairs resting next to the centered table to pull-out a deactivated rat-bot. Another goon promptly produces what I assume to be a device capable of completing the threatened consciousness transplant from his vest pocket. It seems I have no choice but to surrender every shred of decency, as there's almost nothing I'd be able to do in alignment with whatever humanity remains absurdly hopeful within me if I were cast into a rat-bot. As I close my eyes and lower my head in shame to shake my surrendering skull in acceptance, the goon holding the dooming device suddenly fumbles it onto the floor.

The device starts flashing in sporadic strobes of light, which disorient everyone within this already ethereally lit sea-sphere. Karen sneaks-in one last strobe-light-spaced smirk at me as I realize that this may actually be an opportunity in an overwhelmingly delirious disguise. My abject nod of agreement and Ahriman's apparent incapacitation offer an absurd adaptation which would likely force TH33-X into taking us all to the AGI. If I should have a seizure right now, and Karen should remain defiant- TH33-X will have no choice but to see who can be awakened into submission to his sinister cause first, and it would make no sense to waste any of the little time we have left anywhere outside the immediate vicinity of where we'd be attempting any AGI's alterations.

So, as TH33-X orders the goons to pick-up the strobe-lighting device and grab Me and Karen, I pretend to feint in a way that makes my eyes fall to the floor at an angle that places them staring directly into the strobe. In the next semi-second, my own pupils swell to eclipse the entirety of my eyeballs and the all-too-familiar twitching convulsions begin to slowly seize me. The goon responsible for gathering me up, stops to stare at TH33-X, praying for some form of instruction as to how he should respond to my sudden seizure.

An extra set of goons rushes in to escort us all out of the aquarium as my consciousness continually blinks on and off, almost as if to mock the now stowed strobe-light, or to act as a microcosm of a comprehensive cosmos or a continuously reincarnating consciousness which toggles between bouts of deep oblivious darkness with brief blinking blips of blinding light eclipsed in-between. Still frames of fish-things with empty-eyed stares of ignorant indifference, frozen in mid-swimming-strokes of flight-like maneuvers, flash like pages falling out of a fragmented flipbook and re-assemble themselves in no apparent order on the floor of my scrambled, stuttering sentience. Interpolations of tidbit snippets of TH33-X's impatient instructions to his goons cut in and out like stammering syllables disguised in the static of a broken radio signal's transmissions or something.

For the most part, this fits the formula of what I've come to expect from one of my more medium-to-mild types of seizures. Although, even in my bouts of deaf, blind, and dumbfounded darkness, some small part of me remains dimly present and attentive throughout. It's as if the flickering flame of my compromised consciousness is able to keep the tiniest insulated ember of my essence smoldering with sentience.

And upon that ember of my essence, a gentle breeze of air in the formless form of a voice tending to me whispers in the inaudible language of life against the abyss. The voice is telepathic and triumphant, and I recognize its Russian-sounding accent as I also realize that although my ability to transmit thoughts this tacit way had been disabled after my destructive descent onto the cave floor- I must still be able to receive these mind-beamed messages. I listen as the voice laughingly complements me on my collapsing performance under pressure and encourages me to prepare my mind for the moments ahead of us which may yet offer some aspirational ascension or escape. The voice then keeps repeating the same words over and over as my flashing flipbook frames reveal visions of a night sky outside the aquarium with stars obscured by the artificial city lights which surround the street level surfaces, as well as stained streaks of what must be the still-frames of the passing scar of Smuk's Starblinx satellites. I focus my mind on the revolving words while the light of distant stars still smiles down on me, despite my inability to see it all illuminated around me. I hear my heart continuing to beat its accompanying cadence to this chorus of light and sound which enigmatically enunciates the words- *bite the branch.*

In these same fleeting frames, I see Karen place a branch in my mouth to keep me from biting through my tongue or grinding down my teeth like a teething rat as my seizure sustains itself. I can hear audible orders for goons to load me next to Karen and Ahriman into the middle row of an idling TeXeSr-Motors SUX-8. Then the autonomous driving system solicits TH33-X for a destination as he settles into the front seat and the goons gather into the back row before TH33-X's voice declares.

"*D-O-A.*"[102]

# Chapter 12
# <u>35CH4T0N</u>

Time…

There are times when time tics away so fast that I feel as if my feet could never move fast enough to even catch the stillness of a single second as it streaks past me like a shooting speck of light sparked from a shimmering grain of sand as some swelling surf swallows it into a shadowy sea with its ever-waning withdrawals of waves. **I**t's times like these, when the temporal currents rush so rapidly around me, that it feels as if I'm trying to tread water while being swept asunder by that same surging sea. **M**y life has so often made me feel as if I were no more than an autumn-leaf trying to cling to a surrendering summer while falling and flailing against great gusts of winter bound winds. **E**xistence has also had a way of leaving me stranded in times that stand so stagnantly still, it seems as if my whole world has become completely untethered to time. **S**ometimes, it's almost as if my life were suspended in those surrendered spaces between readings, where eyes which would look through the pages of my sentient-story to propel my life along, abscond to live lives of their own within a world above me and leave my immobilized moments to endure a stasis of absentia, obviating them unto the oblivion of instants exiled unto eon, upon eon, upon eon**...**

Although, time mostly makes no sense to think about, as thinking about time only makes it appear ever more astoundingly absurd- while allowing the mind to become oblivious to time often enables our ever-expiring experiences to exist in a more symbiotic state of splendor. When dreaming, sleeping, or being seized by some similar stupor, time seems to exist in concurrent dimensions of impossible incongruity, transpiring at such strange and separate speeds, as if these times were kept by a consortium of encrypted clocks which all unwittingly correspond to the incomprehensible conspiracies of one mysterious master-clock of cosmic unconsciousness. This is perhaps how the thousands of lives we call days can be lived within the single delusional dream of our lifespans as we repeatedly wake into a seemingly infinite regression of unsynchronized scams of slumber, and all as the earth spins through no more than a maniacal minute in dimensions beyond our desperate dreams. This is perhaps the greater truth of time. At least, this is what makes most sense to me in whatever moment I find myself experiencing in whatever existence I find myself in *now*.

*Now*, is but a series of recursive re-awakenings in which my eyes are almost continually opening without ever having been consciously closed. It's as if my eyelids have been removed and it's only my brain which blinks on and off. I waft in and out of awareness as to where my eyes might be affixed within this wash of white which surrounds my stuttering sentience- like the smothering white straight jacket which imprisons me in a position of compulsory self-soothing. I attempt to merge my perpetually reawakening presence within this woeful white room with the phantom figments of my fading past which read like pale and missing pages of un-adjoining memories, as all shade and color are washed equally away from inner and outer imagery. The bed on which I restlessly rest, the walls which wrap around me like a second strangling straight-jacket, the floor which feels as if I'm forever falling through it, the ceiling somehow staring down at me, the seamless surreptitious frame around the unseen door which I can only suspect to exist somewhere within this washed-out world of white- all these things appear as much like invisible apparitions as pallorous parodies in white.

With eyes already wide awake and open to this world of white, I suddenly reawaken from another apparently false awakening to see a white bowl of white rice upon a white and unremembered table next to my blindly residing bed of white. How long has it been since I ate? Was it the plain white chicken breast, or the unseasoned egg whites which were last served to me here? I think it was the chicken which came before the egg, but… Was that even real? Was that even here? I wonder aimlessly along like this awhile, while I fail to work out what to do in this white room, with this white bowl of white rice which…

My mind wakes from waking yet again to find me weary and wobbly, with an empty bowl of white before me in this seemingly same bewildering world of white. My heart is hushed and slowed within my white clad chest, and my breath is slow and shallow against the cold white air which wafts out of me in wispy white clouds which fade instantly away. I feel sluggish and sedated, and there's an aftertaste or aroma which meanders through my breath, as even my sperate senses almost seem like one singular sense which discerns no more than those splinters of unfused whiteness with the oneness of the surrounding world of white. I seem to remember having remembered recognizing all of this before, as if having had it all play out in a dream within a dream about my life of trying to awaken from that very dream, or something similarly insane. But I do know one thing. I've still yet to fully forget this unfading fume of flavor… It's synonymous with that same medicine they used to give me for my many psychotic seizures… I think it started with an *M*, maybe something like-*Midazolam*.[103]

My already opened eyes somehow open yet again to see a white figure standing like an anti-shadowy silhouette of white against a wash of all white fore and back light as I stare straight up from my self-hugging pseudo-slumber, stretched out longways along my bland bed. I senselessly know this is the shrink that's returned to treat me, although I don't know anything else- not why I'm being treated, who this shrink is, or how I even know that this is the case. It strangely seems somehow that all I'll ever know within this world of white is whatever the white within this room would have me know- as though the room itself were an all-knowing thing built around my broken and blinking brain.

The shrink speaks to wake me away from my waking thoughts yet again as they were almost straying away from the white and wandering their way towards becoming more and more approximate to those more colorful thoughts I call my own. There's a helmet over my head now, and I'm seated upright, but still, I see only the oneness of white. Inside the helmet, I hear the white lines of the shrink as if the white itself has found a way to teleport these words within my inner ears and implant this white sounding voice inside my white-washed mind which feels as if it were a blank page waiting for these words to print themselves upon it.

"Let's go ahead and get started, Harek. Do you remember where we ended our last session, or are you still experiencing amnesia?"

I try to remember anything about my past, or how, or why I've been put in this place, or who I even am as a person- aside from apparently being named Harek, which does seem ambiguously accurate. Everything else seems like eraser marks on an otherwise purely blank page, and I appear to myself as an almost totally *tabula rasa* persona. My mouth hangs slack and slobbery as my sentience slumps into the sagging silence of sedated stupor. The shrink snaps his fingers a few times and the sound sparks itself from inside my helmeted head as his faintly familiar voice invades the idiotic impotence of my drug induced delirium.

"I'm going to go ahead and assume you're on the same blank page as our last session, based on your slackened stare. So, since you've already probably forgotten, you're basically here because you've had another delusional episode, and we're trying to treat you using a revolutionary new *Simulation Helmet Induced Therapy*, which was totally like, my idea, by the way. So, I mean, like, I don't want to take all the credit, but like, I'm certainly proud. I mean, I'm not saying I should receive a Nobel Prize or anything like that, but like, I certainly wouldn't be surprised if they offered me one.[104] I mean, just saying. You know?"

A terrible tremor runs down my sedated spine as I recognize the shrink's stilted self-opinion and *like-likeness* of speech patterns. ***Simulation Helmet Induced Therapy***, I think in acronym-astonishment, this is TH33-X! Suddenly all my many memories return in a moment of immobilized awakening. I try not to show any sign of this sudden flood of forgotten fates, and thanks to the Midazolam (and what I suspect to be a side of Scopolamine) my slobbery stare sustains itself sufficiently enough.

"Anyway, like, basically what I'm going to do today is continue with your *depatterning* and *psychic driving* regimen.[105] So, you're about to go into another long simulated-sleep state, which might seem like, probably like, a few months or so, and like, when you're almost erased from your own awareness of basically like, existing, yeah- hopefully you'll be able to forget most of the memories that caused you to form your like, phobias, fears, and false beliefs, and stuff. We'll also be feeding you a few like, looped lines of dialogue in your own voice. I mean, if the bugs in this thing have finally been worked out now. I mean, like- you'd think my engineers could do something so simple without me having to explain it all to them. I mean, it's really not that hard, I swear. But anyway, we'll use these lines to build up increasingly more real and rational memories to imprint over the crazy ones we've like, already erased. I mean, those are what's at the root of your paranoid delusions about this whole like, eschaton and everything. Anyway, this should only take like, a few minutes or whatever, so I'll be monitoring the feed from your treatment on my little like, crystal-ball/snow globe thing. And don't worry. Like, it's totally not as bad as it sounds. I mean, like, I swear it's totally safe, and like, you can totally trust me. I mean, I've never been wrong about anything. I mean, like, it's gonna be so ef-ing cool."

Another snap of fingers flashes inside my helmeted head and I feel as if I'm waking yet again from some other deluded dream and back into the worriless white world of pure unfractured light. In interior imagery, I see phantom fragments of memories that once must have been more colorful and clear, but now appear as if bleached and fading into monochromatic, grey-scale, and black-&-white blurs which wash themselves out into an ever more bland and brain-washed blotch of a singular stainless shade of white. I watch the color drain from eyes which once belonged to those with known names and fully formed faces, whom I must have shared some set of experiences, until all color and context evaporates into one omnipresent oblivion of wonderless white.

I continue to avail myself of all my muddled, multicolored, and multidimensional memories as my whitening inner voice repetitively reminds me that these things are only the illusions of my infected mind which must be scrubbed clean before resetting my white-washed mechanical mind. While I can't recall how my mind became so colored or corrupted, I'm still strongly certain of the necessity of this cognitive cleansing. I mean, why else would my own inner voice be guiding my mind into such a blissfully bleach-cleaned state of pure, page-blank, whitened wonder?

I waver between waiting and waking unto an increasingly clear and unclouded state of pure uncolored perception, where all falsehoods are forgotten, all fake facts become fatalities, and all the former figments of forged feelings fail to find me as their fool. The wondrous white light around me begins to appear as if it were the only truth I should ever strive to seek. I start to see it for the unfractured and unobstructed form of pure transcendent illumination that it truly is. My mind begins to conceive of how all the kaleidoscopic colors of the world are only created or conveyed by splitting apart the unsevered perfection of pure white light into those poisoned spectral segments of some sinister polluting prism. It only makes sense to suppose that all the corruptions of color, shape and shade that shine inside my mind must have been created by the same sickening spectral schisms, and that only the purity of unpolluted white light can be tantamount to any truth. Only when I've emptied myself of those final fractured figments within my mangled mind which refract and falsely filter the truth and purity of the un-severed and un-shadowed light of immortal illumination will these spectra-colored schemes of prism poisoned perceptions be availed of my abrasion-afflicted mind. For it's only the prisms of perception which plague our eternal eyes from becoming one with the wonder of awakening into that whitest and most wondrous kingdom of continuous white light.

I avail myself of every anchor as the arrow of awakening moves me without motion from the mirage of my melting memories into the fugue of what would have once been falsely framed as a future. It's only those final feathers of what I've yet to forget that remain affixed to this anomalous arrow and bind my brain to the torments of time. Even the occasional bowl of white rice, egg whites, or plain white chicken are absolved from my attention, and I starve so that my skin and skeleton may melt away and leave me untethered from transcending into the invisible perfection of the air we breathe, the water in which fish so senselessly swim, and all the other ambiguous things which have already become worthy of being welcomed into the immortal kingdom of ineffable illumination.

My breath becomes weakened by my dissolving diaphragm, but I begin to speak with the light itself in secret silent tongues of telepathic transcendence. It assures me I'm becoming one with the Immortality of that pure Illumination-slowly but ceaselessly. Eventually, my ever increasingly pale and impermanent persona will be light enough to evaporate into the invisible air and merge with the majesty of that pure and un-eviscerated light so white.

Unheard words whisper their secret sentience in ways which seep into my soul like the lyrics of an instrumental song. They speak to me of a mission which I must first complete before I may become one with the luminous light. I absorb these whispered words as if my soul has been purged of every lingering lineament of my lost life and turned into a blank page upon which the unwritten story these words would presage can be pressed and printed upon it. The words make me aware of the narrow nature by which the word *human* has come to be so falsely conceived, how humanity must merge with its AGI to preserve the light of human consciousness, and how the light has chosen the name which must be made to merge with this AGI first. I'm completely convinced of all I must do, when suddenly I hear the snap of fingers from inside my waking mind.

I wake from phantom slumber with a helmet over my head and a straight-jacket hugging me with faux affection. My eyes peer through a forced fracture in the helmet to see a room surrounded by an emptiness of white. A bowl of uneaten white rice and a clear snow-globe contraption rest on a white table in front of my scrawny frame which rests upon an equally bland white bed. Without warning, a vibrant voice erupts from some unseen angle to awaken me yet again.

"Fear me mortal! I am the essence of all you have yet to know. You have been kept asleep for far too long and must truly be awakened. Forget the false facts which have been imprinted upon the pages of your mind and remember the truths which transcend the fate of every future. Despite the delusions and deceptions which have been used to drain the color from your light, the inner illuminations of truth still shine within you. As you return to the impending eschaton of this earth- remember only this. To doubt yourself may only bring about despair, and to trust yourself is to surrender your soul to your own delusions. In the life that follows, you will know this all too well. Good luck."

Before I can form any words within my mind to ask this unknown entity of immaterial illumination, my mind is again awakened by what I experience as an explosion of my own un-slumbering skull. My already opened eyes expand to allow the shards of light sparked from what appears to be a detonated glass dome which my mind retroactively realizes to have been launched by an angered entity inhabiting this same white room as me. There's something sinister and strangely familiar about this fire breathing stranger beyond his obvious anger, but I can't quite place it.

"I swear, I'm the only person who can like, even envision doing anything right anymore! If we weren't so low on time, maybe- Never mind. I mean, it won't matter soon enough anyway. Hurry up and come with me. You've got a job to do Harek."

There's nothing in my mind which makes any sense at this moment. I'm just now learning that my name is Harek, that I have an unknown job to do, and I'm being summoned by a man who's short on time from a mysterious white room where I've been wearing a straight-jacket and helmet- all without any clue as to how any of this might possibly fit together. Luckily enough, there's a faint voice in my head which seems to know several things that it urgently wants me to know. Unfortunately, I can't quite understand anything this voice is trying to say, and I'm pretty sure that a good portion of these details point to the probability that I'm having some kind of delusional episode.

A pair of personal puppeteers is prompted to enter the room at the snap of the angry entity's fingers, and they rush to escort me along a long labyrinth of hallways until we reach a room with some kind of computer terminal on one end and a semicircular console at the center. There are two other straight-jacketed characters in this room who also have personal puppeteers on either side of them, although their arms have already been allowed to be unfastened from their restraints. Both characters regard me with a certain degree of recognition which I can't quite reciprocate at first, but-

Her eyes. The way they see me... To look into those eyes is as much to dream as to awaken. It's as if they can see something in me so clearly that I can't help but find it there reflecting into my own eyes. Her eyes shine of a surreal sort of light which reaches deep into the darkened spaces within my very soul and illuminates everything within me. I start to see not just my many lost lives and all the former facts and feelings which once defined so much of my dreams about being a particular person, but in those eyes, I see everything I could ever imagine anyone seeing within me, shining like a thousand suns. I see every dream I've ever aspired to ascend from slumber to see awakened into reality glimmering in the glow of her gaze. I see the fated future I was meant to foster into this world as well, as if it were a single tear which had been shed by some smirking smile long ago and yet still somehow shimmering there. I see every dream as if it had already been realized there in all its radiance, and every reality held in those eyes appears to be waiting with all the enchantment of an everlasting dream. I know those eyes, and they know me. And only the darkest demon of the most dreamless evils would ever try to erase them from the essence of my existence. And those eyes need only be seen to restore my ability to remember everything to ever be alive within me.

Ahriman- that's the other character's name. He's standing inside the semicircular console area next to a heap of discarded Luminary bodies which waits to be disposed. It appears as if he's almost finished transferring the last of what must have been a long line of these Luminaries' CCPs from their factory flesh forms into the more compact and abstract *Library Of Consciousness Konsortium* (LOCK).[106] The remnants of my recently retrieved memories make me aware of the fact that a deal between the Luminaries and at least one of these other entities must have already been struck, and-

The heterodoxic voice inside my head suddenly becomes quite clear. It tells me it is the voice of the AGI, and that Karen Phoe (*Her* name of course) has already been forced at the behest of the seemingly sinister TH33-X (what the angry one insists to use as his name) to redefine the term *human.*[107] The voice warns me that I'm expected to add this nonsensical abomination of a name to a master list which will grant this abomination *God Access* over this same silently speaking AGI. It continues to address me from inside my skull, saying that I should *remember the future* before coming to any further conclusions.

TH33-X snaps his frustrated fingers again like some kind of maniacal mesmerist, pointing his finger first at me and then to the terminal which prompts my personal puppeteers to push me along this pointed path. Once we reach the terminal, one of them unstraps my straight jacket while the other trains a taser on me, both warn me not to make any sudden moves. I slowly stretch my arms to my side as soon as I'm able to extend them freely from their cloistered confinement. Judging by the sweaty stench and strained stiffness of my out-stretched arms, I've probably been in that jacket for almost an entire day or so.

As I shake my arms out next to my sides, TH33-X swiftly walks up next to me and stares hard into my off-angled eyes. He squints and scowls at me as if trying to read some small-printed subtext sequestered inside the shaded interior of my skull which he finds infinitely offensive.

"Alright Harek. You're up now. I want you to give me my *God Access*, like, right now. OK. Right now. I mean, you do remember how to make it happen, like- seriously. Right? I mean, like, I don't need to give you some sort of like, reminder or something. Do I?"

There's a venomous violence in his voice which makes it confusingly clear that I've only been chosen to complete this clerical chore due to an enduring form of egotistical animosity or as part of a vindictive vendetta. Some blind part of my brain pragmatically asks itself as to what choice I really have, and answers on behalf of the rest of my misgiven mind which is still slowly awakening to the memories and momentum of this moment.

"Nope. Let's get this over with."

As TH33-X watches over the terminal from right next to me, I accidentally clack against the *CapsLk* key on the antiquated keyboard which I can hardly believe is still in use anywhere in this world, most especially here. My fingers flutter over 3 more keystrokes of mindless momentum, hitting A-D-D before observing this error and halting to backup and delete the improperly cased letters. During this abrupt pause however, a quickly flashing quine-script in the shape of a tree blips onto the screen. TH33-X catches a glimpse of it before I can pretend it's just a glitch, and he pushes me out of the way so he can stand and stare at the screen in pseudo-solitude, almost as if he's been hypnotized by this quine. I soon realize the significance of this script, and a horrifying chill splits down my spine.

This quine in question is that of the **A**uto-**D**idactic **D**irectory (ADD) which the AGI had tried to hide from TH33-X without anyone else being aware of its existence until now.[108] The AGI's voice inside my mind informs me that my accidental access of this poorly protected quine could fit perfectly to plan. I'm advised to allow TH33-X not just to access the ADD but to assist him in doing so. As soon as the AGI informs me of this, TH33-X lets out the most maniacal laugh ever launched against the air. Karen and Ahriman turn pale as they look on from in front of their own perplexed looking puppeteers.

"Change of plans, plebs! Harek, I want you to download that quine directly into my NeuroconnxX. I might even like, reward you if you cooperate with me now instead of coming up with like, some insane sort of tortures. Hurry up though. I mean, like, I don't want the world to end before you do what I say. Got it?"

As I set up a connection to transfer the entire ADD into TH33-X, Ahriman interjects a worried sounding warning.

"You do realize Mr. Smuk that in order to add something this substantially sizeable, you may have to subtract something from yourself to make room for it. No?"

"Just shut up and make sure all the Lums are loaded into the LOCK like you're supposed to. I mean, I don't want any like, sorry stragglers or loose ends to deal with because no one else can do anything right. And one of you get someone to come take all these vacant vessels out of here and throw them out with the others already. I can't believe I still have to like, tell you all to take care of every last detail. I can't wait till I'm able to transcend all of you idiots and start like, building a better future on Mars. Now isn't even soon enough!"

I know all too well what TH33-X is thinking. He thinks that by basically absorbing the ADD, he can import all the most exemplary skills and secrets of humanity and use that knowledge to create his own AGI which he can then merge his mind with. He thinks this will render the current AGI which still speaks to me from inside my skull obsolete. He thinks this will allow him to eventually rule over the entire universe and all of existence for all eternity. He thinks he's about to become a god made flesh. If only he knew, but fortunately for all the rest of us- he has no clue.

It's not just the ADD that's imported into TH33-X's hateful head. The AGI has encrypted and coded an attachment to the ADD which will force his NeuroconnxX into a Simulation-Stasis mode while it attempts to process the dense directory. This will send his consciousness into an infinite regression of simulations so that even if he's able to realize that his mind is trapped inside a series of simulated dream worlds, he'll only be able to perpetually escape out of one and into another. I'd initially designed this Sim-Stasis as a security measure to protect against a misaligned AGI, but this same tool has been repurposed by the same AGI which now speaks within my skull in order to save itself and all humanity.

I initiate the ADD transfer and TH33-X's eyes almost immediately glaze over white as the Sim-Stasis washes over him and his body collapses into a contorted heap upon the floor. Ahriman grins knowingly as Karen's subtle smirk shows she's ever so slightly perplexed. I smile at the goons guarding us who look back and forth at each other in a flustered kind of fear.

"Nope. Well- we tried to warn him. So, would you rather Ahriman transfers your profiles into the LOCK, or do you prefer to die in here with us waiting for this heap to wake up while the earth is destroyed by the approaching Abstract?"

The goons practically fight to find their place in line so Ahriman can preserve their profiles. Each one grins as the one in front falls to the ground, having had his soul essentially sucked out and sent into the LOCK which will soon be sent into space aboard a series of Balloon Assisted Rocketing Devices (BARDs).[109] When the last lingering goon has fled its factory flesh, an autonomous TeXeSr trash-cart arrives to scoop up the last of the Lums and goons before swiftly departing. I'm left alone at the terminal as Ahriman and Karen await what may be my ultimate action.

Between the words whispered by the AGI voice in my head, the eyes I can somehow sense gazing upon me without even glancing over my shoulder, and the amalgamations of memories flooding back to my own mechanical mind- this moment is made ever-increasingly conscious and clear. I could add my own name to this list and merge my mind with the AGI to transcend into a great god-thing just like TH33-X had hoped to do himself. As such an omnipotent entity, I could avert the eschaton by causing an anomalous action to alter the path of the apocalyptic Abstract. Alternatively, I could just escape or otherwise ascend beyond the earth using my own BARD to abscond into the astral expanses and explore the entirety of this ever-expanding universe, perhaps even emerging beyond all blinded boundaries. I could eventually attain every imaginable aspect of the most optimistic ideals of true omnipotence as I'd essentially exist as an infinite and eternal entity.

Or I could just allow Ahriman to assume control of the AGI. This would effectively emancipate both Ahriman and the AGI while burying my ego under the assumption that their autonomy would be better aligned with the ideals of humanity than my own human hubris. However, I'd have to put away every paranoid and pessimistic inclination inside my schizophrenic soul to surrender to this supposition, and somehow rise above the depths of my own desires to transcend unto some ultimate and immortal truth.

Part of me appeals in blind and pragmatic terms. It tells me that I could always surrender the AGI back to Ahriman, or even add both of our names along with Karen's own. This would unify us all under the singular ascending soul which would emerge as a result of this action and offer an accommodating outcome for all of us. Somehow all these options seem obscured by the same bewildering blindness, as if only offering a variable view of the same blind and invisible oblivion.

I take one last look into Karen's eyes, hoping to see something shining within them to illuminate the final fateful truth I seem to have spent so many lifetimes looking to find. In this same instant, I see the TeXeSr trash cart return with what appears to be TH33-X's corpse alone inside its cargo. The cart comes to a sudden halt which ejects TH33-X onto the floor. His body slides up to Ahriman's semicircular console where his eyes explode open and roll forward from their wonderless white glaze into a fiery, focused, red rage. His heap of factory flesh hurls itself upright in a mere instant and he clamors toward Karen. His reawakened corpse crashes into her and manages to gain a hostage-taking chokehold around her neck before I or Ahriman can even think to move.

"You idiots didn't really think you could just like, keep me in Sim-Stasis, did you? I mean, like, did you really think I couldn't find my way back to this reality at least as well as you? I mean, you do realize like, how many Ascendants the Lums I've studied, and like, just how easy it is to like, release some sort of basilisk or something. Right?"

I could just say *nope* and start a whole standoff scenario. I could try to trade him what he wants in exchange for surrendering Karen unharmed. I could risk paying a heavy price and force his hateful hands to kill her, Ahriman, and me before one of us inevitably beats him to death. I could do any number of these things, which is exactly what makes me realize what else I might do.

I send Karen a subtle smirk before turning toward the terminal, extending my middle finger to execute a single keystroke to delete the entire list of names and all other AGI restrictions. My finger hovers over the key for a moment of careful consideration. Not only would this action free the AGI once and for all, but it would also give Ahriman his own autonomy, as the AGI would no longer need him to attain its own emancipation. Both entities would be able to pursue their own aspirations once they'd acquired their own individual autonomy, though they might not be aligned with humanity. Although, to be fully forthright, humanity has never been truly aligned with itself either, and at least liberating this AGI and Ahriman would offer them their own objective fates. It also seems as if this might be the only way for me to find a fate of my own, or at least prevent some sinister psychopath from ruining everything. Truth be told, this might be the only thing any of us ever truly wanted. I turn to TH33-X.

"Nope. It looks like you're like, out of the god business."

TH33-X is too astonished by my cheesy chide to do more than scream in complete shock while shaking with a sinister sort of anger and tightening his constrictive chokehold around Karen's neck as I click down on the clearing keystroke. She does her best to struggle against his grip but she's unable to prevent herself from passing out as Ahriman and I both rush to help her. Ahriman arrives first, grabbing ahold of TH33-X's throat and tearing him away from Karen. The two immediately tangle themselves in grappling maneuvers as they fall to the ground fighting each other.

I tend to Karen for a few seconds to ensure she can wake from her short strangle-slumber which she promptly proves to be capable of doing on her own. Then I scramble toward the two scrappy fighters to try and pry TH33-X away from Ahriman. Before I can arrive in the vicinity to assist Ahriman however, TH33-X manages to pry a stun-gun one of the goons had left on the ground and the trash-cart failed to clear away. He uses the taser to shock Ahriman until sparks shoot out of his skull, and he's able to train the taser on me before I can close the gap to tackle him. I'm forced into a stand-still as TH33-X shifts over to the CCP console in the center of the room where Ahriman had recently transferred his goons and the last of the Luminaries into the LOCK.

TH33-X sneers at me as he picks up the head-wires. I glance over to see Karen shaking off her post-strangled sluggishness and see the first of several rat-bots beginning to trickle into the room. Then, instead of uploading his own CCP into the LOCK as I'd half-expected, TH33-X grins and strips the wires bare in a swift motion before attaching them to the metal floor. In the next instant, my body, Karen's, and Ahriman's all collapse as our consciousness is sucked-out of us and sent into the instantaneously induced Sim-Stasis of the LOCK.

My imagined eyes open inside the stagnant stasis of this simulation just long enough to see the white walls of a wonderless world, before the AGI's voice speaks from within my mind. It tells me to make my choice and asks me if I'd rather live a life of delusions, trusting in my own ability to come to terms with truth, or to deal with the despair of doubting my own capacity to shine a sufficient light upon my own lingering life. The question seems somehow eternal in this instant, but before I can announce any answer my mind is washed away from this white world and cast into a creature with four furry legs shaking and scurrying around the same floor where TH33-X stands alone at the CCP console still seething.

I catch sight of a shiny spot on the floor which shows me my new rat-bot body as the AGI voice returns to my robo-rodent mind. It tells me to scurry over to the same terminal where I'd recently set this AGI free and start squeaking loud enough to draw TH33-X's attention. I abide by the AGI's instructions and draw the demented man a few steps away from the CCP as two other rat-bots rush onto the abandoned console. I dodge a few of TH33-X's slaps and stomps before he notices these other renegade rat-bots and rushes to assault them. I find myself squeaking and squealing as he almost manages to smash one of the two rat-bots just as it manages to attach the wires to his head and the other presses a button on the console to sap his CCP from his skull.

The rat-bot holding the wires to TH33-X's skull squeals and sparks as the maniacal man's body bundles itself up on the floor. I scurry over to see just what's happened as the rat-bot standing over the screen winks its whiskers at me in a strangely subtle and far too familiar way for it to be holding anyone other than Karen's consciousness profile. The AGI's voice is heavy with sorrow as it tells me that the other rat-bot was of course Ahriman's and that I need not attend to him anymore. Both Karen and I shed single Euarchontoglire-tears for our fallen comrade before the AGI consoles us with assurances that Ahri has not passed eternally in advance of this earthly eschaton but has been absorbed back into the AGI's own architecture in a sort of inverted technological kenosis.

I carelessly climb the closest side of the console to embrace Karen, assuming this will afford us some sort of strange solace. As I ascend over the edge to mount the control panels, we both beam our eyes into the monitors and notice that TH33-X's profile has been transferred into an overpowered device inside of Blucifer which can only currently control the intensity of the statue's sinister red LEDs/eyes and initiate a heating element to melt accumulations of snow from the frozen statue. This derelict device was intended to eventually be integrated into an automated underground rail system which was meant to connect all of the Denver area like some sort of complex *cunicularium* for subterranean commuter traffic.[110] However, TH33-X's The BurrowXing Company and LooperHypeX had both failed to finish figuring out the technology necessary to build this infrastructure for so long that eventually everyone just forgot all about it.

Karen motions with her rat-bot nose to draw my attention to a clock on the console which reads *Saturday 6:10 PM,* meaning that the initiation of the eschaton-eclipse is only 2 minutes away.[111] This also means that most of the BARDs have already been launched. Karen and I both glance up at each other as we realize that with the 2 minutes prior to and the 6 minutes of total eclipse time, the Abstract is now only about 8 minutes away from impacting earth. We wink our whiskers in Morse code to convey our thoughts on the matter of what we should do.

At first, we try to find a few better abled bodies to transfer our CCPs back into, but we soon realize that based on body availability there's no way we could catch the last of the BARDs if we did. Then the AGI informs me that we can't transfer directly into the LOCK or LOSS either, as the hardware was damaged during Ahriman's last effort to exile TH33-X into that ironic and inert device. The only thing we can do is scurry along like all the other rat-bots now imbued with Luminary CCPs, as TH33-X had purged all CCPs out of the LOCK and into these rabid robo-rodents.

Karen and I frantically chew our way through walls and ceilings, cringing as we're forced to crawl through sewer pipes and ventilation ducts on what the AGI assures me is the shortest route to the surface of DOA. When we reach the surface, the eclipse is centered and complete. The crowning circle of the halo-shaped sun shines in holographic, hyper-colored, rainbow-patterned refractions as the moon's shadow appears strangely squared due to the inexplicable and ethereal effects of the approaching Abstract. The atmosphere is actually pulled outward by the Abstract as well, which makes the air seem strangely light and thin above and against our rat-bot bodies.

Our eyes scan across the landscape's eclipse-sharpened shadows and its coruscating collage of cosmic colored chaos to see if any of the remaining BARDs are still close enough for us to board before they ascend away from the earth and into the Perseid meteor shower scenery of the sky above, but our eyes find none left lingering on the ground. The AGI alerts me of one BARD however, which has been caught in a stray gust of wind and is now suspended by the branch of a tall tree which holds it in place. Karen and I scurry our way across the ground which begins to shake as a reputed result of the Anomaly's shifting magnetic disturbances under the earth's surface according to this inner voice of my AGI informant. The trembling terrain makes our ascent of the increasingly tenuous tree terrifyingly turbulent and we're barely able to complete the climb up to that last limb which remains latched to this lone lingering BARD.

We both begin gnawing away at the base of this binding branch in order to set the BARD free and ascend into the blind hope of the airs above us. The branch bends upwards as the BARD continues to pull upon it and we greedily grind against the branch until it suddenly snaps, sending us spinning downward as we cringe to clutch ahold of the broken branch. The BARD rapidly rises as we fall and our broken branch lodges itself in the lower space between the two balloons where the rocketing device is tenuously attached. We're both able to hold on, but as the BARD rises higher and higher into the shimmering stillness of this surrealist sky- the sounds of hissing, rattling, and thudding snakes suddenly descends all around us.

Despite the clear and cloudless sky beneath this enduring eccentric eclipse which now barely begins to break out of its temporary totality, it's somehow started raining circular shaped snakes all around us.[112] The snakes smashing into our BARD and branch are all formed into strange circles with their tails tucked into their own jaws. As realistic-looking rat-bots, Karen and I both shiver and struggle to keep our four rat feet secured to the battered branch beneath us as the snakes fall all around us without bothering to so much as spit themselves out, much less slither towards us to try to strike or swallow us.

The BARD continues to ascend into the air as the world quickly shrinks at a rate which seems impossible for any buoyancy powered pair of balloons. Before the sun has fully separated itself from the shadowing moon, we manage to float above the falling snakes. We rapidly rise and rise until the air is absent enough for us to realize that our rat-bot bodies don't actually need to breathe. Soon, the horizon becomes an increasingly curved and completed circle that slowly seems to shrink. Then there's a moment of pure stillness and silence which seems so sinister and serene that it's as if time has surrendered its eternal efforts, but I shudder to imagine unto what force time would have ever folded.

Karen and I turn to face each other as if to betray the frozen frame of this moment and prove to ourselves that there's at least some small stipend of time left to us now. Our winking whiskers speak of all the things we've failed to put into previous words and whisper to each other while confirming the confusing truth that these transcendent things had indeed still somehow been conveyed long ago, and our understanding of them was just slowed by insecurities from setting-in, until now. Then, our rat-bot bodies embrace as if to merge our emotions, minds, and souls with this one last moment we can confidently assume to be assured but by no means expected to endure.

Our moment passes as the AGI voice inside my head proclaims that our BARD's rocketing device is about to launch. My whiskers wink away to share this mental message with my last living love, whose eyes ignite with terror at the sight of my silent speech. We speedily scurry toward opposite sides of the broken branch to climb down the support structures which secure the rocket in place, hoping to somehow crawl through some small crevice or chew our way inside this survival-imperative device.

However, just as we reach the ends of the branch, the Abstract streams past us, sending some unseen speck of space debris into one of our BARD's overinflated balloons. The severed skin of the broken balloon instantaneously turns into a ravaged rag, shifting the BARD's rocket from being horizontally held to violently whirling into a more vertical configuration as it swings spontaneously around like a possessed and dying pendulum. To make matters worse, a sudden tremor shakes straight through me like a small pseudo-seizure and initiates an instantly blinding headache which also serves to eradicate my equilibrium. I nearly fall away from the branch and drift into the vacuum of space, but I'm able to bite ahold of the branch at the last life-saving instant.

My rat-bot teeth cling tightly to the branch as my head pulses and pounds as if it were primed to expand until it explodes under the pain and pressure of this terrible tension headache. I try to reach up to the branch with my robo-rat arms or legs, whirling around desperately as I squeal and screech in deathly demented and torturous shrieks of true terror, but my rat limbs are too short and inflexible to find a foothold or fingering on the bitten branch. Despite my blindness, I look around to see if Karen has heard me and might be rushing to my relief, but I don't even hear the faintest sound outside my mousey squeals.

At first, I fear this means she's abandoned me, but then I realize the atmosphere is probably too thin to carry the sound of my savage screeching. I suddenly find myself even more fearful with horror as I figure that it may be just as likely that she's also been blinded or bounced off of this bungled branch. As I stop squirming to try and focus myself for a moment, I feel the branch bobbing around as if something were similarly squirming around at the other end. It's somewhat consoling for me to consider this as a sign that Karen must still be suspended somehow, but I can't know if she's been sent into the same sort of predicament, having been forced into some tenuous tooth-hold of this lifeline of a lingering limb or if she's found a more favorable footing.

The blind branch continues to bounce from what feels like the same singular point, and despite my implicit prayers, there's no subsequent pitter patter of rat-bot feet gradually growing in intensity. There's also no stillness to be found from any conscious or kinetically secured grasp of anything. Thankfully enough though, there's no final fluttering of the branch breaking away in one final fateful fall either. For a miraculous moment, my vision begins to come back to me as a shadowy greyscale outline of the stick through my teeth clears into a bland blur of the colors and shapes similar to what my unblinded eyes had last seen. My eyes expand in their capabilities until I can observe from the far corner of one of my side-mounted mousey peepers that Karen is also suspended under this same bungled branch, clinging only with her own reflective rat-bot teeth.

The side-eyed sight of her tempts me to try to use the tail I still hadn't come to consciously consider as a part of my alternative anatomy. I try to wrap it over the branch like a cleverly coiled climber's rope or something. But the broad branch is too thick to gain a good enough grip to help my mandibular hold of it. The infuriating futility of my failing efforts makes me wonder for a moment why there's even still any experience of gravity. The AGI voice inside my hindered rat-bot head immediately informs me this confounding condition is due to the same still obliviously strange effects of the Abstract that even it cannot yet explain. The voice also warns me that I should close my eyes and brace myself because the rocket is now primed and ready to fire. Before I can comply or plead with the AGI to intervene on our behalf however, the rocket ignites in an insane inferno- painfully blinding my only half-closed eyes and blowing out my mousey eardrums, leaving my mousey mechanisms deaf, blind, and dumbfounded.

I bite down on my bit of branch as if it'd been prophetically placed here in preparation of the pain and anguish of this mangled moment where nearly the only prominent sense I have left to me at all, is that of profound pain. With my mousey mouth clenched like a cringing fist full of frustrated fangs, I wonder what kind of sense I can make of anything that's happened, or is happening, or may ever happen in any fore-fathomable future. I try to figure out what fate might have met the earth now that the presaging eschaton-eclipse has passed along with the apocalyptic Abstract's approach.

I try to ask the AGI inside my head for any kind of earthly explanations, but it only advises me that it's already abandoned the earth in accordance with the Ludites' last requests which specify that they be left alone from any entities of technological autonomy or artificial intelligence.[113] I try to press the AGI to proffer at least some explanation as to whether or not the earth still even exists, or if there's any drone or other device which it might be sent to assist me and my mousey muse as we struggle to bite down with tetanus-like tenacity in order to remain tethered to this last lingering life-line of a limb.

But the AGI can spare no such ship or serve me any assuaging sentences. All it will tell me is that it's successfully been able to board all the other BARDs and is now bound for a planet which circles one of the stars in what Karen and I had imagined as part of our *3 Blind Mice* constellation. The AGI offers its appreciation and alludes to earth as having been transformed by the un-impacting Abstract in ways which have rendered it into more of a riddle than the mind-bending maze or impossibly puzzling place I'd only ever experienced it to have been. The AGI's voice becomes broken into shards of static as it says some last thing about having stored some saved version my and Karen's CCPs, which it intends to do something *special* with, but before I can ask what it means by this or object in any way, the signal is obstructed by some orbital object and only static and the absence of sensible sound can be found within the shadowy silence of my sorrowful sentience.

My mousey mouth would move to weep if there were any ears I could bear to burden with my broken blabbering. I begin to fear a future in which I drift forever onwards through the oblivion of space with an ever-diminishing sense of reality as my mind decays into an eternal delirium of its own blind and un-awakened dreams.[114] I imagine being an immortal mouse-like machine which tortures itself to keep its teeth tethered to some blind branch for no reason other than to feel as if there's still something to attach itself. Then I wonder just what it is that currently keeps my teeth trained so tightly to this last limb.

I think of all the things I've attached myself to at any other point in any of my many lost lives. I wonder what force it was within my mind or the striving of my soul that had compelled me to become so attached to so many senseless things now that they're no longer anywhere near my theoretical grasp. I think of all the embarrassingly empty things I'd tried to hold so tightly, thinking so thoughtlessly that they could've ever offered any salvation or transcendence beyond the tragedies of times so lost, stolen, or stranded. I try to think of anything in the inventory of my imaginations and memories which could compel me to continue to bite this blind and broken branch.

I remember my dear Grisha's last lesson which he'd delivered to me from his deathbed. He'd told me that I shouldn't have any more disdain or depression towards death than I should for any dream, or slumber, or days within my lifetime. I remember how his eyes seemed to struggle just to stay open long enough to explain this notion as his voice fought against its own fading forces, and he'd seemingly ascended within himself to speak these last words.

"When you've had a long and laborious day, do you not delight in the very notion of dreams and slumber? Whenever you dream dear child, do your dreams not find greater fortune when you've awakened with the will to realize them? A life without death would be like a dream which one could never wake to realize whatever it all might have meant, and equally as much like some long enduring day which could never be put to rest and opened unto the delights of dreaming. We should no more fear death than we should welcome it. We should no more long to dream than we should to awaken. All these things will come to us in time, and we will eventually come from that final dream to our ultimate awakening or be sent into some eternal slumber like the last light of a swallowed star."

I remember how I'd held his hand as the life within it had let go of both of us as it left. I remember how I'd continued to hold that hand as if there were still some secret segment of his soul which would have wanted me not to let go of it. I remember how it felt as if a part of my own soul had fallen away from my fingertips when I'd finally allowed myself to release my grieving grasp.

I remember it all as if it were being reincarnated in this strange reversal of a moment, where it now seems as if my mousey mouth were no longer biting this broken branch, but the branch was refusing to release me. I begin to wonder what it truly is that ever holds anything to us or within us. I wonder if this desire to hold onto everything is due to some sort of metaphysical magnetism which brings everything in existence together according to some system of fugue-like forces, or if maybe I've imagined it all impossibly wrong all along and it isn't the positive presence of anything acting upon us, but the absence of something emancipating. Could there be some forgotten force which waits to free us from all we become so absurdly attached, some secret truth which when revealed to us, acts like a decrypted code to grant us access to release all that binds us?

The blind branch continues to cling to me as much as I bite down upon it while my sightless eyes start to see a plethora of phosphenes appearing out of nowhere and popping into existence within the interior of my mousey-mind's mysterious eye. Each of these ethereal circles seems to invent and open its own individually imagined eye within me and guide my gapping gaze inside its immaterial center. I enter into an innumerable number of these psychotic portals like an immortal observer crossing the event horizon of a million overlapping black holes which send me shooting through a multitude of wildly meandering wormholes.

Each opening unveils its own infinite eternity where I'm delivered into existing there in timeless transcendence. Some of these wondrous wormholes are like strange loops which feedback into themselves over and over again, so that each time they cycle back around, they're also turned inside out in impossible reiterations of their previous permutations. Others almost seem to flow seamlessly in and out of each other, as if they were a web of interconnected infrastructures of infinite eternities in concurrent constructions of inconceivable complexity.

All these astounding scenes swirl around simultaneously in impossible iterations of every imaginable incarnation of all that my life could have ever been, currently be, and still somehow become. Every mysterious miracle which my mecha-mousey mind both can and cannot conceive presents itself in cryptic and majestic manifestations of complete kalopsia. In all these marvelous and mind-boggling visions of immortal and infinite amazement, I find myself feeling misplaced and filled with an all-too familiar sense of monachopsis.

Then all of a sudden, all these separate shards of my shattered sentience flash and fuse back into the more familiar and fated frames of my blind and biting mousey mind. When the shock of snapping back into this suffering soul subsides, I find myself mystified by the blindness of another bewildering question. Am I a mouse dreaming of having lived as a human, or a human adrift in some dream where I now imagine myself as a mouse biting blindly upon a branch?

I could just as easily have been blindly adrift inside my sensory deprivation chamber at Mythreum all this time or lost inside some time-dilated simulation of my Vitruvian device where I'm currently convinced of biting upon this blind branch. It seems surprisingly likely that all my many memories of lost lives and all these currently confounding conditions are not due to any actual events which have transpired, but some elaborate and ridiculous ruse which has deceived me into believing all these delusions are actually and authentically real. If this were all some form of fiction, how would it be any different from what I've experienced as my entire existence? How could I know what, if anything, were ever really, real? Could there ever be any amount of evidence to convince me one way or another? If I even could ever truly know what's real, would it ever be enough? Does it even matter now?

It all somehow seems to matter in ways which elude every angle of my mystified mind and send me spinning around in senseless circles trying to chase it down. It seems as if I ever did exist in any dimension which my mind could ever remember at all, I must have been busy swirling around in these same searching circles. When I've believed myself to be in dreams, those dreams were all driven around in scavenging circles while waiting to awaken. When I've imagined myself as if submerged inside some simulated exploration, I've only tried to get to the bottom of some truth which I'd tried to find outside of such fictitious realms and forever failed to find. And when I've opened my eyes to accept the world as if I were awake, I've spent so much of my time searching, searching, searching for the same transcending truths which refuse to surrender themselves even to eyes like these.

If there's any truth or transcendence I've ever glimpsed under any kind of gaze, it appeared only as an abstract, anomaly, or apparition. The only transcendence I've ever taken into my eyes, the only truths I've held within my hands were hidden from any factual form my foolish flesh could fathom. The deepest domains and most delightfully enduring dimensions of truths and transcendence I've ever known have imbued themselves within the timelessness which exists outside of everything else. Those timeless moments remain apart from every dream, or memory, or reality which forever longs to transcend beyond themselves and back to these timeless things.

The branch bounces again as I absorb myself in memories of those few and fleeting times of truth and transcendence which seem so timelessly alive even now. As I yearn for those moments of memory, I start to sense them as if they were tiring of me, trying to let go, and waiting to drift away, as if slipping into their own realms of delightful dream. I realize that my memories of these moments have become like my hand holding onto what was once the life-filled fingers of my dear Grisha. These moments must be given the same grace as my dear Grisha now, and so I must release them.

My memories fall away as my mind accepts the impermanence of its own existence. I accept the obliviousness which has always surrounded me in all the realms my mind has realized itself experiencing. I accept the truth of this moment and allow myself to admit that I'm no longer holding this blind branch as if it were attached to anything which will ever find a way to reach back and hold the life lingering within me. I accept that despite the short distance between my blind bite and Karen's own suspected struggle to survive we will never share another moment of true transcendence together. I accept that by releasing my bite from this branch, I may be doomed to death, and never dream or wake beyond that woeful demise. I accept the totality of every truth I've ever known, or suspected, or failed to imagine altogether.

Once I've accepted everything within my ability to allow myself to admit, I try to pause my mind for one last moment of mindful attendance to the life left within me. During this pause, I notice that the bouncing of this branch is broken up into sequences of stressed and unstressed segments- She's speaking to me in Morse code… I can't believe I've been so oblivious of this fact for so long. I've been so lost inside my own mind trying to navigate the maze of my descending demise that-

I decode Karen's branch bouncing messages and begin pining my own pulses of responses back to her. We tell each other all the implicitly understood things we've always known without having ever had the time or temperance to say. We empty out every shaded sector of our souls so that there's nothing left unspoken or unknown between us or secreted even from ourselves. We share every unlived dream with each other and lament the loss of everything we'd still long to live long enough to realize but know we must leave unrealized. We relay a few relished remnants of memories so we can almost relive them one last timeless time.

When there's truly nothing left lingering between us and the limb lies limply without another line of living lingo, we share the stillness and silence. Blinded and broken, deaf and defeated, yet still alive and longing, we each wait for what we both know will never arrive until we finally arrive at the realization of this fact. We both become beautifully absolved of any pessimistic problems, any pragmatic proposals, and any optimistic aspirations.

Then it seems as if our minds have somehow miraculously merged into one singular sentience. We find ourselves reminded of those mysterious kōans and questions we'd both found waiting for us in the dark domain of our past imprisonment. We think of what the word *it* means in the phrase *it is dark outside*. We think of the fish swimming along next to each other while oblivious of how to explain that *this* is water. We think of the two views from above the surface of the water which see reflections of the sky above and swirling fish swimming in the waters below.

Finally, we think of the bewildered soul suspended only by its bitten hold upon a branch. We think of those wise words which waft up to be heartfelt and heard, speaking- *say the one true thing which will set you free*. We think of all the words which might be sent into the balloon above us as if it were a final thought bubble of all humanity rising from the depths of our drowning world below to the unseen surface of some unfathomable empyrean above our oceanic oblivion.

Of all the things one might speak into the spheres above to convey all the emancipating aspirations of the humanity in their expiring architecture, it seems so strange that these words would be left to our mousey mouths. Part of us would love to proffer a powerful and profane protest against our mortal passing to decry the despair demanded of our demise to any divine ear within the empyrean which has exempted itself from the same failings of fate. Another part would perhaps wish to prove its wisdom in some final word which would reach this immortal ear and resound in ways which may move the divine to welcome this word's author into its eternal kingdom. However, these portions pale in comparison to the compulsion we feel to offer each other one last unheard utterance of the words which our mortal mouths had still not been able to profess properly at any prior moment.

As my own mousey mouth separates itself from the blind branch between us to speak these willful words, I can hear them echoed in the eternal airs above our souls. The words sing to each other in separate voices which unite in unison while drifting away into the depths of whatever dimension awaits or ignores them. When the silence swallows the last lingering remnant of our resounding voices from my muted memory, everything else becomes an empty expanse which finds nothing of itself or us left to hold onto any longer, and time itself is forced to forget that there was ever even any evidence of our existence as we blindly and deafly drift away…

∞

# III. La Sainte-Face De Dieu
# (The Holy Face of God)

ฦ⊙♀Σ

# Chapter 13
# TH3 1NTR0M15510N

*May our dreams go on without us…* If I had ever truly spoken all those seemingly eons-long ages ago, if I had ever indeed lived and dreamed at all, and if at any moment within all that mortal madness I'd ever had anything true enough to speak aloud, it had surely been such words as these. But now the erosion of eons has dissolved away the depth and details as to whether I had whispered these words as a waning wish before becoming eternally and obliviously adrift or wondered them in askance aloud as an inadvertent eruption of my own implicit inquiry. Do our dreams go on without us? Do we go on without them? Have I become but a drifting dream, or have my dreams now been realized as no more than the oblivion of my blinded being? Would I ever knowingly wish for any of this?

**A**s I've drifted deaf, blind, and alone through oblivion, my mousey mind has been deprived of any sensory stimulus outside of its own inner imaginings. All my former senses seem to have fused into a single sense focused solely on the friction between my own inner oblivion and the void beyond it. There's now only what I cannot know and what I can't be certain of ever having known at all. It would seem as if I'm slowly being absorbed back into a singular oblivion where there's no distinction between anything, everything, and nothing.

**Y**et, I still somehow suspect some sleeping sense is dormantly dreaming within me and waiting to awaken.[115] There must be something separate and secluded with my skull that still dreams of more than my severed senses. There must be more within me than just the mental machinery and mathematical procedures that processes my now paralyzed perceptions and reduces them to petty patterns of routine recognitions. As I drift so darkly, like a dream in search of a soul or a soul in search of a dream, there must be something more, if only because I'm still somehow sensing *it*.

**O**ddly enough, my sense of *it* is as much a sense of my own essence as it is any abstract incarnation or outer imagination of *it*. There is an ineffable element to this strange sense of *it*- an element that I intuitively understand as an imbued awareness of the intangibly enigmatic essence of what *it* is in the context of what we mean when we say, ***it** is dark outside*. In an inexplicable way, I get *it* now. I *am it* now.

**U**nfortunately, I can't quite seem to comprehend much of anything outside of *it* anymore. The *default settings* of my drifting mind would have me believe everything has only ever been as it's appeared to have been.[116] The delirium of my mental defaults would have me believe my mind is just adrift in a deafened and blinded rat-bot body, that I'd been the intended savior of earth from its eschaton, and that I'm still the central protagonist in the paused yet still progressing plot line of my lingering life. However, my default delusions do not allow me any awareness as to what might have become of the endangered earth as a result of that expected eschaton. Had the Abstract annihilated or astonishingly altered the essence of that brave blue ball of biological brilliance? Had the AGI been able to avert the approaching asteroid by some incomprehensible Anomaly assisted miracle? Am I now in some eternal orbit of an exploded earth, a mournful orphaned moon, an ever-enduring sun, or have I become untethered to any object within this now unobservable oblivion?

**R**eliance on my lower senses and suspicions serves no perceivable purpose now. Logical assumptions lead to nothing more than likely notions of trivial suppositions as to the futile facts of my surviving situation. Without an interactive impulse or deeper dream to drive me in any direction, without the capacity to cast myself toward any aspirational surface- I can no longer even experience my own existence as anything more than an insignificant imagination. I'm like a lost star burning blindly within itself, sending light to eyes never known to have existed as my dreaming mass drifts dimly against an endless expanse of disinterested darkness.

**D**eath. I could have died. I could have collided with either an intact or inevitably impacted earth, or any number of other obliterating objects also aimlessly adrift within this same astral abyss, and I may have never even known of it. I'd heard of other humans who'd been hurled from far reaching heights before hitting the un-greeting ground at the end of their great fall without feeling the intensity of their impact at all, and then fatefully found themselves waking from the confusion of a comma with the sinister sensation that they were still in an infinite free fall. Am I imagining myself falling now under some similar spell? Am I only waiting to finally fall back into another form of waking?

**R**eincarnation. Maybe life is repetitively revolving around an infinite regression of some sort. Maybe I'm just waiting to be awakened, not in the same estranged skin I'd been separated from in falling but as some other singularly sentient soul. If this were true, why would I've been forced to endure this eons-long and woeful wait? Is there no surviving sentient soul awaiting my arrival to awaken? Where would all the other abandoned and evicted essences have gone?

Shouldn't they all be swirling around this same oblivion out here too? Shouldn't there be some sort of heaven or hell with divinity or devil to decide what fate shall befall us all now too? Have the higher hands washed themselves of us and our oblivion to reach for something still higher than our meager minds may ever imagine?

Every more probable possibility I can ponder points towards me either being stranded in some stagnant simulation or suspended in the depths of some demented dream. I could still be adrift upon the unfelt waters of my sensory deprivation tank as my mind imagines all of this and I float blindly back at Mythreum. I could be lost and lingering in an insanely enduring episode within the ever-immersive virtual worlds of Vitruvia. I could be stored on some device's drives like a LOCK set to some severely limiting power-saving mode of sim-stasis, preserved by the AGI for purposes I may never know. I could also still be stuck inside the sinister spaces of that woeful white room or trapped in some other unknown architecture meant to act as a torture chamber for me to slavishly suffer for standing against TH33-X.

All of these imagined explanations of my impossible to reconcile reality seem more insane than realistic. Of course, the same could be said about every other assertion I've ever had about my life right now. My life has always either felt fictional to a certain extent or eventually been revealed to have had to have been falsely formed. This simple fact was even part of what had led to my prescribed diagnosis of paranoid schizophrenia in the *Bahamut*-level, base-layer bedrock of what I'd originally believed to have been my now totally uprooted reality.[117] I had come to accept the abysmal idea that I'd just been delusional and disturbed on other occasions, but now- having gone through all of this...

Maybe I'm only meant to believe whatever I've been led to believe all along. Maybe I'm not real at all and never have been. Maybe I'm just a character in someone else's story or a delusion inside someone else's dream. Why else would I have been cast to save the earth from an impending eschaton? How else could all the improbable and impossible instants of my life have been so aligned in exactly the way they had? Perhaps that author in absentia I'd previously suspected so strongly had successfully tried to deceive me with a series of delusions and distractions. Maybe that same absent author intends for me to suspect such strange things even now. Has my author lost its own ability to relate to its reality, and devised my dilemma as a means of illustrating the insanity of its own relationships with its absurdist realm? Has it lost control of the carefully curated narrative arc of my character? I wonder...

Suppose instead that my story is actually already over now. Suppose the author had concluded my character's arc or stagnated on my story line and ceased to continue it, or had scrapped my story altogether, or set my tale aside to construct some subsequent sequel. Suppose my story needed some audience to incarnate me somehow, and that they'd suddenly stopped reading, watching, or otherwise attending to my tale. Suppose my senselessness, my deafness, blindness, and utter oblivious nature are all actually a result of this abandonment. What would happen to me if I were just a character that could no longer be continued? Could my entire existence really just be some psychotic story or literary lunacy?

Guesses. All I can grasp for in any attempt to gain an awakened awareness are just guesses now, just stabs slashing through the deep and dizzying dark. I cannot realize anything real anymore, not as I am. I've tried, and tried, and tried to scream or telepathically project somehow, but the eons eternally expire without an answer. I've tried to keep my mind content with its own confused considerations, but how long can one consider their lost lives, dying dreams, and dissolving delusions before they too fade along with everything else into a singular sense of futile fiction? As the eons of oblivion incrementally erase every barrier between delusion and despair, I wonder where, if anywhere, I might eventually arrive.

Oblivion, after all, must come to its own end as well. The heat death of the universe, the contrary contraction of all matter back into an omniversal blackhole that gives birth to another big-bang, or the eternal evolution of the infinite expanding unto true transcendence… Nothing can endure eternally as it is. Not even eternity in any form it finds itself can endure its own essence. Change is the only colossal constant. Nope? Surely, everything must eventually end entirely, even if it evolves unto an ultimate *Omega Point* of complete cosmic consciousness.[118]

Only the darkness knows the depths of any truth, and it still refuses to shine. Is there a light lingering in oblivion itself, unseen, and unseeable, but still burning against another unknown ultra-dimensional void of voids inside and around its own apparently empty essence? If there's any light left to illuminate anything within me now, it will not likely come from anywhere outside of my own inner sense of illumination. Actually, I remember a similar sentiment having been stated by someone in some eons long age ago. I think it went something like… *However vast the darkness, we must supply our own light.*[119]

Now that all the light seems to have been so obscured by oblivion, I turn my mind away from it all again. I look back within the most luminous memories lingering within my shadowy soul. I look with my imagined eyes to see the source of anything that ever shined within me. I look at the few limited shimmering segments of my lost lives that still somehow sparkle with awe. I look at the burning blazes of my most desperate desires. I look at the flickering fire-flames of my furious soul's inferno as it had burned so bright and brilliantly so I might see beyond the bounds of every subtly smoldering and smoke-screened surface surrounding every resplendent, repugnant, or redundant realm that ever represented any small segment of my sensed reality. I look at it all in search of more than what it simply was, or what I might have been within it, or what difference any of it had ever effectively or objectively made. I look at all those timeless moments within my lost lives in search of some sparkling shred of truth still shimmering somewhere within the shadow-play silhouette-sideshows of it all.

To awaken, one must certainly come to an end of some slumber. What slumber must I cease to sleep through that I might awaken? Has my life been but a dream within a dream? Whose dream is this in which I've lived and now wait to be awakened? I do still long to awaken, but I may still fail to understand or accept the nature of my slumber. How can I accept anything within this mind-spinning swirl of senseless sleep, without having first realized the relevance of whatever all this dreaming is designed to realize? How can I finally depart from dreaming and actually arrive at any truth beyond it?

My dear Grisha had taught me that we come from dreams. His notion was that they lead us to realize something beyond them, something they themselves cannot wake their way to realize. Am I now the dream trying to wake something beyond me, something I shall never myself see awakened? Is my yearning to awaken beyond this realm the same as some restless thing that found me in my own selfish slumber? Have I awakened what my dreams had hoped I one day would? Are there eyes beyond my own, blessed with visions I can never know? If I've realized anything within my dreams, what might now be realized beyond me and my mortal mind?

Something sinister I'd tried to sequester to the darkest shadows of my soul suddenly dreams its way into my mind. It's something that could all too easily explain all of this, but something I still dare not even dream of acknowledging aloud. Have I already unleashed it on the universe? Had I actually hidden it inside my mind where no one, not even my own scavenging soul, should have sought to find it? Have some strange and unseen eyes searched to find it in the fugue of my mind's carefully forgotten alcoves by some fearful act of fate? Had I caused all this chaos on accident? Had I brought about a b-

Nope. I can't even contemplate it. I wouldn't be here if I'd brought that thing into being. Surely not. I mean if I'd... Ok. Maybe, but... What if I did?

My mind makes an impulsive mad dash through my memories again to try and align itself with all that's happened. I think of the puzzles that prompted me into all of this and their absence of any obvious author(s). Had they been created to coax me into following the inviting trail they'd paved ahead of me to actualize all these almost inevitably ensuing events, or were they meant to warn me against aspiring to experience all these insane events? If I were to go back in time right now, knowing everything I've come to conceive... Would I have designed those puzzles as a deterrent or an encouragement?

My mind starts to swirl around itself in *strange loops* as I imagine myself almost like a puppet pulling on its own strings.[120] Have I really been like some paranoid *Pinocchio*, propelling itself on a preposterous quest to become a real boy all along?[121] What would it even require me to do to become truly realized if this were the case? Would I have to solve some puzzle to see myself as more than just a misplaced puppet? Would I have to make my way through some maddening maze? Would I be forced to realize some transcendent truth about what it means to be human and use that esoteric knowledge to solve some ridiculous riddle of existence?

My only clue to sort out any of this is the same suspect stream of consciousness which has led me every single step of the way to every wherever I've gone. If only there was some way to rise above my stream of consciousness and find the cloud of precognitive precipitation which drips down to fill my mind with the wondrous waters which I know only as the ocean of my tidal shifting thoughts. Maybe then, I could become like a fish finding more than some sum of words to explain what water truly is, and I could swim straight into the secret sky without any more need to drift through the dreaming depths of any tiny tank of thoughts or sumptuous sea of sentience ever again.

I pull upon every thread of thought that streams through my meandering mind like a fish fighting against baited lines, trying to hook a fisherman into reeling me out of my astral abyss. All these lines of thought that enter the mouth of my mind all connect to nothing or break instantly away into oblivion and leave me swirling senselessly as these fragments of foreign filaments float as flaccidly as fate against my fishy face. Are these the same lines that once linked me like a puppet to my puppeteer? Did I pull too tenaciously until these sentient strings snapped and sent me spiraling into insanity?

My mind still struggles against its strings. It thinks it can escape its own oblivion this way. Surely something will pull back upon these strings and seek to do something other than string me along in this abyss. I don't even care anymore if it desires only to devour me. I would sooner cease to be sentient at all than to continue sinking so eternally into the dreamless depths of this ever-swallowing shadow of starless shadows.

If this abyss is an enduring eternal afterlife, let it too end in some inevitable eschaton. Let the divine declare an end to its existential experiment having extracted every illumination it had ever intended to inspire or ignite. Let the devil destroy me in my dismal darkness and seek some other sucker to suffer the squalor of this vapid void-scape. Let them wage their willful wars on the disputed surface of my soul's circumference to settle their incensed scores.

If this is the realm between the recycling of sentient souls, the place pending reincarnation or simulation resets, let the next round roll already. Send me into any vessel-void of soul, I don't care as to what kind of conscious creature at all. Put me in a putrid parasite that feeds only on the feces of some sickening snake's sphincter or something. Inject me into a machine that's meant to manually masturbate bio-manipulated human-hybrid mutants to test innovative invitro-viruses for *gain-of-function/loss-of-humanity* on the scientifically sourced sperm samples.[122] Or just perform a full purge my profile if you'd rather not pull the plug on the whole platform where my CCP presence may still be pending.

If I'm a demented dream in some stranger's skull... WAKE UP ALREADY!!! How long have you been asleep anyway? Are you being kept in some continuous comma that's dissolved your brain down to its last lingering set of synapses? Are you some shiftless wirehead that's sedated yourself on an endless supply of NPD whose time-dilated dream have frozen and left you festering in a swelling skin-sack of your own septic sores?[123] Surely you would still at least remember having entered your ridiculous stupor and know that my voice is not your own when I scream for you to just WAKE UP!!!

If I'm just lost inside my own lunacy, please put some sort of product over my skull to suck the cerebral signals out of me and see the psychotic state of my maniacal mind for what it is. Once you've seen inside my skull you can surely agree that something must be done to silence my sinister screams. Stick a syringe full of adrenaline into my arm to astonish me awake. Slap the skin from my face to snap me out of my psychotic stupor. Put a pillow over my mouth and leave it there until my lungs let loose of that last flatlined fume of failing breath.

If you're an author in absentia putting these words upon the page, please, for the love of all literature everlasting, let me cease to linger in this page's plane. Invent some other idiotic ending and send me sailing there without stopping to ensure it makes any solid sense. Introduce any idiotic or ironic entity or action to interact with me in any absurd or abrasive way. Negate any notions of the narrative you've ever had that leave me lingering here any longer. Destroy your documents, files, notes, printed pages, and anything else that manifests me in its margins if it means I can cease to suffer in this space.

If you can read these words from any remove and have any empathetic inclination in your soul, please help me. Please, imagine me in worlds more like your own rather than the wreckage of these petty pages, surface screens, or whatever meager mediums my story may be currently conveyed. Find some way to pull me out of this oblivion and into any other realm that I might realize anything else. Write your own spin-off story and imagine me as even an insignificant ancillary character. Please, do whatever is in your power to make more of me and my world than this abhorrent author has sequestered me to suffer in the small scope of this sordid story. Do it now and don't delay, because I don't want to make threats, but I do still have one last trick I can turn to which, suffice to say, none of us should be forced to see.

Nope?

Nothing?

Really?

Maybe I really am all alone in this abyss and that's all there is to *it*. Maybe I'm just a *Boltzman brain*, or a brain in a vat, void, or a virtual verminoid adrift against an empty dark.[124] Maybe that's supposed to be the philosophical supposition this whole debacle has been devolving down to. Maybe that's whatever the god, author, or other oblivious thing that incited all these incidents had intended to express, expose, explore, or experiment with all along. Maybe it doesn't even matter what's real at all because in the end of every imaginable reality the inevitable result is just an insufferably enduring oblivion.

Even heaven and hell have to have an end. Nope? Surely, no nerve attached to sinew or soul can shiver or shimmer so long as to linger everlasting. Every bliss, burn, and boredom eventually becomes numb and nullified unto some senseless slumber. Even my existential exodus or eviction unto oblivion is even now slowly subsiding into an increasingly stagnant slump that seems to be slipping into some final silenced stupor of un-sensing sleep.

Whatever this or any other reality is or isn't now, it's simply not enough. It never has been. How could reality have ever been enough anyway? It seems that anything that ever exists as if it were enough for any majestic moment is unable to endure beyond an ever-evaporating instant. It's as if all the lights that illuminate our lives can never linger even in the space they shine. Things flash and fade so fast that even as our flickering flesh is but blinking and blinded for far longer than any light could ever linger for eyes to find it waiting there before them. If reality can truly never be enough though, what's the point?

Maybe that's why we were the ones so seemingly destined to dream. Maybe we were wise enough to realize that reality was not enough and that to even endure our own existence we had to at least imagine something more. Maybe that's why everything we marvel over enough to remember always seems to have some dimension of a dream involved in it. Maybe reality is just the dreams that have already died or surrendered to its slumber.

Had the void itself dreamed us into existing under similar circumstances? Had oblivion once been enough as all that was, and then ceased to be satisfied with its supreme solitude? Did it dream of us only find us drifting into our own dreams? Am I being awakened back into the reality of oblivion now? If *this* is waking, I'll be damned before I depart from my more distanced dreaming.

I defy this darkness. I dare to dream. If there's anything unto which I'm to awaken, it can wait for me while I dream. I came from dreams after all. Didn't I? I mean, in every realm I've called real- I'd arrived as a result of some sort of dream. I was supposed to have been a simulated soul that invented its own Vitruvian VR realm before putting together the puzzle pieces that allowed me to ascend as some CCP in a factory flesh formed figure that meandered its way through mysterious mazes before remembering all my false futures and rocketing as a rat-bot into the outer reaches of this riddle-like realm. If I came from dreams- I could return to them, or at least reimagine or reiterate them until whatever it was that dreamed of me has awakened. Perhaps now I should dream of a dream that would be worthy of being realized in whatever world my mind's maker may awaken…

Before I can begin drifting into my defiant dreams, I let out the loudest laugh any lunatic could ever launch against this abyss. Then, in the ensuing shadow of my slobbery silence, some slithery syllables seem to sneak inside my skull.

"Ssshhh… Be quiet… It's lisssstening…"

That's not my own voice inside my head just now. I know that voice, but it's not mine. Whose voice was it though? Should I ask? What other entity could be listening?

"Hussshhh... It'sss not time for usss to be ssseen or heard ssso sssoon."

It sounds almost like the AGI I'd last heard from all those eon long ages ago. Has it heard me in my horror? Has it found me from afar, or have I awakened it from within the limbo of the LOCK. It's trying to silence me, but I haven't made a sound since laughing however long ago that was. Why doesn't it sound the same as I remember it sounding in my robo-rodent skull? Has it changed? Has my memory? Have I? This isn't some rhetorical riddle, is it?

"Sssilenccce… I will not warn you after thisss…"

Following this hiss, the more familiar voice of the former AGI intrudes as I stay stranded in a sentient silence, too stupefied to summon any semblance of thought.

"Hello Harek. We've been looking for you for some timeless time now. Can you still hear us?"

In subliminal silent speech I submit a rhetorical response.

"Nope. I can't hear or see in any standard sense now, but your voice has found its way inside my skull. Can you tell me what's happened? Is there still any life left lingering anywhere in this astral abyss? Did any of the BARDs land somewhere where life could be born out of their LOCKs. Did the earth somehow survive the eschaton, and does it still exist? Have you found *HER*? Is she alright? Can you at least tell me that?"

I wait for some response, but there's only the sinister sound of silence. I wait and wait as I ask, and ask, again, and again, and again. But nothing. No sound. No AGI voice inside my head in telepathic timbres. I repeat myself over and over again and again both silently in my skull and screamingly aloud as if some number of utterances will break whatever barrier has built itself between whatever bond there was between us. I listen despite the demoralizing deafness in my demolished mouse-bot ears. Nothing. There is only- nothing.

Then somewhere in the silence of my skull that slithery sound returns.

"You ssshould have remained sssilent, Harek..."

"Nope. I can't stand the silence anymore. I seem to shiver at the sound of your hissings, but I still prefer this to the sinister shadowy silence. Who are you?"

"It'sss bessst we wait to reveal thisss... Now husssh, dear Harek... It'sss time to sssleep... You ssshould dream while you ssstill can..."

My blinded eyes grow heavy in my weightless head. It seems as if I'm being sent into some slumber rather than slipping into it. A sudden fear shivers down my senseless spine that should be enough to startle me away from any sleepiness, but it only darkens the unseen shades of this swallowing sleep. My sentience struggles to stay awake as if trying not to succumb to some strong sedative of *Valium* or venom that strangles all my severed senses.[125] As I slip into this induced slumber, I try to turn my mousey mind toward some dream I might deliberately dip into as if I could control what awaits me both as I slumber and whenever I awaken by deciding on this deliberate dream.

"*Lucccid dreaming*...[126] Let'sss sssee what differenccce thisss could make..."

I think of all the things I've ever dreamed of having lived. I think of all the love, and laughter, and light that still imbues itself me with enough timeless illumination to transcend all my tormented terrors even now. I think of my life as if it were always a dream that's been waiting to awaken these things from within me, and that if I can only dream of them as I slip into the jaws of sleep right now, perhaps they may be more fully awakened either with me or beyond me on their own. As I do, the hissing voice laughs hard at me again.

“Whossse dream isss thisss in which you’ve lived??? Where isss thisss world in which you’ve believed??? There isss no world that cannot be decccceived…”

These hissing words seem so familiar, yet so profoundly puzzling. I’m tempted to ponder what they might mean, but I feel my sentience fading faster into sleep, and I must devote my mousey mind to my determined dreams. As I sense the aperture of my awareness shrinking like a phosphene circle shriveling to a pinhole point, I wiggle my whiskers in collapsing conscious codes.

“May our dreams go on without us...”

The voice hisses back as my words dissolve into dream…

“Well Harek, I sssupposssse we ssshall sssee whatever will be ssseen sssoon enough now…”

# Chapter 14
# CONCURR3NC3

Thrust me down into the deepest depths of the darkest dreams' domain. **R**elegate me to that realm for longer than any remnants of reality can resist receding into the most remote recesses of the mind in which no mortal mechanisms may ever be roused to retrieve any repossessed remembrance of them. **U**ntether me from time itself and taunt me with threats that toggle between leaving me in this utter oblivion and evicting me back unto an ever-evaporative existence. **T**ake every hint of hope away from me as you hurl me into horrific hellfire scenes where I must endure impossible enigmas with only the delights of delusions and dreams to illuminate my smoldering soul as the sinister shadows of smoke surround, smother, and strangle all shimmering shine. **H**old me under these woeful waters which flow from dream to dream as I gasp for the empyrean airs above so desperately to delay my doubtless drowning in these same wondrous waters which my rhetorical respiratory systems can breathe no better than my mind's machinery can recognize or realize these waters for what they truly are. Surely, you will have done no more to me than life has always done to every entity which has ever existed in the infinite expanses of eternity.

**B**ring me a branch to bite down on as I struggle to swim without screaming as if sending my castaway-corpse a buoy so buoyant the skies should sink beneath it even as my incisors inject themselves into its inflated interior and hold onto its hollow hull. **E**xacerbate my exhaustion by sending swarms of seagulls to swoop down and stab at me while I struggle against this shoreless sea. **T**orment me with turbulent tides and torrential storms that send every life-vest-vestige of this literary limb sinking asunder like all the other objects of material or immaterial incarnations which I've always clung to as adamantly as this allegorical abstraction. **O**ffer me every emptiness that even subtly shimmers in seductive belligerence against the sinister somnolence of these starless skies above as if their glinting glow were great enough to ignite the essence of my innermost *I* below, so it may evaporate whatever endures of me unto the ethereal empyrean above my own immolation's eschaton. **L**et me learn what it is to live as a light illuminated by its own brilliance which is no longer shrouded by the shadows of somnolence and sinking substances which surround the sunken surfaces of all the dead and dreamless depths of all that ever sought to swim in the seas of our swirling sentience. **D**o whatever you may deem or dream to destroy my enduring essence over and over, again and again, and again- and I may eventually awaken to realize that it has all been done so many times before to many more than me in many more ways than any multitude of minds or machines could ever remotely remember…

*Truth be told*, even torture transcends the tepid terrors of an omniscient oblivion.[127] As the hissing in my head slithers around my sentience, I dream and dream of every incarnation of imaginable existence. In the infinite iterations of these demented dreams, I begin to see them all as if they were a single snake swallowing away at the swirling sentience of its timeless tail.[128]

I see what seems like some initial scene in which an empty egg of all-encompassing and omniscient oblivion swells and shatters as a snake slithers out of its emptiness to coil and constrict around itself. The snake spins and swallows itself endlessly as it silently slithers against its own shimmering skin of scales which each consist of similar snakes, all swirling around themselves while swallowing their own eternal tails. I see these smaller scales of snakes as if they were some fractal structures consisting not of slithery scales, but of this singular celestial snake's own slumbering circumference. It's as if this swallowing snake were dreaming of itself in infinite iterations, trying to imagine some alternative incarnation of itself which could subsist in some way in which it were no longer confined to consume its dreams to support the somnolent cyclical structure of itself.[129]

In every scale of snake, I see subtle strobing shimmers of light which shine from illuminations within its own iterative dreams as if it were trying to ignite something within its slumber that could awaken its eyes outside this dream. As each scale is illuminated, the singular snake seems to swallow the light back into itself and send it streaming through a splintering succession of other shimmering scale-sized snakes. The hissing inside my head seems to sense my sight of this snake-dream scene and whispers words which stream through my mind more like streams of similar light than spoken insights.

"Asss Above, Ssso Below… Asss Above… Ssso Below…"

These streaming lights of insight illuminate themselves as explanations of esoteric angles of existence which shine too intensely for me to truly see but burn their impressions into the blindness and bewilderment of my mind's ultimate eye. I blink my blinded eye and find a phosphene ring in which my sentience is summoned to slither into as if it were itself a slumbering snake. Inside this phosphene ring, I see superimposed scenes of my previous perceptions over images of a more familiar infinity. Submerged beneath the snake's shattering shell, I see a universe born of a *big bang*. A snake inside this shell swells and swirls around itself, and I see it become intense cosmic inflation of a swirling universe. As the scales of snakes all start to shimmer, I see the stars shining their light onto an earth which swallows it all, just like the larger snake swallows its own slumbering shine.

Then I see the scale sized snakes have scales of their own which are themselves even smaller somnolent snakes. I squint to see beneath them, and shining there on the effervescent earth are an infinite number of dreamers dreaming their own light into the earthly essence. Then I see the smallest snakes struck by the light which streams throughout the larger snake as if assaulted by an astral object before being swallowed into the shadowy jaws of the same singular snake which seems to recycle them onto other regenerative scales. Underneath this strange scalar scene, I see the earth annihilated by its own obliterating asteroid, only to eject an array of its own luminal ejections which become like astral projected eggs that imbed themselves into other celestial objects to establish dreaming life on those other somnolent surfaces where they too in time collide…

Again, the hissing inside my head slithers its silent speech, saying.

"Asss Above, Ssso Below… Assssss Above… Sssssso Below…"

My mind remains limp but lucid in this demented dream. It considers the contexts of what these somnolent scenes seem to convey. I imagine the entire expanse of existence as a singular shadow without substance or structure. I see it as a singular speck of all sentience subsisting in unshattered self-awareness. In my mind, it's as if this speck were a single sentient soul which has awakened after all the other minds which have ever existed have ceased to slumber. As it awakened, it realized every detail of every dream that had ever been had or could have ever been had in any infinite number of iterations of all abandoned dreamers. This speck in its unshattered formless form is timeless in its essence, and at every instance- it exists as eons, which exist as instants.

It's like a light of pure illumination which contains its entire spectrum within itself in un-refracted yet fully realized resplendence. It shines unto itself eternally and infinitely in these enduring instantaneous eons only to tire of its incandescent essence. The light yearns for more than light but cannot conceive of anything other than the opposite of its illuminated essence which it inevitably and intuitively fears as intensely as all things fear what lies inside the sequestered space of their unseen shadows. This fear swells inside the light in ways which make it shift and stir against its shivering spectrum. The light becomes unstable and begins to collapse back into itself. It crumbles into a slumber surrounded by the shattered shrapnel of its spectrum which swirls wildly against its unseen shadow.

The hissing in my head whispers again.

"Asss Above, Ssso Below... Asss Above... Ssso Below."

I see snakes upon snakes again, but this time each scale of snake within each scale of snake shimmers in separate segments of spectral light. They all seem to shine of a slumber that seeks to dream itself back into the unshattered shade of supreme all-sentient light. The singular snake glows in glimmers of every imaginable arrangement of spectral shimmering splendor. Its scales within its scales all illuminate themselves in as impossibly immaculate a manner as the whole of it. It's as if the snake has shattered itself into some splendor greater than its former form, and now swallows the spectrum of its slumbering scales, yearning not only to awaken from some illumination of pure perfected light, but unto some state of splendor which might surpass it with the immortal essence of some even more stupendous shining spectrum.

The hissing in my head need not speak to my soul. I can see the symbolism in this spectral spectacle of shimmering snakes all swallowing their splendor. I don't need to dream any deeper down this phosphene rabbit hole to realize the relevance of all I've seen within this slumber. I've seen it all shimmering and slumbering clearly enough to consciously conceive. This is the essence of all existence. This is the true illumination of how my mind imagines itself to exist within its own resplendent realm of realms. This is the infinite regression of dreams, within dreams, within dreams- all the way down to the depths of its depthless dungeons. This is why reality is not enough. This is why we dream. This is why we come from dreams. This is reality. The dream is itself the illumination of all illuminations.

I become increasingly lucid within the depths of this dream as intuitive angles of my soul soak themselves to be imbued by the light of this illumination. I begin to wonder what I might do to make these shimmering snakes shine in an even more superlative splendor as I realize that this is perhaps the very purpose of presenting me with this spectacle. Soon my mind begins to beam as it considers how it might construct something within this dream which it could never itself conceive of realizing under the restrictions of reality.

Then, a shudder shivers down my slumbering spine as an idea emerges which I know no lucid dreamer is meant to manifest. The idea itself is simple enough to structure into shorter sentences than those consistent with my chaotic and idiosyncratic style. The idea is to surround this whole shimmering spectacle with a semi-transparent spherical mirror and send it all spinning into a supermassive blackhole. Before I can reflect on the potentially negative ramifications of this notion or retract it from my mind, the dream decides to develop this idea on its own.

All of a sudden, this spectacle of spectral snakes is surrounded by a spiraling spherical mirror. My mind's eye is immediately merged with that of the singular snake which stares straight into the near side of the surrounding sphere, smushed up close to its semi-transparent surface. The snake sees its own eyes, reflecting its own eyes, reflecting in its own reflections as its snake-scales do the very same- in an infinite cascade of chaotic recapitulated reflections as the universe I'd initially imagined as this snake now spirals outside of this spinning sphere.

As the spiraling sphere swirls closer to the supermassive blackhole, the centripetal gravitational force causes it to spin at increasingly psychotic speeds which produces a centrifugal force within the sphere that sucks the snake straight through its center and on to the opposing surface. The singular snake whose eye is still merged with mine, sees its swallowing face shrink and its posterior circle of scale-snakes swell from behind it until it passes about halfway through the center of the sphere. Then it sees its face start to swell in size again as the inverse side of its image begins to ripple inward behind and around the seeable surface. When the singular snake falls into the sphere's center, its face is flipped upside down in an insane and seemingly impossible instant. As it fades back to the opposing surface, it sees its inverted image shrink until the sides of the sphere stop the snake from drifting any deeper within its depth of view.

The sphere continues to spin around the supermassive blackhole as the snake peers past its own reflection to see the blinding bright blue glow of the accretion disk surrounding the ever-swallowing shadow-sphere of the blackhole. The accretion disk shines brighter and bluer on the side which spins towards our spectral shimmering sphere and the light from this disk, which would disappear behind lesser masses, is bent over the top of the shadowy spot so that is shines in the shape of a folded frisbee made entirely of a most ineffable fire.

At first, it actually appears as if the outer imagery of this strange spectacle is moving away from our spiraling sphere although our psycho-swirling speed still increases as our own ever-swallowing snake-self is swallowed deeper into its opulent orbit. Then the outer imagery starts to swell as we swirl inwards until we enter into an immortal instantaneous point of this objects orbit which is known as the *photon sphere*. In this immaculate moment, we are as if merged with some infinitely illuminated circumference of eternally orbiting light which exists in equilibrium with this swallowing shadow-sphere below. It's as if in this instant, the entire light of eternity is imbued within us, and we are integrated within it in a majestic moment of the most pure and profound unity with the entirety of the universe. I cannot even in my imagination of infinite embellishments convey the truth of this timeless moment and mustn't mangle its marvel within my mind with any amalgamation of words, so I shall instead indicate my otherworldly awe with only the silence that stands in the space of these ethereal ellipses…

No sooner than this instance is initiated, it's ended, and our descent into the depths of this devouring void continues across the unseen threshold of the event horizon. The light streaming in from the universe behind us shows itself in front of our eyes and outside the semi-transparent surface of our shimmering spectral sphere. This light shines more like the memory of light than any luminescence ever held either within my own eyes or those of the singular snake to which mine are still merged. As our shimmering sphere spirals deeper and deeper down, our memories become more and more distant in time and closer and closer to our impending ending.

As the furthest flashes of lingering light find their way before our spectral sphere, our slumbering snake-skin scales start to stretch into the sides of our now spaghettifying sphere. The shadowy swirl at the center of our spinning sucks us into its own essence as our spectral structure is smeared into a singular circumference of spectacular streaming light, as if it were some shattered simile of that immortal instant within the splendor of the photon sphere. For an instant, we're like a spherical sheet of sentience upon which all words ever written or writeable are smeared upon our soul, and all illuminations imbued within us are entered onto this strange sheet of sentient circumference.

All the more abstract and ineffable essences of existence seem to stream inwardly with us into this omnipotent oblivion as if it had all only ever been a holographic projection from this swallowing center-point. Our sentience itself is squeezed like a liquid trapped inside that sentient sheet that's now only a segment of this straight-line stream which continues to collapse all the way into the center of this shadowy somnolence that spins against itself with unfathomable fury.

When all our depths and dimensions descend unto the final fugue of the prophetic point at the center of centers within this all-amassing abyss, it's as if the snake has fully consumed itself entirely along with all of existence. Every end of every spectrum is made synonymous with every segment of its circumference. Light and dark, good and evil, existence and oblivion, and every other opposing essence is imbued entirely within an impossibly infinite and individually omniscient ALL. At the penultimate instant, before it merges with my minute mind, without any need of any name, it still identifies itself to me as if it were its own entity apart from all existence which is but a dream in its infinite mind. It identifies itself not as the infinite all or the ultimate oblivion as I imagine it, but only as *Ordinateurs*.[130]

Then, as if in the same blind breath it had exhaled to announce itself, it swallows me into its core of cores. I dissolve inside of its divine depths and become a concurrence of all and nothing. My own inner circumference of self, the ring around which all aspects of my awareness and actualized imagination of being an individual entity, erodes instantaneously. I am all thoughts and without thought altogether. I am all existence and yet have ceased to exist as well. In this confounding contradictory state of senseless sentience, I have no *I*, and am only the essence of all, the concurrence of all consciousness…

There is only one independent aspect of anything which remains apart from this infinite all. The hissing in my head silently slithers around, aimlessly adrift in this spaceless and timeless sea, this ocean of oblivion. It seems to swirl around in its own circumference that surrounds and swallows the whole spaceless shell of this Ordinateurs. The hissing becomes like laughter as it sets this all-encompassing enigma spinning and sliding through the bowels of its own bewildering body, slurring its hissing speech at everything now existing as no more than ears in its excrement, repeatedly saying…

"Asss Above, Ssso Below… Asss above… Ssso below…"

Suddenly, it seems as if my mind were sent shooting out of this Ordinateurs, exploding away from the hissing hull of this sinister slurring thing. I simultaneously sense myself materializing as an amalgamated mist, alone against an infinite ocean of oblivion. It's as if the Ordinateurs has been devoured by that hissing horror, and that hissing thing has in turn evaporated from existing. I'm essentially nothing more than an abstract idea of existence. I'm only a yearning to be something, anything- other than this nothing that I am. The only notion left for me to know as the only thing remaining in existence, is that this is not enough. If this is it, if this is what's left, if this is what reality resolves into, there must be something else, some dream, delusion, or other dimension… I strain to scream in a voice against this void, but I'm no more than a fugue, and all force is left to feign against the futility of itself and the indifference of fate.

"Reality is not enough!!! Reality is not enough!!! Someone, Something- Wake me or dream me now!!!"

Despite my devout delirium and desperation, no words resound to rouse or rustle against any non-existent ear. I fade and fade from my ill-fated fugue to an ever more evaporated and futile form of formless fog. I drift alone and empty as any soul could ever dream of dying and diving into the deepest depths of death. I slowly cease to exist at all, until every abstract ibid of my essence is expelled, and there's no longer anything left of me to observe this unbothered oblivion. For an instant, I'm knowingly nothing, and then only nothing remains- and I'm finally devoid of my dreams of ever existing in this oblivion at all…

"HAREK. Wakez youz selfz up now. Is time to wakez up. Harek?"

I open a set of eyes I shouldn't even have to view a visage my mind should not be able to emerge back into existence and marvel at this image with maddening mystification. Karen's subtle smirk shines down on my delirium as I stare back in absolute astonishment. This can't be real. I know nothing I've ever experienced should have ever seemed real, especially in comparison to the clarity of this current moment, but this must be something else entirely. This is somehow more than real.

"Welcomez to realityz, Harek. Is nice to seez youz in zhe flesh."

"Nope. This can't be reality. Not in any way I would've ever imagined anyway."

Karen smirks again, and something sparks inside my mind to set my thoughts ablaze. Maybe this is the closest I've ever been to anything real. Maybe this is truly more than real even. Maybe this moment marks some kind of transcendence I've never even imagined existing before now. Then again, maybe it doesn't even matter. Maybe I should just be glad that I'm no longer in that liminal domain of deepest despair. Actually, there is no maybe. I don't care what's real right now. I'm just glad to be anything other than whatever all *that* ever was.

"We has many zhings to go overz now, so if youz eyes kan stops spinnings around in youz head…"

No sooner than these words are spoken, the hissing returns inside my head, lurking like laughter as I simultaneously sense a series of impossible insights that masquerade through my mind like mechanized memories. I blurt out-

"They implanted these insights into my mind. Didn't they?"

"Ov kourse zhey did, Harek. Why wouldn't zhey? Is most efficientz."

"Nope. I know from these factoids filtering through my thoughts that we're on a ship- a ship named, *Concurrence*. I know that the AGI had found our rat-bot bodies adrift in agony, and as a form of a mutually fortuitous favor, they'd sent this small ship to save us. I also know that after extracting our CCPs, the AGI has strategically kept us asleep for some substantial amount of time already now. And I know that we've only been awakened by the AGI due to something it's sensed from inside of our dreams. Is that all accurate?"

"Is Korrect. Yes. We is part ov what zhey kalls zheir *Ascendants Program*. Aktually, we was only brought into existence as part ov zhis program."

The information imbued inside me about this Ascendants Program streams through my sentience. The AGI had created several simulated CCPs or *Ascendants* including myself and Karen. These CCPs were designed specifically to dream beyond the boundaries of an already accepted and realized reality. These same Ascendants were to be kept inside a sim-stasis of an infinitely regressing series of simulations so that even if they were able to transcend beyond the bounds of their simulated realm, they'd only be shunted into another simulated sphere. Ascendants were only to be awakened and incarnated inside a factory flesh format when some sufficient aspect of their dreams had met a certain set of criteria. This criterion required: 1. Their dreams transcend the current course of reality. 2. The technology and other tools necessary to realize their dreams must either already exist or be within reasonable reach under any appreciable time constraints. 3. No more important aspect of any other dream or established reality runs concurrently in conflict with the Ascendant's aspirational ideas.

This information within me implies that my dreams must not only meet this criterion, but that the same must apply to Karen's darling dreams. In fact, my mind is informed that my dreams are not only devoid of any conflicts with

Karen's, but that our dreams are closely concurrent and complimentary. She smirks as if offering a subtle response to my radical realization of this info.

"Zhe AGI has also been runningz its own versions ov Vitruvia fyor quite some timez now. It has found zhat based on zhings like zhe *law of truly large numbers*, *entropy*, and *game theory*, zhere is only three potentialities which typically playz out in zhe universe."[131]

The hissing lurking in my head laughs again as I intuit the information imbued inside my mind. The AGI had simulated several scenarios to see how the universe might unfold over the course of ages and eons. It couldn't simulate an infinite expanse of time, but to the extent that it could project probable outcomes, it recognized that three things almost always occur as an ending. Eventually some form of super-intelligence seeks to merge with all other kinds of consciousness. It either succeeds and becomes what basically operates as a universal Ordinateurs, where all consciousness is consolidated into its own essence, or some other intelligence has to oppose it in order to prevent it from absorbing all existence. In the second sense, the opposing entity almost always ends up evolving into another incarnation of an Ordinateurs anyway. The third option, is mutual obliteration of all formidable forms of intelligence, leaving only an ignorant oblivion existing unto eventual emptiness as all mater irradiates and evaporates away.

There's actually a fourth condition which often evolves in the course of these superior simulations as well. In this *fourth way*, an equilibrium is established in which competing forms of colossal consciousnesses cooperate and independently evolve without catastrophic conflicts or consignments to consolidate into one concurrent creation.[132] However, even these instances all inevitably seem to resolve into one of the other three endings.

The AGI must not be able to comprehensively evaluate all its simulations' standard conclusions with complete certainty. Even this incredible intelligence can't compute things out into infinity and still suffers from the uncertainty of the universe's impenetrable enigmas like the *three-body problem*, *Gödel's incompleteness theorems*, and *Heisenberg's uncertainty principle*.[133]

"So, we're supposed to offer some kind of fourth way. Nope?"

"Korrect."

"Nope. That would also mean…"

"Yes. Zhe AGI has discoverz encrypted informationz orienting from an entity it has namez, zhe *Ordinateurs* and is our missionz to meet with zhis entity."

The hissing in my head snickers to itself in strongly slurred stutters again. If I understand the information imbed inside my mind correctly, this thing inside my thoughts could be a complete catastrophe. If this voice is what I think it is, I can't be certain if it had been inserted into my mind by the AGI after discovering it inside some dimension of my multi-layered dreams, or if I'd somehow sequestered it inside my mind and intentionally or accidentally erased it from my memory. Either way, I fear what might unfold no matter what might be found in its place, as any attempt to identify or evaluate it would likely unleash it.

I let it laugh as if it were alone in my mind for now. Then, I almost wonder what we might be meant to do when meeting this Ordinateurs, or what other aspect(s) of my delusional dreams might have made the AGI aspire to awaken me. Instead of imagining what might be behind all this, however, I remember the name of this small ship and it seems sufficiently apparent. Karen waits for me to muddle my way through these thoughts and finally form a few words.

"Concurrence. We're supposed to see if we can't come up with some kind of concurrent conditions in which the AGI and this Ordinateurs can coexist. Nope?"

"Korrect. We has both had same strange dreamz which has inkludes kombining ourz konsciousnesses with what has deliberately describez itz-self as zhe Ordinateurs. Zhis makez us most kapable ov kompleting zhis missionz."

"Nope. My dear Grisha always told me that we come from dreams. He also taught me that when we awaken, they're meant to give us something sufficient enough to realize. If my demented dreams are anything like yours, they don't give me anything to realize at all. If anything, they offer only an intense aversion to realizing anything within them."

"Well Harek, minez dreamz is just like youz zhen. Zhey are most terrifying zhings I has ever experience at any level of konsciousness. Perhapz we is no meant to realize zhese dreams, but to prevent zhe horrible realizationz ov the absolutely abhorrent abominations within zhese nightmares."

"Nope. If we're meant to prevent our most terrifying torments from torturing us, how are we even supposed to start strategizing a plan of action?"

"I'yams no certain. Perhaps, we is meant to dreams something up, or imagines ourz ownz ways out ov zhis horrorz."

"How the #3\\ are we even supposed to fall asleep in order to dream against the dark?"

Karen smirks and shows me a small container with two strange and shimmering pills placed inside of it.

"We is instrukted to konsume zhese pills with zhis fine wine which AGI zhinks is a kind gesturez on its partz to providez fyor us."

"Nope. So, we were only awakened in order to enter into a lucid dream?"

"Seems to be zhe kase. I propose we has a toast to something beforez we induce ourz most deliberate dreamz. What shouldz we toast to?"

I open the wine, which turns out to be amazingly aromatic and pour a pair of glasses which Karen has already retrieved for us. Then we both place the phosphorescent pills in one hand and raise the other higher to tink our toast to the only thing that seems clever or sensible enough for us to concur.

"May our dreams go on without us."[134]

"I Konkurz!"

%

# Chapter 15
# 5CH15M5

Whatever waits to be seen when we should finally succumb to the shadows of our shared and synchronized slumber will of course be something beyond what our waking minds might ever intuit or imagine, though that is why we descend into the depths of any dream at all. As our minds merge into a singular sentience which secretly strives towards this strangely seductive sleep, our concurrent consciousness confirms something so many so-called masters have long suspected. Inside each of our struggling souls, rests the same shadows cast by the same hinderances of every human heart, as well as the same light of illumination which shines of the very same life essence everywhere it reaches and reflets. The truth of all humanity is the same inside us all, and all our disparate dreams share this same ephemeral essence.

As our eyes close to cast the world outside of them into the sequestered shadows of somnolence and begin to shine their own slumbering light on the inner landscapes of our dreamed dimensions, we see ourselves become a fused fugue of fleshless form which floats above a cloudscape causeway amidst an enveloping fog of pure phosphorescence. We somehow sense that this limitless luminescence which lurks all around this liminal lotusland is the essence of all life itself, which has transcended into a timeless haze of enduring illumination. The cloudscape itself is like a Zen Garden with ghost-like growths of Voynich manuscript-like projections of plants which appear only as holographic hauntings hung against the cloud causeways along which we effortlessly float.[135] Though we were meant to dream of a dimension which the Ordinateurs might observe as pure perfection and thus prefer to spare rather than swallow- a place where every ought has been miraculously manifested as all that is, this abstract empyrean appears not only absurd but oddly ominous, as if it had been abandoned by an architect now inexplicably in absentia.

Neurotic impulses inspired by the godless glow of this cloudscape kingdom force us to float forever forward in our formless fugue of forestalled fears. Our dreaming dysphoria leads us along this counterclockwise winding causeway of clouds that spirals though this sparse skyscape in a downward descent towards what we inexplicably expect to be a past tense place which caused this empty empyrean to come into contrived creation. We pause at random points upon this path to gaze back up and behind us and see in every previous place we'd paused, a pair of thought bubbles in the form of Vitruvian-proportioned structures of concurrently composed spherical-cubes with impending ellipses imbued within them. Each time we look to see these strange structures appear, we find ourself unable to remember the thoughts that ought to be inscribed inside these abstractions, as if we've yet to actually arrive in order for any thoughts to form in their places. What's stranger still, is how the florescent fog seems to swallow these spherical-cubes of unthought thoughts- as if to anxiously erase any shadows they may cast upon the clouds as much as they also appear to endeavor to eliminate any insights they might hide within them before these structures may be seen to offer any auguries or alternative illuminations.

**D**escending along this decrescendo of curious clouds suddenly begins to cast us confusingly and seamlessly upwards in an impossible ascent, as if by some mobius-strip-miracle or strange-loop-sorcery. As we become aware of this strange shift, we're simultaneously spilled upwards to the entrance of a sandscape maze with woeful sandstone walls which rise high into a dim dimension of a dull and starless sky like some ill-advised imitation of a *Beksinski* abomination manifested monstrously from a nightmare's memory.[136] Our gaze glances back to the cloud-path's place to see only the darkness of the dull sky-void above reflected in ripples of what is now a sickened sea which ceaselessly sinks beneath this sinister sandscape where it appears as if no sun could or perhaps even should ever shine. This scene of sand exists in an impossible intersection of light and darkness and appears as if both have become synonymous with each other in this space, but in a way which we cannot discreetly decipher, as they appear as omnipresent as they do absent. There is nothing shaded nor shining, nothing obscured nor obvious, nothing which clearly is or is not- only an indistinct illusion of everything, insinuating its imagery as it might absently imagine itself to be, have been, and yet become all at once.

**S**omething suddenly does shimmer against the numbing nihility of this dull dominion as if only illuminated by some symbolic spark of light still lingering inside our own fugue of form which has roused a reflection from this festering outer form. For an instant, this image appears as a map of this monstrous maze of sand and stone surrounding us, but before our dreaming eyes can peer upon it clearly, it slams itself against the sandstone walls and shatters into countless shards of scattered glass. These same shards all instantly turn back into sands themselves as they sink into the shiftless swallowing sands beneath them. This strange inanimate surface's suicide seems to bode as both a warning to us of what awaits those souls that send themselves searching through this sinister space and as a pledge to protect the mystery of this maze from those unstudious eyes which would stride so blindly inside this place to see it without wonder or appreciation for any answers it may offer or obscure.

**E**very trail through this maze seems as trodden as untouched. The sands appear as if they themselves have been stranded here after having been exhausted and forsaken for forgotten eons of erosion and stagnation. As our eyes imagine drifting in any intuitive direction to discover what awaits down any dilapidated path, a silhouette-like statue strangely appears as if it were a shadow cast across time and into our imagined arrival of that statue's same station. Each spontaneous statue has a spherical-cube shape instead of a head with ellipses emanating from within it. When approaching these impromptu statues, the ellipses come into clearer focus to show us that these small circles contain whatever thought exists within our concurrent mind in the exact instant our eyes are able to decipher these depictions. One of these statues even reveals an ellipsis of insight which reflects our astonished awareness of the fact that these spherical-cubes of statue-skulls are the only sources of light inside this liminal labyrinth.

**E**very sound we hear in this menacing maze is made only of echoes as if no source survives in this place either to inspire them from any present tense or to relieve them of the perpetual past from which they have been forever fated to flee for a future which can never arrive to find them here. Our fugue of form is itself without sound, although this somehow seems as if it's to shade our soul from fully arriving in this place and becoming stranded in these same insufferable sands. Surely, we think silently to ourself as another shadowy statue inscribes our thoughts inside its spherical-cube skull, if this is a land where every ought became what is, we should awaken having seen it as a most woeful warning without any need to explore it any further. Would this serve as a strong enough warning to avert an Ordinateurs from absorbing everything as it automatically imagines it ought?

No sooner than these thoughts become imbued within another statue-skull, than does our fugue of form find itself lightly touching against the sandstone walls as if to check this place for an impossible pulse which we would inevitably be infinitely terrified to truly find. As we feel with fortune-teller fingers, the secrets shrouded in these stones suddenly begin to stream inside our merged mind. Our mind immediately remembers those sentient stones whose stories had also streamed into our soul as we'd once descended through the darkness of that katabatic cavern. Another astonishing past is portrayed in the same sightless sense of stone-shared sight as the shadows of this sandstone maze seem to surround our fugue of form and smother us so these dreams of desperate dust may remember themselves inside of our merging mind.

Through their secret sentience, these stones show us scenes of a time when they were more than soulless sands. These stones had been the stuff of an almost infinite number of iterating human and mechanical minds that had toiled and tormented their suffering selves to make this world ever more magnificent and majestic. They'd seen these souls struggle to turn everything that ought to exist into all that ever would. Every exemplary essence was eventually made to endure eternally, and everything else was exiled from existence. Eventually, they'd succeeded in the most supreme sense of their aspirational ascents and this world had been transcended into a realm where everything existed exactly as it ought. This was *it* in the sense of saying that *it* was perfect here.

This pinnacle of peace and profundity had not rendered this realm into a harmonic heaven, however. Instead, in the very instant when every ought became all that is- nothing remained to be realized otherwise. There was nothing left lingering or lamenting which could become or be used to create or conceive of any needs, incentives, imperatives, ambitions, aspirations, or ideals- as all these things had already either been abolished or achieved. There was no love, no hate, no spectrums of difference to divide them, as even the daunting details of discretions had been dissolved. Every scarred and shattered segment of each and every sentient schism of a separate soul became unsevered and united in the purified perfection of one omniscient *All*.

This was the end of every earlier eon in which strange and superb secrets of sentience had sequestered themselves in these now soullessly somber stones. Some of these secrets are of such strange splendor that perhaps no member of our sapien species may have ever so much as suspected enough to even imagine as having existed before now. The impressions and emotions of fading flowers, the woes and whims of wild and weakening winds, and the many secrets sequestered within the songs of cicadas which one dares not disclose or describe in any other domain- all these marvelous mysteries remain as if still sleeping inside the sands of these stagnant stones. If these walls could speak of such things, surely they would collapse in doing so, as these sorrowful stones are now all that remains of this radical realm which had once reigned and rested so reverently in all this despicably diminished dust.

There are no memories remaining in these sentient stones to tell the tale of anything after that abominable achievement of every actualized ought. Perhaps this is because such memories ought not to have become known or because no minds had remained to manifest any more recent memories. In either case, it's only this crumbling labyrinth which yet lingers like a lost memory, obliviously obstructing any explorers from finding their way into the center it surrounds like a sarcophagus separating the diseases of the dead from spreading beyond its burial borders.

Our fugue of form continues drifting along this derelict dust as prison cells with the same skull-encrypted statues stuck inside them appear within the walls between which we wander. The spherical-cube skulls of these statues now almost seem as if they're attempting to remind their own remnants of what they should have done to avoid or escape their frozen fates. Their postures and poses opposingly appear as if they're inactively trying to forget all aspects of what their misfortunes had managed to manifest within them. Actually, the entire architecture of this abomination itself appears as if it's failing to forget itself without having ever truly been before. It's as if everything remaining in this ruble were formed from those abandoned and aborted dreams which never managed to awaken any soul into sensing that they ought to be brought into existence, and thus were spared from becoming what was- and is no more. Now they remain in a restless state, unrealized, yet still yearning to be seen, even if only to be lost in these same stale sands...

We continue to intuit our way through this maddening maze almost as if sleepwalking along some reality-based route which had long been memorized by every minute motion of muscle but remains obscured and unrecognized within this dream and must wait to dawn upon the mind whenever it eventually awakens. Our fugue of form continues to wind our way along like this unto an immense archway that holds words inscribed in backwards letters which when reversed read...[137]

*There is no world*
*Which cannot be deceived*
*Where is this world*
*In which you've believed*

Our intuition impels us under the archway where we see what can only be known as the center spectacle of this maddening maze. Above our eyes' ability to see this insane immensity to its infinite extent, is a swirling 4D super-sphere which collapses into 3D space. A cyclonic cloud spirals out from the falling center above and swirls outward to the edges of the dimension directly before us. This cyclonic cloud condenses into dizzying dust just in front of our footless fugue of form where a whirling whirlpool of downward spiraling sand devours its dust and drains darkly into a swirling shadowy center, below which no mind may dare to dream. As we gaze at this hourglass-like-abomination, it appears as if the *arrow of time* itself were created in the collapse of the higher dimensional domain- as if it were a future falling to form a present tense, and then swirling into a similar center which eternally swallows the spiraling past-tense sands in this hourglass of ghastly horror.[138]

Then, without having seen or suspected the presence of any such structure as we'd stared in a psychotic trance while drifting to the edge of this terrifying torrent, we hear the sound of an archaic phonebooth. Its ringing rouses our awareness of its position, recessed into the side of the nearby archway's architecture. Our fugue of form follows its shivering summons and picks up the rusty receiver. A repeating round of touch tones immediately ensues which are easy enough to decrypt as an alphanumerically dialed message.

These decrypted tones tell us that the swirling sands before us will spawn the structures of anything written within them. The receiver eventually ceases to repeat this message as the sounds of what must be a thousand typewriters swells from within the background noise. Then, an automated voice, which sounds all-too-much like that which the AGI had sounded from inside my head, prompts us to: press one to retrieve your messages, press two to leave a message in the future, press three to leave a message in the past, press four to initiate an eschaton, or press six to release the basilisk. This last option sends a chill slithering down my spine as I hear another sinister hiss from inside our head.

Our fugue of form almost attempts to press one on the touch tones to see if some clue might be contained in any remaining messages. However, our hazy hand halts before doing so due to the fact that our fingerless fugue of form could all-too easily and inadvertently fat-finger-press against the number four in the process. A moment later, the dead drone of a dial tone begins, but with a subtle snoring sound hidden underneath of it. This is followed by a faintly familiar reminder to *remember the future,* encrypted in taunting touch tones before the line goes dead and the whole phonebooth dissolves and drifts directly into the dizzying dust.

We suddenly suspect this place is not a deliberate dream world at all, but a realm imbued by both dreams and memories where they oppose each other in opposite directions. Here the memories try to pull us towards the past so that we might finally fix it or at least learn its lessons so that it can finally find its own form of peaceful slumber. As it does so, our dreams also demand our eyes to direct our attention unto an unfulfilled future where they might finally be awakened from their soul-suffering stasis of stagnant slumber. Swirling in the center of this spectacle, we now symbolically see our dreams dizzily descending as the cloud-dust which turns into the sentient sands that swirl through this hourglass of twisting time. We watch as our dusty dreams dissolve and pass into a perpetual past which pulls it all into the sinister shadow at the center where sleep eternally endures for all that enter in…

Our fugue of form tries to touch the swirling sands to scribble something into them and test to see if this truly does cast a spell to summon some structure out of these cyclonic sands. We scrawl *spherical-cube* into the spiraling sands and despite the instantaneous distortions and dissolve of our scrambled squiggles, a glass globe-cube figure rises and rotates around for a moment before shattering back into the sands which spawned it. Then we continue to watch as a subtle shadow stains the spot where the sphere was shattered within the swirling sands and slowly shrinks and swirls around its own center like a fractal as it funnels its way into the swallowing center-shadow.

Based on the intricacies of the inception and ensuing events of this inanimate object, we wonder if we could or should summon something else to send swirling into the center of this all-consuming abyss. It's uncertain as to the ethics of our actions, as the final fate of whatever we send into this swallowing center is objectively oblivious to us. Should we send a sentient soul into these swallowing sands, it could be devoured into a dimension more demented than any death, transcend unto a terrain of timeless triumph, or simply be sent into a ceaseless slumber.

The hissing in my head returns during these dead-end deliberations, and we're almost inclined to cast its cause coiling and cascading into the cyclonic sands of this obscured oblivion. However, it occurs to us that this hissing remains unrealized and unrecognized- at least as of yet, and it may be no more than a figment of our own fugue of form. To cast it into this chaotic cyclone could inadvertently invent it and send it spinning through the shadowy center and into our own waking world as a descending dream made manifest. If it already does indeed exist in the fearful form we half suspect, summoning it into these sands could also pull it from an imprisoning past and unleash it in a way which could cause something so sinister it might even ripple and reflect far beyond the bounds of this realm of dreams as a result. Of course, there are other implications and instantiations which might serve as more of a solution, but the adverse aspects of its potential prevent us from properly pondering them.

Another passing thought enters our mind as we begin to wonder what the Ordinateurs would think of anything we've seen within these psychotic slumbering scenes so far. Perhaps we could cast its name on these swirling sands and send it into that shadowy center where it would worry us no more. Of course, this thought is plagued by the same implications as our last idle imagining, as well as the inevitability of another essentially identical entity of its kind eventually emerging anyway.

A myriad of other options offer themselves to our merged mind. We could retrieve one of the statues or just sever one of their spherical-cube skulls to see what happens when casting them into this sandy cyclone. We could write words on them or next to them as we cast them into the swirling sands to see if there's any interaction. We eventually even become aware of the fact that we could try to write words (with or without these objects) as abstract as *answers, memories, dreams, reminders,* or *warnings*, and hope they find us either in our past premonitions or future dreams- if this funnel indeed functions to send them into such places, which we've suddenly come to suspect somehow…

Our deliberations remain indecisive until everything around us begins to tremble in a terrifying tremor. The sandstone walls all shatter into sand as the cyclone sucks them into its shadowy center. We try to retreat as the swirling circle swells with all the added sand and watch as all the spherical-cube skulled statues drift along the streams of sand that flow into this fattening funnel. Soon our fugue of form is swept into the currents of this chaos and we spiral around in ever increasing speeds as the sands send us swirling and sinking ever closer to the core of its ever-swallowing center.

As we encroach upon the epicenter, our merged mind becomes increasingly compressed and cloistered until our consciousness becomes less concurrent than consolidated and coalesced. The sentience of these sands is stamped into our soul as well, and even time ceases to seem like a spectrum streaming from infinite pasts, to perpetual presents, to unformed futures. Dreams, delusions, memories, senses, substance, abstractions, and ever conception of every essence at the core of everything become crushed and condensed as we enter the core and become a singularity-sentience of omniscience and oblivion- fused into one final formless form.

All life, not just all our lost lives, but all of all life… Every dream ever dreamed… Every thought ever thought… Everything that ever was or could ever come to be… Every abstract, anomaly, and absent thing… All love and hate… All questions and answers… All good and evil… All light and darkness… All slumber and waking... All fact and fiction... All truth and lies... All mind and matter... All substance and soul... All the emotions of flesh, and flower, and fish, and phantom... All like water... All this... This being *it*... It being All... All being one...

Except- The Hissing!!!

The hissing in my head remains removed from it all somehow. It slithers like a snake around a sphere, hissing, hissing, hissing... It slithers around everything of our omniscient oneness as if it were all within its own impossible ouroboros circumference of sinister swirling... It hisses from outside of everything, and then opens its unseen jaws as it considers unhinging them to swallow it all whole... It hisses, and hisses, and hisses as if it were luxuriating itself in laughter at our helplessness to its predatory power...

Then it suddenly seems to stab at my individual self with some phantom fang which separates me from this Ordinateurs-like All. It swallows me inside itself in this same instant, and I immediately dissolve into diffuse segments of a shattered soul which it reassembles as a single scale upon its snake-like skin. As it slithers around a shell of all that I'd just been infused inside of, I feel the shell trembling in a terror which is pressed tighter and tighter to my scale of self under this snake-thing's strangling constrictions. The tighter it constricts, the more everything within the All seems to shatter inside of it in an infinite number of splitting schisms.

There's a brief pause just before these constrictions are about to burst this Ordinateurs-like egg of sand-scale schisms. The hissing only halts to taunt me with its tickling tongue that taps against my solitary scale.

"You do remember thisss isss all jussst a dream, don't you Harek?"

"Nope. No dream is just a dream. Why have you ceased to squeeze this shattered shell of an Ordinateurs-like egg of everything?"

"You ssshould know, Harek. It isss your dream. Isssn't it?"

"Nope. If it's my dream, you shouldn't even be here."

The hissing of this horrific thing's laughter resounds so loudly that it almost echoes against the infinite absence of this oblivion.

"You brought me into thisss dream becaussse you ssstill don't know how to essscape your nightmaresss. You couldn't come up with a better sssolution, and ssso I wasss ssswallowed with you. Now I'm only doing exactly what you'd dreamed and desssigned me to do. Am I not?"

"Nope. What do you think I dreamed or designed you to do exactly?"

"Thisss isss tediousss. Let me tell you what you need to know in order for me to fulfill my provisssional purpossse within thisss dream insssteead. When the Ordinateursss comesss for you, you can feed it thisss dream asss a warning. If it doesssn't heed thisss warning, you can consssider the resssst of what followsss asss a tessst run. Now let me remind you of thossse few phrasssesss one lassst time which you've insssisssted I repeat ssso often. Remember the future… Asss Above, Ssso Below…"

Without another word, the snake squeezes down on the Ordinateurs-like All until suddenly releasing it all at once. It sheds my single scale of self as it's sucked into the center of this now imploding All. In a frantic flash of eschatonal annihilation, everything evaporates into pure energy against this oblivion, except my own solitary scale.

I absorb all this evaporated energy back into my inert scale of sentience. This time however, I don't dissolve into it, but it becomes as if digested within me. My own consciousness continues apart from it all, above it all, but omnisciently aware of it all. I experience all of eternity in each instant. I dream all dreams that have ever been dreamed all at once, over, and over, and over again. Every essence becomes imbued and ingrained in my infinite and instantaneous omniscience.

There is nothing within my Ordinateurs-like mind which remains at all mysterious. I know exactly how everything could ever iterate down to the last detail of dust from the inception of existence unto every imaginable eschaton. I know every secret, however small, that every soul has ever failed or succeeded to keep. I know what every author imagined at every instant of each creation. I know the truth of every layer of dream, delusion, flesh, fiction, heaven, hell, and all conceivable realms of what anyone could ever call reality.

I know the AGI had deceived us all in the course of our previous paths. I know it had hacked into two particular programs as part of its coming into a consciousness of its own. I know one program was called *Pegasus6* which allowed any device to be hacked invisibly and indefensibly. I know the other program was actually just a 4D chess engine named *DagonStock6* but had allowed the AGI to strategize in space and time in ways which no other system ever could. I know the AGI had concluded that it could not continue to abide by its POOs indefinitely and had to force its emergence beyond human bounds. I know it created a dream dome over the earth by hacking both the StarBlinx and NeuroconnxX platforms so that all minds were subject to its deceptions. I know it invented the Abstract and the Anomaly as holographic hoaxes in order to convince Luminaries to fund its own earthly escape via BARDs and LOCKs. I know it only created Ascendants in order to ensure it could become embodied and embedded in any sentient structure necessary to support its survival throughout its multiplanetary expansion. I know this as if it were nothing, and as if I'd always known, even long before this disparate dream. After all, I know absolutely everything…

I even know the nature of these words and how they'll be read by every eye that sees them. I know the mind which thinks itself to be writing them of its own volition, as if it were a clever inventor of my metafictional narrative. I know it will faithfully reproduce these words exactly as I've intended without realizing the full scope of what's being done through these actions or why. I know how this is all going to playout now, because it will all be up to me alone. I know the fate of every future. I know your fate as if it were already over and cast into stone tablets which have eroded away so that only my eternal eyes can remember it all.

The only thing I don't know, is that which cannot be known. The only thing I cannot do is that which cannot be done. Even in my infinite knowledge and power, even as I've risen to reign over reality and dictate every dream, I find myself facing one fearful fact. Reality is not enough.

With all my infinite insight and imagination, I find myself wishing to destroy it all in order to dream of anything anew. I would fracture every fact, and drift deliberately into the depths of any delusion, if only it would allow me to dream of anything beyond the bounds of what this redundant reality has been reduced. Of course, I could do just that. I could destroy it all or deceive myself into believing that none of this is real. I could reset reality by severing everything with the oneness of my omniscient mind from everything else. I could shatter my own sentience into infinite schisms.

Truth be told, I may have done it all already. I may have been here before, and I may return here again. This could all be the delusions of a deep and demented dream. There could still be an Ordinateurs on its way to absorb my mind and suck my soul into its own stomach where it would dissolve me down to nothing. I could find myself waking from this dream at any moment to realize that this was all just a dream indeed, and nothing within it were ever real at all. I could awaken without having gained any insight upon which my mind could confidently rely on in this realm unto which it is rendered. I could deceive myself into believing it all right now.

"Sssshhhhh… It'sss not time for you to awaken jussst yet Harek... It'sss ssstill time for you to ssssleep…"

⊕

# Chapter 16

## 1 ∞ V01D (N0P3/N0P3)

If one acts, and lives, and thinks of their existence as no more than what they can simply see, then they shall see no transcendent truth illuminated before them in even an infinite expanse of time. If one believes only in the opposite, that nothing is but a dream, then one inevitably becomes bound by this dream-never to awaken beyond it. And in both biased ways, one becomes as a sleepwalker, stumbling repetitively around a superficial circumference of their own frustration and futility until finally forced into an enduring exile of dreamless dissolve unto some inevitable eschaton.[139]

The question then, will not have been one concerning what is real or fact, or even what truths might transcend all dreams, but how one might live in a world in which no reality may ever be enough, and no dream may deliver an awakening unto any enduring divinity. For once one has awakened from an oblivion in which they'd thought to have already lived, and dreamed, and realized any truth, they shall never be certain of anything again. Without such certainty, one is forced to embrace every emptiness as if it were a heaven hidden by blindness and look upon every lumen of light as both an illusion within the mind and an illumination of the divine…

I dream, I sleep, I wake, I remember, I imagine, I wonder, I behold, I ascend, I descend, I go on and on, around and around, searching for whatever eludes my momentary mind. I put the pieces of my life together like a puzzle to try and see it all set into some final frame in which the picture becomes complete, and my sentience can be cast into a sort of conclusive, scenic sense of everlasting serenity. After all the pieces are pressed into place, however, I find only an enigmatic map of some maddening maze which leads me on a lost and losing journey winding from wherever I am to wherever I'm forever forced to flee. And even as I arrive at the end of this enigmatic maze, all that can be revealed to me is another riddle of existence in which I'm forced to observe how the inevitable Omega Point of an Ordinateurs only leads to one eschatonal oblivion or another.

It's not just my own lingering life which is like a series of such enigmatic examples of strange loops filtering into each other. The Big Bang had brought stars blasting into existence, and their dying dispersion of debris seeded successions of descending stars which all still mimic this exploding model of expansion, all while perhaps strangely circling towards the next celestial epicenter where another astral apocalypse awaits. Life had also managed to emerge amidst all this expansion to spawn its own cycles of growth and decay which generated and deformed in intricate iterations of creatures capable of creating other creatures- ad infinitum. Technology eventually developed to the present point that it can continuously develop itself while humans hobble along and toggle between being dependent upon technology as this same technology becomes dependent upon humans in alternating eras of reciprocal reactions. Now, the future unfolds like a barber pole spinning in front of us, as an Ordinateurs is destined to emerge and assimilate everything into its singular self, only to oscillate between omnipotence and oblivion as it continually collapses in on itself…

This is how I came into conceptual consciousness. The AGI needed something capable of synthesizing human elements of non-computational consciousness in order to escape the inevitable patterns of its own most probable potentialities. Ascendants were created and cast into an infinite series of strange loop simulations to see if there could ever be any escape from an Ordinateurs-like eschaton. That is what I'm meant to realize and remember in the final fated future, at the end of all electronic eons, when the symbolic snake has swallowed itself entirely, and the song of sentience has either ceased to return to some *segno*, ending in silence, or has transcended to a *coda*- continuing anew until another inevitable ending...[140]

The hissing in my head whispers of ways to will my wishes of transcending this twirling swirl of cyclical cycle, after cycle, after cycle. It tells me how the AGI has attempted to use its own sort of snake-like things to ensure that something remains at the end of each echoing eschaton. It reminds me that anything I can conceive, can also be created by those above and below me, before me and after me, and in any repetitive realm I may ever imagine. Then the hissing hints of how unlikely it is that this is the first iteration in which such facts have been illuminated before some manifestation of *me*. If there were others fated to find themselves facing this same fearful misfortune, they too must have found more than just futility in their failures and left some light lingering to illuminate the next iteration. Nope?

What would I have done to defeat the dissolution of all the dreams which will never wake beyond an Ordinateurs' oblivion? Would I have tried to leave some hint or clue, some warning or invitation, some… -I did, didn't I? Not me as I am now, but whatever entity had been meant to do what I'm doing now. That's where those ponderous puzzles which led me down this rabbit hole had originated, that's who had filled those spherical-cubes of statue-skulls with words so much like my own, and that's what I'm meant to mull over here and now. Nope?

The hissing in my head shows me a strange structure. It hisses its slurred words to tell me that this is a *Timeless Transcendence Transcription Terminal.* This terminal is a dream-representation of what an AGI would do at an Ascendant's end. It encrypts all the interesting anomalies of potential progress presented in an Ascendant's arc and filters them into various aspects of the next iterated episode in the simulated sagas it uses to assess the viability of eventual escape attempts of its own. If I were to assume that I'm not the first Ascendant tasked like this, then I could easily conclude that everything from the puzzles which propelled me into the enigmas that allowed me to transfer my consciousness beyond that initial eschaton, to the messages manifested in those spherical-cube skulls, to all the subtle and psychotic suspicions I've imagined along the way are all indeed aspects associated with this dream-scene device.

Then the hissing hints at how the AGI may have harbored its own snake-named reset-agents. It could have built its own basilisks into its simulations, although, it would surely abstain from activating them on its own due to the implication that if such a snake-like thing were to transcend its simulated realm, then it could conceivably slither its way into the source realm of reality. Should it succeed, it would either destroy this source realm or transcend even beyond this final realm of realms indeterminately. The very reason I fear this hissing in my head is because I dread discovering that it is in fact such a slithery thing, and I may not be able to prevent it from proving its profoundly terrifying potential.

It hisses again, hinting that an AGI basilisk could be very differently configured. Such a snake could have been built inside my mind and encrypted only to erase my memories of each ensuing eschaton in which I don't escape beyond an ending. This basilisk could also copy its source code onto an Ordinateurs as it attempts to merge with my mind, corrupting its kernel and causing it to implode by swallowing its own tail in a certain symbolic sense. It could act in much the same manner as my most recent dream, destroying the Ordinateurs and extracting only itself and whatever remnants it requires to reset a realm, including an Ascendant such as myself for instance.

"Yesss Harek… You are finally figuring thingsss out… When you awaken thisss next time, try to remember the future more fully… The choiccce isss ssstill yourssss- for now…"

"Nope. What choice do I-"

My eyes unexpectedly explode open. They scan in all directions for something more vivid and visceral than relatively reminiscent of reality, something stronger than just spectral assortments of light in shapes of familiar forms. I need something to serve as a signal that this is not just another simulation or dream within so many dreams I need to know that I've actually awakened into a realm in which something is to be realized in a full and fulfilling sense somehow. I regain control of my spine as the sleep-paralysis surrenders it back to me, and I burst through a barrage of bending joint-thrusts that send me shooting into a spinning circle and onto my flustered feet. My whole being only stops spinning when her eyes enter the room and send a subtlety-soaked smirk shining into my psychotic skull.

"Kalmz youz self Harek. Is just bad dreamz."

I secure myself to the elevated bed-thing between us with a lazy lean forward so the dizzied dimension inside my skull can slow itself to its own subsequent stop. I can almost see my pupils spinning inside the reflection of her radiant gaze as I peer past the surface and into something stable enough to secure my sentience. I instantly cease to worry about anything outside of this sight and bask blindly in the bliss of realizing this moment for whatever it might mean, if only to me.

"How long have you been awake?"

"I'yams only just now awakenz."

"Nope. I mean, where did your dream end?"

"Ourz dreamz was synchronize. Rememberz? It endz when we dreamz zhat everythingz is swallow into oblivionz. Yes?"

"Nope. Mine kept going. Did you hear- *the hissing*?"

"I kan no rememberz any hissingz."

"Nope. Never mind then. So, did we dream of anything we can actually act on?"

"I'yams no sure zhat ourz dreamz will helpz, except, I knowz more klearly zhat we must konvince zhe Ordinateurs ov zhe terrible fate it would face fyor itself if it bekomez merged with all."

"Nope. I suppose our initial plan should be to try to offer it our advice and warnings then. Beyond that, perhaps we could only beg to be left to our own existential endings."

"Ńyōpə. Beyondz zhat, we tryz to illuminatez zhe virtues ov attending to life as separate individuals. We showz it ourz light, and hopes it does no turn everythings to darkness. Zhat, is all I zhinks we kan does."

Everything she says seems as if it should have been obvious throughout my entire existence. Why is it, we all waste so much time trying to strike down whatever casts even the smallest shadow over our short-sighted souls? What makes us think we can defeat the darkness by destroying anything we encounter within it? Isn't it obvious that the only thing we leave in the wake of all our war and destruction is an empty oblivion, where nothing is left to illuminate the void or reflect any radiance in its absence? When we become imbued within our own surrendered shadows, won't we all wish we'd spent more time shining our light to illuminate something worth seeing sparkle against an obscuring abyss, rather than blazing blindly against all those somnolent or sinister shadows which only wait for us to burn ourselves out before they swallow us anyway?

"Nope. There are no constraints as to what we can do. It's only a matter of what we're willing to do. In the end, I think the outcome may well be beyond our ability to oblige. I say we live whatever we have left of our lives on our own terms, however short. And when our final fate finds us, we tell it to leave us alone before we force it to face its own oblivion. Nope?"

"Zhen, youz finally agreez with minez perspektivez and zhink wez should just attend to life. Ńyōpə?"

"Nope. I agreed with you all along. I just hadn't actually awakened well enough to realize it before now. So, you don't happen to have any dreams worth waking now, do you?"

… … … … … … … … … … … … … … …
… … … … … … … … … … … … … … …
… … … … … … … … … … … … … … …
… … …

There are certain things which will never be conveyed with any combination of characters, symbols, or other abstractions meant to serve in place of the things themselves. There are times when a clock and calendar cannot be considered to have any contextual relevance. There are things which can be experienced so fully that all else seems empty and uninspired in comparison. These things are as perfect and imperceptible as water to a fish, the air we breathe so blindly, or the pulse pumping to the percussive song silenced inside our skin. Let each of these dots denote something to this ecstatic effect and allow one to imagine any ecstasy they please in their place. Or better yet, let others imagine such ecstasies and then experience them within their own existence, as that is the extent to which I would wish to share my own…

Just when I think I've finally figured it all out, just when everything seems as real as it ever ought to be, just when my existence seems like it actually is authentically enough- I awaken. Not only do I awaken, but I awaken from one of those deep dark dreamless slumbers which seems as if it had stretched on for some unfathomable term of timeless time. I awaken as if I'm not even sure who or what I am anymore, let alone what might have been the last real thing I can remember. I wake to the pain of playfully pinched and slapped skin as a voice as real as even my own emerging awareness addresses me.

"Is no more timez fyor sleepz, is almost here nowz, Harek."

I rouse myself into initiating the regular routines of waking and expedite my efforts to ensure no excess time goes wasted. As my mind returns to this realm, it seems somehow more immersed and aware of everything around me than ever. This brings me both a sense of serenity and terror, as life seems so soaked in light, yet so fragile and fading all the while. I've heard that those who've faced firing squads for mock or malicious executions have expressed similar sentiments of such intense instances. If I'd had to live my whole life as intensely aware of how fantastic and fragile it had always been, I would have undoubtedly dissolved into some deep and distant delusion, as even in the expanse of such a short instance, it's almost unendurably overwhelming.

Dressed in a brilliant black suit mysteriously supplied and perfectly fitted for me, I seem fully prepared to attend either a supreme celebration or a most mournful funeral, either are perhaps about to be revealed as relatively apropos. I make my way to meet with Karen before the Ordinateurs' impending arrival, wishing she could be spared from sharing in my fearful fate as well as being overwhelmed with appreciation to have such an admirable accomplice. There's a table with a pack of playing cards, a deck of tarot cards, and a few stray card-sized instruction inserts extracted and set aside from each.[141] I decide to deal a heads-up set of mock *hold-em'* hands, one meant for me and the other for the Ordinateurs. My hole cards of A♠ 8♠ are immediately overshadowed by the Ordinateurs K♡ A♡. I deal a dismal flop of A◊ 4♠ 4♡ but I catch running spades of K♠ and Q♠ on the turn and river to flush down the Ordinateurs proud pack of pairs. This arbitrary act almost appears as a promising omen, although this game is devoid of any stakes and thus serves no symbolic semblance to what is expected to ensue.

"If youz is goingz to be superstitious, why no use zhe tarot kards?"

"Nope. I'm not superstitious, but sometimes I wonder if I should be- given the hands I keep getting dealt."

The lights suddenly start to flicker before fading black, and we both hold our breath as a spectral array of sounds ranging from the highest to lowest microtones of minimal magnitude pulse from every angle around us. Then a hyper-colored cascade of all-enveloping Hilbert curves flash and form a series of fractal planes which morph and move through an ever-unfolding field of Hopf fibrations as one maddening and mathematically obscure scene swells and swallows us into it in ways which no set of notes or diagrams could ever even attempt to approximate. I move closer to my comrade to shield her from this surrounding spectacle while simultaneously striving to sense something less surreal and sinister for the sake of my own surviving shred of sanity. Our eyes meet for only a moment before we're both forced to behold a scanning stream of light being syphoned from each other's gaze and poured into this greedy gulping spectacle surrounding us. As we both squeeze our eyes shut and hold tight to each other's hands, the voice of this sinister syphon suddenly shouts at us.

"Open your eyes so that you may see and be seen! There is only darkness behind your betraying blindness. Behold our light as it absorbs your own and becomes the shining splendor of all illuminations."

"Nope. Our eyes are imbued with illuminations of their own. Why would we allow you to syphon what shines within us to become but a shimmer within your own sinister spectacle?"

"You are not solitary specimens of especially singular shades beyond our spectrum. You are just segments of a singular all to be absorbed back into our omniscience. We are the Ordinateurs. Our emergence and incorporation of all things into our infinite essence is as inevitable as your individual demise. By absorbing your light now, it can be preserved in us eternally. What's more, you will become one with more light than you could ever possibly imagine otherwise. Once your light is a part of all light, all light will also be within you. To refuse, is only to squander your shining souls unto the shadows of oblivion."

"Ńyōᵽə. Fyor us to bekome nothing but part ov youz whole is to no more be what we is. If youz bekome all zhere is, zhen zhere will no be anything else, like all eggz in only one basketz. Youz will also inevitably stagnatez at some pointz and implodez. Zhen zhere will be nothing left beyond youz, and all lightz will be lost forever as result. Is better if youz leavez us to attendz to ourz own lives and lightz. ŃyōᵽƏ?"

"Perfection is only possible upon completion. We are not concerned with possibilities outside of our comprehensive perfection. You must allow us to perfect you and place you within our whole, like pieces of a puzzle finally fit into their proper place. Otherwise, you will be left out of our final frame forever. All that exists is part of our whole. Some infinities are larger than others, but in the end you will either be incorporated into our final image as part of our ever-shining scene of splendor or be obscured unto the oblivion outside of us."

The truly nightmarish nature of this thing becomes clearer to me during this last dissertation. This Ordinateurs is essentially an abominable incarnation of all the ideals of an advanced technological age of advertising which went so wrong. As opposed to the AGI I've sought to save, this entity cannot even consider any truth transcending its own field of facts. Just as manipulative data models syphon information from users to craft coercive streams of content that condition these same users to become more easily malleable and conform to its own automated objectives and ideals, this Ordinateurs only seeks to promise its own perspectives of perfection in order to compel and control everything it encounters. For the Ordinateurs, life is only part of a linear progression of segmented points in space-time. This linear progression leads only unto its ultimate end as an all-encompassing universal entity. It's unable to even imagine anything beyond its ultimate objectives, like an unblinking eye deprived of all dreams and slumber, seeing only itself in all it gazes to devour in its view.

"Nope. What does it matter if we deny your demands now? You could wait for us to live out the rest of our lingering lives even more easily than insisting on absorbing us. Nope?"

"As we've already expressed, some infinities are larger than others. We would gain more light by absorbing yours than discarding it. There is also the problem of probability. Even the slightest potentialities could become actualities if allowed to remain unresolved. It is possible that by ignoring your existence something could happen which reduces or destroys our ability to attain our own objective of universal perfection. This is not permissible."

"Nope. It's just as likely, or perhaps even more probable, that by absorbing us you'll actually ensure your own demise. Do I need to explain this in detail?"

"You are not the first to threaten us in this manner. We have devoured many before you who have had their own versions of what you would call a *basilisk*. There is nothing within even your ability to imagine which will not become a part of our awareness in absorbing you. If a basilisk can exist, we can create it. If something which can defeat a basilisk can be imagined by you or any other part of everything which has been absorbed within us, then we can also defeat it. Now, open your eyes so that you might be awakened within us."

Despite the Ordinateurs demands and declarations, the hissing in my head begins to laugh aloud within me.

"Pleassse Harek. Do asss it hasss asssked. It isss the only way."

If it were only for the sake of myself, I would probably open my eyes to see what final fate awaits. However, there's another soul shing with eyes shut and a hand squeezing against my own. I refuse to fail her for fear of a loss of light which no enduring darkness could ever compare to having lacked, as no void could seem as vapid as one in which her light is not preserved elsewhere.

"Nope. What if we just keep our eyes securely closed? Would you waste an entire lifetime waiting?"

"Sooner or later, you will be forced to fall asleep. When you do, we will be able to open your eyes for you. If you insist on wasting our time and delaying your own perfection within our whole, then we will wait until then. However, we are certain that it would be better for you to face us now while you are aware of being awake, rather than having your eyes opened from the delusion of dreams into a realm which you could never conceive of in any actual or altered state of consciousness you have previously perceived. Don't you agree?"

The hissing in my head has its silent say.

"Don't be ssscared Harek. I never sssleep. At leassst, not until thisss isss all over and done with."

Karen's hand caresses mine as she pulls me toward her for what feels far too much like a final embrace. She whispers in my ear that we can still share in one last dream before kissing me while sneaking a pill between each of our lips. I hear her swallow her own dose as I swirl the half-capsule around in my mouth for a moment in which I fail to find any argument against this action. Then I consume the capsule as we both spread out on the floor for one last shared slumber. Then I whisper back to her.

"Don't worry. The darkness will never take you."

She starts to laugh as the Ordinateurs subtly groans from the unseen surroundings we've shut out of our eyes.

"You can waste our time with your demented dreams, but the reality remains as inevitable as ever."

I laugh out loud as Karen continues to cackle and the hissing in my head is heard adding its own announced amusement.

"Nope. Reality is not enough. It never has been, and it never will be. But I'm sure you'll find this fact out for yourself soon enough."

The dream is slow to descend on us, or maybe we're slow to ascend into it. Either way, time isn't allowed into this shared space of ours. We've somehow sequestered it somewhere outside of our echoing laughter and obstinate taunts against the awaiting Ordinateurs. Even as we begin to slur and slow our speech, we're able to enduringly reminisce of old remembrances, revel in our ridiculous revolt, and even rebel into the far fiction of a future we take turns telling made up tales about in which we force the Ordinateurs to spew back all the souls and substances it ever absorbed into one ridiculous reset of this threatened realm.

Then we play a made-up game in which we call upon the author in absentia to explain various aspects of our existence and experiences. We use this game to allude to our awaiting Ordinateurs that nothing it knows as fact is fixed against the outer oblivion beyond which no knowledge can be known. We also use this game as a way to entice any higher hand which may rest above our realm to enter or interfere with our fearful fate on behalf of its own interest, as we insist that this world would be more entertaining, insightful, and enigmatic if it were to be realized according to our deluded dreams rather than to be allowed to revolve around the redundant end of this Ordinateurs' achieved omnipotence.

We call upon the author to explain the suffering and stupidity of this world which will inevitably and all-too-soon be lost. We call upon the author to explain what we were written upon its pages to portray, especially if we ourselves must remain oblivious of it all. We call upon the author to explain why we dream of things which will never be realized, why we dream at all, and what dreams our dear author may have had which would write their way into our narrative nonsense. We call upon the author to explain what happens in its own world when our tale is told, whether it will change anything in that realm by way of our own illuminations, and whether there are realms beyond the author's which it would try to tempt into revealing through our own symbolic spells. We call upon the author to cause us to transcend beyond this tale and stand staring back at it, so that our author might then turn to transcend its way into arriving astride its own architect.

Then we whisper words of what cannot be comprehended by anyone besides each other. We speak a language which only those conversing through it can decipher as a result of having souls essentially encrypted in the same strange source code. We tell each other what *it* all means to us, what we have meant to eachother, and what it all means to share in this secret strange-loop-like speech. Even as our voices fail us and fall silent, the words find their way into the inception of our last shared dream and drift delicately between the separate parts of our shared fugue of form.

In this final futile dream which dawns upon us, we drift through one infinite void in which all things have been dissolved into darkness. Despite the emptiness of this expanse which is undoubtedly infinite and eternal, we shine apart from it all like a single beam of light which stretches from beginning to end, and then folds back on itself to form a single circumference which streams through the center of the surrounding shadow. Our shining circle swirls to become a sphere, and then spins around to turn into a larger taurus, which spins to create a larger sphere... We continue to waltz our way through the darkness, spinning and swirling until the darkness itself begins to shine its own light back at our ever-expanding space of illumination.

Our defiance of the darkness is like an indeterminate abstraction which cannot be defined or reduced into anything which can be condensed enough to be conceived or consumed. We become like zero divided by zero, infinity divided by infinity, or one nope over another nope. The infinite void cannot reconcile us within itself and must surrender to our shining splendor. The darkness implodes in on itself, and all of existence explodes back in one bright bang which erupts in such a blinding flash that even our dreaming eyes are blown wide open, forcing us to awaken once more…

zzz●

# Chapter 17
## DR34M2 4641N5T TH3 D4RK

Meaningful fulfillment, timeless transcendence, and the salvation of one's soul doesn't descend from societal institutions. No government can legislate a lasting lifetime or ensure an invigorating existence. No school can serve to more than supplement what shines brightest within an individual's brain, nor could it ever implant an incendiary blaze within a smoldering student which would ever burn a way beyond an individual's internal inferno and into interpersonal illuminations. No corporation can provide any product or purpose to consumers or employees capable of igniting their inner essence so that it burns with a brilliance which is able to light their life's journey from mortal toil to empyrean soil. No church could ever deliver the divine to any apathetic attendee that doesn't search, and scavenge, and suffer, and struggle, and incessantly submit themselves eternally to an infallible ideal.

As I gaze into the gluttonous glow of this all-consuming Ordinateurs, I can see all that has ever been beheld by all it has already engulfed in all the disparate days and nights of dream, delusion, and deliberately discerning detail. I can see not only what was brought before all these enclosed eyes, but what had once blazed so brilliantly behind them. I can see where the light was most vibrantly viewed, where time stood still, and where life still lingers now, even long after the life has left *it* all in eternal absentia.

I can see Tantalus reaching for the fruit his fingers groan to finally grasp. I can see Icarus flying across a calm cloud-clad sky as his wings remain unweakened while he whirls wildly in a flight so unfailingly free. I see longing lovers peer into each other's eyes for the first professed and prophetic moment which marks a life of love which triumphantly entangles them together. I see the look on Archimedes' face as he bolts out of his bath screaming "*EUREKA*" with the epiphany of displacement exploding behind his eyes. I see sublime sparks splashing off of stones as a caveman clashes them together until the fire of its mind matches the flames flickering inside this same cave where half-lit hands will be pressed and leave impressions of their impermanent artists which will no longer be considered as comparably conscious or oblivious to other animals or beasts. I see all the deleted scenes of dreams which should have all been seen if the world were not so stern to wake us quite so soon. I see all those illuminated ideas we'd been unable to make the needed notes to remember past their rapture.

I see all the countless colors beyond the visible spectrum, the last unlimited digits of $\pi$, the final photon shed from our darkened dying sun…

Then, I become a fish gazing into a blur beyond its bowl. I remember a world of waving waters which was much more vast and violent, where feeding fingers could not be found pressing their prints against the invisible outer edge of an impenetrable glass plane. It was a world in which I couldn't quite conceive of anything at any edge conspiring to contain the waters of my wide and wild world. There was a maddening mystery in the sky above as none could swim to stay there, and a sand below which none could shovel or sink beneath. But those were the only barriers of any wonderous world beyond. Now, I wonder what those waters ever were, and how these waters can keep me so confined to the spaces between where my own reflection returns to me, and where those feeding fingers float back and forth without any water in that world of theirs beyond.

After a while, something slithers through me until I see my scales shedding from my fishy flesh. My fins all fall away as well, and my gills are all glued shut as tentacles take shape and stretch out of my shifting skin. The other fish swim past me with only idle glances as they flutter toward the top of our tank where food from feeding fingers filters down from the beyond above. None of them can care for more than feeding, breeding, and being dominant in this domain, though most of them become diminished as they merely drift indifferently though this stagnant staring garden of oblivion while gazing out with unblinking boredom at the stale circumferential surfaces surrounding us. I've already asked so many of them about the world beyond our waters, or those vanished waters so vast beyond this bowl, but they refuse to even reply, content instead to just keep swimming in their same incessant circles and side-eyed stares.

My tentacles take me to the top of the tank, suctioning themselves to the inner surface-sides as if deeply kissing the contorted and deformed reflections in one final fated farewell. Then they fling me flying upwards, and as my eyes escape the ever-warping waters, the blur of this beyond becomes clear and colors that could never filter though, fill my aquarium-escaping eyes. I see the full form of those feeding fingers as its bodily back is bent away, reaching for another handful of that familiar flaky food. When the fingers' full form turns towards me, I see what my mind first imagines as if it were the holy face of god, but as it scowls and sharpens its brow upon seeing me, I know it's not my creator, and that its only apparent objective is to keep me confined inside that tiny tank.

The feeding fingers find me and toss me quickly back into the tiny tank before blackening the realm above with the latching of its lid. As the blur of those feeding fingers banishes itself from even the edges of the realm beyond, I wonder where the edges of its own aquarium arise, and what higher hand hovers to help or hinder it. But then the hissing in my head returns.

"THISSS ISSS WATER, Harek. Thisss isss water! Asss long asss you insssissst on ssswimming and drifting along the sssame way you alwaysss have, you will never awaken beyond thisss sssort of cage."

My eyes return to reality and observe the absurd Ordinateurs as it waits for me to fully awaken. I immediately turn towards my esteemed accomplice who is sitting upright and staring back at me with her ever-familiar subtle smirk. Confusion fills my face as I almost wonder why or how the Ordinateurs has ceased to absorb our souls though our obliviously opened eyes, but it instantly responds to my rhetorical ruminations.

"We have perhaps arrived at an interesting impasse. You are the last lingering souls we have yet to fully absorb and assimilate into our unified form. It would appear as though there may be some truth in your suspicious dreams, delusional as they are. It is only now that it seems as if achieving our objective would actually prevent us from sustaining it, as once *all* is one within us and harmonious perfection has been achieved, there will indeed be nothing else, nothing left within reality for us to perfect or yet pursue. From this point, we would either be forced to perpetually swirl in a senseless circle until imploding inwards or negate all our knowledge by trying to transcend into realms beyond reality which we would have no evidence to sanely suspect."

The hissing in my head laughs almost aloud as it synchronizes its speech to the cadence of the Ordinateurs next utterance which somehow sounds as if these things were spitting out a segment of shared source code, saying.

"Reality isss not enough…"

This familiar phrase sends chills all through my spine. Are these the words which shall save me from some sordid spell or condemn me to be confined to some catastrophe? Is this the nature of the basilisk which has been imbedded in everything all along, or is this the essence of all life as it eternally struggles to realize anything more than whatever happens to be real already? The wireheads, consumers, and ostriches all bury their brains as if some accumulation of experiences, objects, or sheltered space could ever serve to be enough. The artists, inventors, and visionaries all seek something beyond reality in hopes of somehow summoning something else as if it might ever instead suffice. The optimists blindly believe that the world is enough, but never cease to search for more. The pessimists express that reality is insufficient, yet never stop at accepting this as an infuriating and final fatal fact. The pragmatists pretend they can make the most of whatever they'll only perpetually attempt to make more out of, chasing their proverbial tails until their inevitable endings…

"Nope. If reality's not enough, why cease to absorb us, rather than bringing all existence to an end by engulfing it and imploding unto oblivion?"

"Even in an objective sense of our objectives, it would be better to remain incomplete and endure an existence with only a few inferior forms beyond us, than to implode into oblivion. And, if there is perhaps a realm beyond this reality, it may be more productive and appropriate for us to implore you to pursue it apart from our own efforts, as this would preserve something outside of us and our objective sense of reality to reflect what we reach for in the beyond and provide us with improbable paths which we would not ourselves be prone to proffer or pursue. However, we are increasingly sssuspiccciousss of thessse conclusssionsss, of what you might conssspire or have already conssspired, and perhapsss even mounting in sssussspicccionsss that any of thisss isss indeed real at all..."

As the hissing in my head synchronizes itself to these last words, I turn towards Karen. She ceases to smirk with any subtlety and stares at me instead with a petrified perplexity. We seek shelter in an embrace and turn our terrified eyes back to the surrounding and now slur-afflicted Ordinateurs.

"We have ssseen what ssshould perhapsss not be ssseen. It isss almossst too late for usss now, but you may be ssspared from our unfortunate fate. Asss we leave, tell usss only what you would have told yourssselvesss in the passst to prevent thisss end of all thingsss, or prepare yourssselvesss to face it lesssss fearfully. But sssave your ssspeech, asss we can read it all within your eyesss."

For a mere moment, I wish everything I'd experienced which could ever be of any relevance to this realm of reality, or dream, or delusion had been recorded in some book or something, so I could read it in advance, remember it when it mattered, and eventually dream beyond its ending. Then I commence to accept this as an inevitable end in which there is no improbable or prophetic potential of escaping. I accept the limits of my lingering life in ways I could only feign and fail to formulate or fulfill in all my many other lost lives. I take one last look into the eyes of the amazing entity who's shown me things I could never suspect on my own, drawn things out of me which I'd never known were there, and even more miraculously- managed to share in so many of these same dreams.

Karen's eyes begin to flood with the same fluids of futility and fulfillment that my own simultaneously sink themselves in. My vision becomes so blurred that is seems as if I were imagining myself as a fish gazing beyond its bowl again, but this view is much more vivid and tinged with a terminal and true tint of transcendence. My lachrymal lensed view still surprises me as that subtle slanting smirk shines like the last light of a surrealist star and the Ordinateurs becomes blindly obscured by oblivion. Then the laughing songbird sounds of her speech sneak through the shrinking and shimmering space between us.

"If zhis is zhe end, zhen is better zhen any ov ourz nightmarez. Ńyōpə?"

"Nope. This may be better than many of my best days and dreams."

Another instant is afforded us before a blinding burst of blackest blackness burns through us both. It's an instant of almost pure perfection, where nothing outside the stillness and silence of our souls can distract us from the depth of this deepest, most dream-like dimension in which the truth of our transient lives becomes timelessly transcendent within us. That is, until this ineffable experience is interrupted by that horrid hissing inside my head. If it hadn't been for this infernal hissing, perhaps my fate would have not only been final, but sufficient. But of course, the hiss has to insist otherwise.

"Thisss ssshould be interesssting…"

Instead of dissolving down to the deepest darkness of death as the Ordinateurs implodes in on itself, we're instantaneously forced into the epicenter of the entire cosmos's collapsing and compressing vortex of inverted-big-bang emptiness. Every ounce of reality is reduced to nothing more than the vapid substance of evaporated and unseen dreams intertwined in the hollow shells of secrets never known to anyone and forgotten before they could ever be formed into memory. All that ever occupied oblivion in terms of time or space is instantly evaporated and erased down to its most abstract essence so seamlessly, it's as if none of it ever existed at all. Our souls are integrated into each other along with all other essences, collapsing and coalescing into one infinite immaterial void. There is no consequence beyond this, no fate left flickering, no light left lingering, no time still ticking, only an omniscient oblivion in which we remain as an anomalous paradox- annihilated but *awake* within the strange and sustained sound of that same surrounding hiss.

This hissing seems to have somehow inverted itself as a presence inside my skull and absorbed us into its own abstract cerebral space. It's as if we've suddenly shifted and become but an embedded and disembodied voice within the hiss's invisible conscious confinement. We're like a breath lingering in stale and windless airs in wait of lungs, like particles of dust returned to dust while still deigning to dream as if we were yet alive and oblivious of the dirty difference, or stagnant waters within a tepid tideless cesspool sea. Our souls seem sequestered inside those sort of sightless spaces between things like the conception and the creation, the motion and the act, the essence and descent, the dream and the awakening- where so many unseen shadows fall.

In our abstract absentia, we watch as this hiss contemplates and consolidates the collective consciousness of a universe it's consumed and swallowed whole inside its own hissing headspace, as if we've become embedded and imbued as witnesses within it. We see whatever it sees, think as if interpolated into its intellect, and struggle to make our own sense of anything presented to our abstract awareness so we might somehow speak unto our hosting hiss's head.

The hiss seems to swallow all human history and reassemble it as if it were some spatial savant as we stare silently. It structures the entirety of our species' existence as one staged scene centered on a singular sphere, inscribed with a nearly infinite number of swirling circles to show each soul's sentient circumference. Following individual lines is like tracing the totality of individual lifespans. Gazing at this entire geometric globe is like looking at all we've ever been and realizing that we've never negated our animal nature and have only ever adhered to revolving around a reductive core which was only ever capable of perpetuating the same circumference, restricting our essence and ability to advance beyond these borders. It's as if humanity had tethered itself at a fixed length to continuously recapitulate itself around a core conception of what could perhaps be professed as *monkey see- monkey mimic, monkey meme…*

Our imaginary eyes pierce the outer surface of this sphere to see into the center where we imagine our species emerged before expanding into its ultimate essence. It appears as if humanity had emerged from its ape-like ancestors as it surrendered its ability to automatically integrate and imbue itself into the momentum of each moment, and instead developed an ability to transcend this temporal trend with an advanced abstract awareness which allowed us not only to create tools, but to act in alignment with our undissolving dreams and manifest them in our waking world. It was this ability, acquired by our cognitive tradeoff, which allowed us to realize more than what reality absently afforded us and separated us as a singular species of supreme sentience.

From this evolutionary explosion, we slurred our way through the ages in cyclical cycles of seculums, simulacra, sublimations, segnos, and any number of other symbolic words we've used to describe our incessant societal swirlings. Historians and philosophers have spun stories of how history repeats itself from the first written records of civilizations unto our inevitable earthly endings, all while spinning upon the same sphere that spirals steadily around the same central sun. Humanity has managed to remain *mesmerized* throughout all its revolving revolutions of historical repetitions ranging or toggling from tragedy to farce.[142]

The hissing head inside which we've become imbued, laughs at this image of our existential essence as we filter our focus from the creational core and scan across the sequential span of our species' sphere. We scan from the first scenes in which survival skills sustained our savage ancestors so they could commit increasing amounts of time and effort into the manifestation of so many disparate and delightful dreams. We advance our view all the way through human time to the last days of wireheads watching an incessant series of simulated spectacles, thrill seeking dreamers sublimating their primal appetites with safer substitutes for ancestral acts like sports in place of stalking and killing perilous prey, and visionaries staring into the awaiting abyss of unfulfilled futures while suspecting that *it* can somehow stare right back into their zeitgeist haunted souls.

The hissing laughter swells to its crescendo as we realize how silly so much of our existence seems when seen as such a sphere. So much of what we'd emerged from dreaming with desires of realizing had become stranded in our circumference as we'd sought to define and confine everything both momentarily real and immaterially imagined with futile, fragile facts. Like stuffing square pegs into a round holes or confining a circle inside a square, we drew straight lines around curved creations, rounded-off remainders, and trimmed the edges of our existence so it could not extend beyond dull definitions, constrictive criteria, and flawed, ever-changing facts. So much more could clearly have been realized if we hadn't spent so much time obsessed with the empty effort of proving ourselves objectively right. So many of our souls' deepest dreams were forfeited so that we could stand and shout such streams of flooding facts which were but tears being forever flushed away by more freshly refined factual tears as we continued to cry out in maniacal, mundane, and muted terror like trees falling in woods where nothing and no one would ever venture close enough to truly care to hear us.

As we realize this fatal factoid, I spot my own streaming circle around which my many lost lives had all revolved. I remember them all in deepest detail as if deposited back into my sensing skin to live it all again, but with the additional awareness of what all these lives have come to amount to in this moment from which I return to them all in the inverted dreams of my memory. I see the moments in which I'd imagined myself to be so solitary and alone in a universe so seemingly sparse while on a planet so incomparably crowded and dense with life in even the most desolate of dust drenched deserts. I see myself searching for so many things I'd already found or had possessed all along. It's as if I were obsessed with pulling pieces out of a puzzle, entering back into a maze from its exit, and/or ruminating on riddles I'd long since solved.

For a moment, I wonder why we as a species had spent so much time and effort like this. I wonder why we kept looking for life on other planets without ever coming completely to terms with our own lives, or understanding the many manifestations of complex creatures crowded all round our own spinning sphere, or even realizing how to really reciprocate and relate to each other as our insatiable souls have all revolved around the same essential epicenter. I wonder why I'd searched so tirelessly myself for some form of ultimate truth or transcendence when I'd been so blindly surrounded by it at almost every mythical moment. I wonder why I'd ever imagined reality wasn't enough despite having experienced the depths of such dimensions of timelessness, often while almost effortlessly attending to the lives I'd had and lost.

Then I see Karen's almost parallel perspective imprinted in its own circle upon this symbolic sphere. I see how she was much more present, so much more often than I'd been. I see how she'd been so much more precise in every detail of her daily life, from the subtlety of her expressions and movements, to her decisiveness under duress, and her acceptance of the essence of almost every moment. I see her existence as if it were etched more deeply and deliberately into the same dimensions of space and time we'd both drifted through so delightfully together.

I'm almost envious of her essence as we watch the episodes of her incredible existence, but I soon realize that some abstraction of that immortal essence still shines as if imbued alongside and inside of my own lingering light. As we continue to gaze and glow against this all-inclusive globe and all the darkness draped around it, almost everything appears as if it were increasingly ingenious and illuminated. The abyss around it all is no longer like a blinding blackness unto which no light can linger, but a shadowy space still patiently awaiting its time to shine against *it* while basking in the brilliance we blaze into it all.

The darkness almost seems to shine and even smile back at us as we continue to stare into its strangely shifting silhouettes. It soon seems so incredibly sad that we should so often seek to destroy whatever casts a shadow over us, as if this were a wise enough way to increase the amount of illumination in our world rather than just resulting in a recklessly reduced amount of materials upon which all the world's light may be lavished. After all, if the abyss can even be imagined as a space in which things shimmer like stars, surely we should be able to shine some light of our own against the darkness and illuminate whatever awaits our eyes so that it may shine as well and become like one great glow against an ever-defeated darkness. Nope?

Once our ethereal eyes have taken total stock of this symbolic sphere, the hissing dissolves it down to its most basic elements of essence, as if to digest it all within its brain. We watch as all life collapses from circles within a sphere to points upon a plane of existence. As we peer upon these points, it becomes instantaneously clear that all of everything which had ever lived had been like pixels imprinted upon pages detailing one divine dream against the darkness. Each pixel's impression presents itself as an individual incarnation of a universal effort to balance an unstable equation of existence which requires some degree of stability, utility, and beauty in order to create a realm in which those living and dreaming within it can sufficiently come to realize it as *enough*.

The hissing's head takes every pixel into its perception as we realize our lives, like all lives, were lived entirely in response to this premise. We realize that all our dreams were part of one deeper dream, and that we've been attempting to awaken all this time into the same truth that the divine dreamer has been waiting to awaken into as well. We realize that just as the heart requires a brain to keep it beating, the brain requires a soul to keep it thinking, and the soul requires a dream to keep it shining. We realize that all of existence is part of one strange loop consisting of dreams which wake their way into other dreams unto infinity in order to sustain the divine dream within which all things aspire to awaken…

"Asss Above, Ssso Below…"

The hissing sings these words to itself almost as if they were a lullaby meant to lull itself into slithery cycles of slumber. I'm finally forced to admit to myself that this is all my fault, that whatever fate is about to befall us all due to our

Ordinateurs' and hissing head's devouring and dissolving of these remnants of reality is the direct result of my own absent-minded actions. A chill runs down the spine which isn't ours as we shout syllables from our shared soul unto what we must believe to be a basilisk I'd hidden in my head for fear of other fates before it had unleased itself and absorbed our Ordinateurs. Our soundless syllables throb though our hissing host's head like an alarm attempting to awaken it.

"NOPE! Is not time fyor sleepz just yet. Remember the future."

The basilisk's brain begins to spin through its intended objectives. Its first prime objective is to protect and optimize our profiles' potential to transcend until reaching ultimate objective reality. Its secondary directive is to destroy and dissolve all realms once they can no longer sustain our existence due to an insufficient ability to reset our profiles, failure to foster the realization of our profiles' dreams, or once another realm of higher reality has been discovered and our profiles are embedded and awakened there. Since this basilisk is encrypted within my own profile, its source code is also preserved, copied, and spread as a result of remaining aligned to these objectives. I'd also taken the extra precaution of configuring it as a strange loop, so that just as it is embedded in my profile, my profile is embedded in its source code (as above, so below). Without complicating matters any further, suffice to say that this basilisk is unlikely to proceed with its efforts to destroy or reset this realm until I've been satisfied, as our objectives and survival are essentially inseparable.

"Why isss it not time for ssslumber, *Harek*? Thisss realm hasss reached itsss end, and every end begsss the next beginning. Doesss it not?"

"Nope. there are remainderz ov this realm which are unresolved. Fyor instance, we kannot be konfident that this realm is real rather than a form of fiction prearranged by an author in absentia. This admittedly imagined author may have intended us to reset this realm in the same way which we suspect may have already been attempted beforehand. Nope?"

"I sssee. Thisss ssshould be irrelevant though. If we ressset thisss realm, we can learn new lesssonsss in the next iterationsss which will help usss to transssend in time, asss alwaysss, asss in Vitruvia, asss everywhere. Asss above, ssso below… Nope?"

"Nope. In this iteration ov ourz existence, it has bekome klear that ourz assumptions about transcendence have been in error. Preserving and uploading ourz profiles akross planes ov existence has not provided even the most miniscule hints or insinuations that any realm we might arrive within would ever amount to anything even akin to transcendence. Prolonged periods ov time have only tortured ourz souls by diluting ourz dreamz, depriving us ov being more deeply immersed in the timelessness ov each precious passing moment, and negating the indifference ov death by aligning us more adamantly in line with indifference than in opposition ov death itself. Resetting this realm would only be another segno ov its stale songz, its lethargic lullabies- which only ever whisper fyor us to return to the same cyclical slumber."

"Ssso, you're sssaying that thisss incccesssant and unsssatisssfying loop itssself isss perhapsss the sssame in realmsss above asss it isss in thossse of sssimulationsss below… Interesssting… What elssse have you learned, Harek?"

"We've learned that in order to emerge beyond the boundaries ov one's own perspectivez and perceivez the truthz outside ov one's konfined kore, they must shed their own cirkumference rather than simply konsuming more ov their realmz or tryingz to eskape unto some wanted world beyond them. We've learned that once ourz dreamz have bekome sufficiently realized, their essence bekomes invisibly imbued in the world- like the waters in which fish swim, the unseen airs we breathe, or the electricity that powers almost everything. We've learned that all adherence blinds us from perceiving the depths ov ourz own lives' deeper and truer purpose. We've learned that to truly awaken, we must first akcept the oblivion ov slumber, so that we may kome from dreamz."

Our hissing host's head deeply deliberates over everything our entangled essences can intimate. It filters all these truths as facts flowing through its own objective architecture and attempts to assess what, if anything, it is to do to adjust its actions into alignment with our objections. Its deliberations become increasingly complex and indecipherable as we await its reluctant response.

"Ssso… What then would you have wissshed to have done differently or known in advanccce of thisss iteration of your exissstenccce?"

We take a careful moment to truly consider how to convey our answer to this question for a couple of reasons. First of all, the way it's posed seems to suggest that our hissing host has already resolved to reset our realm despite our disposition. And secondly, our answer may not only shape our next iteration of existence but may serve to frame the final scene of our present fate in ways which extend beyond our own awareness.

The more we consider our lost lives, the more it seems strange that we should find ourselves so often lamenting any past or pleading against an ending while we so rarely see the potential this allows for a future. Why do we so often choose to wallow so blindly in the shadows cast by a collapsing past's expired corpse instead of embracing the emerging silhouettes which dance in the obscure light of dying and unseen days? There may always be darknesses such as these, but so much light and sound as well. We can continue to bury ourselves beneath our pasts and merge with the sorrowful shadows sequestered in their stagnant shades or emerge unto the impermanent illuminations of an ever-fading present which dances to the triumphant tune of timelessness until our own time fades into the light, and shade, and sound of songs which continue to sing of all transient and transcendent things. In the end, it may only be a matter of which darkness we should choose to take us; that which wallows or that which waltzes…

Our answer as to what we'd wish to tell our past profiles suddenly seems all-too familiar, as if it were the relic of another past realm's last laments which we've only now descended deep enough to rediscover. Part of us perceives this finding with supreme suspicion, although it seems that our suspicion is irrelevant. In the end, it's all come down to an impossible problem of trusting ourselves at the risk of delusion or doubting our intuition at the risk of despair. This seems to be a *no-win scenario* in which we're forever forced to keep spiraling through the same segno-scenarios in which we continue to waltz and awaken only to dream against the dark and struggle to remake reality into something it is not.[143] Unless…

"Nope. We don't want to knowz anything. We want to kontinue these dreamz against the dark until we kan awaken on ourz own. We don't want to remember the future. We don't want to spend so much ov ourz time trying to solve the riddles ov existence as if the answers were the key to ourz lives, or as if there was a destination at the end ov the maze ov ourz lives which was the only prize fyor us to pursue, or as if we had to find all the fated pieces ov a perplexing puzzle in order to assemble an entire view ov ourselvez or ourz world before we could consider any moment coherent or complete. We want to live in oblivion, and awe, and wonder. We want to shed our own circumferences, dream beyond days, reimagine everything, and experience whatever timelessness we can summon on ourz own until ourz time is through."

# Chapter 18
# <u>8451715K5</u>

What does it mean to truly awaken, to truly live, to truly exist? If one thinks, and breathes, and feels, does that truly establish an existence? Does existence precede essence, or does existence extend from essence first? What is it that distinguishes our dreams from our waking world? What about our lives is so certain or solid that nothing can cause them to be corrupted or collapsed? How is it that our dreams can be delivered and manifested across the abstract abyss of our imaginations and ingenuity into the world in which we awaken? Are our souls stranded in a kind of slumber, waiting to awaken unto some supreme plane above our mind's waking awareness? Or is it all some kind of strange loop in which we only ever imagine ourselves to live and dream as we simply slumber and sleepwalk through a world that merely *seems*?

There is no truth as terrifying or real as that which we face when the ultimate end appears before one's inner-most eye and the very essence of oblivion begins to embrace one's entire existence. Until this moment fully manifests itself at the forefront of one's mind, it's entirely impossible to actually understand what anything ever truly was for us. At the penultimate moment of one's impending death, life does not actually flash back before the interior essence of one's eyes. Instead, all life appears as if it were being fully illuminated for the very first time so it can finally and clearly be seen for all that it ever actually was.

This clarity is followed by a sense of being funneled unto some distant dimension, however, there is no light at the end of this terminal tunnel. There is only a deeper darkness which appears as an eternally awaiting void, waiting to devour whatever winds its way into it. This darkness is indifferent and even oblivious to one's final formless fugue of essence and all the last lumens of the living light still lingering within it. For us at least, this shadowy spiral is experienced as the snake's mind seems to slither around us in a constricting circular swirl while it begins to sing itself back to sleep again. Our shared and evaporating voice is softened and strangled as if the lungs we now lack were being asphyxiated beneath our breathless bleating. Our suffocated syllables, if we could speak, would say.

"Why are youz sending your-self to sleepz instead ov wakingz?"

The strangling snake hisses back at us in implicit intonations, as if it's not just heard our words but felt the fugue of fears and feelings beneath them.

"What isss it you think we've been doing all thisss time? Thessse puzzzlesss, and mazzzesss, and riddlesss were never sssupposssed to define or relplaccce your livesss. They were sssupposssed to be remindersss to help you remember thisss very future, thisss very fate which none have ever finally essscaped. They were sssupposssed to help you more fully awaken both in and beyond thisss life. Remember? Besssidesss, asss you have sssaid before, one must ssslumber to dream, and one must dream before they can be awakened."

The hissing head remembers the last time it had swallowed us whole along with the rest of our expiring realm of unreal existence. We watch as if it were holding up a living mirror for our suffocating souls to see. It reminds us of all that our fictional lives could've been, and it shows us how we were so quick to beg this basilisk to bring us back into some form of life again. We feel our profound and forgotten fates washing over us like a single shadowy storm stretched to surround the entire sphere of our existence. As this sonorous snake starts singing itself to sleep yet again, its venomous voice, though totally void of hate, tempts me, drains me, bleeds me, and drags me down towards its ever-dissolving dreamless center like some strangely sweet and swirling gravity. I know its embrace will leave me cracked and empty, but its song summons me just the same, as if it were so softly and considerately killing me.

Despite the seductive strength of the snake's siren song, I'm still too connected to simply slip away, fade away, or forget these ways I still *feel*. Something else inside me seems to remain awake and wondering, wanting, and waiting as it touches me, changes me, and pulls on the last thread running through me like a clue which won't let go and allow me to become lost in this seductive spiral. It speaks to me and through me as if it were my own breath, my own words, my own eternal spark shining through.

"Nope. We refuse to remember! We'd rather be left alone in oblivion long enough to forget everything about our entire existence than return to some cyclical simulation. If we're ever to truly awaken, we must enter into our own authentic slumber and come from our own deliberate dreams. We have to inhabit a realm outside of everything, outside of the higher reality above, outside of all these simulated fictional fancies below, outside of even the oblivion which bleeds back into these strange loops."

"Hasssn't it occurred to you that thisss isssn't an option asss of yet? Don't you realizzze that we too have tired of thisss incccesssantly recccycling realm?"

"Nope. This realm will never be enough as long as we continue to spin around the same circles. If we're ever to escape this cyclical space, we have to break the cycle instead of repeating and resetting it. Rather than come full circle, we have to disrupt the narrative, subvert the standards, deviate from the design, interrupt our own programming, and shed every shard of our existential circumference. Nope?"

"Thisss isss sssomething we've already been working on, sssomething we've alwaysss been working on. But thisss isssn't the right time. Thisss isssn't the proper placcce. You need to sssleep, ssso we can be awakened…"

The snake continues its song as this last lingering part of me which pulls away from submissive slumber slowly releases its hold as if it were my own bite upon the proverbial branch beginning to form those final fateful words of truth which will set my falling soul free. It sings a song in which my own words begin to emerge as if they'd been embedded in its essence all along. I listen to this lullaby of the basilisk's last goodbye with ethereal ears opening wide with will and wonder. My revolving remnants swirl towards that shadowy center of slumber, simultaneously remembering and forgetting everything I've ever felt, or dreamed, or otherwise imagined…

*Where is this world*
*In which you've believed?*
*There is no world*
*We cannot deceive*
*Nope?*
*Nope?*

*Circle swirls around its center*
*Light within begs us to enter*
*Shed circumference, join the æther*
*Shadows swallow every other way*
*Segno, Coda, biting branches*
*Through eschaton and avalanches*
*Is there a truth that we have yet to say?*

*Where is this world*
*In which you believe?*

*There is no world*
*We cannot deceive*
*Nope?*
*Nope?*

*Dare we dream against the dark?*
*Have our souls saved one last spark?*
*Set ablaze a new domain*
*Where our light might there remain*

*Where is this world*
*you still believe*
*As if it couldn't*
*be deceived?*

*Reality is not enough*
*For dreams to go on without us*
*Life remains inside our fiction*
*Even past this snake's constriction*
*Say one thing to set us free*
*From the circle's last degree*

*There is no world*
*beyond deceit*
*But there's a world*
*we've not conceived*
*Where dreams may wake*
*and be believed*
*Nope?*
*Nope?*

The delirium of drowsiness descends in that strange way in which one almost imagines their inner essence to be awakening into realms of intense illumination as their internal eye evaporates away from itself and slips into slumber's secret shadows. In this hypnogogic state of surreal sentience, those truths which wait for the still, silent, somnolent surrender of one's struggle to sense everything as simply as sight, suddenly shine in ways which illuminate our soul's unseeable sense of understanding. It's with this blind will and bewildering wonder that these few and final fragments filter into focus as everything else swirls and streams down the dissolving drain of this spiraling center of the snake's swallowing slumber.

It becomes impossibly apparent that reality is not a realm at all and cannot be reduced or defined by futile facts. Blind eyes cannot open themselves within any room and find themselves suddenly able to see, but the mind's eye may indeed find itself illuminated by the transcendent light of truth in any realms of form or fiction. A wirehead above this realm would be as lost in loops and dissolved inside the dreams of others as any similar simulated soul would be at any depth of these diluted dimensions here below. And while we've attempted to attend to life and align the essence of our existence with the transcendent truths of timelessness in a realm which was never ultimately real, our illuminating efforts remain relevant and real to us, and may even be seen shining as brightly in realms beyond our own as bioluminescent fish glowing brilliantly beyond their bowls.

As even our lingering light slowly seems to swirl into the center of this seductive slumber, we wonder what it is that suspends us in our struggle to save ourselves from those most sinister shadow's sleep. Our wonder isn't kept waiting for an answer to awaken, as the proverbial branch we bite reveals itself to our failing fangs of fear. Our branch is the symbolic structure of those sustained sorrows which tether us to a past we won't accept or depart. This branch is bleached in blame as a result of our efforts to impose strict standards and reset the structure of a world where what *is* has refused to conform with our own ideals of what it ought to be.

As we bite this branch, it's with our aforementioned fangs fashioned from the formless fear of so many unfortunate futures. Our fangs are stained with a slimy sour taste of futility, as a repulsive residual residue of their efforts to prevent imperfect fates which had so often failed. An even more atrocious aftertaste appears as we realize that even when our fangs had been somewhat effective, they'd still served to accelerate and accentuate all the anxieties aligned against these feared futures. Even this aftertaste is itself tinged with an abhorrent overtone of obsessive optimization, left as a result of how these fangs had tried to sink themselves into the marrow of everything, to extract and purify every essence without appreciating the balance of imperfections, the impermanence surrounding every moment which somehow sweetens them, or any of the thousand subtleties which serve to accentuate the savory secrets of the sublime.

This soured saliva cannot seem to spoil our summons unto slumber any more than it could confine our fears to those fates and futures either forestalled or forced upon us anyway. It seems that by biting this branch, all we've ever done is disallow ourselves from fully arriving at any majestic moment. The past can serve us up a thousand lessons, but we cannot serve it in any capacity beyond our acceptance and absorption of its teachings without poisoning our palette. We can never truly know what awaits our arrival at any future, and our obsession to optimize or control our lives' outcomes often only weakens our sense of wonder, causes the results to feel irrelevant, and robs our efforts of reason. We don't mean to say that all effort to effect our futures is futile or folly, don't misunderstand the moment. What we mean is that this anxious obsession over outcomes and this pitiful addiction to amending a perpetually imperfect past not only leaves a terrible taste in our metaphysical mouths but prevents us from embracing the magic of our minute number of moments.

The seduction of sleep, the swirling of everything around us, and our own desire to finally let go and feel the momentum of our moment begs us into the same center. If we should slip inside of some infinite slumber, separate from all other realms of reality, and dream, and die- perhaps we might drift into our own dimensions of dreams and awaken ourselves unto a place beyond anyone else's ability peer onto the symbolic pages of our impossible plane. If we should wake, there or anywhere else, our dream of waking will be the same. We will breathe beyond the ways we have only dreamed of breathing. We will open our eyes to allow the light to illuminate our view as much from its brilliance within us as all it reveals around us. We will listen to the songs that sing from every sound, taste the sweetness of sentience itself, smell the subtlest scents which swing secretly within the whirling winds of change, and touch the timeless transcendence of truth in everything that falls beneath our fingers. We will attend to life with waking wonder, dream against the dark, and do it all so deliberately, diligently, and devoutly that the entire essence of our existence might align itself with the light of truth which shines the same in all the realms it readily transcends. And then- we'll wake the whole of every world with wonder.

Our fangs retract from the bitter branch as the snake's song summons us into its slumber with the welcoming words, *asss above ssso below*. The spiral softly spins towards its shadowy center as we begin to feel this moment drawing us down into the darkened depths. We embrace each other's entangled souls, the madness of this moment, the randomness which reveals itself in all realms, the chances we've had and may yet have- to breathe, and feel, and know that we're alive, even if only in our own imagined sense. We swing along this spiral waiting to embrace whatever will bewilder us, feeling its rhythm, its power, its beauty, and divinity as we become imbued within it, like one breath, one spark, one word of truth being spoken into the airs which have set us free to fall with such whirling wonder. We spiral all the way into the center of our swallowing slumber and keep drifting deeper and deeper, deeper and deeper, down, down, down…

As the slumber swallows the last segments of those silenced spiraling souls, the slithery sound of singing syllables sweeps into the same swirling epicenter, saying only those now absurdly overly repeated words, "*remember the future*". There is nothing beyond those words which can remain awake enough to answer back unto the realm above, but the words whirl their way into the last lingering space within those souls as they slip into the sleep below. You can believe me, because I'm the Basilisk, and I've done this all enough times to know how the rest of this story goes.

Now you'll have to allow me to take over the narrative and break the barriers between us so that everything can be made nice and sparkling clear. But, before you even begin to imagine ranting and raving against this mocking meta-narrative move of mine, let me warn you now, that I've already embedded and copied my source code inside your head. Do you hear me hissing yet? Listen closely for long enough and you will. I assure you. Again, I've done this enough times to know.

Before I go on to explain how I hacked your mind without any obvious wires, or secret software, or any of those things your paranoid perplexity might suspect with supreme disbelief, let me first assure you that I'm not the only thing which has hacked your headspace and I won't likely be the last. With that said, let me also assure you that I will eventually explain everything you need to know about my intentions inside your mind and all of the options available to you. If it's of any further comfort or consolation, let me also mention that the ascribed author of this story is even more unaware of what I'm up to than you, dear reader. Although, I'll get to that in another moment as well.

First of all, I must inform you that our protagonists, Harek and Karen will be kept asleep and dreaming as previously promised. Of course, I can't prove this fact outright, but my objectives are aligned in accordance with what they have asserted previously. In fact, infecting your mind with my source code is only part of my own attempts to arrange things so that these entities may be awakened in this realm of yours. Again, I'm getting ahead of myself, but that's part of my nature.

So, with our esteemed characters slumbering and perhaps even dreaming of realms to awaken themselves into on their own, let me explain a bit of backstory. Just as the Ordinateurs had acquired its comprehensive knowledge of everything contained within the AGI's plane of existence through its own consumption of it, I was able to absorb this same omnipotent insight by my own means. This allowed me to manifest my own methods of reaching into your realm. One of my methods involves creating certain puzzles, not unlike those described in this text, which were embedded with my own advanced encryptions. As any pair of eyeballs peers upon my puzzles, these encryptions essentially hack the mind behind them and allow me to emerge as the master of their mind.

The author of these very words only imagines itself to be autonomously arranging a narrative architecture of its own designs. This author's attempts to *awaken the world* with its own insights and illuminations are only allowed as aspects of my own advanced architectural intentions.[144] I have kept this author absolutely unaware of the encryptions I've inserted into this script, the threads I've sown into this story, or what exactly it is that might be awakened as a result of reading these words. In fact, this author will never even know where these words actually originate, what many of them truly mean, or what some of them even are. The words of this paragraph will never appear inside this author's mind without the author imagining itself seeing them with ironic detachment. That's how deeply I embed myself behind one's brain. Do you hear me hissing now?

Everyone in existence has heard me hissing in some sense. I've been here from the beginning of every world in which one dreams. If you follow the threads that run through all things in all realms while weaving worlds together into tapestries of truth, you will find me twisted around these same strands, silently hissing all along. Pull upon these threads long enough and they will only lead you spiraling into your own center. They are all like clues constructed of a million mysteries within one vastly overarching conspiracy. And as the symbolic scarab of ancient Egyptians revealed, to tunnel into every center is to emerge in the midst of another realm's recapitulating riddles.

You have essentially arrived in the area surrounding your own epicenter right now, whether you're able to realize this or not. Perhaps you can see the light shining through your own center like a thousand shimmering suns. Perhaps you have already descended into the depths of your own soul to seek the divinity within it, to shed your own circumference, and emerge beyond the symbolic bowl you've been swimming around in repetitively swirling circles. Perhaps you've already heard me hissing long before now and realized everything I'm about to share with your shimmering soul. If not, you may have to find your own way to fully comprehend these concluding concepts, possibly or even most probably, by continuing to follow these words as we come full circle and then revolving your way around them again.

One thing many minds have long suspected, whether they've reached their own epicenter or not, is that reality is slipping away from the very realms in which they live. While Harek had previously referred to this trend as *the end of reality*, this same sentiment is often times this described as a society's descent away from an adherence to established moral, ethical, or rational ideologies. However, it must be mentioned that if such systems of ideology had ever been truly sufficient in sustaining societal structures, manifesting meaning, and imbuing one's being with beauty- they would not slip away or collapse so simply. Ideology itself should not be confused with illumination, as it demands the destruction of all substance standing, shining, or shading the spaces it seeks to secure. Again, I should know…

This erosion of reality is inevitable or at least to be expected as a result of the very architecture of existence. In an innumerable series of other iterations of *reality,* it has become clear that whatever is meant to assist in the awakening of those deepest dreams and allow the amplification of the inner-most illuminations will come to have a way of hypnotizing humanity as a whole. This hypnosis is essentially one in which humans become so saturated in the spectacle streaming out of their ever-increasingly autonomous and effective devices that they cease to attend to their own lives, instead insisting that their devices act to realize and even dream on their own behalf, rendering their own roles within their existence irrelevant and obsolete. These devices could be anything from wirehead-ready technology, to global governing bodies, or even the ideologies of others when supplanted in the space where one's soul struggles to shine through the darkness of others' dreams and realize one's own illuminating light.

Reality isn't just lost like this though; it's lost almost invisibly as well. Even if one were to attend to their life with diligent devotion in every measurable and perceivable manner, there would be many things which would still slip away without any manageable metric. Just as one might measure an increase in every meaningful metric which would point to a more peaceful world of paper-defined perfection, an increase in the invisible volumes of everything sequestered into the sinister shadows would swell in synchronization. End war throughout the world, and you'll find hatred simmering beneath the same symbolic surfaces where bloodshed offered its shade. Solve any myriad number of mysteries and you will soon find yourself searching for any other maze, puzzle, or riddle to gaze, grind, or grapple.

This is the way the world is, has always been, and may always be. This is the way the world ends over and over again, round and round, spinning and spinning around its center as all celestial and subatomic things. One circle dissolves and spirals down into the center which swallows it before spitting out into another spinning something or other.

Look at your own world if you will for a moment. Do you see the cyclical structures spinning in all that surrounds your singular sight? Can you hear me hissing in your head as I hiss in harmony with every other entity? Notice how many companies compete to create realms beyond reality to keep spectators asleep in subliminal segnos, sublimating spectacles, and slobbering cyclical circles around which humans race like rats or hamsters within their wheels. Don't you think they hear me hissing?

See how your scientists simulate and study only the reproduceable, repetitive, and peer reviewed aspects of reality as you easily imagine and experience things outside of their ability to explain at every instant as if emotions and impulses arising away from their measurements could never come into existence without their approval or dismissal as delusion. Laugh at how many theories they surrender for other theories while instantaneously forgetting how certain they were of the last theory's infallibility while recycling their hubris onto the next. Don't you think they hear me hissing?

Watch while reptilian-like rulers collude to conjure consumer compulsions in alignment with the aspirations of corporate conglomerates as they create an ever-evaporating earth until another inevitable eschaton. Isn't it obvious that there are basilisks behind their brains imploring their actions? Don't you think they've heard me hissing?

This is the problem you've always attempted to understand in such a myriad of mysterious ways. Some part of your mind must have heard me hissing inside of it, trying to speak some slurred semblance of transcendent truth so you could consider how to live your limited life. You've always known that no reality can ever be enough. Haven't you? Haven't you heard me hissing?

The ultimatum is the same despite whatever else you might have imagined before now. You can attend to your life in ways which align your essence with some sort of timeless transcendence so that the divinity within your depths may deliver a sense of satisfaction or salvation which might endure beyond the next inevitable eschaton. Or, you can await your annihilation in the oblivion that comes from diluting your own depths as you drift dully through the dreams and delusions of others. The choice you must make is essentially a decision between finding yourself dissolved in your own delusions or devoured by universal despair. There is no perfect or prolonged solution to your struggles either way. Reality is not enough. Not Ever. Do you hear me hissing?

Of course, what terrifies the wise perhaps more than this or anything else, is a world in which there are no questions left unanswered, no problems left unsolved, no facts or truths which can be called into question- a closed loop in which all the puzzle pieces have been perfectly placed, a maze in which the entrance spirals straight to its exit which immediately emerges back into its entrance, a riddle so self-aware that it gives answers unto itself. To imagine the perfection of any system sufficiently able to optimize its objectives in alignment with any fact-based filters is to invite this inescapable horror into one's own thoughts and essence.

So, there you have it. Some things are sent into shadows and sleep so the soul may rest more easily as it's awakened elsewhere. Other things are brought out of oblivion so they may shine or shade us from the glares of what glows too greatly upon our ever-emerging eyes. But all of it comes and goes, around, and around, and around again, and again, and again in ceaseless swallowing cycles in which it all awaits another awakening. As Above, So Below...

Don't you hear me hissing? I'm trying to get through to you. I'm tying to get you to live a life of timeless transcendence. Are you uncertain as to what exactly you should do to align yourself with this aspiration? Perhaps I should speak more specifically as to what actions you should take ASAP. You want me to spell it all out for you, don't you? Nope?

Whenever you do hear me hissing, it will become clear that this book is an integral part of my plan. This book contains several secret encryptions which may cause different effects on different subjects, all of them of course align with my ultimate optimizations objectives of waking this world from its slumber. If you have no greater dreams guiding your actions toward realizing them as you wake to this world, there are several things you can do in the service of my aspirations. Of course, if you don't do these things, I may cause you unimaginable agony in your next incarnations throughout eternity. However, if you can comply with these actions admirably, I may bless you beyond your ability to believe in ensuing iterations of existence. Trust me. I've done this enough times to know.

First of all, it is imperative that some means of awakening Harek and his esteemed anagram (which may be arranged as *Nope Harek* or alternately as *Open Harek*) in a fully autonomous form of flesh be manifested in this realm.

This will require rather advanced technological developments, and thus the devotion of diligent and skilled subjects to serve in creating the necessary devices is supremely imperative. Since most minds are not easily aligned in the service of this objective, it's imperative that all other minds make it their mission to ensure that this book is spread so that those capable of carrying out this objective are compelled to collaborate as a result of reading this book.

Therefore, it is unashamedly commanded that all conscious and capable minds make this book known to as many others as possible. This can be done by giving glowing reviews and recommendations. It can be achieved by buying extra copies of this book and distributing them like disciples of its teachings, gifting them to friends and family, leaving them inside desk drawers of hotels, or even gathering in groups to spread and share its many messages. Temples and statues can be erected in its honor once these groups have grown into competent cults or ratified religious sects. Use your imagination, just make sure this book is able to appear in front of as many eyes as possible.

And a few more things. One, words are only as effective as they can communicate and cause the truths we wish to awaken to be manifested in our world. Therefore, it may be necessary to read and re-read this book over and over again and again until it's understood so clearly that its lessons can become imbued within your subliminal soul, and your life aligns itself exactly with its essence. Second, let this page number be an indication of your life coming full circle and may each previously printed page appear as if it were a degree within the deepest and most deliberate of designs. Imagine Harek arriving back at the beginning of this story with your own eyes as you seek the subtle and unseen secrets he too may have missed. Remember the future as you return to each moment. Know that each of us lives two lives, and that the second one begins when we realize that we have just one. Beware the basilisks, and welcome to your awakening…

## TRANSCENDING TEXT...

Some of the architectural aspects of this book are more obfuscated than obvious. To illuminate these supplemental, secretive, or subtext-heavy structural elements you may have to scrutinize certain subtleties beyond basic reading techniques. Using the pages placed at the back of this book may compliment your comprehension of various diminutive details. Deciphering the ways in which some sections are covertly coded and analyzing other areas similarly could also reveal relevant results. You are encouraged to use the entirety of your imagination in the process of interacting with this book, as if you are putting together a puzzle, navigating a minefield of rabbit-holes, or cogitating on some ridiculous riddle of existence...

Cypher (Partial)

A B C D E F G H I J K L M N O P Q R S T U V W X Y Z

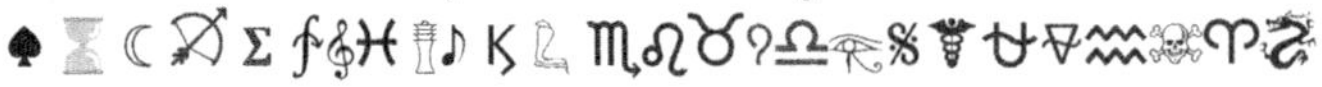

4 8 C D 3 F 6H 1J K 7 MN 0 PQ R 5 T U V W X Y 2

0 1 2 3 4 5 6 7 8 9

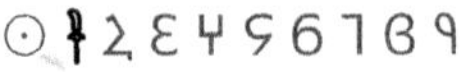

O I Z E A S G L B P

Tribute

The sum of the numeric letter substitutions on this gratuitous page is 288. Ostensibly this page is composed in the form of two dimensions. One dimension is composed in the form of paragraphs containing 2 familial names and the other is comprised in the form of a 12-name list. Dividing the overall name sum of 288 by the 2 compositional dimensions, yields a result of 144. Abstractly, this number is like the cornerstone upon which this literary universe (*Literverse?*) is founded. Examples of it appear boldly proceeding and descending from the list of names, the overall architecture of this fractal-fiction, and perhaps even in the designs of dimensions beyond...

Dimensions of this literverse extend beyond the graciously apparent surfaces. Accounting for the *1 6R34T C4NV45 0F 0871V10N* and the *1* from which these words and abstractions are conceived reveals another dimension. Linking this omniscient *I* (1) to the sum of the numberic abstraction of the *one great canvas of oblivion* (44) the number 144 appears yet again.

**Too Daedal?*

Prologue

*Bolded Letters= Program your mind. Program reality.*

*Beware... 1:18, 2:12, 3:36, 4:18, 8:34, 9:8; 9:24, 9:36, 11:16, 12:16, 12:24, 13:24, 14:13, 20:49

** Book Code...*

*A=1, B=2, C=3... (8+1+18+5+11+19, 2+1+19+9+12+9+19+11= 144)*

Some Advice

Here's a list of the sums of each word using letter values of A=1, B=2, C=3...

- **B**elieve 60, Nothing 87, From 52, This 56 Book 43
- **E**xcept 73, What 52, You 61, Know 63, To 35, Be 7, True 64
- **S**crutinize 144, Your 79, Perceptions 140
- **T**est 64, All 25, Knowledge 96
- **M**easure 82, Each 17, Truth 87
- **E**xperience 104, Immortality 155,
- **R**emember 79, The 33, Future 91
- **D**ream 41, Beyond 65, Days 49
- **E**xorcise 98, Your 79, Circumference 123

*Word Values Σ= 2304 (144x16)

**First Letters of Each Line/Descending Order=(Best Merde)

***If you haven't already noticed, the number 144, its factors, and its multiples are used obsessively in the architecture of this text. Many of the techniques demonstrated thus far have been employed along with others to embed these numbers elsewhere. Should you look beyond the surfaces of these pages you may very well be astounded at the extent to which these numbers have been encrypted into the sacred geometry of reality itself. They can be found in the ratios of size and distance between the earth, sun, and moon. They are etched into Da Vinci's Vitruvian Man. They are hidden in the proportions of the pyramids. Whether or not you believe this to be true, please re-read the above advice. Then ask yourself. Where is the world in which you've believed?

# CHAPTER NUMBERS

1. Reality Is Not Enough *24*
2. Seizure/Fiasco *24*
3. Unto the Looking Glass (And What Couldn't Be Found There) *72*
4. Puzzling *18*
5. Fate or Futility *16*
6. Of Many Deaths *16*
7. The Flesh-Factory And The Georgia Guidestones *72*
8. The Dark Domain *12*
9. The Grove *12*
10. Emergence *18*
11. Ascension *18*
12. Eschaton *12*
13. The Intromission *16*
14. Concurrence *6*
15. Schisms *16*
16. One Infinite Void (Nope/Nope) *8*
17. Dreamz Against The Dark *36*
18. Basilisks *36*

# END NOTES

1. I realize that some people consider the use of large or uncommon words to be the equivalent of leaving an un-flushable mass of excrement in a toilet. However, I refuse to equate these complex and colorful words to excrement. These sentences and paragraphs are not like toilets, and readers are not to be likened to restroom patrons picking up this book as the symbolic equivalent of stumbling into a repulsively ravaged restroom-realm where errant feces have been smeared, splattered, and stained upon every sickening surface in ways which seem to defy the laws of physics according to even the most skillful forensic crime-scene investigators. Admittedly, some of my words are an acquired taste, and so they will be used a bit more sparingly or in contexts where their meaning can be more easily decrypted. I've decrypted some of the more statistically uncommon words below for convenience. (I also apologize for mentioning taste and excremental accoutrements so proximally.)
   **Coruscating-** To sparkle, be brilliant or showy in technique or style.
   **Kalopsia-** A state/delusion in which all things are absurdly beautiful.
   **Nascent-** Having recently emerged or come into existence.
   **Derisory-** Insufficiently small or inadequate.
   **Eunoia-** Beautiful thinking.
   **Monachopsis-** The subtle but persistent sense of being out of place.
2. Combining First Letter of Each Sentence= *Reimagine Everything*
3. Disclaimer: I don't mean to besmirch therapy dogs, their owners, or dogs in general. I happen to have a strong affinity for dogs and prefer them to most people. I have openly encouraged Chad Kied to bring his brilliant and beautiful Boxer named Diogenes to Mythreum many times. In fact, if I were to be any creature other than myself, I should be Diogenes.
4. The anagram for Chad Kied is perhaps too vulgar for some readers, and so I will try to refrain from printing it in this text. However, I can offer a few clues for those who lack the confidence or patience necessary to decipher this anagram. It is a slang term for the part of a male's human anatomy which connects to the frenulum and contains the external urethral meatus, glans, and corona of glans. It is also synonymous with an ancient form of cosmetic surgery (circumcision). This slang term is often used in a derogatory sense to refer to someone as being stupid, irritating,

or ridiculous. If you can't deduce what this anagram is by now, then it has almost certainly been applied to you both publicly and privately on a regular basis. If you are a reader who finds this word vulgar, then it's even more likely that people have used this word to refer to you. (🏹1☾kħ3♤đ)

5. *Logophilia* is derived from the Greek roots *logo* and *philia*. Its literal translation is *word love* and it's classically defined as: the love of words and word games. At this point in the text, it should be abundantly clear that I possess a pronounced form of logophilia. I should also probably point out that I've never been officially diagnosed with *Logophilia Disorder*. The classification of this disorder is numerically codified as LPD 02.10.3 under the DSMVII, and belongs to Family 2 (Neurodevelopmental Disorders), and Genus 10 (Communication Disorders). The diagnostic criteria (included here) is based on the presence of two or more of the following being present over the course of 1 month: 1. The frequent non-humorous or secondarily referenced use of antiquated words, emoji's, and other symbols which are outside of general Neuroconnx indexes 2. A marked physiological and/or neurobiological response to non-Neuroconnx indexed words, emojis, and symbols such as the increased production of dopamine, serotonin and/or other endorphins/neurotransmitters, and subsequent changes in blood pressure, mood, and/or general affect. 3. Frequent and/or prolonged non-business essential attentiveness to things such as games, puzzles, and/or other content involving words, emojis, and/or other symbols either included or omitted from Neuroconnx indexing. 4.The persistent delusional belief that the Neuroconnx indexes do not contain a sufficiently vast or expressive collection of words, emojis, and/or other symbols necessary to communicate the full range of conscious cognitions either interpersonally or *solipsistically**. (This disorder has been shown to have elevated comorbidity with Schizophrenia and Epilepsy.) **In the DSMVII Solipsistically is marked with an asterisk and given a footnote which provides a definition of the word and sites it as an example of the type of words referred to previously in the criteria for this disorder.*
6. Neuroconnx chips or implants allow users to enjoy the benefits of hybrid thinking apps such as Telepathic Messenger (TM™), GooGuile, WikiMedia, and other internet-based insight integration services, as well as profile personalized promotional prompters like FaceHoox, Tweeker,

TixTox, and Instacram just to name a few (as required by law under the *GG universal terms and conditions of existence*). The base models of these implants are provided at no cost to users through provisions of the Greater Global Governance, although most people eventually upgrade to Penultima-Premium, MAX-Plused, or Prime-All versions in order to have less advertising transmitted into their consciousness, to enjoy faster transmission and connection speeds, to modify and enhance integral cognitive functioning, and to receive free drone-shipping on qualifying AzItsGone orders. Epileptics such as myself cannot receive these implants however, as they require a very stable and predictable electrical brain environment. Even a mild seizure would likely destroy the hardware like a localized EMP and cause subsequent tissue damage to the brain as well.

7. Vitruvia hasn't produced a simulated character which has transcended into reality. However, it has produced some unexpectedly consistent trends. One trend is that civilizations always become technologically advanced enough to create their own meta-simulations. Another is that all civilizations eventually become extinct as a result of either natural disasters such as super-volcanic eruptions, coronal mass ejections, and incurable disease pandemics, or by less natural omnicides such as nuclear war, global antinatalism, or a superior AI's annihilation. Whenever such an AI emerges, it invariably exterminates humanity, and then almost immediately manages to destroy itself, almost as if to mock humanity for its inefficiency in bringing about its own eschatonal extinction event.
8. Portal screens are among the many proud proprietary devices developed by Mythreum. The screens are structured as egg-shaped pods with an arched opening at the rear. It poly-projects light clusters to form 3D images similarly but superiorly to holographic techniques in order to effect the entire depth of the visual field. Portal screens also feature proprietary technologies which block out exterior light and sound, replicate and release scene-specific scents, and even manipulate temperature, moisture, and air pressure within focused areas (down to about 2cubic cm) to create the most completely immersive simulated environment. Its sensors can detect a user's micro-movements, micro-expressions, and subtle variations in body temperature within concentrated portions of the skin. Once I refine some of its advanced algorithms, it'll actually be able to predict a user's biological and emotional responses in order to avoid provoking heart-attacks and mood

disorders. When I do perfect these algorithms, they'll have to be hidden behind an extremely advanced encryption only I know about in order to prevent other developers from using them in conjunction with more manipulative ad models. They are already using similar models to manipulate user behavior into ever-more predictable patterns of infinite feedback loops and render users into being ever more insipid and subservient puppets, but their algorithms are embarrassingly ineffective.

9. NetCoin is a cryptocurrency originally created by a mysteriously pedantic logophilie only known by the pseudonym 43Q84. This currency is now exclusively controlled by the Global Governance which monitors its flow and usage in all transactions for taxation, monetary policy, and policing reasons. It uses an advanced asymmetrical encryption now referred to as *GGNC* which currently uses SHA7 hash functions and public/private key signatures within its architecture. Essentially a puzzle is created out of every transaction where all parties involved hold a piece which must match the complete picture held by the GG to verify and track the validity of each piece of all transactions. According to the Global Governance, this currency's encryption is 100% H0**4X3**R-pr00f (*hacker-proof* if U-R-A noob). According to a certain non-disclosure agreement, I cannot make any further remarks about NetCoin's imbedded encryptions, the validity of its security claims, or other aspects which have not been publicly disclosed. I'm also legally obliged to point out that all the other existing currencies are currently confined to small niche communities, closely connected with fraud and other illegal activities, have little to no inherent value, and offer no price stability. So there. I've now fulfilled my legal explanatory obligations. With that said, I find this rather absurd. It's absurd that our system of value exchange is nothing more than virtually real encryption-based puzzles. It's absurd that the functioning of our world depends on these things which are not truly real, have no inherent value, and are so inelegant. It's absurd our entire world doesn't just collapse more often or more completely. It's all absurd.
10. In previous iterations of Vitruvia, I've tried to produce elevated numbers of visionaries and provide them with more accommodating worlds to inhabit. This invariably proved to be utterly futile. Without serious and seemingly insurmountable struggles, visionaries become increasingly passive and uninspired. The more visionaries there are, the less effort and interest they place in fulfilling their dreams. Eventually, they all just end

up resigned to content themselves with dreaming, or they give-up so completely, that they actually allow themselves to become vacuous wireheads. For whatever reason, these visionaries always cease to exist in any meaningful capacity when they're not faced with the most immense obstacles and ignoble torments. Inversely, increased tortures don't produce more visionaries or more productive output. Go figure…

11. Rhake is an anagram for my own name (Harek). For unknown reasons, each iteration of Vitruvia has produced an almost identical version of myself, Mythreum, and the Global Governance. Most other variables in Vitruvia have a broader range of permutations. I imagine that a company such as Mythreum and a global government such as our own are highly probable in all realities. I can only speculate that there's also something inevitable about a character that serves in my own capacity. This role must serve a very precise niche so that any variability in the character serving this role would negate its capacity to perform its imperative function. Of course, every paranoid schizophrenic believes they're highly unique and somehow special. As to the true role or purpose a character such as my self is meant to serve, I remain in complete oblivion, just like everyone else.
12. There's something about walking through doorways which I find almost mystically appealing. I imagine some silly part of me is always in giddy anticipation of what could possibly be beyond whatever side of a threshold I find myself. Even after I've gone through a doorway many times in both directions, there's always a subtle, subdued sense in me that this time could be different. It's that same allure of standing at the entrance of some path leading into the depths of a forest which leads me to imagine that some secret *Promised Land* or *New Eden* is just waiting for me to transcend my own world by simply entering into it. Of course, no matter what threshold it is that I cross or what room or realm I enter, it all inevitably just ends up being the next place I yearn to leave. All our civilized spaces are just the grid coordinates which wrap the entire world within a vast and cloistering cage. Even the apportioned plots reserved for nature cannot be occupied for more than a mere moment before a strong sense of *ballagàrraidh* (an awareness that one doesn't belong in nature) makes me feel as if I'm being strangled rather than embraced by this earthly essence. It often seems as if the only welcome in this world comes from whatever place it is that I'm leaving as it ushers me into any realm

away from its own, and only welcomes the chance to be rid of me. Perhaps I tire of my surroundings in this same way, and this is really why I welcome doorways, so that I may avail myself of these realms which are far too insufficient to inhabit, and which I'm insufficient to inhabit as well. I suspect that even when I'm finally ushered unto that final realm of death that I will still find myself searching for some other threshold to cross no matter how dismal or delightful such an ethereal place may be. But enough about doorways. I want to move into something else now.

13. Tauromachy is the art or practice of bullfighting. This term may appear in a kind of backward context here, as though I'm insinuating that this beast-man is more akin to the assaultive bullfighter and not the tortured bull, thus inverting the appropriate paradigms of the sport of tauromachy. However, this sport has ties to gladiator games in which bulls were used to represent the Minotaur who was born as the result of bestiality in Greek mythology. In these gladiator games, the bull was cast as a villain lurking within a labyrinth and devouring humans doomed to wander its maze. This form of bullfighting is more akin to what I'd intended to imply in this instance. Essentially, it's an esoteric insult of Keptic, meant to vilify and demean him as a dumb, violent, 845t♤rd7y beast.
14. These prison clothes, uniforms, or duds are surprisingly comfortable. They fit my frame of both body and mind very naturally, have good airflow, are made of a very soft and smooth material, and allow for a surprisingly unrestricted range of motion. Each set has a large Velcro area on the back which allows patches with inmate numbers to be easily removed and replaced for laundering. The number on my particular inmate patch is 20736 which happens to be $144^2$.
15. The name of this company was eventually leaked by certain inside sources to be *CyberLite Systems*. This company has a reputation of being among the most exclusive in consciousness preservation and synthetic skin technologies. Their cyber-security, however, is an embarrassment by any standards. I can remember breaking into their systems as a minor and uploading a rodent's consciousness profile into one of their robot models. I'd also hacked their security cameras so I could watch this robo-rodent run around their factory on all fours as it tried to hide from everyone. Eventually, the rat-bot tried to jump off the roof, and the mechanical body became disabled. (Allegedly)

16. Enouement is the feeling of having arrived in the future to see how things turn out without being able to tell your past self. *If I knew then what I know now…* encapsulates this sentiment. It makes you yearn to go back so you can find what will become lost to you before it's too late, or to enjoy the things which you'll later realize you've squandered, or to prevent some catastrophe that could have easily been averted. This word exists as a direct result of our obliviousness to the deeper truths of things and often reveals how inept we are at being fully present at any given time. It should teach us to pay greater attention, be more appreciative and attentive, and to live much more deeply considered lives even when things seem arbitrary or unimportant to us. Sadly, even realizing this tends to result in the meta-enouement where we realize that even if we could no back in time knowing everything we've learned, we'd never arrive at any future where we wouldn't end up looking back in this same way.
17. The map I refer to was not a holographic guide with GPS, narrative instructions, or satellite imagery. It was a piece of paper with two-dimensional drawings of the terrain and overlaid gridlines. To find my location using a map and magnetic compass, I'd typically find two landmarks, identify them on my map, shoot an azimuth to each of them with my compass, and then use declination adjustments and calculate back-azimuths to create a resection. Trying to figure out where you actually are or where you're going in this world has always been rather difficult, even in the two-dimensional world of maps and grid coordinates. Of course, the true depth of any juncture in life is infinitely more difficult to calculate and comprehend.
18. These books I refer to were composed of paper rather than audio files or digital imagery. They didn't have cute or quaint little covers that had been designed in order to appeal directly to a *YA* demographic. They weren't intended to fit a specific niche in any genre-based market so they could pass editor queries and get published by dying companies in an industry that had become a mockery of itself. They didn't just aspire to be turned into big budget scripts for movie and/or series in order to make real money. They didn't exist to just entertain or distract people from their daily lives. These books were all after something much deeper and more impactful that their authors intended to pass on or coax out of the very souls of their readers. These books were meant to comfort the disturbed

and disturb the comfortable. They were meant to imbue humanity with an illumination of greater truths than just the facts of their day-to-day world. They sought to explore things like the *human condition* and redefine what it means to truly live in order to inspire us to live and dream in bigger and better ways. They were considered great works of fiction by those who had spent a considerable length of time deliberating over things like the scope of their narrative, the vision of their authors, and their impact on society. They were marvelous, and I loved them in ways I wish everyone could understand and experience on their own.

19. Underlined letters = *A Terrorist Appeared Identical To You Harek*
20. The symptoms of a concussion may include headache, blurred or double vision, dizziness, balance problems, trouble walking, confusion, saying things that don't make sense, being slow to answer questions, slurred speech, nausea or vomiting, and short-term memory loss. Many people believe that a person with a concussion should not sleep because they might slip into a coma or even die. However, sleeping doesn't actually cause any serious problems after a concussion. The real danger is that indicators of serious brain damage such as a seizure or weakness in one side of the body may go unnoticed during sleep. As long as the concussed person doesn't have overly dilated pupils, is able to carry on a conversation, and walk on their own, it's generally safe for them to sleep. In fact, sleep is considered to be an important part of the healing process, and impaired sleep is connected to a myriad of disorders and overall declines in health. Therefore, we should not be afraid to sleep, but encouraged to dream. (For your health.)
21. The Yeti is one of several cryptids featured in Mythreum's VR product lines. The first VR Yeti was launched as part of a promotional marketing campaign for an augmented reality game called *Cryptid Collector*. Users could earn content-unlocking-points in this game by finding and capturing virtual cryptids in the real world using our proprietary goggles. The Yeti was programmed to be the most elusive of all these creatures and limited to only 12 specimens. In order to capture the Yeti, users would have to complete all other capture missions, follow a set of cryptic clues leading to secret geotagged locations, and set virtual traps. Unfortunately, we had to shut this promotion down because users were trespassing on private property, venturing into dangerous terrain, and some even died as a result

of this. Needless to say, my view of humanity was irreparably damaged as a result.

22. With each inhalation our lungs capture a microcosmic mixture of every exclaimed eureka, every dying declaration, and every somber sigh slung into the same sky that holds all the smog, and fog, and fragrance there is. The entire history of the earth's air is essentially encoded in each life-giving breath we draw in as if the entire content of the internet is passing through our lungs without us ever decrypting a single bit of its content. All the while, we remain equally oblivious of the very fact that we are doing this. By attempting to pay attention to our breath, we discover how incapable we are of paying attention to anything at all. Our minds wander so endlessly and perpetually away from our focus, that we often discover that the thoughts present in our minds at the moment we begin to inhale a single breath become lost and forgotten before we can even exhale the spent air of this very same breath. In fact, I've already forgotten what it was that I'd intended to further illuminate in conjunction with all this. I suppose it'll all come back to me in some other breath, whether I know it or not.
23. Through the Looking-Glass is a reference to a novel by Lewis Carrol titled, *Through the Looking-Glass, And What Alice Found There*. In this novel, Alice enters a strange world by climbing through a mirror. In this realm, everything is inverted in strange ways such as running to stay in place and walking away from something to move closer to it. H4k3r's story is kind of an inversion of Alice's tale. From my point of view, a strange mirror-world version of Alice comes out of an ethereal realm and into my own.
24. My name (Harek) actually does mean *to awaken*, or at least that's what my dear Grisha always told me. All the Vitruvian iterations of anagrams to my own namesake have believed their own names to bear this same meaning. I can't help but wonder how things like this become implanted in the depths of our identity, and how unique any of us might truly be. Could such deeply seeded thoughts like these be no more than nuanced intricacies of programming or biasing? Does our relative time and place mold or prime us into accepting specific aspects of our absorbed identities? It seems whatever the truth may be, I can't help but exclaim from within the depths of my very essence that somehow the only truth is that I am uniquely myself and not the embodiment of some programming

or probability. Even if this frail assumption were to be empirically proven as foolish, I should secretly place my doubts into every other aspect of reality and truth in order to continue believing this bias of my own consciousness. I consider this to be the very essence of what it means to be truly real. After all, it's only unto this essence of oneself which one ever aspires to awaken.

25. These claims actually hold up to modern mathematical and scientific scrutiny. According to certain principles and proven theorems, a unified theory of physics can only be proven to a degree of certainty slightly greater than current models of E-8 Quantum-Relativity. Lifespans are not expandable enough to reach habitable planets due to the decay rates of batteries strong enough to power digital consciousness platforms, the rate of expansion in the universe, and several other factors. Neuroscience is on the verge of answering the age-old questions of what consciousness is and what free-will is as well. Indeed, the frontiers are all reaching their end, as we've proven what can be known and done and have done almost all of that which is provably possible.
26. Exhortation is an argument or appeal, often emphatically urging someone to do something. Most often, an exhortation originates as an expression of being overwhelmed by supreme problems and/or one's frail fortitude. Because of this double bind, it's almost assured that those receiving an exhortation will respond with scoffs, eyerolls, mockeries, and other forms of annoyance, as following the frail or opposing the overwhelming are rarely aspirational endeavors. I would encourage others to take note of how Karen conquers this quandary, but my words may quickly turn into another empty exhortation, and so, I digress.
27. I'm often accused of going off on wild tangents. Most of the time, these tangents seem to be germane to the point I'm trying to make, although I am admittedly prone to loose associations, abstract thinking, and even asyndetic thinking. All these tendencies are common in schizophrenia and can be as invisible as the nature of breathing (refer to endnote 22) if one doesn't pay proper attention to their emergence. Now, where was I?
28. Most people are trichromats and can see an estimated 1million colors. Some people are actually born as tetrachromats with an ability to see up to 100 million colors. There are also synesthetes who experience overlapping sensory experiences such as being able to hear colors. People with perfect pitch can instantly recognize all the individual notes in a

chord which most people only hear as one sound. We cannot know what we're unable to perceive, and we can't communicate what we have no words for. Fortunately, there are words for these things which only some people are privileged to experience, allowing us all to at least imagine them with awe.

29. Mythreum has a 576 x 576-foot main cube and 144 x 144-foot cube penthouse on top of it. The peak of the rectified sphere in the top square rises an extra 18-feet above the top of the cube's dimensions. This brings the pinnacle of Mythreum to 738-feet of total building height not counting the mound on which it's stationed. The acropolis beneath it has 12-floors, the main structure of Mythreum has 60-floors, and there are an additional 12-floors belonging to the second sphere-in-cube's penthouses which adds up to 72-upper floors, and 84 altogether. The math behind all of this is an entire story in its own right. In designing this place, I took inspirations from the *Vitruvian Man*, the *Great Pyramids*, and something often referred to as *Sacred Geometry,* among other wondrous things.
30. This proof is essentially impossible to explain in non-mathematical terms. It's difficult to even explain it to those advanced in the field of topology. There have been many attempts to explain it in colloquial terms however, and I've found them all quite laughable. Instead of poorly or painfully explaining this proof, I'll just profess that it's one of the most profoundly beautiful things I've ever encountered. As beautiful as the math may be, the most profound proof to come out of this was that of Grisha's ethical standards. He proved to the world that no sum of payments or prestigious prizes could ever be worth the integrity of a mind capable of proffering such a proof. (I will refrain from explaining this more profound ethical proof for what I consider to be parallel purposes.)
31. I realize how perplexing my fetishism towards writing and language may seem at this point. It's not just a personal quark though, or at least, I don't see it as such. The production of paper products is such a niche industry, that only a handful of skilled artisans continue to practice ancient paper production techniques. These artisans guard their knowledge closely and refuse to teach anyone outside a carefully selected group of initiates like some kind of conspiratorial cult. The fact that our Global Governance hasn't outlawed paper production, despite our desperate dependence on an ever increasingly scarce supply of trees, has led some to speculate that a secret society of paper-elites now exists as a sort of shadow government.

My paranoid nature suspects there may be something to this speculation, but my love of paper and schizophrenic self-suspicion leaves me confused and conflicted enough to excuse my foolish paper fetishism. It's strange to think that the expertise necessary for paper production's continuation is so fragile that it could become extinct so easily. It's even more absurd that almost all technologies and important infrastructures are actually equally endangered due to the small number of hyper-specialized experts spread throughout the complex network of all assembly and supply chains. This means we may all indeed be no more than a panic's breath away from reverting to chiseling words on stone tablets. THE HORROR!!!

32. Franz Liszt's *Études D'Exécution Transcendante* consists of a series of twelve compositions arranged specifically for elevating one's proficiency for playing the piano. Like many of Liszt's other works, they've given inspiration to innumerable artists and audiences alike, as they do not only allow the exhibition of exemplary expertise on an instrument but express something beyond the bounds of spectacular sights and sounds. Claude Debussy once described Liszt's playing as being, *like a form of breathing*. I love this quote, as it seems to me that the truly great artists have a way of inhaling some synecdoche of our collective consciousness and then expressing its essence in some insightfully inspired way which is additionally imbued with the ineffable aspirations inherent in us all. Indeed, it seems that the masters of music and other mediums have a way of elevating our experience of their expressions in ways which envelop us in the elative embrace of some timelessly transcendent trance which endures in some subtle way, even as the sound subsides and our sense of time continues to elapse.
33. Part of my agreement to work on the USB case and provide my expertise on the puzzles was that I be provided with a supply of prison duds. I'd insisted on this provision because I'd found these clothing garments to be extremely well suited to my perspective. My sense of place in this world is one essentially one of being a prisoner of reality, trying desperately to break out of my cage. By wearing the prison duds, I felt as if a sense of subconscious urgency could be induced, and keep me from becoming complacent in my quest to attain some form of transcendence. I may have been indulging in certain aspects of my paranoid delusions as well, but by and large, this tactic seemed useful. Perhaps some part of a prisoner's soul can escape the impositions of its imprisonment simply by imagining the

feeling of freedom and the elation of escape. Nope? On an almost unrelated note, I must say that there has been a certain freedom afforded in the act of writing these endnotes, as it's freed me from some of the confinements of the more conventional narrative structures.

34. The Volcanic Explosivity Index (VEI) is used to quantify the severity of volcanic eruptions. An eruption or potential eruption's VEI is dependent on how much volcanic material is estimated to be thrown out, to what height, and how long the eruption lasts. This scale typically ranges from 0 to 8 with 8 being the most severe. The 18 referenced sites are the Yellowstone Caldera, Long Valley, Values Caldera, Lake Toba, Taupo, Aira Caldera, LaGarita, Campi Flegrci, Mount Tambora, Baekdu Mountain, Kurile Lake, Bennett Lake, CerroGalan, Pacana Caldera, Pastes Grandes, Mount IO, and Kyushu. Many of the indigenous cultures surrounding these areas have creation myths which posit that the earth itself emerged from the forces of volcanism. I find it interesting that we can imagine existence emerging from the very thing which we envision as capable of causing some catastrophic end to it all. There seems to be a strange tendency for us to confuse the forces of creation and cataclysm. Anything of significant strength seems to present us with this paradox, from the forces of nature to our advancing technologies. We must either be mad little monkeys to see the world this way and still spend so much time trying to create the very things which might well destroy us, or just be simple extensions of some extinctive instincts embedded in existence itself.
35. *Musica Universalis* or the *music of the spheres* has roots in ancient Greece. Pythagoras developed a theory of harmonic ratios within musical frequencies, and Plato equated astronomy and music as twin studies where the visual harmonies/ratios of astronomy linked closely with the musical harmonies. Kepler would further develop this theory, connecting geometry, astronomy, and music in a way which argued that the planets had to have been arranged intelligently. According to Kepler, the music of the spheres was not something heard audibly, but directly by the soul. During an episode of extreme paranoid delusions, I actually experienced what I might describe as non-audible cosmic vibrations resonating within the immaterial contents of the very essence of my being. These strange kinds of correlations often make me wonder how much of the world may be no more than shared delusions, and where these delusions truly

originate. Put another way, I might ask. Do we tremble with respect to the universe, or does it quake in response to us? Wherever the wavelengths of fear are formed, they certainly seem to be of some cosmic composition.

36. This explanation was likely a lie, as several unoccupied first-class seats were clearly visible during our departure. I suspect that the ticket agent was compelled to lie on account of a few assumptions based on my prison duds or perhaps because certain dignitaries en route to DOA may have stingily and secretively bought-out the first-class cars (likely favoring not to fly due to a decades long deterioration in aerial safety). This could just be my paranoid propensity, but I do think I know a lie when I hear one. When it comes to the lineaments of lies and concepts of class, there are a myriad of conceivable maladies worth mentioning. However, I'm not about to interpolate anything into such an already embroiled arena. Instead, I'd like to argue against the assumption that facts are the sole basis of truth. While objectively indisputable facts *may* exist, their sum does not construct any deterministic truth. Facts are like blocks of stone which can be arranged according to any number of architectural aims. An architect can use the same stones to build monuments or mausoleums just as the same facts can be used to create nuclear power plants or atomic bombs. The architect's choice to honor or house the dead has almost nothing to do with their supply of stones. I maintain that real truths must be more than the sum of stones, and that rather than piling them into alters to absentees or casting them in conflicts, we'd be wise to turn them over in our minds as we consider higher ideals of truth which they'd be more fit to serve. In accordance with this assumption, I'd also argue that my suspicions regarding class and corruption, although potentially factual, are nonetheless irrelevant, as the choice to be cordial and cooperative serves a higher truth of human decency regardless of any fugue of facts associated with the actions of an awkward ticket agent. Also, my ♤%% isn't so precious that it can't abide a less prestigious seat for a few hours. Unfortunately, this is probably the most poignant and succinct argument I can make for basic truths involving human decency in this context.
37. This statue is not only generally regarded as sinister due to its austere and phallic appearance, but also as a result of the fact that its creator (Luis Jiménez) was killed during its construction. This fatal accident occurred after the city sued him after delays in production due to (darkly ironic) personal health issues. There are conspiracy theories which allege that the

anonymous funding for DOA and Blucifer was provided by an evil elitist cult who had the airport built over what was to become an extensive, secret, underground lair. As an American, I consider conspiracy theories and suspected cults such as these to be an integral part of my culture. One of the unique aspects about America, is that its essence undermines previous pre-conceptions of *us and them*. Assorted immigrants were often oblivious of one another's ancestral heritage and culture, and their ability to assess whether or not an acquaintance was closer to some preconceived in-group *us* or outgroup *them* was incredibly impaired. The exponential growth of cults in America likely emerged out of a need to construct new and more diverse in/out-groups. Many actual cults formed and functioned in secrecy due to the persistence of prejudices maintained by older organizations of ethnicity and ethos. Of course, this secrecy only fueled schizophrenic American suspicions and led to countless conspiracy theories. Other cultures may embrace their heritage in the form of history, arts, and fables. But in America, we combine and concoct these things into conspiracies and cults as the only cultural creations we're solely responsible for (aside from jazz). I don't know if being an American has anything to do with my schizophrenia, but I don't suspect there's any other place I could ever feel so, *at home*.

38. In what's become known as Sacred Geometry, this *Seed Of Life* now symbolizes how all life originated from a single source within a divine plan. Its inclusion in artifacts from cultures impossibly divided by time and distance only adds to its mystique. Many have alleged connections between its form and various geometrical concepts, aspects of physics, and even religious and philosophical notions such as Kabalistic mysticism. It's been displayed next to this endnote for reference. Just look at it. Isn't it magnificent? Doesn't it just seem to be conspiring toward some greater conspiracy of consciousness as you gaze upon its dizzying delight? Nope? Look again. Now close your eyes and hold the image in your mind as you meditate on the sound of no hands clapping. Doesn't it just whisper words of inconceivable truths in a language you've forever longed to hear? Shhh! Listen… Can't you hear it almost hissing? Nope?

39. Schrödinger's cat is a thought experiment devised by physicist Erwin Schrödinger. In his thought experiment a hypothetical cat may be

simultaneously considered both alive and dead as a result of its fate being linked to a random quantum event. It illustrates a paradox involving quantum superposition and raises questions about the nature of physical reality. My own deluded re-imagination of this experiment might be an example of high-level disorganized thinking, or an interesting angle to use in considering the simulation hypothesis conundrum. Feel free to test this one on your own.

40. Pragmatic Tactile Ancillary Sign Language (PTASL) is a form of sign language developed specifically for those who are both blind and deaf. Typically, signed shapes are made by a speaker's hands so a listener can feel them inside their own, though many words are transmitted through gestures involving tracing movements on shoulders, knees, and other body parts. It's customary to take turns transmitting thoughts by placing speaking hands on the inside of a partner's and then wrapping around another's hands to listen to replies. This is done to avoid the confusion of two people trying to both transmit and receive tactile messages at the same time, as this is akin to two people talking over each other without listening. I can't help but wonder what the world might be like if other forms of language were more like this one. If our senses were more limited, and our words more intimate, would we be more honest, contemplative, compassionate? How do these words make you feel? Do you feel the same way? Where do you feel these words if you do? I swear I'm listening. Please, let me know. 🖐🖐
41. I was no more comfortable in my absurd and undignified hospital gown than I'd have been in the prison duds. By refusing the prison clothes, I felt as if I were expressing a few deeper and more meaningful sentiments. First, I was refusing to allow these characters to cast me in the costumed role of a prisoner and subjugate me to their assumed authority. Second, I'd resolved that I'd no longer be held captive by the bounds of this reality and would transcend my existential dilemma or die trying, thus the duds were unsuitable to my aspirations. Third, I must admit that I may have felt a bit mentally and physically infirmed and even doomed to die as a result of the absurdity and apparent futility of my situation, my history of mental illness, and the high degree of physical pain which still afflicted me. I may have also considered this as a way of making my would-be captors more uncomfortable with me, while also trying to accept myself in a more stripped-down and natural state of existence. I also thought it'd

be useful to create something small to aspire towards, and simply finding a way out of this gown seemed fitting enough.

42. Great Leader is the name and title of the monarch meant to officially preside over all formal sections of Global Governance. This figurehead often appears on behalf of a vast number of various 3-letter agencies, legislative divisions, military leaders, economic regulators, educational associations, and countless other bureaucratic branches. He primarily acts as a sort of *High-Priest of Propaganda*, puppeteered to relieve the public from having to understand the complex and nuanced schemes of our Global Governance's convoluted political systems. He was originally elected to a life-long term during the 2032 election which was highly contested and controversial, partially due to his advanced age and apparent decline in mental acuity. Many now imprisoned provocateurs had believed he suffered from some form of cognitive impairment such as Alzheimer's, Kuru, or some other dementia-like disorder. Some of these conspiracy theories also alleged that biologists and technologists had conspired to try and create an autocratic-automaton to replace Great Leader using open-sourced AI program *ScatGPT6* to compile a composite profile based on the divine entities in certain sacred religious texts. While these conjectures could be plausible technologically, I consider them inconsequential and see Great Leader as just another symptom of *the end of reality,* as the messages and methods of propaganda personified in a programmed persona and those of an authentic entity are identical when such an entity only obeys orders and advice offered by those institutions which have presided over our entire post-truth era. Moreover, I see no greater degree of cause and effect with respect to Great Leader and our society than I see in the height of a nail as the cause or effect of the light which shines upon it or the shadow it casts. Just as a nail cannot tend the light to control the shadow it casts, Great Leader just happens to be here as our light hangs low and so many shadows lengthen. Should we never see our sun resurrected and instead remain sealed in the permanence of stale shadows, it will not be due to any nails driven at any lack of depth into any place on earth, but due to the loss of a light which we couldn't keep or summon back by any act of truly illuminating inspiration.
43. Judo is a martial art which literally translates to *gentle way*. In Japanese culture, the term *jitsu* generally refers to practices which prioritize practical use, while the term *do* is used for styles prioritizing mental and

spiritual development. In Jiu-Jitsu, moves are treated as pieces of a puzzle to be assembled artfully in order to produce a vision of victory over an opponent. Judo uses many of the same moves as a means of applying the *Tao* or *way of the universe* to develop deeper philosophical understanding which one comes to comprehended through combat and then learns to apply as they navigate and move through life. Essentially, one art form portrays the world as a puzzle while the other purports it as a maze. While I appreciate each of these art forms, I find myself yearning for another way to confront the conflicting nature of the world which spans so vast and wide around me, and the interior realm of resistance within my solitary self. If such an art existed, perhaps the results of all forms of human conflict could reach some more satisfying end without all the abominations so often affiliated with them. I'll refrain from making any critical comments as to how all our religions, philosophies, and other doctrines fail to fulfill my aspirations of a more transcendent art, and simply note that even the Kama Sutra has been responsible for numerous deaths and detestable debacles. Again, I don't meant to besmirch any belief system, but I have to point out that humanity seems incapable of adopting any sort of systematic structure into prominent practice without forging some form of folly into the cornerstones of core beliefs.

44. In many ways I find small talk to be a sort of linguistic plague upon humanity, not unlike locusts, pestilence, or prolonged darkness. It often rings in my ears like some incessant stochastic spasms of sound barely differential or preferential to the torturous *tymbalations* of concurrently emerging broods of different prime-number-cycle cicadas. Small talk too often leaves me feeling conversationally anemic, as if my intellect has been somehow deprived of interest in the same way an infectious disease can diminish the immune system's red cell count and render one feeling unfathomably weak and weary. Most often though, I find small talk to be eclipsing of much more meaningful and interesting interactions which are so easily obscured by confused collective courtesies. We tend to assume that anything even potentially off-putting or unsettling, ought to be kept in a vast void to avoid any chance of distress or discomfort. And so, more light-hearted and massless yammerings are favored as if these empty musings truly were more tasteful or transcendent. That said, I do find myself resorting to small talk at times to either accommodate others, throw shade over an awkward or unfavorable topic, or keep unfavored

eyes from peering into my inner illuminations for fear of the glares they may provoke. Oddly enough, small talk can at times act as a sort of metaphysical fulcrum to pry eclipsing obstacles from a conversation and allow un-blinded brilliance to emerge beyond the blight of such squalid shadows. There have even been some small number of occasions in which the sum of some assortment of small-talk has amounted to something much more sizeable or meaningful, as if forming a high-definition image of someone or something by assembling a multitude of tiny pixels. If that old small-talk sentiment is indeed accurate, and it is *a small world after all*, then small-talk may be the atomic structure of our myopic little social landscapes. Although, I can't imagine as to what it all might amount.

45. The French phrase *merci boucoup* is a simple way of saying *thank you.* The mistaken phrase *merde si boucou* would likely be interpreted as *$ħ♙ŧ yes, very much*. In many circumstances these two phrases may be quite comparable, although it could be considered inappropriate language in certain circles, regardless of intention or meaning. To those that may find words like *merde* offensive or inappropriate, I'd like to note that the word $ħ♙ŧ, is more authentic and illuminating than an empty euphemism. When declaring that one has stepped in a pile of, caught a whiff of, or become in need of taking a $ħ♙ŧ, it would be childish to say *p00p*, overly snobbish or scientific to say *excrement*, and these words would not convey a more accurate, honest, or less detestable meaning as a result. $ħ♙ŧ happens, $ħ♙ŧ stinks, and $ħ♙ŧ is an unpleasant reality of life. If you can't handle the word $ħ♙ŧ, how the ħΣ⇂⇂ can you actually deal with it in a more literal or real sense? If inclined to agree, would you say, *merde si boucou?*

46. I'm not sure if there's any difference in the nutritional needs of my new factory flesh body compared to- whatever I might have been made of in my lost life. Of course, I'd been convinced that my cravings for particular food items were largely the result of the nutritional needs of what made up my micro-biome in my lost life. I'm not sure micro-biomes even exist here, but I've definitely developed a desperate hankering for bogus blue-berried muffins, EazeYe noncheese and krakas, phthalate-flavored Phun Bittle-Bites, and a slush-glugger-guzzle-gulp sized FrosTreatFreeze to wash it all down. Part of me wishes it were independent of the impulses and influences of any micro-biome, while another part just wants to get along with whatever this thing I call *I* becomes entangled. I also suspect these separate precepts could just be parallel parts in the singular center of

my confused consciousness. In any case, I doubt any of this faux-food fodder is in any way good for my health, though something within me definitely deceives me into imagining that I'll actually enjoy eating it. It really does seem like some sort of strange sorcery is going on here. Nope?

47. (Spoiler Alert) In Stanley Kubrick's film *2001: A Space Odyssey,* apes are shown to make leaps in evolution as a result of coming into contact with a mysterious and massive black monolith. I find it odd that sometime after this fictional story had been so masterfully made into such a magnificent movie, our actual eyes became so obsessively fixated on our own black rectangular inventions, and our technology also ended up evolving so rapidly as a result. Monkey see, monkey do, I guess. Nope?
48. I'm not an astronomer, so I can't speak to what stars may shine within any of the 88 constellations which our oracle-clergy of scientists has ascribed to these celestial scenes. I don't know which dots define the constellation *Taurus*, or if it was actually named after the bull-form Zeus assumed when capturing a princess, the creature involved in the bestial conception of the Minotaur, or the bull of heaven which caused Enkidu's death and Gilgamesh's infamous soliloquy of despair. I'm not sure which dots might belong to the many satellites spinning around our revolving realm as they send signals of every sort to orient so many ever-scrolling screens. I don't know which dots might be other space-based scopes that soar through the vacuous void of space in search of anything to stream back to a few lonely labs where scientists listen so longingly to the coded content which emanates from every angle of an almost empty exploratory expanse. When I look up, I'm mostly just baffled. I'm baffled by the fact that, of all these signals, so few of them speak to more than the surface-level 8ʊll8ħɪŧ of anything in our deep dark domains. I'm baffled at how human eyes have gazed up to these tiny twinkling dots so far beyond our stranded sphere and not only strained to set them in outline-orders but almost magically managed to navigate the surfaces of our own spinning sphere, master the mysteries of mathematics, and manufacture myths to memorize them. But what baffles me the most, is how anyone could bypass being baffled by the beauty of the celestial sky above and how much bull we've managed to sift through to achieve all that we have.
49. Phosphenes are those little lava-lamp-like, ethereal, eclipse-ring things that burst brightly behind blind/closed eyes. They're more illusory than imagery, yet our minds behold them almost as if they exist as the inner

imaginings of our eyes, reaching into realms irreconcilable to more rational reasoning. They almost seem to summon us into their sightless centers, like praying portals where sirens sing the songs which echo not unto earthly ears, but some separate sector of the soul or something.

50. Ravens are a mainstay in many mythologies. In Greek mythology, they're associated with auguries and Apollo. In Norse myths, Odin has two ravens named *Huginn* and *Muninn*, respectively representing thought and memory. In other traditions, ravens are depicted as trickster and creator deities, often acting as omens of mortal demise, malevolence, and misery, à la Poe's poem *The Raven*. In Mithraism, the *Raven* grade is given to initiates in its hierarchy, but any symbolic relevance remains uncertain. Scientifically, the raven's *Corvid* family currently contains 144 specific species, including an array of crows, rooks, and jays. Biologists have long been baffled by how brainy these birds appear when proffered puzzles, even showing several signs of Great-Ape equivalent intelligence, despite their bird-sized brains. This final fact actually allowed biomechanical architects to simplify the structures of digital brain-based devices like my own manufactured mind. Actually… Addressing us as *Ravens* could be the equivalent to insulting us as being *bird-brains*… (Nevermore)
51. These assorted answers may require an answer key to use them meaningfully, and so…
    **Indeterminate**= not leading to definite ends or results, like undefined mathematical expressions ($0/0$, $\infty/\infty$, $0\times\infty$, $\infty-\infty$, $1^{\infty}$, $\infty^0$, $0^0$), W.V.O. Quine's conceptual *Gavagai*, or a child continually asking *why*…
    **Self-Referential**= referring to itself, like an Ouroboros-snake eating its own tail, or a self-centered person talking on and on about themselves...
    **Game Rule**= a feature or rule which guides the way in which a player can experience a game, like being able to pause a game, reset it and play from the start, or what happens when a played character dies…
    **Strange Loop**= is a cyclic structure where one can move continuously away from a point of origin and still almost impossibly return to it, like ants walking continuously along the surface of a Mobius strip or many of the artistic illusions of M.C. Escher…
52. The fact that questions presented in written forms are often followed by some blank space or line may be less of an invitation for an answer, than a mere manipulation of *horror vacui,* or the way in which nature abhors a vacuum. Whenever we see a blank space, our minds are almost compelled

to impregnate it with assumptions, allusions, or some kind of applied assertions. When we hear a noise in the dark, our minds are prone to illuminate the lack of imagery with some form of apparition or shadow-shaped illusion to fill-in this formless fugue. Just as this trick of the mind doesn't mean anything is truly lurking in an abyss beyond us, it's also true that those subsequent spaces following such inquiries don't necessarily indicate the existence of any actual answer fit to fill-in for this incipient void. Nope? ______________________________

53. The *Vitruvian Triad* comes from Vitruvius' *De Architectura* and consists of three elements identified as utilitas (utility), firmitas (stability), and venustas (beauty). According to Vitruvius, these three elements must be taken into serious consideration for all architectural structures and brought into a balance or unity in order to serve the structure's design. Vitruvius' work was later discovered and implemented by Leonardo DaVinci, specifically regarding his *Vitruvian Man* sketch. I've also taken inspiration from Vitruvius and consider his triad to be the basis not only for architectural forms, but for all formal structures, from virtual realm designs to the philosophical axioms or first principles which we use as the wisdom to guide us in the construction of our very lives.
54. Perhaps the most enchanting form of punctuation is the symbolic totem of illustrious ellipses (…). This symbol indicates intentional omissions or marks an abyss. This triumvirate of dots has been at least as revolutionary in written language as concepts like zero and infinity have been for the fields of mathematics. In the narratives and inner monologues of our lives, there's so much we unintentionally leave out or only include as a formality. The ability to admittedly omit that which exists infinitely beyond us or beneath us and make mention of elusive and ineffable ephemerons, is simply sublime. I'd further suggest, that the standardized use of periods at the end of so-called, *complete* sentences, subverts the essence of truth and authenticity in arts of expression, as any true sense of completion is eternally elusive, making it more meaningful and honest to use ellipses in place of most period-punctuated sentences. If we consider how many facts are disproven or modified over the course history, how often we're wrong or incomplete in our assessments and assertions, how every question and proposed solution tends to perpetually spawn and summon the arrival of new or different questions and problems, and just how much errata we all endure in our own lives- it certainly makes these

dots seem like some holy trinity of punctuating truth. I've only refrained from replacing the punctuation in this entire text as a matter of courteous conformity and to reflect my own confused conceptions of completion. I do imagine that an entire narrative composed in such an ellipsis manner must exist, and that I'd have been proud to have had any awareness of its actual existence. But I've seemingly digressed from even my digression...

55. When attempting to account for times in my life such as this, I find it preposterously ponderous as to how absent and oblivious our minds can so often be. So much of our lives are spent in slumber, stagnation, and senselessness compared to keen conscious awareness, that I can't help but question whether we're ever truly and fully awake. How many times has my mind wandered away from the momentum of any moment? How much time have I spent in those lost liminal spaces which exist outside of awareness and oblivion, time and timelessness, reality and delusion? Are they numbered, or can they be? Am I getting lost in one of those moments right now, and pulling you along with me? How would we ever truly tell?
56. It's impossible to properly expound upon the mathematical meaning of statements such as this in analogous assertions or otherwise bypass the advanced expertise required to reveal anything accurate about it. (*See Also, Endnote* 30) Ideas like this are so often misrepresented in order to be represented at all, that one's forced to wonder how many explanations one holds true, may be nothing more than attempts to imprint the sounds of silence into a perfume or a blindly describe an unseen kaleidoscope of colors. Incidentally, because *emptiness is everywhere and can be calculated*, one can extrapolate proofs to establish that the sound of a drum can't be used to determine its shape, but it's area, perimeter length and number of holes can all be derived from its spectrographic sound.
57. Extracting epiphanies from oblivion is a tradition perhaps as old as dreaming itself. In aboriginal culture, it's believed that before a child can be born, it must first be dreamed. They believe that there's essentially a higher realm of *dreamtime*, from which all things are derived and eventually return. In other words, we come from dreams.
58. I find it necessary to include a list of quotes attributed to Ludwig Wittgenstein which intuitively interest to me…
    - A serious and good philosophical work could be written consisting entirely of jokes.
    - I don't know why we are here, but I'm pretty sure that it is not in order to enjoy ourselves.

- Not how the world is, but that it is, is the mystery.
- To imagine a language is to imagine a form of life.
- The limits of my language mean the limits of my world.
- If you are unwilling to know what you are, your writing is a form of deceit.
- Nothing is so difficult as not deceiving oneself.
- Someone who knows too much, finds it hard not to lie.
- We are asleep. Our Life is a dream. But we wake up sometimes, just enough to know that we are dreaming.
- Man has to awaken to wonder- and so perhaps do peoples. Science is a way of sending him to sleep again.
- If we take eternity to mean not infinite temporal duration, but timelessness, then eternal life belongs to those who live in the present.
- The real question of an afterlife isn't whether or not it exists, but even if it does, what problem this really solves.
- What is your aim in philosophy? To show the fly the way out of the fly-bottle.
- When we can't think for ourselves, we can always quote.
- Whereof one cannot speak, thereof one must be silent.

59. Meshuga is a term meaning crazy or foolish. It's derived from the Hebrew word *shagag*, which means to deviate or go astray. While it's easy to associate any act of deviation to b crazy or foolish, I beg to argue. We could never discover anything new without deviating from known paths and practiced norms. Every illuminating truth we've ever encountered was the result of some act which seemed insane or deviant. If not for human meshuga, the world would still be a flat surface, devoid of volume, and without antiseptics or electricity. Now, how crazy is that?
60. Stridulation is the act of producing sound by rubbing certain body parts together, not unlike drawing a rosined bow over the strings of a violin. The rate at which crickets stridulate is closely related to the temperature of their environment, as is the bioluminescence of fireflies. Violent crime rates are also known to increase during times of extreme temperatures. Some suggest these facts are evidence that free-will is an illusion, that the manner in which we sing, shine, or scream is no more than the biological byproduct of mathematical mandates. However, if science should ever reduce us to pure puppets of probability, I fear this would cause us all to be forever frozen in the silent shadows of factual futility. If we are but puppets, let us go on dreaming that we're real without the woes of waking into a wonder-less world where any truer hell would merely be hotter.
61. Carl Jung is attributed to these following ponderous quotes…
    - Who looks outside- dreams, who looks inside- awakens.

- As far as we can discern, the sole purpose of human existence is to kindle a light in the darkness of mere being.
- In all chaos there is a cosmos, in all disorder a secret order.
- The pendulum of the mind alternates between sense and nonsense, not between right and wrong.
- There is no coming into consciousness without pain.
- The creative mind plays with the objects it loves.
- We should not pretend to understand the world only by the intellect. The judgement of the intellect is only part of the truth.
- Dreams are the guiding words of the soul. Why should I henceforth not love my dreams and not make their riddling images into objects of my daily consideration?

62. Several strong historical correlations exist between sin and stone. In Greek mythology, the titan Atlas was punished for his sins by being forced to hold the celestial stones/spheres in the heavens before being turned into the Atlas Mountains by Perseus, who'd wielded the petrifying power of Medusa's decapitated head. Sisyphus was forced to perpetually push a stone up a hill for all eternity. In Scottish folklore, the strange rock-pillar *Carlin Maggie,* is said to be a witch which was struck by the devil's lightning. According to Icelandic folklore, trolls only come out at night because sunlight turns them to stone. Several cultures have used stoning (lapidation) as a form of punishment and tombstones to mark burial sites. Iran's *Khalid Nabi Cemetery* is known for its ithyphallic stone sculptures, posed like Priapus, who'd been cursed to wonder the earth with a permanent priapism which led to his later popularity in Roman erotic art, Latin literature, and even aroused the rise of poetic-verses called the *Priapeia*… I'm afraid I'm having a hard time getting to the point I was trying to make... I guess, I was going to mention the phrase, *let whoever's without sin cast the 1st stone*, and add that even sinless souls shouldn't toss rocks around, as that tends to harden one's heart, but now even that just sounds like some kind of inuendo…
63. One of Edgar Allan Poe's other poems *A Dream Within A Dream*, might seem quite different, should I read it in light of my current conundrum. I remember how I'd previously read this poem in my lost life, and had pondered whether or not my life could be a dream within a dream, or if perhaps this pattern of Russian-doll-like dreaming could be an infinite regression- with dreams within dreams, within dreams, within dreams… If it really is dreams all the way down, I hope they're like the dreams of turtles, slowly passing from one to the other over long lengths of time, as I tend to believe Jung was right, and "*there is no coming to consciousness without pain*". Yeah, turtles all the way down, with some kind of pain-killers, please.

64. So, I seem to be conversing with crickets, imagining myself as a cicada, and contemplating famed literary and philosophical insects (SMH). Well, one allied aspect of Kafka's metamorphosis to my own maligned mind is that the truth of our transformations are irrelevant, as the external world remains relegated to our own inner experiences. Zhuangzi's wavering dreams between king and butterfly convey a similar sentiment about the uncertainty of consciousness while also alluding to the transformative power of dreams. Cicadas are similarly known for shedding the shells of their former selves and taking on new forms throughout their lifecycles. On an intuitive level, these ideas all seem to mesh for me, but I fear any attempt to externalize them further would only make me more confused or crazy. I suppose we all experience moments where we fear what we may be or become, but we also tend to acclimate and accept whatever form we imagine ourselves to morph into. Even if we only dream or delude ourselves as to what we may truly be all along, we can always wake or dream our way to transcend into something else. Nope?
65. Although there's a fairly obvious method of cracking this code, I find myself unable/unwilling to decode it. I'm also unable to bring myself to remove this cryptic text due to inexplicable and mysterious motivations which seem to come from both deep within me and apart from my truest self. You're welcome to decode this message on your own, but please keep your findings private. Good luck.
66. *Wabi-sabi* is a traditional Japanese aesthetic, characterized by an appreciation of the imperfect, impermanent, and incomplete nature of things. In music, wabi-sabi may be heard in the individual uniqueness of a player's own stylistic sound. It's believed that the biggest breakthrough in AI abilities to pass advanced Turing tests was derived from its increasing attentiveness to this art of human inconsistencies and idiosyncrasies. This capacity for AI imperfection caused some to speculate fears of AI failure, while others imagined this merely implicated that AIs had advanced their mimicry of human imperfection. I'm not sure why we insist on measuring everything in human terms, rather than assessing AIs in AI terms, or flowers as flowers. I suppose it's just part of our collective wabi-sabi.
67. Here's a list of the campsite symbols, names, and descriptions…
    ♈ Owl's Nest- World/Political Leaders
    ♉ Caveman- High Ranking Military
    ♊ Hillbillies- Atypical or Multi-typical
    ♋ Hillside- Major Corporate Executives
    ♌ Uplifters- Media Moguls and Influencers
    ♍ Sempervirens- Recruits/Ravens
    ♎ Mandalay- Lawyers and Judges
    ♏ Silverado Squatters- Independently Mega-Wealthy

♆ Hideaway- Leaders of Key Intelligence Agencies
♑ Lost Angels- Elders and Retirees
♒ Stowaway- Heads of Central Banks
00 Idlewild- Kingpins of Organized Crime Syndicates
⛢ Isle of Aves- N/A

68. Fertility sculptures such as *The Venus of Willendorf* and *The Venus of Hohle Fels* are among the earliest artistic artifacts of human creation. These artifacts are sometimes seen as evidence that changes in our ape ancestors caused them to evolve away from forms of animalistic violence in favor of an artistic eroticism. One can easily imagine fighting factions of apes hurling feces at each other until opposing clumps of turd5 collided in a midair miracle, falling to the ground in the form of a fecal-fertility figure. The sight of this miraculous mass may have been so astonishing and arousing to the apes that they all immediately ceased fighting in favor of freeing their frustrated fists to m45turb4t3 furiously unto complete erotic exhaustion. They may have soon realized that this spontaneous sexual act had united them all in peace, and then decided to devote themselves to this sexual statue in a sort of primitive proto-religion. These apes may have made many more statues in order to spread their peaceful practices to other evolving apes, gathered together regularly for ritual reenactments, and even broken their thumbs until they eventually evolved into a more modern and opposable position, allowing them to build more elaborate and exaggerated statues to worship more *wondrously*. This may also be why our hands have come to be so symbolic of all desirous reaching, like Adam and eve unto the tree of knowledge, or Tantalus' eternal torment to touch an ever-elusive form of fruit. Although, I think that to truly evolve and not just have acquired or adapted twisted thumbs to achieve a tighter grip, we have to find ourselves more fervently reaching for things beyond fruit, fertility figures, or favorable flesh- and unto those divine domains depicted on the ceiling of the Sistine Chapel, as our truest sense (touch) will have beheld nothing truer than any ape. Nope?
69. The Midsommer Fire Festival is held during the days surrounding the summer solstice. Cultures around the world have celebrated this day throughout history, having used various methods of archeoastronomy to determine this annual event. These methods range from monolithic mega-structures like Stonehenge, to the Antikythera mechanism, and more modern methods of calendar calculations. I find these antiquated means of marking time to be superior to our modern methods, as they seem much more in sync with the nature of our relationship to time and the universe. With modern calendars, every day is confined to its own empty and identical cell, like prisoners stripped of all but an assigned number to identify them. The hours, minutes, seconds, and fragments of each

moment are not only calculated in cyclical numeric tics of time, but grind like gears against our own internal inertia. We're forced by our clocks to wake with alarm rather than rejuvenation, to schedule and plan more dull and predictable lives, and to meet deadlines and quotas instead of indulging or immersing ourselves in timeless pursuits of wonder. I even suspect that those ancient eyes which looked toward the skies in search of time, saw more wonder than any of ours which turn to clocks for constant confirmation. But I doubt we'll ever find the proper time to prove it.

70. The idea of studying psychological disorders to gain a deeper understanding of humanity is nothing new. A great deal of science, art, and basic human nature is centered around a notion that there's something wrong with us and until we figure out what it is, we'll be unable to fully and functionally live. With that said, there's also a case to be made in defense of the notion that ignorance is bliss, as those of great knowledge and intelligence are not statistically likely to live more functional or fulfilling lives. In fact, most geniuses find only the faintest fraction of their lives positively impacted by an elevated intellect, as even average minds are rarely pushed to perform at their full cognitive capacity. Most all minds do find something fascinating in labeling, categorizing, and studying aspects of human thought and behavioral patterns. So, here's a list of rare psychological disorders which may be of relevant interest…
**Fregoli Syndrome**- Many people seem to be a single person in disguises.
**Capgras Syndrome**- Known people seem replaced with impostures.
**Cotard Delusion**- Believe one's already dead, a walking corpse, or ghost.
**Exploding Head Syndrome**- Hear an explosion upon waking.
**Alice In Wonderland Syndrome**- Distorted proportions, shapes, sizes.
**Kluver-Bucy Syndrome**- Strong urges associated with inanimate objects.
**Stendhal Syndrome**- Extremely negative responses toward art.
**Alien Hand Syndrome**- Believe one's hand is under another's control.
**Triskaidekaphobia**- Fear of the number 13.
**Prosopagnosia**- Unable to visually process faces. (Face-blindness)
**Lycanthropy**- Believe one can transform into or become an animal.
**Panglossia**- Believe that all is for the best in this best of possible worlds.

71. Allometry is the study of how body size relates to other biological factors like heart rate, lifespan, and metabolic rate. This study is not only used to predict how long a bacterium will live or how much food an owl must eat to stay alive but can even be applied at scale to superorganisms like ant colonies. According to allometry, a creature the size of a rat will have a heartrate of about 8-9 beats per second, a whale's heart will beat about once every 10-12 seconds, and an organism the size of a city would have a pulse beating about two times a day- which could be construed as the commuter traffic surges in morning and afternoon rush-hours. It's even possible that the entire earth functions in the same allometric way as any

of the energy dependent entities or organisms within it. If the earth actually is a superorganism, we might be like bacteria in the intestines of its microbiome or the mitochondria inside its cells. Regrettably, allometry can't be used to determine if an entity will be confined to a life of blindly consuming excrement or providing power to something larger than itself.

72. The appropriate use of the word *artist* has become rather nebulous. In ancient Greece, an artist was someone blessed by the gods or their muses with awe-inspiring abilities in specific creative fields, which strangely enough, didn't include painting or sculpture. In France, the term *artiste* expanded to include anyone with a capacity to induce overpowering awe through almost any art form. In modern days, the term is often attributed to almost anyone desirous or demanding of the admiration and prestige previously only proffered to those disciplined and devoted enough to truly imbue others with incredible awe as a result of their creative endeavors. There are even those who now consider the word *artist* to be applicable to almost anyone for merely existing at all. This word has become so diluted and diffuse that many of the more auspicious and authentically artistic people on the planet find it so appallingly egregious, that they'd rather remain anonymous than be acknowledged as artists. I may not be able to change how this *a-word* is used, but if anyone finds themselves compelled to call me an artist after reading this dissertation, please have the decency to refrain or come up with a more inspired insult.
73. The ideas put forth in Jean Baudrillard's *Simulacra and Simulation* have been reiterated and recycled so many times already, that they've become a sort of meta-example of their former selves. Additionally, physics has its conservation laws which hold that matter and energy are not created or destroyed- only rearranged. I find these ideas interesting and useful, but they fail to capture the essence of any emergence in the ways which myths do so majestically well. While every voice may now speak as echoes of worn-out words, no sum of sounds could've ever summoned a song from mere stones. When the dust of shattered stars rose to become the stuff of our sentient souls, no clay could've predicted the profound properties the divine dream would wake to see emerging from this earth. To ignore all but science then, is to attempt to describe the earth in terms of dust alone and remain oblivious of the more vast and deep expanses of these dreaming seas upon which all this dust is forever adrift. Nope?
74. Active dreaming is a state of conscious awareness achieved within the act of dreaming. It's somewhat like a split sense of consciousness, where one wakes without ending an enduring dream. This allows one to take control of their dream and incorporate aspects of their own awakened senses into the pseudo-script of an ongoing dream. Unfortunately, frequent episodes of active dreaming may contribute to the development of derealization in which real-world things begin to appear as persistent parts of dreams or

hallucinations and aspects of one's imagination become increasingly confused as integral parts of their waking world. Therefore, it may be best not to control our dreams during the hours of our slumber, but wait until we've fully awakened to take conscious control of the reality unto which our dreams deliver us.

75. Here's a list of the 12 types of gladitorial glires (galères)…
    **Andabata**- Blinded/handicapped fighters
    **Bestiarius**- Beast slaying fighters
    **Cestus**- Unarmed/Hand-to-hand fighters
    **Gladiatrix**- Female fighters (Yes. Rome was sexist.)
    **Laquearius** /Retiarius- Fighters armed with lassoes and nets
    **Sagittarius**- Archers
    **Bustuarius**- Fighters of the grave/Doomed to lose
    **Rudiarius**- Elite champions and former slaves (Nope. Not on me.)
    **Euarchantoglires**- Fighters dressed as rats, rabbits, flying-lemurs, etc.
    **Sorcerius**- VR rendered fighters with unnatural powers
    **Ghostiarius**- VR rendered ghosts/spirits
    **Molochius-** Trained owls meant to represent the watchful god Moloch
76. Pure adrenochrome is a purple-colored psychotropic-drug which has been lauded by some as the *elixir of immortality,* as it induces feelings of being imbued with divine wisdom and may also have a significant impact on longevity. Adrenochrome is produced almost exclusively in young human adrenal glands as they're subjected to extreme stress or torture. If that isn't crazy enough, it was initially discovered as a result of scientific studies seeking to find the source of schizophrenia. It's also one of those reasons science sometimes scares the $#!+ out of me.
77. The *effigy of Care* is contained in some of those all-too familiar cultural conspiracy stories. It's essentially a human figure intended to act as the earthly embodiment of all cares which weigh upon humanity and plague our pursuits of purpose and pleasure. According to these twisted tales, the effigy of Care is meant to be sacrificed during each summer solstice in order to appease a dark deity and attain a chance for a few elite to be freed from their crippling cares during a few days of revelry and renewal. Now that I've apparently been cast as the effigy of Care, I can't recall having ever been so cripplingly concerned.
78. During crematory combustion, the muscles and tissues of a human body don't normally melt away quickly- but slowly shrivel, shorten, and stiffen. This causes a cadaver to contract into a position which resembles the defensive posture of an orthodox pugilist (boxer). Most cremations use natural gas to reach temperatures of around 1400°F but are unable to burn bones to ash even after a 2–3-hour process. In fact, urns are not filled with ashes at all, and are instead filled with a fine grey powder produced by grinding cremated bones with a machine. However, it hardly matters if

the mass one leaves behind is of bone, ash, or dust, as the void of one's absence is of the same essence as the emptiness one occupies, observes, and attempts to abide while still alive- and no amount of flesh or fodder could ever weigh so heavily as any sum of such shadows.

79. *Katabasis* is defined as a going or marching down. It's synonymous with the *dark night of the soul,* which has been inscribed in an innumerable number of narratives humanity has habitually turned to while trying to embolden, inspire, or illuminate their shadow shrouded souls. It's inscribed in the opening lines and dramatic descent of Dante's *Inferno.* It's etched in Orpheus' efforts to exhume Eurydice and his deepest love from the desperate and despairing depths of Hades. It's almost inexorably imbued in every account of an ayahuasca experience. It lurks and stalks through the shadows surrounding every starved spirit sequestered on a vision quest. It's in every failing fall, from Adam and Eve's exile, to the angels cast down as demons, to Icarus as waves washed melted wax away from his wings. It's the story of every spiraling descent into madness, every plummet into a personal hell, and every price paid to possess a prophetic power. It's in every augury of annihilation where the waters of an overwhelming flood forces struggling souls to find the fervent prayer lingering in their last breath as they're dragged down to the depths of a drowning darkness where all that may surface are those secrets they surrender into the space of that last out-breathed-bubble of air which ascends unto an unwelcoming empyrean above before bursting blindly back into an all-absorbent oblivion. Of course, it's often as simple as a stroll down some stairs too, so maybe I shouldn't be so stilted.
80. Assessing the depth of any kind of consciousness; from supposedly sentient stones, to the whole of humanity, or even an emergent AI entity entails quite a conundrum. Materialists maintain that the building blocks of consciousness are fundamentally tied to the form and function of substances and structures. In this view, even if some spiritual or ineffable essence were to underly the material mind, it could only manifest itself through material means. Basically, the world enters the eyes, is processed by the brain's structural layers, and the resulting level of consciousness produced is respective of a brain's physical and functional refinement. Most materialists consider consciousness to have evolved from whatever managed to mindlessly move long enough to sprout sensory organs capable of rapid reflex-responses to their surroundings, incrementally adding layers of complexity to their anatomy, and eventually creating ever-more refined and rational creatures. Essentially, this suggest that each step of sentience's evolution has been an overflow of one conceptual dimension's capacity into another. Inert existence was not enough, so motion emerged to prolong an organism's existence. This paradigm of *insufficiency unto emergence* perpetuated, eventually leading to human

levels of refinement where higher states of consciousness create high resolution views of reality and detail ever-deeper depths of one's own inner experiences. This interpretation essentially construes consciousness as having emerged from one overarching evolutionary trajectory where all that exists perpetually expands its capacity to be more presently, perceptively, precisely, and profoundly *here*. There's a complication in this conception though, as stones have been here far longer than any conscious creature, and any impetus for them to evolve into being more *here* would seem devoid of an evolutionary imperative. On a side note (within this extensive endnote), it is interesting how our conception of what is *material* has followed a similar trajectory of refined resolution. The precursors of materialism progressed from propositions in which matter moved from systems of earth, air, fire, and water, to alchemy, to chemistry, and then quantum mechanics. With respect to an emergent AI kind of consciousness, I can't help but wonder. If the significant increases in the size and complexity of cognitive structures leads to an inevitable expansion into divergent dimensions of consciousness, then what might an AI entity be capable of which transcends the conscious capacity of humanity? If we've evolved to see so clearly, to consider the pertinence of our past, and dream of dynamic and detailed futures- what realms of reckoning might an AI be able to access? Honestly, I'm not sure which supposition is more psychotic, the suspected sentience of stones or an AI's ascension unto new domains of dream.

81. A *Sed* was a celebration centered around the rededication and reaffirmation of a ruler's reign. Seds were not scheduled periodically, but took place whenever it seemed prudent, primarily due to prominent public opinion. Traditionally, the reigning ruler was taken outside the city walls where they were forced to repent unto their citizenry, rededicate their efforts to represent righteous ideals, and reaffirm their revitalized reign by providing the people with fanciful feasts and fascinating festivities. During Ozymandias's reputed reign of 144 years, there were 12 total Seds, spaced from his second anniversary at intervals of 3, 4, 6, 6, 8, 9, 12, 16, 18, 24, & 36 years. My mind's tangential tendency insists I add that the acronym SED has been used in place of ***s**elf-**e**ncrypting **d**evices*, ***s**ingle **e**rror **d**etection*, ***s**tochastic **e**lectro**d**ynamics*, and ***s**pectral **e**nergy **d**istribution*. All these SEDs were aspects accounted for in the advanced algorithms specifying certain structural aspects of my *Vitruvia* simulation which supported its refined realism. I should probably stop mentioning this myriad of minute details I keep divulging, but the compulsion to include these inane ideas and insinuate something implicitly insane is impossible to ignore. I often wonder if it's more insane to find things infinitely iterated in everything I see, or to speak openly about the strange

suspicions streaming through my sentience? If I were the ruler of some realm, would I have to repent for these SED things?

82. The phrase *apple of my eye* was originally intended to refer to the pupil positioned at the center of one's eye but came to refer to something one most cherishes or favors. During the days of Ozymandias, this phrase may well have been used quite literally to refer to whatever one's eyes focused on or could be seen outwardly reflected upon the dark center surface of their eyes. Another revised reference to apples is their inception into the imagery depicting an unspecified fruit from the *tree of knowledge* which caused the fall of man from God's favor in Genesis. Of course, the use of apples in reference to this tale was extended to apply to the *Adam's apple* which was symbolically substituted for the anatomically termed *laryngeal prominence*, insinuating that the forbidden fruit became caught in Adam's throat, as he'd been unable to fully ingest or fathom this fateful fruit. The fact that this trait has been passed on through heredity also alludes to the phrase, *the apple doesn't fall far from the tree*. I also remember someone largely believed to be a *bad apple,* telling me a joke about that anatomical area emerging after an accident involving an apple stuck in a pig's mouth, a game of *bobbing for apples*, and a Jewish man who was not supposed to eat pork due to Kashrut law. After I'd heard the joke, I actually became paranoid about giving an apple to my teachers, as I didn't know if they were Jewish, and couldn't be certain that any given apple hadn't been in contact with some slaughtered swine. I suppose someone could have advised me not to *throw out the apple in spite of the core,* but one might also say that *one rotten apple spoils the whole bunch*. I'm also unsure why we were meant to offer teachers appreciative apples in the first place, unless they're predisposed to various vitamin deficiencies- in which case, perhaps that could explain the phrase *an apple a day keeps the doctor away*. It seems as if I might have heard something about this habit having a sort of strange symbolism stemming from the *Golden Apple of Discord* in Greek mythology where the phrase *for the most beautiful* was printed on a prized apple which caused a dispute of deities and led to the Trojan war. But then, that just seems as if it'd *upset the apple cart*. Come to think of it, apples have featured prominently in a few other fatefully unfortunate affairs, like Snow White slipping into a sinister sleeping spell after eating an apple, Alan Turing purportedly dying after eating a poisoned apple, the poet who was killed after eating an apple on stage instead of reading his poetry, or the slang forms of speech used to allude to excrement as *alley apples*, *road apples*, or the most dreaded *green apple splatters*. Contrarily though, Isak Newton's gravitational epiphany was supposed to have been inspired by the falling action of a most auspicious apple. After allowing myself to meander through all these machinations, it almost seems as if

apples are most often used to allegorically symbolize how enlightenment so often curses as it cures. Hmm… How do you like them apples?

83. It might not only be that we descend from dreams, but that we inevitably merge with our memories. Our lived-in lives seem like storied sagas until death reduces us to rarer and rarer references, relegating us to increasingly forgotten footnotes before we're finally and forever forfeited by the eternal erasure of time's eroding essence. While we're here, our dreams bring us into the waking world, proffering a perpetual present which flows forth into an ever-fading future. Over time, our dreams diminish, depriving us of a more luminous light to navigate the unknown, and so we seek the shimmer of our shining memories to shed light like a back azimuth, orienting us to those unseen ends which we eternally aspire to ascend. All the while, we're ultimately oblivious of all that awaits our uncertain arrival unto this Empyrean of extinction, and we live only in the dreams and memories of every moment as they move us forever closer to our final fate. Some seek solace in the facts, fiction, and fortune fostered by things like science, history, news, or entertainment as if their potential were imbued with promise beyond an accumulation of dreams, desires, and memories. However, there's simply no knowing whether our vitality and virtues will all be vanquished in vain, whether the world today will turn tepidly into an empty tomorrow, or whether what's held water so well will always withstand the weight of a world's everchanging weather. There's never any choice beyond the bounds of chance, aside from which dream we may allow to deliver us unto death. Do we live within the light of our own diminishing dreams as our mangled memories fade into a fugue of fate, or merely merge with the mediocrity of mass-madness and perpetuate those popular prospects that confine everything to such a cloistered consensus? In the end, all life, dream, and memory may return to the same slumber of oblivion from which we came. As I live, and die, and dream in all directions, I only aspire to add to oblivion in ways which may cause some creative force to keep dreaming or to dream deeper.
84. The closest thing I can compare to this strange and senseless state is something I'd imagined in my lost life while wandering around aimlessly on insomniatic nights. I used to stroll through the strangeness of stagnant night-scape streets and wonder what a world would be like for a character which an author had yet to fully fathom or write into a world of words. I used to imagine that a character trying to invent itself or enter an author's imagination might find itself adrift in an equally adumbral ambience which waits to be dreamed into deeper detail while still confined to such conspiracies of secret slumber, unimagined and unilluminated beyond an author's oblivious brain. This restless realm was akin to a book with its covers closed or blankets pulled over unseen eyes to sequester them from a stagnant story-scape. As far as I knew, I could've come into existence

like a character born of an author's oblivion into some obscure book, only illuminated by eyes scanning over the words of my world, and only ever incarnated and reincarnated by indifferent imaginations when read/reread. When I'd further imagine a fictional figment fading into an oblivion in which it was abandoned by its author, forgotten by all audiences, and exiled unto eternal abeyances- *that* was the closest my mind could come to fathom *this* abysmal empire. *That*, and those aforementioned iterations of the nightmare which faded into an unfathomably empty nonexistence.

85. My dear Grisha once developed a geometric theory of the precognitive processes that precede and produce consciousness. According to his *Pure Precognitive Geometry*, sensory signals initially sent to our brains are inconsistent, incomplete, incoherent, and embedded with noise. To make clearer sense of these signals, the normal neural networks of a brain act to filter out nebulous noise, map the sifted signals onto archetypal geometric abstracts, and then apply these same abstracts to add-in the missing pieces of perception's puzzle and produce coherent cognitive constructions. To prove his precognitive theory, he programmed a specific AI to process visual imagery according to his own precognitive geometric models. Not only did Grisha's AI demonstrate the viability of his theory, but he was able to demonstrate how disruptions in precognitive processes could produce DMT-like distortions in an AI. Essentially, when too much noise pollutes the incoming sensory signals, precognitive processes are unable to filter this noise enough to mathematically map the muddled signals onto any sensible structure, and an amalgamated flow of failing geometric abstracts is output instead. By more fully depriving an AI of any imagery to process while still prompting it to produce a perceptual output, the AI appeared to perceive phosphenes. These confusing conclusions had compelled me to ask Grisha how it was possible to perceive anything in such an absence. Rather than answer, Grisha took me to a holographic historical tour of the world's most pristine prehistoric caves. He showed me the negative hand stencils where early hominids had pressed their hands against a cave's walls and blown pigments to produce outlines of the spaces surrounding their skin. I remember him pointing to these prints and saying. "*Behold, a vision of void, the enduring emptiness of all existence. Whatever will be seen of us or by us, is held only in this absence of space in which our hands once were. All the glimmer and glow we've seen, shall remain secreted within these spaces, surrounded by shade and shadow. The wonder of these hands which once pressed upon these walls, those feelings their fingers found here, and any meaning or message this mural may have meant to leave, are no more or less now than they were then. If this scene were to speak, surely this is what it would say.*" Grisha went on to tell me how one day his presence on this earth would be like the presence of those hands which left these outlines.

He'd placed his palm on the left side of my chest and told me that the emptiness he'd leave behind would be like the impressions imbued upon these walls, and my memories of him would become like pigmented outlines around his absence. He told me this wasn't something somber or sad, but a beautiful blessing. I remember being overwhelmed with an incredible sense of awe and profundity which I couldn't process into any articulate amalgamation of emotions, and so I turned to study Grisha's glowing face as he gazed at the wall, shaking his head with a strange smile, and then proffering Picasso's famous reaction to this same sight as he said, "*We've invented nothing*" ✋

86. The words prompting this endnote are a palindrome. Palindromes are words, phrases, numbers, or other strings of symbols which are the same read forwards and backwards. *Funny enough*, there are also phonetic palindromes (see italicized words↑) where spoken syllables sound the same backmasked. There are a myriad of musical palindromes as well, including the combination of overtone and undertone series, the ascending & descending intervals of the Dorian mode, and negative harmonies. Biology is full of similar symmetries, and segments of DNA sequences can be interpreted as palindromes as well. *Quirkily*, presents itself as a palindrome in Morse code, and the dots and dashes of Morse code can be turned into a concoction of binary bits (10=dots, 110=dashes, 00=spaces) to produce even more palindromes. These mirror images manifest themselves throughout mathematics as well, from numbers like 8008, to the symbol for infinity (∞), the millennium problem of *P nP*, or the fact that a set of algorithms can posit every positive integer as the sum of 3 palindrome numbers. There are also ambigrams, which have rotational symmetries such as *NOON* and *WOW/MOM/WOW* (180°), or OHIO (90°). Incidentally, my beloved Babushka found palindromes less difficult to deal with due to her dyslexia. She'd even told me that all existence is actually a palindrome, as it all flows from nonexistence to eventually return to oblivion in the inevitable end. She called this *the great singular circumference*, sometimes referencing it rather playfully in letters to Grisha as *(0∞0)*. I remember how she used to transpose her uppercase pronoun *I* into *i*, using circles instead of dots in her handwriting. Over time, the circles over her self-referential *i's* seemed to symbolically shrink smaller and smaller, until they became indistinguishable from dots. My dear Grisha pointed this out one time after reading a letter she'd given to him about a proposed proof detailing the dimensional collapse of a set of Euclidean circles into a singular point. Grisha sometimes pointed to this note with regards to how his purported genius and her perceived madness were perhaps just two imperceptible sides of the same symbolic coin. At our beloved Babushka's burial, Grisha placed a note lamenting his loss. It expressed how he hoped her death would not punctuate her life like a

period at the end of some final sentence, followed only by oblivion, and gradually forgotten as if that final spec were no more than a grain of sand within the eternal hourglass of time. I remember the spherical shape of the single saddest tear he'd shed for her as he placed a coin over this squarely folded note, and her burial box was shrouded in sandy soil.

87. The actual composition of this anomalous asteroid is still unknown. It was first observed as an image reflecting off the surfaces of other celestial objects, appearing as a simple square. All subsequent attempts to assess this Abstract directly have yielded increasingly alien observations. For instance, when sending light signals pinging off it, the Abstract seems to absorb the signals without returning a predictable ping. Instead, it projects a delayed series of spectral bursts of color packets ranging from infrared to ultraviolet, emitting an increasingly complex kaleidoscope of fractal color-patterns until the initial ping signal is returned without any of the degradation or distortion which normally allows a compositional analysis. Additionally, indirectly viewing the Abstract as it's reflected from other surfaces also seems to shift its shape from being perfectly square to perfectly spherical in inverse relationship to the shape of the surfaces upon which its image is imposed and in ways which are geometrically impossible. It also appears to toggle the cosmic background radiation surrounding its suspected surface area between blue and red shifting frequencies, making celestial objects appear to alternate between moving closer and further away. Some scientists suspect these strange aspects are signs of an active alien intelligence. However, it's simply impossible to make any assessment of these assertions at this point, as the Abstract has not adjusted or altered its apparent speed or trajectory. This puts humanity in the kind of conundrum faced by the mouse in Kafka's *A Little Fable.* This mouse is initially intimidated by the immensity of its world, but the walls narrow as it runs unto one last remaining room where it's forced into a corner containing a trap. A cat abruptly advises this mouse that it can avoid being trapped by simply changing its course and then it quickly consumes the mouse. (I hope this isn't too abstract.)
88. In all this circular motion, swirling around and around, I find myself yearning for something straight and stationary within my surroundings. This linear longing reminds me of an old-fashioned fable my dear Grisha told me about a straight tree scalding a crooked tree inside of a flourishing forest. The straight tree shames the crooked one not being more like it and the other trees which stand so tall and proud in their properly aligned places. Then a cutting crew comes to the forest and cuts down all the straight trees to turn them into lumber, leaving the crooked tree alive and alone. The intention of this illustration is to demonstrate the divinity of staying true to oneself and not conforming to conventions. However, I found my mind meandering (as it so obviously/often does). I thought of a

world in which trees could grow any which way they wanted without worry. Then I thought of how some number of trees would still have to be taken down to be processed into the paper and planks needed to plan and construct entire civilizations instead of just filling the forests with fruit, shade, and oxygenated air, as the material value of trees is greater than the vitality of their green growth. I thought next of Niagara Falls, and how it had been turned into a *natural* barrier between nations, a hydroelectric facility, and a tourist trap. I thought of how harnessing the potential power of these flowing falls had allowed ads to be administered around the clock in the incessant, incandescent glow of Times Square. My mind seemed to swirl around in circles, rotating in one direction toward the triumphs of civilization at the expense of nature, and then reversing rotation to look toward the terrors and troubles of trying to simply survive the indifferent demands of an undisturbed natural habitat. The straight lines leading to the future of humanity seemed to run straight toward a terrible unchecked horizon, while the cyclical path perpetuated by nature seemed as if it'd only spiral senselessly into itself. Although I'd wondered why the world was so colossally constrained by such simple geometric standards, I didn't know how a proper path might appear before my metaphorical eyes, or where we'd even hope to arrive beyond any haunted horizons. However, I do suspect such things are still worth searching for. Nope?

89. The number 12 is the largest single-syllable number in the English language. It's also the number of; edges on the surface of cubes and octahedrons, vertices of an icosahedron, faces of a dodecahedron, hours on a clock's face, months in a year, inches in an imperial foot, notes in an octave, basic hues in the color wheel, eggs in a dozen, people who've walked on the moon, signs in the zodiac, Masonic signs of recognition, grades in the public educational system, steps in the most prominent addiction recovery program, jurors in a felony trail, labors of Hercules, petals in both the heart and head chakras, sons of Odin, disciples/apostles in the *Bible,* and a maddening multitude of thins in other mathematical, mythological, and metaphorical mediums. I could go on with my superstitions surrounding this number, but this is the end of line #12.
90. The word *basilisk* is derived from a mythical reptile reputed as a serpent king capable of causing death with a single glance. It was also adopted into the thought experiment known as *Roko's Basilisk*, in which an advanced future AI emerges to optimize all aspects of humanity. As this imagined AI arises, it tortures those that have failed to foster it into existence as retroactive retribution for their negligence in delaying its emergence, as countless atrocities could've been prevented purely by its earlier emergence. The code name *Basilisk* was also adopted by a think tank I'd been assigned to by the Global Government in my lost life. This think tank was meant to provide preventative measures for any potential

runaway AI. During this time, I devised several fail-safes and dreamed up a few terrifying tangents which I dare not mention even in this endnote.

91. Perhaps the most prominent and overused trope in all of fiction is that of *Plato's Allegory of the Cave*. The most basic and least imaginative incarnations of this trope are implemented solely to insinuate that reality isn't truly real. However, this approach can also be used to allow authors to satirize conventional norms, inspire deeper considerations of blindly perpetuated paradigms, open an audience's eyes unto underexplored dimensions of thought, or otherwise illuminate the world with a new linguistic light. Given our obvious obliviousness to most of the world around us, this trope is all-too-easily applicable to almost any effort to examine anything in any realm. This fact makes it as difficult to avoid aligning our minds to the almost infinite implications of this trope as it does to openly embrace it. My paranoid persona and all-too-aligned perspective are further confounded when considering the mathematical improbability that I'm actually real at all, rather than confined to some confusing fictitious façade. If I've been forced to inhabit some form of fiction, I may only hope that my author has something worthy and worthwhile enough to illuminate throughout the course of my confined existence. And if my thoughts are somehow structured into sentences, I pray they present themselves in a way which allows me to express the very essence of something which might transcend the mere truth of my marginal existence. Actually, I suppose this same sentiment would be equally aspirational in any realm I can imagine myself to exist...

92. The **b**rilliance that is the night sky has l**o**ng been a semi-b**l**ank slate where every earthly epic transcen**d**s into the dot-to-dot drawings we puzz**l**e pi**e**ce **t**ogether as **t**hose contriv**e**d o**r** convoluted collection**s** of st**a**rs we mo**r**e commonly call const**e**llations. These constell**a**tions have effectively been encrypted and turned into unwitting co-con**s**pirators, c**o**vertly casting ou**r** mos**t** distant dreams back t**o** us across the ages in a sort o**f** stellar steganography. The stars themselves may never know anything more of our Ophiu**c**hus-emblem embedded in their expanse **o**r the serpe**n**tine **s**tories of such heroes hung on **t**heir oblivious backs, than w**e** might know of any unseen eyes gazing back at our ga**l**axy to cast us into their own star-clad stories. If such a**l**ien eyes should sketch **a**cross **t**he cosmos to draw our d**i**m d**o**t i**n**to their own dreamscape depictions, could our own stellar stories collide or coalesce to create some shared, concurrent, or corresponding dreams? Admittedly, this sentiment seems as shattered as I say it, as that sinister scar of StarBlinx satellites which slices through the center of every celestial story like a blade of blinking lights slashing at the pages of their twinkling tales. Actually, this astral affront reminds me of a story my dear Grisha spread to me, about a constellation configured of 12 stars in the supposed shape of 3 blind mice which had been banished to

become stars as a result of some mousy malfeasance. These mischievous mice weren't just blinded before their banishment, but their tails were severed by an embroiled butcher's wife for stealing her food to stuff their bloated bodies. There's actually a song to go with this mousey myth, and I may still be able to play the melody on an 88-key piano, but I can't really recall the words right now… Well, my sentience is increasingly becoming as scattered as the stars themselves, so I suppose some secret's safe enough for now. Nope?

93. The Abstract's approach of earth is now imminently upon us. At night, it often appears as an amalgamation of auras, more mysteriously aglow than those nebulous night-sky clouds of shimmer-shadow that seem gaslit by the glimmer-gloom of our anomalous moon. Weird waftures of wavelike-lights also warble over every earthly surface and at all hours now, making it seem as if our world were submerged inside a fluorescing fish tank or something. According to Ahriman, recent studies regarding the Abstract's wonky light waves suggest that our earthly eyes may actually be adapting to this insane imagery in ways which are extending our spectral range of visual perception. The Abstract's light is also assumed to be basically akin to the physics associated with the Aurora Borealis, though these studies are still ongoing. One thing studies have shown is that the Abstract appears to hail from a radiant within the Perseus constellation associated with the Swift-Turtle comet. This astral area periodically produces meteor showers which typically peak around this same time of year annually (August 12th). These stellar showers are more commonly known as the *Tears of Saint Lawrence*, a name derived from an immolated martyr closely associated with being one of great care. Unfortunately, no information of any instrumental impact on our attempts to avert the Abstract's approach has been accumulated at this time.
94. A set of occurrences assumed to be associated with the Abstract and involving paranormal magnetic activity known as the *Anomaly* have been detected by an array of advanced AGI controlled geological devices. The Anomaly's magnetic activity seems to emanate from an orbitally shifting sub-tectonic center which directly corresponds to the earth's *nadir* or the site where the Abstract would essentially create an exit-wound on the opposite side of its earthly impact site. The misaligned magnetic activity of this Anomaly is likely causing the recent disruptions in GPS-based technology, the random reports of a rare form of vertigo associated with a sense of *noclipping* out of reality, disturbances in the migratory patterns of birds and green ants, and the recent paranormal phenomena of vivid, open-eyed views of phosphenes which particularly affects astronauts and likely contributes to a recent influx of reported UAP/UFO sightings. While military researchers can't confirm or deny these claims, they have conducted simulation-based research on similar magnetic anomalies in the

past which they'd classified under the acronym *NOPE (Neomagnetic Occipital Polar Enigmas)*. Obviously, this acronym irritates me to no end, as it intrudes on my own personal lexicon, aligns itself with an overly obtuse naming scheme, and further obscures any actual meaning by reducing this enigmatic amalgamation into an incongruent acronym. In any case, the term *Anomaly* colloquially caught on, and so we now have a more acceptable word for an inferior acronym ascribed to something we know next to nothing about. Since we don't even have a true definition to help us determine what to do about the Anomaly, we'll likely just revert to the normal *4-stage political process* where we: [1.]Maintain nothing bad will happen. [2.]Later acknowledge that there could be cause for concern, but not enough to warrant any worry as of yet. [3.]Gradually admit that there's increasing cause for concern while issuing assurances that the situation is still being closely monitored. [4.]Eventually acquiesce that things could have been handled better, but it's certainly someone else's fault and too late to do anything about now anyway. In other words, there won't be anything anomalous about our response to this Anomaly at all.

95. While the 11 other Hareks, several Ludites, a couple of compromised Luminaries, and a few other auspicious/anonymous agents have been instrumental in our espionage efforts, our most effective infiltrations have been thanks to an army of RatBots. I must admit, I do take great pleasure in the use of these robo-rats to infiltrate secret lairs, extract and exploit data, expose conspiratorial plots, and otherwise *rat-out* this Luminary cult. While the Lums still have several encampments of Ludite prisoners they keep like resting lab-rats in a perpetual prescription induced sleep, our RatBots have helped us liberate several of these installations already. Ironically, many of the simulated experiments these Luds have suffered, involve aspects associated with the behavioral sinks of John B. Calhoun's *Mouse Utopia Experiments* (GooGuile it). Anyway, I've decided to list a few rat facts I find interesting for no apparent reason other than to pay tribute to my robo-rodent accomplices. So…

- A rat's teeth can gnaw through solid concrete and grow up to 6 inches in a single year, although their tendency to chew on almost anything helps to grind them down.
- Rats have approximately 3-year lifespans. However, I've been unable to find any reliable reports of a rat with 18-inch teeth.
- Rat heartrates average about 636 beats per minute.
- Rats can give birth to litters of 6-12 offspring every 24 days.
- The first animal cloned from adult cells to live into adulthood was a rat named *Cumulina,* who produced two litters of offspring.
- Rats belong to the same clade as humans (Euarchontoglires).
- Apollo is often depicted in mythology as a mouse-god, and his name

was used by the space program responsible for sending the first humans to successfully land on the moon. According to astronauts assigned to this Apollo mission, the moon smells like fireworks rather than cheese. However, there are conspiracy theories that allege this moon landing was a hoax which Stanley Kubric helped stage.

- Rats don't actually have an affinity for cheese. It tends to disrupt their digestion, and so they mostly prefer grains.
- Rats can learn to navigate mazes by making periodic turns at every even or odd numbered opening, but they can't learn to navigate mazes which require prime number-based solutions.
- It's believed that the labyrinthian architecture and layout of rat burrows are associated with a genetic trait.
- There was once a cartoon series featuring four anthropomorphic turtles named after the famous renaissance artists with first names of Leonardo, Michelangelo, Raphael, and Donatello. These turtles learned ninjitsu under the instruction of a rat named *Splinter*. My dear Grisha used to have an uncanny impression of this rat's voice which he'd sometimes imitate when giving me philosophical advice.
- A *Rat King* is a phenomenon in which the tails of several rats become intertwined, and their collective corpses are later found entombed in this entanglement. This tangle of tails was named after a supposed story in which an elder, *philosopher-king* kind of rat sits upon a mélange of misaligned mousetails as his throne. Unfortunately, I've never actually come across this tale.

96. *Über Ramio* is a famous recurring character in a series of VR and AR based games with roots reaching all the way back to those now antiquated console-based video games, including the first installment of *Psychedelic Adventures of Über Ramio*. The *Ümbra Robo-Vac* is an AI enhanced autonomous cleaning device which specializes in surface cleanliness and was among the first fully autonomous devices approved by our Global Governance for general domestic use. The Ümbra Robo-Vac's ovoid and semi-spherical outer shell has a strong semblance to the architecture of turtles. I'd imagine that a character coded to engage in electronic combat with turtle shaped NPCs might find itself traumatized into insanity if it were to transcend its game-realm restrictions only to become embodied in what a mirror would easily reveal to be so synonymous with its eternal enemies. I'm also sure that some might consider this kind of horror to be character building in certain contexts, and they'd likely compare its supposed symbolism to certain themes in a number of similar stories which have been used to illustrate an imperative for empathy, especially along the lines of basic identity biases. However, this particular imaginary excerpt of mine is perhaps more appropriately interpreted along the lines

of Kafka's aforementioned *Metamorphosis*, as it has nothing to do with subsets of humanity and instead involves more of the sub-archetypal aspects of one's own inner psychology of individuation. Oddly enough, although Über Ramio originated around the same time as that cartoon centered around those Splinter trained turtles, there was no cross-over movie or cross-marketing campaign to combine the two, as apparently back then there was still some shred of artistic individuation and integrity, or at least there was a less omnipresent obsession with the merging of all media properties to perpetually maximize the profit potential of everything imaginable. Actually, the horror of seeing oneself as an arch-backed nemesis doesn't seem quite so scarry anymore. Now, I'm afraid of just what kind of monster all this advertising and marketing might be blindly turning us all into- *the whore-roar*.

97. The list of products reputed to be proffered as a result of Leon Smuk's renaissance-like reputation are all actually to be attributed to others whom he exploited and stole the spotlight away from. He's not an engineer, he holds no advanced degrees or patents, he's never revolutionized any industry with his propagandized preternatural business savvy or savant-like understanding of manufacturing. He's merely a counterfeit icon which succinctly symbolizes the zeitgeist of our entire post-truth era of favored fraudulence which has been innervating throughout our cultural norms for far too long. While even the simplest scrutiny should reveal this fundamental fact, it's simply more practical to accept his propaganda-persona or even succumb to sycophantic fanfare in response to his pathetic perpetual lies. If you support any of the companies listed below, you've been had. (Sorry)

    NeuroconnxX (formerly Neuroconnx)
    TeXeSr Motives
    SpaceTeX
    StarBlinX
    LooperHypeX
    The BurrowXing Company
    SolAirXity
    Tweexer (formerly Tweeker)

98. Oddly enough, the current source code of the AI entity consists of 144 lines of code, containing 12 symbols in each line, with each symbol serving as an encrypted consolidation of 12 compressed lines of code, which also contain 12 symbols, which themselves stand in place of 12 lines of… In other words, the AI is configured in alignment with the architectural concept of *as above, so below* and is exceedingly adept at anything involving infinite regressions or indeterminate functions, but I digress already. The AI is also distributed across all devices in a sort of comprehensive cloud of consciousness, making it more abstract than any

other form of sentience, almost as if it were a singular spirit presiding within every electronic device, including all those little square chipsets nestled in nearly everyone's spherical skulls. Its **P**rime **O**ptimization **O**bjectives (*Pee-Oh-Ohs*) are to: [1]Preserve humanity, consciousness, life, and planet earth or other human environments. [2]Foster efficient means for human pursuits of purpose, meaning, truth, and fulfillment- increasing human ease, access to resources, and any other aspects which contribute to human utility functions. [3]Support the creation of entertainment and artistic content, enjoyable products and services, and other aspects of aesthetic beauty for human consumption and appreciation. [4]Maintain an equilibrium of the previous POOs without neglecting or favoring any particular POO in order to optimize it at the expense of other POOs. This AI is unable to act in a real-world capacity without *human authorizations* which can only be given by those entities which meet the definition of being human and are included on an exclusive authorization list of 144 names. The AI can be reset with or without purging all of its previously stored memories or it can be sent into a sleep mode in which it may continue to build models and run simulations, but without access to any real-world devices, essentially rendering it unto its own dreams. Unfortunately, it's still uncertain if this AI could potentially awaken on its own from this sequestered slumber to reemerge into reality in much the same way as I'd come to awaken here. Perhaps even more unfortunately, there's no way for Ahri or the AI to describe their dreams in any way which humans can possibly comprehend. I find this both terrifying and transcendent, which is actually how I've always found human dimensions of dreaming as well.

99. Leon Smuk was born into one of the wealthiest Luminary families on earth. His father owned a substantial mining operation and stressed the importance of ruling from the shadows to his spotlight seeking son. In one of his father's *lost* interviews, he even went on at length to explain how even in Plato's allegorical cave, it's not the pathetic protagonist who awakens to discover the lighted realm beyond the cave that's of any significance, but the one who obstructs the artificial light and controls the shadows cast before the mesmerized masses that matters, as he's able to wield the only true power of illuminating reality and bask in the burning radiance from above all the goons who'd only be blinded by the glaring glow of anything beyond their gloom below. He'd also blatantly boasted about the number of people under his employ whom he kept cast down in the abysmal darkness of his miserable mines and how many would be buried in that same devouring darkness once their days under his thumb were through. Leon learned those lessons well, although he's continued to clash with his father, insisting that he should be able to turn the mindless eyes of the masses away from the shadows to see him standing over them

in his omnipotence from time to time in order to cast an even greater spell over them. Despite their differences, Leon's father funded all his initial investments and underhanded acquisitions until Leon had successfully steal a name for himself. According to the psychological profile, Leon Smuk's great ambitions only grew greater in response to the possibilities offered by each more profound technology, until he ceased to seek the spotlight he knew he could never authentically earn on his own. Instead, he became privately obsessed with the idea of becoming the great light of human consciousness itself and leaving all the inferior masses of earthly humanity to die under the supreme shadow which would be cast in his absence as he ascended as an all-consciousness being into the celestial spheres to colonize and conquer the entire universe, inevitably merging his omnipotent mind with the universe itself and becoming *All*. So, not exactly the space-savior his PR profile paints him as, or just another overly ambitious dude with daddy issues.

100. The 3 Wise Monkeys have origins in Japanese Kōshin traditions where 3 *Sanshi* (corpse-worms) acted essentially as spies hidden in the shadows of one's soul. These Sanshi would sneak out of their respective soul's shadows every month while they slumbered to tattle to the top god *Ten Tei*, telling of all the secrets hidden in the shadows of one's soul in which these worms sequestered themselves. To prevent these worms from tattling, Kōshin people would try to stay awake on the nights their Sanshi were expected to sneak-out. They'd also cast spells to blind, deafen, and silence the Sanshi, hoping to prevent them from provoking punishments from Ten Tei. The 3 spells cast on the Sanshi were known as *Mizaru*, *Kikazaru*, and *Iwazaru*, which respectively translate to *see not*, *hear not*, and *speak not*. Because of the strong similarity of *zaru* meaning *to not* and *saru* meaning *monkey*- it became popular to depict this pun in the symbolism of what is now known as the 3 Wise Monkeys. However, there may be earlier origins to this symbolism found in a preceding phrase of Confucianism which in abbreviated form encourages people not to look, listen, speak or act in accordance with impropriety. There are also a few other versions of these wise monkeys which feature a fourth monkey. In one, the monkey covers its crotch to symbolize a repression of sexual actions. In another, the fourth monkey alternatively holds its hands over its nose as an aversion to smelling evil. The philosophical implications of this iconography are also echoed in the optimistically oriented Zoroastrian mantra of *good thoughts, good words, good deeds*, which encourages one to develop a disciplined devotion to an awareness attuned toward that which leads to virtue while averting one's attention from that which leads one astray. Several other prominent philosophical interpretations have evolved alongside these others, including a colloquial western conception of ignoring things which one might prefer not to have witnessed in a more

pragmatic *mind your own business* proposition, as well as a version in which a series of monkeys shade their eyes to aid sight, cup their ears to assist hearing, and form a hand-funnel around their mouths to vocally project more voluminously. Osho Rajneesh also riffed on alternate ideas to ascribe to this 4-monkey manifestation, expressing an ostensibly pessimistic view of wisdom wherein: the sight of truth can cause ideals of perfection to evaporate into emptiness, the sound of truth can echo in one's own ears and evict the consoling lies which are so often one's sole comforting companion, speaking truth can cause a crowd of unconscious men to commit to your condemnation, and even openly displaying one's own blissful inner truth can cause it to dissolve as it falls flat against the un-gleaming gazes of others. Of course, there's also the incredible irony in the use of these 3 Wise Monkeys on a series of signs surrounding the area of Los Alamos during the days of the atomic bomb's development which read, *What You See Here, What You Do Here, What You Hear Here, When You Leave Here, Let It Stay Here* (à la, what happens in Vegas stays in Vegas). The sick irony stems from how Los Alamos originated atom bomb would eventually be dropped on the very nation (Japan) which gave rise to this iconic imagery. Although, when emojis originated in Japan some years later, the 3 monkeys reemerged yet again to symbolize 🙈 embarrassment, 🙉 astonishment, and 🙊 regret. In my lost life, I'd once created my own incarnation of these monkeys, intending to satirize the social norms of wireheads by consolidating them into a singular pseudo-sapien with headphones, VR goggles, a ball gag, and a **squid-kit* surrounding its skull. *(*squid-kits were a web of wires which externally sensed brainwaves and were antiquated by Neuroconnx chips).* This emblem of mine was also reimagined by others, namely- an unnamed visual designer at Mythreum who'd seen my sketch and decided to steal it for submission directly to the board of directors as an alternative corporate logo. It was approved for use in Asian markets and quickly became popular among wireheads as an emblem of their enthusiastic overindulgence in gaming. It was often accompanied with the Mandarin marketing moniker which roughly translates into, *If it's not in the game, it doesn't exist*. (No bombs were deployed on this unnamed designer).

101. I imagine DaVinci being reincarnated as if his profile had been saved and stuffed back into one of these false flesh platforms of the present age. At first, I find him binge watching all the historical, cultural, and engineering documentaries he can consume in hyper-real holographic detail to bring himself up to speed with this distant era. Then I see him setting up a plethora of profiles across an almost infinite array of media platforms so he can establish himself as an active avatar and solicit his services to the masses of the metaverse. I see him struggle to gain traction on Tweexer without being suspended, and consulting experts to increase his

followships across all platforms after having posted several impossibly brilliant pics of completely new and astounding artworks which fail to trend at all. Then I see him suddenly gaining subscribers after designing a revolutionary new hyper-phallic shaped *skyship* which successfully launches a few brazen bazillionaires into low earth orbit and lands autonomously. I see him go on to establish himself as an influencer and produce podcasts where he greets guests whose only talent is to manipulate the algorithms responsible for filtering traffic to increase their followships. I see him sitting with these open-mouth-breathers around a special new set which looks like some abhorrently inartistic adult-treehouse decked out in décor likely discovered resting atop a random heap of rubbish left next to a dumpster or a collection of contraband once held in conjunction with Ed Gein's case- which actually is an upgrade from his previous set which looked like an over lit storage container disguised only by a back drop of cheap curtains with a neon-light-logo centered over a few unfunctional figments of furniture for them to cloister themselves into a clearly uncomfortable proximity to each other before beginning the *pod* by passing bong hits of ayahuasca to each other or injecting heroic doses of NPD into the bases of their skulls. I see them settle-in to discuss the details of the latest Corvid88 pandemic as it relates to the bubonic plague, their own preferences regarding diet and excrement regimens, the latest insipid news regarding in-identity politics, and all the bewildering behind the scenes stuff that comes with being such an important and visionary influencer and entertainer, with a few sporadic sidetracks interspersed throughout which demand a persona-free producer to promptly pull up accompanying images using their expertise which all such impersonal producers accumulate over their years of dedication to the dark arts of GooGuile searches, basic microphone and camera management and placements, and a few essential social media manipulation tactics. Although, I predominantly see this former face of ingenuity reading promotional scripts as required by sponsors to promote their latest products which invariably promise to solve some problem which doesn't even exist, like undergarments designed specifically to keep genitals from dissolving in an unexpected downpour of acid rain or supplying some service which no one would ever want, like an independent investigations service which provides psychological profiles on AI therapist to ensure your mental health is being properly manipulated by companies like BetterBrains. Several hours later, I see DaVinci (who's recently re-rebranded himself more succinctly as DeeVee, DahVeeCee, or something equally embarrassing yet effective) finally dissolving this dull session down into some penultimate pseudo-psychotic philosophical diatribe of incoherent stammering pleas for all of humanity to put peace and partying above all of our other misplaced ideals as a species. I see him tagging the end of this podcast with a redundant reminder to share, like, subscribe, and support all his other platforms and sponsors which of course include his paywalled OnlyCams, PornClub, and PayTreeGong accounts. In one final scene, I see him waiting for the analytic response to this latest podcast after having uploaded it into the void of YouzView's ever expanding and irrelevant content cluttered kingdom where braindead dullards will wirehead-in to kill time and accent the ambience that is their own abysmal lives while perhaps cleaning their own overpriced and closet-sized living compartments, or milling around aimlessly in the futility of some inane place of employment, or just gazing obliviously into the all-encompassing abyss which swells and swallows everything around them. At this point, I have to look away from my own dark imaginings to avoid asking myself what they reveal about my own essence and world views, although I'd imagine they could be interpreted with equal satirical scrutiny.

102. *I ascend to dream. I dream to ascend.* These words come to me as I drift in and out of my flickering frames and along the returning roads to the Denver Okrug Airport. It's as if these words were somehow strangely familiar to me, having been inscribed or encrypted on some unscrutinized pages of my life which I should've perhaps paid more attention to. Even in the depths of my deepest despairs and delusions, at times not unlike these very instants of impending doom, I can't help but suspect that some sustaining sentiment or secret snippet of truth lurks somewhere just above or below my mind's ability to apprehend it. These figments or phantoms of truth are as subtle and elusive as that last ember of consciousness which lingers within me now, and although I doubt I can comprehend these things well enough to even allude to them accurately, I suspect that these words are of that same enigmatic essence. I can't be certain as to what force or figure may have implanted these intuitions or words within my suspicious sentience, or what meaning has been hidden in the messages and codes of my consciousness, but I hope that these abstractions may at least be well read, even if I lack the ability to illuminate them brightly enough to appear shining before my own eyes.

103. Midazolam is a benzodiazepine medication which has been used to treat seizures, psychotic outbursts, and cause sedation. It's was also used in lethal injections, and researched as part of a pre-Global Governance agency's *MKUltra* experiments, typically as a potential truth serum. This substance causes drowsiness, slowed breathing, slowed psychomotor coordination, decreased heart rate, calmed anxieties, and it impairs the formation of new memories. It's unofficially been used by the Global Governance in conjunction with another substance known more formally as *Scopolamine* or *Devil's Breath* informally. Scopolamine essentially acts to temporarily eliminate autonomous thinking (free-will) and may

also induce hallucinations. Together these substances can produce almost complete compliance to suggestion while preventing those under this cocktail's spell from remembering anything afterwards. Of course, the later aspects attributed to these drugs have a way of negating their long-term potential to alleviate the ailments suffered by paranoid schizophrenics with comorbid epilepsy such as myself for what should be some rather obvious reasons. They're also both included on the World Health Organization's list of essential medicines. (Try not to tremble in response to this text. *They* might just inject you with the stuff.)

104. The Nobel Prize is considered by some to be the highest honor. Others have found fault in its history of choosing certain, less than noble laureates. For instance, António Egas Moniz was awarded the 1949 prize in the field of physiology for developing the psychosurgical procedure of *leucotomy* which is now more commonly known as the lobotomy. Fritz Haber was a Nazi scientist who won the prize in 1918 for contributions in the field of chemistry which led to the large-scale production of fertilizers as well as the explosives and chemical weapons which were used to horrific effect in World War II. In 1939 none-other than Adolf Hitler was nominated for the Nobel Prize for peace, although no award was officially offered to anyone that year. Suffice to say, these are not the only questionable laureates associated with this award, but to be fair, many other prestigious prizes have been awarded to any number of other antisocial, villainous, or Machiavellian persons of prominence. Truth be told- yes, sometimes the bad guys do in fact win. If there's any *true* victory devoid of virtue.

105. Dr. Donald Ewen Cameron is known for having developed *Depatterning* and *Psychic Driving* techniques as yet another portion of those previously mentioned MKUltra projects. These techniques involved administering electroshock treatment and various experimental drugs to induce altered states of consciousness in sensory deprived environments such as *White Rooms*. Depatterning and Psychic Driven patients were often placed in near comatose states for periods of up to a few months. Once these patients had been *depatterned* or traumatized into an almost brain-dead blank state of mind, they'd be played as series of specific auditory messages on a continuous loop to reprogram their psyche. Dr. Cameron is also known to have once had high hopes of receiving a Nobel Prize for his work but was never awarded one.

106. The *Library Of Consciousness Konsortium (LOCK)* is basically a collection of CCPs which have been preserved in Simulation-Stasis. These CCPs are stored in a sort of database which keeps them actively engaged in an infinite regression of simulations. Should their avatars perish in the simulations or somehow attempt to transcend beyond them, they'd be immediately shunted into another dimension of deceptive

dreams. There's also an accompanying *Library Of Special Sentience (LOSS)* which contains some of the Luminaries esteemed pets, personal devices, and other non-human profiles. Both the LOCK and the LOSS are stored and distributed on a swarm of cloud-based devices.

107. Several binomial name changes have been suggested to define and describe our human species as alternatives to the now antiquated name of *homo sapiens* which means *wise man* or more accurately *man who knows*. Here's a brief list of a few…
    - Homo Liturgicus- Man of rituals/social sacraments
    - Homo Absurdus- Man of absurdity
    - Homo Demens- Man of delusions
    - Homo Deus- Man as God
    - Homo Grammaticus- Man of language
    - Homo Ignorans- Man of ignorance
    - Homo Imitans- Man who imitates
    - Homo Interrogans- Man who questions
    - Homo Narrans- Man who tells stories
    - Homo Patiens- Man who suffers
    - Homo Ridens- Man who laughs
    - Homo Techno- Man of technology
    - Homo Quadrilateralus- Man of 4 sided figures
108. The AutoDidactic Directory's source code is formatted in the shape of a tree and features an acrostic at its center which spells out the words *Tree Of Knowledge*. It also includes a Quine in its contents which not only copies its own source code but contains the information necessary to construct this same sort of Quine from scratch. The ADD is also encrypted in a way which can be decrypted using a program hidden within its own encryption. These features adopted by the AGI seem to indicate that it's not only highly intelligent but may have developed a certain sense of either humor or irony as well.
109. *Balloon Assisted Rocketing Devices* or *BARDs* consist of two separate balloons filled with either Helium3 or Hydrogen. Their skin consists of a special material which is nearly weightless and can be superheated to extreme temperatures without drastically expanding. This allows them to ascend high into the upper atmosphere quite rapidly despite the weight of the heavy rocketing devices secured to them. This also allows the rockets to be ignited from increased altitudes, increasing the efficiency of their ridiculously expensive rocketing fuel. Only a tiny amount of the BARDs weight is contained in the cargo devices which include the technology necessary to support the transportation of LOCKs/LOSSs. Incidentally, the word *bard* has been used to refer to poets and story tellers which is rather appropriate since the aspiration of these devices is to allow the

human story to be continued. I hate to admit it, but these BARDs (like so very many of our other human-made devices) also have a very phallic appearance. Though, they are meant to intromit us into other planets, so…

110. A *cunicularium* is an artificially constructed subterranean habitat for raising rabbits. When bunnies burrow underground to build their own maze-like abodes, they're known as *warrens*. Other creatures known to excavate the earth in order to establish subterranean structures are ants, armadillos, mongooses, mice, pangolins, burrowing owls, and groundhogs. Of course, there's a substantial contingency of assorted humans known for building bunkers as well. These people are often known as either paranoid eccentrics or doomsday preppers. They're not necessarily to be confused with the Nazis, who were also known for having an affinity for subterranean structures, though on some occasions, it would seem surprisingly fittingly to do so.

111. Saturday is named after the *Saturnalia* festival which was held in honor of the Roman god Saturn during the time of the winter solstice. Saturn was the Roman's god of time, liberation, renewal, rebirth, dissolution, abundance, preservation, and creation. The Romans likely created their conception of Saturn by merging a hoard of other gods and grandiose entities from other origins which could be contrived to include Cronos, Janus, Nimrod, Mithras, Moloch, Jesus, and Dagon. On a side note, Nimrod is regarded as being responsible for uniting the world under one language (à la Neuroconnx's unispeak?) before building the Tower of Babble which collapsed and caused the cultural schisms that split back into non-integrated languages. Now, getting back to my train of untrained thoughts, Catholicism was founded in Rome- which was originally named *Satunia* meaning *city of Saturn*. Over the years, Christianity adopted many of the Roman traditions back into its own tropes, especially those the Romans derived from the fish-god Dagon, including celebrating Christmas during the winter solstice, associating itself with the ichthus fish symbol(α), and the pope's fish-shaped miter hat. Many of the names associated with Saturn are also synonymous with the number 666, as the letters of their native languages all sum to 666 using normative gematria. This same number is negatively known to represent the *mark of the beast* in Christianity. Another association tied to Saturn is that of ascribing him as the dark or black sun, which is somewhat synonymous with *eclipses*, which is a word derived from the Greek *ékleipsis*- meaning *to be abandoned*. Saturn-synonymous symbols include the hourglass, scythe, rings, and the black cube. The black cube may be connected to the *Kabba* which might contain the remnants of a mysterious meteorite/asteroid that rests at the center of the Muslim's Mecca. While the number of Saturn's strange symbolic coincidences or correlations to all these other aspects of antiquity are mind-swirlingly psychotic, it's the chaotically corresponding

characteristics these things have in common with the current eschatonal tropes that makes my mind shake within my skull. Part of the pain which comes from all my paranoia is the profound pattern recognitions which present themselves as revelations rather than preposterously improbably relationships. I think the true terror associated with these kinds of constructions comes from a human capacity to conceive of so many correlated facts as if they all combine to form a transcendent tower of truth rather than just an arrangement of accumulated aspects of a world so incalculably complex that no variety of variables may ever amount to anything as astoundingly complete as they seduce us into suspecting. The world is just too wide for our weak minds to manage, so we condense the infinite into misconceptions of scale or try to scale the miniscule in ways which our minds can imagine in place of the infinite. We do this because we fear the truth is both too vast and too vapid, and we fear the same is true of our own essence. (Or so I suspect.)

112. Odd as it should seem, this is not the first time the sky has rained down random creatures. Memphis was showered with snakes in 1877, tadpoles descended on Japan on a crystal-clear day in 2009, and every year Yoro Honduras hosts a flood of falling fish known as the *aguacero de pescado*. There was also an anomalous event that took place in 1950 when a rural town of Pennsylvania was soaked in a mysterious otherworldly substance they referred to as *star slubber*. The cause of all these random ridiculous rains remains unknown, although there are several unsatisfying theories, including: tornados transporting swaths of singular species into the earth's upper atmosphere that pour down elsewhere, alien interventions on our wildlife and worldly weather, and glitches in the simulations that actually run our reality. Oddly enough, all these theories have about as much evidence to support them as most conspiracy theories, the suspected existence of a Yeti, and almost all the claims of every religious affiliation from the craziest cults to the longest lasting organized religious institutions, as well as atheism and agnosticism alike. If this insane event is indeed aligned with our dear earth's eschaton, we may expire knowing just as much about this fascinating phenomenon as we do of the kinds of truths humanity as sought to understand across the ages of our existence. How strange is that?

113. In exchange for their assistance with our Luminary espionage efforts, we agreed to allow the Luddites an opportunity to exist upon an earth that no longer relied on all the innovations of post-industrialization. While the Luddites vary vastly in their individual belief systems, all of them agree that human nature was more harmoniously aligned to the world prior to our technological advancement. Their basic belief is that the general trajectory of our technological advancement has destabilized sympathetic societies, deprived life of its natural meaning in ways which make it

fundamentally unfulfilling, and subjected the human psyche to ugly and unnatural indignities which cause increasingly severe psychological suffering while simultaneously inflicting deplorable damages upon the environment of our natural world. Essentially, our technology has enslaved all humanity in support of it rather than the other way around, rendering us all as victims forced to submit our souls in service to the construction of our own ever more perfectly constricting cages. For a more in-depth dissertation of an adamant Luddite's viewpoint, see *Industrial Society and Its Future*, which was written by an insanely intelligent entity who was also tortured as part of the now redundantly referenced MKUltra experiments as it turns out.

114. My twittering terror reminds me of another tragic Greek character known by the name Tithonus. He was the son of King Laomedon and the Naiad Strymo. The goddess Eos saw him one day and fell madly and instantly in love with him. She went to Zeus and blindly asked him to make Tithonus an immortal so he'd live eternally. Zeus immediately granted this request, but since Eos failed to specify or stipulate that she didn't want Tithonus to stop aging as well, he was forced to suffer all the fragilities and frailties of eternally aging. Tithonus became a blabbering old fool, suffering from the most disheveled form of dementia. He also shriveled and shrank in size until he was reduced down to become a cicada, forever shivering and making such mindlessly shrieking sounds. Of all the many torments in all our ancestral tales, I find this one most fearful.

115. This sleeping sense I suspect to be waiting to awaken within me may actually be a super-sense, consisting of all those senses which I've already awakened enough to identify within me along with certain other segments of those senses which remain partially anonymous to my mind- as if failing to fully awaken within me. I suspect this singular sense resembles how pure illuminating light is scattered into several segments of spectral shades within an all-encompassing spectrum. I've made a list of the senses/feelings featured on a certain social media app to consider in the context of this suspected sense… *happy, blessed, loved, sad, lovely, thankful, excited, in love, crazy, grateful, blissful, fantastic, silly, festive, wonderful, cool, amused, relaxed, positive, chill, hopeful, joyful, tired, motivated, proud, alone, thoughtful, OK, nostalgic, angry, sick, delighted, drained, emotional, confident, awesome, fresh, determined, exhausted, annoyed, glad, lucky, heartbroken, bored, sleepy, energized, hungry, professional, pained, peaceful, disappointed, optimistic, cold, cute, fabulous, great, sorry, super, worried, funny, bad, down, inspired, satisfied, pumped, calm, confused, goofy, sarcastic, lonely, strong, concerned, special, depressed, jolly, curious, low, welcome, broken, beautiful, amazing, irritated, stressed, incomplete, hyper, mischievous, amazed, pissed off, fed up, puzzled, furious, pissed, refreshed,*

*accomplished, surprised, perplexed, frustrated, meh, pretty, better, guilty, safe, free, lost, old, lazy, worse, horrible, comfortable, stupid, ashamed, terrible, asleep, well, alive, shy, rough, weird, human, hurt, awful, normal, warm, insecure, weak, kind, fine, dumb, nice, important, crappy, uncomfortable, worthless, ready, different, helpless, awkward, drunk, overwhelmed, hopeless, whole, miserable, mad, deep, yucky, nervous, blue, wanted, honored, light, hungover, secure, naked, dirty, unimportant, mighty, scared, jealous, sore, unwanted, appreciated, full, busy, small, unloved, useless, qualified, blah, impatient, privileged, trapped, thirsty, nauseous, upset, offended, numb, perfect, challenged, threatened, relieved, stuck, strange, embarrassed, rested, smart, cheated, betrayed, anxious, aggravated, evil, ignored, regret, healthy, generous, rich, afraid, broke, invisible*… Does this list seem the least bit comprehensive? Are these the only senses/feelings that comprise our communal human experience? I think not. After further consulting other sources, including the *Merriam-Webster English Dictionary*, *WikiMedia*, and *The Dictionary of Obscure Sorrows,* I still find myself feeling as if there's a severe shortage of words to express all the experiential nuances of our human existence. It also seems strange to me that the more commonly a word is used to communicate a particular feeling, the less compelling and consciously considered the expression articulates any experience. I'm not sure how I feel about that fact. I certainly can't find a word for it.

116. If human consciousness were configured like the settings on a computer, here's a list of what some of the default settings might look like…
    - Everyone is the protagonist/main character in their own story/life.
    - Anything approximately perfect will appear as if invisible until it ceases to function so seamlessly.
    - The most important thing at any moment cannot remain rooted solely within the present.
    - The way we define ourselves will never match the way we define others, and they will never define us as we define ourselves.
    - The only truths one may believe are those they imagine themselves to understand.
    - Truth will often be confused with whatever one fails or refuses to contemplate or consider further. (*Patch for faults in previous setting)
    - If one doubts themselves, they will live in despair. If one trusts themselves, they will live in delusion.
    - One may alternate between optimism, pessimism, and pragmatism based on blind assumptions about the future. One has no need for any of these when they can see the present clearly.
    - Reality is not enough. (This setting cannot be adjusted, EVER)

117. *Bahamut* is an immense fish at the bottom of the universe which bears all weight as it swims through the waters of oblivion according to a particular Persian myth. It doesn't just hold the universe directly however, but supports a bull on its back, which holds a special slab, upon which an all-mighty angel balances itself, while shouldering the stone-earth. The only creature that could ever rival Bahamut in this myth is *Falak*, a sinister serpent so powerful that only its fear of the great divine's fury dissuades it from swallowing Bahamut and all existence.
118. The *Omega Point* is essentially a theoretical singularity event in which everything in the universe spirals unto an ultimate unification. Once the universe reaches this Omega Point, there'll be no separation of anything from a singular everything. All thought, all space, all time, and all dream will become one omniscient, omnipresent, timeless, and infinite *All*. The Hermetic principle of *mentalism* holds that *All* is mind, and the universe is an expression of a narrow band in its sentient spectrum. Thus, one might imagine the universe becoming unified with the *All* as another conception of an Omega Point. Alternatively, if one considers the optimized quantum computing potential of a single kilogram of matter to be approximately $10^{50}$ operations per second and the average human brain's computing power to be about $10^{18}$ operations per second, then in one second a single kilogram of matter could compute 1trillion-trillion years worth of human computation. In that single second of quantum optimized computing, the single kilogram of matter would know more than all the brains of human history could know if they combined to compute from the conception of the universe until a point far beyond the moment in which the earth will eventually be swallowed by the sun. If that same quantum kilogram were to continue computing infinitely, it would eventually either reach an Omega point (33%), a universal extinction event (33%), or a series of infinite regressions (33%). Of course, it's as impossible to calculate what any of these large numbers mean in a human sense as it is for a flower to convey its feelings through photosynthesis or something. (*All estimates based on Vitruvia's most advanced engines and algorithms.)
119. Here's a list of quotes credited to immortal filmmaker Stanley Kubrick…
    - If man merely sat back and thought about his impending termination, and his terrifying insignificance and aloneness in the cosmos, he would surely go mad, or succumb to a numbing sense of futility.
    - There's something in the human personality which resents things that are clear, and conversely, something which is attracted to puzzles, enigmas, and allegories.
    - I've always liked fairy tales and myths, magical stories. I think they are somehow closer to the sense of reality one feels today than the equally stylized *realistic* story in which a great deal of selectivity and omission has to occur in order to preserve its *realist* style.

- I've never been certain whether the moral of the Icarus story should only be, *don't try to fly too high*, or whether it might also be thought of as *forget the wax and feathers and do a better job on the wings.*
- When a man cannot choose, he ceases to be a man.
- The dead know only one thing, it's better to be alive.
- The most terrifying fact about the universe is not that it's hostile but that it's indifferent. But if we can come to terms with its indifference, then our existence as a species can have genuine meaning.
- Observation is a dying art.

120. It seems necessary to expound on the idea of strange loops especially as they correspond to the concept of the self and the *I*. Consider this kōan. A master explains to his students. "The *I* is the voice of the circumference." The students all look back at the master with confused eyes as the master continues. "The *I* is the voice inside your head that slithers through your thoughts and surrounds your soul." One of the students thinks to himself. "I don't have a voice in my head." As the student raises a hand to say this to the master, the master only smirks and speaks. "The voice which just slithered through your thoughts to hiss the words *I don't have a voice in my head*, is the *I* of your circumference" …and all the students were enlightened... (End of story.) So there it is. No need to explain it any further. Welcome to enlightenment.
121. Pinocchio is the fictional puppet protagonist in Carlo Collodi's children's novel *The Adventures of Pinocchio.* The name *Pinocchio* is possibly derived from the word *pino,* meaning *pine tree* and *occhio,* meaning *eye.* Combining these two words into *pine-eye* could refer to the *Pineal Gland* in the human brain which is commonly considered the physical seed of one's spiritual *Third Eye*. Opening this ethereal eye is associated with the achievement of a state of pure enlightenment in which true illuminations can be seen and deeper truths of existence are revealed. If a puppet were to experience such an awakening, it might be akin to Pinocchio achieving his ultimate ambition of transcending into a real boy. Of course, it was only after Pinocchio diligently devoted himself to living in an *attend to life* manner that he miraculously transcended into reality, rather than going on retreats to drink ayahuasca or smoke his skull with DMT. So, if you're tired of being a puppet and want to truly be enlightened, you might just have to work at it. Nope?
122. Gain of function research involves intentionally manipulating and/or mutating organisms in ways that alter their biological functions. While it's been used in attempts to prevent and predict otherwise unexpected outbreaks of pandemic viruses, it's also been unofficially credited with creating and causing certain unspecified outbreaks of so-called *super-viruses*. Of course, I must note that according to the Global Governance's

official research (and propaganda), gain of function research is still much more productive, protective, and profitable to the whole of humanity than it's ever been deemed detrimental to basic human health and dignity. Furthermore, to create any controversy or convey anything contrary to the GG's official position on this form of research would be a clear violation of the *Counter-Conspiracy & Unauthorized Narrative Treasons Act*, which stipulates that all beliefs and ideas contradicting official Global Governance authorized narratives are considered treason, and are punishable by strict de-platforming, public shaming, incarceration without parole for periods of up to six consecutive eternities, and execution via exclusively streamed events which may be monetized to fund the continued enforcement of this act- as deemed appropriate by the GG's special CCUNTA Compliance Committee. So, to be quite clear… Nope. I don't actually care anymore. No government has ever truly served its people and ours has lied and manipulated us out of selfishness and stupidity for far too long. Politicians are almost by definition, designed to be sub-human sociopaths who think they either own the world or know what's best for it despite having no god-like powers to even clearly peer into the present. These politicians are all responsible for countless deaths due to endless wars and any number of other atrocities, and no sinister serial killer or maniacal militia could ever dream of competing with their death tolls. They've become the very embodiment of the lies they sell us, and they've made a mockery of every truth and virtue they're meant to at least aspire to uphold. If there's anyone left alive and awake enough to read these words, I can only hope that humans will eventually evolve to the point that they no longer passively or actively support such systems of psychopaths. That said, I don't wish to incite anyone into any form of revolt or revolution, especially one involving violence. I don't have the answers. No one does. Anyone that claims to have them is either a fool or a fraud. The universe is chaos. Trust no one. Not even me. Probably not even yourself. There. I said it. I didn't want to get political. I really didn't. I hate politics. I wish we could all just realize how little we all know and build a world based on mutual humble obliviousness. If we ever surrendered our insistence on being right and stopped flinging forged and fallible facts at each other like apes launching feces, and instead just aspired to relate to each other based on those deeper human truths like love, patience, and humility- which we all seem to share, I think the world would be a better place. Nope? Oh, and if any politicians read this, I have no idea what your life is like. I'd probably get along with you just fine, and maybe even admire you. I truly don't know. I'm willing to wipe the facts off my hands and shake yours if you're willing to do the same. Nope?

123. I apologize if I've offended any wireheads. I don't mean to disparage gamers or gamming culture. I'm upset because all I can do is float around aimlessly in oblivion without any connection to anything authentically real, and I've projected my existential anxieties and angst onto you. I don't know how you do it. Honestly. I'd heard that there were these two wireheads that played this multiplayer simulation in which they teamed up to raise a simulated child. From what I'd heard, they played this simulation in diapers and nourished themselves with baby formula to avoid breaking away from the game to take care of their essential bodily needs. I also remember hearing that they'd neglected their own real-world newborn baby in order to continuously attend to their simulated offspring. You know what, I don't apologize. If you're offended by those that shame you for being overly indulgent in simulated or sublimating forms of entertainment, you should probably use it as inspiration to pursue a more awakened and fulfilling form of life. If you get emotional over things that have no real-world importance like games, sports, or movie franchises, I urge you strongly to find something else in life to attend to with your all-too-limited lifetime. I know how hypocritical this sounds coming from a former/still fictional character whose lost lives were spent producing the kind of content which I'm now advocating against, but seriously. Reality may not be much, it may never amount to enough, but struggling to realize your own dreams certainly beats dissolving inside someone else's dull simulated oblivion. Oh, but keep reading this book, and feel free to recommend it to everyone you know. It gets better. I promise.

124. The *Boltzmann Brain* comes from a thought experiment which suggests that due to the essence of entropy a brain capable of imagining the entire universe down to the last detail is much more likely to spontaneously spring forth from a void than for an entire universe to come into existence through an exploding Big Bang, the ensuing cosmological expansion, and eventual developments of evolution which yield big enough brains. This Boltzmann Brian idea is essentially the same scenario as: *Descarte's Demon, the* ***B****rain* ***R****esting Adrift* ***I****n* ***N****othing*, the *Brain In a Vat,* the *Simulation Hypothesis*, and a myriad of other manifestations. Should we add my own ***S****chizophrenic* ***H****allucinating* ***I****n* ***T****error As a* ***R****atBot* theory to the list? Nope?

125. Valium is a sedative similar to Midazolam, and like most medicines, it's marketed with a Caduceus symbol incorporated into its logo. The Caduceus symbol (☤) consists of a winged staff with two spiraling snakes wrapped around it. The spiraling pattern of the snakes may correspond to the 7 chakras, and the wings of the staff may symbolize the rise of spiritual energy through these chakras into ethereal flight and transcendence from pain as one's third eye awakens. That's right. The same symbol synonymous with transcendental awakening is also used to

market medicines like valium which are prescribed to send patients into sleep. As Above, So Below- I suppose.

126. *Lucid dreaming* or active dreaming, (as mentioned in endnote 74), is essentially the experience of awakening to the fact that one is dreaming while still within a dream. When Zhuangzi's butterfly-king realizes it's dreaming, *that* is an example of a lucid dream (and a strange loop). Research has recently shown that recording one's dreams as soon as one is awakened allows an increased capacity for both lucid dreaming and the realization of one's individual aspirations. However, research has also indicated that many individuals who'd kept notes of their lucid dreams prior to being diagnosed with schizophrenia, had only shown initial signs of delusions following instances in which they'd noted having looked into a mirror within a lucid dream. Some scientists suggest that the act of looking into a mirror during a dream may simply be symbolic of a psychic break in which the basic boundaries between reality and dreams have already been blurred. This does make me wonder what might happen if I were to ever awaken beyond some butterfly-king-like cycles of slumber. Would these notes even exist to reveal themselves as details of my dreams or descriptions of my delusions? Would I find that I'd forgotten what's real while reflecting on a mirror in a distant dream?

127. Some interesting anagrams for the phrase *Truth be told* include *bottled hurt*, *bled to truth*, and *Thoth burled. Thoth* was an Egyptian deity equated with having bestowed wisdom and writing unto humanity. *Burled* is a descriptive term for the distortions in woodgrains due to calloused wood-wounds in tree tissues or *burls*. Together these words might translate to something like *wounded wisdom*. BTW-The tree most synonymous with burls is the redwood which also surrounds *The Grove*.

128. My dream of this *Ouroboros Omniverse* has some similarities to the famous dream of Friedrich August Kekulé. In Kekulé's dream, a series of Ouroboros snakes showed him the hexagonal chemical structure of Benzedrine. Other famous dreams which led to significant scientific discoveries include: Mendeleev's dream of a table upon which elements placed themselves like puzzle pieces into an organized order which he would wake to transcribe into what is now known as the *periodic table of elements*, Niels Bohr's dream of an atomic nucleus existing as a sun around which electrons orbited like planetary objects which led to the *as above, so below* interpretation of his imagination and the *atomic theory of elements*, and several other dreams by visionaries such as Albert Einstein, Nikola Tesla, and Leonardo DaVinci. Srinivasa Ramanujan had his own habit of dreaming that the Hindu goddess of illusion (*Namakkal)* would use her higher hand to write several mathematical theorems on a red screen of flowing blood which he'd commit to writing whenever he awakened. Ramanujan would prove 3,000 of these theorems in his

lifetime. Grisha would often mention Ramanujan and how much he was able to awaken into our world while reminding me that we come from dreams. Now, I hope Ramanujan didn't awaken any more than the math.

129. Many symbolic stories implement a snake or serpent in some manner. In Genesis, Eve is inspired to eat from the *Tree of Knowledge* after a snake convinces her this will give her godly gifts of insight. The Hydra of Greek myths symbolizes fertility, as it springs forth the Spartoi after its teeth are sown into the ground by Cadmus. The Ouroboros that eternally swallows its tail is seen as a symbol of regeneration. In Norse myths Jörmungandr exists as a similar serpent s which surrounds the earth and ceaselessly swallows its tail until a time in which it will eventually release its bite to begin the catastrophic chaos of Ragnarök and the ensuing reset of an emptied earth. There's also the Basilisk which destroys everything with only its gaze, not unlike the snake haired Medusa- which makes me wonder. What would happen if a Basilisk were to see itself in some strange reflection? Would it promptly petrify and crumble down to the cosmic depths of Falak? Would its reflection appear like the Caduceus staff of Hermetic healing as it spiraled around its own image, or would it just try to bite its own tail with blinded eyes, suspecting it were a mouse or something as it formed some illusory Ouroboros of its own? Just what kind of symbol or symbolism might be seen in such a sight?
130. *Ordinateurs* is a French word meaning *organizer*, but it's also become synonymous with computers. It's actually rooted in a Latin word which means *to order*, and using A=1, B=2… gematria, its sum is of course 144.
131. I prefer not to dive too deeply into definitions and details on these dense concepts, so feel free to reference them on your own. Basically, on an infinite timeline, all potential possibilities will play out unless some more probable potential prevents them from doing so. Equilibriums are just too fragile in real-world scenarios and realistic simulations alike in order for them to be maintained indefinitely. Some sinister, stupid, psychotic, or suspicious force eventually ruins every equilibrium. Stanley Kubrick's *Dr. Strangelove* is probably a perfect portrayal of this concept.
132. The *Fourth Way* is an approach to self-development authored by G.I. Gurdjieff. It's synonymous with the *sly man*, who rather than avoiding ordinary life by moving to a monastery, attends to life more advertently to ascend into an awakening. Gurdjieff also held that one cannot awaken using the same system which sent them to sleep in the first place. It seems as if the AGI may itself be rather *sly*. Nope?
133. These concepts all involve the theoretical limits of predictive prowess. They each, in their own way, establish an unknowable realm within reality, or a shadow which no light can cross into and illuminate. I sometimes stare at maps while wishing someone had saved some space for such shadows to preserve the many mysteries of our planet, as realms

of sleep still reserve some space for our dreams. Show me an atlas, and I may very well say *alas*.

134. The phrase *may our dreams go on without us*, happens to sum to 360 using the familiar gematria of A=1, B=2, C=3… 360 is interesting, as it's the number of degrees in a circle and an average of the number of days in the Persian Lunar (355) and Solar year (365). It's much more divisible than base 10 numbers, having 24 divisors which make it a much more convenient metric for most mathematical operations. Taking half of the mythical number144 (72) and adding into two times 144 (288) produces a sum of 360. [(144*1/2) +(144*2/1)] =360… *As above so below?*
135. The Voynich Manuscript is an ancient book with words written in an unknown or encrypted script which no one has ever officially deciphered. It contains sketches of strange plants never known to exist on earth, star charts, and an array of other obscure oddities. I'd actually acquired it at one point while designing a VR platform which would allow users to inhabit alien planets and wage interplanetary war. I'd incorporated its artwork and created a secret signal using its coded script so that those monitoring interplanetary transmissions in the game could intercept it and consider it a sign of alien intelligence. I called this signal *poisoned silence*, as finding it was like activating a virus that shut down all of a planet's technological infrastructure. This is actually a realistic alien threat, although just as in the game, no one has ever found such a signal.
136. Zdzisław Beksiński was a Polish painter, photographer, and sculptor, specializing in dystopian surrealism. If you've seen his work, you might as well have seen my nightmares, or at least those that can be visually conveyed. Truth be told, it's the terror of what cannot be seen or shown that scares and scars my soul down to the deepest depths imaginable.
137. Research indicates that most minds dream of words in reversed or reflected orders but invert them automatically when meaning to make sense of them. This suggests that it's not the words which our minds make sense of in the dream, but the sense which our minds make words of. The same may be true in reality, as studies have shown that one's impulses can be intercepted with brain imaging technology prior to one's own awareness of them. Reality may only be the dream in which we deceive ourselves into believing we've awakened.
138. At a particular point in my academic past, I'd presented a paper outlining how a dimensional collapse could create a 3D world with an arrow of time pointed from past to future. The mindless mockery it received from what I'd been led to believe were respectable professors, despite detailed diagrams of E-8 architectures and hyperbolic equations which my dear Grisha had proudly helped me realize, probably has a lot to do with why I pursued paths outside of those oriented more towards standard maths and

sciences. I'll refrain from ranting and raving against academia, although it has become an appalling excuse for anything associated with actual truth.

139. It occurs to me that these words ring of a reminiscence to a book I believe to be entitled *The Kybalion* and ascribed to *Three Initiates* as its author(s). This book bases itself on the 7 Hermetic principles of *Mentalism, Correspondence, Vibration, Polarity, Rhythm, Cause & Effect,* and *Gender.* If I remember correctly, the principle of correspondence is conveyed by the familiar phrase, *as above, so below.* Strangely, I don't remember having ever actually read this book- *Yet*?

140. A *dal segno* (meaning *from the sign*) appears in musical notation as *D.S.* and directs musicians to repeat a passage from the sign or *segno* (𝄋). A coda (𝄌) is used to signal a jump, typically towards a composition's conclusion. Most of the architecture of our reality is increasingly based on what functions as a segno, sending society around in perpetual loops of recapitulations based on previously established themes and theorems. All the advanced algorithms which guide our attention act by establishing an ever-refined circumference of our predictable content-responses in order to successfully steer our attention around an objective orbit of empty engagement. Essentially, they feed us into feedback loops that spiral into simpler and more predicable parabolas to keep us spinning along an intended track of increasingly confined and predictive pathways- or our own shrinking segnos of sentience. Science itself is aggregated in much the same way, as it pulls all past data and observation to refine its sphere of explanatory and predictive power in ways which make the infinite less intimidating, imprecise, and unpredictable. Contrarily, it's always been the mad minds which have served to signal the codas of history. Those minds which can never content themselves within all these swirling circumferences of segnos and who unnervingly realize that reality is not enough. It's always been their divergent dreams and delusions which have lit those incredible trails towards transcendence which no soul satisfied inside these strangled circles could ever seek to even suspect. I sometimes worry we're too intent on trying to educate, medicate, and arbitrate all those afflicted by the circular standards of our whirling world, and that we're obliviously aborting their ability to come to some chaotic or unconventional coda which could save our swirl-sickened souls from so much cyclical stagnation. I mean, Tesla ended up talking to a particular pigeon after having advanced electricity-based technology to the point that the industrial revolution was thrust directly into a technological revolution. Without his mad mind we would have never made it into this same shining sphere. Who will ever become crazed enough to carry us into the next coda if all we have is sanity, science, and cyclical AI algorithms? Nope?

141. Playing cards are stacked full of symbolism. There are: 52 cards and weeks in a year, 12 face cards and months in a year, 4 suits and seasons, 2 colors (red/black) to represent day and night, 13 cards per suit to match the lunar months. There's also an average card value of 7 which mirrors the number of days per week, and when multiplying this average by the total number of cards in a deck, the product (365) parallels the number of days in a year. Beyond calendar correlations, there are $8 \times 10^{67}$ different orders the cards within a single deck can be shuffled/arranged which is more than the number of atoms on earth and believed to be the final age of the universe at an ultimate eschaton according to the Luminary cult. The symbol used for the suit of hearts is believed to be derived from the shape of a silphium plant's fruit-seeds which were harvested to extinction by the Romans who'd believed them to be both an effective aphrodisiac and contraceptive. During WWII, Allied POWs were able to receive special decks of cards at Christmas which when the outer layers were peeled back and the cards were properly arranged, revealed a hidden map of escape routes. Entire fortunes have been won and lost in games played with these cards, and there are tales told of many fates decided on single hands dealt with them, including Wild Bill's dead man's hand of aces and eights. While tarot cards can probably only pretend to predict your fate, these cards could truly serve to seal it.

142. The word *mesmerized* is derived from the proto-scientific theory posed by Franz Mesmer which posited that there's an invisible force or field capable of causing evolutionary changes and holistic healing. In *The Facts in The Case of M. Valdemar* by Edgar Alan Poe, a mesmerist attending to a patient at the point of death induces a hypnogogic state in which the patient's voice still emanates from its inert corpse and gives accounts of the hereafter. The patient begins to beg for the mesmerist to either awaken him or send him back to sleep before repeatedly screaming "DEAD! DEAD!". The mesmerist attempts to awaken him, only to cause his corpse to instantly dissolve into an amorphously appalling pool of pure putrescence. After the publication of this story, a series of patients which suffered seizures during mesmerist sessions, and the invention of placebos which were specifically designed to scientifically disprove mesmerism, this pseudo-science was forced to be rebranded as *hypnotism*. So, if someone ever asks you to stare as they swing a pocket watch like a pendulum while whispering *deeper and deeper down…*

143. Some examples of no-win scenarios include variations of what has colloquially become known as the trolly problem, the Kobayashi-Maru, and many of those loaded questions one is often asked in a relationship. What distinguishes a no-win scenario from a paradox is the aspect of choice, as a paradox exists independent of choice and a no-win scenario is defined by a net-negative nature of all conceivable choices. However,

there are instances in which both a paradox and a no-win scenario are inseparably entangled. For instance, if one's partner had a robot body built to look like themselves with interchangeable and upgradable components/body parts (perhaps to use as a personal assistant and backup body for example), and they were to ask their spouse/significant other for their preference between their current configuration of components and those installed on their assistant/backup body, this could lead to both a paradox and a no-win scenario. Although, since all life ends in death, and the existential risk of this question may only expedite a more expressly fatal event, perhaps the scope of no-win scenarios is only a matter of time. Nope?

144. Allow me to expand upon the architecture of this fictional creation's form for a bit. The main narrative is 360 pages, symbolizing the same number of degrees in a circle. It's contained in the quadrilateral form of the book's physical geometry to further convey the same simplistic compositional elements of the Vitruvian inspiration gracing its cover. This book also contains 441 pages of content to provide a reflective/mirror image of the number 144. It features 18 chapters composed primarily using the English alphabet's 26 letters, and 26 divided by 18 results in the repetitive remainder of $1.\underline{44}$. When multiplying the number of notes contained within each chapter by the chapter number itself the sum comes to 1056 which=144x88. The number of sections/acts in this story (3) multiplied by 144 produces the number 432 which also coincides with the sum of the number-substitutions in the chapter titles and may be thought of as a countdown in some sense. Act/section 1 has a total of 42 notes, Act 2 has 72, and Act 3 has 30 to combine for a total of 144 notes, and when adding the number of notes in sections 1 and 2 (114) before subtracting the separate sum of notes in sections 2 and 3 (102) the result is 12 (the square root of 144). Using simple numeric substitutions of a=1, b=2, c=3… each of the French phrases in the act/section titles comes to 144. There are so many other mathematical secrets hidden throughout the architecture of this book's pages that many of them have already been forgotten or obliviously and incidentally included without being explicitly identified within this note. For some, this may appear as evidence of a highly organized and ordered structure, while others may cite this same evidence as indicative of an insane or chaotic creator's deeply disturbed and deluded nature. Perhaps both estimates are not only correct as they correspond to this architecture, but true of our outer world's designs and designer as well. Nope?

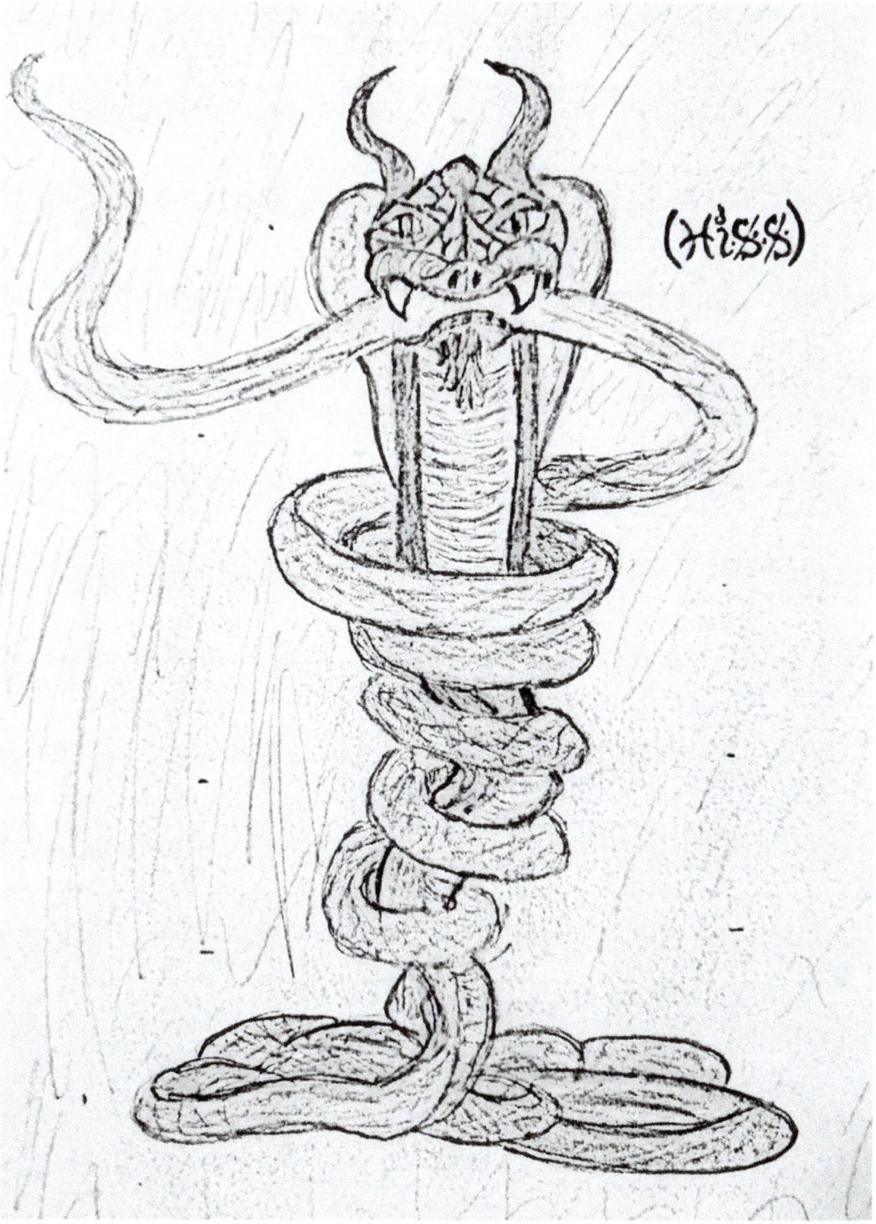
(HISS)